Great American Love Stories

Great American Love Stories

SELECTED AND WITH AN
INTRODUCTION BY
LUCY ROSENTHAL

Galahad Books • New York

First Galahad Books edition published in 1995.

Galahad Books
A division of Budget Book Service, Inc.
386 Park Avenue South
New York, NY 10016

Galahad Books is a registered trademark of Budget Book Service, Inc.

Published by arrangement with Lucy Rosenthal.

Library of Congress Catalog Card Number: 95-79465

ISBN: 0-88365-918-2

Printed in the United States of America.

Contents

Love is all the land we need.

— June Jordan,
His Own Where

Great American Love Stories

Introduction

by Lucy Rosenthal

$\mathcal{P}$ICTURE THE BRIDE, her unwanted groom beside her, rubbing "the palm of her right hand down the side of her satin wedding gown." The meaning of this "odd gesture," we learn, is that the bride — forgetful both of her gown and of the occasion for it — is reaching for something familiar, "the pocket of her overalls, and being unable to find it her face became impatient, bored, and exasperated." These bridal jitters, perhaps distinctively American in their down-to-earth practicality, are drawn from Carson McCullers's "Ballad of the Sad Café." For a fuller account of the marriage's outcome, as well as a luminous essay on love itself, I refer you to the splendid story.

Another image comes into focus: We're in Larry McMurtry's Thalia, Texas, a town that's gone — courtesy of the fluctuating price of oil — from bust to boom and back again. The Centennial Committee meeting has just broken up. Committee-person Duane Moore, having surreptitiously removed his boots and pants, lurks in the shadows half-concealed. Duane is wondering how he will get around further impediments to making love (illicit variety) to fellow committee member Suzie Nolan, now inconveniently stationed behind the wheel of her car. Half-mindful of the need not to be seen — they're in the town square — he steals toward her. She greets him pleasantly: "Hi, you rat." It's a come-hither signal. "He considered trying to go through the window," McMurtry writes, "but he decided to be mature." What follows might be subtitled *Love as Mishap*. Certainly it

affords an entertaining view of one of the more vital theaters of operation for love in America — the automobile.

And on the subject of American love's indispensable props, consider the anguished monologue delivered by a woman waiting devoutly
for her phone to ring in Dorothy Parker's "A Telephone Call": "It
would be so little to You, God, such a little, little thing. Only let him
telephone now. Please, God. Please, please, please."

The language of love given voice in this collection is manifold. Its
accents and idiom vary with the lovers' region, occupation, interests,
station in life, and country of origin. "Drink," says McCullers's Miss
Amelia tenderly to her beloved. "It will liven your gizzard." In Harold
Brodkey's "Innocence," narrator Wiley, Harvard man and dazzled
student of Orra Perkins's charms, announces: "To see her in sunlight
was to see Marxism die." Bobbie Ann Mason's daffy and languorous
heroine in "Residents and Transients," made slightly more flaky with
love, confides in a Kentucky twang: "One day I was counting the cats
and I absentmindedly counted myself."

In Damon Runyon's "Idyll of Miss Sarah Brown," we hear the
voices of characters from *Guys and Dolls*, denizens of the sidewalks and
gambling dens of New York. Sky Masterson, card shark and gambler
extraordinaire, is trying to win the favor of Miss Sarah Brown, the
mission worker who has incongruously won his heart. "And after a
couple of ganders at this young doll, The Sky is a goner, for this is one
of the most beautiful young dolls anybody ever sees on Broadway, and
especially as a mission worker. . . . Many citizens claim it is a great
shame that such a beautiful doll is wasting her time being good." The
smitten Sky muses: " 'I wish I can think of some way to help this little
doll,' he says, 'especially,' he says, 'in saving a few souls to build up her
mob at the mission.' "

From a window of a house overlooking Market Street in a Warsaw
shtetl early in this century, Isaac Bashevis Singer's Dr. Fischelson, no
less ardent than Sky, addresses Spinoza with prayerlike words of
thanksgiving for love. (American love stories are not consistently set
at home; the melting pot is reflected in our literature.) And back in
this country's untamed rural landscape, in a story very nearly operatic,
with cadences reminiscent of D. H. Lawrence, Wilbur Daniel Steele
has a lovesick escapee from an asylum quote Lovelace and the Song of
Solomon to the girl he holds hostage ("*Amarantha sweet and fair —*

Ah, braid no more that shining hair . . ."). As the title, "How Beautiful with Shoes," suggests, the story is in love with literature as well. Brodkey's Wiley, as "Innocence" draws to a close, makes his own poetry: "She was an angel as brilliant as a beautiful insect infinitely enlarged and irrevocably foreign: she was unlike me: she was a girl. . . ." (As Shakespeare observed in a related connection, "Age cannot wither her, nor custom stale her infinite variety.") Brodkey and the other writers in this collection would seem to be right on the money. To love someone is to take on also the myriad values he or she embodies — philosophic, literary, erotic — really, to fulfill one's self by embracing the other person's world.

The thirty-one stories collected here reflect a nearly infinite American diversity — economic, regional, racial, ethnic — as well as some common themes. Any number of the selections feature gardens, often with snakes. The turning points of many of these stories seem to depend on Eden's being near. In the garden tended by Rappaccini's daughter, "strange flowers" grew and the foliage, in Hawthorne's words, "crept serpent-like along the ground." In the invented landscape of Melville's "Piazza" — an account of love as pure illusion — we encounter another version of the serpent: "a Chinese creeper . . . had burst out in starry bloom, but now, if you removed the leaves a little, showed millions of strange, cankerous worms, which, feeding upon those blossoms, so shared their blessed hue as to make it unblessed evermore." Edith Wharton's Lydia, in a moment of capitulation toward the close of "Souls Belated," is seen "with slow steps, . . . walking toward the garden." In Scott Fitzgerald's " 'The Sensible Thing,' " the lovers (her name is Jonquil), at a key moment in the story, "saw each other's eyes, and both took a short, faintly accelerated breath, and then they went on into the second garden. That was all." June Jordan's teenage Buddy, longing to be free from the ghetto and reunited with the girl he loves, tempers his impatience and lightens his despair: "He start a garden." The references to gardens can also be figurative, allusive. Willa Cather's lovers, for instance, in "Coming, Aphrodite!" are named Eden Bower and Don Hedger. The garden where it all began remains in this literature a central setting for love, idyllic or catastrophic or both.

Many of these stories suggest that love in our culture is at odds with various other codes, such as fidelity or the work ethic. A particularly entertaining example of the latter is the last scene of Dashiell Hammett's *The Maltese Falcon*, in which Sam Spade explains to Brigid O'Shaughnessy that while there are many things a man in love can do, he can't cover up for the woman who killed his partner. He says — "tenderly" — "I hope to Christ they don't hang you, precious, by that sweet neck." Cather's story puts the lovers at competitive cross-purposes. In John Cheever's "Pot of Gold," that the lovers' initial meeting is in the workplace does them no good at all. In Mark Helprin's story "The Pacific," however, the setting is a defense plant, America is at war (the title is a piercing irony), and love and work become powerfully fused in the mind of a woman welder trying to forge an unbreakable connection with her husband fighting overseas. (Her name, Paulette Ferry, might be a subtle reminder of another body of water, and the passage across the River Styx.) Brodkey's story, for all the ardency of its idealism and romance, can be read as a salute to love *as* work, with explicitness of detail that is not so much prurient as illustrative of the American emphasis on technique — the how-to preoccupation that says if you're going to do it at all, you better do it right.

Still other of these stories deal with the magical and transforming properties of love. Sometimes transfiguration is to be found, literally, in potions or poisons, sometimes in the simple alterations of body chemistry or the glands. Hawthorne's "Rappaccini's Daughter" comes naturally to mind as an example of the former, along with the demonically witty tale told by Susan Fromberg Schaeffer in her richly imagined "Bluebeard's Second Wife." Peter Beagle's fantastical and comic "Lila the Werewolf" belongs here too, though strictly speaking, its transformations happen unaided by any elixir; they appear rather to be regulated by the calendar. In Gail Godwin's immensely appealing "St. George," the heroine's loneliness takes the form of a mythical beast. Love's expansion of the heart can take gentler and more realistic guises too: Cather likens love's flight to the behavior of a "sail, that has been filled by a strong breeze . . . when the wind suddenly dies" — and she describes the altered features of a lover's face accordingly.

To be under the spell of love is to be ruled by the possibilities of the unknown. In the shtetl of Singer's "Spinoza of Market Street," the events of love give rise to talk of bewitchment and intoxication. In Eudora Welty's "No Place for You, My Love," the man and woman are changed by a drive through a wild and strange no-man's-land south of New Orleans that seems to take them backward along the evolutionary scale — to a primeval site, perhaps the site of creation. Stories as disparate as John O'Hara's masterly "Imagine Kissing Pete" and Grace Paley's rueful and exuberant "Interest in Life" surprise us — the O'Hara nearly stuns — not least by the transforming agent they have in common. In Cheever's story, the alchemy of love is such that it converts poverty and disappointment and even failure into gold. For better or worse, love is bewitching.

For Americans wearing, however restlessly, the mantle of our Puritan heritage, it appears also that love often happens in a foreign country. James's Daisy Miller unforgettably and definitively comes to grief abroad, Rappaccini's garden grows in Italy, Edith Wharton's clandestine lovers in "Souls Belated" have their wanderings abroad likened to "the flight of outlaws," and even Fitzgerald's George O'Kelly is made readier for love's travail by a detour to Peru. It's almost as if love itself were an exotic and mysterious land. Certainly the authors of the earlier stories in this collection showed, in relation to their subject matter, the hesitancies and tentativeness of courtship. Not until Cather's "Coming, Aphrodite!" does the drama of love get staged at home. As our own century winds down, however, our puritanical skittishness seems to subside with it, or at least takes less drastic forms. Though the discomfort level remains high, it's gratifying to note that only rarely do contemporary characters die of love or find it solely overseas.

The stories are arranged in a very loose chronological order. I departed from chronology either for the sake of variety or for compatibility of tone and themes. Thus, Beagle's "Lila the Werewolf" and Hammett's "If They Hang You" are paired for having in common the suspicion with which they both view the female of the species. The John Cheever and Bernard Malamud stories are at once hopeful and autumnal — love is tenacious and can flourish, they seem to be saying, even in arid or unlikely soil. If Brodkey's story proceeds from lust to innocence, Susan Minot's "Lust" travels a thorny path from innocence to lust — posing an intriguing question: What would happen if the two stories exchanged titles?

Schaeffer's biting and astonishing variation on the theme of sisterhood as powerful, love as both ecstatic and a snare, is followed by Ian

Frazier's equally satiric (though perhaps more laid-back) suggestion in "Dating Your Mom" that love's vistas are inexhaustible. Gloria Kurian Broder's poignant and wise "Elena, Unfaithful" offers a portrait of death as the ultimate infidelity, while in Nicholas Delbanco's "Consolation of Philosophy" Robert Lewin's reveries of defection (recalling Fitzgerald in their delicacy of style and insight) bring him full circle back to the warmth of his waking life and his marriage.

My criteria in selecting these stories were readability, literary quality, and an original and alive rendering of themes. In "Here Come the Maples," John Updike's bittersweet tribute to divorce, marriage is presented as divorce running backward. It appears that we are being told that divorce is an honorable condition, having its own claim to dignified ritual. And what startles on a fresh reading of Ernest Hemingway's "Up in Michigan" is to find the writer whose life and reputation have come to be almost emblematic of the word *machismo* writing with compassion and understanding of the double standard, the sexual plight of a woman.

What else do these stories have in common? With few exceptions, humor. Their authors seem to be saying that when all else fails, or even when it doesn't, comedy can be counted on for consolation, to soothe love's fevers.

I close this collection with Paley. Like O'Hara before her, she suggests that to be in love is to take an interest in life — an interest that often includes, though it is not confined to, the begetting of children.

One further word: Rereading these accounts of beautiful flowers and fearsome underbrush, of foreign cities where love flourishes and wilts, of natural and magical transformations, I was struck by the gaiety I was experiencing, increasingly. Very simply, the stories were making me happy. It seems, then, altogether fair to say that the relationship between author and reader, linked by pleasures shared, is a lovers' compact too.

Rappaccini's Daughter

by Nathaniel Hawthorne

(From the Writings of Aubépine)

WE DO NOT REMEMBER to have seen any translated specimens of the productions of M. de l'Aubépine — a fact the less to be wondered at, as his very name is unknown to many of his own countrymen as well as to the student of foreign literature. As a writer, he seems to occupy an unfortunate position between the Transcendentalists (who, under one name or another, have their share in all the current literature of the world) and the great body of pen-and-ink men who address the intellect and sympathies of the multitude. If not too refined, at all events too remote, too shadowy, and unsubstantial in his modes of development to suit the taste of the latter class, and yet too popular to satisfy the spiritual or metaphysical requisitions of the former, he must necessarily find himself without an audience, except here and there an individual or possibly an isolated clique. His writings, to do them justice, are not altogether destitute of fancy and originality; they might have won him greater reputation but for an inveterate love of allegory, which is apt to invest his plots and characters with the aspect of scenery and people in the clouds, and to steal away the human warmth out of his conceptions. His fictions are sometimes historical, sometimes of the present day, and sometimes, so far as can be discovered, have little or no reference either to time or space. In any case, he generally contents himself with a very slight embroidery of outward manners, — the faintest possible counterfeit of real life, — and endeavors to create an interest by some less obvious peculiarity of the subject. Occasionally a breath of Nature, a raindrop of pathos and tenderness, or a gleam of humor, will find its way into the midst of his fantastic imagery, and make us feel as if, after all, we were yet within the limits of our native earth. We will only add to this very cursory notice that M. de l'Aubépine's productions, if the reader chance to take them in precisely the proper point of view, may amuse a leisure hour as well as those of a brighter man; if otherwise, they can hardly fail to look excessively like nonsense.

Our author is voluminous; he continues to write and publish with as much praiseworthy and indefatigable prolixity as if his efforts were crowned with the brilliant success that so justly attends those of Eugene Sue. His first appearance was by a collection of stories in a long series of volumes entitled "Contes deux fois racontées." The titles of some of his more recent works (we quote from memory) are as follows: "Le Voyage Céleste à Chemin de Fer," 3 tom., 1838; "Le nouveau Père Adam et la nouvelle Mère Eve," 2 tom., 1839; "Roderic; ou le Serpent à l'estomac," 2 tom., 1840; "Le Culte du Feu," a folio volume of ponderous research into the religion and ritual of the old Persian Ghebers, published in 1841; "La Soirée du Château en Espagne," 1 tom., 8vo, 1842; and "L'Artiste du Beau; ou le Papillon Mécanique," 5 tom., 4to, 1843. Our somewhat wearisome perusal of this startling catalogue of volumes has left behind it a certain personal affection and sympathy, though by no means admiration, for M. de l'Aubépine; and we would fain do the little in our power towards introducing him favorably to the American public. The ensuing tale is a translation of his "Beatrice; ou la Belle Empoisonneuse," recently published in "La Revue Anti-Aristocratique." This journal, edited by the Comte de Bearhaven, has for some years past led the defence of liberal principles and popular rights with a faithfulness and ability worthy of all praise.

A young man, named Giovanni Guasconti, came, very long ago, from the more southern region of Italy, to pursue his studies at the University of Padua. Giovanni, who had but a scanty supply of gold ducats in his pocket, took lodgings in a high and gloomy chamber of an old edifice which looked not unworthy to have been the palace of a Paduan noble, and which, in fact, exhibited over its entrance the armorial bearings of a family long since extinct. The young stranger, who was not unstudied in the great poem of his country, recollected that one of the ancestors of this family, and perhaps an occupant of this very mansion, had been pictured by Dante as a partaker of the immortal agonies of his Inferno. These reminiscences and associations, together with the tendency to heartbreak natural to a young man for the first time out of his native sphere, caused Giovanni to sigh heavily as he looked around the desolate and ill-furnished apartment.

"Holy Virgin, signor!" cried old Dame Lisabetta, who, won by the youth's remarkable beauty of person, was kindly endeavoring to give the chamber a habitable air, "what a sigh was that to come out of a young man's heart! Do you find this old mansion gloomy? For the love of Heaven, then, put your head out of the window, and you will see as bright sunshine as you have left in Naples."

Guasconti mechanically did as the old woman advised, but could not quite agree with her that the Paduan sunshine was as cheerful as that of southern Italy. Such as it was, however, it fell upon a garden beneath the window and expended its fostering influences on a variety of plants, which seemed to have been cultivated with exceeding care.

"Does this garden belong to the house?" asked Giovanni.

"Heaven forbid, signor, unless it were fruitful of better pot herbs than any that grow there now," answered old Lisabetta. "No; that garden is cultivated by the own hands of Signor Giacomo Rappaccini, the famous doctor, who, I warrant him, has been heard of as far as Naples. It is said that he distils these plants into medicines that are as potent as a charm. Oftentimes you may see the signor doctor at work, and perchance the signora, his daughter, too, gathering the strange flowers that grow in the garden."

The old woman had now done what she could for the aspect of the chamber; and, commending the young man to the protection of the saints, took her departure.

Giovanni still found no better occupation than to look down into the garden beneath his window. From its appearance, he judged it to be one of those botanic gardens which were of earlier date in Padua than elsewhere in Italy or in the world. Or, not improbably, it might once have been the pleasure-place of an opulent family; for there was the ruin of a marble fountain in the centre, sculptured with rare art, but so wofully shattered that it was impossible to trace the original design from the chaos of remaining fragments. The water, however, continued to gush and sparkle into the sunbeams as cheerfully as ever.

A little gurgling sound ascended to the young man's window, and made him feel as if the fountain were an immortal spirit that sung its song unceasingly and without heeding the vicissitudes around it, while one century imbodied it in marble and another scattered the perishable garniture on the soil. All about the pool into which the water subsided grew various plants, that seemed to require a plentiful supply of moisture for the nourishment of gigantic leaves, and, in some instances, flowers gorgeously magnificent. There was one shrub in particular, set in a marble vase in the midst of the pool, that bore a profusion of purple blossoms, each of which had the lustre and richness of a gem; and the whole together made a show so resplendent that it seemed enough to illuminate the garden, even had there been no sunshine. Every portion of the soil was peopled with plants and herbs, which, if less beautiful, still bore tokens of assiduous care, as if all had their individual virtues, known to the scientific mind that fostered them. Some were placed in urns, rich with old carving, and others in common garden pots; some crept serpent-like along the ground or climbed on high, using whatever means of ascent was offered them. One plant had wreathed itself round a statue of Vertumnus, which was thus quite veiled and shrouded in a drapery of hanging foliage, so happily arranged that it might have served a sculptor for a study.

While Giovanni stood at the window he heard a rustling behind a screen of leaves, and became aware that a person was at work in the garden. His figure soon emerged into view, and showed itself to be that of no common laborer, but a tall, emaciated, sallow, and sickly-looking man, dressed in a scholar's garb of black. He was beyond the middle term of life, with gray hair, a thin, gray beard, and a face singularly marked with intellect and cultivation, but which could never, even in his more youthful days, have expressed much warmth of heart.

Nothing could exceed the intentness with which this scientific gardener examined every shrub which grew in his path: it seemed as if he was looking into their inmost nature, making observations in regard to their creative essence, and discovering why one leaf grew in this shape and another in that, and wherefore such and such flowers differed among themselves in hue and perfume. Nevertheless, in spite of this deep intelligence on his part, there was no approach to intimacy between himself and these vegetable existences. On the contrary, he avoided their actual touch or the direct inhaling of their odors with a caution that impressed Giovanni most disagreeably; for the man's demeanor was that of one walking among malignant influences, such as savage beasts, or deadly snakes, or evil spirits, which, should he allow them one moment of license, would wreak upon him some terrible fatality. It was strangely frightful to the young man's imagination to see this air of insecurity in a person cultivating a garden, that most simple and innocent of human toils, and which had been alike the joy and labor of the unfallen parents of the race. Was this garden, then, the Eden of the present world? And this man, with such a perception of harm in what his own hands caused to grow, — was he the Adam?

The distrustful gardener, while plucking away the dead leaves or pruning the too luxuriant growth of the shrubs, defended his hands with a pair of thick gloves. Nor were these his only armor. When, in his walk through the garden, he came to the magnificent plant that hung its purple gems beside the marble fountain, he placed a kind of mask over his mouth and nostrils, as if all this beauty did but conceal a deadlier malice; but, finding his task still too dangerous, he drew back, removed the mask, and called loudly, but in the infirm voice of a person affected with inward disease, —

"Beatrice! Beatrice!"

"Here am I, my father. What would you?" cried a rich and youthful voice from the window of the opposite house — a voice as rich as a tropical sunset, and which made Giovanni, though he knew not why, think of deep hues of purple or crimson and of perfumes heavily delectable. "Are you in the garden?"

"Yes, Beatrice," answered the gardener, "and I need your help."

Soon there emerged from under a sculptured portal the figure of a young girl, arrayed with as much richness of taste as the most splendid of the flowers, beautiful as the day, and with a bloom so deep and vivid that one shade more would have been too much. She looked redundant with life, health, and energy; all of which attributes were bound down and compressed, as it were, and girdled tensely, in their luxuriance, by her virgin zone. Yet Giovanni's fancy must have grown morbid while he looked down into the garden; for the impression which the fair stranger made upon him was as if here were another flower, the human sister of those vegetable ones, as beautiful as they, more beautiful than the richest of them, but still to be touched only with a glove, nor to be approached without a mask. As Beatrice came down the garden path, it was observable that she handled and inhaled the odor of several of the plants which her father had most sedulously avoided.

"Here, Beatrice," said the latter, "see how many needful offices require to be done to our chief treasure. Yet, shattered as I am, my life might pay the penalty of approaching it so closely as circumstances demand. Henceforth, I fear, this plant must be consigned to your sole charge."

"And gladly will I undertake it," cried again the rich tones of the young lady, as she bent towards the magnificent plant and opened her arms as if to embrace it. "Yes, my sister, my splendor, it shall be Beatrice's task to nurse and serve thee; and thou shalt reward her with thy kisses and perfumed breath, which to her is as the breath of life."

Then, with all the tenderness in her manner that was so strikingly expressed in her words, she busied herself with such attentions as the plant seemed to require; and Giovanni, at his lofty window, rubbed his eyes and almost doubted whether it were a girl tending her favorite flower, or one sister performing the duties of affection to another. The scene soon terminated. Whether Dr. Rappaccini had finished his labors in the garden, or that his watchful eye had caught the stranger's face, he now took his daughter's arm and retired. Night was already closing in; oppressive exhalations seemed to proceed from the plants and steal upward past the open window; and Giovanni, closing the lattice, went to his couch and dreamed of a rich flower and beautiful girl. Flower and maiden were different, and yet the same, and fraught with some strange peril in either shape.

But there is an influence in the light of morning that tends to rectify whatever errors of fancy, or even of judgment, we may have incurred during the sun's decline, or among the shadows of the night, or in the less wholesome glow of moonshine. Giovanni's first movement, on starting from sleep, was to throw open the window and gaze down into the garden which his dreams had made so fertile of mysteries. He was surprised and a little ashamed to find how real and matter-of-fact an affair it proved to be, in the first rays of the sun which gilded the dew-drops that hung upon leaf and blossom, and, while giving a brighter beauty to each rare flower, brought everything within the limits of ordinary experience. The young man rejoiced that, in the heart of the barren city, he had the privilege of overlooking this spot of lovely and luxuriant vegetation. It would serve, he said to himself, as a symbolic language to keep him in communion with Nature. Neither the sickly and thoughtworn Dr. Giacomo Rappaccini, it is true, nor his brilliant daughter, were now visible; so that Giovanni could not determine how much of the singularity which he attributed to both was due to their own qualities and how much to his wonder-working fancy; but he was inclined to take a most rational view of the whole matter.

In the course of the day he paid his respects to Signor Pietro Baglioni, professor of medicine in the university, a physician of eminent repute, to whom Giovanni had brought a letter of introduction. The professor was an elderly personage, apparently of genial nature, and habits that might almost be called jovial. He kept the young man to dinner, and made himself very agreeable by the freedom and liveliness of his conversation, especially when warmed by a flask or two of Tuscan wine. Giovanni, conceiving that men of science, inhabitants of the same city, must needs be on familiar terms with one another, took an opportunity to mention the name of Dr. Rappaccini. But the professor did not respond with so much cordiality as he had anticipated.

"Ill would it become a teacher of the divine art of medicine," said Professor Pietro Baglioni, in answer to a question of Giovanni, "to withhold due and well-considered praise of a physician so eminently skilled as Rappaccini; but, on the other hand, I should answer it but scantily to my conscience were I to permit a worthy youth like yourself, Signor Giovanni, the son of an ancient friend, to imbibe erroneous ideas respecting a man who might hereafter chance to hold your life and death in his hands. The truth is, our worshipful Dr. Rappaccini has as much science as any member of the faculty — with perhaps one single exception — in Padua, or all Italy; but there are certain grave objections to his professional character."

"And what are they?" asked the young man.

"Has my friend Giovanni any disease of body or heart, that he is so inquisitive about physicians?" said the professor, with a smile. "But as for Rappaccini, it is said of him — and I, who know the man well, can answer for its truth — that he cares infinitely more for science than for mankind. His patients are interesting to him only as subjects for some new experiment. He would sacrifice human life, his own among the rest, or whatever else was dearest to him, for the sake of adding so much as a grain of mustard seed to the great heap of his accumulated knowledge."

"Methinks he is an awful man indeed," remarked Guasconti, mentally recalling the cold and purely intellectual aspect of Rappaccini. "And yet, worshipful professor, is it not a noble spirit? Are there many men capable of so spiritual a love of science?"

"God forbid," answered the professor, somewhat testily; "at least, unless they take sounder views of the healing art than those adopted by Rappaccini. It is his theory that all medicinal virtues are comprised within those substances which we term vegetable poisons. These he cultivates with his own hands, and is said even to have produced new varieties of poison, more horribly deleterious than Nature, without the assistance of this learned person, would ever have plagued the world withal. That the signor doctor does less mischief than might be expected with such dangerous substances is undeniable. Now and then, it must be owned, he has effected, or seemed to effect, a marvellous cure; but, to tell you my private mind, Signor Giovanni, he should receive little credit for such instances of success, — they being probably the work of chance, — but should be held strictly accountable for his failures, which may justly be considered his own work."

The youth might have taken Baglioni's opinions with many grains of allowance had he known that there was a professional warfare of long continuance between him and Dr. Rappaccini, in which the latter was generally thought to have gained the advantage. If the reader be inclined to judge for himself, we refer him to certain black-letter tracts on both sides, preserved in the medical department of the University of Padua.

"I know not, most learned professor," returned Giovanni, after musing on what had been said of Rappaccini's exclusive zeal for science, — "I know not how dearly this physician may love his art; but surely there is one object more dear to him. He has a daughter."

"Aha!" cried the professor, with a laugh. "So now our friend Giovanni's secret is out. You have heard of this daughter, whom all the young men in Padua are wild about, though not half a dozen have ever had the good hap to see her face. I know little of the Signora Beatrice save that Rappaccini is said to have instructed her deeply in his science, and that, young and beautiful as fame reports her, she is already qualified to fill a professor's chair. Perchance her father destines her for mine! Other absurd rumors there be, not worth talking about or listening to. So now, Signor Giovanni, drink off your glass of lachryma."

Guasconti returned to his lodgings somewhat heated with the wine he had quaffed, and which caused his brain to swim with strange fantasies in reference to Dr. Rappaccini and the beautiful Beatrice. On his way, happening to pass by a florist's, he bought a fresh bouquet of flowers.

Ascending to his chamber, he seated himself near the window, but within the shadow thrown by the depth of the wall, so that he could look down into the garden with little risk of being discovered. All beneath his eye was a solitude. The strange plants were basking in the sunshine, and now and then nodding gently to one another, as if in acknowledgment of sympathy and kindred. In the midst, by the shattered fountain, grew the magnificent shrub, with its purple gems clustering all over it; they glowed in the air, and gleamed back again out of the depths of the pool, which thus seemed to overflow with colored radiance from the rich reflection that was steeped in it. At first, as we have said, the garden was a solitude. Soon, however, — as Giovanni had half hoped, half feared, would be the case, — a figure appeared beneath the antique sculptured portal, and came down between the rows of plants, inhaling their various perfumes as if she were one of those beings of old classic fable that lived upon sweet odors. On again beholding Beatrice, the young man was even startled to perceive how much her beauty exceeded his recollection of it; so brilliant, so vivid, was its character, that she glowed amid the sunlight, and, as Giovanni whispered to himself, positively illuminated the more shadowy intervals of the garden path. Her face being now more revealed than on the former occasion, he was struck by its expression of simplicity and sweetness, — qualities that had not entered into his idea of her character, and which made him ask anew what manner of mortal she might be. Nor did he fail again to observe, or imagine, an analogy between the beautiful girl and the gorgeous shrub that hung its gemlike flowers over the fountain, — a resemblance which Beatrice seemed to have indulged a fantastic humor in heightening, both by the arrangement of her dress and the selection of its hues.

Approaching the shrub, she threw open her arms, as with a passionate ardor, and drew its branches into an intimate embrace — so intimate that her features were hidden in its leafy bosom and her glistening ringlets all intermingled with the flowers.

"Give me thy breath, my sister," exclaimed Beatrice; "for I am faint with common air. And give me this flower of thine, which I separate with gentlest fingers from the stem and place it close beside my heart."

With these words the beautiful daughter of Rappaccini plucked one of the richest blossoms of the shrub, and was about to fasten it in her bosom. But now, unless Giovanni's draughts of wine had bewildered his senses, a singular incident occurred. A small orange-colored reptile, of the lizard or chameleon species, chanced to be creeping along the path, just at the feet of Beatrice. It appeared to Giovanni, — but, at the distance from which he gazed, he could scarcely have seen anything so minute, — it appeared to him, however, that a drop or two of moisture from the broken stem of the flower descended upon the lizard's head. For an instant the reptile contorted itself violently, and then lay motionless in the sunshine. Beatrice observed this remarkable phenomenon, and crossed herself, sadly, but without surprise; nor did she therefore hesitate to arrange the fatal flower in her bosom. There it blushed, and almost glimmered with the dazzling effect of a precious stone, adding to her dress and aspect the one appropriate charm which nothing else in the world could have supplied. But Giovanni, out of the shadow of his window, bent forward and shrank back, and murmured and trembled.

"Am I awake? Have I my senses?" said he to himself. "What is this being? Beautiful shall I call her, or inexpressibly terrible?"

Beatrice now strayed carelessly through the garden, approaching closer beneath Giovanni's window, so that he was compelled to thrust his head quite out of its concealment in order to gratify the intense and painful curiosity which she excited. At this moment there came a beautiful insect over the garden wall; it had, perhaps, wandered through the city, and found no flowers or verdure among those antique haunts of men until the heavy perfumes of Dr. Rappaccini's shrubs had lured it from afar. Without alighting on the flowers, this winged brightness seemed to be attracted by Beatrice, and lingered in the air and fluttered about her head. Now, here it could not be but that Giovanni Guasconti's eyes deceived him. Be that as it might, he fancied that, while Beatrice was gazing at the insect with childish delight, it

grew faint and fell at her feet; its bright wings shivered; it was dead —
from no cause that he could discern, unless it were the atmosphere of
her breath. Again Beatrice crossed herself and sighed heavily as she
bent over the dead insect.

An impulsive movement of Giovanni drew her eyes to the window.
There she beheld the beautiful head of the young man — rather a
Grecian than an Italian head, with fair, regular features, and a glistening of gold among his ringlets — gazing down upon her like a being
that hovered in mid air. Scarcely knowing what he did, Giovanni
threw down the bouquet which he had hitherto held in his hand.

"Signora," said he, "there are pure and healthful flowers. Wear
them for the sake of Giovanni Guasconti."

"Thanks, signor," replied Beatrice, with her rich voice, that came
forth as it were like a gush of music, and with a mirthful expression
half childish and half woman-like. "I accept your gift, and would fain
recompense it with this precious purple flower; but if I toss it into the
air it will not reach you. So Signor Guasconti must even content
himself with my thanks."

She lifted the bouquet from the ground, and then, as if inwardly
ashamed at having stepped aside from her maidenly reserve to respond
to a stranger's greeting, passed swiftly homeward through the garden.
But few as the moments were, it seemed to Giovanni, when she was
on the point of vanishing beneath the sculptured portal, that his
beautiful bouquet was already beginning to wither in her grasp. It was
an idle thought; there could be no possibility of distinguishing a faded
flower from a fresh one at so great a distance.

For many days after this incident the young man avoided the window that looked into Dr. Rappaccini's garden, as if something ugly
and monstrous would have blasted his eyesight had he been betrayed
into a glance. He felt conscious of having put himself, to a certain
extent, within the influence of an unintelligible power by the communication which he had opened with Beatrice. The wisest course
would have been, if his heart were in any real danger, to quit his
lodgings and Padua itself at once; the next wiser, to have accustomed
himself, as far as possible, to the familiar and daylight view of Beatrice
— thus bringing her rigidly and systematically within the limits of ordinary experience. Least of all, while avoiding her sight, ought
Giovanni to have remained so near this extraordinary being that the

proximity and possibility even of intercourse should give a kind of substance and reality to the wild vagaries which his imagination ran riot continually in producing. Guasconti had not a deep heart — or, at all events, its depths were not sounded now; but he had a quick fancy, and an ardent southern temperament, which rose every instant to a higher fever pitch. Whether or no Beatrice possessed those terrible attributes, that fatal breath, the affinity with those so beautiful and deadly flowers which were indicated by what Giovanni had witnessed, she had at least instilled a fierce and subtle poison into his system. It was not love, although her rich beauty was a madness to him; nor horror, even while he fancied her spirit to be imbued with the same baneful essence that seemed to pervade her physical frame; but a wild offspring of both love and horror that had each parent in it, and burned like one and shivered like the other. Giovanni knew not what to dread; still less did he know what to hope; yet hope and dread kept a continual warfare in his breast, alternately vanquishing one another and starting up afresh to renew the contest. Blessed are all simple emotions, be they dark or bright! It is the lurid intermixture of the two that produces the illuminating blaze of the infernal regions.

Sometimes he endeavored to assuage the fever of his spirit by a rapid walk through the streets of Padua or beyond its gates: his footsteps kept time with the throbbings of his brain, so that the walk was apt to accelerate itself to a race. One day he found himself arrested; his arm was seized by a portly personage, who had turned back on recognizing the young man and expended much breath in overtaking him.

"Signor Giovanni! Stay, my young friend!" cried he. "Have you forgotten me? That might well be the case if I were as much altered as yourself."

It was Baglioni, whom Giovanni had avoided ever since their first meeting, from a doubt that the professor's sagacity would look too deeply into his secrets. Endeavoring to recover himself, he stared forth wildly from his inner world into the outer one and spoke like a man in a dream.

"Yes; I am Giovanni Guasconti. You are Professor Pietro Baglioni. Now let me pass!"

"Not yet, not yet, Signor Giovanni Guasconti," said the professor, smiling, but at the same time scrutinizing the youth with an earnest glance. "What! did I grow up side by side with your father? and shall his son pass me like a stranger in these old streets of Padua? Stand still, Signor Giovanni; for we must have a word or two before we part."

"Speedily, then, most worshipful professor, speedily," said Giovanni, with feverish impatience. "Does not your worship see that I am in haste?"

Now, while he was speaking there came a man in black along the street, stooping and moving feebly like a person in inferior health. His face was all overspread with a most sickly and sallow hue, but yet so pervaded with an expression of piercing and active intellect that an observer might easily have overlooked the merely physical attributes and have seen only this wonderful energy. As he passed, this person exchanged a cold and distant salutation with Baglioni, but fixed his eyes upon Giovanni with an intentness that seemed to bring out whatever was within him worthy of notice. Nevertheless, there was a peculiar quietness in the look, as if taking merely a speculative, not a human, interest in the young man.

"It is Dr. Rappaccini!" whispered the professor when the stranger had passed. "Has he ever seen your face before?"

"Not that I know," answered Giovanni, starting at the name.

"He *has* seen you! he must have seen you!" said Baglioni, hastily. "For some purpose or other, this man of science is making a study of you. I know that look of his! It is the same that coldly illuminates his face as he bends over a bird, a mouse, or a butterfly, which, in pursuance of some experiment, he has killed by the perfume of a flower; a look as deep as Nature itself, but without Nature's warmth of love. Signor Giovanni, I will stake my life upon it, you are the subject of one of Rappaccini's experiments!"

"Will you make a fool of me?" cried Giovanni, passionately. "*That*, signor professor, were an untoward experiment."

"Patience! patience!" replied the imperturbable professor. "I tell thee, my poor Giovanni, that Rappaccini has a scientific interest in thee. Thou hast fallen into fearful hands! And the Signora Beatrice, — what part does she act in this mystery?"

But Guasconti, finding Baglioni's pertinacity intolerable, here broke away, and was gone before the professor could again seize his arm. He looked after the young man intently and shook his head.

"This must not be," said Baglioni to himself. "The youth is the son of my old friend, and shall not come to any harm from which the arcana of medical science can preserve him. Besides, it is too insufferable an impertinence in Rappaccini, thus to snatch the lad out of my own hands, as I may say, and make use of him for his infernal experiments. This daughter of his! It shall be looked to. Perchance, most learned Rappaccini, I may foil you where you little dream of it!"

Meanwhile Giovanni had pursued a circuitous route, and at length found himself at the door of his lodgings. As he crossed the threshold he was met by old Lisabetta, who smirked and smiled, and was evidently desirous to attract his attention; vainly, however, as the ebullition of his feelings had momentarily subsided into a cold and dull vacuity. He turned his eyes full upon the withered face that was puckering itself into a smile, but seemed to behold it not. The old dame, therefore, laid her grasp upon his cloak.

"Signor! signor!" whispered she, still with a smile over the whole breadth of her visage, so that it looked not unlike a grotesque carving in wood, darkened by centuries. "Listen, signor! There is a private entrance into the garden!"

"What do you say?" exclaimed Giovanni, turning quickly about, as if an inanimate thing should start into feverish life. "A private entrance into Dr. Rappaccini's garden?"

"Hush! hush! not so loud!" whispered Lisabetta, putting her hand over his mouth. "Yes; into the worshipful doctor's garden, where you may see all his fine shrubbery. Many a young man in Padua would give gold to be admitted among those flowers."

Giovanni put a piece of gold into her hand.

"Show me the way," said he.

A surmise, probably excited by his conversation with Baglioni, crossed his mind, that this interposition of old Lisabetta might perchance be connected with the intrigue, whatever were its nature, in which the professor seemed to suppose that Dr. Rappaccini was involving him. But such a suspicion, though it disturbed Giovanni, was inadequate to restrain him. The instant that he was aware of the possibility of approaching Beatrice, it seemed an absolute necessity of his existence to do so. It mattered not whether she were angel or demon; he was irrevocably within her sphere, and must obey the law that whirled him onward, in ever-lessening circles, towards a result which he did not attempt to foreshadow; and yet, strange to say, there came across him a sudden doubt whether this intense interest on his part were not delusory; whether it were really of so deep and positive a nature as to justify him in now thrusting himself into an incalculable position; whether it were not merely the fantasy of a young man's brain, only slightly or not at all connected with his heart.

He paused, hesitated, turned half about, but again went on. His withered guide led him along several obscure passages, and finally undid a door, through which, as it was opened, there came the sight and sound of rustling leaves, with the broken sunshine glimmering among them. Giovanni stepped forth, and, forcing himself through the entanglement of a shrub that wreathed its tendrils over the hidden entrance, stood beneath his own window in the open area of Dr. Rappaccini's garden.

How often is it the case that, when impossibilities have come to pass and dreams have condensed their misty substance into tangible realities, we find ourselves calm, and even coldly self-possessed, amid circumstances which it would have been a delirium of joy or agony to anticipate! Fate delights to thwart us thus. Passion will choose his own time to rush upon the scene, and lingers sluggishly behind when an appropriate adjustment of events would seem to summon his appearance. So was it now with Giovanni. Day after day his pulses had throbbed with feverish blood at the improbable idea of an interview with Beatrice, and of standing with her, face to face, in this very garden, basking in the Oriental sunshine of her beauty, and snatching from her full gaze the mystery which he deemed the riddle of his own existence. But now there was a singular and untimely equanimity within his breast. He threw a glance around the garden to discover if Beatrice or her father were present, and, perceiving that he was alone, began a critical observation of the plants.

The aspect of one and all of them dissatisfied him; their gorgeousness seemed fierce, passionate, and even unnatural. There was hardly an individual shrub which a wanderer, straying by himself through a forest, would not have been startled to find growing wild, as if an unearthly face had glared at him out of the thicket. Several also would have shocked a delicate instinct by an appearance of artificialness indicating that there had been such commixture, and, as it were, adultery, of various vegetable species, that the production was no longer of God's making, but the monstrous offspring of man's depraved fancy, glowing with only an evil mockery of beauty. They were probably the result of experiment, which in one or two cases had succeeded in mingling plants individually lovely into a compound possessing the questionable and ominous character that distinguished the whole growth of the garden. In fine, Giovanni recognized but two or three plants in the collection, and those of a kind that he well knew to be poisonous. While busy with these contemplations he heard the rustling of a silken garment, and, turning, beheld Beatrice emerging from beneath the sculptured portal.

Giovanni had not considered with himself what should be his deportment; whether he should apologize for his intrusion into the garden, or assume that he was there with the privity at least, if not by the desire, of Dr. Rappaccini or his daughter; but Beatrice's manner placed him at his ease, though leaving him still in doubt by what agency he had gained admittance. She came lightly along the path and met him near the broken fountain. There was surprise in her face, but brightened by a simple and kind expression of pleasure.

"You are a connoisseur in flowers, signor," said Beatrice, with a smile, alluding to the bouquet which he had flung her from the window. "It is no marvel, therefore, if the sight of my father's rare collection has tempted you to take a nearer view. If he were here, he could tell you many strange and interesting facts as to the nature and habits of these shrubs; for he has spent a lifetime in such studies, and this garden is his world."

"And yourself, lady," observed Giovanni, "if fame says true, — you likewise are deeply skilled in the virtues indicated by these rich blossoms and these spicy perfumes. Would you deign to be my instructress, I should prove an apter scholar than if taught by Signor Rappaccini himself."

"Are there such idle rumors?" asked Beatrice, with the music of a pleasant laugh. "Do people say that I am skilled in my father's science of plants? What a jest is there! No; though I have grown up among these flowers, I know no more of them than their hues and perfume; and sometimes methinks I would fain rid myself of even that small knowledge. There are many flowers here, and those not the least brilliant, that shock and offend me when they meet my eye. But pray, signor, do not believe these stories about my science. Believe nothing of me save what you see with your own eyes."

"And must I believe all that I have seen with my own eyes?" asked

Giovanni, pointedly, while the recollection of former scenes made him shrink. "No, signora; you demand too little of me. Bid me believe nothing save what comes from your own lips."

It would appear that Beatrice understood him. There came a deep flush to her cheek; but she looked full into Giovanni's eyes, and responded to his gaze of uneasy suspicion with a queenlike haughtiness.

"I do so bid you, signor," she replied. "Forget whatever you may have fancied in regard to me. If true to the outward senses, still it may be false in its essence; but the words of Beatrice Rappaccini's lips are true from the depths of the heart outward. Those you may believe."

A fervor glowed in her whole aspect and beamed upon Giovanni's consciousness like the light of truth itself; but while she spoke there was a fragrance in the atmosphere around her, rich and delightful, though evanescent, yet which the young man, from an indefinable reluctance, scarcely dared to draw into his lungs. It might be the odor of the flowers. Could it be Beatrice's breath which thus embalmed her words with a strange richness, as if by steeping them in her heart? A faintness passed like a shadow over Giovanni and flitted away; he seemed to gaze through the beautiful girl's eyes into her transparent soul, and felt no more doubt or fear.

The tinge of passion that had colored Beatrice's manner vanished; she became gay, and appeared to derive a pure delight from her communion with the youth not unlike what the maiden of a lonely island might have felt conversing with a voyager from the civilized world. Evidently her experience of life had been confined within the limits of that garden. She talked now about matters as simple as the daylight or summer clouds, and now asked questions in reference to the city, or Giovanni's distant home, his friends, his mother, and his sisters — questions indicating such seclusion, and such lack of familiarity with modes and forms, that Giovanni responded as if to an infant. Her spirit gushed out before him like a fresh rill that was just catching its first glimpse of the sunlight and wondering at the reflections of earth and sky which were flung into its bosom. There came thoughts, too, from a deep source, and fantasies of a gemlike brilliancy, as if diamonds and rubies sparkled upward among the bubbles of the fountain. Ever and anon there gleamed across the young man's mind a sense of wonder that he should be walking side by side with the being who had so wrought upon his imagination, whom he had idealized in such hues of terror, in whom he had positively witnessed such manifestations of dreadful attributes, — that he should be conversing with Beatrice like a brother, and should find her so human and so maidenlike. But such reflections were only momentary; the effect of her character was too real not to make itself familiar at once.

In this free intercourse they had strayed through the garden, and now, after many turns among its avenues, were come to the shattered fountain, beside which grew the magnificent shrub, with its treasury of glowing blossoms. A fragrance was diffused from it which Giovanni recognized as identical with that which he had attributed to Beatrice's breath, but incomparably more powerful. As her eyes fell upon it, Giovanni beheld her press her hand to her bosom as if her heart were throbbing suddenly and painfully.

"For the first time in my life," murmured she, addressing the shrub, "I had forgotten thee."

"I remember, signora," said Giovanni, "that you once promised to reward me with one of these living gems for the bouquet which I had the happy boldness to fling to your feet. Permit me now to pluck it as a memorial of this interview."

He made a step towards the shrub with extended hand; but Beatrice darted forward, uttering a shriek that went through his heart like a dagger. She caught his hand and drew it back with the whole force of her slender figure. Giovanni felt her touch thrilling through his fibres.

"Touch it not!" exclaimed she, in a voice of agony. "Not for thy life! It is fatal!"

Then, hiding her face, she fled from him and vanished beneath the sculptured portal. As Giovanni followed her with his eyes, he beheld the emaciated figure and pale intelligence of Dr. Rappaccini, who had been watching the scene, he knew not how long, within the shadow of the entrance.

No sooner was Guasconti alone in his chamber than the image of Beatrice came back to his passionate musings, invested with all the witchery that had been gathering around it ever since his first glimpse of her, and now likewise imbued with a tender warmth of girlish womanhood. She was human; her nature was endowed with all gentle and feminine qualities; she was worthiest to be worshipped; she was capable, surely, on her part, of the height and heroism of love. Those

tokens which he had hitherto considered as proofs of a frightful peculiarity in her physical and moral system were now either forgotten, or,
by the subtle sophistry of passion transmitted into a golden crown of
enchantment, rendering Beatrice the more admirable by so much as
she was the more unique. Whatever had looked ugly was now beautiful; or, if incapable of such a change, it stole away and hid itself among
those shapeless half ideas which throng the dim region beyond the
daylight of our perfect consciousness. Thus did he spend the night,
nor fell asleep until the dawn had begun to awake the slumbering
flowers in Dr. Rappaccini's garden, whither Giovanni's dreams doubtless led him. Up rose the sun in his due season, and, flinging his beams
upon the young man's eyelids, awoke him to a sense of pain. When
thoroughly aroused, he became sensible of a burning and tingling
agony in his hand — in his right hand — the very hand which
Beatrice had grasped in her own when he was on the point of plucking
one of the gemlike flowers. On the back of that hand there was now a
purple print like that of four small fingers, and the likeness of a slender
thumb upon his wrist.

Oh, how stubbornly does love, — or even that cunning semblance
of love which flourishes in the imagination, but strikes no depth of
root into the heart, — how stubbornly does it hold its faith until the
moment comes when it is doomed to vanish into thin mist! Giovanni
wrapped a handkerchief about his hand and wondered what evil thing
had stung him, and soon forgot his pain in a reverie of Beatrice.

After the first interview, a second was in the inevitable course of
what we call fate. A third; a fourth; and a meeting with Beatrice in the
garden was no longer an incident in Giovanni's daily life, but the
whole space in which he might be said to live; for the anticipation and
memory of that ecstatic hour made up the remainder. Nor was it
otherwise with the daughter of Rappaccini. She watched for the
youth's appearance, and flew to his side with confidence as unreserved
as if they had been playmates from early infancy — as if they were such
playmates still. If, by any unwonted chance, he failed to come at the
appointed moment, she stood beneath the window and sent up the
rich sweetness of her tones to float around him in his chamber and
echo and reverberate throughout his heart: "Giovanni! Giovanni!
Why tarriest thou? Come down!" And down he hastened into that
Eden of poisonous flowers.

But, with all this intimate familiarity, there was still a reserve in Beatrice's demeanor, so rigidly and invariably sustained that the idea of infringing it scarcely occurred to his imagination. By all appreciable signs, they loved; they had looked love with eyes that conveyed the holy secret from the depths of one soul into the depths of the other, as if it were too sacred to be whispered by the way; they had even spoken love in those gushes of passion when their spirits darted forth in articulated breath like tongues of long-hidden flame; and yet there had been no seal of lips, no clasp of hands, nor any slightest caress such as love claims and hallows. He had never touched one of the gleaming ringlets of her hair; her garment — so marked was the physical barrier between them — had never been waved against him by a breeze. On the few occasions when Giovanni had seemed tempted to overstep the limit, Beatrice grew so sad, so stern, and withal wore such a look of desolate separation, shuddering at itself, that not a spoken word was requisite to repel him. At such times he was startled at the horrible suspicions that rose, monster-like, out of the caverns of his heart and stared him in the face; his love grew thin and faint as the morning mist, his doubts alone had substance. But, when Beatrice's face brightened again after the momentary shadow, she was transformed at once from the mysterious, questionable being whom he had watched with so much awe and horror; she was now the beautiful and unsophisticated girl whom he felt that his spirit knew with a certainty beyond all other knowledge.

A considerable time had now passed since Giovanni's last meeting with Baglioni. One morning, however, he was disagreeably surprised by a visit from the professor, whom he had scarcely thought of for whole weeks, and would willingly have forgotten still longer. Given up as he had long been to a pervading excitement, he could tolerate no companions except upon condition of their perfect sympathy with his present state of feeling. Such sympathy was not to be expected from Professor Baglioni.

The visitor chatted carelessly for a few moments about the gossip of the city and the university, and then took up another topic.

"I have been reading an old classic author lately," said he, "and met with a story that strangely interested me. Possibly you may remember it. It is of an Indian prince, who sent a beautiful woman as a present to Alexander the Great. She was as lovely as the dawn and gorgeous as the sunset; but what especially distinguished her was a certain rich perfume in her breath — richer than a garden of Persian roses. Alexander, as was natural to a youthful conqueror, fell in love at first sight with this magnificent stranger; but a certain sage physician, happening to be present, discovered a terrible secret in regard to her."

"And what was that?" asked Giovanni, turning his eyes downward to avoid those of the professor.

"That this lovely woman," continued Baglioni, with emphasis, "had been nourished with poisons from her birth upward, until her whole nature was so imbued with them that she herself had become the deadliest poison in existence. Poison was her element of life. With that rich perfume of her breath she blasted the very air. Her love would have been poison — her embrace death. Is not this a marvellous tale?"

"A childish fable," answered Giovanni, nervously starting from his chair. "I marvel how your worship finds time to read such nonsense among your graver studies."

"By the by," said the professor, looking uneasily about him, "what singular fragrance is this in your apartment? Is it the perfume of your gloves? It is faint, but delicious; and yet, after all, by no means agreeable. Were I to breathe it long, methinks it would make me ill. It is like the breath of a flower; but I see no flowers in the chamber."

"Nor are there any," replied Giovanni, who had turned pale as the professor spoke; "nor, I think, is there any fragrance except in your worship's imagination. Odors, being a sort of element combined of the sensual and the spiritual, are apt to deceive us in this manner. The recollection of a perfume, the bare idea of it, may easily be mistaken for a present reality."

"Ay; but my sober imagination does not often play such tricks," said Baglioni; "and, were I to fancy any kind of odor, it would be that of some vile apothecary drug, wherewith my fingers are likely enough to be imbued. Our worshipful friend Rappaccini, as I have heard, tinctures his medicaments with odors richer than those of Araby. Doubtless, likewise, the fair and learned Signora Beatrice would minister to her patients with draughts as sweet as a maiden's breath; but woe to him that sips them!"

Giovanni's face evinced many contending emotions. The tone in which the professor alluded to the pure and lovely daughter of Rappaccini was a torture to his soul; and yet the intimation of a view of her character, opposite to his own, gave instantaneous distinctness to a thousand dim suspicions, which now grinned at him like so many demons. But he strove hard to quell them and to respond to Baglioni with a true lover's perfect faith.

"Signor professor," said he, "you were my father's friend; perchance, too, it is your purpose to act a friendly part towards his son. I would fain feel nothing towards you save respect and deference; but I pray you to observe, signor, that there is one subject on which we must not speak. You know not the Signora Beatrice. You cannot, therefore, estimate the wrong — the blasphemy, I may even say — that is offered to her character by a light or injurious word."

"Giovanni! my poor Giovanni!" answered the professor, with a calm expression of pity, "I know this wretched girl far better than yourself. You shall hear the truth in respect to the poisoner Rappaccini and his poisonous daughter; yes, poisonous as she is beautiful. Listen; for, even should you do violence to my gray hairs, it shall not silence me. That old fable of the Indian woman has become a truth by the deep and deadly science of Rappaccini and in the person of the lovely Beatrice."

Giovanni groaned and hid his face.

"Her father," continued Baglioni, "was not restrained by natural affection from offering up his child in this horrible manner as the victim of his insane zeal for science; for, let us do him justice, he is as true a man of science as ever distilled his own heart in an alembic. What, then, will be your fate? Beyond a doubt you are selected as the material of some new experiment. Perhaps the result is to be death; perhaps a fate more awful still. Rappaccini, with what he calls the interest of science before his eyes, will hesitate at nothing."

"It is a dream," muttered Giovanni to himself; "surely it is a dream."

"But," resumed the professor, "be of good cheer, son of my friend. It is not yet too late for the rescue. Possibly we may even succeed in bringing back this miserable child within the limits of ordinary nature, from which her father's madness has estranged her. Behold this little silver vase! It was wrought by the hands of the renowned Benvenuto Cellini, and is well worthy to be a love gift to the fairest dame in Italy. But its contents are invaluable. One little sip of this antidote would have rendered the most virulent poisons of the Borgias innocuous. Doubt not that it will be as efficacious against those of Rappaccini. Bestow the vase, and the precious liquid within it, on your Beatrice, and hopefully await the result."

Baglioni laid a small, exquisitely wrought silver vial on the table and withdrew, leaving what he had said to produce its effect upon the young man's mind.

"We will thwart Rappaccini yet," thought he, chuckling to himself, as he descended the stairs; "but, let us confess the truth of him, he is a wonderful man — a wonderful man indeed; a vile empiric, however, in his practice, and therefore not to be tolerated by those who respect the good old rules of the medical profession."

Throughout Giovanni's whole acquaintance with Beatrice, he had occasionally, as we have said, been haunted by dark surmises as to her character; yet so thoroughly had she made herself felt by him as a simple, natural, most affectionate, and guileless creature, that the image now held up by Professor Baglioni looked as strange and incredible as if it were not in accordance with his own original conception. True, there were ugly recollections connected with his first glimpses of the beautiful girl; he could not quite forget the bouquet that withered in her grasp, and the insect that perished amid the sunny air, by no ostensible agency save the fragrance of her breath. These incidents, however, dissolving in the pure light of her character, had no longer the efficacy of facts, but were acknowledged as mistaken fantasies, by whatever testimony of the senses they might appear to be substantiated. There is something truer and more real than what we can see with the eyes and touch with the finger. On such better evidence had Giovanni founded his confidence in Beatrice, though rather by the necessary force of her high attributes than by any deep and generous faith on his part. But now his spirit was incapable of sustaining itself at the height to which the early enthusiasm of passion had exalted it; he fell down, grovelling among earthly doubts, and defiled therewith the pure whiteness of Beatrice's image. Not that he gave her up; he did but distrust. He resolved to institute some decisive test that should satisfy him, once for all, whether there were those dreadful peculiarities in her physical nature which could not be supposed to exist without some corresponding monstrosity of soul. His eyes, gazing down afar, might have deceived him as to the lizard, the insect, and the flowers; but if he could witness, at the distance of a few paces, the sudden blight of one fresh and healthful flower in Beatrice's hand, there would be room for no further question. With this idea he hastened to the florist's and purchased a bouquet that was still gemmed with the morning dew-drops.

It was now the customary hour of his daily interview with Beatrice. Before descending into the garden, Giovanni failed not to look at his figure in the mirror, — a vanity to be expected in a beautiful young man, yet, as displaying itself at that troubled and feverish moment, the token of a certain shallowness of feeling and insincerity of charac-ter. He did gaze, however, and said to himself that his features had never before possessed so rich a grace, nor his eyes such vivacity, nor his cheeks so warm a hue of superabundant life.

"At least," thought he, "her poison has not yet insinuated itself into my system. I am no flower to perish in her grasp."

With that thought he turned his eyes on the bouquet, which he had never once laid aside from his hand. A thrill of indefinable horror shot through his frame on perceiving that those dewy flowers were already beginning to droop; they wore the aspect of things that had been fresh and lovely yesterday. Giovanni grew white as marble, and stood motionless before the mirror, staring at his own reflection there as at the likeness of something frightful. He remembered Baglioni's remark about the fragrance that seemed to pervade the chamber. It must have been the poison in his breath! Then he shuddered — shuddered at himself. Recovering from his stupor, he began to watch with curious eye a spider that was busily at work hanging its web from the antique cornice of the apartment, crossing and recrossing the artful system of interwoven lines — as vigorous and active a spider as ever dangled from an old ceiling. Giovanni bent towards the insect, and emitted a deep, long breath. The spider suddenly ceased its toil; the web vi-brated with a tremor originating in the body of the small artisan. Again Giovanni sent forth a breath, deeper, longer, and imbued with a venomous feeling out of his heart: he knew not whether he were wicked, or only desperate. The spider made a convulsive gripe with his limbs and hung dead across the window.

"Accursed! accursed!" muttered Giovanni, addressing himself. "Hast thou grown so poisonous that this deadly insect perishes by thy breath?"

At that moment a rich, sweet voice came floating up from the garden.

"Giovanni! Giovanni! It is past the hour! Why tarriest thou? Come down!"

"Yes," muttered Giovanni again. "She is the only being whom my breath may not slay! Would that it might!"

He rushed down, and in an instant was standing before the bright and loving eyes of Beatrice. A moment ago his wrath and despair had been so fierce that he could have desired nothing so much as to wither her by a glance; but with her actual presence there came influences which had too real an existence to be at once shaken off: recollections of the delicate and benign power of her feminine nature, which had so often enveloped him in a religious calm; recollections of many a holy and passionate outgush of her heart, when the pure fountain had been unsealed from its depths and made visible in its transparency to his mental eye; recollections which, had Giovanni known how to estimate them, would have assured him that all this ugly mystery was but an earthly illusion, and that, whatever mist of evil might seem to have gathered over her, the real Beatrice was a heavenly angel. Incapable as he was of such high faith, still her presence had not utterly lost its magic. Giovanni's rage was quelled into an aspect of sullen insensibility. Beatrice, with a quick spiritual sense, immediately felt that there was a gulf of blackness between them which neither he nor she could pass. They walked on together, sad and silent, and came thus to the marble fountain and to its pool of water on the ground, in the midst of which grew the shrub that bore gem-like blossoms. Giovanni was affrighted at the eager enjoyment — the appetite, as it were — with which he found himself inhaling the fragrance of the flowers.

"Beatrice," asked he, abruptly, "whence came this shrub?"

"My father created it," answered she, with simplicity.

"Created it! created it!" repeated Giovanni. "What mean you, Beatrice?"

"He is a man fearfully acquainted with the secrets of Nature," replied Beatrice; "and, at the hour when I first drew breath, this plant sprang from the soil, the offspring of his science, of his intellect, while I was but his earthly child. Approach it not!" continued she, observing with terror that Giovanni was drawing nearer to the shrub. "It has qualities that you little dream of. But I, dearest Giovanni, — I grew up and blossomed with the plant and was nourished with its breath. It was my sister, and I loved it with a human affection; for, alas! — hast thou not suspected it? — there was an awful doom."

Here Giovanni frowned so darkly upon her that Beatrice paused and trembled. But her faith in his tenderness reassured her, and made her blush that she had doubted for an instant.

"There was an awful doom," she continued, "the effect of my father's fatal love of science, which estranged me from all society of my kind. Until Heaven sent thee, dearest Giovanni, oh, how lonely was thy poor Beatrice!"

"Was it a hard doom?" asked Giovanni, fixing his eyes upon her.

"Only of late have I known how hard it was," answered she, tenderly. "Oh, yes; but my heart was torpid, and therefore quiet."

Giovanni's rage broke forth from his sullen gloom like a lightning flash out of a dark cloud.

"Accursed one!" cried he, with venomous scorn and anger. "And, finding thy solitude wearisome, thou hast severed me likewise from all the warmth of life and enticed me into thy region of unspeakable horror!"

"Giovanni!" exclaimed Beatrice, turning her large bright eyes upon his face. The force of his words had not found its way into her mind; she was merely thunderstruck.

"Yes, poisonous thing!" repeated Giovanni, beside himself with passion. "Thou hast done it! Thou hast blasted me! Thou hast filled my veins with poison! Thou hast made me as hateful, as ugly, as loathsome and deadly a creature as thyself — a world's wonder of hideous monstrosity! Now, if our breath be happily as fatal to ourselves as to all others, let us join our lips in one kiss of unutterable hatred, and so die!"

"What has befallen me?" murmured Beatrice, with a low moan out of her heart. "Holy Virgin, pity me, a poor heart-broken child!"

"Thou, — dost thou pray?" cried Giovanni, still with the same fiendish scorn. "Thy very prayers, as they come from thy lips, taint the atmosphere with death. Yes, yes; let us pray! Let us to church and dip our fingers in the holy water at the portal! They that come after us will perish as by a pestilence! Let us sign crosses in the air! It will be scattering curses abroad in the likeness of holy symbols!"

"Giovanni," said Beatrice, calmly, for her grief was beyond passion, "why dost thou join thyself with me thus in those terrible words? I, it is true, am the horrible thing thou namest me. But thou, — what hast thou to do, save with one other shudder at my hideous misery to go forth out of the garden and mingle with thy race, and forget that there ever crawled on earth such a monster as poor Beatrice?"

"Dost thou pretend ignorance?" asked Giovanni, scowling upon her. "Behold! this power have I gained from the pure daughter of Rappaccini."

There was a swarm of summer insects flitting through the air in search of the food promised by the flower odors of the fatal garden. They circled round Giovanni's head, and were evidently attracted towards him by the same influence which had drawn them for an instant within the sphere of several of the shrubs. He sent forth a breath among them, and smiled bitterly at Beatrice as at least a score of the insects fell dead upon the ground.

"I see it! I see it!" shrieked Beatrice. "It is my father's fatal science! No, no, Giovanni; it was not I! Never! never! I dreamed only to love thee and be with thee a little time, and so to let thee pass away, leaving but thine image in mine heart; for, Giovanni, believe it, though my body be nourished with poison, my spirit is God's creature, and craves love as its daily food. But my father, — he has united us in this fearful sympathy. Yes; spurn me, tread upon me, kill me! Oh, what is death after such words as thine? But it was not I. Not for a world of bliss would I have done it."

Giovanni's passion had exhausted itself in its outburst from his lips. There now came across him a sense, mournful, and not without tenderness, of the intimate and peculiar relationship between Beatrice and himself. They stood, as it were, in an utter solitude, which would be made none the less solitary by the densest throng of human life. Ought not, then, the desert of humanity around them to press this insulated pair closer together? If they should be cruel to one another, who was there to be kind to them? Besides, thought Giovanni, might there not still be a hope of his returning within the limits of ordinary nature, and leading Beatrice, the redeemed Beatrice, by the hand? O, weak, and selfish, and unworthy spirit, that could dream of an earthly union and earthly happiness as possible, after such deep love had been so bitterly wronged as was Beatrice's love by Giovanni's blighting words! No, no; there could be no such hope. She must pass heavily, with that broken heart, across the borders of Time — she must bathe her hurts in some fount of paradise, and forget her grief in the light of immortality, and *there* be well.

But Giovanni did not know it.

"Dear Beatrice," said he, approaching her, while she shrank away as always at his approach, but now with a different impulse, "dearest Beatrice, our fate is not yet so desperate. Behold! there is a medicine, potent, as a wise physician has assured me, and almost divine in its efficacy. It is composed of ingredients the most opposite to those by which thy awful father has brought this calamity upon thee and me. It is distilled of blessed herbs. Shall we not quaff it together, and thus be purified from evil?"

"Give it me!" said Beatrice, extending her hand to receive the little silver vial which Giovanni took from his bosom. She added, with a peculiar emphasis, "I will drink; but do thou await the result."

She put Baglioni's antidote to her lips; and, at the same moment, the figure of Rappaccini emerged from the portal and came slowly towards the marble fountain. As he drew near, the pale man of science seemed to gaze with a triumphant expression at the beautiful youth and maiden, as might an artist who should spend his life in achieving a picture or a group of statuary and finally be satisfied with his success. He paused; his bent form grew erect with conscious power; he spread out his hands over them in the attitude of a father imploring a blessing upon his children; but those were the same hands that had thrown poison into the stream of their lives. Giovanni trembled. Beatrice shuddered nervously, and pressed her hand upon her heart.

"My daughter," said Rappaccini, "thou art no longer lonely in the world. Pluck one of those precious gems from thy sister shrub and bid thy bridegroom wear it in his bosom. It will not harm him now. My science and the sympathy between thee and him have so wrought within his system that he now stands apart from common men, as thou dost, daughter of my pride and triumph, from ordinary women. Pass on, then, through the world, most dear to one another and dreadful to all besides!"

"My father," said Beatrice, feebly, — and still as she spoke she kept her hand upon her heart, — "wherefore didst thou inflict this miserable doom upon thy child?"

"Miserable!" exclaimed Rappaccini. "What mean you, foolish girl? Dost thou deem it misery to be endowed with marvellous gifts against which no power nor strength could avail an enemy — misery, to be able to quell the mightiest with a breath — misery, to be as terrible as thou art beautiful? Wouldst thou, then, have preferred the condition of a weak woman, exposed to all evil and capable of none?"

"I would fain have been loved, not feared," murmured Beatrice, sinking down upon the ground. "But now it matters not. I am going, father, where the evil which thou hast striven to mingle with my being will pass away like a dream — like the fragrance of these poisonous flowers, which will no longer taint my breath among the flowers of Eden. Farewell, Giovanni! Thy words of hatred are like lead within my heart; but they, too, will fall away as I ascend. Oh, was there not, from the first, more poison in thy nature than in mine?"

To Beatrice, — so radically had her earthly part been wrought upon by Rappaccini's skill, — as poison had been life, so the powerful antidote was death; and thus the poor victim of man's ingenuity and of thwarted nature, and of the fatality that attends all such efforts of perverted wisdom, perished there, at the feet of her father and Giovanni. Just at that moment Professor Pietro Baglioni looked forth from the window, and called loudly, in a tone of triumph mixed with horror, to the thunderstricken man of science, —

"Rappaccini! Rappaccini! and is *this* the upshot of your experiment!"

The Piazza

by Herman Melville

"With fairest flowers,
Whilst summer lasts, and I live here, Fidele —"

WHEN I REMOVED into the country, it was to occupy an old-fashioned farmhouse, which had no piazza — a deficiency the more regretted because not only did I like piazzas, as somehow combining the coziness of indoors with the freedom of outdoors, and it is so pleasant to inspect your thermometer there, but the country round about was such a picture that in berry time no boy climbs hill or crosses vale without coming upon easels planted in every nook, and sunburnt painters painting there. A very paradise of painters. The circle of the stars cut by the circle of the mountains. At least, so looks it from the house; though, once upon the mountains, no circle of them can you see. Had the site been chosen five rods off, this charmed ring would not have been.

The house is old. Seventy years since, from the heart of the Hearth Stone Hills, they quarried the Kaaba, or Holy Stone, to which, each Thanksgiving, the social pilgrims used to come. So long ago that, in digging for the foundation, the workmen used both spade and ax, fighting the troglodytes of those subterranean parts — sturdy roots of a sturdy wood, encamped upon what is now a long landslide of sleeping meadow, sloping away off from my poppybed. Of that knit wood but one survivor stands — an elm, lonely through steadfastness.

Whoever built the house, he builded better than he knew, or else

Orion in the zenith flashed down his Damocles' sword to him some starry night and said, "Build there." For how, otherwise, could it have entered the builder's mind, that, upon the clearing being made, such a purple prospect would be his? — nothing less than Greylock, with all his hills about him, like Charlemagne among his peers.

Now, for a house, so situated in such a country, to have no piazza for the convenience of those who might desire to feast upon the view, and take their time and ease about it, seemed as much of an omission as if a picture gallery should have no bench; for what but picture galleries are the marble halls of these same limestone hills? — galleries hung, month after month anew, with pictures ever fading into pictures ever fresh. And beauty is like piety — you cannot run and read it; tranquillity and constancy, with, nowadays, an easy chair, are needed. For though, of old, when reverence was in vogue and indolence was not, the devotees of Nature doubtless used to stand and adore — just as, in the cathedrals of those ages, the worshipers of a higher Power did — yet, in these times of failing faith and feeble knees, we have the piazza and the pew.

During the first year of my residence, the more leisurely to witness the coronation of Charlemagne (weather permitting, they crown him every sunrise and sunset), I chose me, on the hillside bank near by, a royal lounge of turf — a green velvet lounge, with long, moss-padded back; while at the head, strangely enough, there grew (but, I suppose, for heraldry) three tufts of blue violets in a field argent of wild strawberries; and a trellis, with honeysuckle, I set for canopy. Very majestical lounge, indeed. So much so that here, as with the reclining majesty of Denmark in his orchard, a sly earache invaded me. But, if damps abound at times in Westminster Abbey because it is so old, why not within this monastery of mountains, which is older?

A piazza must be had.

The house was wide, my fortune narrow, so that, to build a panoramic piazza, one round and round, it could not be — although, indeed, considering the matter by rule and square, the carpenters, in the kindest way, were anxious to gratify my furthest wishes, at I've forgotten how much a foot.

Upon but one of the four sides would prudence grant me what I wanted. Now, which side?

To the east, that long camp of the Hearth Stone Hills, fading far away towards Quito, and every fall, a small white flake of something peering suddenly, of a coolish morning, from the topmost cliff — the season's new-dropped lamb, its earliest fleece; and then the Christmas dawn, draping those dun highlands with red-barred plaids and tartans — goodly sight from your piazza, that. Goodly sight; but, to the north is Charlemagne — can't have the Hearth Stone Hills with Charlemagne.

Well, the south side. Apple trees are there. Pleasant, of a balmy morning in the month of May, to sit and see that orchard, white-budded, as for a bridal; and, in October, one green arsenal yard, such piles of ruddy shot. Very fine, I grant; but, to the north is Charlemagne.

The west side, look. An upland pasture, alleying away into a maple wood at top. Sweet, in opening spring, to trace upon the hillside, otherwise gray and bare — to trace, I say, the oldest paths by their streaks of earliest green. Sweet, indeed, I can't deny; but, to the north is Charlemagne.

So Charlemagne, he carried it. It was not long after 1848, and, somehow, about that time, all round the world these kings, they had the casting vote, and voted for themselves.

No sooner was ground broken than all the neighborhood, neighbor Dives, in particular, broke, too — into a laugh. Piazza to the north! Winter piazza! Wants, of winter midnights, to watch the Aurora Borealis, I suppose; hope he's laid in good store of polar muffs and mittens.

That was in the lion month of March. Not forgotten are the blue noses of the carpenters, and how they scouted at the greenness of the cit, who would build his sole piazza to the north. But March don't last forever; patience, and August comes. And then, in the cool elysium of my northern bower, I, Lazarus in Abraham's bosom, cast down the hill a pitying glance on poor old Dives, tormented in the purgatory of his piazza to the south.

But, even in December, this northern piazza does not repel — nipping cold and gusty though it be, and the north wind, like any miller, bolting by the snow in finest flour — for then, once more, with frosted beard, I pace the sleety deck, weathering Cape Horn.

In summer, too, Canute-like, sitting here, one is often reminded of the sea. For not only do long ground swells roll the slanting grain, and little wavelets of the grass ripple over upon the low piazza, as their beach, and the blown down of dandelions is wafted like the spray, and the purple of the mountains is just the purple of the billows, and a still August noon broods upon the deep meadows as a calm upon the Line, but the vastness and the lonesomeness are so oceanic, and the silence and the sameness, too, that the first peep of a strange house, rising beyond the trees, is for all the world like spying, on the Barbary coast, an unknown sail.

And this recalls my inland voyage to fairyland. A true voyage, but, take it all in all, interesting as if invented.

From the piazza, some uncertain object I had caught, mysteriously snugged away, to all appearance, in a sort of purpled breast pocket, high up in a hopperlike hollow or sunken angle among the northwestern mountains — yet, whether, really, it was on a mountainside or a mountaintop could not be determined; because, though, viewed from favorable points, a blue summit, peering up away behind the rest, will, as it were, talk to you over their heads, and plainly tell you, that, though he (the blue summit) seems among them, he is not of them (God forbid!), and, indeed, would have you know that he considers himself — as, to say truth, he has good right — by several cubits their superior, nevertheless, certain ranges, here and there double-filed, as in platoons, so shoulder and follow up upon one another, with their irregular shapes and heights, that, from the piazza, a nigher and lower mountain will, in most states of the atmosphere, effacingly shade itself away into a higher and further one; that an object, bleak on the former's crest, will, for all that, appear nested in the latter's flank. These mountains, somehow, they play at hide-and-seek, and all before one's eyes.

But, be that as it may, the spot in question was, at all events, so situated as to be only visible, and then but vaguely, under certain witching conditions of light and shadow.

Indeed, for a year or more, I knew not there was such a spot, and might, perhaps, have never known, had it not been for a wizard afternoon in autumn — late in autumn — a mad poet's afternoon, when the turned maple woods in the broad basin below me, having lost their first vermilion tint, dully smoked, like smoldering towns, when flames expire upon their prey; and rumor had it that this smokiness in the general air was not all Indian summer — which was not used to be so sick a thing, however mild — but, in great part, was blown from far-off forests, for weeks on fire, in Vermont; so that no wonder the sky was ominous as Hecate's caldron — and two sports-men, crossing a red stubble buckwheat field, seemed guilty Macbeth and foreboding Banquo; and the hermit sun, hutted in an Adullum cave, well towards the south, according to his season, did little else but, by indirect reflection of narrow rays shot down a Simplon Pass among the clouds, just steadily paint one small, round strawberry mole upon the wan cheek of northwestern hills. Signal as a candle. One spot of radiance, where all else was shade.

Fairies there, thought I; some haunted ring where fairies dance.

Time passed, and the following May, after a gentle shower upon the mountains — a little shower islanded in misty seas of sunshine; such a distant shower — and sometimes two, and three, and four of them, all visible together in different parts — as I love to watch from the piazza, instead of thunderstorms as I used to, which wrap old Greylock like a Sinai, till one thinks swart Moses must be climbing among scathed hemlocks there; after, I say, that gentle shower, I saw a rainbow, resting its further end just where, in autumn, I had marked the mole. Fairies there, thought I; remembering that rainbows bring out the blooms, and that, if one can but get to the rainbow's end, his fortune is made in a bag of gold. Yon rainbow's end, would I were there, thought I. And none the less I wished it, for now first noticing what seemed some sort of glen, or grotto, in the mountainside; at least, whatever it was, viewed through the rainbow's medium it glowed like the Potosi mine. But a workaday neighbor said no doubt it was but some old barn — an abandoned one, its broadside beaten in, the acclivity its background. But I, though I had never been there, I knew better.

A few days after, a cheery sunrise kindled a golden sparkle in the same spot as before. The sparkle was of that vividness it seemed as if it could only come from glass. The building, then — if building, after all, it was — could, at least, not be a barn, much less an abandoned one, stale hay ten years musting in it. No; if aught built by mortal, it must be a cottage; perhaps long vacant and dismantled, but this very spring magically fitted up and glazed.

Again, one noon, in the same direction, I marked, over dimmed tops of terraced foliage, a broader gleam, as of a silver buckler held sunwards over some croucher's head; which gleam, experience in like cases taught, must come from a roof newly shingled. This, to me, made pretty sure the recent occupancy of that far cot in fairyland.

Day after day, now, full of interest in my discovery, what time I could spare from reading the *Midsummer Night's Dream*, and all about Titania, wishfully I gazed off towards the hills; but in vain. Either troops of shadows, and imperial guard, with slow pace and solemn, defiled along the steeps, or, routed by pursuing light, fled broadcast from east to west — old wars of Lucifer and Michael; or the mountains, though unvexed by these mirrored sham fights in the sky, had an atmosphere otherwise unfavorable for fairy views. I was sorry, the more so because I had to keep my chamber for some time after — which chamber did not face those hills.

At length, when pretty well again, and sitting out in the September morning upon the piazza and thinking to myself, when, just after a little flock of sheep, the farmer's banded children passed, a-nutting, and said, "How sweet a day" — it was, after all, but what their fathers call a weather-breeder — and, indeed, was become so sensitive through my illness as that I could not bear to look upon a Chinese creeper of my adoption, and which, to my delight, climbing a post of the piazza, had burst out in starry bloom, but now, if you removed the leaves a little, showed millions of strange, cankerous worms, which, feeding upon those blossoms, so shared their blessed hue as to make it unblessed evermore — worms whose germs had doubtless lurked in the very bulb which, so hopefully, I had planted: in this ingrate peevishness of my weary convalescence was I sitting there, when, suddenly looking off, I saw the golden mountain window, dazzling like a deep-sea dolphin. Fairies there, thought I, once more, the queen of fairies at her fairy-window, at any rate, some glad mountain girl; it will do me good, it will cure this weariness, to look on her. No more; I'll launch my yawl — ho, cheerly, heart! — and push away for fairyland, for rainbow's end, in fairyland.

How to get to fairyland, by what road, I did not know, nor could any one inform me, not even one Edmund Spenser, who had been there — so he wrote me — further than that to reach fairyland it must be voyaged to, and with faith. I took the fairy-mountain's bearings, and the first fine day, when strength permitted, got into my yawl — high-pommeled, leather one — cast off the fast, and away I sailed, free voyager as an autumn leaf. Early dawn, and, sallying westward, I sowed the morning before me.

Some miles brought me nigh the hills, but out of present sight of them. I was not lost, for roadside goldenrods, as guideposts, pointed, I doubted not, the way to the golden window. Following them, I came to a lone and languid region, where the grass-grown ways were traveled but by drowsy cattle, that, less waked than stirred by day, seemed to walk in sleep. Browse they did not — the enchanted never eat. At least, so says Don Quixote, that sagest sage that ever lived.

On I went, and gained at last the fairy-mountain's base, but saw yet no fairy ring. A pasture rose before me. Letting down five moldering bars — so moistly green they seemed fished up from some sunken wreck — a wigged old Aries, long-visaged and with crumpled horn, came snuffing up, and then, retreating, decorously led on along a milky-way of whiteweed, past dim-clustering Pleiades and Hyades, of small forget-me-nots, and would have led me further still his astral path but for golden flights of yellowbirds — pilots, surely, to the golden window, to one side flying before me, from bush to bush, toward deep woods — which woods themselves were luring — and, somehow, lured, too, by their fence, banning a dark road, which, however dark, led up. I pushed through, when Aries, renouncing me now for some lost soul, wheeled, and went his wiser way. Forbidding and forbidden ground — to him.

A winter wood road, matted all along with wintergreen. By the side of pebbly waters — waters the cheerier for their solitude; beneath swaying fir boughs, petted by no season but still green in all, on I journeyed — my horse and I; on, by an old sawmill bound down and hushed with vines that his grating voice no more was heard; on, by a deep flume clove through snowy marble, vernal-tinted, where freshet eddies had, on each side, spun out empty chapels in the living rock; on, where Jacks-in-the-pulpit, like their Baptist namesake, preached but to the wilderness; on, where a huge, criss-grain block, fern-bedded, showed where, in forgotten times, man after man had tried to split it, but lost his wedges for his pains — which wedges yet rusted in their holes; on, where, ages past, in steplike ledges of a cascade, skull-hollow pots had been churned out by ceaseless whirling of a flintstone — ever wearing, but itself unworn; on, by wild rapids pouring into a secret pool, but, soothed by circling there awhile, issued forth serenely; on, to less broken ground and by a little ring, where, truly, fairies must have danced, or else some wheel-tire been heated — for all was bare; still on, and up, and out into a hanging orchard, where maidenly looked down upon me a crescent moon, from morning.

My horse hitched low his head. Red apples rolled before him — Eve's apples, seek-no-furthers. He tasted one, I another; it tasted of the ground. Fairyland not yet, thought I, flinging my bridle to a humped old tree, that crooked out an arm to catch it. For the way now lay where path was none, and none might go but by himself, and only go by daring. Through blackberry brakes that tried to pluck me back, though I but strained toward fruitless growths of mountain laurel, up slippery steeps to barren heights, where stood none to welcome. Fairy-land not yet, thought I, though the morning is here before me.

Footsore enough and weary, I gained not then my journey's end, but came erelong to a craggy pass, dipping towards growing regions still beyond. A zigzag road, half overgrown with blueberry bushes, here turned among the cliffs. A rent was in their ragged sides; through it a little track branched off, which, upwards threading that short defile, came breezily out above, to where the mountaintop, part sheltered northward by a taller brother, sloped gently off a space ere darkly plunging; and here, among fantastic rocks, reposing in a herd, the foot track wound, half beaten, up to a little, low-storied, grayish cottage, capped, nunlike, with a peaked roof.

On one slope the roof was deeply weather-stained, and, nigh the turfy eaves-trough, all velvet-napped; no doubt the snail-monks founded mossy priories there. The other slope was newly shingled. On the north side, doorless and windowless, the clapboards, innocent of paint, were yet green as the north side of lichened pines, or copperless hulls of Japanese junks becalmed. The whole base, like those of the neighboring rocks, was rimmed about with shaded streaks of richest sod; for, with hearthstones in fairyland, the natural rock, though housed, preserves to the last, just as in open fields, its fertilizing charm; only, by necessity, working now at a remove, to the sward without. So, at least, says Oberon, grave authority in fairy lore. Though, setting Oberon aside, certain it is that, even in the common world, the soil close up to farmhouses, as close up to pasture rocks, is, even though untended, ever richer than it is a few rods off — such gentle, nurturing heat is radiated there.

But with this cottage the shaded streaks were richest in its front and about its entrance, where the groundsill, and especially the doorsill, had, through long eld, quietly settled down.

No fence was seen, no inclosure. Near by — ferns, ferns, ferns; further — woods, woods, woods; beyond — mountains, mountains, mountains; then — sky, sky, sky. Turned out in aerial commons, pasture for the mountain moon. Nature, and but nature, house and all; even a low cross-pile of silver birch, piled openly, to season; up among whose silvery sticks, as through the fencing of some sequestered grave, sprang vagrant raspberry bushes — willful assertors of their right of way.

The foot track, so dainty narrow, just like a sheep track, led through long ferns that lodged. Fairyland at last, thought I; Una and her lamb dwell here. Truly, a small abode — mere palanquin, set down on the summit, in a pass between two worlds, participant of neither.

A sultry hour, and I wore a light hat, of yellow sinnet, with white duck trousers — both relics of my tropic seagoing. Clogged in the muffling ferns, I softly stumbled, staining the knees a sea green.

Pausing at the threshold, or rather where threshold once had been, I saw, through the open doorway, a lonely girl, sewing at a lonely window. A pale-cheeked girl and fly-specked window, with wasps about the mended upper panes. I spoke. She shyly started, like some Tahiti girl, secreted for a sacrifice, first catching sight, through palms, of Captain Cook. Recovering, she bade me enter; with her apron brushed off a stool; then silently resumed her own. With thanks I took the stool; but now, for a space, I, too, was mute. This, then, is the fairy-mountain house, and here the fairy queen sitting at her fairy-window.

I went up to it. Downwards, directed by the tunneled pass, as through a leveled telescope, I caught sight of a far-off, soft, azure world. I hardly knew it, though I came from it.

"You must find this view very pleasant," said I, at last.

"Oh, sir," tears starting in her eyes, "the first time I looked out of this window, I said 'never, never shall I weary of this.' "

"And what wearies you of it now?"

"I don't know," while a tear fell; "but it is not the view, it is Marianna."

Some months back, her brother, only seventeen, had come hither, a long way from the other side, to cut wood and burn coal, and she, elder sister, had accompanied him. Long had they been orphans, and now sole inhabitants of the sole house upon the mountain. No guest came, no traveler passed. The zigzag, perilous road was only used at seasons by the coal wagons. The brother was absent the entire day, sometimes the entire night. When, at evening, fagged out, he did come home, he soon left his bench, poor fellow, for his bed, just as one, at last, wearily quits that, too, for still deeper rest. The bench, the bed, the grave.

Silent I stood by the fairy-window, while these things were being told.

"Do you know," said she at last, as stealing from her story, "do you know who lives yonder? — I have never been down into that country — away off there, I mean; that house, that marble one," pointing far across the lower landscape; "have you not caught it? there, on the long hillside: the field before, the woods behind; the white shines out against their blue; don't you mark it? the only house in sight."

I looked, and, after a time, to my surprise, recognized, more by its position than its aspect or Marianna's description, my own abode, glimmering much like this mountain one from the piazza. The mirage haze made it appear less a farmhouse than King Charming's palace.

"I have often wondered who lives there; but it must be some happy one; again this morning was I thinking so."

"Some happy one," returned I, starting; "and why do you think that? You judge some rich one lives there?"

"Rich or not, I never thought, but it looks so happy, I can't tell how, and it is so far away. Sometimes I think I do but dream it is there. You should see it in a sunset."

"No doubt the sunset gilds it finely, but not more than the sunrise does this house, perhaps."

"This house? The sun is a good sun, but it never gilds this house. Why should it? This old house is rotting. That makes it so mossy. In the morning, the sun comes in at this old window, to be sure — boarded up, when first we came; a window I can't keep clean, do what I may — and half burns, and nearly blinds me at my sewing, besides setting the flies and wasps astir — such flies and wasps as only lone mountain houses know. See, here is the curtain — this apron — I try to shut it out with then. It fades it, you see. Sun gild this house? not that ever Marianna saw."

"Because when this roof is gilded most, then you stay here within."

"The hottest, weariest hour of day, you mean? Sir, the sun gilds not this roof. It leaked so, brother newly shingled all one side. Did you not see it? The north side, where the sun strikes most on what the rain has wetted. The sun is a good sun, but this roof, it first scorches, and then rots. An old house. They went West, and are long dead, they say, who built it. A mountain house. In winter no fox could den in it. That chimney-place has been blocked up with snow, just like a hollow stump."

"Yours are strange fancies, Marianna."

"They but reflect the things."

"Then I should have said, 'These are strange things,' rather than, 'Yours are strange fancies.' "

"As you will," and took up her sewing.

Something in those quiet words, or in that quiet act, it made me mute again; while, noting through the fairy-window a broad shadow stealing on, as cast by some gigantic condor floating at brooding poise on outstretched wings, I marked how, by its deeper and inclusive dusk, it wiped away into itself all lesser shades of rock or fern.

"You watch the cloud," said Marianna.

"No, a shadow; a cloud's, no doubt — though that I cannot see. How did you know it? Your eyes are on your work."

"It dusked my work. There, now the cloud is gone, Tray comes back."

"How?"

"The dog, the shaggy dog. At noon, he steals off, of himself, to change his shape — returns, and lies down awhile, nigh the door. Don't you see him? His head is turned round at you, though when you came he looked before him."

"Your eyes rest but on your work; what do you speak of?"

"By the window, crossing."

"You mean this shaggy shadow — the nigh one? And, yes, now that I mark it, it is not unlike a large, black Newfoundland dog. The invading shadow gone, the invaded one returns. But I do not see what casts it."

"For that, you must go without."

"One of those grassy rocks, no doubt."

"You see his head, his face?"

"The shadow's? You speak as if *you* saw it, and all the time your eyes are on your work."

"Tray looks at you," still without glancing up; "this is his hour; I see him."

"Have you, then, so long sat at this mountain window, where but clouds and vapors pass, that to you shadows are as things, though you speak of them as of phantoms; that, by familiar knowledge working like a second sight, you can, without looking for them, tell just where they are, though, as having micelike feet, they creep about, and come and go; that to you these lifeless shadows are as living friends, who, though out of sight, are not out of mind, even in their faces — is it so?"

"That way I never thought of it. But the friendliest one, that used to soothe my weariness so much, coolly quivering on the ferns, it was taken from me, never to return, as Tray did just now. The shadow of a birch. The tree was struck by lightning, and brother cut it up. You saw the cross-pile outdoors — the buried root lies under it, but not the shadow. That is flown, and never will come back, nor ever anywhere stir again."

Another cloud here stole along, once more blotting out the dog, and blackening all the mountain; while the stillness was so still deafness might have forgot itself, or else believed that noiseless shadow spoke.

"Birds, Marianna, singing birds, I hear none; I hear nothing. Boys and bobolinks, do they never come a-berrying up here?"

"Birds I seldom hear; boys, never. The berries mostly ripe and fall — few but me the wiser."

"But yellowbirds showed me the way — part way, at least."

"And then flew back. I guess they play about the mountainside but don't make the top their home. And no doubt you think that, living so lonesome here, knowing nothing, hearing nothing — little, at least, but sound of thunder and the fall of trees — never reading, seldom speaking, yet ever wakeful, this is what gives me my strange thoughts — for so you call them — this weariness and wakefulness together. Brother, who stands and works in open air, would I could rest like him; but mine is mostly but dull woman's work — sitting, sitting, restless sitting."

"But do you not go walk at times? These woods are wide."

"And lonesome; lonesome, because so wide. Sometimes, 'tis true, of afternoons, I go a little way, but soon come back again. Better feel lone by hearth than rock. The shadows hereabouts I know — those in the woods are strangers."

"But the night?"

"Just like the day. Thinking, thinking — a wheel I cannot stop; pure want of sleep it is that turns it."

"I have heard that, for this wakeful weariness, to say one's prayers, and then lay one's head upon a fresh hop pillow ——"

"Look!"

Through the fairy-window, she pointed down the steep to a small garden patch near by — mere pot of rifled loam, half rounded in by sheltering rocks — where, side by side, some feet apart, nipped and puny, two hopvines climbed two poles, and, gaining their tip ends, would have then joined over in an upward clasp, but the baffled shoots, groping awhile in empty air, trailed back whence they sprung.

"You have tried the pillow, then?"

"Yes."

"And prayer?"

"Prayer and pillow."

"Is there no other cure, or charm?"

"Oh, if I could but once get to yonder house, and but look upon whoever the happy being is that lives there! A foolish thought: why do I think it? Is it that I live so lonesome, and know nothing?"

"I, too, know nothing, and therefore cannot answer; but for your sake, Marianna, well could wish that I were that happy one of the happy house you dream you see; for then you would behold him now, and, as you say, this weariness might leave you."

— Enough. Launching my yawl no more for fairyland, I stick to the piazza. It is my box-royal, and this amphitheater, my theater of San Carlo. Yes, the scenery is magical — the illusion so complete. And Madam Meadow Lark, my prima donna, plays her grand engagement here; and, drinking in her sunrise note, which, Memnon-like, seems struck from the golden window, how far from me the weary face behind it.

But every night when the curtain falls, truth comes in with darkness. No light shows from the mountain. To and fro I walk the piazza deck, haunted by Marianna's face, and many as real a story.

Daisy Miller

by Henry James

1

At the little town of Vevey, in Switzerland, there is a particularly comfortable hotel. There are, indeed, many hotels, for the entertainment of tourists is the business of the place, which, as many travelers will remember, is seated upon the edge of a remarkably blue lake — a lake that it behooves every tourist to visit. The shore of the lake presents an unbroken array of establishments of this order, of every category, from the "grand hotel" of the newest fashion, with a chalk-white front, a hundred balconies, and a dozen flags flying from its roof, to the little Swiss pension of an elder day, with its name inscribed in German-looking lettering upon a pink or yellow wall and an awkward summerhouse in the angle of the garden. One of the hotels at Vevey, however, is famous, even classical, being distinguished from many of its upstart neighbors by an air both of luxury and of maturity. In this region, in the month of June, American travelers are extremely numerous; it may be said, indeed, that Vevey assumes at this period some of the characteristics of an American watering place. There are sights and sounds which evoke a vision, an echo, of Newport and Saratoga. There is a flitting hither and thither of "stylish" young girls, a rustling of muslin flounces, a rattle of dance music in the morning hours, a sound of high-pitched voices at all times. You receive an impression of these things at the excellent inn of the "Trois Couronnes" and are transported in fancy to the Ocean House or to Congress Hall. But at

the "Trois Couronnes," it must be added, there are other features that
are much at variance with these suggestions: neat German waiters,
who look like secretaries of legation; Russian princesses sitting in the
garden; little Polish boys walking about, held by the hand, with their
governors; a view of the sunny crest of the Dent du Midi and the
picturesque towers of the Castle of Chillon.

I hardly know whether it was the analogies or the differences that
were uppermost in the mind of a young American, who, two or three
years ago, sat in the garden of the "Trois Couronnes," looking about
him, rather idly, at some of the graceful objects I have mentioned. It
was a beautiful summer morning, and in whatever fashion the young
American looked at things, they must have seemed to him charming.
He had come from Geneva the day before by the little steamer, to see
his aunt, who was staying at the hotel — Geneva having been for a
long time his place of residence. But his aunt had a headache — his
aunt had almost always a headache — and now she was shut up in her
room, smelling camphor, so that he was at liberty to wander about. He
was some seven-and-twenty years of age; when his friends spoke of
him, they usually said that he was at Geneva "studying." When his
enemies spoke of him, they said — but, after all, he had no enemies;
he was an extremely amiable fellow, and universally liked. What I
should say is, simply, that when certain persons spoke of him they
affirmed that the reason of his spending so much time at Geneva was
that he was extremely devoted to a lady who lived there — a foreign
lady — a person older than himself. Very few Americans — indeed, I
think none — had ever seen this lady, about whom there were some
singular stories. But Winterbourne had an old attachment for the little
metropolis of Calvinism; he had been put to school there as a boy, and
he had afterward gone to college there — circumstances which had led
to his forming a great many youthful friendships. Many of these he had
kept, and they were a source of great satisfaction to him.

After knocking at his aunt's door and learning that she was indis-
posed, he had taken a walk about the town, and then he had come in
to his breakfast. He had now finished his breakfast; but he was drinking a small cup of coffee, which had been served to him on a little
table in the garden by one of the waiters who looked like an attaché.
At last he finished his coffee and lit a cigarette. Presently a small boy
came walking along the path — an urchin of nine or ten. The child,

who was diminutive for his years, had an aged expression of countenance, a pale complexion, and sharp little features. He was dressed in knickerbockers, with red stockings, which displayed his poor little spindle-shanks; he also wore a brilliant red cravat. He carried in his hand a long alpenstock, the sharp point of which he thrust into everything that he approached — the flowerbeds, the garden benches, the trains of the ladies' dresses. In front of Winterbourne he paused, looking at him with a pair of bright, penetrating little eyes.

"Will you give me a lump of sugar?" he asked in a sharp, hard little voice — a voice immature and yet, somehow, not young.

Winterbourne glanced at the small table near him, on which his coffee service rested, and saw that several morsels of sugar remained. "Yes, you may take one," he answered; "but I don't think sugar is good for little boys."

This little boy stepped forward and carefully selected three of the coveted fragments, two of which he buried in the pocket of his knickerbockers, depositing the other as promptly in another place. He poked his alpenstock, lance-fashion, into Winterbourne's bench and tried to crack the lump of sugar with his teeth.

"Oh, blazes; it's har-r-d!" he exclaimed, pronouncing the adjective in a peculiar manner.

Winterbourne had immediately perceived that he might have the honor of claiming him as a fellow countryman. "Take care you don't hurt your teeth," he said, paternally.

"I haven't got any teeth to hurt. They have all come out. I have only got seven teeth. My mother counted them last night, and one came out right afterward. She said she'd slap me if any more came out. I can't help it. It's this old Europe. It's the climate that makes them come out. In America they didn't come out. It's these hotels."

Winterbourne was much amused. "If you eat three lumps of sugar, your mother will certainly slap you," he said.

"She's got to give me some candy, then," rejoined his young interlocutor. "I can't get any candy here — any American candy. American candy's the best candy."

"And are American little boys the best little boys?" asked Winterbourne.

"I don't know. I'm an American boy," said the child.

"I see you are one of the best!" laughed Winterbourne.

"Are you an American man?" pursued this vivacious infant. And then, on Winterbourne's affirmative reply — "American men are the best," he declared.

His companion thanked him for the compliment, and the child, who had now got astride of his alpenstock, stood looking about him, while he attacked a second lump of sugar. Winterbourne wondered if he himself had been like this in his infancy, for he had been brought to Europe at about this age.

"Here comes my sister!" cried the child in a moment. "She's an American girl."

Winterbourne looked along the path and saw a beautiful young lady advancing. "American girls are the best girls," he said cheerfully to his young companion.

"My sister ain't the best!" the child declared. "She's always blowing at me."

"I imagine that is your fault, not hers," said Winterbourne. The young lady meanwhile had drawn near. She was dressed in white muslin, with a hundred frills and flounces, and knots of pale-colored ribbon. She was bareheaded, but she balanced in her hand a large parasol, with a deep border of embroidery; and she was strikingly, admirably pretty. "How pretty they are!" thought Winterbourne, straightening himself in his seat, as if he were prepared to rise.

The young lady paused in front of his bench, near the parapet of the garden, which overlooked the lake. The little boy had now converted his alpenstock into a vaulting pole, by the aid of which he was springing about in the gravel and kicking it up not a little.

"Randolph," said the young lady, "what *are* you doing?"

"I'm going up the Alps," replied Randolph. "This is the way!" And he gave another little jump, scattering the pebbles about Winterbourne's ears.

"That's the way they come down," said Winterbourne.

"He's an American man!" cried Randolph, in his little hard voice.

The young lady gave no heed to this announcement, but looked straight at her brother. "Well, I guess you had better be quiet," she simply observed.

It seemed to Winterbourne that he had been in a manner presented. He got up and stepped slowly toward the young girl, throwing away his cigarette. "This little boy and I have made acquaintance," he said, with great civility. In Geneva, as he had been perfectly aware, a young man was not at liberty to speak to a young unmarried lady except under certain rarely occurring conditions; but here at Vevey, what conditions could be better than these? — a pretty American girl coming and standing in front of you in a garden. This pretty American girl, however, on hearing Winterbourne's observation, simply glanced at him; she then turned her head and looked over the parapet, at the lake and the opposite mountains. He wondered whether he had gone too far, but he decided that he must advance farther, rather than retreat. While he was thinking of something else to say, the young lady turned to the little boy again.

"I should like to know where you got that pole," she said.

"I bought it," responded Randolph.

"You don't mean to say you're going to take it to Italy?"

"Yes, I am going to take it to Italy," the child declared.

The young girl glanced over the front of her dress and smoothed out a knot or two of ribbon. Then she rested her eyes upon the prospect again. "Well, I guess you had better leave it somewhere," she said after a moment.

"Are you going to Italy?" Winterbourne inquired in a tone of great respect.

The young lady glanced at him again. "Yes, sir," she replied. And she said nothing more.

"Are you — a — going over the Simplon?" Winterbourne pursued, a little embarrassed.

"I don't know," she said. "I suppose it's some mountain. Randolph, what mountain are we going over?"

"Going where?" the child demanded.

"To Italy," Winterbourne explained.

"I don't know," said Randolph. "I don't want to go to Italy. I want to go to America."

"Oh, Italy is a beautiful place!" rejoined the young man.

"Can you get candy there?" Randolph loudly inquired.

"I hope not," said his sister. "I guess you have had enough candy, and mother thinks so too."

"I haven't had any for ever so long — for a hundred weeks!" cried the boy, still jumping about.

The young lady inspected her flounces and smoothed her ribbons again; and Winterbourne presently risked an observation upon the beauty of the view. He was ceasing to be embarrassed, for he had begun to perceive that she was not in the least embarrassed herself. There had not been the slightest alteration in her charming complexion; she was evidently neither offended nor flattered. If she looked another way when he spoke to her, and seemed not particularly to hear him, this was simply her habit, her manner. Yet, as he talked a little more and pointed out some of the objects of interest in the view, with which she appeared quite unacquainted, she gradually gave him more of the benefit of her glance; and then he saw that this glance was perfectly direct and unshrinking. It was not, however, what would have been called an immodest glance, for the young girl's eyes were singularly honest and fresh. They were wonderfully pretty eyes; and, indeed, Winterbourne had not seen for a long time anything prettier than his fair countrywoman's various features — her complexion, her nose, her ears, her teeth. He had a great relish for feminine beauty; he was addicted to observing and analyzing it; and as regards this young lady's face he made several observations. It was not at all insipid, but it was not exactly expressive; and though it was eminently delicate, Winterbourne mentally accused it — very forgivingly — of a want of finish. He thought it very possible that Master Randolph's sister was a coquette; he was sure she had a spirit of her own; but in her bright, sweet, superficial little visage there was no mockery, no irony. Before long it became obvious that she was much disposed toward conversation. She told him that they were going to Rome for the winter — she and her mother and Randolph. She asked him if he was a "real American"; she shouldn't have taken him for one; he seemed more like a German — this was said after a little hesitation — especially when he spoke. Winterbourne, laughing, answered that he had met Germans who spoke like Americans, but that he had not, so far as he remembered, met an American who spoke like a German. Then he asked her if she should not be more comfortable in sitting upon the bench which he had just quitted. She answered that she liked standing up and walking about; but she presently sat down. She told him she was from New York State — "if you know where that is." Winterbourne learned more about her by catching hold of her small, slippery brother and making him stand a few minutes by his side.

"Tell me your name, my boy," he said.

"Randolph C. Miller," said the boy sharply. "And I'll tell you her name"; and he leveled his alpenstock at his sister.

"You had better wait till you are asked!" said this young lady calmly.

"I should like very much to know your name," said Winterbourne.

"Her name is Daisy Miller!" cried the child. "But that isn't her real name; that isn't her name on her cards."

"It's a pity you haven't got one of my cards!" said Miss Miller.

"Her real name is Annie P. Miller," the boy went on.

"Ask him *his* name," said his sister, indicating Winterbourne.

But on this point Randolph seemed perfectly indifferent; he continued to supply information with regard to his own family. "My father's name is Ezra B. Miller," he announced. "My father ain't in Europe; my father's in a better place than Europe."

Winterbourne imagined for a moment that this was the manner in which the child had been taught to intimate that Mr. Miller had been removed to the sphere of celestial reward. But Randolph immediately added, "My father's in Schenectady. He's got a big business. My father's rich, you bet!"

"Well!" ejaculated Miss Miller, lowering her parasol and looking at the embroidered border. Winterbourne presently released the child, who departed, dragging his alpenstock along the path. "He doesn't like Europe," said the young girl. "He wants to go back."

"To Schenectady, you mean?"

"Yes; he wants to go right home. He hasn't got any boys here. There is one boy here, but he always goes round with a teacher; they won't let him play."

"And your brother hasn't any teacher?" Winterbourne inquired.

"Mother thought of getting him one, to travel round with us. There was a lady told her of a very good teacher; an American lady — perhaps you know her — Mrs. Sanders. I think she came from Boston. She told her of this teacher, and we thought of getting him to travel round with us. But Randolph said he didn't want a teacher traveling round with us. He said he wouldn't have lessons when he was in the cars. And we *are* in the cars about half the time. There was an English lady we met in the cars — I think her name was Miss Featherstone; perhaps you know her. She wanted to know why I didn't give Randolph lessons — give him 'instruction,' she called it. I guess he could give me more instruction than I could give him. He's very smart."

"Yes," said Winterbourne; "he seems very smart."

"Mother's going to get a teacher for him as soon as we get to Italy. Can you get good teachers in Italy?"

"Very good, I should think," said Winterbourne.

"Or else she's going to find some school. He ought to learn some more. He's only nine. He's going to college." And in this way Miss Miller continued to converse upon the affairs of her family and upon other topics. She sat there with her extremely pretty hands, ornamented with very brilliant rings, folded in her lap, and with her pretty eyes now resting upon those of Winterbourne, now wandering over the garden, the people who passed by, and the beautiful view. She talked to Winterbourne as if she had known him a long time. He found it very pleasant. It was many years since he had heard a young girl talk so much. It might have been said of this unknown young lady, who had come and sat down beside him upon a bench, that she chattered. She was very quiet; she sat in a charming, tranquil attitude; but her lips and her eyes were constantly moving. She had a soft, slender, agreeable voice, and her tone was decidedly sociable. She gave Winterbourne a history of her movements and intentions and those of her mother and brother, in Europe, and enumerated, in particular, the various hotels at which they had stopped. "That English lady in the cars," she said — "Miss Featherstone — asked me if we didn't all live in hotels in America. I told her I had never been in so many hotels in my life as since I came to Europe. I have never seen so many — it's nothing but hotels." But Miss Miller did not make this remark with a querulous accent; she appeared to be in the best humor with everything. She declared that the hotels were very good, when once you got used to their ways, and that Europe was perfectly sweet. She was not disappointed — not a bit. Perhaps it was because she had heard so much about it before. She had ever so many intimate friends that had been there ever so many times. And then she had had ever so many dresses and things from Paris. Whenever she put on a Paris dress she felt as if she were in Europe.

"It was a kind of a wishing cap," said Winterbourne.

"Yes," said Miss Miller without examining this analogy; "it always made me wish I was here. But I needn't have done that for dresses. I am sure they send all the pretty ones to America; you see the most frightful things here. The only thing I don't like," she proceeded, "is the society. There isn't any society; or, if there is, I don't know where it keeps itself. Do you? I suppose there is some society somewhere, but I haven't seen anything of it. I'm very fond of society, and I have always had a great deal of it. I don't mean only in Schenectady, but in New York. I used to go to New York every winter. In New York I had lots of society. Last winter I had seventeen dinners given me; and three of them were by gentlemen," added Daisy Miller. "I have more friends in New York than in Schenectady — more gentleman friends; and more young lady friends too," she resumed in a moment. She paused again for an instant; she was looking at Winterbourne with all her prettiness in her lively eyes and in her light, slightly monotonous smile. "I have always had," she said, "a great deal of gentlemen's society."

Poor Winterbourne was amused, perplexed, and decidedly charmed. He had never yet heard a young girl express herself in just this fashion; never, at least, save in cases where to say such things seemed a kind of demonstrative evidence of a certain laxity of deportment. And yet was he to accuse Miss Daisy Miller of actual or potential *inconduite*, as they said at Geneva? He felt that he had lived at Geneva so long that he had lost a good deal; he had become dishabituated to the American tone. Never, indeed, since he had grown old enough to appreciate things, had he encountered a young American girl of so pronounced a type as this. Certainly she was very charming, but how deucedly sociable! Was she simply a pretty girl from New York State? Were they all like that, the pretty girls who had a good deal of gentlemen's society? Or was she also a designing, an audacious, an unscrupulous young person? Winterbourne had lost his instinct in this matter, and his reason could not help him. Miss Daisy Miller looked extremely innocent. Some people had told him that, after all, American girls were exceedingly innocent; and others had told him that, after all, they were not. He was inclined to think Miss Daisy Miller was a flirt — a pretty American flirt. He had never, as yet, had any relations with young ladies of this category. He had known, here in Europe, two or three women — persons older than Miss Daisy Miller, and provided, for respectability's sake, with husbands — who were great coquettes — dangerous, terrible women, with whom one's relations were liable to take a serious turn. But this young girl was not a coquette in that sense; she was very unsophisticated; she was only a pretty American flirt. Winterbourne was almost grateful for having found the formula that applied to Miss Daisy Miller. He leaned back in his seat; he remarked to himself that she had the most charming nose he had ever seen; he wondered what were the regular conditions and limitations of one's intercourse with a pretty American flirt. It presently became apparent that he was on the way to learn.

"Have you been to that old castle?" asked the young girl, pointing with her parasol to the far-gleaming walls of the Château de Chillon.

"Yes, formerly, more than once," said Winterbourne. "You too, I suppose, have seen it?"

"No; we haven't been there. I want to go there dreadfully. Of course I mean to go there. I wouldn't go away from here without having seen that old castle."

"It's a very pretty excursion," said Winterbourne, "and very easy to make. You can drive, you know, or you can go by the little steamer."

"You can go in the cars," said Miss Miller.

"Yes; you can go in the cars," Winterbourne assented.

"Our courier says they take you right up to the castle," the young girl continued. "We were going last week, but my mother gave out. She suffers dreadfully from dyspepsia. She said she couldn't go. Randolph wouldn't go either; he says he doesn't think much of old castles. But I guess we'll go this week, if we can get Randolph."

"Your brother is not interested in ancient monuments?" Winterbourne inquired, smiling.

"He says he don't care much about old castles. He's only nine. He wants to stay at the hotel. Mother's afraid to leave him alone, and the courier won't stay with him; so we haven't been to many places. But it will be too bad if we don't go up there." And Miss Miller pointed again at the Château de Chillon.

"I should think it might be arranged," said Winterbourne. "Couldn't you get some one to stay for the afternoon with Randolph?"

Miss Miller looked at him a moment, and then, very placidly, "I wish *you* would stay with him!" she said.

Winterbourne hesitated a moment. "I should much rather go to Chillon with you."

"With me?" asked the young girl with the same placidity.

She didn't rise, blushing, as a young girl at Geneva would have done; and yet Winterbourne, conscious that he had been very bold, thought it possible she was offended. "With your mother," he answered very respectfully.

But it seemed that both his audacity and his respect were lost upon Miss Daisy Miller. "I guess my mother won't go, after all," she said. "She don't like to ride round in the afternoon. But did you really mean what you said just now — that you would like to go up there?"

"Most earnestly," Winterbourne declared.

"Then we may arrange it. If mother will stay with Randolph, I guess Eugenio will."

"Eugenio?" the young man inquired.

"Eugenio's our courier. He doesn't like to stay with Randolph; he's the most fastidious man I ever saw. But he's a splendid courier. I guess he'll stay at home with Randolph if mother does, and then we can go to the castle."

Winterbourne reflected for an instant as lucidly as possible — "we" could only mean Miss Daisy Miller and himself. This program seemed almost too agreeable for credence; he felt as if he ought to kiss the young lady's hand. Possibly he would have done so and quite spoiled the project, but at this moment another person, presumably Eugenio, appeared. A tall, handsome man, with superb whiskers, wearing a velvet morning coat and a brilliant watch chain, approached Miss Miller, looking sharply at her companion. "Oh, Eugenio!" said Miss Miller with the friendliest accent.

Eugenio had looked at Winterbourne from head to foot; he now bowed gravely to the young lady. "I have the honor to inform mademoiselle that luncheon is upon the table."

Miss Miller slowly rose. "See here, Eugenio!" she said; "I'm going to that old castle, anyway."

"To the Château de Chillon, mademoiselle?" the courier inquired. "Mademoiselle has made arrangements?" he added in a tone which struck Winterbourne as very impertinent.

Eugenio's tone apparently threw, even to Miss Miller's own apprehension, a slightly ironical light upon the young girl's situation. She turned to Winterbourne, blushing a little — a very little. "You won't back out?" she said.

"I shall not be happy till we go!" he protested.

"And you are staying in this hotel?" she went on. "And you are really an American?"

The courier stood looking at Winterbourne offensively. The young man, at least, thought his manner of looking an offense to Miss Miller; it conveyed an imputation that she "picked up" acquaintances. "I shall have the honor of presenting to you a person who will tell you all about me," he said, smiling and referring to his aunt.

"Oh, well, we'll go some day," said Miss Miller. And she gave him a smile and turned away. She put up her parasol and walked back to the inn beside Eugenio. Winterbourne stood looking after her; and as she moved away, drawing her muslin furbelows over the gravel, said to himself that she had the *tournure* of a princess.

He had, however, engaged to do more than proved feasible, in promising to present his aunt, Mrs. Costello, to Miss Daisy Miller. As soon as the former lady had got better of her headache, he waited upon her in her apartment; and, after the proper inquiries in regard to her health, he asked her if she had observed in the hotel an American family — a mamma, a daughter, and a little boy.

"And a courier?" said Mrs. Costello. "Oh yes, I have observed them. Seen them — heard them — and kept out of their way." Mrs. Costello was a widow with a fortune; a person of much distinction, who frequently intimated that, if she were not so dreadfully liable to sick headaches, she would probably have left a deeper impress upon her time. She had a long, pale face, a high nose, and a great deal of very striking white hair, which she wore in large puffs and *rouleaux* over the top of her head. She had two sons married in New York and another who was now in Europe. This young man was amusing himself at Hamburg, and, though he was on his travels, was rarely perceived to visit any particular city at the moment selected by his mother for her own appearance there. Her nephew, who had come up to Vevey expressly to see her, was therefore more attentive than those who, as she said, were nearer to her. He had imbibed at Geneva the idea that one must always be attentive to one's aunt. Mrs. Costello had not seen him for many years, and she was greatly pleased with him, manifesting her approbation by initiating him into many of the secrets of that social sway which, as she gave him to understand, she exerted in the American capital. She admitted that she was very exclusive; but, if he were acquainted with New York, he would see that one had to be. And her picture of the minutely hierarchical constitution of the society of that city, which she presented to him in many different lights, was, to Winterbourne's imagination, almost oppressively striking.

He immediately perceived, from her tone, that Miss Daisy Miller's place in the social scale was low. "I am afraid you don't approve of them," he said.

"They are very common," Mrs. Costello declared. "They are the sort of Americans that one does one's duty by not — not accepting."

"Ah, you don't accept them?" said the young man.

"I can't, my dear Frederick. I would if I could, but I can't."

"The young girl is very pretty," said Winterbourne in a moment.

"Of course she's pretty. But she is very common."

"I see what you mean, of course," said Winterbourne after another pause.

"She has that charming look that they all have," his aunt resumed. "I can't think where they pick it up; and she dresses in perfection — no, you don't know how well she dresses. I can't think where they get their taste."

"But, my dear aunt, she is not, after all, a Comanche savage."

"She is a young lady," said Mrs. Costello, "who has an intimacy with her mamma's courier."

"An intimacy with the courier?" the young man demanded.

"Oh, the mother is just as bad! They treat the courier like a familiar friend — like a gentleman. I shouldn't wonder if he dines with them. Very likely they have never seen a man with such good manners, such fine clothes, so like a gentleman. He probably corresponds to the young lady's idea of a count. He sits with them in the garden in the evening. I think he smokes."

Winterbourne listened with interest to these disclosures; they helped him to make up his mind about Miss Daisy. Evidently she was rather wild. "Well," he said, "I am not a courier, and yet she was very charming to me."

"You had better have said at first," said Mrs. Costello with dignity, "that you had made her acquaintance."

"We simply met in the garden, and we talked a bit."

"*Tout bonnement!* And pray what did you say?"

"I said I should take the liberty of introducing her to my admirable aunt."

"I am much obliged to you."

"It was to guarantee my respectability," said Winterbourne.

"And pray who is to guarantee hers?"

"Ah, you are cruel!" said the young man. "She's a very nice young girl."

"You don't say that as if you believed it," Mrs. Costello observed.

"She is completely uncultivated," Winterbourne went on. "But she is wonderfully pretty, and, in short, she is very nice. To prove that I believe it, I am going to take her to the Château de Chillon."

"You two are going off there together? I should say it proved just the contrary. How long had you known her, may I ask, when this interesting project was formed? You haven't been twenty-four hours in the house."

"I have known her half an hour!" said Winterbourne, smiling.

"Dear me!" cried Mrs. Costello. "What a dreadful girl!"

Her nephew was silent for some moments. "You really think, then," he began earnestly, and with a desire for trustworthy information — "you really think that ——" But he paused again.

"Think what, sir?" said his aunt.

"That she is the sort of young lady who expects a man, sooner or later, to carry her off?"

"I haven't the least idea what such young ladies expect a man to do. But I really think that you had better not meddle with little American girls that are uncultivated, as you call them. You have lived too long out of the country. You will be sure to make some great mistake. You are too innocent."

"My dear aunt, I am not so innocent," said Winterbourne, smiling and curling his mustache.

"You are guilty too, then!"

Winterbourne continued to curl his mustache meditatively. "You won't let the poor girl know you then?" he asked at last.

"Is it literally true that she is going to the Château de Chillon with you?"

"I think that she fully intends it."

"Then, my dear Frederick," said Mrs. Costello, "I must decline the honor of her acquaintance. I am an old woman, but I am not too old, thank Heaven, to be shocked!"

"But don't they all do these things — the young girls in America?" Winterbourne inquired.

Mrs. Costello stared a moment. "I should like to see my grand-daughters do them!" she declared grimly.

This seemed to throw some light upon the matter, for Winter-bourne remembered to have heard that his pretty cousins in New York were "tremendous flirts." If, therefore, Miss Daisy Miller exceeded the liberal margin allowed to these young ladies, it was probable that anything might be expected of her. Winterbourne was impatient to see her again, and he was vexed with himself that, by instinct, he should not appreciate her justly.

Though he was impatient to see her, he hardly knew what he should say to her about his aunt's refusal to become acquainted with her; but he discovered, promptly enough, that with Miss Daisy Miller there was no great need of walking on tiptoe. He found her that evening in the garden, wandering about in the warm starlight like an indolent sylph, and swinging to and fro the largest fan he had ever beheld. It was ten o'clock. He had dined with his aunt, had been sitting with her since dinner, and had just taken leave of her till the morrow. Miss Daisy Miller seemed very glad to see him; she declared it was the longest evening she had ever passed.

"Have you been all alone?" he asked.

"I have been walking round with mother. But mother gets tired walking round," she answered.

"Has she gone to bed?"

"No; she doesn't like to go to bed," said the young girl. "She doesn't sleep — not three hours. She says she doesn't know how she lives. She's dreadfully nervous. I guess she sleeps more than she thinks. She's gone somewhere after Randolph; she wants to try to get him to go to bed. He doesn't like to go to bed."

"Let us hope she will persuade him," observed Winterbourne.

"She will talk to him all she can; but he doesn't like her to talk to him," said Miss Daisy, opening her fan. "She's going to try to get Eugenio to talk to him. But he isn't afraid of Eugenio. Eugenio's a splendid courier, but he can't make much impression on Randolph! I don't believe he'll go to bed before eleven." It appeared that Ran-dolph's vigil was in fact triumphantly prolonged, for Winterbourne strolled about with the young girl for some time without meeting her mother. "I have been looking round for that lady you want to introduce me to," his companion resumed. "She's your aunt." Then, on Winterbourne's admitting the fact and expressing some curiosity as to how she had learned it, she said she had heard all about Mrs. Costello from the chambermaid. She was very quiet and very *comme il faut*; she wore white puffs; she spoke to no one, and she never dined at the table d'hôte. Every two days she had a headache. "I think that's a lovely description, headache and all!" said Miss Daisy, chattering along in her thin, gay voice. "I want to know her ever so much. I know just what *your* aunt would be; I know I should like her. She would be very exclusive. I like a lady to be exclusive; I'm dying to be exclusive myself. Well, we *are* exclusive, mother and I. We don't speak to everyone — or they don't speak to us. I suppose it's about the same thing. Anyway, I shall be ever so glad to know your aunt."

Winterbourne was embarrassed. "She would be most happy," he said; "but I am afraid those headaches will interfere."

The young girl looked at him through the dusk. "But I suppose she doesn't have a headache every day," she said sympathetically.

Winterbourne was silent a moment. "She tells me she does," he answered at last, not knowing what to say.

Miss Daisy Miller stopped and stood looking at him. Her prettiness was still visible in the darkness; she was opening and closing her enormous fan. "She doesn't want to know me!" she said suddenly. "Why don't you say so? You needn't be afraid. I'm not afraid!" And she gave a little laugh.

Winterbourne fancied there was a tremor in her voice; he was touched, shocked, mortified by it. "My dear young lady," he protested, "she knows no one. It's her wretched health."

The young girl walked on a few steps, laughing still. "You needn't be afraid," she repeated. "Why should she want to know me?" Then she paused again; she was close to the parapet of the garden, and in front of her was the starlit lake. There was a vague sheen upon its surface, and in the distance were dimly seen mountain forms. Daisy Miller looked out upon the mysterious prospect and then she gave another little laugh. "Gracious! she *is* exclusive!" she said. Winterbourne wondered whether she was seriously wounded, and for a moment almost wished that her sense of injury might be such as to make it becoming in him to attempt to reassure and comfort her. He had a pleasant sense that she would be very approachable for consolatory purposes. He felt then, for the instant, quite ready to sacrifice his aunt, conversationally; to admit that she was a proud, rude woman, and to declare that they needn't mind her. But before he had time to commit himself to this perilous mixture of gallantry and impiety, the young lady, resuming her walk, gave an exclamation in quite another tone. "Well, here's Mother! I guess she hasn't got Randolph to go to bed." The figure of a lady appeared, at a distance, very indistinct in the darkness, and advancing with a slow and wavering movement. Suddenly it seemed to pause.

"Are you sure it is your mother? Can you distinguish her in this thick dusk?" Winterbourne asked.

"Well!" cried Miss Daisy Miller with a laugh; "I guess I know my own mother. And when she has got on my shawl, too! She is always wearing my things."

The lady in question, ceasing to advance, hovered vaguely about the spot at which she had checked her steps.

"I am afraid your mother doesn't see you," said Winterbourne. "Or perhaps," he added, thinking, with Miss Miller, the joke permissible — "perhaps she feels guilty about your shawl."

"Oh, it's a fearful old thing!" the young girl replied serenely. "I told her she could wear it. She won't come here because she sees you."

"Ah, then," said Winterbourne, "I had better leave you."

"Oh, no; come on!" urged Miss Daisy Miller.

"I'm afraid your mother doesn't approve of my walking with you."

Miss Miller gave him a serious glance. "It isn't for me; it's for you — that is, it's for *her*. Well, I don't know who it's for! But mother doesn't like any of my gentlemen friends. She's right down timid. She always makes a fuss if I introduce a gentleman. But I *do* introduce them — almost always. If I didn't introduce my gentlemen friends to Mother," the young girl added in her little soft, flat monotone, "I shouldn't think I was natural."

"To introduce me," said Winterbourne, "you must know my name." And he proceeded to pronounce it.

"Oh, dear, I can't say all that!" said his companion with a laugh. But by this time they had come up to Mrs. Miller, who, as they drew near, walked to the parapet of the garden and leaned upon it, looking intently at the lake and turning her back to them. "Mother!" said the young girl in a tone of decision. Upon this the elder lady turned round. "Mr. Winterbourne," said Miss Daisy Miller, introducing the young man very frankly and prettily. "Common," she was, as Mrs. Costello had pronounced her; yet it was a wonder to Winterbourne that, with her commonness, she had a singularly delicate grace.

Her mother was a small, spare, light person, with a wandering eye, a very exiguous nose, and a large forehead, decorated with a certain amount of thin, much frizzled hair. Like her daughter, Mrs. Miller was dressed with extreme elegance; she had enormous diamonds in her ears. So far as Winterbourne could observe, she gave him no greeting — she certainly was not looking at him. Daisy was near her, pulling her shawl straight. "What are you doing, poking round here?" this young lady inquired, but by no means with that harshness of accent which her choice of words may imply.

"I don't know," said her mother, turning toward the lake again.

"I shouldn't think you'd want that shawl!" Daisy exclaimed.

"Well, I do!" her mother answered with a little laugh.

"Did you get Randolph to go to bed?" asked the young girl.

"No; I couldn't induce him," said Mrs. Miller very gently. "He wants to talk to the waiter. He likes to talk to that waiter."

"I was telling Mr. Winterbourne," the young girl went on; and to the young man's ear her tone might have indicated that she had been uttering his name all her life.

"Oh, yes!" said Winterbourne; "I have the pleasure of knowing your son."

Randolph's mamma was silent; she turned her attention to the lake. But at last she spoke. "Well, I don't see how he lives!"

"Anyhow, it isn't so bad as it was at Dover," said Daisy Miller.

"And what occurred at Dover?" Winterbourne asked.

"He wouldn't go to bed at all. I guess he sat up all night in the public parlor. He wasn't in bed at twelve o'clock: I know that."

"It was half-past twelve," declared Mrs. Miller with mild emphasis.

"Does he sleep much during the day?" Winterbourne demanded.

"I guess he doesn't sleep much," Daisy rejoined.

"I wish he would!" said her mother. "It seems as if he couldn't."

"I think he's real tiresome," Daisy pursued.

Then, for some moments, there was silence. "Well, Daisy Miller," said the elder lady, presently, "I shouldn't think you'd want to talk against your own brother!"

"Well, he *is* tiresome, Mother," said Daisy, quite without the asperity of a retort.

"He's only nine," urged Mrs. Miller.

"Well, he wouldn't go to that castle," said the young girl. "I'm going there with Mr. Winterbourne."

To this announcement, very placidly made, Daisy's mamma offered no response. Winterbourne took for granted that she deeply disapproved of the projected excursion; but he said to himself that she was a simple, easily managed person, and that a few deferential protestations would take the edge from her displeasure. "Yes," he began; "your daughter has kindly allowed me the honor of being her guide."

Mrs. Miller's wandering eyes attached themselves, with a sort of appealing air, to Daisy, who, however, strolled a few steps farther, gently humming to herself. "I presume you will go in the cars," said her mother.

"Yes, or in the boat," said Winterbourne.

"Well, of course, I don't know," Mrs. Miller rejoined. "I have never been to that castle."

"It is a pity you shouldn't go," said Winterbourne, beginning to feel reassured as to her opposition. And yet he was quite prepared to find that, as a matter of course, she meant to accompany her daughter.

"We've been thinking ever so much about going," she pursued; "but it seems as if we couldn't. Of course Daisy — she wants to go round. But there's a lady here — I don't know her name — she says she shouldn't think we'd want to go to see castles *here*; she should think we'd want to wait till we got to Italy. It seems as if there would be so many there," continued Mrs. Miller with an air of increasing confidence. "Of course we only want to see the principal ones. We visited several in England," she presently added.

"Ah yes! in England there are beautiful castles," said Winterbourne. "But Chillon, here, is very well worth seeing."

"Well, if Daisy feels up to it —" said Mrs. Miller, in a tone impregnated with a sense of the magnitude of the enterprise. "It seems as if there was nothing she wouldn't undertake."

"Oh, I think she'll enjoy it!" Winterbourne declared. And he desired more and more to make it a certainty that he was to have the privilege of a tête-à-tête with the young lady, who was still strolling along in front of them, softly vocalizing. "You are not disposed, madam," he inquired, "to undertake it yourself?"

Daisy's mother looked at him an instant askance, and then walked forward in silence. Then — "I guess she had better go alone," she said simply. Winterbourne observed to himself that this was a very different type of maternity from that of the vigilant matrons who massed themselves in the forefront of social intercourse in the dark old city at the other end of the lake. But his meditations were interrupted by hearing his name very distinctly pronounced by Mrs. Miller's unprotected daughter.

"Mr. Winterbourne!" murmured Daisy.

"Mademoiselle!" said the young man.

"Don't you want to take me out in a boat?"

"At present?" he asked.

"Of course!" said Daisy.

"Well, Annie Miller!" exclaimed her mother.

"I beg you, madam, to let her go," said Winterbourne ardently; for he had never yet enjoyed the sensation of guiding through the summer starlight a skiff freighted with a fresh and beautiful young girl.

"I shouldn't think she'd want to," said her mother. "I should think she'd rather go indoors."

"I'm sure Mr. Winterbourne wants to take me," Daisy declared. "He's so awfully devoted!"

"I will row you over to Chillon in the starlight."

"I don't believe it!" said Daisy.

"Well!" ejaculated the elder lady again.

"You haven't spoken to me for half an hour," her daughter went on.

"I have been having some very pleasant conversation with your mother," said Winterbourne.

"Well, I want you to take me out in a boat!" Daisy repeated. They had all stopped, and she had turned round and was looking at Winterbourne. Her face wore a charming smile, her pretty eyes were gleaming, she was swinging her great fan about. No; it's impossible to be prettier than that, thought Winterbourne.

"There are half a dozen boats moored at that landing place," he said, pointing to certain steps which descended from the garden to the lake. "If you will do me the honor to accept my arm, we will go and select one of them."

Daisy stood there smiling; she threw back her head and gave a little, light laugh. "I like a gentleman to be formal!" she declared.

"I assure you it's a formal offer."

"I was bound I would make you say something," Daisy went on.

"You see, it's not very difficult," said Winterbourne. "But I am afraid you are chaffing me."

"I think not, sir," remarked Mrs. Miller very gently.

"Do, then, let me give you a row," he said to the young girl.

"It's quite lovely, the way you say that!" cried Daisy.

"It will be still more lovely to do it."

"Yes, it would be lovely!" said Daisy. But she made no movement to accompany him; she only stood there laughing.

"I should think you had better find out what time it is," interposed her mother.

"It is eleven o'clock, madam," said a voice, with a foreign accent, out of the neighboring darkness; and Winterbourne, turning, perceived the florid personage who was in attendance upon the two ladies. He had apparently just approached.

"Oh, Eugenio," said Daisy, "I am going out in a boat!"

Eugenio bowed. "At eleven o'clock, mademoiselle?"

"I am going with Mr. Winterbourne — this very minute."

"Do tell her she can't," said Mrs. Miller to the courier.

"I think you had better not go out in a boat, mademoiselle," Eugenio declared.

Winterbourne wished to Heaven this pretty girl were not so familiar with her courier; but he said nothing.

"I suppose you don't think it's proper!" Daisy exclaimed. "Eugenio doesn't think anything's proper."

"I am at your service," said Winterbourne.

"Does mademoiselle propose to go alone?" asked Eugenio of Mrs. Miller.

"Oh, no; with this gentleman!" answered Daisy's mamma.

The courier looked for a moment at Winterbourne — the latter thought he was smiling — and then, solemnly, with a bow, "As mademoiselle pleases!" he said.

"Oh, I hoped you would make a fuss!" said Daisy. "I don't care to go now."

"I myself shall make a fuss if you don't go," said Winterbourne.

"That's all I want — a little fuss!" And the young girl began to laugh again.

"Mr. Randolph has gone to bed!" the courier announced frigidly.

"Oh, Daisy; now we can go!" said Mrs. Miller.

Daisy turned away from Winterbourne, looking at him, smiling and fanning herself. "Good night," she said; "I hope you are disappointed, or disgusted, or something!"

He looked at her, taking the hand she offered him. "I am puzzled," he answered.

"Well, I hope it won't keep you awake!" she said very smartly; and, under the escort of the privileged Eugenio, the two ladies passed toward the house.

Winterbourne stood looking after them; he was indeed puzzled. He lingered beside the lake for a quarter of an hour, turning over the mystery of the young girl's sudden familiarities and caprices. But the only very definite conclusion he came to was that he should enjoy deucedly "going off" with her somewhere.

Two days afterward he went off with her to the Castle of Chillon. He waited for her in the large hall of the hotel, where the couriers, the servants, the foreign tourists, were lounging about and staring. It was not the place he should have chosen, but she had appointed it. She came tripping downstairs, buttoning her long gloves, squeezing her folded parasol against her pretty figure, dressed in the perfection of a soberly elegant traveling costume. Winterbourne was a man of imagination and, as our ancestors used to say, sensibility; as he looked at her dress and, on the great staircase, her little rapid, confiding step, he felt as if there were something romantic going forward. He could have believed he was going to elope with her. He passed out with her among all the idle people that were assembled there; they were all looking at her very hard; she had begun to chatter as soon as she joined him. Winterbourne's preference had been that they should be conveyed to Chillon in a carriage; but she expressed a lively wish to go in the little steamer; she declared that she had a passion for steamboats. There was always such a lovely breeze upon the water, and you saw such lots of people. The sail was not long, but Winterbourne's companion found time to say a great many things. To the young man himself their little excursion was so much of an escapade — an adventure — that, even allowing for her habitual sense of freedom, he had some expectation of seeing her regard it in the same way. But it must be confessed that, in this particular, he was disappointed. Daisy Miller was extremely animated, she was in charming spirits; but she was apparently not at all excited; she was not fluttered; she avoided neither his eyes nor those of anyone else; she blushed neither when she looked at him nor when she felt that people were looking at her. People continued to look at her a great deal, and Winterbourne took much satisfaction in his pretty companion's distinguished air. He had been a little afraid that she would talk loud, laugh overmuch, and even, perhaps, desire to move about the boat a good deal. But he quite forgot his fears; he sat smiling, with his eyes upon her face, while, without moving from her place, she delivered herself of a great number of original reflections. It was the most charming garrulity he had ever heard. He had assented to the idea that she was "common"; but was she so, after all, or was he simply getting used to her commonness? Her conversation was chiefly of what metaphysicians term the objective cast, but every now and then it took a subjective turn.

"What on *earth* are you so grave about?" she suddenly demanded, fixing her agreeable eyes upon Winterbourne's.

"Am I grave?" he asked. "I had an idea I was grinning from ear to ear."

"You look as if you were taking me to a funeral. If that's a grin, your ears are very near together."

"Should you like me to dance a hornpipe on the deck?"

"Pray do, and I'll carry round your hat. It will pay the expenses of our journey."

"I never was better pleased in my life," murmured Winterbourne.

She looked at him a moment and then burst into a little laugh. "I like to make you say those things! You're a queer mixture!"

In the castle, after they had landed, the subjective element decidedly prevailed. Daisy tripped about the vaulted chambers, rustled her skirts in the corkscrew staircases, flirted back with a pretty little cry and a shudder from the edge of the *oubliettes*, and turned a singularly well-shaped ear to everything that Winterbourne told her about the place. But he saw that she cared very little for feudal antiquities and that the dusky traditions of Chillon made but a slight impression upon her. They had the good fortune to have been able to walk about without other companionship than that of the custodian; and Winterbourne arranged with this functionary that they should not be hurried — that they should linger and pause wherever they chose. The custodian interpreted the bargain generously — Winterbourne, on his side, had been generous — and ended by leaving them quite to themselves. Miss Miller's observations were not remarkable for logical consistency; for anything she wanted to say she was sure to find a pretext. She found a great many pretexts in the rugged embrasures of Chillon for asking Winterbourne sudden questions about himself — his family, his previous history, his tastes, his habits, his intentions — and for supplying information upon corresponding points in her own personality. Of her own tastes, habits, and intentions Miss Miller was prepared to give the most definite, and indeed the most favorable account.

"Well, I hope you know enough!" she said to her companion, after he had told her the history of the unhappy Bonivard. "I never saw a man that knew so much!" The history of Bonivard had evidently, as they say, gone into one ear and out of the other. But Daisy went on to say that she wished Winterbourne would travel with them and "go round" with them; they might know something, in that case. "Don't you want to come and teach Randolph?" she asked. Winterbourne said that nothing could possibly please him so much, but that he had unfortunately other occupations. "Other occupations? I don't believe it!" said Miss Daisy. "What do you mean? You are not in business." The young man admitted that he was not in business; but he had engagements which, even within a day or two, would force him to go back to Geneva. "Oh, bother!" she said; "I don't believe it!" and she began to talk about something else. But a few moments later, when he was pointing out to her the pretty design of an antique fireplace, she broke out irrelevantly, "You don't mean to say you are going back to Geneva?"

"It is a melancholy fact that I shall have to return to Geneva tomorrow."

"Well, Mr. Winterbourne," said Daisy, "I think you're horrid!"

"Oh, don't say such dreadful things!" said Winterbourne — "just at the last!"

"The last!" cried the young girl; "I call it the first. I have half a mind to leave you here and go straight back to the hotel alone." And for the next ten minutes she did nothing but call him horrid. Poor Winterbourne was fairly bewildered; no young lady had as yet done him the honor to be so agitated by the announcement of his movements. His companion, after this, ceased to pay any attention to the curiosities of Chillon or the beauties of the lake; she opened fire upon the mysterious charmer in Geneva whom she appeared to have instantly taken it for granted that he was hurrying back to see. How did Miss Daisy Miller know that there was a charmer in Geneva? Winterbourne, who denied the existence of such a person, was quite unable to discover, and he was divided between amazement at the rapidity of her induction and amusement at the frankness of her *persiflage*. She seemed to him, in all this, an extraordinary mixture of innocence and crudity. "Does she never allow you more than three days at a time?" asked Daisy ironically. "Doesn't she give you a vacation in summer? There's no one so hard worked but they can get leave to go off somewhere at this season. I suppose, if you stay another day, she'll come after you in the boat. Do wait over till Friday, and I will go down to the landing to see her arrive!" Winterbourne began to think he had been wrong to feel disappointed in the temper in which the young lady had embarked. If he had missed the personal accent, the personal accent was now making its appearance. It sounded very distinctly, at last, in her telling him she would stop "teasing" him if he would promise her solemnly to come down to Rome in the winter.

"That's not a difficult promise to make," said Winterbourne. "My aunt has taken an apartment in Rome for the winter and has already asked me to come and see her."

"I don't want you to come for your aunt," said Daisy; "I want you to come for me." And this was the only allusion that the young man was ever to hear her make to his invidious kinswoman. He declared that, at any rate, he would certainly come. After this Daisy stopped teasing. Winterbourne took a carriage, and they drove back to Vevey in the dusk; the young girl was very quiet.

In the evening Winterbourne mentioned to Mrs. Costello that he had spent the afternoon at Chillon with Miss Daisy Miller.

"The Americans — of the courier?" asked this lady.

"Ah, happily," said Winterbourne, "the courier stayed at home."

"She went with you all alone?"

"All alone."

Mrs. Costello sniffed a little at her smelling bottle. "And that," she exclaimed, "is the young person whom you wanted me to know!"

2

Winterbourne, who had returned to Geneva the day after his excursion to Chillon, went to Rome toward the end of January. His aunt had been established there for several weeks, and he had received a couple of letters from her. "Those people you were so devoted to last summer at Vevey have turned up here, courier and all," she wrote. "They seem to have made several acquaintances, but the courier continues to be the most intime. The young lady, however, is also very intimate with some third-rate Italians, with whom she rackets about in a way that makes much talk. Bring me that pretty novel of Cherbuliez's — *Paule Méré* — and don't come later than the 23rd."

In the natural course of events, Winterbourne, on arriving in Rome, would presently have ascertained Mrs. Miller's address at the American banker's and have gone to pay his compliments to Miss Daisy. "After what happened at Vevey, I think I may certainly call upon them," he said to Mrs. Costello.

"If, after what happens — at Vevey and everywhere — you desire to keep up the acquaintance, you are very welcome. Of course a man may know everyone. Men are welcome to the privilege!"

"Pray what is it that happens — here, for instance?" Winterbourne demanded.

"The girl goes about alone with her foreigners. As to what happens further, you must apply elsewhere for information. She has picked up half a dozen of the regular Roman fortune hunters, and she takes them about to people's houses. When she comes to a party she brings with her a gentleman with a good deal of manner and a wonderful mustache."

"And where is the mother?"

"I haven't the least idea. They are very dreadful people."

Winterbourne meditated a moment. "They are very ignorant — very innocent only. Depend upon it they are not bad."

"They are hopelessly vulgar," said Mrs. Costello. "Whether or no being hopelessly vulgar is being 'bad' is a question for the metaphysicians. They are bad enough to dislike, at any rate; and for this short life that is quite enough."

The news that Daisy Miller was surrounded by half a dozen wonderful mustaches checked Winterbourne's impulse to go straightway to see her. He had, perhaps, not definitely flattered himself that he had made an ineffaceable impression upon her heart, but he was annoyed at hearing of a state of affairs so little in harmony with an image that had lately flitted in and out of his own meditations; the image of a very pretty girl looking out of an old Roman window and asking herself urgently when Mr. Winterbourne would arrive. If, however, he determined to wait a little before reminding Miss Miller of his claims to her consideration, he went very soon to call upon two or three other friends. One of these friends was an American lady who had spent several winters at Geneva, where she had placed her children at school. She was a very accomplished woman, and she lived in the Via Gregoriana. Winterbourne found her in a little crimson drawing room on a third floor; the room was filled with southern sunshine. He had not been there ten minutes when the servant came in, announcing "Madame Mila!" This announcement was presently followed by the entrance of little Randolph Miller, who stopped in the middle of the room and stood staring at Winterbourne. An instant later his pretty sister crossed the threshold; and then, after a considerable interval, Mrs. Miller slowly advanced.

"I know you!" said Randolph.

"I'm sure you know a great many things," exclaimed Winterbourne, taking him by the hand. "How is your education coming on?"

Daisy was exchanging greetings very prettily with her hostess, but when she heard Winterbourne's voice she quickly turned her head. "Well, I declare!" she said.

"I told you I should come, you know," Winterbourne rejoined, smiling.

"Well, I didn't believe it," said Miss Daisy.

"I am much obliged to you," laughed the young man.

"You might have come to see me!" said Daisy.

"I arrived only yesterday."

"I don't believe that!" the young girl declared.

Winterbourne turned with a protesting smile to her mother, but this lady evaded his glance, and, seating herself, fixed her eyes upon her son. "We've got a bigger place than this," said Randolph. "It's all gold on the walls."

Mrs. Miller turned uneasily in her chair. "I told you if I were to bring you, you would say something!" she murmured.

"I told *you!*" Randolph exclaimed. "I tell *you*, sir!" he added jocosely, giving Winterbourne a thump on the knee. "It *is* bigger, too!"

Daisy had entered upon a lively conversation with her hostess; Winterbourne judged it becoming to address a few words to her mother. "I hope you have been well since we parted at Vevey," he said.

Mrs. Miller now certainly looked at him — at his chin. "Not very well, sir," she answered.

"She's got the dyspepsia," said Randolph. "I've got it too. Father's got it. I've got it most!"

This announcement, instead of embarrassing Mrs. Miller, seemed to relieve her. "I suffer from the liver," she said. "I think it's this climate; it's less bracing than Schenectady, especially in the winter season. I don't know whether you know we reside at Schenectady. I was saying to Daisy that I certainly hadn't found any one like Dr. Davis, and I didn't believe I should. Oh, at Schenectady he stands first; they think everything of him. He has so much to do, and yet there was nothing he wouldn't do for me. He said he never saw anything like my dyspepsia, but he was bound to cure it. I'm sure there was nothing he wouldn't try. He was just going to try something new when we came off. Mr. Miller wanted Daisy to see Europe for herself. But I wrote to Mr. Miller that it seems as if I couldn't get on without Dr. Davis. At Schenectady he stands at the very top; and there's a great deal of sickness there, too. It affects my sleep."

Winterbourne had a good deal of pathological gossip with Dr. Davis's patient, during which Daisy chattered unremittingly to her own companion. The young man asked Mrs. Miller how she was pleased with Rome. "Well, I must say I am disappointed," she answered. "We had heard so much about it; I suppose we had heard too much. But we couldn't help that. We had been led to expect something different."

"Ah, wait a little, and you will become very fond of it," said Winterbourne.

"I hate it worse and worse every day!" cried Randolph.

"You are like the infant Hannibal," said Winterbourne.

"No, I ain't!" Randolph declared at a venture.

"You are not much like an infant," said his mother. "But we have seen places," she resumed, "that I should put a long way before Rome." And in reply to Winterbourne's interrogation, "There's Zürich," she concluded, "I think Zürich is lovely; and we hadn't heard half so much about it."

"The best place we've seen is the City of Richmond!" said Randolph.

"He means the ship," his mother explained. "We crossed in that ship. Randolph had a good time on the *City of Richmond*."

"It's the best place I've seen," the child repeated. "Only it was turned the wrong way."

"Well, we've got to turn the right way some time," said Mrs. Miller with a little laugh. Winterbourne expressed the hope that her daughter at least found some gratification in Rome, and she declared that Daisy was quite carried away. "It's on account of the society — the society's splendid. She goes round everywhere; she has made a great number of acquaintances. Of course she goes round more than I do. I must say they have been very sociable; they have taken her right in. And then she knows a great many gentlemen. Oh, she thinks there's nothing like Rome. Of course, it's a great deal pleasanter for a young lady if she knows plenty of gentlemen."

By this time Daisy had turned her attention again to Winterbourne. "I've been telling Mrs. Walker how mean you were!" the young girl announced.

"And what is the evidence you have offered?" asked Winterbourne, rather annoyed at Miss Miller's want of appreciation of the zeal of an admirer who on his way down to Rome had stopped neither at Bologna nor at Florence, simply because of a certain sentimental impatience. He remembered that a cynical compatriot had once told him that American women — the pretty ones, and this gave a largeness to the axiom — were at once the most exacting in the world and the least endowed with a sense of indebtedness.

"Why, you were awfully mean at Vevey," said Daisy. "You wouldn't do anything. You wouldn't stay there when I asked you."

"My dearest young lady," cried Winterbourne, with eloquence, "have I come all the way to Rome to encounter your reproaches?"

"Just hear him say that!" said Daisy to her hostess, giving a twist to a bow on this lady's dress. "Did you ever hear anything so quaint?"

"So quaint, my dear?" murmured Mrs. Walker in the tone of a partisan of Winterbourne.

"Well, I don't know," said Daisy, fingering Mrs. Walker's ribbons. "Mrs. Walker, I want to tell you something."

"Mother-r," interposed Randolph, with his rough ends to his words, "I tell you you've got to go. Eugenio'll raise — something!"

"I'm not afraid of Eugenio," said Daisy with a toss of her head. "Look here, Mrs. Walker," she went on, "you know I'm coming to your party."

"I am delighted to hear it."

"I've got a lovely dress!"

"I am very sure of that."

"But I want to ask a favor — permission to bring a friend."

"I shall be happy to see any of your friends," said Mrs. Walker, turning with a smile to Mrs. Miller.

"Oh, they are not my friends," answered Daisy's mamma, smiling shyly in her own fashion. "I never spoke to them."

"It's an intimate friend of mine — Mr. Giovanelli," said Daisy without a tremor in her clear little voice or a shadow on her brilliant little face.

Mrs. Walker was silent a moment; she gave a rapid glance at Winterbourne. "I shall be glad to see Mr. Giovanelli," she then said.

"He's an Italian," Daisy pursued with the prettiest serenity. "He's a great friend of mine; he's the handsomest man in the world — except Mr. Winterbourne! He knows plenty of Italians, but he wants to know some Americans. He thinks ever so much of Americans. He's tremendously clever. He's perfectly lovely!"

It was settled that this brilliant personage should be brought to Mrs. Walker's party, and then Mrs. Miller prepared to take her leave. "I guess we'll go back to the hotel," she said.

"You may go back to the hotel, Mother, but I'm going to take a walk," said Daisy.

"She's going to walk with Mr. Giovanelli," Randolph proclaimed.

"I am going to the Pincio," said Daisy, smiling.

"Alone, my dear — at this hour?" Mrs. Walker asked. The afternoon was drawing to a close — it was the hour for the throng of carriages and of contemplative pedestrians. "I don't think it's safe, my dear," said Mrs. Walker.

"Neither do I," subjoined Mrs. Miller. "You'll get the fever, as sure as you live. Remember what Dr. Davis told you!"

"Give her some medicine before she goes," said Randolph.

The company had risen to its feet; Daisy, still showing her pretty teeth, bent over and kissed her hostess. "Mrs. Walker, you are too perfect," she said. "I'm not going alone; I am going to meet a friend."

"Your friend won't keep you from getting the fever," Mrs. Miller observed.

"Is it Mr. Giovanelli?" asked the hostess.

Winterbourne was watching the young girl; at this question his attention quickened. She stood there, smiling and smoothing her bonnet ribbons; she glanced at Winterbourne. Then, while she glanced and smiled, she answered, without a shade of hesitation, "Mr. Giovanelli — the beautiful Giovanelli."

"My dear young friend," said Mrs. Walker, taking her hand pleadingly, "don't walk off to the Pincio at this hour to meet a beautiful Italian."

"Well, he speaks English," said Mrs. Miller.

"Gracious me!" Daisy exclaimed, "I don't want to do anything improper. There's an easy way to settle it." She continued to glance at Winterbourne. "The Pincio is only a hundred yards distant; and if Mr. Winterbourne were as polite as he pretends, he would offer to walk with me!"

Winterbourne's politeness hastened to affirm itself, and the young girl gave him gracious leave to accompany her. They passed downstairs before her mother, and at the door Winterbourne perceived Mrs. Miller's carriage drawn up, with the ornamental courier whose acquaintance he had made at Vevey seated within. "Goodbye, Eugenio!" cried Daisy; "I'm going to take a walk." The distance from the Via Gregoriana to the beautiful garden at the other end of the Pincian Hill is, in fact, rapidly traversed. As the day was splendid, however, and the concourse of vehicles, walkers, and loungers numerous, the young Americans found their progress much delayed. This fact was highly agreeable to Winterbourne, in spite of his consciousness of his singular situation. The slow-moving, idly gazing Roman crowd bestowed much attention upon the extremely pretty young

foreign lady who was passing through it upon his arm; and he wondered what on earth had been in Daisy's mind when she proposed to
expose herself, unattended, to its appreciation. His own mission, to
her sense, apparently, was to consign her to the hands of Mr.
Giovanelli; but Winterbourne, at once annoyed and gratified, resolved that he would do no such thing.

"Why haven't you been to see me?" asked Daisy. "You can't get out
of that."

"I have had the honor of telling you that I have only just stepped
out of the train."

"You must have stayed in the train a good while after it stopped!"
cried the young girl with her little laugh. "I suppose you were asleep.
You have had time to go to see Mrs. Walker."

"I knew Mrs. Walker ——" Winterbourne began to explain.

"I know where you knew her. You knew her at Geneva. She told
me so. Well, you knew me at Vevey. That's just as good. So you ought
to have come." She asked him no other question than this; she began
to prattle about her own affairs. "We've got splendid rooms at the
hotel; Eugenio says they're the best rooms in Rome. We are going to
stay all winter, if we don't die of the fever; and I guess we'll stay then.
It's a great deal nicer than I thought; I thought it would be fearfully
quiet; I was sure it would be awfully poky. I was sure we should be
going round all the time with one of those dreadful old men that
explain about the pictures and things. But we only had about a week
of that, and now I'm enjoying myself. I know ever so many people,
and they are all so charming. The society's extremely select. There are
all kinds — English, and Germans, and Italians. I think I like the
English best. I like their style of conversation. But there are some
lovely Americans. I never saw anything so hospitable. There's something or other every day. There's not much dancing; but I must say I
never thought dancing was everything. I was always fond of conversation. I guess I shall have plenty at Mrs. Walker's, her rooms are so
small." When they had passed the gate of the Pincian Gardens, Miss
Miller began to wonder where Mr. Giovanelli might be. "We had
better go straight to that place in front," she said, "where you look at
the view."

"I certainly shall not help you to find him," Winterbourne declared.

"Then I shall find him without you," said Miss Daisy.

"You certainly won't leave me!" cried Winterbourne.

She burst into her little laugh. "Are you afraid you'll get lost — or run over? But there's Giovanelli, leaning against that tree. He's staring at the women in the carriages: did you ever see anything so cool?"

Winterbourne perceived at some distance a little man standing with folded arms nursing his cane. He had a handsome face, an artfully poised hat, a glass in one eye, and a nosegay in his buttonhole. Winterbourne looked at him a moment and then said, "Do you mean to speak to that man?"

"Do I mean to speak to him? Why, you don't suppose I mean to communicate by signs?"

"Pray understand, then," said Winterbourne, "that I intend to remain with you."

Daisy stopped and looked at him, without a sign of troubled consciousness in her face, with nothing but the presence of her charming eyes and her happy dimples. "Well, she's a cool one!" thought the young man.

"I don't like the way you say that," said Daisy. "It's too imperious."

"I beg your pardon if I say it wrong. The main point is to give you an idea of my meaning."

The young girl looked at him more gravely, but with eyes that were prettier than ever. "I have never allowed a gentleman to dictate to me, or to interfere with anything I do."

"I think you have made a mistake," said Winterbourne. "You should sometimes listen to a gentleman — the right one."

Daisy began to laugh again. "I do nothing but listen to gentlemen!" she exclaimed. "Tell me if Mr. Giovanelli is the right one?"

The gentleman with the nosegay in his bosom had now perceived our two friends, and was approaching the young girl with obsequious rapidity. He bowed to Winterbourne as well as to the latter's companion; he had a brilliant smile, an intelligent eye; Winterbourne thought him not a bad-looking fellow. But he nevertheless said to Daisy, "No, he's not the right one."

Daisy evidently had a natural talent for performing introductions; she mentioned the name of each of her companions to the other. She strolled along with one of them on each side of her; Mr. Giovanelli, who spoke English very cleverly — Winterbourne afterward learned that he had practiced the idiom upon a great many American heiresses

— addressed her a great deal of very polite nonsense; he was extremely urbane, and the young American, who said nothing, reflected upon that profundity of Italian cleverness which enables people to appear more gracious in proportion as they are more acutely disappointed. Giovanelli, of course, had counted upon something more intimate; he had not bargained for a party of three. But he kept his temper in a manner which suggested far-stretching intentions. Winterbourne flattered himself that he had taken his measure. "He is not a gentleman," said the young American; "he is only a clever imitation of one. He is a music master, or a penny-a-liner, or a third-rate artist. D—n his good looks!" Mr. Giovanelli had certainly a very pretty face; but Winterbourne felt a superior indignation at his own lovely fellow countrywoman's not knowing the difference between a spurious gentleman and a real one. Giovanelli chattered and jested and made himself wonderfully agreeable. It was true that, if he was an imitation, the imitation was brilliant. "Nevertheless," Winterbourne said to himself, "a nice girl ought to know!" And then he came back to the question whether this was, in fact, a nice girl. Would a nice girl, even allowing for her being a little American flirt, make a rendezvous with a presumably low-lived foreigner? The rendezvous in this case, indeed, had been in broad daylight and in the most crowded corner of Rome, but was it not impossible to regard the choice of these circumstances as a proof of extreme cynicism? Singular though it may seem, Winterbourne was vexed that the young girl, in joining her *amoroso*, should not appear more impatient of his own company, and he was vexed because of his inclination. It was impossible to regard her as a perfectly well-conducted young lady; she was wanting in a certain indispensable delicacy. It would therefore simplify matters greatly to be able to treat her as the object of one of those sentiments which are called by romancers "lawless passions." That she should seem to wish to get rid of him would help him to think more lightly of her, and to be able to think more lightly of her would make her much less perplexing. But Daisy, on this occasion, continued to present herself as an inscrutable combination of audacity and innocence.

She had been walking some quarter of an hour, attended by her two cavaliers, and responding in a tone of very childish gaiety, as it seemed to Winterbourne, to the pretty speeches of Mr. Giovanelli, when a carriage that had detached itself from the revolving train drew up beside the path. At the same moment Winterbourne perceived that his friend Mrs. Walker — the lady whose house he had lately left — was seated in the vehicle and was beckoning to him. Leaving Miss Miller's side, he hastened to obey her summons. Mrs. Walker was flushed; she wore an excited air. "It is really too dreadful," she said. "That girl must not do this sort of thing. She must not walk here with you two men. Fifty people have noticed her."

Winterbourne raised his eyebrows. "I think it's a pity to make too much fuss about it."

"It's a pity to let the girl ruin herself!"

"She is very innocent," said Winterbourne.

"She's very crazy!" cried Mrs. Walker. "Did you ever see anything so imbecile as her mother? After you had all left me just now, I could not sit still for thinking of it. It seemed too pitiful, not even to attempt to save her. I ordered the carriage and put on my bonnet, and came here as quickly as possible. Thank Heaven I have found you!"

"What do you propose to do with us?" asked Winterbourne, smiling.

"To ask her to get in, to drive her about here for half an hour, so that the world may see she is not running absolutely wild, and then to take her safely home."

"I don't think it's a very happy thought," said Winterbourne; "but you can try."

Mrs. Walker tried. The young man went in pursuit of Miss Miller, who had simply nodded and smiled at his interlocutor in the carriage and had gone her way with her companion. Daisy, on learning that Mrs. Walker wished to speak to her, retraced her steps with a perfect good grace and with Mr. Giovanelli at her side. She declared that she was delighted to have a chance to present this gentleman to Mrs. Walker. She immediately achieved the introduction, and declared that she had never in her life seen anything so lovely as Mrs. Walker's carriage rug.

"I am glad you admire it," said this lady, smiling sweetly. "Will you get in and let me put it over you?"

"Oh, no, thank you," said Daisy. "I shall admire it much more as I see you driving round with it."

"Do get in and drive with me!" said Mrs. Walker.

"That would be charming, but it's so enchanting just as I am!" and Daisy gave a brilliant glance at the gentlemen on either side of her.

"It may be enchanting, dear child, but it is not the custom here," urged Mrs. Walker, leaning forward in her victoria, with her hands devoutly clasped.

"Well, it ought to be, then!" said Daisy. "If I didn't walk I should expire."

"You should walk with your mother, dear," cried the lady from Geneva, losing patience.

"With my mother dear!" exclaimed the young girl. Winterbourne saw that she scented interference. "My mother never walked ten steps in her life. And then, you know," she added with a laugh, "I am more than five years old."

"You are old enough to be more reasonable. You are old enough, dear Miss Miller, to be talked about."

Daisy looked at Mrs. Walker, smiling intensely. "Talked about? What do you mean?"

"Come into my carriage, and I will tell you."

Daisy turned her quickened glance again from one of the gentlemen beside her to the other. Mr. Giovanelli was bowing to and fro, rubbing down his gloves and laughing very agreeably; Winterbourne thought it a most unpleasant scene. "I don't think I want to know what you mean," said Daisy presently. "I don't think I should like it."

Winterbourne wished that Mrs. Walker would tuck in her carriage rug and drive away, but this lady did not enjoy being defied, as she afterward told him. "Should you prefer being thought a very reckless girl?" she demanded.

"Gracious!" exclaimed Daisy. She looked again at Mr. Giovanelli, then she turned to Winterbourne. There was a little pink flush in her cheek; she was tremendously pretty. "Does Mr. Winterbourne think," she asked slowly, smiling, throwing back her head, and glancing at him from head to foot, "that, to save my reputation, I ought to get into the carriage?"

Winterbourne colored; for an instant he hesitated greatly. It seemed so strange to hear her speak that way of her "reputation." But he himself, in fact, must speak in accordance with gallantry. The finest gallantry, here, was simply to tell her the truth; and the truth, for Winterbourne, as the few indications I have been able to give have made him known to the reader, was that Daisy Miller should take Mrs. Walker's advice. He looked at her exquisite prettiness, and then he said, very gently, "I think you should get into the carriage."

Daisy gave a violent laugh. "I never heard anything so stiff! If this is improper, Mrs. Walker," she pursued, "then I am all improper, and you must give me up. Goodbye; I hope you'll have a lovely ride!" and, with Mr. Giovanelli, who made a triumphantly obsequious salute, she turned away.

Mrs. Walker sat looking after her, and there were tears in Mrs. Walker's eyes. "Get in here, sir," she said to Winterbourne, indicating the place beside her. The young man answered that he felt bound to accompany Miss Miller, whereupon Mrs. Walker declared that if he refused her this favor she would never speak to him again. She was evidently in earnest. Winterbourne overtook Daisy and her companion, and, offering the young girl his hand, told her that Mrs. Walker had made an imperious claim upon his society. He expected that in answer she would say something rather free, something to commit herself still further to that "recklessness" from which Mrs. Walker had so charitably endeavored to dissuade her. But she only shook his hand, hardly looking at him, while Mr. Giovanelli bade him farewell with a too emphatic flourish of the hat.

Winterbourne was not in the best possible humor as he took his seat in Mrs. Walker's victoria. "That was not clever of you," he said candidly, while the vehicle mingled again with the throng of carriages.

"In such a case," his companion answered, "I don't wish to be clever; I wish to be *earnest!*"

"Well, your earnestness has only offended her and put her off."

"It has happened very well," said Mrs. Walker. "If she is so perfectly determined to compromise herself, the sooner one knows it the better; one can act accordingly."

"I suspect she meant no harm," Winterbourne rejoined.

"So I thought a month ago. But she has been going too far."

"What has she been doing?"

"Everything that is not done here. Flirting with any man she could pick up; sitting in corners with mysterious Italians; dancing all the evening with the same partners; receiving visits at eleven o'clock at night. Her mother goes away when visitors come."

"But her brother," said Winterbourne, laughing, "sits up till midnight."

"He must be edified by what he sees. I'm told that at their hotel everyone is talking about her, and that a smile goes round among all the servants when a gentleman comes and asks for Miss Miller."

"The servants be hanged!" said Winterbourne angrily. "The poor girl's only fault," he presently added, "is that she is very uncultivated."

"She is naturally indelicate," Mrs. Walker declared. "Take that example this morning. How long had you known her at Vevey?"

"A couple of days."

"Fancy, then, her making it a personal matter that you should have left the place!"

Winterbourne was silent for some moments; then he said, "I suspect, Mrs. Walker, that you and I have lived too long at Geneva!" And he added a request that she should inform him with what particular design she had made him enter her carriage.

"I wished to beg you to cease your relations with Miss Miller — not to flirt with her — to give her no further opportunity to expose herself — to let her alone, in short."

"I'm afraid I can't do that," said Winterbourne. "I like her extremely."

"All the more reason that you shouldn't help her to make a scandal."

"There shall be nothing scandalous in my attentions to her."

"There certainly will be in the way she takes them. But I have said what I had on my conscience," Mrs. Walker pursued. "If you wish to rejoin the young lady I will put you down. Here, by the way, you have a chance."

The carriage was traversing that part of the Pincian Garden that overhangs the wall of Rome and overlooks the beautiful Villa Borghese. It is bordered by a large parapet, near which there are several seats. One of the seats at a distance was occupied by a gentleman and a lady, toward whom Mrs. Walker gave a toss of her head. At the same moment these persons rose and walked toward the parapet. Winterbourne had asked the coachman to stop; he now descended from the carriage. His companion looked at him a moment in silence; then, while he raised his hat, she drove majestically away. Winterbourne stood there; he had turned his eyes toward Daisy and her cavalier. They evidently saw no one; they were too deeply occupied with each other. When they reached the low garden wall, they stood a moment looking off at the great flat-topped pine clusters of the Villa Borghese; then Giovanelli seated himself, familiarly, upon the broad ledge of the wall. The western sun in the opposite sky sent out a brilliant shaft through a couple of cloud bars, whereupon Daisy's companion took her parasol out of her hands and opened it. She came a little nearer, and he held the parasol over her; then, still holding it, he let it rest upon her shoulder, so that both of their heads were hidden from Winterbourne. This young man lingered a moment, then he began to walk. But he walked — not toward the couple with the parasol; toward the residence of his aunt, Mrs. Costello.

He flattered himself on the following day that there was no smiling among the servants when he, at least, asked for Mrs. Miller at her hotel. This lady and her daughter, however, were not at home; and on the next day after, repeating his visit, Winterbourne again had the misfortune not to find them. Mrs. Walker's party took place on the evening of the third day, and, in spite of the frigidity of his last interview with the hostess, Winterbourne was among the guests. Mrs. Walker was one of those American ladies who, while residing abroad, make a point, in their own phrase, of studying European society, and she had on this occasion collected several specimens of her diversely born fellow mortals to serve, as it were, as textbooks. When Winterbourne arrived, Daisy Miller was not there, but in a few moments he saw her mother come in alone, very shyly and ruefully. Mrs. Miller's hair above her exposed-looking temples was more frizzled than ever. As she approached Mrs. Walker, Winterbourne also drew near.

"You see, I've come all alone," said poor Mrs. Miller. "I'm so frightened; I don't know what to do. It's the first time I've ever been to a party alone, especially in this country. I wanted to bring Randolph or Eugenio, or someone, but Daisy just pushed me off by myself. I ain't used to going round alone."

"And does not your daughter intend to favor us with her society?" demanded Mrs. Walker impressively.

"Well, Daisy's all dressed," said Mrs. Miller with that accent of the dispassionate, if not of the philosophic, historian with which she always recorded the current incidents of her daughter's career. "She got dressed on purpose before dinner. But she's got a friend of hers there; that gentleman — the Italian — that she wanted to bring. They've got going at the piano; it seems as if they couldn't leave off. Mr. Giovanelli sings splendidly. But I guess they'll come before very long," concluded Mrs. Miller hopefully.

"I'm sorry she should come in that way," said Mrs. Walker.

"Well, I told her that there was no use in her getting dressed before dinner if she was going to wait three hours," responded Daisy's mamma. "I didn't see the use of her putting on such a dress as that to sit round with Mr. Giovanelli."

"This is most horrible!" said Mrs. Walker, turning away and addressing herself to Winterbourne. "*Elle s'affiche.* It's her revenge for my having ventured to remonstrate with her. When she comes, I shall not speak to her."

Daisy came after eleven o'clock; but she was not, on such an occasion, a young lady to wait to be spoken to. She rustled forward in radiant loveliness, smiling and chattering, carrying a large bouquet, and attended by Mr. Giovanelli. Everyone stopped talking and turned and looked at her. She came straight to Mrs. Walker. "I'm afraid you thought I never was coming, so I sent mother off to tell you. I wanted to make Mr. Giovanelli practice some things before he came; you know he sings beautifully, and I want you to ask him to sing. This is Mr. Giovanelli; you know I introduced him to you; he's got the most lovely voice, and he knows the most charming set of songs. I made him go over them this evening on purpose; we had the greatest time at the hotel." Of all this Daisy delivered herself with the sweetest, brightest audibleness, looking now at her hostess and now round the room, while she gave a series of little pats, round her shoulders, to the edges of her dress. "Is there anyone I know?" she asked.

"I think every one knows you!" said Mrs. Walker pregnantly, and she gave a very cursory greeting to Mr. Giovanelli. This gentleman bore himself gallantly. He smiled and bowed and showed his white teeth; he curled his mustaches and rolled his eyes and performed all the proper functions of a handsome Italian at an evening party. He sang very prettily half a dozen songs, though Mrs. Walker afterward declared that she had been quite unable to find out who asked him. It was apparently not Daisy who had given him his orders. Daisy sat at a distance from the piano, and though she had publicly, as it were, professed a high admiration for his singing, talked, not inaudibly, while it was going on.

"It's a pity these rooms are so small; we can't dance," she said to Winterbourne, as if she had seen him five minutes before.

"I am not sorry we can't dance," Winterbourne answered; "I don't dance."

"Of course you don't dance; you're too stiff," said Miss Daisy. "I hope you enjoyed your drive with Mrs. Walker!"

"No, I didn't enjoy it; I preferred walking with you."

"We paired off: that was much better," said Daisy. "But did you ever hear anything so cool as Mrs. Walker's wanting me to get into her carriage and drop poor Mr. Giovanelli, and under the pretext that it was proper? People have different ideas! It would have been most unkind; he had been talking about that walk for ten days."

"He should not have talked about it at all," said Winterbourne; "he would never have proposed to a young lady of this country to walk about the streets with him."

"About the streets?" cried Daisy with her pretty stare. "Where, then, would he have proposed to her to walk? The Pincio is not the streets, either; and I, thank goodness, am not a young lady of this country. The young ladies of this country have a dreadfully poky time of it, so far as I can learn; I don't see why I should change my habits for *them.*"

"I am afraid your habits are those of a flirt," said Winterbourne gravely.

"Of course they are," she cried, giving him her little smiling stare again. "I'm a fearful, frightful flirt! Did you ever hear of a nice girl that was not? But I suppose you will tell me now that I am not a nice girl."

"You're a very nice girl; but I wish you would flirt with me, and me only," said Winterbourne.

"Ah! thank you — thank you very much; you are the last man I should think of flirting with. As I have had the pleasure of informing you, you are too stiff."

"You say that too often," said Winterbourne.

Daisy gave a delighted laugh. "If I could have the sweet hope of making you angry, I should say it again."

"Don't do that; when I am angry I'm stiffer than ever. But if you won't flirt with me, do cease, at least, to flirt with your friend at the piano; they don't understand that sort of thing here."

"I thought they understood nothing else!" exclaimed Daisy.

"Not in young unmarried women."

"It seems to me much more proper in young unmarried women than in old married ones," Daisy declared.

"Well," said Winterbourne, "when you deal with natives you must go by the custom of the place. Flirting is a purely American custom; it doesn't exist here. So when you show yourself in public with Mr. Giovanelli, and without your mother ——"

"Gracious! poor Mother!" interposed Daisy.

"Though you may be flirting, Mr. Giovanelli is not; he means something else."

"He isn't preaching, at any rate," said Daisy with vivacity. "And if you want very much to know, we are neither of us flirting; we are too good friends for that: we are very intimate friends."

"Ah!" rejoined Winterbourne, "if you are in love with each other, it is another affair."

She had allowed him up to this point to talk so frankly that he had no expectation of shocking her by this ejaculation; but she immediately got up, blushing visibly, and leaving him to exclaim mentally that little American flirts were the queerest creatures in the world. "Mr. Giovanelli, at least," she said, giving her interlocutor a single glance, "never says such very disagreeable things to me."

Winterbourne was bewildered; he stood, staring. Mr. Giovanelli had finished singing. He left the piano and came over to Daisy. "Won't you come into the other room and have some tea?" he asked, bending before her with his ornamental smile.

Daisy turned to Winterbourne, beginning to smile again. He was still more perplexed, for this inconsequent smile made nothing clear, though it seemed to prove, indeed, that she had a sweetness and softness that reverted instinctively to the pardon of offenses. "It has never occurred to Mr. Winterbourne to offer me any tea," she said with her little tormenting manner.

"I have offered you advice," Winterbourne rejoined.

"I prefer weak tea!" cried Daisy, and she went off with the brilliant Giovanelli. She sat with him in the adjoining room, in the embrasure of the window, for the rest of the evening. There was an interesting performance at the piano, but neither of these young people gave heed to it. When Daisy came to take leave of Mrs. Walker, this lady conscientiously repaired the weakness of which she had been guilty at the moment of the young girl's arrival. She turned her back straight upon Miss Miller and left her to depart with what grace she might. Winterbourne was standing near the door; he saw it all. Daisy turned very pale and looked at her mother, but Mrs. Miller was humbly unconscious of any violation of the usual social forms. She appeared, indeed, to have felt an incongruous impulse to draw attention to her own striking observance of them. "Good night, Mrs. Walker," she said; "we've had a beautiful evening. You see, if I let Daisy come to parties without me, I don't want her to go away without me." Daisy turned away, looking with a pale, grave face at the circle near the door; Winterbourne saw that, for the first moment, she was too much shocked and puzzled even for indignation. He on his side was greatly touched.

"That was very cruel," he said to Mrs. Walker.

"She never enters my drawing room again!" replied his hostess.

Since Winterbourne was not to meet her in Mrs. Walker's drawing room, he went as often as possible to Mrs. Miller's hotel. The ladies were rarely at home, but when he found them, the devoted Giovanelli was always present. Very often the brilliant little Roman was in the drawing room with Daisy alone, Mrs. Miller being apparently constantly of the opinion that discretion is the better part of surveillance. Winterbourne noted, at first with surprise, that Daisy on these occasions was never embarrassed or annoyed by his own entrance; but he very presently began to feel that she had no more surprises for him; the unexpected in her behavior was the only thing to expect. She showed no displeasure at her tête-à-tête with Giovanelli being interrupted; she could chatter as freshly and freely with two gentlemen as with one; there was always, in her conversation, the same odd mixture of audacity and puerility. Winterbourne remarked to himself that if she was seriously interested in Giovanelli, it was very singular that she should not take more trouble to preserve the sanctity of their interviews; and he liked her the more for her innocent-looking indifference and her apparently inexhaustible good humor. He could hardly have said why, but she seemed to him a girl who would never be jealous. At the risk of exciting a somewhat derisive smile on the reader's part, I may affirm that with regard to the women who had hitherto interested him, it very often seemed to Winterbourne among the possibilities that, given certain contingencies, he should be afraid — literally afraid — of these ladies; he had a pleasant sense that he should never be afraid of Daisy Miller. It must be added that this sentiment was not altogether flattering to Daisy; it was part of his conviction, or rather of his apprehension, that she would prove a very light young person.

But she was evidently very much interested in Giovanelli. She looked at him whenever he spoke; she was perpetually telling him to do this and to do that; she was constantly "chaffing" and abusing him. She appeared completely to have forgotten that Winterbourne had said anything to displease her at Mrs. Walker's little party. One Sunday afternoon, having gone to St. Peter's with his aunt, Winterbourne perceived Daisy strolling about the great church in company with the inevitable Giovanelli. Presently he pointed out the young girl and her cavalier to Mrs. Costello. This lady looked at them a moment through her eyeglass, and then she said:

"That's what makes you so pensive in these days, eh?"

"I had not the least idea I was pensive," said the young man.

"You are very much preoccupied; you are thinking of something."

"And what is it," he asked, "that you accuse me of thinking of?"

"Of that young lady's — Miss Baker's, Miss Chandler's — what's her name? — Miss Miller's intrigue with that little barber's block."

"Do you call it an intrigue," Winterbourne asked — "an affair that goes on with such peculiar publicity?"

"That's their folly," said Mrs. Costello; "it's not their merit."

"No," rejoined Winterbourne, with something of that pensiveness to which his aunt had alluded. "I don't believe that there is anything to be called an intrigue."

"I have heard a dozen people speak of it; they say she is quite carried away by him."

"They are certainly very intimate," said Winterbourne.

Mrs. Costello inspected the young couple again with her optical instrument. "He is very handsome. One easily sees how it is. She thinks him the most elegant man in the world, the finest gentleman. She has never seen anything like him; he is better, even, than the courier. It was the courier probably who introduced him; and if he succeeds in marrying the young lady, the courier will come in for a magnificent commission."

"I don't believe she thinks of marrying him," said Winterbourne, "and I don't believe he hopes to marry her."

"You may be very sure she thinks of nothing. She goes on from day to day, from hour to hour, as they did in the Golden Age. I can imagine nothing more vulgar. And at the same time," added Mrs. Costello, "depend upon it that she may tell you any moment that she is 'engaged.' "

"I think that is more than Giovanelli expects," said Winterbourne.

"Who is Giovanelli?"

"The little Italian. I have asked questions about him and learned something. He is apparently a perfectly respectable little man. I believe he is, in a small way, a *cavaliere avvocato*. But he doesn't move in what are called the first circles. I think it is really not absolutely impossible that the courier introduced him. He is evidently immensely charmed with Miss Miller. If she thinks him the finest gentleman in the world, he, on his side, has never found himself in personal contact with such splendor, such opulence, such expensiveness as this young lady's. And then she must seem to him wonderfully pretty and interesting. I rather doubt that he dreams of marrying her. That must appear to him too impossible a piece of luck. He has nothing but his handsome face to offer, and there is a substantial Mr. Miller in that mysterious land of dollars. Giovanelli knows that he hasn't a title to offer. If he were only a count or a *marchese!* He must wonder at his luck, at the way they have taken him up."

"He accounts for it by his handsome face and thinks Miss Miller a young lady *qui se passe ses fantaisies!*" said Mrs. Costello.

"It is very true," Winterbourne pursued, "that Daisy and her mamma have not yet risen to that stage of — what shall I call it? — of culture at which the idea of catching a count or a *marchese* begins. I believe that they are intellectually incapable of that conception."

"Ah! but the *avvocato* can't believe it," said Mrs. Costello.

Of the observation excited by Daisy's "intrigue," Winterbourne gathered that day at St. Peter's sufficient evidence. A dozen of the

American colonists in Rome came to talk with Mrs. Costello, who sat on a little portable stool at the base of one of the great pilasters. The vesper service was going forward in splendid chants and organ tones in the adjacent choir, and meanwhile, between Mrs. Costello and her friends, there was a great deal said about poor little Miss Miller's going really "too far." Winterbourne was not pleased with what he heard, but when, coming out upon the great steps of the church, he saw Daisy, who had emerged before him, get into an open cab with her accomplice and roll away through the cynical streets of Rome, he could not deny to himself that she was going very far indeed. He felt very sorry for her — not exactly that he believed that she had completely lost her head, but because it was painful to hear so much that was pretty, and undefended, and natural assigned to a vulgar place among the categories of disorder. He made an attempt after this to give a hint to Mrs. Miller. He met one day in the Corso a friend, a tourist like himself, who had just come out of the Doria Palace, where he had been walking through the beautiful gallery. His friend talked for a moment about the superb portrait of Innocent X by Velasquez which hangs in one of the cabinets of the palace, and then said, "And in the same cabinet, by the way, I had the pleasure of contemplating a picture of a different kind — that pretty American girl whom you pointed out to me last week." In answer to Winterbourne's inquiries, his friend narrated that the pretty American girl — prettier than ever — was seated with a companion in the secluded nook in which the great papal portrait was enshrined.

"Who was her companion?" asked Winterbourne.

"A little Italian with a bouquet in his buttonhole. The girl is delightfully pretty, but I thought I understood from you the other day that she was a young lady *du meilleur monde.*"

"So she is!" answered Winterbourne; and having assured himself that his informant had seen Daisy and her companion but five minutes before, he jumped into a cab and went to call on Mrs. Miller. She was at home; but she apologized to him for receiving him in Daisy's absence.

"She's gone out somewhere with Mr. Giovanelli," said Mrs. Miller. "She's always going round with Mr. Giovanelli."

"I have noticed that they are very intimate," Winterbourne observed.

"Oh, it seems as if they couldn't live without each other!" said Mrs. Miller. "Well, he's a real gentleman, anyhow. I keep telling Daisy she's engaged!"

"And what does Daisy say?"

"Oh, she says she isn't engaged. But she might as well be!" this impartial parent resumed; "she goes on as if she was. But I've made Mr. Giovanelli promise to tell me, if *she* doesn't. I should want to write to Mr. Miller about it — shouldn't you?"

Winterbourne replied that he certainly should; and the state of mind of Daisy's mamma struck him as so unprecedented in the annals of parental vigilance that he gave up as utterly irrelevant the attempt to place her upon her guard.

After this Daisy was never at home, and Winterbourne ceased to meet her at the houses of their common acquaintance, because, as he perceived, these shrewd people had quite made up their minds that she was going too far. They ceased to invite her; and they intimated that they desired to express to observant Europeans the great truth that, though Miss Daisy Miller was a young American lady, her behavior was not representative — was regarded by her compatriots as abnormal. Winterbourne wondered how she felt about all the cold shoulders that were turned toward her, and sometimes it annoyed him to suspect that she did not feel at all. He said to himself that she was too light and childish, too uncultivated and unreasoning, too provincial, to have reflected upon her ostracism, or even to have perceived it. Then at other moments he believed that she carried about in her elegant and irresponsible little organism a defiant, passionate, perfectly observant consciousness of the impression she produced. He asked himself whether Daisy's defiance came from the consciousness of innocence, or from her being, essentially, a young person of the reckless class. It must be admitted that holding one's self to a belief in Daisy's "innocence" came to seem to Winterbourne more and more a matter of fine-spun gallantry. As I have already had occasion to relate, he was angry at finding himself reduced to chopping logic about this young lady; he was vexed at his want of instinctive certitude as to how far her eccentricities were generic, national, and how far they were personal. From either view of them he had somehow missed her, and now it was too late. She was "carried away" by Mr. Giovanelli.

A few days after his brief interview with her mother, he encountered her in that beautiful abode of flowering desolation known as the Palace of the Caesars. The early Roman spring had filled the air with bloom and perfume, and the rugged surface of the Palatine was muffled with tender verdure. Daisy was strolling along the top of one of those great mounds of ruin that are embanked with mossy marble and paved with monumental inscriptions. It seemed to him that Rome had never been so lovely as just then. He stood, looking off at the enchanting harmony of line and color that remotely encircles the city, inhaling the softly humid odors, and feeling the freshness of the year and the antiquity of the place reaffirm themselves in mysterious interfusion. It seemed to him also that Daisy had never looked so pretty, but this had been an observation of his whenever he met her. Giovanelli was at her side, and Giovanelli, too, wore an aspect of even unwonted brilliancy.

"Well," said Daisy, "I should think you would be lonesome!"

"Lonesome?" asked Winterbourne.

"You are always going round by yourself. Can't you get anyone to walk with you?"

"I am not so fortunate," said Winterbourne, "as your companion."

Giovanelli, from the first, had treated Winterbourne with distinguished politeness. He listened with a deferential air to his remarks; he laughed punctiliously at his pleasantries; he seemed disposed to testify to his belief that Winterbourne was a superior young man. He carried himself in no degree like a jealous wooer; he had obviously a great deal of tact; he had no objection to your expecting a little humility of him. It even seemed to Winterbourne at times that Giovanelli would find a certain mental relief in being able to have a private understanding with him — to say to him, as an intelligent man, that, bless you, *he* knew how extraordinary was this young lady, and didn't flatter himself with delusive — or at least *too* delusive — hopes of matrimony and dollars. On this occasion he strolled away from his companion to pluck a sprig of almond blossom, which he carefully arranged in his buttonhole.

"I know why you say that," said Daisy, watching Giovanelli. "Because you think I go round too much with *him*." And she nodded at her attendant.

"Every one thinks so — if you care to know," said Winterbourne.

"Of course I care to know!" Daisy exclaimed seriously. "But I don't believe it. They are only pretending to be shocked. They don't really care a straw what I do. Besides, I don't go round so much."

"I think you will find they do care. They will show it disagreeably."

Daisy looked at him a moment. "How disagreeably?"

"Haven't you noticed anything?" Winterbourne asked.

"I have noticed you. But I noticed you were as stiff as an umbrella the first time I saw you."

"You will find I am not so stiff as several others," said Winterbourne, smiling.

"How shall I find it?"

"By going to see the others."

"What will they do to me?"

"They will give you the cold shoulder. Do you know what that means?"

Daisy was looking at him intently; she began to color. "Do you mean as Mrs. Walker did the other night?"

"Exactly!" said Winterbourne.

She looked away at Giovanelli, who was decorating himself with his almond blossom. Then looking back at Winterbourne, "I shouldn't think you would let people be so unkind!" she said.

"How can I help it?" he asked.

"I should think you would say something."

"I do say something"; and he paused a moment. "I say that your mother tells me that she believes you are engaged."

"Well, she does," said Daisy very simply.

Winterbourne began to laugh. "And does Randolph believe it?" he asked.

"I guess Randolph doesn't believe anything," said Daisy. Randolph's skepticism excited Winterbourne to further hilarity, and he observed that Giovanelli was coming back to them. Daisy, observing it too, addressed herself again to her countryman. "Since you have mentioned it," she said, "I *am* engaged." . . . Winterbourne looked at her; he had stopped laughing. "You don't believe!" she added.

He was silent a moment; and then, "Yes, I believe it," he said.

"Oh, no, you don't!" she answered. "Well, then — I am not!"

The young girl and her cicerone were on their way to the gate of the enclosure, so that Winterbourne, who had but lately entered, presently took leave of them. A week afterward he went to dine at a beautiful villa on the Caelian Hill, and, on arriving, dismissed his hired vehicle. The evening was charming, and he promised himself the satisfaction of walking home beneath the Arch of Constantine and past the vaguely lighted monuments of the Forum. There was a waning moon in the sky, and her radiance was not brilliant, but she was veiled in a thin cloud curtain which seemed to diffuse and equalize it. When, on his return from the villa (it was eleven o'clock), Winterbourne approached the dusky circle of the Colosseum, it recurred to him, as a lover of the picturesque, that the interior, in the pale moonshine, would be well worth a glance. He turned aside and walked to one of the empty arches, near which, as he observed, an open carriage — one of the little Roman streetcabs — was stationed. Then he passed in, among the cavernous shadows of the great structure, and emerged upon the clear and silent arena. The place had never seemed to him more impressive. One-half of the gigantic circus was in deep shade, the other was sleeping in the luminous dusk. As he stood there he began to murmur Byron's famous lines, out of "Manfred," but before he had finished his quotation he remembered that if nocturnal meditations in the Colosseum are recommended by the poets, they are deprecated by the doctors. The historic atmosphere was there, certainly; but the historic atmosphere, scientifically considered, was no better than a villainous miasma. Winterbourne walked to the middle of the arena, to take a more general glance, intending thereafter to make a hasty retreat. The great cross in the center was covered with shadow; it was only as he drew near it that he made it out distinctly. Then he saw that two persons were stationed upon the low steps which formed its base. One of these was a woman, seated; her companion was standing in front of her.

Presently the sound of the woman's voice came to him distinctly in the warm night air. "Well, he looks at us as one of the old lions or tigers may have looked at the Christian martyrs!" These were the words he heard, in the familiar accent of Miss Daisy Miller.

"Let us hope he is not very hungry," responded the ingenious Giovanelli. "He will have to take me first; you will serve for dessert!"

Winterbourne stopped, with a sort of horror, and, it must be added, with a sort of relief. It was as if a sudden illumination had been flashed upon the ambiguity of Daisy's behavior, and the riddle had become easy to read. She was a young lady whom a gentleman need no longer be at pains to respect. He stood there, looking at her — looking at her companion and not reflecting that though he saw them vaguely, he himself must have been more brightly visible. He felt angry with himself that he had bothered so much about the right way of regarding Miss Daisy Miller. Then, as he was going to advance again, he checked himself, not from the fear that he was doing her injustice, but from a sense of the danger of appearing unbecomingly exhilarated by this sudden revulsion from cautious criticism. He turned away toward the entrance of the place, but, as he did so, he heard Daisy speak again.

"Why, it was Mr. Winterbourne! He saw me, and he cuts me!"

What a clever little reprobate she was, and how smartly she played at injured innocence! But he wouldn't cut her. Winterbourne came forward again and went toward the great cross. Daisy had got up; Giovanelli lifted his hat. Winterbourne had now begun to think simply of the craziness, from a sanitary point of view, of a delicate young girl lounging away the evening in this nest of malaria. What if she *were* a clever little reprobate? that was no reason for her dying of the *perniciosa*. "How long have you been here?" he asked almost brutally.

Daisy, lovely in the flattering moonlight, looked at him a moment. Then — "All the evening," she answered, gently. . . . "I never saw anything so pretty."

"I am afraid," said Winterbourne, "that you will not think Roman fever very pretty. This is the way people catch it. I wonder," he added, turning to Giovanelli, "that you, a native Roman, should countenance such a terrible indiscretion."

"Ah," said the handsome native, "for myself I am not afraid."

"Neither am I — for you! I am speaking for this young lady."

Giovanelli lifted his well-shaped eyebrows and showed his brilliant teeth. But he took Winterbourne's rebuke with docility. "I told the signorina it was a grave indiscretion, but when was the signorina ever prudent?"

"I never was sick, and I don't mean to be!" the signorina declared. "I don't look like much, but I'm healthy! I was bound to see the Colosseum by moonlight; I shouldn't have wanted to go home without that; and we have had the most beautiful time, haven't we, Mr. Giovanelli? If there has been any danger, Eugenio can give me some pills. He has got some splendid pills."

"I should advise you," said Winterbourne, "to drive home as fast as possible and take one!"

"What you say is very wise," Giovanelli rejoined. "I will go and make sure the carriage is at hand." And he went forward rapidly.

Daisy followed with Winterbourne. He kept looking at her; she seemed not in the least embarrassed. Winterbourne said nothing; Daisy chattered about the beauty of the place. "Well, I *have* seen the Colosseum by moonlight!" she exclaimed. "That's one good thing." Then, noticing Winterbourne's silence, she asked him why he didn't speak. He made no answer; he only began to laugh. They passed under one of the dark archways; Giovanelli was in front with the carriage. Here Daisy stopped a moment, looking at the young American. "*Did* you believe I was engaged, the other day?" she asked.

"It doesn't matter what I believed the other day," said Winterbourne, still laughing.

"Well, what do you believe now?"

"I believe that it makes very little difference whether you are engaged or not!"

He felt the young girl's pretty eyes fixed upon him through the thick gloom of the archway; she was apparently going to answer. But Giovanelli hurried her forward. "Quick! quick!" he said; "if we get in by midnight we are quite safe."

Daisy took her seat in the carriage, and the fortunate Italian placed himself beside her. "Don't forget Eugenio's pills!" said Winterbourne as he lifted his hat.

"I don't care," said Daisy in a little strange tone, "whether I have Roman fever or not!" Upon this the cab driver cracked his whip, and they rolled away over the desultory patches of the antique pavement.

Winterbourne, to do him justice, as it were, mentioned to no one that he had encountered Miss Miller, at midnight, in the Colosseum with a gentleman; but nevertheless, a couple of days later, the fact of her having been there under these circumstances was known to every member of the little American circle, and commented accordingly. Winterbourne reflected that they had of course known it at the hotel, and that, after Daisy's return, there had been an exchange of remarks between the porter and the cab driver. But the young man was conscious, at the same moment, that it had ceased to be a matter of serious regret to him that the little American flirt should be "talked about" by low-minded menials. These people, a day or two later, had serious information to give: the little American flirt was alarmingly ill. Winterbourne, when the rumor came to him, immediately went to the hotel for more news. He found that two or three charitable friends had preceded him, and that they were being entertained in Mrs. Miller's salon by Randolph.

"It's going round at night," said Randolph — "that's what made her sick. She's always going round at night. I shouldn't think she'd want to, it's so plaguy dark. You can't see anything here at night, except when there's a moon. In America there's always a moon!" Mrs. Miller was invisible; she was now, at least, giving her daughter the advantage of her society. It was evident that Daisy was dangerously ill.

Winterbourne went often to ask for news of her, and once he saw Mrs. Miller, who, though deeply alarmed, was, rather to his surprise, perfectly composed, and, as it appeared, a most efficient and judicious nurse. She talked a good deal about Dr. Davis, but Winterbourne paid her the compliment of saying to himself that she was not, after all, such a monstrous goose. "Daisy spoke of you the other day," she said to him. "Half the time she doesn't know what she's saying, but that time I think she did. She gave me a message she told me to tell you. She told me to tell you that she never was engaged to that handsome Italian. I am sure I am very glad; Mr. Giovanelli hasn't been near us since she was taken ill. I thought he was so much of a gentleman; but I don't call that very polite! A lady told me that he was afraid I was angry with him for taking Daisy round at night. Well, so I am, but I suppose he knows I'm a lady. I would scorn to scold him. Anyway, she says she's not engaged. I don't know why she wanted you to know, but she said to me three times, 'Mind you tell Mr. Winterbourne.' And then she told me to ask if you remembered the time you went to that castle in Switzerland. But I said I wouldn't give any such messages as that. Only, if she is not engaged, I'm sure I'm glad to know it."

But, as Winterbourne had said, it mattered very little. A week after this, the poor girl died; it had been a terrible case of the fever. Daisy's grave was in the little Protestant cemetery, in an angle of the wall of imperial Rome, beneath the cypresses and the thick spring flowers.

Winterbourne stood there beside it, with a number of other mourners, a number larger than the scandal excited by the young lady's career would have led you to expect. Near him stood Giovanelli, who came nearer still before Winterbourne turned away. Giovanelli was very pale: on this occasion he had no flower in his buttonhole; he seemed to wish to say something. At last he said, "She was the most beautiful young lady I ever saw, and the most amiable"; and then he added in a moment, "and she was the most innocent."

Winterbourne looked at him and presently repeated his words, "And the most innocent?"

"The most innocent!"

Winterbourne felt sore and angry. "Why the devil," he asked, "did you take her to that fatal place?"

Mr. Giovanelli's urbanity was apparently imperturbable. He looked on the ground a moment, and then he said, "For myself I had no fear; and she wanted to go."

"That was no reason!" Winterbourne declared.

The subtle Roman again dropped his eyes. "If she had lived, I should have got nothing. She would never have married me, I am sure."

"She would never have married you?"

"For a moment I hoped so. But no. I am sure."

Winterbourne listened to him: he stood staring at the raw protuberance among the April daisies. When he turned away again, Mr. Giovanelli, with his light, slow step, had retired.

Winterbourne almost immediately left Rome; but the following summer he again met his aunt, Mrs. Costello at Vevey. Mrs. Costello was fond of Vevey. In the interval Winterbourne had often thought of Daisy Miller and her mystifying manners. One day he spoke of her to his aunt — said it was on his conscience that he had done her injustice.

"I am sure I don't know," said Mrs. Costello. "How did your injustice affect her?"

"She sent me a message before her death which I didn't understand at the time; but I have understood it since. She would have appreciated one's esteem."

"Is that a modest way," asked Mrs. Costello, "of saying that she would have reciprocated one's affection?"

Winterbourne offered no answer to this question; but he presently said, "You were right in that remark that you made last summer. I was booked to make a mistake. I have lived too long in foreign parts."

Nevertheless, he went back to live at Geneva, whence there continue to come the most contradictory accounts of his motives of sojourn: a report that he is "studying" hard — an intimation that he is much interested in a very clever foreign lady.

Souls Belated

by Edith Wharton

1

Their railway-carriage had been full when the train left Bologna; but at the first station beyond Milan their only remaining companion — a courtly person who ate garlic out of a carpet-bag — had left his crumb-strewn seat with a bow.

Lydia's eye regretfully followed the shiny broadcloth of his retreating back till it lost itself in the cloud of touts and cab-drivers hanging about the station; then she glanced across at Gannett and caught the same regret in his look. They were both sorry to be alone.

"*Par-ten-za!*" shouted the guard. The train vibrated to a sudden slamming of doors; a waiter ran along the platform with a tray of fossilized sandwiches; a belated porter flung a bundle of shawls and band-boxes into a third-class carriage; the guard snapped out a brief *Partenza!* which indicated the purely ornamental nature of his first shout; and the train swung out of the station.

The direction of the road had changed, and a shaft of sunlight struck across the dusty red velvet seats into Lydia's corner. Gannett did not notice it. He had returned to his *Revue de Paris*, and she had to rise and lower the shade of the farther window. Against the vast horizon of their leisure such incidents stood out sharply.

Having lowered the shade, Lydia sat down, leaving the length of the carriage between herself and Gannett. At length he missed her and looked up.

"I moved out of the sun," she hastily explained.

He looked at her curiously: the sun was beating on her through the shade.

"Very well," he said pleasantly; adding, "You don't mind?" as he drew a cigarette-case from his pocket.

It was a refreshing touch, relieving the tension of her spirit with the suggestion that, after all, if he could *smoke* —! The relief was only momentary. Her experience of smokers was limited (her husband had disapproved of the use of tobacco) but she knew from hearsay that men sometimes smoked to get away from things; that a cigar might be the masculine equivalent of darkened windows and a headache. Gannett, after a puff or two, returned to his review.

It was just as she had foreseen; he feared to speak as much as she did. It was one of the misfortunes of their situation that they were never busy enough to necessitate, or even to justify, the postponement of unpleasant discussions. If they avoided a question it was obviously, unconcealably because the question was disagreeable. They had unlimited leisure and an accumulation of mental energy to devote to any subject that presented itself; new topics were in fact at a premium. Lydia sometimes had premonitions of a famine-stricken period when there would be nothing left to talk about, and she had already caught herself doling out piecemeal what, in the first prodigality of their confidences, she would have flung to him in a breath. Their silence therefore might simply mean that they had nothing to say; but it was another disadvantage of their position that it allowed infinite opportunity for the classification of minute differences. Lydia had learned to distinguish between real and factitious silences; and under Gannett's she now detected a hum of speech to which her own thoughts made breathless answer.

How could it be otherwise, with that thing between them? She glanced up at the rack overhead. The *thing* was there, in her dressing-bag, symbolically suspended over her head and his. He was thinking of it now, just as she was; they had been thinking of it in unison ever since they had entered the train. While the carriage had held other travellers they had screened her from his thoughts; but now that he and she were alone she knew exactly what was passing through his mind; she could almost hear him asking himself what he should say to her. . . .

The thing had come that morning, brought up to her in an innocent-looking envelope with the rest of their letters, as they were leaving the hotel at Bologna. As she tore it open, she and Gannett were laughing over some ineptitude of the local guide-book — they had been driven, of late, to make the most of such incidental humors of travel. Even when she had unfolded the document she took it for some unimportant business paper sent abroad for her signature, and her eye travelled inattentively over the curly *Whereases* of the preamble until a word arrested her: — Divorce. There it stood, an impassable barrier, between her husband's name and hers.

She had been prepared for it, of course, as healthy people are said to be prepared for death, in the sense of knowing it must come without in the least expecting that it will. She had known from the first that Tillotson meant to divorce her — but what did it matter? Nothing mattered, in those first days of supreme deliverance, but the fact that she was free; and not so much (she had begun to be aware) that freedom had released her from Tillotson as that it had given her to Gannett. This discovery had not been agreeable to her self-esteem. She had preferred to think that Tillotson had himself embodied all her reasons for leaving him; and those he represented had seemed cogent enough to stand in no need of reinforcement. Yet she had not left him till she met Gannett. It was her love for Gannett that had made life with Tillotson so poor and incomplete a business. If she had never, from the first, regarded her marriage as a full cancelling of her claims upon life, she had at least, for a number of years, accepted it as a provisional compensation, — she had made it "do." Existence in the commodious Tillotson mansion in Fifth Avenue — with Mrs. Tillotson senior commanding the approaches from the second-story front windows — had been reduced to a series of purely automatic acts. The moral atmosphere of the Tillotson interior was as carefully screened and curtained as the house itself: Mrs. Tillotson senior dreaded ideas as much as a draught on her back. Prudent people liked an even temperature; and to do anything unexpected was as foolish as going out in the rain. One of the chief advantages of being rich was that one need not be exposed to unforeseen contingencies: by the use of ordinary firmness and common sense one could make sure of doing exactly the same thing every day at the same hour. These doctrines, reverentially imbibed with his mother's milk, Tillotson (a model son who had never given his parents an hour's anxiety) complacently expounded to his wife, testifying to his sense of their importance by the regularity with which he wore goloshes on damp days, his punctuality at meals, and his elaborate precautions against burglars and contagious diseases. Lydia, coming from a smaller town, and entering New York life through the portals of the Tillotson mansion, had mechanically accepted this point of view as inseparable from having a front pew in church and a parterre box at the opera. All the people who came to the house revolved in the same small circle of prejudices. It was the kind of society in which, after dinner, the ladies compared the exorbitant charges of their children's teachers, and agreed that, even with the new duties on French clothes, it was cheaper in the end to get everything from Worth; while the husbands, over their cigars, lamented municipal corruption, and decided that the men to start a reform were those who had no private interests at stake.

To Lydia this view of life had become a matter of course, just as lumbering about in her mother-in-law's landau had come to seem the only possible means of locomotion, and listening every Sunday to a fashionable Presbyterian divine the inevitable atonement for having thought oneself bored on the other six days of the week. Before she met Gannett her life had seemed merely dull: his coming made it appear like one of those dismal Cruikshank prints in which the people are all ugly and all engaged in occupations that are either vulgar or stupid.

It was natural that Tillotson should be the chief sufferer from this readjustment of focus. Gannett's nearness had made her husband ridiculous, and a part of the ridicule had been reflected on herself. Her tolerance laid her open to a suspicion of obtuseness from which she must, at all costs, clear herself in Gannett's eyes.

She did not understand this until afterwards. At the time she fancied that she had merely reached the limits of endurance. In so large a charter of liberties as the mere act of leaving Tillotson seemed to confer, the small question of divorce or no divorce did not count. It was when she saw that she had left her husband only to be with

Gannett that she perceived the significance of anything affecting their relations. Her husband, in casting her off, had virtually flung her at Gannett: it was thus that the world viewed it. The measure of alacrity with which Gannett would receive her would be the subject of curious speculation over afternoon-tea tables and in club corners. She knew what would be said — she had heard it so often of others! The recollection bathed her in misery. The men would probably back Gannett to "do the decent thing"; but the ladies' eyebrows would emphasize the worthlessness of such enforced fidelity; and after all, they would be right. She had put herself in a position where Gannett "owed" her something; where, as a gentleman, he was bound to "stand the damage." The idea of accepting such compensation had never crossed her mind; the so-called rehabilitation of such a marriage had always seemed to her the only real disgrace. What she dreaded was the necessity of having to explain herself; of having to combat his arguments; of calculating, in spite of herself, the exact measure of insistence with which he pressed them. She knew not whether she most shrank from his insisting too much or too little. In such a case the nicest sense of proportion might be at fault; and how easy to fall into the error of taking her resistance for a test of his sincerity! Whichever way she turned, an ironical implication confronted her: she had the exasperated sense of having walked into the trap of some stupid practical joke.

Beneath all these preoccupations lurked the dread of what he was thinking. Sooner or later, of course, he would have to speak; but that, in the meantime, he should think, even for a moment, that there was any use in speaking, seemed to her simply unendurable. Her sensitiveness on this point was aggravated by another fear, as yet barely on the level of consciousness; the fear of unwillingly involving Gannett in the trammels of her dependence. To look upon him as the instrument of her liberation; to resist in herself the least tendency to a wifely taking possession of his future; had seemed to Lydia the one way of maintaining the dignity of their relation. Her view had not changed, but she was aware of a growing inability to keep her thoughts fixed on the essential point — the point of parting with Gannett. It was easy to face as long as she kept it sufficiently far off: but what was this act of mental postponement but a gradual encroachment on his future? What was needful was the courage to recognize the moment when, by some word or look, their voluntary fellowship should be transformed into a bondage the more wearing that it was based on none of those common obligations which make the most imperfect marriage in some sort a centre of gravity.

When the porter, at the next station, threw the door open, Lydia drew back, making way for the hoped-for intruder, but none came, and the train took up its leisurely progress through the spring wheat-fields and budding copses. She now began to hope that Gannett would speak before the next station. She watched him furtively, half-disposed to return to the seat opposite his, but there was an artificiality about his absorption that restrained her. She had never before seen him read with so conspicuous an air of warding off interruption. What could he be thinking of? Why should he be afraid to speak? Or was it her answer that he dreaded?

The train paused for the passing of an express, and he put down his book and leaned out of the window. Presently he turned to her with a smile.

"There's a jolly old villa out here," he said.

His easy tone relieved her, and she smiled back at him as she crossed over to his corner.

Beyond the embankment, through the opening in a mossy wall, she caught sight of the villa, with its broken balustrades, its stagnant fountains, and the stone satyr closing the perspective of a dusky grass-walk.

"How should you like to live there?" he asked as the train moved on.

"There?"

"In some such place, I mean. One might do worse, don't you think so? There must be at least two centuries of solitude under those yew-trees. Shouldn't you like it?"

"I — I don't know," she faltered. She knew now that he meant to speak.

He lit another cigarette. "We shall have to live somewhere, you know," he said as he bent above the match.

Lydia tried to speak carelessly. "*Je n'en vois pas la nécessité!* Why not live everywhere, as we have been doing?"

"But we can't travel forever, can we?"

"Oh, forever's a long word," she objected, picking up the review he had thrown aside.

"For the rest of our lives then," he said, moving nearer.

She made a slight gesture which caused his hand to slip from hers. "Why should we make plans? I thought you agreed with me that it's pleasanter to drift."

He looked at her hesitatingly. "It's been pleasant, certainly; but I suppose I shall have to get at my work again some day. You know I haven't written a line since — all this time," he hastily emended.

She flamed with sympathy and self-reproach. "Oh, if you mean *that* — if you want to write — of course we must settle down. How stupid of me not to have thought of it sooner! Where shall we go? Where do you think you could work best? We oughtn't to lose any more time."

He hesitated again. "I had thought of a villa in these parts. It's quiet; we shouldn't be bothered. Should you like it?"

"Of course I should like it." She paused and looked away. "But I thought — I remember your telling me once that your best work had been done in a crowd — in big cities. Why should you shut yourself up in a desert?"

Gannett, for a moment, made no reply. At length he said, avoiding her eye as carefully as she avoided his: "It might be different now; I can't tell, of course, till I try. A writer ought not to be dependent on his *milieu*; it's a mistake to humor oneself in that way; and I thought that just at first you might prefer to be —"

She faced him. "To be what?"

"Well — quiet. I mean —"

"What do you mean by 'at first'?" she interrupted.

He paused again. "I mean after we are married."

She thrust up her chin and turned toward the window. "Thank you!" she tossed back at him.

"Lydia!" he exclaimed blankly; and she felt in every fibre of her averted person that he had made the inconceivable, the unpardonable mistake of anticipating her acquiescence.

The train rattled on and he groped for a third cigarette. Lydia remained silent.

"I haven't offended you?" he ventured at length, in the tone of a man who feels his way.

She shook her head with a sigh. "I thought you understood," she moaned. Their eyes met and she moved back to his side.

"Do you want to know how not to offend me? By taking it for granted, once for all, that you've said your say on this odious question and that I've said mine, and that we stand just where we did this morning before that — that hateful paper came to spoil everything between us!"

"To spoil everything between us? What on earth do you mean? Aren't you glad to be free?"

"I was free before."

"Not to marry me," he suggested.

"But I don't *want* to marry you!" she cried.

She saw that he turned pale. "I'm obtuse, I suppose," he said slowly. "I confess I don't see what you're driving at. Are you tired of the whole business? Or was I simply a — an excuse for getting away? Perhaps you didn't care to travel alone? Was that it? And now you want to chuck me?" His voice had grown harsh. "You owe me a straight answer, you know; don't be tenderhearted!"

Her eyes swam as she leaned to him. "Don't you see it's because I care — because I care so much? Oh, Ralph! Can't you see how it would humiliate me? Try to feel it as a woman would! Don't you see the misery of being made your wife in this way? If I'd known you as a girl — that would have been a real marriage! But now — this vulgar fraud upon society — and upon a society we despised and laughed at — this sneaking back into a position that we've voluntarily forfeited: don't you see what a cheap compromise it is? We neither of us believe in the abstract 'sacredness' of marriage; we both know that no ceremony is needed to consecrate our love for each other; what object can we have in marrying, except the secret fear of each that the other may escape, or the secret longing to work our way back gradually — oh, very gradually — into the esteem of the people whose conventional morality we have always ridiculed and hated? And the very fact that, after a decent interval, these same people would come and dine with us — the women who talk about the indissolubility of marriage, and who would let me die in a gutter to-day because I am 'leading a life of sin' — doesn't that disgust you more than their turning their backs on us now? I can stand being cut by them, but I couldn't stand their coming to call and asking what I meant to do about visiting that unfortunate Mrs. So-and-so!"

She paused, and Gannett maintained a perplexed silence.

"You judge things too theoretically," he said at length, slowly. "Life is made up of compromises."

"The life we ran away from — yes! If we had been willing to accept them" — she flushed — "we might have gone on meeting each other at Mrs. Tillotson's dinners."

He smiled slightly. "I didn't know that we ran away to found a new system of ethics. I supposed it was because we loved each other."

"Life is complex, of course; isn't it the very recognition of that fact that separates us from the people who see it *tout d'une pièce*? If *they* are right — if marriage is sacred in itself and the individual must always be sacrificed to the family — then there can be no real marriage between us, since our — our being together is a protest against the sacrifice of the individual to the family." She interrupted herself with a laugh. "You'll say now that I'm giving you a lecture on sociology! Of course one acts as one can — as one must, perhaps — pulled by all sorts of invisible threads; but at least one needn't pretend, for social advantages, to subscribe to a creed that ignores the complexity of human motives — that classifies people by arbitrary signs, and puts it in everybody's reach to be on Mrs. Tillotson's visiting-list. It may be necessary that the world should be ruled by conventions — but if we believed in them, why did we break through them? And if we don't believe in them, is it honest to take advantage of the protection they afford?"

Gannett hesitated. "One may believe in them or not; but as long as they do rule the world it is only by taking advantage of their protection that one can find a *modus vivendi*."

"Do outlaws need a *modus vivendi*?"

He looked at her hopelessly. Nothing is more perplexing to man than the mental process of a woman who reasons her emotions.

She thought she had scored a point and followed it up passionately. "You do understand, don't you? You see how the very thought of the thing humiliates me! We are together to-day because we choose to be — don't let us look any farther than that!" She caught his hands.

"*Promise* me you'll never speak of it again; promise me you'll never *think* of it even," she implored, with a tearful prodigality of italics.

Through what followed — his protests, his arguments, his final unconvinced submission to her wishes — she had a sense of his but half-discerning all that, for her, had made the moment so tumultuous. They had reached that memorable point in every heart-history when, for the first time, the man seems obtuse and the woman irrational. It was the abundance of his intentions that consoled her, on reflection, for what they lacked in quality. After all, it would have been worse, incalculably worse, to have detected any overreadiness to understand her.

2

When the train at night-fall brought them to their journey's end at the edge of one of the lakes, Lydia was glad that they were not, as usual, to pass from one solitude to another. Their wanderings, during the year had indeed been like the flight of outlaws: through Sicily, Dalmatia, Transylvania and Southern Italy they had persisted in their tacit avoidance of their kind. Isolation, at first, had deepened the flavor of their happiness, as night intensifies the scent of certain flowers; but in the new phase on which they were entering, Lydia's chief wish was that they should be less abnormally exposed to the action of each other's thoughts.

She shrank, nevertheless, as the brightly-looming bulk of the fashionable Anglo-American hotel on the water's brink began to radiate toward their advancing boat its vivid suggestion of social order, visitors' lists, Church services, and the bland inquisition of the *table-d'hôte*. The mere fact that in a moment or two she must take her place on the hotel register as Mrs. Gannett seemed to weaken the springs of her resistance.

They had meant to stay for a night only, on their way to a lofty village among the glaciers of Monte Rosa; but after the first plunge into publicity, when they entered the dining-room, Lydia felt the relief of being lost in a crowd, of ceasing for a moment to be the centre of Gannett's scrutiny; and in his face she caught the reflection of her feeling. After dinner, when she went upstairs, he strolled into the smoking-room, and an hour or two later, sitting in the darkness of her window, she heard his voice below and saw him walking up and down the terrace with a companion cigar at his side. When he came up he told her he had been talking to the hotel chaplain — a very good sort of fellow.

"Queer little microcosms, these hotels! Most of these people live here all summer and then migrate to Italy or the Riviera. The English are the only people who can lead that kind of life with dignity — those soft-voiced old ladies in Shetland shawls somehow carry the British Empire under their caps. *Civis Romanus sum.* It's a curious study — there might be some good things to work up here."

He stood before her with the vivid preoccupied stare of the novelist on the trail of a "subject." With a relief that was half painful she noticed that, for the first time since they had been together, he was hardly aware of her presence.

"Do you think you could write here?"

"Here? I don't know." His stare dropped. "After being out of things so long one's first impressions are bound to be tremendously vivid, you know. I see a dozen threads already that one might follow —"

He broke off with a touch of embarrassment.

"Then follow them. We'll stay," she said with sudden decision.

"Stay here?" He glanced at her in surprise, and then, walking to the window, looked out upon the dusky slumber of the garden.

"Why not?" she said at length, in a tone of veiled irritation.

"The place is full of old cats in caps who gossip with the chaplain. Shall you like — I mean, it would be different if —"

She flamed up.

"Do you suppose I care? It's none of their business."

"Of course not; but you won't get them to think so."

"They may think what they please."

He looked at her doubtfully.

"It's for you to decide."

"We'll stay," she repeated.

Gannett, before they met, had made himself known as a successful writer of short stories and of a novel which had achieved the distinction of being widely discussed. The reviewers called him "promising," and Lydia now accused herself of having too long interfered with the fulfilment of his promise. There was a special irony in the fact, since his passionate assurances that only the stimulus of her companionship could bring out his latent faculty had almost given the dignity of a "vocation" to her course: there had been moments when she had felt unable to assume, before posterity, the responsibility of thwarting his career. And, after all, he had not written a line since they had been together: his first desire to write had come from renewed contact with the world! Was it all a mistake then? Must the most intelligent choice work more disastrously than the blundering combinations of chance? Or was there a still more humiliating answer to her perplexities? His sudden impulse of activity so exactly coincided with her own wish to withdraw, for a time, from the range of his observation, that she wondered if he too were not seeking sanctuary from intolerable problems.

"You must begin to-morrow!" she cried, hiding a tremor under the laugh with which she added, "I wonder if there's any ink in the inkstand?"

Whatever else they had at the Hotel Bellosguardo, they had, as Miss Pinsent said, "a certain tone." It was to Lady Susan Condit that they owed this inestimable benefit; an advantage ranking in Miss Pinsent's opinion above even the lawn tennis courts and the resident chaplain. It was the fact of Lady Susan's annual visit that made the hotel what it was. Miss Pinsent was certainly the last to underrate such a privilege: — "It's so important, my dear, forming as we do a little family, that there should be some one to give *the tone*; and no one could do it better than Lady Susan — an earl's daughter and a person of such determination. Dear Mrs. Ainger now — who really *ought*, you know, when Lady Susan's away — absolutely refuses to assert herself." Miss Pinsent sniffed derisively. "A bishop's niece! — my dear, I saw her once actually give in to some South Americans — and before us all. She gave up her seat at table to oblige them — such a lack of dignity! Lady Susan spoke to her very plainly about it afterwards."

Miss Pinsent glanced across the lake and adjusted her auburn front.

"But of course I don't deny that the stand Lady Susan takes is not always easy to live up to — for the rest of us, I mean. Monsieur Grossart, our good proprietor, finds it trying at times, I know — he has said as much, privately, to Mrs. Ainger and me. After all, the poor man is not to blame for wanting to fill his hotel, is he? And Lady Susan is so difficult — so very difficult — about new people. One might almost say that she disapproves of them beforehand, on principle. And yet she's had warnings — she very nearly made a dreadful mistake once with the Duchess of Levens, who dyed her hair and — well, swore and smoked. One would have thought that might have been a lesson to Lady Susan." Miss Pinsent resumed her knitting with a sigh. "There are exceptions, of course. She took at once to you and Mr. Gannett — it was quite remarkable, really. Oh, I don't mean that either — of course not! It was perfectly natural — we *all* thought you so charming and interesting from the first day — we knew at once that Mr. Gannett was intellectual, by the magazines you took in; but you know what I mean. Lady Susan is so very — well, I won't say prejudiced, as Mrs. Ainger does — but so prepared *not* to like new people, that her taking to you in that way was a surprise to us all, I confess."

Miss Pinsent sent a significant glance down the long laurustinus alley from the other end of which two people — a lady and gentleman — were strolling toward them through the smiling neglect of the garden.

"In this case, of course, it's very different; that I'm willing to admit. Their looks are against them; but, as Mrs. Ainger says, one can't exactly tell them so."

"She's very handsome," Lydia ventured, with her eyes on the lady, who showed, under the dome of a vivid sunshade, the hour-glass figure and superlative coloring of a Christmas chromo.

"That's the worst of it. She's too handsome."

"Well, after all, she can't help that."

"Other people manage to," said Miss Pinsent skeptically.

"But isn't it rather unfair of Lady Susan — considering that nothing is known about them?"

"But, my dear, that's the very thing that's against them. It's infinitely worse than any actual knowledge."

Lydia mentally agreed that, in the case of Mrs. Linton, it possibly might be.

"I wonder why they came here?" she mused.

"That's against them too. It's always a bad sign when loud people come to a quiet place. And they've brought van-loads of boxes — her maid told Mrs. Ainger's that they meant to stop indefinitely."

"And Lady Susan actually turned her back on her in the *salon?*"

"My dear, she said it was for our sakes; that makes it so unanswerable! But poor Grossart *is* in a way! The Lintons have taken his most expensive *suite*, you know — the yellow damask drawing-room above the portico — and they have champagne with every meal!"

They were silent as Mr. and Mrs. Linton sauntered by; the lady with tempestuous brows and challenging chin; the gentleman, a blond stripling, trailing after her, head downward, like a reluctant child dragged by his nurse.

"What does your husband think of them, my dear?" Miss Pinsent whispered as they passed out of earshot.

Lydia stooped to pick a violet in the border.

"He hasn't told me."

"Of your speaking to them, I mean. Would he approve of that? I know how very particular nice Americans are. I think your action might make a difference; it would certainly carry weight with Lady Susan."

"Dear Miss Pinsent, you flatter me!"

Lydia rose and gathered up her book and sunshade.

"Well, if you're asked for an opinion — if Lady Susan asks you for one — I think you ought to be prepared," Miss Pinsent admonished her as she moved away.

3

Lady Susan held her own. She ignored the Lintons, and her little family, as Miss Pinsent phrased it, followed suit. Even Mrs. Ainger agreed that it was obligatory. If Lady Susan owed it to the others not to speak to the Lintons, the others clearly owed it to Lady Susan to back her up. It was generally found expedient, at the Hotel Bellosguardo, to adopt this form of reasoning.

Whatever effect this combined action might have had upon the Lintons, it did not at least have that of driving them away. Monsieur Grossart, after a few days of suspense, had the satisfaction of seeing them settle down in his yellow damask *premier* with what looked like a permanent installation of palm-trees and silk sofa-cushions, and a gratifying continuance in the consumption of champagne. Mrs. Linton trailed her Doucet draperies up and down the garden with the same challenging air, while her husband, smoking innumerable cigarettes, dragged himself dejectedly in her wake; but neither of them, after the first encounter with Lady Susan, made any attempt to extend their acquaintance. They simply ignored their ignorers. As Miss Pinsent resentfully observed, they behaved exactly as though the hotel were empty.

It was therefore a matter of surprise, as well as of displeasure, to Lydia, to find, on glancing up one day from her seat in the garden, that the shadow which had fallen across her book was that of the enigmatic Mrs. Linton.

"I want to speak to you," that lady said, in a rich hard voice that seemed the audible expression of her gown and her complexion.

Lydia started. She certainly did not want to speak to Mrs. Linton.

"Shall I sit down here?" the latter continued, fixing her intensely-shaded eyes on Lydia's face, "or are you afraid of being seen with me?"

"Afraid?" Lydia colored. "Sit down, please. What is it that you wish to say?"

Mrs. Linton, with a smile, drew up a garden-chair and crossed one open-work ankle above the other.

"I want you to tell me what my husband said to your husband last night."

Lydia turned pale.

"My husband — to yours?" she faltered, staring at the other.

"Didn't you know they were closeted together for hours in the smoking-room after you went upstairs? My man didn't get to bed until nearly two o'clock and when he did I couldn't get a word out of him. When he wants to be aggravating I'll back him against anybody living!" Her teeth and eyes flashed persuasively upon Lydia. "But you'll tell me what they were talking about, won't you? I know I can trust you — you look so awfully kind. And it's for his own good. He's such a precious donkey and I'm so afraid he's got into some beastly scrape or other. If he'd only trust his own old woman! But they're always writing to him and setting him against me. And I've got nobody to turn to." She laid her hand on Lydia's with a rattle of bracelets. "You'll help me, won't you?"

Lydia drew back from the smiling fierceness of her brows.

"I'm sorry — but I don't think I understand. My husband has said nothing to me of — of yours."

The great black crescents above Mrs. Linton's eyes met angrily.

"I say — is that true?" she demanded.

Lydia rose from her seat.

"Oh, look here, I didn't mean that, you know — you mustn't take one up so! Can't you see how rattled I am?"

Lydia saw that, in fact, her beautiful mouth was quivering beneath softened eyes.

"I'm beside myself!" the splendid creature wailed, dropping into her seat.

"I'm so sorry," Lydia repeated, forcing herself to speak kindly; "but how can I help you?"

Mrs. Linton raised her head sharply.

"By finding out — there's a darling!"

"Finding what out?"

"What Trevenna told him."

"Trevenna —?" Lydia echoed in bewilderment.

Mrs. Linton clapped her hand to her mouth.

"Oh, Lord — there, it's out! What a fool I am! But I supposed of course you knew; I supposed everybody knew." She dried her eyes and bridled. "Didn't you know that he's Lord Trevenna? I'm Mrs. Cope."

Lydia recognized the names. They had figured in a flamboyant elopement which had thrilled fashionable London some six months earlier.

"Now you see how it is — you understand, don't you?" Mrs. Cope continued on a note of appeal. "I knew you would — that's the reason I came to you. I suppose *he* felt the same thing about your husband; he's not spoken to another soul in the place." Her face grew anxious again. "He's awfully sensitive, generally — he feels our position, he says — as if it wasn't *my* place to feel that! But when he does get talking there's no knowing what he'll say. I know he's been brooding over something lately, and I *must* find out what it is — it's to his interest that I should. I always tell him that I think only of his interest; if he'd only trust me! But he's been so odd lately — I can't think what he's plotting. You will help me, dear?"

Lydia, who had remained standing, looked away uncomfortably.

"If you mean by finding out what Lord Trevenna has told my husband, I'm afraid it's impossible."

"Why impossible?"

"Because I infer that it was told in confidence."

Mrs. Cope stared incredulously.

"Well, what of that? Your husband looks such a dear — any one can see he's awfully gone on you. What's to prevent your getting it out of him?"

Lydia flushed.

"I'm not a spy!" she exclaimed.

"A spy — a spy? How dare you?" Mrs. Cope flamed out. "Oh, I don't mean that either! Don't be angry with me — I'm so miserable." She essayed a softer note. "Do you call that spying — for one woman to help out another? I do need help so dreadfully! I'm at my wits' end with Trevenna, I am indeed. He's such a boy — a mere baby, you know; he's only two-and-twenty." She dropped her orbed lids. "He's younger than me — only fancy! a few months younger. I tell him he ought to listen to me as if I was his mother; oughtn't he now? But he won't, he won't! All his people are at him, you see — oh, I know *their* little game! Trying to get him away from me before I can get my divorce — that's what they're up to. At first he wouldn't listen to them; he used to toss their letters over to me to read; but now he reads them himself, and answers 'em too, I fancy; he's always shut up in his room, writing. If I only knew what his plan is I could stop him fast enough — he's such a simpleton. But he's dreadfully deep too — at times I can't make him out. But I know he's told your husband everything — I knew that last night the minute I laid eyes on him. And I *must* find out — you must help me — I've got no one else to turn to!"

She caught Lydia's fingers in a stormy pressure.

"Say you'll help me — you and your husband."

Lydia tried to free herself.

"What you ask is impossible; you must see that it is. No one could interfere in — in the way you ask."

Mrs. Cope's clutch tightened.

"You won't, then? You won't?"

"Certainly not. Let me go, please."

Mrs. Cope released her with a laugh.

"Oh, go by all means — pray don't let me detain you! Shall you go and tell Lady Susan Condit that there's a pair of us — or shall I save you the trouble of enlightening her?"

Lydia stood still in the middle of the path, seeing her antagonist through a mist of terror. Mrs. Cope was still laughing.

"Oh, I'm not spiteful by nature, my dear; but you're a little more than flesh and blood can stand! It's impossible, is it? Let you go, indeed! You're too good to be mixed up in my affairs, are you? Why, you little fool, the first day I laid eyes on you I saw that you and I were both in the same box — that's the reason I spoke to you."

She stepped nearer, her smile dilating on Lydia like a lamp through a fog.

"You can take your choice, you know; I always play fair. If you'll tell I'll promise not to. Now then, which is it to be?"

Lydia, involuntarily, had begun to move away from the pelting storm of words; but at this she turned and sat down again.

"You may go," she said simply. "I shall stay here."

4

She stayed there for a long time, in the hypnotized contemplation, not of Mrs. Cope's present, but of her own past. Gannett, early that morning, had gone off on a long walk — he had fallen into the habit of taking these mountain-tramps with various fellow-lodgers; but even had he been within reach she could not have gone to him just then. She had to deal with herself first. She was surprised to find how, in the last months, she had lost the habit of introspection. Since their coming to the Hotel Bellosguardo she and Gannett had tacitly avoided themselves and each other.

She was aroused by the whistle of the three o'clock steamboat as it neared the landing just beyond the hotel gates. Three o'clock! Then Gannett would soon be back — he had told her to expect him before four. She rose hurriedly, her face averted from the inquisitorial façade of the hotel. She could not see him just yet; she could not go indoors. She slipped through one of the overgrown garden-alleys and climbed a steep path to the hills.

It was dark when she opened their sitting-room door. Gannett was sitting on the window-ledge smoking a cigarette. Cigarettes were now his chief resource: he had not written a line during the two months they had spent at the Hotel Bellosguardo. In that respect, it had turned out not to be the right *milieu* after all.

He started up at Lydia's entrance.

"Where have you been? I was getting anxious."

She sat down in a chair near the door.

"Up the mountain," she said wearily.

"Alone?"

"Yes."

Gannett threw away his cigarette: the sound of her voice made him want to see her face.

"Shall we have a little light?" he suggested.

She made no answer and he lifted the globe from the lamp and put a match to the wick. Then he looked at her.

"Anything wrong? You look done up."

She sat glancing vaguely about the little sitting-room, dimly lit by the pallid-globed lamp, which left in twilight the outlines of the furniture, of his writing-table heaped with books and papers, of the tea-roses and jasmine drooping on the mantel-piece. How like home it had all grown — how like home!

"Lydia, what is wrong?" he repeated.

She moved away from him, feeling for her hatpins and turning to lay her hat and sunshade on the table.

Suddenly she said: "That woman has been talking to me."

Gannett stared.

"That woman? What woman?"

"Mrs. Linton — Mrs. Cope."

He gave a start of annoyance, still, as she perceived, not grasping the full import of her words.

"The deuce! She told you —?"

"She told me everything."

Gannett looked at her anxiously.

"What impudence! I'm so sorry that you should have been exposed to this, dear."

"Exposed!" Lydia laughed.

Gannett's brow clouded and they looked away from each other.

"Do you know *why* she told me? She had the best of reasons. The first time she laid eyes on me she saw that we were both in the same box."

"Lydia!"

"So it was natural, of course, that she should turn to me in a difficulty."

"What difficulty?"

"It seems she has reason to think that Lord Trevenna's people are trying to get him away from her before she gets her divorce —"

"Well?"

"And she fancied he had been consulting with you last night as to — as to the best way of escaping from her."

Gannett stood up with an angry forehead.

"Well — what concern of yours was all this dirty business? Why should she go to you?"

"Don't you see? It's so simple. I was to wheedle his secret out of you."

"To oblige that woman?"

"Yes; or, if I was unwilling to oblige her, then to protect myself."

"To protect yourself? Against whom?"

"Against her telling everyone in the hotel that she and I are in the same box."

"She threatened that?"

"She left me the choice of telling it myself or of doing it for me."

"The beast!"

There was a long silence. Lydia had seated herself on the sofa, beyond the radius of the lamp, and he leaned against the window. His next question surprised her.

"When did this happen? At what time, I mean?"

She looked at him vaguely.

"I don't know — after luncheon, I think. Yes, I remember; it must have been at about three o'clock."

He stepped into the middle of the room and as he approached the light she saw that his brow had cleared.

"Why do you ask?" she said.

"Because when I came in, at about half-past three, the mail was just being distributed, and Mrs. Cope was waiting as usual to pounce on her letters; you know she was always watching for the postman. She was standing so close to me that I couldn't help seeing a big official-looking envelope that was handed to her. She tore it open, gave one look at the inside, and rushed off upstairs like a whirlwind, with the director shouting after her that she had left all her other letters behind. I don't believe she ever thought of you again after that paper was put into her hand."

"Why?"

"Because she was too busy. I was sitting in the window, watching for you, when the five o'clock boat left, and who should go on board, bag and baggage, valet and maid, dressing-bags and poodle, but Mrs.

Cope and Trevenna. Just an hour and a half to pack up in! And you should have seen her when they started. She was radiant — shaking hands with everybody — waving her handkerchief from the deck — distributing bows and smiles like an empress. If ever a woman got what she wanted just in the nick of time that woman did. She'll be Lady Trevenna within a week, I'll wager."

"You think she has her divorce?"

"I'm sure of it. And she must have got it just after her talk with you."

Lydia was silent.

At length she said, with a kind of reluctance, "She was horribly angry when she left me. It wouldn't have taken long to tell Lady Susan Condit."

"Lady Susan Condit has not been told."

"How do you know?"

"Because when I went downstairs half an hour ago I met Lady Susan on the way —"

He stopped, half smiling.

"Well?"

"And she stopped to ask if I thought you would act as patroness to a charity concert she is getting up."

In spite of themselves they both broke into a laugh. Lydia's ended in sobs and she sank down with her face hidden. Gannett bent over her, seeking her hands.

"That vile woman — I ought to have warned you to keep away from her; I can't forgive myself! But he spoke to me in confidence; and I never dreamed — well, it's all over now."

Lydia lifted her head.

"Not for me. It's only just beginning."

"What do you mean?"

She put him gently aside and moved in her turn to the window. Then she went on, with her face turned toward the shimmering blackness of the lake, "You see of course that it might happen again at any moment."

"What?"

"This — this risk of being found out. And we could hardly count again on such a lucky combination of chances, could we?"

He sat down with a groan.

Still keeping her face toward the darkness, she said, "I want you to go and tell Lady Susan — and the others."

Gannett, who had moved towards her, paused a few feet off.

"Why do you wish me to do this?" he said at length, with less surprise in his voice than she had been prepared for.

"Because I've behaved basely, abominably, since we came here: letting these people believe we were married — lying with every breath I drew —"

"Yes, I've felt that too," Gannett exclaimed with sudden energy.

The words shook her like a tempest: all her thoughts seemed to fall about her in ruins.

"You — you've felt so?"

"Of course I have." He spoke with low-voiced vehemence. "Do you suppose I like playing the sneak any better than you do? It's damnable."

He had dropped on the arm of a chair, and they stared at each other like blind people who suddenly see.

"But you have liked it here," she faltered.

"Oh, I've liked it — I've liked it." He moved impatiently. "Haven't you?"

"Yes," she burst out; "that's the worst of it — that's what I can't bear. I fancied it was for your sake that I insisted on staying — because you thought you could write here; and perhaps just at first that really was the reason. But afterwards I wanted to stay myself — I loved it." She broke into a laugh. "Oh, do you see the full derision of it? These people — the very prototypes of the bores you took me away from, with the same fenced-in view of life, the same keep-off-the-grass morality, the same little cautious virtues and the same little frightened vices — well, I've clung to them, I've delighted in them, I've done my best to please them. I've toadied Lady Susan, I've gossipped with Miss Pinsent, I've pretended to be shocked with Mrs. Ainger. Respectability! It was the one thing in life that I was sure I didn't care about, and it's grown so precious to me that I've stolen it because I couldn't get it in any other way."

She moved across the room and returned to his side with another laugh.

"I who used to fancy myself unconventional! I must have been born with a card-case in my hand. You should have seen me with that poor woman in the garden. She came to me for help, poor creature, because she fancied that, having 'sinned,' as they call it, I might feel some pity for others who had been tempted in the same way. Not I! She didn't know me. Lady Susan would have been kinder, because Lady Susan wouldn't have been afraid. I hated the woman — my one thought was not to be seen with her — I could have killed her for guessing my secret. The one thing that mattered to me at that moment was my standing with Lady Susan!"

Gannett did not speak.

"And you — you've felt it too!" she broke out accusingly. "You've enjoyed being with these people as much as I have; you've let the chaplain talk to you by the hour about 'The Reign of Law' and Professor Drummond. When they asked you to hand the plate in church I was watching you — *you wanted to accept.*"

She stepped close, laying her hand on his arm.

"Do you know, I begin to see what marriage is for. It's to keep people away from each other. Sometimes I think that two people who love each other can be saved from madness only by the things that come between them — children, duties, visits, bores, relations — the things that protect married people from each other. We've been too close together — that has been our sin. We've seen the nakedness of each other's souls."

She sank again on the sofa, hiding her face in her hands.

Gannett stood above her perplexedly: he felt as though she were being swept away by some implacable current while he stood helpless on its bank.

At length he said, "Lydia, don't think me a brute — but don't you see yourself that it won't do?"

"Yes, I see it won't do," she said without raising her head.

His face cleared.

"Then we'll go to-morrow."

"Go — where?"

"To Paris; to be married."

For a long time she made no answer; then she asked slowly, "Would they have us here if we were married?"

"Have us here?"

"I mean Lady Susan — and the others."

"Have us here? Of course they would."

"Not if they knew — at least, not unless they could pretend not to know."

He made an impatient gesture.

"We shouldn't come back here, of course; and other people needn't know — no one need know."

She sighed. "Then it's only another form of deception and a meaner one. Don't you see that?"

"I see that we're not accountable to any Lady Susans on earth!"

"Then why are you ashamed of what we are doing here?"

"Because I'm sick of pretending that you're my wife when you're not — when you won't be."

She looked at him sadly.

"If I were your wife you'd have to go on pretending. You'd have to pretend that I'd never been — anything else. And our friends would have to pretend that they believed what you pretended."

Gannett pulled off the sofa-tassel and flung it away.

"You're impossible," he groaned.

"It's not I — it's our being together that's impossible. I only want you to see that marriage won't help it."

"What will help it then?"

She raised her head.

"My leaving you."

"Your leaving me?" He sat motionless, staring at the tassel which lay at the other end of the room. At length some impulse of retaliation for the pain she was inflicting made him say deliberately:

"And where would you go if you left me?"

"Oh!" she cried, wincing.

He was at her side in an instant.

"Lydia — Lydia — you know I didn't mean it; I couldn't mean it! But you've driven me out of my senses; I don't know what I'm saying. Can't you get out of this labyrinth of self-torture? It's destroying us both."

"That's why I must leave you."

"How easily you say it!" He drew her hands down and made her face him. "You're very scrupulous about yourself — and others. But have you thought of me? You have no right to leave me unless you've ceased to care —"

"It's because I care —"

"Then I have a right to be heard. If you love me you can't leave me."

Her eyes defied him.

"Why not?"

He dropped her hands and rose from her side.

"Can you?" he said sadly.

The hour was late and the lamp flickered and sank. She stood up with a shiver and turned toward the door of her room.

5

At daylight a sound in Lydia's room woke Gannett from a troubled sleep. He sat up and listened. She was moving about softly, as though fearful of disturbing him. He heard her push back one of the creaking shutters; then there was a moment's silence, which seemed to indicate that she was waiting to see if the noise had roused him.

Presently she began to move again. She had spent a sleepless night, probably, and was dressing to go down to the garden for a breath of air. Gannett rose also; but some undefinable instinct made his movements as cautious as hers. He stole to his window and looked out through the slats of the shutter.

It had rained in the night and the dawn was gray and lifeless. The cloud-muffled hills across the lake were reflected in its surface as in a tarnished mirror. In the garden, the birds were beginning to shake the drops from the motionless laurustinus-boughs.

An immense pity for Lydia filled Gannett's soul. Her seeming intellectual independence had blinded him for a time to the feminine cast of her mind. He had never thought of her as a woman who wept and clung: there was a lucidity in her intuitions that made them appear to be the result of reasoning. Now he saw the cruelty he had committed in detaching her from the normal conditions of life; he felt, too, the insight with which she had hit upon the real cause of their suffering. Their life was "impossible," as she had said — and its worst penalty was that it had made any other life impossible for them. Even had his love lessened, he was bound to her now by a hundred ties of pity and self-reproach; and she, poor child! must turn back to him as Latude returned to his cell . . .

A new sound startled him: it was the stealthy closing of Lydia's door. He crept to his own and heard her footsteps passing down the corridor. Then he went back to the window and looked out.

A minute or two later he saw her go down the steps of the porch and enter the garden. From his post of observation her face was invisible, but something about her appearance struck him. She wore a long travelling cloak and under its folds he detected the outline of a bag or bundle. He drew a deep breath and stood watching her.

She walked quickly down the laurustinus alley toward the gate; there she paused a moment, glancing about the little shady square. The stone benches under the trees were empty, and she seemed to gather resolution from the solitude about her, for she crossed the square to the steam-boat landing, and he saw her pause before the ticket-office at the head of the wharf. Now she was buying her ticket. Gannett turned his head a moment to look at the clock: the boat was due in five minutes. He had time to jump into his clothes and overtake her —

He made no attempt to move; an obscure reluctance restrained him. If any thought emerged from the tumult of his sensations, it was that he must let her go if she wished it. He had spoken last night of his rights: what were they? At the last issue, he and she were two separate beings, not made one by the miracle of common forebearances, duties, abnegations, but bound together in a *noyade* of passion that left them resisting yet clinging as they went down.

After buying her ticket, Lydia had stood for a moment looking out across the lake; then he saw her seat herself on one of the benches near the landing. He and she, at that moment, were both listening for the same sound: the whistle of the boat as it rounded the nearest promontory. Gannett turned again to glance at the clock: the boat was due now.

Where would she go? What would her life be when she had left him? She had no near relations and few friends. There was money enough . . . but she asked so much of life, in ways so complex and immaterial. He thought of her as walking barefooted through a stony waste. No one would understand her — no one would pity her — and he, who did both, was powerless to come to her aid . . .

He saw that she had risen from the bench and walked toward the edge of the lake. She stood looking in the direction from which the steamboat was to come; then she turned to the ticket-office, doubtless to ask the cause of the delay. After that she went back to the bench and sat down with bent head. What was she thinking of?

The whistle sounded; she started up, and Gannett involuntarily made a movement toward the door. But he turned back and continued to watch her. She stood motionless, her eyes on the trail of smoke that preceded the appearance of the boat. Then the little craft rounded the point, a dead-white object on the leaden water: a minute later it was puffing and backing at the wharf.

The few passengers who were waiting — two or three peasants and a snuffy priest — were clustered near the ticket-office. Lydia stood apart under the trees.

The boat lay alongside now; the gang-plank was run out and the peasants went on board with their baskets of vegetables, followed by the priest. Still Lydia did not move. A bell began to ring querulously; there was a shriek of steam, and someone must have called to her that she would be late, for she started forward, as though in answer to a summons. She moved waveringly, and at the edge of the wharf she paused. Gannett saw a sailor beckon to her; the bell rang again and she stepped upon the gang-plank.

Half-way down the short incline to the deck she stopped again; then she turned and ran back to the land. The gang-plank was drawn in, the bell ceased to ring, and the boat backed out into the lake. Lydia, with slow steps, was walking toward the garden . . .

As she approached the hotel she looked up furtively and Gannett drew back into the room. He sat down beside a table; a Bradshaw lay at his elbow, and mechanically, without knowing what he did, he began looking out the trains to Paris . . .

Coming, Aphrodite!

by Willa Cather

1

Don Hedger had lived for four years on the top floor of an old house on
the south side of Washington Square, and nobody had ever disturbed
him. He occupied one big room with no outside exposure except on
the north, where he had built in a many-paned studio window that
looked upon a court and upon the roofs and walls of other buildings.
His room was very cheerless, since he never got a ray of direct sunlight; the south corners were always in shadow. In one of the corners
was a clothes closet, built against the partition, in another a wide divan,
serving as a seat by day and a bed by night. In the front corner, the
one farther from the window, was a sink, and a table with two gas
burners where he sometimes cooked his food. There, too, in the
perpetual dusk, was the dog's bed, and often a bone or two for his
comfort.

The dog was a Boston bull terrier, and Hedger explained his surly
disposition by the fact that he had been bred to the point where it told
on his nerves. His name was Caesar III, and he had taken prizes at
very exclusive dog shows. When he and his master went out to prowl
about University Place or to promenade along West Street, Caesar III
was invariably fresh and shining. His pink skin showed through his
mottled coat, which glistened as if it had just been rubbed with olive
oil, and he wore a brass-studded collar, bought at the smartest sad-
dler's. Hedger, as often as not, was hunched up in an old striped

blanket coat, with a shapeless felt hat pulled over his bushy hair, wearing black shoes that had become grey, or brown ones that had become black, and he never put on gloves unless the day was biting cold.

Early in May, Hedger learned that he was to have a new neighbour in the rear apartment — two rooms, one large and one small, that faced the west. His studio was shut off from the larger of these rooms by double doors, which, though they were fairly tight, left him a good deal at the mercy of the occupant. The rooms had been leased, long before he came there, by a trained nurse who considered herself knowing in old furniture. She went to auction sales and bought up mahogany and dirty brass and stored it away here, where she meant to live when she retired from nursing. Meanwhile, she sub-let her rooms, with their precious furniture, to young people who came to New York to "write" or to "paint" — who proposed to live by the sweat of the brow rather than of the hand, and who desired artistic surroundings. When Hedger first moved in, these rooms were occupied by a young man who tried to write plays, — and who kept on trying until a week ago, when the nurse had put him out for unpaid rent.

A few days after the playwright left, Hedger heard an ominous murmur of voices through the bolted double doors: the lady-like intonation of the nurse — doubtless exhibiting her treasures — and another voice, also a woman's, but very different; young, fresh, unguarded, confident. All the same, it would be very annoying to have a woman in there. The only bath-room on the floor was at the top of the stairs in the front hall, and he would always be running into her as he came or went from his bath. He would have to be more careful to see that Caesar didn't leave bones about the hall, too; and she might object when he cooked steak and onions on his gas burner.

As soon as the talking ceased and the women left, he forgot them. He was absorbed in a study of paradise fish at the Aquarium, staring out at people through the glass and green water of their tank. It was a highly gratifying idea; the incommunicability of one stratum of animal life with another, — though Hedger pretended it was only an experiment in unusual lighting. When he heard trunks knocking against the sides of the narrow hall, then he realized that she was moving in at once. Toward noon, groans and deep gasps and the creaking of ropes, made him aware that a piano was arriving. After the tramp of the movers died away down the stairs, somebody touched off a few scales and chords on the instrument, and then there was peace. Presently he heard her lock her door and go down the hall humming something; going out to lunch, probably. He stuck his brushes in a can of turpentine and put on his hat, not stopping to wash his hands. Caesar was smelling along the crack under the bolted doors; his bony tail stuck out hard as a hickory withe, and the hair was standing up about his elegant collar.

Hedger encouraged him. "Come along, Caesar. You'll soon get used to a new smell."

In the hall stood an enormous trunk, behind the ladder that led to the roof, just opposite Hedger's door. The dog flew at it with a growl of hurt amazement. They went down three flights of stairs and out into the brilliant May afternoon.

Behind the Square, Hedger and his dog descended into a basement oyster house where there were no tablecloths on the tables and no handles on the coffee cups, and the floor was covered with sawdust, and Caesar was always welcome, — not that he needed any such precautionary flooring. All the carpets of Persia would have been safe for him. Hedger ordered steak and onions absentmindedly, not realizing why he had an apprehension that this dish might be less readily at hand hereafter. While he ate, Caesar sat beside his chair, gravely disturbing the sawdust with his tail.

After lunch Hedger strolled about the Square for the dog's health and watched the stages pull out; — that was almost the very last summer of the old horse stages on Fifth Avenue. The fountain had but lately begun operations for the season and was throwing up a mist of rainbow water which now and then blew south and sprayed a bunch of Italian babies that were being supported on the outer rim by older, very little older, brothers and sisters. Plump robins were hopping about on the soil; the grass was newly cut and blindingly green. Looking up the Avenue through the Arch, one could see the young poplars with their bright, sticky leaves, and the Brevoort glistening in its spring coat of paint, and shining horses and carriages, — occasionally an automobile, mis-shapen and sullen, like an ugly threat in a stream of things that were bright and beautiful and alive.

While Caesar and his master were standing by the fountain, a girl approached them, crossing the Square. Hedger noticed her because she wore a lavender cloth suit and carried in her arms a big bunch of fresh lilacs. He saw that she was young and handsome, — beautiful, in fact, with a splendid figure and good action. She, too, paused by the fountain and looked back through the Arch up the Avenue. She smiled rather patronizingly as she looked, and at the same time seemed delighted. Her slowly curving upper lip and half-closed eyes seemed to say: "You're gay, you're exciting, you are quite the right sort of thing; but you're none too fine for me!"

In the moment she tarried, Caesar stealthily approached her and sniffed at the hem of her lavender skirt, then, when she went south like an arrow, he ran back to his master and lifted a face full of emotion and alarm, his lower lip twitching under his sharp white teeth and his hazel eyes pointed with a very definite discovery. He stood thus, motionless, while Hedger watched the lavender girl go up the steps and through the door of the house in which he lived.

"You're right, my boy, it's she! She might be worse looking, you know."

When they mounted to the studio, the new lodger's door, at the back of the hall, was a little ajar, and Hedger caught the warm perfume of lilacs just brought in out of the sun. He was used to the musty smell of the old hall carpet. (The nurse-lessee had once knocked at his studio door and complained that Caesar must be somewhat responsible for the particular flavour of that mustiness, and Hedger had never spoken to her since.) He was used to the old smell, and he preferred it to that of the lilacs, and so did his companion, whose nose was so much more discriminating. Hedger shut his door vehemently, and fell to work.

Most young men who dwell in obscure studios in New York have had a beginning, come out of something, have somewhere a home town, a family, a paternal roof. But Don Hedger had no such background. He was a foundling, and had grown up in a school for homeless boys, where book-learning was a negligible part of the curriculum. When he was sixteen, a Catholic priest took him to Greensburg, Pennsylvania, to keep house for him. The priest did something to fill in the large gaps in the boy's education, — taught him to like "Don Quixote" and "The Golden Legend," and encouraged him to mess with paints and crayons in his room up under the slope of the mansard. When Don wanted to go to New York to study at the Art

League, the priest got him a night job as packer in one of the big department stores. Since then, Hedger had taken care of himself; that was his only responsibility. He was singularly unencumbered; had no family duties, no social ties, no obligations toward any one but his landlord. Since he travelled light, he had travelled rather far. He had got over a good deal of the earth's surface, in spite of the fact that he never in his life had more than three hundred dollars ahead at any one time, and he had already outlived a succession of convictions and revelations about his art.

Though he was not but twenty-six years old, he had twice been on the verge of becoming a marketable product; once through some studies of New York streets he did for a magazine, and once through a collection of pastels he brought home from New Mexico, which Remington, then at the height of his popularity, happened to see, and generously tried to push. But on both occasions Hedger decided that this was something he didn't wish to carry further, — simply the old thing over again and got nowhere, — so he took enquiring dealers experiments in a "later manner," that made them put him out of the shop. When he ran short of money, he could always get any amount of commercial work; he was an expert draughtsman and worked with lightning speed. The rest of his time he spent in groping his way from one kind of painting into another, or travelling about without luggage, like a tramp, and he was chiefly occupied with getting rid of ideas he had once thought very fine.

Hedger's circumstances, since he had moved to Washington Square, were affluent compared to anything he had ever known before. He was now able to pay advance rent and turn the key on his studio when he went away for four months at a stretch. It didn't occur to him to wish to be richer than this. To be sure, he did without a great many things other people think necessary, but he didn't miss them, because he had never had them. He belonged to no clubs, visited no houses, had no studio friends, and he ate his dinner alone in some decent little restaurant, even on Christmas and New Year's. For days together he talked to nobody but his dog and the janitress and the lame oysterman.

After he shut the door and settled down to his paradise fish on that first Tuesday in May, Hedger forgot all about his new neighbour. When the light failed, he took Caesar out for a walk. On the way home he did his marketing on West Houston Street, with a one-eyed Italian woman who always cheated him. After he had cooked his beans and scallopini, and drunk half a bottle of Chianti, he put his dishes in the sink and went up on the roof to smoke. He was the only person in the house who ever went to the roof, and he had a secret understanding with the janitress about it. He was to have "the privilege of the roof," as she said, if he opened the heavy trapdoor on sunny days to air out the upper hall, and was watchful to close it when rain threatened. Mrs. Foley was fat and dirty and hated to climb stairs, — besides, the roof was reached by a perpendicular iron ladder, definitely inaccessible to a woman of her bulk, and the iron door at the top of it was too heavy for any but Hedger's strong arm to lift. Hedger was not above medium height, but he practised with weights and dumb-bells, and in the shoulders he was as strong as a gorilla.

So Hedger had the roof to himself. He and Caesar often slept up there on hot nights, rolled in blankets he had brought home from Arizona. He mounted with Caesar under his left arm. The dog had never learned to climb a perpendicular ladder, and never did he feel so much his master's greatness and his own dependence upon him, as when he crept under his arm for this perilous ascent. Up there was even gravel to scratch in, and a dog could do whatever he liked, so long as he did not bark. It was a kind of Heaven, which no one was strong enough to reach but his great, paint-smelling master.

On this blue May night there was a slender, girlish looking young moon in the west, playing with a whole company of silver stars. Now and then one of them darted away from the group and shot off into the gauzy blue with a soft little trail of light, like laughter. Hedger and his dog were delighted when a star did this. They were quite lost in watching the glittering game, when they were suddenly diverted by a sound, — not from the stars, though it was music. It was not the Prologue to Pagliacci, which rose ever and anon on hot evenings from an Italian tenement on Thompson Street, with the gasps of the corpulent baritone who got behind it; nor was it the hurdy-gurdy man, who often played at the corner in the balmy twilight. No, this was a woman's voice, singing the tempestuous, over-lapping phrases of Signor Puccini, then comparatively new in the world, but already so popular that even Hedger recognized his unmistakable gusts of breath. He looked about over the roofs; all was blue and still, with the well-built chimneys that were never used now standing up dark and mournful. He moved softly toward the yellow quadrangle where the gas from the hall shone up through the half-lifted trapdoor. Oh yes! It came up through the hole like a strong draught, a big, beautiful voice, and it sounded rather like a professional's. A piano had arrived in the morning, Hedger remembered. This might be a very great nuisance. It would be pleasant enough to listen to, if you could turn it on and off as you wished; but you couldn't. Caesar, with the gas light shining on his collar and his ugly but sensitive face, panted and looked up for information. Hedger put down a reassuring hand.

"I don't know. We can't tell yet. It may not be so bad."

He stayed on the roof until all was still below, and finally descended, with quite a new feeling about his neighbour. Her voice, like her figure, inspired respect, — if one did not choose to call it admiration. Her door was shut, the transom was dark; nothing remained of her but the obtrusive trunk, unrightfully taking up room in the narrow hall.

2

For two days Hedger didn't see her. He was painting eight hours a day just then, and only went out to hunt for food. He noticed that she practised scales and exercises for about an hour in the morning; then she locked her door, went humming down the hall, and left him in peace. He heard her getting her coffee ready at about the same time he got his. Earlier still, she passed his room on her way to her bath. In the evening she sometimes sang, but on the whole she didn't bother him. When he was working well he did not notice anything much. The morning paper lay before his door until he reached out for his milk bottle, then he kicked the sheet inside and it lay on the floor until evening. Sometimes he read it and sometimes he did not. He forgot there was anything of importance going on in the world outside of his third floor studio. Nobody had ever taught him that he ought to be interested in other people; in the Pittsburgh steel strike, in the Fresh Air Fund, in the scandal about the Babies' Hospital. A grey wolf, living in a Wyoming canyon, would hardly have been less concerned about these things than was Don Hedger.

One morning he was coming out of the bath-room at the front end of the hall, having just given Caesar his bath and rubbed him into a glow with a heavy towel. Before the door, lying in wait for him, as it were, stood a tall figure in a flowing blue silk dressing gown that fell away from her marble arms. In her hands she carried various accessories of the bath.

"I wish," she said distinctly, standing in his way, "I wish you wouldn't wash your dog in the tub. I never heard of such a thing! I've found his hair in the tub, and I've smelled a doggy smell, and now I've caught you at it. It's an outrage!"

Hedger was badly frightened. She was so tall and positive, and was fairly blazing with beauty and anger. He stood blinking, holding on to his sponge and dog-soap, feeling that he ought to bow very low to her. But what he actually said was:

"Nobody has ever objected before. I always wash the tub, — and, anyhow, he's cleaner than most people."

"Cleaner than me?" her eyebrows went up, her white arms and neck and her fragrant person seemed to scream at him like a band of outraged nymphs. Something flashed through his mind about a man who was turned into a dog, or was pursued by dogs, because he unwittingly intruded upon the bath of beauty.

"No, I didn't mean that," he muttered, turning scarlet under the bluish stubble of his muscular jaws. "But I know he's cleaner than I am."

"That I don't doubt!" Her voice sounded like a soft shivering of crystal, and with a smile of pity she drew the folds of her voluminous blue robe close about her and allowed the wretched man to pass. Even Caesar was frightened; he darted like a streak down the hall, through the door and to his own bed in the corner among the bones.

Hedger stood still in the doorway, listening to indignant sniffs and coughs and a great swishing of water about the sides of the tub. He had washed it; but as he had washed it with Caesar's sponge, it was quite possible that a few bristles remained; the dog was shedding now. The playwright had never objected, nor had the jovial illustrator who occupied the front apartment, — but he, as he admitted, "was usually pye-eyed, when he wasn't in Buffalo." He went home to Buffalo sometimes to rest his nerves.

It had never occurred to Hedger that any one would mind using the tub after Caesar; — but then, he had never seen a beautiful girl caparisoned for the bath before. As soon as he beheld her standing there, he realized the unfitness of it. For that matter, she ought not to step into a tub that any other mortal had bathed in; the illustrator was sloppy and left cigarette ends on the moulding.

All morning as he worked he was gnawed by a spiteful desire to get back at her. It rankled that he had been so vanquished by her disdain. When he heard her locking her door to go out for lunch, he stepped quickly into the hall in his messy painting coat, and addressed her.

"I don't wish to be exigent, Miss," — he had certain grand words that he used upon occasion — "but if this is your trunk, it's rather in the way here."

"Oh, very well!" she exclaimed carelessly, dropping her keys into her handbag. "I'll have it moved when I can get a man to do it," and she went down the hall with her free, roving stride.

Her name, Hedger discovered from her letters, which the postman left on the table in the lower hall, was Eden Bower.

3

In the closet that was built against the partition separating his room from Miss Bower's, Hedger kept all his wearing apparel, some of it on hooks and hangers, some of it on the floor. When he opened his closet door now-a-days, little dust-coloured insects flew out on downy wing, and he suspected that a brood of moths were hatching in his winter overcoat. Mrs. Foley, the janitress, told him to bring down all his heavy clothes and she would give them a beating and hang them in the court. The closet was in such disorder that he shunned the encounter, but one hot afternoon he set himself to the task. First he threw out a pile of forgotten laundry and tied it up in a sheet. The bundle stood as high as his middle when he had knotted the corners. Then he got his shoes and overshoes together. When he took his overcoat from its place against the partition, a long ray of yellow light shot across the dark enclosure, — a knot hole, evidently, in the high wainscoting of the west room. He had never noticed it before, and without realizing what he was doing, he stooped and squinted through it.

Yonder, in a pool of sunlight, stood his new neighbour, wholly unclad, doing exercises of some sort before a long gilt mirror. Hedger did not happen to think how unpardonable it was of him to watch her. Nudity was not improper to any one who had worked so much from the figure, and he continued to look, simply because he had never seen a woman's body so beautiful as this one, — positively glorious in action. As she swung her arms and changed from one pivot of motion to another, muscular energy seemed to flow through her from her toes to her finger-tips. The soft flush of exercise and the gold of afternoon sun played over her flesh together, enveloped her in a luminous mist which, as she turned and twisted, made now an arm, now a shoulder, now a thigh, dissolve in pure light and instantly recover its outline with the next gesture. Hedger's fingers curved as if he were holding a crayon; mentally he was doing the whole figure in a single running line, and the charcoal seemed to explode in his hand at the point where the energy of each gesture was discharged into the whirling disc of light, from a foot or shoulder, from the up-thrust chin or the lifted breasts.

He could not have told whether he watched her for six minutes or sixteen. When her gymnastics were over, she paused to catch up a lock of hair that had come down, and examined with solicitude a little reddish mole that grew under her left arm-pit. Then, with her hand on her hip, she walked unconcernedly across the room and disappeared through the door into her bedchamber.

Disappeared — Don Hedger was crouching on his knees, staring at the golden shower which poured in through the west windows, at the lake of gold sleeping on the faded Turkish carpet. The spot was enchanted; a vision out of Alexandria, out of the remote pagan past, had bathed itself there in Helianthine fire.

When he crawled out of his closet, he stood blinking at the grey sheet stuffed with laundry, not knowing what had happened to him. He felt a little sick as he contemplated the bundle. Everything here was different; he hated the disorder of the place, the grey prison light, his old shoes and himself and all his slovenly habits. The black calico curtains that ran on wires over his big window were white with dust. There were three greasy frying pans in the sink, and the sink itself — He felt desperate. He couldn't stand this another minute. He took up an armful of winter clothes and ran down four flights into the basement.

"Mrs. Foley," he began, "I want my room cleaned this afternoon, thoroughly cleaned. Can you get a woman for me right away?"

"Is it company you're having?" the fat, dirty janitress enquired.

Mrs. Foley was the widow of a useful Tammany man, and she owned real estate in Flatbush. She was huge and soft as a feather bed. Her face and arms were permanently coated with dust, grained like wood where the sweat had trickled.

"Yes, company. That's it."

"Well, this is a queer time of the day to be asking for a cleaning woman. It's likely I can get you old Lizzie, if she's not drunk. I'll send Willy round to see."

Willy, the son of fourteen, roused from the stupor and stain of his fifth box of cigarettes by the gleam of a quarter, went out. In five minutes he returned with old Lizzie, — she smelling strong of spirits and wearing several jackets which she had put on one over the other, and a number of skirts, long and short, which made her resemble an animated dish-clout. She had, of course, to borrow her equipment from Mrs. Foley, and toiled up the long flights, dragging mop and pail and broom. She told Hedger to be of good cheer, for he had got the right woman for the job, and showed him a great leather strap she wore about her wrist to prevent dislocation of tendons. She swished about the place, scattering dust and splashing soapsuds, while he watched her in nervous despair. He stood over Lizzie and made her scour the sink, directing her roughly, then paid her and got rid of her. Shutting the door on his failure, he hurried off with his dog to lose himself among the stevedores and dock labourers on West Street.

A strange chapter began for Don Hedger. Day after day, at that hour in the afternoon, the hour before his neighbour dressed for dinner, he crouched down in his closet to watch her go through her mysterious exercises. It did not occur to him that his conduct was detestable; there was nothing shy or retreating about this unclad girl, — a bold body, studying itself quite coolly and evidently well pleased with itself, doing all this for a purpose. Hedger scarcely regarded his action as conduct at all; it was something that had happened to him. More than once he went out and tried to stay away for the whole afternoon, but at about five o'clock he was sure to find himself among his old shoes in the dark. The pull of that aperture was stronger than his will, — and he had always considered his will the strongest thing about him. When she threw herself upon the divan and lay resting, he still stared, holding his breath. His nerves were so on edge that a sudden noise made him start and brought out the sweat on his forehead. The dog would come and tug at his sleeve, knowing that something was wrong with his master. If he attempted a mournful whine, those strong hands closed about his throat.

When Hedger came slinking out of his closet, he sat down on the edge of the couch, sat for hours without moving. He was not painting at all now. This thing, whatever it was, drank him up as ideas had sometimes done, and he sank into a stupor of idleness as deep and dark as the stupor of work. He could not understand it; he was no boy, he had worked from models for years, and a woman's body was no mystery to him. Yet now he did nothing but sit and think about one. He slept very little, and with the first light of morning he awoke as completely possessed by this woman as if he had been with her all the night before. The unconscious operations of life went on in him only to perpetuate this excitement. His brain held but one image now — vibrated, burned with it. It was a heathenish feeling; without friendliness, almost without tenderness.

Women had come and gone in Hedger's life. Not having had a mother to begin with, his relations with them, whether amorous or friendly, had been casual. He got on well with janitresses and washwomen, with Indians and with the peasant women of foreign countries. He had friends among the silk-skirt factory girls who came to eat their lunch in Washington Square, and he sometimes took a model for a day in the country. He felt an unreasoning antipathy toward the well-dressed women he saw coming out of big shops, or driving in the Park. If, on his way to the Art Museum, he noticed a pretty girl standing on the steps of one of the houses on upper Fifth Avenue, he frowned at her and went by with his shoulders hunched up as if he were cold. He had never known such girls, or heard them talk, or seen the inside of the houses in which they lived; but he believed them all to be artificial and, in an aesthetic sense, perverted. He saw them enslaved by desire of merchandise and manufactured articles, effective only in making life complicated and insincere and in embroidering it with ugly and meaningless trivialities. They were enough, he thought, to make one almost forget woman as she existed in art, in thought, and in the universe.

He had no desire to know the woman who had, for the time at least, so broken up his life, — no curiosity about her every-day personality. He shunned any revelation of it, and he listened for Miss Bower's coming and going, not to encounter, but to avoid her. He wished that the girl who wore shirt-waists and got letters from Chicago would keep out of his way, that she did not exist. With her he had naught to make. But in a room full of sun, before an old mirror, on a little enchanted rug of sleeping colours, he had seen a woman who emerged naked through a door, and disappeared naked. He thought of that body as never having been clad, or as having worn the stuffs and dyes of all the centuries but his own. And for him she had no geographical associations; unless with Crete, or Alexandria, or Veronese's Venice. She was the immortal conception, the perennial theme.

The first break in Hedger's lethargy occurred one afternoon when two young men came to take Eden Bower out to dine. They went into her music room, laughed and talked for a few minutes, and then took her away with them. They were gone a long while, but he did not go out for food himself; he waited for them to come back. At last he heard them coming down the hall, gayer and more talkative than when they left. One of them sat down at the piano, and they all began to sing. This Hedger found absolutely unendurable. He snatched up his hat and went running down the stairs. Caesar leaped beside him, hoping that old times were coming back. They had supper in the oysterman's basement and then sat down in front of their own doorway. The moon stood full over the Square, a thing of regal glory; but Hedger did not see the moon; he was looking, murderously, for men. Presently two, wearing straw hats and white trousers and carrying canes, came down the steps from his house. He rose and dogged them across the Square. They were laughing and seemed very much elated about something. As one stopped to light a cigarette, Hedger caught from the other:

"Don't you think she has a beautiful talent?"

His companion threw away his match. "She has a beautiful figure." They both ran to catch the stage.

Hedger went back to his studio. The light was shining from her transom. For the first time he violated her privacy at night, and peered through that fatal aperture. She was sitting, fully dressed, in the window, smoking a cigarette and looking out over the housetops. He watched her until she rose, looked about her with a disdainful, crafty smile, and turned out the light.

The next morning, when Miss Bower went out, Hedger followed

her. Her white skirt gleamed ahead of him as she sauntered about the Square. She sat down behind the Garibaldi statue and opened a music book she carried. She turned the leaves carelessly, and several times glanced in his direction. He was on the point of going over to her, when she rose quickly and looked up at the sky. A flock of pigeons had risen from somewhere in the crowded Italian quarter to the south, and were wheeling rapidly up through the morning air, soaring and dropping, scattering and coming together, now grey, now white as silver, as they caught or intercepted the sunlight. She put up her hand to shade her eyes and followed them with a kind of defiant delight in her face.

Hedger came and stood beside her. "You've surely seen them before?"

"Oh, yes," she replied, still looking up. "I see them every day from my windows. They always come home about five o'clock. Where do they live?"

"I don't know. Probably some Italian raises them for the market. They were here long before I came, and I've been here four years."

"In that same gloomy room? Why didn't you take mine when it was vacant?"

"It isn't gloomy. That's the best light for painting."

"Oh, is it? I don't know anything about painting. I'd like to see your pictures sometime. You have such a lot in there. Don't they get dusty, piled up against the wall like that?"

"Not very. I'd be glad to show them to you. Is your name really Eden Bower? I've seen your letters on the table."

"Well, it's the name I'm going to sing under. My father's name is Bowers, but my friend Mr. Jones, a Chicago newspaper man who writes about music, told me to drop the 's.' He's crazy about my voice."

Miss Bower didn't usually tell the whole story, — about anything. Her first name, when she lived in Huntington, Illinois, was Edna, but Mr. Jones had persuaded her to change it to one which he felt would be worthy of her future. She was quick to take suggestions, though she told him she "didn't see what was the matter with 'Edna.' "

She explained to Hedger that she was going to Paris to study. She was waiting in New York for Chicago friends who were to take her over, but who had been detained. "Did you study in Paris?" she asked.

"No, I've never been in Paris. But I was in the south of France all last summer, studying with C——. He's the biggest man among the moderns, — at least I think so."

Miss Bower sat down and made room for him on the bench. "Do tell me about it. I expected to be there by this time, and I can't wait to find out what it's like."

Hedger began to relate how he had seen some of this Frenchman's work in an exhibition, and deciding at once that this was the man for him, he had taken a boat for Marseilles the next week, going over steerage. He proceeded at once to the little town on the coast where his painter lived, and presented himself. The man never took pupils, but because Hedger had come so far, he let him stay. Hedger lived at the master's house and every day they went out together to paint, sometimes on the blazing rocks down by the sea. They wrapped themselves in light woollen blankets and didn't feel the heat. Being there and working with C—— was being in Paradise, Hedger concluded; he learned more in three months than in all his life before.

Eden Bower laughed. "You're a funny fellow. Didn't you do anything but work? Are the women very beautiful? Did you have awfully good things to eat and drink?"

Hedger said some of the women were fine looking, especially one girl who went about selling fish and lobsters. About the food there was nothing remarkable, — except the ripe figs, he liked those. They drank sour wine, and used goat-butter, which was strong and full of hair, as it was churned in a goat skin.

"But don't they have parties or banquets? Aren't there any fine hotels down there?"

"Yes, but they are all closed in summer, and the country people are poor. It's a beautiful country, though."

"How, beautiful?" she persisted.

"If you want to go in, I'll show you some sketches, and you'll see."

Miss Bower rose. "All right. I won't go to my fencing lesson this morning. Do you fence? Here comes your dog. You can't move but he's after you. He always makes a face at me when I meet him in the hall, and shows his nasty little teeth as if he wanted to bite me."

In the studio Hedger got out his sketches, but to Miss Bower, whose favourite pictures were Christ Before Pilate and a redhaired Magdalen of Henner, these landscapes were not at all beautiful, and they gave her no idea of any country whatsoever. She was careful not to commit herself, however. Her vocal teacher had already convinced her that she had a great deal to learn about many things.

"Why don't we go out to lunch somewhere?" Hedger asked, and began to dust his fingers with a handkerchief — which he got out of sight as swiftly as possible.

"All right, the Brevoort," she said carelessly. "I think that's a good place, and they have good wine. I don't care for cocktails."

Hedger felt his chin uneasily. "I'm afraid I haven't shaved this morning. If you could wait for me in the Square? It won't take me ten minutes."

Left alone, he found a clean collar and handkerchief, brushed his coat and blacked his shoes, and last of all dug up ten dollars from the bottom of an old copper kettle he had brought from Spain. His winter hat was of such a complexion that the Brevoort hall boy winked at the porter as he took it and placed it on the rack in a row of fresh straw ones.

4

That afternoon Eden Bower was lying on the couch in her music room, her face turned to the window, watching the pigeons. Reclining thus she could see none of the neighbouring roofs, only the sky itself and the birds that crossed and recrossed her field of vision, white as scraps of paper blowing in the wind. She was thinking that she was young and handsome and had had a good lunch, that a very easy-going, light-hearted city lay in the streets below her; and she was wondering why she found this queer painter chap, with his lean, bluish cheeks and heavy black eyebrows, more interesting than the smart young men she met at her teacher's studio.

Eden Bower was, at twenty, very much the same person that we all know her to be at forty, except that she knew a great deal less. But one thing she knew: that she was to be Eden Bower. She was like some one standing before a great show window full of beautiful and costly things, deciding which she will order. She understands that they will not all be delivered immediately, but one by one they will arrive at her door. She already knew some of the many things that were to happen to her; for instance, that the Chicago millionaire who was going to take her abroad with his sister as chaperone, would eventually press his claim in quite another manner. He was the most circumspect of bachelors, afraid of everything obvious, even of women who were too flagrantly handsome. He was a nervous collector of pictures and furniture, a nervous patron of music, and a nervous host; very cautious about his health, and about any course of conduct that might make him ridiculous. But she knew that he would at last throw all his precautions to the winds.

People like Eden Bower are inexplicable. Her father sold farming machinery in Huntington, Illinois, and she had grown up with no acquaintances or experiences outside of that prairie town. Yet from her earliest childhood she had not one conviction or opinion in common with the people about her, — the only people she knew. Before she was out of short dresses she had made up her mind that she was going to be an actress, that she would live far away in great cities, that she would be much admired by men and would have everything she wanted. When she was thirteen, and was already singing and reciting for church entertainments, she read in some illustrated magazine a long article about the late Czar of Russia, then just come to the throne or about to come to it. After that, lying in the hammock on the front porch on summer evenings, or sitting through a long sermon in the family pew, she amused herself by trying to make up her mind whether she would or would not be the Czar's mistress when she played in his Capital. Now Eden had met this fascinating world only in the novels of Ouida, — her hard-worked little mother kept a long row of them in the upstairs storeroom, behind the linen chest. In Huntington, women who bore that relation to men were called by a very different name, and their lot was not an enviable one; of all the shabby and poor, they were the shabbiest. But then, Eden had never lived in Huntington, not even before she began to find books like "Sappho" and "Mademoiselle de Maupin," secretly sold in paper covers throughout Illinois. It was as if she had come into Huntington, into the Bowers family, on one of the trains that puffed over the marshes behind their back fence all day long, and was waiting for another train to take her out.

As she grew older and handsomer, she had many beaux, but these small-town boys didn't interest her. If a lad kissed her when he brought her home from a dance, she was indulgent and she rather liked it. But if he pressed her further, she slipped away from him laughing. After she began to sing in Chicago, she was consistently discreet. She stayed as a guest in rich people's houses, and she knew that she was being watched like a rabbit in a laboratory. Covered up in bed, with the lights out, she thought her own thoughts, and laughed.

This summer in New York was her first taste of freedom. The Chicago capitalist, after all his arrangements were made for sailing, had been compelled to go to Mexico to look after oil interests. His sister knew an excellent singing master in New York. Why should not a discreet, well-balanced girl like Miss Bower spend the summer there, studying quietly? The capitalist suggested that his sister might enjoy a summer on Long Island; he would rent the Griffith's place for her, with all the servants, and Eden could stay there. But his sister met this proposal with a cold stare. So it fell out, that between selfishness and greed, Eden got a summer all her own, — which really did a great deal toward making her an artist and whatever else she was afterward to become. She had time to look about, to watch without being watched; to select diamonds in one window and furs in another, to select shoulders and moustaches in the big hotels where she went to lunch. She had the easy freedom of obscurity and the consciousness of power. She enjoyed both. She was in no hurry.

While Eden Bower watched the pigeons, Don Hedger sat on the other side of the bolted doors, looking into a pool of dark turpentine, at his idle brushes, wondering why a woman could do this to him. He, too, was sure of his future and knew that he was a chosen man. He could not know, of course, that he was merely the first to fall under a fascination which was to be disastrous to a few men and pleasantly stimulating to many thousands. Each of these two young people sensed the future, but not completely. Don Hedger knew that nothing much would ever happen to him. Eden Bower understood that to her a great deal would happen. But she did not guess that her neighbour would have more tempestuous adventures sitting in his dark studio than she would find in all the capitals of Europe, or in all the latitude of conduct she was prepared to permit herself.

5

One Sunday morning Eden was crossing the Square with a spruce young man in a white flannel suit and a panama hat. They had been breakfasting at the Brevoort and he was coaxing her to let him come up to her rooms and sing for an hour.

"No, I've got to write letters. You must run along now. I see a friend of mine over there, and I want to ask him about something before I go up."

"That fellow with the dog? Where did you pick him up?" the young man glanced toward the seat under a sycamore where Hedger was reading the morning paper.

"Oh, he's an old friend from the West," said Eden easily. "I won't introduce you, because he doesn't like people. He's a recluse. Goodbye. I can't be sure about Tuesday. I'll go with you if I have time after my lesson." She nodded, left him, and went over to the seat littered with newspapers. The young man went up the Avenue without looking back.

"Well, what are you going to do today? Shampoo this animal all morning?" Eden enquired teasingly.

Hedger made room for her on the seat. "No, at twelve o'clock I'm going out to Coney Island. One of my models is going up in a balloon this afternoon. I've often promised to go and see her, and now I'm going."

Eden asked if models usually did such stunts. No, Hedger told her, but Molly Welch added to her earnings in that way. "I believe," he added, "she likes the excitement of it. She's got a good deal of spirit. That's why I like to paint her. So many models have flaccid bodies."

"And she hasn't, eh? Is she the one who comes to see you? I can't help hearing her, she talks so loud."

"Yes, she has a rough voice, but she's a fine girl. I don't suppose you'd be interested in going?"

"I don't know," Eden sat tracing patterns on the asphalt with the end of her parasol. "Is it any fun? I got up feeling I'd like to do something different today. It's the first Sunday I've not had to sing in church. I had that engagement for breakfast at the Brevoort, but it wasn't very exciting. That chap can't talk about anything but himself."

Hedger warmed a little. "If you've never been to Coney Island, you ought to go. It's nice to see all the people; tailors and bar-tenders and prize-fighters with their best girls, and all sorts of folks taking a holiday."

Eden looked sidewise at him. So one ought to be interested in people of that kind, ought one? He was certainly a funny fellow. Yet he was never, somehow, tiresome. She had seen a good deal of him lately, but she kept wanting to know him better, to find out what made him different from men like the one she had just left — whether he really was as different as he seemed. "I'll go with you," she said at last, "if you'll leave that at home." She pointed to Caesar's flickering ears with her sunshade.

"But he's half the fun. You'd like to hear him bark at the waves when they come in."

"No, I wouldn't. He's jealous and disagreeable if he sees you talking to any one else. Look at him now."

"Of course, if you make a face at him. He knows what that means, and he makes a worse face. He likes Molly Welch, and she'll be disappointed if I don't bring him."

Eden said decidedly that he couldn't take both of them. So at twelve o'clock when she and Hedger got on the boat at Desbrosses Street, Caesar was lying on his pallet, with a bone.

Eden enjoyed the boat-ride. It was the first time she had been on the water, and she felt as if she were embarking for France. The light warm breeze and the plunge of the waves made her very wide awake, and she liked crowds of any kind. They went to the balcony of a big, noisy restaurant and had a shore dinner, with tall steins of beer. Hedger had got a big advance from his advertising firm since he first lunched with Miss Bower ten days ago, and he was ready for anything.

After dinner they went to the tent behind the bathing beach, where the tops of two balloons bulged out over the canvas. A red-faced man in a linen suit stood in front of the tent, shouting in a hoarse voice and telling the people that if the crowd was good for five dollars more, a beautiful young woman would risk her life for their entertainment. Four little boys in dirty red uniforms ran about taking contributions in their pill-box hats. One of the balloons was bobbing up and down in its tether and people were shoving forward to get nearer the tent.

"Is it dangerous, as he pretends?" Eden asked.

"Molly says it's simple enough if nothing goes wrong with the balloon. Then it would be all over, I suppose."

"Wouldn't you like to go up with her?"

"I? Of course not. I'm not fond of taking foolish risks."

Eden sniffed. "I shouldn't think sensible risks would be very much fun."

Hedger did not answer, for just then every one began to shove the other way and shout, "Look out. There she goes!" and a band of six pieces commenced playing furiously.

As the balloon rose from its tent enclosure, they saw a girl in green tights standing in the basket, holding carelessly to one of the ropes with one hand and with the other waving to the spectators. A long rope trailed behind to keep the balloon from blowing out to sea.

As it soared, the figure in green tights in the basket diminished to a mere spot, and the balloon itself, in the brilliant light, looked like a big silver-grey bat, with its wings folded. When it began to sink, the girl stepped through the hole in the basket to a trapeze that hung below, and gracefully descended through the air, holding to the rod with both hands, keeping her body taut and her feet close together. The crowd, which had grown very large by this time, cheered vociferously. The men took off their hats and waved, little boys shouted, and fat old women, shining with the heat and a beer lunch, murmured admiring comments upon the balloonist's figure. "Beautiful legs, she has!"

"That's so," Hedger whispered. "Not many girls would look well in that position." Then, for some reason, he blushed a slow, dark, painful crimson.

The balloon descended slowly, a little way from the tent, and the red-faced man in the linen suit caught Molly Welch before her feet touched the ground, and pulled her to one side. The band struck up "Blue Bell" by way of welcome, and one of the sweaty pages ran forward and presented the balloonist with a large bouquet of artificial flowers. She smiled and thanked him, and ran back across the sand to the tent.

"Can't we go inside and see her?" Eden asked. "You can explain to the door man. I want to meet her." Edging forward, she herself addressed the man in the linen suit and slipped something from her purse into his hand.

They found Molly seated before a trunk that had a mirror in the lid and a "make-up" outfit spread upon the tray. She was wiping the cold cream and powder from her neck with a discarded chemise.

"Hello, Don," she said cordially. "Brought a friend?"

Eden liked her. She had an easy, friendly manner, and there was something boyish and devil-may-care about her.

"Yes, it's fun. I'm mad about it," she said in reply to Eden's questions. "I always want to let go, when I come down on the bar. You don't feel your weight at all, as you would on a stationary trapeze."

The big drum boomed outside, and the publicity man began shouting to newly arrived boatloads. Miss Welch took a last pull at her cigarette. "Now you'll have to get out, Don. I change for the next act. This time I go up in a black evening dress, and lose the skirt in the basket before I start down."

"Yes, go along," said Eden. "Wait for me outside the door. I'll stay and help her dress."

Hedger waited and waited, while women of every build bumped into him and begged his pardon, and the red pages ran about holding out their caps for coins, and the people ate and perspired and shifted parasols against the sun. When the band began to play a two-step, all the bathers ran up out of the surf to watch the ascent. The second balloon bumped and rose, and the crowd began shouting to the girl in a black evening dress who stood leaning against the ropes and smiling. "It's a new girl," they called. "It ain't the Countess this time. You're a peach, girlie!"

The balloonist acknowledged these compliments, bowing and looking down over the sea of upturned faces, — but Hedger was determined she should not see him, and he darted behind the tent-fly. He was suddenly dripping with cold sweat, his mouth was full of the bitter taste of anger and his tongue felt stiff behind his teeth. Molly Welch, in a shirt-waist and a white tam-o'-shanter cap, slipped out from the tent under his arm and laughed up in his face. "She's a crazy one you brought along. She'll get what she wants!"

"Oh, I'll settle with you, all right!" Hedger brought out with difficulty.

"It's not my fault, Donnie. I couldn't do anything with her. She bought me off. What's the matter with you? Are you soft on her? She's safe enough. It's as easy as rolling off a log, if you keep cool." Molly Welch was rather excited herself, and she was chewing gum at a high speed as she stood beside him, looking up at the floating silver cone. "Now watch," she exclaimed suddenly. "She's coming down on the bar. I advised her to cut that out, but you see she does it first-rate. And she got rid of the skirt, too. Those black tights show off her legs very well. She keeps her feet together like I told her, and makes a good line along the back. See the light on those silver slippers, — that was a good idea I had. Come along to meet her. Don't be a grouch; she's done it fine!"

Molly tweaked his elbow, and then left him standing like a stump, while she ran down the beach with the crowd.

Though Hedger was sulking, his eye could not help seeing the low blue welter of the sea, the arrested bathers, standing in the surf, their arms and legs stained red by the dropping sun, all shading their eyes and gazing upward at the slowly falling silver star.

Molly Welch and the manager caught Eden under the arms and lifted her aside, a red page dashed up with a bouquet, and the band struck up "Blue Bell." Eden laughed and bowed, took Molly's arm, and ran up the sand in her black tights and silver slippers, dodging the friendly old women, and the gallant sports who wanted to offer their homage on the spot.

When she emerged from the tent, dressed in her own clothes, that part of the beach was almost deserted. She stepped to her companion's side and said carelessly: "Hadn't we better try to catch this boat? I hope you're not sore at me. Really, it was lots of fun."

Hedger looked at his watch. "Yes, we have fifteen minutes to get to the boat," he said politely.

As they walked toward the pier, one of the pages ran up panting. "Lady, you're carrying off the bouquet," he said, aggrievedly.

Eden stopped and looked at the bunch of spotty cotton roses in her hand. "Of course. I want them for a souvenir. You gave them to me yourself."

"I give 'em to you for looks, but you can't take 'em away. They belong to the show."

"Oh, you always use the same bunch?"

"Sure we do. There ain't too much money in this business."

She laughed and tossed them back to him. "Why are you angry?" she asked Hedger. "I wouldn't have done it if I'd been with some fellows, but I thought you were the sort who wouldn't mind. Molly didn't for a minute think you would."

"What possessed you to do such a fool thing?" he asked roughly.

"I don't know. When I saw her coming down, I wanted to try it. It looked exciting. Didn't I hold myself as well as she did?"

Hedger shrugged his shoulders, but in his heart he forgave her.

The return boat was not crowded, though the boats that passed them, going out, were packed to the rails. The sun was setting. Boys and girls sat on the long benches with their arms about each other, singing. Eden felt a strong wish to propitiate her companion, to be alone with him. She had been curiously wrought up by her balloon trip; it was a lark, but not very satisfying unless one came back to something after the flight. She wanted to be admired and adored. Though Eden said nothing, and sat with her arms limp on the rail in front of her, looking languidly at the rising silhouette of the city and the bright path of the sun, Hedger felt a strange drawing near to her. If he but brushed her white skirt with his knee, there was an instant communication between them, such as there had never been before. They did not talk at all, but when they went over the gangplank she took his arm and kept her shoulder close to his. He felt as if they were enveloped in a highly charged atmosphere, an invisible network of subtle, almost painful sensibility. They had somehow taken hold of each other.

An hour later, they were dining in the back garden of a little French hotel on Ninth Street, long since passed away. It was cool and leafy there, and the mosquitoes were not very numerous. A party of South Americans at another table were drinking champagne, and Eden murmured that she thought she would like some, if it were not too expensive. "Perhaps it will make me think I am in the balloon again. That was a very nice feeling. You've forgiven me, haven't you?"

Hedger gave her a quick straight look from under his black eyebrows, and something went over her that was like a chill, except that it was warm and feathery. She drank most of the wine; her companion was indifferent to it. He was talking more to her tonight than he had ever done before. She asked him about a new picture she had seen in his room; a queer thing full of stiff, supplicating female figures. "It's Indian, isn't it?"

"Yes. I call it Rain Spirits, or maybe, Indian Rain. In the Southwest, where I've been a good deal, the Indian traditions make women have to do with the rain-fall. They were supposed to control it, somehow, and to be able to find springs, and make moisture come out of the earth. You see I'm trying to learn to paint what people think and feel; to get away from all that photographic stuff. When I look at you, I don't see what a camera would see, do I?"

"How can I tell?"

"Well, if I should paint you, I could make you understand what I see." For the second time that day Hedger crimsoned unexpectedly, and his eyes fell and steadily contemplated a dish of little radishes. "That particular picture I got from a story a Mexican priest told me; he said he found it in an old manuscript book in a monastery down there, written by some Spanish Missionary, who got his stories from the Aztecs. This one he called 'The Forty Lovers of the Queen,' and it was more or less about rain-making."

"Aren't you going to tell it to me?" Eden asked.

Hedger fumbled among the radishes. "I don't know if it's the proper kind of story to tell a girl."

She smiled; "Oh, forget about that! I've been balloon riding today. I like to hear you talk."

Her low voice was flattering. She had seemed like clay in his hands ever since they got on the boat to come home. He leaned back in his chair, forgot his food, and, looking at her intently, began to tell his story, the theme of which he somehow felt was dangerous tonight.

The tale began, he said, somewhere in Ancient Mexico, and concerned the daughter of a king. The birth of this Princess was preceded by unusual portents. Three times her mother dreamed that she was delivered of serpents, which betokened that the child she carried would have power with the rain gods. The serpent was the symbol of water. The Princess grew up dedicated to the gods, and wise men taught her the rain-making mysteries. She was with difficulty restrained from men and was guarded at all times, for it was the law of the Thunder that she be maiden until her marriage. In the years of her adolescence, rain was abundant with her people. The oldest man could not remember such fertility. When the Princess had counted eighteen summers, her father went to drive out a war party that harried his borders on the north and troubled his prosperity. The King destroyed the invaders and brought home many prisoners. Among the prisoners was a young chief, taller than any of his captors, of such strength and ferocity that the King's people came a day's journey to

look at him. When the Princess beheld his great stature, and saw that
his arms and breast were covered with the figures of wild animals,
bitten into the skin and coloured, she begged his life from her father.
She desired that he should practise his art upon her, and prick upon
her skin the signs of Rain and Lightning and Thunder, and stain the
wounds with herb-juices, as they were upon his own body. For many
days, upon the roof of the King's house, the Princess submitted herself
to the bone needle, and the women with her marvelled at her fortitude. But the Princess was without shame before the Captive, and it
came about that he threw from him his needles and his stains, and fell
upon the Princess to violate her honour; and her women ran down
from the roof screaming, to call the guard which stood at the gateway
of the King's house, and none stayed to protect their mistress. When
the guard came, the Captive was thrown into bonds, and he was
gelded, and his tongue was torn out, and he was given for a slave to
the Rain Princess.

The country of the Aztecs to the east was tormented by thirst, and
their King, hearing much of the rain-making arts of the Princess, sent
an embassy to her father, with presents and an offer of marriage. So
the Princess went from her father to be the Queen of the Aztecs, and
she took with her the Captive, who served her in everything with
entire fidelity and slept upon a mat before her door.

The King gave his bride a fortress on the outskirts of the city,
whither she retired to entreat the rain gods. This fortress was called
the Queen's House, and on the night of the new moon the Queen
came to it from the palace. But when the moon waxed and grew
toward the round, because the god of Thunder had had his will of her,
then the Queen returned to the King. Drought abated in the country
and rain fell abundantly by reason of the Queen's power with the stars.

When the Queen went to her own house she took with her no
servant but the Captive, and he slept outside her door and brought her
food after she had fasted. The Queen had a jewel of great value, a
turquoise that had fallen from the sun, and had the image of the sun
upon it. And when she desired a young man whom she had seen in the
army or among the slaves, she sent the Captive to him with the jewel,
for a sign that he should come to her secretly at the Queen's House
upon business concerning the welfare of all. And some, after she had
talked with them, she sent away with rewards; and some she took into

her chamber and kept them by her for one night or two. Afterward she called the Captive and bade him conduct the youth by the secret way he had come, underneath the chambers of the fortress. But for the going away of the Queen's lovers the Captive took out the bar that was beneath a stone in the floor of the passage, and put in its stead a rush-reed, and the youth stepped upon it and fell through into a cavern that was the bed of an underground river, and whatever was thrown into it was not seen again. In this service nor in any other did the Captive fail the Queen.

But when the Queen sent for the Captain of the Archers, she detained him four days in her chamber, calling often for food and wine, and was greatly content with him. On the fourth day she went to the Captive outside her door and said: "Tomorrow take this man up by the sure way, by which the King comes, and let him live."

In the Queen's door were arrows, purple and white. When she desired the King to come to her publicly, with his guard, she sent him a white arrow; but when she sent the purple, he came secretly, and covered himself with his mantle to be hidden from the stone gods at the gate. On the fifth night that the Queen was with her lover, the Captive took a purple arrow to the King, and the King came secretly and found them together. He killed the Captain with his own hand, but the Queen he brought to public trial. The Captive, when he was put to the question, told on his fingers forty men that he had let through the underground passage into the river. The Captive and the Queen were put to death by fire, both on the same day, and afterward there was scarcity of rain.

Eden Bower sat shivering a little as she listened. Hedger was not trying to please her, she thought, but to antagonize and frighten her by his brutal story. She had often told herself that his lean, big-boned lower jaw was like his bull-dog's, but tonight his face made Caesar's most savage and determined expression seem an affectation. Now she was looking at the man he really was. Nobody's eyes had ever defied her like this. They were searching her and seeing everything; all she had concealed from Livingston, and from the millionaire and his friends, and from the newspaper men. He was testing her, trying her out, and she was more ill at ease than she wished to show.

"That's quite a thrilling story," she said at last, rising and winding her scarf about her throat. "It must be getting late. Almost every one has gone."

They walked down the Avenue like people who have quarrelled, or who wish to get rid of each other. Hedger did not take her arm at the street crossings, and they did not linger in the Square. At her door he tried none of the old devices of the Livingston boys. He stood like a post, having forgotten to take off his hat, gave her a harsh, threatening glance, muttered "goodnight," and shut his own door noisily.

There was no question of sleep for Eden Bower. Her brain was working like a machine that would never stop. After she undressed, she tried to calm her nerves by smoking a cigarette, lying on the divan by the open window. But she grew wider and wider awake, combating the challenge that had flamed all evening in Hedger's eyes. The balloon had been one kind of excitement, the wine another; but the thing that had roused her, as a blow rouses a proud man, was the doubt, the contempt, the sneering hostility with which the painter had looked at her when he told his savage story. Crowds and balloons were all very well, she reflected, but woman's chief adventure is man. With a mind over active and a sense of life over strong, she wanted to walk across the roofs in the starlight, to sail over the sea and face at once a world of which she had never been afraid.

Hedger must be asleep; his dog had stopped sniffing under the double doors. Eden put on her wrapper and slippers and stole softly down the hall over the old carpet; one loose board creaked just as she reached the ladder. The trapdoor was open, as always on hot nights. When she stepped out on the roof she drew a long breath and walked across it, looking up at the sky. Her foot touched something soft; she heard a low growl, and on the instant Caesar's sharp little teeth caught her ankle and waited. His breath was like steam on her leg. Nobody had ever intruded upon his roof before, and he panted for the movement or the word that would let him spring his jaw. Instead, Hedger's hand seized his throat.

"Wait a minute. I'll settle with him," he said grimly. He dragged the dog toward the manhole and disappeared. When he came back, he found Eden standing over by the dark chimney, looking away in an offended attitude.

"I caned him unmercifully," he panted. "Of course you didn't hear anything; he never whines when I beat him. He didn't nip you, did he?"

"I don't know whether he broke the skin or not," she answered aggrievedly, still looking off into the west.

"If I were one of your friends in white pants, I'd strike a match to find whether you were hurt, though I know you are not, and then I'd see your ankle, wouldn't I?"

"I suppose so."

He shook his head and stood with his hands in the pockets of his old painting jacket. "I'm not up to such boy-tricks. If you want the place to yourself, I'll clear out. There are plenty of places where I can spend the night, what's left of it. But if you stay here and I stay here —" He shrugged his shoulders.

Eden did not stir, and she made no reply. Her head drooped slightly, as if she were considering. But the moment he put his arms about her they began to talk, both at once, as people do in an opera. The instant avowal brought out a flood of trivial admissions. Hedger confessed his crime, was reproached and forgiven, and now Eden knew what it was in his look that she had found so disturbing of late.

Standing against the black chimney, with the sky behind and blue shadows before, they looked like one of Hedger's own paintings of that period; two figures, one white and one dark, and nothing whatever distinguishable about them but that they were male and female. The faces were lost, the contours blurred in shadow, but the figures were a man and a woman, and that was their whole concern and their mysterious beauty, — it was the rhythm in which they moved, at last, along the roof and down into the dark hole; he first, drawing her gently after him. She came down very slowly. The excitement and bravado and uncertainty of that long day and night seemed all at once to tell upon her. When his feet were on the carpet and he reached up to lift her down, she twined her arms about his neck as after a long separation, and turned her face to him, and her lips, with their perfume of youth and passion.

One Saturday afternoon Hedger was sitting in the window of Eden's music room. They had been watching the pigeons come wheeling over the roofs from their unknown feeding grounds.

"Why," said Eden suddenly, "don't we fix those big doors into your studio so they will open? Then, if I want you, I won't have to go through the hall. That illustrator is loafing about a good deal of late."

"I'll open them, if you wish. The bolt is on your side."

"Isn't there one on yours, too?"

"No. I believe a man lived there for years before I came in, and the nurse used to have these rooms herself. Naturally, the lock was on the lady's side."

Eden laughed and began to examine the bolt. "It's all stuck up with paint." Looking about, her eye lighted upon a bronze Buddha which was one of the nurse's treasures. Taking him by his head, she struck the bolt a blow with his squatting posteriors. The two doors creaked, sagged, and swung weakly inward a little way, as if they were too old for such escapades. Eden tossed the heavy idol into a stuffed chair. "That's better," she exclaimed exultantly. "So the bolts are always on the lady's side? What a lot society takes for granted!"

Hedger laughed, sprang up and caught her arms roughly. "Whoever takes you for granted — Did anybody, ever?"

"Everybody does. That's why I'm here. You are the only one who knows anything about me. Now I'll have to dress if we're going out for dinner."

He lingered, keeping his hold on her. "But I won't always be the only one, Eden Bower. I won't be the last."

"No, I suppose not," she said carelessly. "But what does that matter? You are the first."

As a long, despairing whine broke in the warm stillness, they drew apart. Caesar, lying on his bed in the dark corner, had lifted his head at this invasion of sunlight, and realized that the side of his room was broken open, and his whole world shattered by change. There stood his master and this woman, laughing at him! The woman was pulling the long black hair of this mightiest of men, who bowed his head and permitted it.

6

In time they quarrelled, of course, and about an abstraction, — as young people often do, as mature people almost never do. Eden came in late one afternoon. She had been with some of her musical friends to lunch at Burton Ives' studio, and she began telling Hedger about its splendours. He listened a moment and then threw down his brushes. "I know exactly what it's like," he said impatiently. "A very good department-store conception of a studio. It's one of the show places."

"Well, it's gorgeous, and he said I could bring you to see him. The boys tell me he's awfully kind about giving people a lift, and you might get something out of it."

Hedger started up and pushed his canvas out of the way. "What could I possibly get from Burton Ives? He's almost the worst painter in the world; the stupidest, I mean."

Eden was annoyed. Burton Ives had been very nice to her and had begged her to sit for him. "You must admit that he's a very successful one," she said coldly.

"Of course he is! Anybody can be successful who will do that sort of thing. I wouldn't paint his pictures for all the money in New York."

"Well, I saw a lot of them, and I think they are beautiful."

Hedger bowed stiffly.

"What's the use of being a great painter if nobody knows about you?" Eden went on persuasively. "Why don't you paint the kind of pictures people can understand, and then, after you're successful, do whatever you like?"

"As I look at it," said Hedger brusquely, "I am successful."

Eden glanced about. "Well, I don't see any evidences of it," she said, biting her lip. "He has a Japanese servant and a wine cellar, and keeps a riding horse."

Hedger melted a little. "My dear, I have the most expensive luxury in the world, and I am much more extravagant than Burton Ives, for I work to please nobody but myself."

"You mean you could make money and don't? That you don't try to get a public?"

"Exactly. A public only wants what has been done over and over. I'm painting for painters, — who haven't been born."

"What would you do if I brought Mr. Ives down here to see your things?"

"Well, for God's sake, don't! Before he left I'd probably tell him what I thought of him."

Eden rose. "I give you up. You know very well there's only one kind of success that's real."

"Yes, but it's not the kind you mean. So you've been thinking me a scrub painter, who needs a helping hand from some fashionable studio man? What the devil have you had anything to do with me for, then?"

"There's no use talking to you," said Eden walking slowly toward the door. "I've been trying to pull wires for you all afternoon, and this is what it comes to." She had expected that the tidings of a prospective call from the great man would be received very differently, and had been thinking as she came home in the stage how, as with a magic wand, she might gild Hedger's future, float him out of his dark hole on a tide of prosperity, see his name in the papers and his pictures in the windows on Fifth Avenue.

Hedger mechanically snapped the midsummer leash on Caesar's collar and they ran downstairs and hurried through Sullivan Street off toward the river. He wanted to be among rough, honest people, to get down where the big drays bumped over stone paving blocks and the men wore corduroy trousers and kept their shirts open at the neck. He stopped for a drink in one of the sagging bar-rooms on the water front. He had never in his life been so deeply wounded; he did not know he could be so hurt. He had told this girl all his secrets. On the roof, in these warm, heavy summer nights, with her hands locked in his, he had been able to explain all his misty ideas about an unborn art the world was waiting for; had been able to explain them better than he had ever done to himself. And she had looked away to the chattels of this uptown studio and coveted them for him! To her he was only an unsuccessful Burton Ives.

Then why, as he had put it to her, did she take up with him? Young, beautiful, talented as she was, why had she wasted herself on a scrub? Pity? Hardly; she wasn't sentimental. There was no explaining her. But in this passion that had seemed so fearless and so fated to be, his own position now looked to him ridiculous; a poor dauber without money or fame, — it was her caprice to load him with favours. Hedger ground his teeth so loud that his dog, trotting beside him, heard him and looked up.

While they were having supper at the oysterman's, he planned his escape. Whenever he saw her again, everything he had told her, that he should never have told any one, would come back to him; ideas he had never whispered even to the painter whom he worshipped and had gone all the way to France to see. To her they must seem his apology for not having horses and a valet, or merely the puerile boastfulness of a weak man. Yet if she slipped the bolt tonight and came through the doors and said, "Oh, weak man, I belong to you!" what could he do? That was the danger. He would catch the train out to Long Beach tonight, and tomorrow he would go on to the north end of Long Island, where an old friend of his had a summer studio among the sand dunes. He would stay until things came right in his mind. And she could find a smart painter, or take her punishment.

When he went home, Eden's room was dark; she was dining out somewhere. He threw his things into a hold-all he had carried about the world with him, strapped up some colours and canvases, and ran downstairs.

7

Five days later Hedger was a restless passenger on a dirty, crowded Sunday train, coming back to town. Of course he saw now how unreasonable he had been in expecting a Huntington girl to know anything about pictures; here was a whole continent of people who knew nothing about pictures and he didn't hold it against them. What had such things to do with him and Eden Bower? When he lay out on the dunes, watching the moon come up out of the sea, it had seemed to him that there was no wonder in the world like the wonder of Eden Bower. He was going back to her because she was older than art, because she was the most overwhelming thing that had ever come into his life.

He had written her yesterday, begging her to be at home this evening, telling her that he was contrite, and wretched enough.

Now that he was on his way to her, his stronger feeling unaccountably changed to a mood that was playful and tender. He wanted to share everything with her, even the most trivial things. He wanted to tell her about the people on the train, coming back tired from their holiday with bunches of wilted flowers and dirty daisies; to tell her that the fish-man, to whom she had often sent him for lobsters, was among the passengers, disguised in a silk shirt and a spotted tie, and how his wife looked exactly like a fish, even to her eyes, on which cataracts were forming. He could tell her, too, that he hadn't as much as unstrapped his canvases, — that ought to convince her.

In those days passengers from Long Island came into New York by ferry. Hedger had to be quick about getting his dog out of the express car in order to catch the first boat. The East River, and the bridges, and the city to the west, were burning in the conflagration of the sunset; there was that great home-coming reach of evening in the air.

The car changes from Thirty-fourth Street were too many and too perplexing; for the first time in his life Hedger took a hansom cab for Washington Square. Caesar sat bolt upright on the worn leather cushion beside him, and they jogged off, looking down on the rest of the world.

It was twilight when they drove down lower Fifth Avenue into the Square, and through the Arch behind them were the two long rows of pale violet lights that used to bloom so beautifully against the grey stone and asphalt. Here and yonder about the Square hung globes that shed a radiance not unlike the blue mists of evening, emerging softly when daylight died, as the stars emerged in the thin blue sky. Under them the sharp shadows of the trees fell on the cracked pavement and the sleeping grass. The first stars and the first lights were growing silver against the gradual darkening, when Hedger paid his driver and went into the house, — which, thank God, was still there! On the hall table lay his letter of yesterday, unopened.

He went upstairs, with every sort of fear and every sort of hope clutching at his heart; it was as if tigers were tearing him. Why was there no gas burning in the top hall? He found matches and the gas bracket. He knocked, but got no answer; nobody was there. Before his own door were exactly five bottles of milk, standing in a row. The milk-boy had taken spiteful pleasure in thus reminding him that he forgot to stop his order.

Hedger went down to the basement; it, too, was dark. The janitress was taking her evening airing on the basement steps. She sat waving a palm-leaf fan majestically, her dirty calico dress open at the neck. She told him at once that there had been "changes." Miss Bower's room was to let again, and the piano would go tomorrow. Yes, she left yesterday, she sailed for Europe with friends from Chicago. They arrived on Friday, heralded by many telegrams. Very rich people they were said to be, though the man had refused to pay the nurse a month's rent in lieu of notice, — which would have been only right, as the young lady had agreed to take the rooms until October. Mrs. Foley had observed, too, that he didn't overpay her or Willy for their trouble, and a great deal of trouble they had been put to, certainly.

Yes, the young lady was very pleasant, but the nurse said there were rings on the mahogany table where she had put tumblers and wine glasses. It was just as well she was gone. The Chicago man was uppish in his ways, but not much to look at. She supposed he had poor health, for there was nothing to him inside his clothes.

Hedger went slowly up the stairs — never had they seemed so long, or his legs so heavy. The upper floor was emptiness and silence. He unlocked his room, lit the gas, and opened the windows. When he went to put his coat in the closet, he found, hanging among his clothes, a pale, flesh-tinted dressing gown he had liked to see her wear, with a perfume — oh, a perfume that was still Eden Bower! He shut the door behind him and there, in the dark, for a moment he lost his manliness. It was when he held this garment to him that he found a letter in the pocket.

The note was written with a lead pencil, in haste: She was sorry that he was angry, but she still didn't know just what she had done. She had thought Mr. Ives would be useful to him; she guessed he was too proud. She wanted awfully to see him again, but Fate came knocking at her door after he had left her. She believed in Fate. She would never forget him, and she knew he would become the greatest painter in the world. Now she must pack. She hoped he wouldn't mind her leaving the dressing gown; somehow, she could never wear it again.

After Hedger read this, standing under the gas, he went back into the closet and knelt down before the wall; the knot hole had been plugged up with a ball of wet paper, — the same blue note-paper on which her letter was written.

He was hard hit. Tonight he had to bear the loneliness of a whole lifetime. Knowing himself so well, he could hardly believe that such a thing had ever happened to him, that such a woman had lain happy and contented in his arms. And now it was over. He turned out the light and sat down on his painter's stool before the big window. Caesar, on the floor beside him, rested his head on his master's knee. We must leave Hedger thus, sitting in his tank with his dog, looking up at the stars.

COMING, APHRODITE! This legend, in electric lights over the Lexington Opera House, had long announced the return of Eden Bower to New York after years of spectacular success in Paris. She came at last, under the management of an American Opera Company, but bringing her own *chef d'orchestre.*

One bright December afternoon Eden Bower was going down Fifth Avenue in her car, on the way to her broker, in Williams Street. Her thoughts were entirely upon stocks, — Cerro de Pasco, and how much she should buy of it, — when she suddenly looked up and realized that she was skirting Washington Square. She had not seen the place since she rolled out of it in an old-fashioned four-wheeler to seek her fortune, eighteen years ago.

"*Arrêtez, Alphonse. Attendez moi,*" she called, and opened the door before he could reach it. The children who were streaking over the asphalt on roller skates saw a lady in a long fur coat, and short, high-heeled shoes, alight from a French car and pace slowly about the Square, holding her muff to her chin. This spot, at least, had changed very little, she reflected; the same trees, the same fountain, the white arch, and over yonder, Garibaldi, drawing the sword for freedom. There, just opposite her, was the old red brick house.

"Yes, that is the place," she was thinking. "I can smell the carpets now, and the dog, — what was his name? That grubby bathroom at the end of the hall, and that dreadful Hedger — still, there was something about him, you know —" She glanced up and blinked against the sun. From somewhere in the crowded quarter south of the Square a flock of pigeons rose, wheeling quickly upward into the brilliant blue sky. She threw back her head, pressed her muff closer to her chin, and watched them with a smile of amazement and delight. So they still rose, out of all that dirt and noise and squalor, fleet and silvery, just as they used to rise that summer when she was twenty and went up in a balloon on Coney Island!

Alphonse opened the door and tucked her robes about her. All the way down town her mind wandered from Cerro de Pasco, and she kept smiling and looking up at the sky.

When she had finished her business with the broker, she asked him to look in the telephone book for the address of M. Gaston Jules, the picture dealer, and slipped the paper on which he wrote it into her glove. It was five o'clock when she reached the French Galleries, as they were called. On entering she gave the attendant her card, asking him to take it to M. Jules. The dealer appeared very promptly and begged her to come into his private office, where he pushed a great chair toward his desk for her and signalled his secretary to leave the room.

"How good your lighting is in here," she observed, glancing about. "I met you at Simon's studio, didn't I? Oh, no! I never forget anybody who interests me." She threw her muff on his writing table and sank into the deep chair. "I have come to you for some information that's not in my line. Do you know anything about an American painter named Hedger?"

He took the seat opposite her. "Don Hedger? But, certainly! There are some very interesting things of his in an exhibition at V——'s. If you would care to —"

She held up her hand. "No, no. I've no time to go to exhibitions. Is he a man of any importance?"

"Certainly. He is one of the first men among the moderns. That is to say, among the very moderns. He is always coming up with something different. He often exhibits in Paris, you must have seen —"

"No, I tell you I don't go to exhibitions. Has he had great success? That is what I want to know."

M. Jules pulled at his short grey moustache. "But, Madame, there are many kinds of success," he began cautiously.

Madame gave a dry laugh. "Yes, so he used to say. We once quarrelled on that issue. And how would you define his particular kind?"

M. Jules grew thoughtful. "He is a great name with all the young men, and he is decidedly an influence in art. But one can't definitely place a man who is original, erratic, and who is changing all the time."

She cut him short. "Is he much talked about at home? In Paris, I mean? Thanks. That's all I want to know." She rose and began buttoning her coat. "One doesn't like to have been an utter fool, even at twenty."

"*Mais, non!*" M. Jules handed her her muff with a quick, sympathetic glance. He followed her out through the carpeted show-room, now closed to the public and draped in cheesecloth, and put her into her car with words appreciative of the honour she had done him in calling.

Leaning back in the cushions, Eden Bower closed her eyes, and her face, as the street lamps flashed their ugly orange light upon it, became hard and settled, like a plaster cast; so a sail, that has been filled by a strong breeze, behaves when the wind suddenly dies. Tomorrow night the wind would blow again, and this mask would be the golden face of Aphrodite. But a "big" career takes its toll, even with the best of luck.

Up in Michigan

by Ernest Hemingway

JIM GILMORE came to Hortons Bay from Canada. He bought the blacksmith shop from old man Horton. Jim was short and dark with big mustaches and big hands. He was a good horseshoer and did not look much like a blacksmith even with his leather apron on. He lived upstairs above the blacksmith shop and took his meals at D. J. Smith's.

Liz Coates worked for Smith's. Mrs. Smith, who was a very large clean woman, said Liz Coates was the neatest girl she'd ever seen. Liz had good legs and always wore clean gingham aprons and Jim noticed that her hair was always neat behind. He liked her face because it was so jolly but he never thought about her.

Liz liked Jim very much. She liked it the way he walked over from the shop and often went to the kitchen door to watch for him to start down the road. She liked it about his mustache. She liked it about how white his teeth were when he smiled. She liked it very much that he didn't look like a blacksmith. She liked it how much D. J. Smith and Mrs. Smith liked Jim. One day she found that she liked it the way the hair was black on his arms and how white they were above the tanned line when he washed up in the washbasin outside the house. Liking that made her feel funny.

Hortons Bay, the town, was only five houses on the main road between Boyne City and Charlevoix. There was the general store and post office with a high false front and maybe a wagon hitched out in front, Smith's house, Stroud's house, Dillworth's house, Horton's house and Van Hoosen's house. The houses were in a big grove of elm trees and the road was very sandy. There was farming country and timber each way up the road. Up the road a ways was the Methodist church and down the road the other direction was the township school. The blacksmith shop was painted red and faced the school.

A steep sandy road ran down the hill to the bay through the timber. From Smith's back door you could look out across the woods that ran down to the lake and across the bay. It was very beautiful in the spring and summer, the bay blue and bright and usually whitecaps on the lake out beyond the point from the breeze blowing from Charlevoix and Lake Michigan. From Smith's back door Liz could see ore barges way out in the lake going toward Boyne City. When she looked at them they didn't seem to be moving at all but if she went in and dried some more dishes and then came out again they would be out of sight beyond the point.

All the time now Liz was thinking about Jim Gilmore. He didn't seem to notice her much. He talked about the shop to D. J. Smith and about the Republican Party and about James G. Blaine. In the evenings he read *The Toledo Blade* and the Grand Rapids paper by the lamp in the front room or went out spearing fish in the bay with a jacklight with D. J. Smith. In the fall he and Smith and Charley Wyman took a wagon and tent, grub, axes, their rifles and two dogs and went on a trip to the pine plains beyond Vanderbilt deer hunting. Liz and Mrs. Smith were cooking for four days for them before they started. Liz wanted to make something special for Jim to take but she didn't finally because she was afraid to ask Mrs. Smith for the eggs and flour and afraid if she bought them Mrs. Smith would catch her cooking. It would have been all right with Mrs. Smith but Liz was afraid.

All the time Jim was gone on the deer hunting trip Liz thought about him. It was awful while he was gone. She couldn't sleep well from thinking about him but she discovered it was fun to think about him too. If she let herself go it was better. The night before they were to come back she didn't sleep at all, that is she didn't think she slept because it was all mixed up in a dream about not sleeping and really not sleeping. When she saw the wagon coming down the road she felt weak and sick sort of inside. She couldn't wait till she saw Jim and it seemed as though everything would be all right when he came. The wagon stopped outside under the big elm and Mrs. Smith and Liz went out. All the men had beards and there were three deer in the back of the wagon, their thin legs sticking stiff over the edge of the wagon box. Mrs. Smith kissed D. J. and he hugged her. Jim said "Hello, Liz," and grinned. Liz hadn't known just what would happen when Jim got back but she was sure it would be something. Nothing had happened. The men were just home, that was all. Jim pulled the burlap sacks off the deer and Liz looked at them. One was a big buck. It was stiff and hard to lift out of the wagon.

"Did you shoot it, Jim?" Liz asked.

"Yeah. Ain't it a beauty?" Jim got it onto his back to carry to the smokehouse.

That night Charley Wyman stayed to supper at Smith's. It was too late to get back to Charlevoix. The men washed up and waited in the front room for supper.

"Ain't there something left in that crock, Jimmy?" D. J. Smith asked, and Jim went out to the wagon in the barn and fetched in the jug of whiskey the men had taken hunting with them. It was a four-gallon jug and there was quite a little slopped back and forth in the bottom. Jim took a long pull on his way back to the house. It was hard to lift such a big jug up to drink out of it. Some of the whiskey ran down on his shirt front. The two men smiled when Jim came in with the jug. D. J. Smith sent for glasses and Liz brought them. D. J. poured out three big shots.

"Well, here's looking at you, D. J.," said Charley Wyman.

"That damn big buck, Jimmy," said D. J.

"Here's all the ones we missed, D. J.," said Jim, and downed his liquor.

"Tastes good to a man."

"Nothing like it this time of year for what ails you."

"How about another, boys?"

"Here's how, D. J."

"Down the creek, boys."

"Here's to next year."

Jim began to feel great. He loved the taste and the feel of whiskey. He was glad to be back to a comfortable bed and warm food and the shop. He had another drink. The men came in to supper feeling hilarious but acting very respectable. Liz sat at the table after she put on the food and ate with the family. It was a good dinner. The men ate seriously. After supper they went into the front room again and Liz cleaned off with Mrs. Smith. Then Mrs. Smith went upstairs and pretty soon Smith came out and went upstairs too. Jim and Charley were still in the front room. Liz was sitting in the kitchen next to the stove pretending to read a book and thinking about Jim. She didn't want to go to bed yet because she knew Jim would be coming out and she wanted to see him as he went out so she could take the way he looked up to bed with her.

She was thinking about him hard and then Jim came out. His eyes were shining and his hair was a little rumpled. Liz looked down at her book. Jim came over back of her chair and stood there and she could feel him breathing and then he put his arms around her. Her breasts felt plump and firm and the nipples were erect under his hands. Liz was terribly frightened, no one had ever touched her, but she thought, "He's come to me finally. He's really come."

She held herself stiff because she was so frightened and did not know anything else to do and then Jim held her tight against the chair and kissed her. It was such a sharp, aching, hurting feeling that she thought she couldn't stand it. She felt Jim right through the back of the chair and she couldn't stand it and then something clicked inside of her and the feeling was warmer and softer. Jim held her tight hard against the chair and she wanted it now and Jim whispered, "Come on for a walk."

Liz took her coat off the peg on the kitchen wall and they went out the door. Jim had his arm around her and every little way they stopped and pressed against each other and Jim kissed her. There was no moon and they walked ankle-deep in the sandy road through the trees down to the dock and the warehouse on the bay. The water was lapping in the piles and the point was dark across the bay. It was cold but Liz was hot all over from being with Jim. They sat down in the shelter of the warehouse and Jim pulled Liz close to him. She was frightened. One of Jim's hands went inside her dress and stroked over her breast and the other hand was in her lap. She was very frightened and didn't know how he was going to go about things but she snuggled close to him. Then the hand that felt so big in her lap went away and was on her leg and started to move up it.

"Don't, Jim," Liz said. Jim slid the hand further up.

"You mustn't, Jim. You mustn't." Neither Jim nor Jim's big hand paid any attention to her.

The boards were hard. Jim had her dress up and was trying to do something to her. She was frightened but she wanted it. She had to have it but it frightened her.

"You mustn't do it, Jim. You mustn't."

"I got to. I'm going to. You know we got to."

"No we haven't, Jim. We ain't got to. Oh, it isn't right. Oh, it's so big and it hurts so. You can't. Oh, Jim. Jim. Oh."

The hemlock planks of the dock were hard and splintery and cold and Jim was heavy on her and he had hurt her. Liz pushed him, she was so uncomfortable and cramped. Jim was asleep. He wouldn't move. She worked out from under him and sat up and straightened her skirt and coat and tried to do something with her hair. Jim was sleeping with his mouth a little open. Liz leaned over and kissed him on the cheek. He was still asleep. She lifted his head a little and shook it. He rolled his head over and swallowed. Liz started to cry. She walked over to the edge of the dock and looked down to the water. There was a mist coming up from the bay. She was cold and miserable and everything felt gone. She walked back to where Jim was lying and shook him once more to make sure. She was crying.

"Jim," she said, "Jim. Please, Jim."

Jim stirred and curled a little tighter. Liz took off her coat and leaned over and covered him with it. She tucked it around him neatly and carefully. Then she walked across the dock and up the steep sandy road to go to bed. A cold mist was coming up through the woods from the bay.

"The Sensible Thing"

by F. Scott Fitzgerald

1

At the Great American Lunch Hour young George O'Kelly straightened his desk deliberately and with an assumed air of interest. No one in the office must know that he was in a hurry, for success is a matter of atmosphere, and it is not well to advertise the fact that your mind is separated from your work by a distance of seven hundred miles.

But once out of the building he set his teeth and began to run, glancing now and then at the gay noon of early spring which filled Times Square and loitered less than twenty feet over the heads of the crowd. The crowd all looked slightly upward and took deep March breaths, and the sun dazzled their eyes so that scarcely any one saw any one else but only their own reflection on the sky.

George O'Kelly, whose mind was over seven hundred miles away, thought that all outdoors was horrible. He rushed into the subway, and for ninety-five blocks bent a frenzied glance on a car-card which showed vividly how he had only one chance in five of keeping his teeth for ten years. At 137th Street he broke off his study of commercial art, left the subway, and began to run again, a tireless, anxious run that brought him this time to his home — one room in a high, horrible apartment-house in the middle of nowhere.

There it was on the bureau, the letter — in sacred ink, on blessed paper — all over the city, people, if they listened, could hear the beating of George O'Kelly's heart. He read the commas, the blots, and the thumb-smudge on the margin — then he threw himself hopelessly upon his bed.

He was in a mess, one of those terrific messes which are ordinary incidents in the life of the poor, which follow poverty like birds of prey. The poor go under or go up or go wrong or even go on, somehow, in a way the poor have — but George O'Kelly was so new to poverty that had any one denied the uniqueness of his case he would have been astounded.

Less than two years ago he had been graduated with honors from The Massachusetts Institute of Technology and had taken a position with a firm of construction engineers in southern Tennessee. All his life he had thought in terms of tunnels and skyscrapers and great squat dams and tall, three-towered bridges, that were like dancers holding hands in a row, with heads as tall as cities and skirts of cable strand. It had seemed romantic to George O'Kelly to change the sweep of rivers and the shape of mountains so that life could flourish in the old bad lands of the world where it had never taken root before. He loved steel, and there was always steel near him in his dreams, liquid steel, steel in bars, and blocks and beams and formless plastic masses, waiting for him, as paint and canvas to his hand. Steel inexhaustible, to be made lovely and austere in his imaginative fire . . .

At present he was an insurance clerk at forty dollars a week with his dream slipping fast behind him. The dark little girl who had made this mess, this terrible and intolerable mess, was waiting to be sent for in a town in Tennessee.

In fifteen minutes the woman from whom he sublet his room knocked and asked him with maddening kindness if, since he was home, he would have some lunch. He shook his head, but the interruption aroused him, and getting up from the bed he wrote a telegram.

"Letter depressed me have you lost your nerve you are foolish and just upset to think of breaking off why not marry me immediately sure we can make it all right ——"

He hesitated for a wild minute, and then added in a hand that could scarcely be recognized as his own: "In any case I will arrive to-morrow at six o'clock."

When he finished he ran out of the apartment and down to the telegraph office near the subway stop. He possessed in this world not quite one hundred dollars, but the letter showed that she was "nervous" and this left him no choice. He knew what "nervous" meant — that she was emotionally depressed, that the prospect of marrying into a life of poverty and struggle was putting too much strain upon her love.

George O'Kelly reached the insurance company at his usual run, the run that had become almost second nature to him, that seemed best to express the tension under which he lived. He went straight to the manager's office.

"I want to see you, Mr. Chambers," he announced breathlessly.

"Well?" Two eyes, eyes like winter windows, glared at him with ruthless impersonality.

"I want to get four days' vacation."

"Why, you had a vacation just two weeks ago!" said Mr. Chambers in surprise.

"That's true," admitted the distraught young man, "but now I've got to have another."

"Where'd you go last time? To your home?"

"No, I went to — a place in Tennessee."

"Well, where do you want to go this time?"

"Well, this time I want to go to — a place in Tennessee."

"You're consistent, anyhow," said the manager dryly. "But I didn't realize you were employed here as a travelling salesman."

"I'm not," cried George desperately, "but I've got to go."

"All right," agreed Mr. Chambers, "but you don't have to come back. So don't!"

"I won't." And to his own astonishment as well as Mr. Chambers' George's face grew pink with pleasure. He felt happy, exultant — for the first time in six months he was absolutely free. Tears of gratitude stood in his eyes, and he seized Mr. Chambers warmly by the hand.

"I want to thank you," he said with a rush of emotion, "I don't want to come back. I think I'd have gone crazy if you'd said that I could come back. Only I couldn't quit myself, you see, and I want to thank you for — for quitting for me."

He waved his hand magnanimously, shouted aloud, "You owe me three days' salary but you can keep it!" and rushed from the office. Mr. Chambers rang for his stenographer to ask if O'Kelly had seemed queer lately. He had fired many men in the course of his career, and they had taken it in many different ways, but none of them had thanked him — ever before.

2

Jonquil Cary was her name, and to George O'Kelly nothing had ever looked so fresh and pale as her face when she saw him and fled to him eagerly along the station platform. Her arms were raised to him, her mouth was half parted for his kiss, when she held him off suddenly and lightly and, with a touch of embarrassment, looked around. Two boys, somewhat younger than George, were standing in the background.

"This is Mr. Craddock and Mr. Holt," she announced cheerfully. "You met them when you were here before."

Disturbed by the transition of a kiss into an introduction and suspecting some hidden significance, George was more confused when he found that the automobile which was to carry them to Jonquil's house belonged to one of the two young men. It seemed to put him at a disadvantage. On the way Jonquil chattered between the front and back seats, and when he tried to slip his arm around her under cover of the twilight she compelled him with a quick movement to take her hand instead.

"Is this street on the way to your house?" he whispered. "I don't recognize it."

"It's the new boulevard. Jerry just got this car to-day, and he wants to show it to me before he takes us home."

When, after twenty minutes, they were deposited at Jonquil's house, George felt that the first happiness of the meeting, the joy he had recognized so surely in her eyes back in the station, had been dissipated by the intrusion of the ride. Something that he had looked forward to had been rather casually lost, and he was brooding on this as he said good night stiffly to the two young men. Then his ill-humor faded as Jonquil drew him into a familiar embrace under the dim light of the front hall and told him in a dozen ways, of which the best was without words, how she had missed him. Her emotion reassured him, promised his anxious heart that everything would be all right.

They sat together on the sofa, overcome by each other's presence, beyond all except fragmentary endearments. At the supper hour Jonquil's father and mother appeared and were glad to see George. They liked him, and had been interested in his engineering career when he had first come to Tennessee over a year before. They had been sorry when he had given it up and gone to New York to look for something more immediately profitable, but while they deplored the curtailment of his career they sympathized with him and were ready to recognize the engagement. During dinner they asked about his progress in New York.

"Everything's going fine," he told them with enthusiasm. "I've been promoted — better salary."

He was miserable as he said this — but they were all *so* glad.

"They must like you," said Mrs. Cary, "that's certain — or they wouldn't let you off twice in three weeks to come down here."

"I told them they had to," explained George hastily; "I told them if they didn't I wouldn't work for them any more."

"But you ought to save your money," Mrs. Cary reproached him gently. "Not spend it all on this expensive trip."

Dinner was over — he and Jonquil were alone and she came back into his arms.

"So glad you're here," she sighed. "Wish you never were going away again, darling."

"Do you miss me?"

"Oh, so much, so much."

"Do you — do other men come to see you often? Like those two kids?"

The question surprised her. The dark velvet eyes stared at him.

"Why, of course they do. All the time. Why — I've told you in letters that they did, dearest."

This was true — when he had first come to the city there had been already a dozen boys around her, responding to her picturesque fragility with adolescent worship, and a few of them perceiving that her beautiful eyes were also sane and kind.

"Do you expect me never to go anywhere" — Jonquil demanded, leaning back against the sofa-pillows until she seemed to look at him from many miles away — "and just fold my hands and sit still — forever?"

"What do you mean?" he blurted out in a panic. "Do you mean you think I'll never have enough money to marry you?"

"Oh, don't jump at conclusions so, George."

"I'm not jumping at conclusions. That's what you said."

George decided suddenly that he was on dangerous grounds. He had not intended to let anything spoil this night. He tried to take her again in his arms, but she resisted unexpectedly, saying:

"It's hot. I'm going to get the electric fan."

When the fan was adjusted they sat down again, but he was in a supersensitive mood and involuntarily he plunged into the specific world he had intended to avoid.

"When will you marry me?"

"Are you ready for me to marry you?"

All at once his nerves gave way, and he sprang to his feet.

"Let's shut off that damned fan," he cried, "it drives me wild. It's like a clock ticking away all the time I'll be with you. I came here to be happy and forget everything about New York and time ———"

He sank down on the sofa as suddenly as he had risen. Jonquil turned off the fan, and drawing his head down into her lap began stroking his hair.

"Let's sit like this," she said softly, "just sit quiet like this, and I'll put you to sleep. You're all tired and nervous and your sweetheart'll take care of you."

"But I don't want to sit like this," he complained, jerking up suddenly, "I don't want to sit like this at all. I want you to kiss me. That's the only thing that makes me rest. And anyways I'm not nervous — it's you that's nervous. I'm not nervous at all."

To prove that he wasn't nervous he left the couch and plumped himself into a rocking-chair across the room.

"Just when I'm ready to marry you you write me the most nervous letters, as if you're going to back out, and I have to come rushing down here ———"

"You don't have to come if you don't want to."

"But I *do* want to!" insisted George.

It seemed to him that he was being very cool and logical and that she was putting him deliberately in the wrong. With every word they were drawing farther and farther apart — and he was unable to stop himself or to keep worry and pain out of his voice.

But in a minute Jonquil began to cry sorrowfully and he came back to the sofa and put his arm around her. He was the comforter now, drawing her head close to his shoulder, murmuring old familiar things until she grew calmer and only trembled a little, spasmodically, in his arms. For over an hour they sat there, while the evening pianos thumped their last cadences into the street outside. George did not move, or think, or hope, lulled into numbness by the premonition of disaster. The clock would tick on, past eleven, past twelve, and then Mrs. Cary would call down gently over the banister — beyond that he saw only to-morrow and despair.

3

In the heat of the next day the breaking-point came. They had each guessed the truth about the other, but of the two she was the more ready to admit the situation.

"There's no use going on," she said miserably, "you know you hate the insurance business, and you'll never do well in it."

"That's not it," he insisted stubbornly; "I hate going on alone. If you'll marry me and come with me and take a chance with me, I can make good at anything, but not while I'm worrying about you down here."

She was silent a long time before she answered, not thinking — for she had seen the end — but only waiting, because she knew that every word would seem more cruel than the last. Finally she spoke:

"George, I love you with all my heart, and I don't see how I can ever love any one else but you. If you'd been ready for me two months ago I'd have married you — now I can't because it doesn't seem to be the sensible thing."

He made wild accusations — there was some one else — she was keeping something from him!

"No, there's no one else."

This was true. But reacting from the strain of this affair she had found relief in the company of young boys like Jerry Holt, who had the merit of meaning absolutely nothing in her life.

George didn't take the situation well, at all. He seized her in his arms and tried literally to kiss her into marrying him at once. When this failed, he broke into a long monologue of self-pity, and ceased only when he saw that he was making himself despicable in her sight. He threatened to leave when he had no intention of leaving, and refused to go when she told him that, after all, it was best that he should.

For a while she was sorry, then for another while she was merely kind.

"You'd better go now," she cried at last, so loud that Mrs. Cary came down-stairs in alarm.

"Is something the matter?"

"I'm going away, Mrs. Cary," said George brokenly. Jonquil had left the room.

"Don't feel so badly, George." Mrs. Cary blinked at him in helpless sympathy — sorry and, in the same breath, glad that the little tragedy was almost done. "If I were you I'd go home to your mother for a week or so. Perhaps after all this is the sensible thing ——"

"Please don't talk," he cried. "Please don't say anything to me now!"

Jonquil came into the room again, her sorrow and her nervousness alike tucked under powder and rouge and hat.

"I've ordered a taxicab," she said impersonally. "We can drive around until your train leaves."

She walked out on the front porch. George put on his coat and hat and stood for a minute exhausted in the hall — he had eaten scarcely a bite since he had left New York. Mrs. Cary came over, drew his head down and kissed him on the cheek, and he felt very ridiculous and weak in his knowledge that the scene had been ridiculous and weak at the end. If he had only gone the night before — left her for the last time with a decent pride.

The taxi had come, and for an hour these two that had been lovers rode along the less-frequented streets. He held her hand and grew calmer in the sunshine, seeing too late that there had been nothing all along to do or say.

"I'll come back," he told her.

"I know you will," she answered, trying to put a cheery faith into her voice. "And we'll write each other — sometimes."

"No," he said, "we won't write. I couldn't stand that. Some day I'll come back."

"I'll never forget you, George."

They reached the station, and she went with him while he bought his ticket. . . .

"Why, George O'Kelly and Jonquil Cary!"

It was a man and a girl whom George had known when he had

worked in town, and Jonquil seemed to greet their presence with relief. For an interminable five minutes they all stood there talking; then the train roared into the station, and with ill-concealed agony in his face George held out his arms toward Jonquil. She took an uncertain step toward him, faltered, and then pressed his hand quickly as if she were taking leave of a chance friend.

"Good-by, George," she was saying, "I hope you have a pleasant trip."

"Good-by, George. Come back and see us all again."

Dumb, almost blind with pain, he seized his suitcase, and in some dazed way got himself aboard the train.

Past clanging street-crossings, gathering speed through wide suburban spaces toward the sunset. Perhaps she too would see the sunset and pause for a moment, turning, remembering, before he faded with her sleep into the past. This night's dusk would cover up forever the sun and the trees and the flowers and laughter of his young world.

4

On a damp afternoon in September of the following year a young man with his face burned to a deep copper glow got off a train at a city in Tennessee. He looked around anxiously, and seemed relieved when he found that there was no one in the station to meet him. He taxied to the best hotel in the city where he registered with some satisfaction as George O'Kelly, Cuzco, Peru.

Up in his room he sat for a few minutes at the window looking down into the familiar street below. Then with his hand trembling faintly he took off the telephone receiver and called a number.

"Is Miss Jonquil in?"

"This is she."

"Oh —" His voice after overcoming a faint tendency to waver went on with friendly formality.

"This is George O'Kelly. Did you get my letter?"

"Yes. I thought you'd be in to-day."

Her voice, cool and unmoved, disturbed him, but not as he had expected. This was the voice of a stranger, unexcited, pleasantly glad to see him — that was all. He wanted to put down the telephone and catch his breath.

"I haven't seen you for — a long time." He succeeded in making this sound offhand. "Over a year."

He knew how long it had been — to the day.

"It'll be awfully nice to talk to you again."

"I'll be there in about an hour."

He hung up. For four long seasons every minute of his leisure had been crowded with anticipation of this hour, and now this hour was here. He had thought of finding her married, engaged, in love — he had not thought she would be unstirred at his return.

There would never again in his life, he felt, be another ten months like these he had just gone through. He had made an admittedly remarkable showing for a young engineer — stumbled into two un-usual opportunities, one in Peru, whence he had just returned, and another, consequent upon it, in New York, whither he was bound. In this short time he had risen from poverty into a position of unlimited opportunity.

He looked at himself in the dressing-table mirror. He was almost black with tan, but it was a romantic black, and in the last week, since he had had time to think about it, it had given him considerable pleasure. The hardiness of his frame, too, he appraised with a sort of fascination. He had lost part of an eyebrow somewhere, and he still wore an elastic bandage on his knee, but he was too young not to realize that on the steamer many women had looked at him with unusual tributary interest.

His clothes, of course, were frightful. They had been made for him by a Greek tailor in Lima — in two days. He was young enough, too, to have explained this sartorial deficiency to Jonquil in his otherwise laconic note. The only further detail it contained was a request that he should *not* be met at the station.

George O'Kelly, of Cuzco, Peru, waited an hour and a half in the hotel, until, to be exact, the sun had reached a midway position in the sky. Then, freshly shaven and talcum-powdered toward a somewhat more Caucasian hue, for vanity at the last minute had overcome ro-mance, he engaged a taxicab and set out for the house he knew so well.

He was breathing hard — he noticed this but he told himself that it was excitement, not emotion. He was here; she was not married — that was enough. He was not even sure what he had to say to her. But this was the moment of his life that he felt he could least easily have dispensed with. There was no triumph, after all, without a girl concerned, and if he did not lay his spoils at her feet he could at least hold them for a passing moment before her eyes.

The house loomed up suddenly beside him, and his first thought was that it had assumed a strange unreality. There was nothing changed — only everything was changed. It was smaller and it seemed shabbier than before — there was no cloud of magic hovering over its roof and issuing from the windows of the upper floor. He rang the door-bell and an unfamiliar colored maid appeared. Miss Jonquil would be down in a moment. He wet his lips nervously and walked into the sitting-room — and the feeling of unreality increased. After all, he saw, this was only a room, and not the enchanted chamber where he had passed those poignant hours. He sat in a chair, amazed to find it a chair, realizing that his imagination had distorted and colored all these simple familiar things.

Then the door opened and Jonquil came into the room — and it was as though everything in it suddenly blurred before his eyes. He had not remembered how beautiful she was, and he felt his face grow pale and his voice diminish to a poor sigh in his throat.

She was dressed in pale green, and a gold ribbon bound back her dark, straight hair like a crown. The familiar velvet eyes caught his as she came through the door, and a spasm of fright went through him at her beauty's power of inflicting pain.

He said "Hello," and they each took a few steps forward and shook hands. Then they sat in chairs quite far apart and gazed at each other across the room.

"You've come back," she said, and he answered just as tritely: "I wanted to stop in and see you as I came through."

He tried to neutralize the tremor in his voice by looking anywhere but at her face. The obligation to speak was on him, but, unless he immediately began to boast, it seemed that there was nothing to say. There had never been anything casual in their previous relations — it didn't seem possible that people in this position would talk about the weather.

"This is ridiculous," he broke out in sudden embarrassment. "I don't know exactly what to do. Does my being here bother you?"

"No." The answer was both reticent and impersonally sad. It depressed him.

"Are you engaged?" he demanded.

"No."

"Are you in love with some one?"

She shook her head.

"Oh." He leaned back in his chair. Another subject seemed exhausted — the interview was not taking the course he had intended.

"Jonquil," he began, this time on a softer key, "after all that's happened between us, I wanted to come back and see you. Whatever I do in the future I'll never love another girl as I've loved you."

This was one of the speeches he had rehearsed. On the steamer it had seemed to have just the right note — a reference to the tenderness he would always feel for her combined with a non-committal attitude toward his present state of mind. Here with the past around him, beside him, growing minute by minute more heavy on the air, it seemed theatrical and stale.

She made no comment, sat without moving, her eyes fixed on him with an expression that might have meant everything or nothing.

"You don't love me any more, do you?" he asked her in a level voice.

"No."

When Mrs. Cary came in a minute later, and spoke to him about his success — there had been a half-column about him in the local paper — he was a mixture of emotions. He knew now that he still wanted this girl, and he knew that the past sometimes comes back — that was all. For the rest he must be strong and watchful and he would see.

"And now," Mrs. Cary was saying, "I want you two to go and see the lady who has the chrysanthemums. She particularly told me she wanted to see you because she'd read about you in the paper."

They went to see the lady with the chrysanthemums. They walked along the street, and he recognized with a sort of excitement just how her shorter footsteps always fell in between his own. The lady turned out to be nice, and the chrysanthemums were enormous and extraordinarily beautiful. The lady's gardens were full of them, white and pink and yellow, so that to be among them was a trip back into the heart of summer. There were two gardens full, and a gate between them; when they strolled toward the second garden the lady went first through the gate.

And then a curious thing happened. George stepped aside to let

Jonquil pass, but instead of going through she stood still and stared at him for a minute. It was not so much the look, which was not a smile, as it was the moment of silence. They saw each other's eyes, and both took a short, faintly accelerated breath, and then they went on into the second garden. That was all.

The afternoon waned. They thanked the lady and walked home slowly, thoughtfully, side by side. Through dinner, too, they were silent. George told Mr. Cary something of what had happened in South America, and managed to let it be known that everything would be plain sailing for him in the future.

Then dinner was over, and he and Jonquil were alone in the room which had seen the beginning of their love affair and the end. It seemed to him long ago and inexpressibly sad. On that sofa he had felt agony and grief such as he would never feel again. He would never be so weak or so tired and miserable and poor. Yet he knew that that boy of fifteen months before had had something, a trust, a warmth that was gone forever. The sensible thing — they had done the sensible thing. He had traded his first youth for strength and carved success out of despair. But with his youth, life had carried away the freshness of his love.

"You won't marry me, will you?" he said quietly.

Jonquil shook her dark head.

"I'm never going to marry," she answered.

He nodded.

"I'm going on to Washington in the morning," he said.

"Oh ——"

"I have to go. I've got to be in New York by the first, and meanwhile I want to stop off in Washington."

"Business!"

"No-o," he said as if reluctantly. "There's some one there I must see who was very kind to me when I was so — down and out."

This was invented. There was no one in Washington for him to see — but he was watching Jonquil narrowly, and he was sure that she winced a little, that her eyes closed and then opened wide again.

"But before I go I want to tell you the things that happened to me since I saw you, and, as maybe we won't meet again, I wonder if — if just this once you'd sit in my lap like you used to. I wouldn't ask except since there's no one else — yet — perhaps it doesn't matter."

She nodded, and in a moment was sitting in his lap as she had sat so often in that vanished spring. The feel of her head against his shoulder, of her familiar body, sent a shock of emotion over him. His arms holding her had a tendency to tighten around her, so he leaned back and began to talk thoughtfully into the air.

He told her of a despairing two weeks in New York which had terminated with an attractive if not very profitable job in a construction plant in Jersey City. When the Peru business had first presented itself it had not seemed an extraordinary opportunity. He was to be third assistant engineer on the expedition, but only ten of the American party, including eight rodmen and surveyors, had ever reached Cuzco. Ten days later the chief of the expedition was dead of yellow fever. That had been his chance, a chance for anybody but a fool, a marvellous chance ——

"A chance for anybody but a fool?" she interrupted innocently.

"Even for a fool," he continued. "It was wonderful. Well, I wired New York ——"

"And so," she interrupted again, "they wired that you ought to take a chance?"

"Ought to!" he exclaimed, still leaning back. "That I *had* to. There was no time to lose ——"

"Not a minute?"

"Not a minute."

"Not even time for ——" she paused.

"For what?"

"Look."

He bent his head forward suddenly, and she drew herself to him in the same moment, her lips half open like a flower.

"Yes," he whispered into her lips. "There's all the time in the world. . . ."

All the time in the world — his life and hers. But for an instant as he kissed her he knew that though he search through eternity he could never recapture those lost April hours. He might press her close now till the muscles knotted on his arms — she was something desirable and rare that he had fought for and made his own — but never again an intangible whisper in the dusk, or on the breeze of night. . . .

Well, let it pass, he thought; April is over, April is over. There are all kinds of love in the world, but never the same love twice.

A Telephone Call

by Dorothy Parker

PLEASE, God, let him telephone me now. Dear God, let him call me now. I won't ask anything else of You, truly I won't. It isn't very much to ask. It would be so little to You, God, such a little, little thing. Only let him telephone now. Please, God. Please, please, please.

If I didn't think about it, maybe the telephone might ring. Sometimes it does that. If I could think of something else. If I could think of something else. Maybe if I counted five hundred by fives, it might ring by that time. I'll count slowly. I won't cheat. And if it rings when I get to three hundred, I won't stop; I won't answer it until I get to five hundred. Five, ten, fifteen, twenty, twenty-five, thirty, thirty-five, forty, forty-five, fifty. . . . Oh, please ring. Please.

This is the last time I'll look at the clock. I will not look at it again. It's ten minutes past seven. He said he would telephone at five o'clock. "I'll call you at five, darling." I think that's where he said "darling." I'm almost sure he said it there. I know he called me "darling" twice, and the other time was when he said good-bye. "Good-bye, darling." He was busy, and he can't say much in the office, but he called me "darling" twice. He couldn't have minded my calling him up. I know you shouldn't keep telephoning them — I know they don't like that. When you do that, they know you are thinking about them and wanting them, and that makes them hate you. But I hadn't talked to him in three days — not in three days. And all I did was ask him how he was; it was just the way anybody might have called him up. He couldn't have minded that. He couldn't have thought I was bothering him. "No, of course you're not," he said. And he said he'd telephone me. He didn't have to say that. I didn't ask him to, truly I didn't. I'm sure I didn't. I don't think he would say he'd telephone me, and then just never do it. Please don't let him do that, God. Please don't.

"I'll call you at five, darling." "Good-bye, darling." He was busy, and he was in a hurry, and there were people around him, but he called me "darling" twice. That's mine, that's mine. I have that, even if I never see him again. Oh, but that's so little. That isn't enough. Nothing's enough, if I never see him again. Please let me see him again, God. Please, I want him so much. I want him so much. I'll be good, God. I will try to be better, I will, if You will let me see him again. If You will let him telephone me. Oh, let him telephone me now.

Ah, don't let my prayer seem too little to You, God. You sit up there, so white and old, with all the angels about You and the stars slipping by. And I come to You with a prayer about a telephone call. Ah, don't laugh, God. You see, You don't know how it feels. You're so safe, there on Your throne, with the blue swirling under You. Nothing can touch You; no one can twist Your heart in his hands. This is suffering, God, this is bad, bad suffering. Won't you help me? For Your Son's sake, help me. You said You would do whatever was asked of You in His name. Oh, God, in the name of Thine only beloved Son, Jesus Christ, our Lord, let him telephone me now.

I must stop this. I mustn't be this way. Look. Suppose a young man says he'll call a girl up, and then something happens, and he doesn't. That isn't so terrible, is it? Why, it's going on all over the world, right this minute. Oh, what do I care what's going on all over the world? Why can't that telephone ring? Why can't it, why can't it? Couldn't you ring? Ah, please, couldn't you? You damned, ugly, shiny thing. It would hurt you to ring, wouldn't it? Oh, that would hurt you. Damn you, I'll pull your filthy roots out of the wall, I'll smash your smug black face in little bits. Damn you to hell.

No, no, no. I must stop. I must think about something else. This is what I'll do. I'll put the clock in the other room. Then I can't look at it. If I do have to look at it, then I'll have to walk into the bedroom, and that will be something to do. Maybe, before I look at it again, he will call me. I'll be so sweet to him, if he calls me. If he says he can't see me tonight, I'll say, "Why, that's all right, dear. Why, of course it's all right." I'll be the way I was when I first met him. Then maybe he'll like me again. I was always sweet, at first. Oh, it's so easy to be sweet to people before you love them.

I think he must still like me a little. He couldn't have called me "darling" twice today, if he didn't still like me a little. It isn't all gone, if he still likes me a little; even if it's only a little, little bit. You see, God, if You would just let him telephone me, I wouldn't have to ask You anything more. I would be sweet to him, I would be gay, I would be just the way I used to be, and then he would love me again. And then I would never have to ask You for anything more. Don't You see, God? So won't You please let him telephone me? Won't You please, please, please?

Are You punishing me, God, because I've been bad? Are You angry with me because I did that? Oh, but, God, there are so many bad people — You could not be hard only to me. And it wasn't very bad; it couldn't have been bad. We didn't hurt anybody, God. Things are only bad when they hurt people. We didn't hurt one single soul; You know that. You know it wasn't bad, don't You, God? So won't You let him telephone me now?

If he doesn't telephone me, I'll know God is angry with me. I'll count five hundred by fives, and if he hasn't called me then, I will know God isn't going to help me, ever again. That will be the sign. Five, ten, fifteen, twenty, twenty-five, thirty, thirty-five, forty, forty-five, fifty, fifty-five. . . . It was bad. I knew it was bad. All right, God, send me to hell. You think You're frightening me with Your hell, don't You? You think Your hell is worse than mine.

I mustn't. I mustn't do this. Suppose he's a little late calling me up — that's nothing to get hysterical about. Maybe he isn't going to call — maybe he's coming straight up here without telephoning. He'll be cross if he sees I have been crying. They don't like you to cry. He doesn't cry. I wish to God I could make him cry. I wish I could make him cry and tread the floor and feel his heart heavy and big and festering in him. I wish I could hurt him like hell.

He doesn't wish that about me. I don't think he even knows how he makes me feel. I wish he could know, without my telling him. They don't like you to tell them they've made you cry. They don't like you to tell them you're unhappy because of them. If you do, they think you're possessive and exacting. And then they hate you. They hate you whenever you say anything you really think. You always have to keep playing little games. Oh, I thought we didn't have to; I thought this was so big I could say whatever I meant. I guess you can't, ever. I guess there isn't ever anything big enough for that. Oh, if he would just telephone, I wouldn't tell him I had been sad about him. They hate sad people. I would be so sweet and so gay, he couldn't help but like me. If he would only telephone. If he would only telephone.

Maybe that's what he is doing. Maybe he is coming up here without calling me up. Maybe he's on his way now. Something might have happened to him. No, nothing could ever happen to him. I can't picture anything happening to him. I never picture him run over. I never see him lying still and long and dead. I wish he were dead. That's a terrible wish. That's a lovely wish. If he were dead, he would be mine. If he were dead, I would never think of now and the last few weeks. I would remember only the lovely times. It would be all beautiful. I wish he were dead. I wish he were dead, dead, dead.

This is silly. It's silly to go wishing people were dead just because they don't call you up the very minute they said they would. Maybe the clock's fast; I don't know whether it's right. Maybe he's hardly late at all. Anything could have made him a little late. Maybe he had to stay at his office. Maybe he went home, to call me up from there, and somebody came in. He doesn't like to telephone me in front of people. Maybe he's worried, just a little, little bit, about keeping me waiting. He might even hope that I would call him up. I could do that. I could telephone him.

I mustn't. I mustn't, I mustn't. Oh, God, please don't let me telephone him. Please keep me from doing that. I know, God, just as well as You do, that if he were worried about me, he'd telephone no matter where he was or how many people there were around him. Please make me know that, God. I don't ask You to make it easy for me — You can't do that, for all that You could make a world. Only let me know it, God. Don't let me go on hoping. Don't let me say comforting things to myself. Please don't let me hope, dear God. Please don't.

I won't telephone him. I'll never telephone him again as long as I live. He'll rot in hell, before I'll call him up. You don't have to give me strength, God; I have it myself. If he wanted me, he could get me. He knows where I am. He knows I'm waiting here. He's so sure of me, so sure. I wonder why they hate you, as soon as they are sure of you. I should think it would be so sweet to be sure.

It would be so easy to telephone him. Then I'd know. Maybe it wouldn't be a foolish thing to do. Maybe he wouldn't mind. Maybe he'd like it. Maybe he has been trying to get me. Sometimes people try and try to get you on the telephone, and they say the number doesn't answer. I'm not just saying that to help myself; that really happens. You know that really happens, God. Oh, God, keep me away from that telephone. Keep me away. Let me still have just a little bit of pride. I think I'm going to need it, God. I think it will be all I'll have.

Oh, what does pride matter, when I can't stand it if I don't talk to him? Pride like that is such a silly, shabby little thing. The real pride, the big pride, is in having no pride. I'm not saying that just because I want to call him. I am not. That's true, I know that's true. I will be big. I will be beyond little prides.

Please, God, keep me from telephoning him. Please, God.

I don't see what pride has to do with it. This is such a little thing, for me to be bringing in pride, for me to be making such a fuss about. I may have misunderstood him. Maybe he said for me to call him up, at five. "Call me at five, darling." He could have said that, perfectly well. It's so possible that I didn't hear him right. "Call me at five, darling." I'm almost sure that's what he said. God, don't let me talk this way to myself. Make me know, please make me know.

I'll think about something else. I'll just sit quietly. If I could sit still. If I could sit still. Maybe I could read. Oh, all the books are about people who love each other, truly and sweetly. What do they want to write about that for? Don't they know it isn't true? Don't they know it's a lie, it's a God damned lie? What do they have to tell about that for, when they know how it hurts? Damn them, damn them, damn them.

I won't. I'll be quiet. This is nothing to get excited about. Look. Suppose he were someone I didn't know very well. Suppose he were another girl. Then I'd just telephone and say, "Well, for goodness' sake, what happened to you?" That's what I'd do, and I'd never even think about it. Why can't I be casual and natural, just because I love him? I can be. Honestly, I can be. I'll call him up, and be so easy and pleasant. You see if I won't, God. Oh, don't let me call him. Don't, don't, don't.

God, aren't You really going to let him call me? Are You sure, God? Couldn't You please relent? Couldn't You? I don't even ask You to let him telephone me now, God; only let him do it in a little while. I'll count five hundred by fives. I'll do it so slowly and so fairly. If he hasn't telephoned then, I'll call him. I will. Oh, please, dear God, dear kind God, my blessed Father in Heaven, let him call before then. Please, God. Please.

Five, ten, fifteen, twenty, twenty-five, thirty, thirty-five. . . .

How Beautiful with Shoes

by Wilbur Daniel Steele

BY THE TIME the milking was finished, the sow, which had far-rowed the past week, was making such a row that the girl spilled a pint of warm milk down the trough lead to quiet the animal before taking the pail to the well house. Then in the quiet she heard a sound of hoofs on the bridge, where the road crossed the creek a hundred yards below the house, and she set the pail down on the ground beside her bare, barn-soiled feet. She picked it up again. She set it down. It was as if she calculated its weight.

That was what she was doing, as a matter of fact, setting off against its pull toward the well house the pull of that wagon team in the road, with little more of personal will or wish in the matter than has a wooden weathervane between two currents in the wind. And as with the vane, so with the wooden girl — the added behest of a whiplash cracking in the distance was enough; leaving the pail at the barn door, she set off in a deliberate, docile beeline through the cowyard, over the fence, and down in a diagonal across the farm's one tilled field toward the willow brake that walled the road at the dip. And once under way, though her mother came to the kitchen door and called in her high, flat voice, "Amarantha, where you goin', Amarantha?" the girl went on apparently unmoved, as though she had been as deaf as the woman in the doorway; indeed, if there was emotion in her it was the purely sensuous one of feeling the clods of the furrows breaking softly between her toes. It was springtime in the mountains.

"Amarantha, why don't you answer me, Amarantha?"

For moments after the girl had disappeared beyond the willows the widow continued to call, unaware through long habit of how absurd it sounded, the name which that strange man her husband had put upon their daughter in one of his moods. Mrs. Doggett had been deaf so long she did not realize that nobody else ever thought of it for the broad-fleshed, slow-minded girl, but called her Mary, or even more simply, Mare.

Ruby Herter had stopped his team this side of the bridge, the mules' heads turned into the lane to his father's farm beyond the road. A big-barreled, heavy-limbed fellow with a square, sallow, not unhandsome face, he took out youth in ponderous gestures of masterfulness; it was like him to have cracked his whip above his animals' ears the moment before he pulled them to a halt. When he saw the girl getting over the fence under the willows he tongued the wad of tobacco out of his mouth into his palm, threw it away beyond the road, and drew a sleeve of his jumper across his lips.

"Don't run yourself out o' breath, Mare; I got all night."

"I was comin'." It sounded sullen only because it was matter of fact.

"Well, keep a-comin' and give us a smack." Hunched on the wagon seat, he remained motionless for some time after she had arrived at the hub, and when he stirred it was but to cut a fresh bit of tobacco, as if already he had forgotten why he threw the old one away. Having satisfied his humor, he unbent, climbed down, kissed her passive mouth, and hugged her up to him, roughly and loosely, his hands careless of contours. It was not out of the way; they were used to handling animals both of them; and it was spring. A slow warmth pervaded the girl, formless, nameless, almost impersonal.

Her betrothed pulled her head back by the braid of her yellow hair. He studied her face, his brows gathered and his chin out.

"Listen, Mare, you wouldn't leave nobody else hug and kiss you, dang you!"

She shook her head, without vehemence or anxiety.

"Who's that?" She harkened up the road. "Pull your team out," she added, as a Ford came in sight around the bend above the house, driven at speed. "Geddap!" she said to the mules herself.

But the car came to a halt near them, and one of the five men crowded in it called, "Come on, Ruby, climb in. They's a loony loose out o' Dayville Asylum, and they got him trailed over somewhere on

Split Ridge, and Judge North phoned up to Slosson's store for ever'-body come help circle him — come on, hop the runnin'-board!"

Ruby hesitated, an eye on his team.

"Scared, Ruby?" The driver raced his engine. "They say this boy's a killer."

"Mare, take the team in and tell Pa." The car was already moving when Ruby jumped it. A moment after it had sounded on the bridge it was out of sight.

"Amarantha, Amarantha, why don't you come, Amarantha?"

Returning from her errand, fifteen minutes later, Mare heard the plaint lifted in the twilight. The sun had dipped behind the back ridge, though the sky was still bright with day, the dusk began to smoke up out of the plowed field like a ground fog. The girl had returned through it, got the milk, and started toward the well house before the widow saw her.

"Daughter, seems to me you might!" she expostulated without change of key. "Here's some young man friend o' yourn stopped to say howdy, and I been rackin' my lungs out after you. . . . Put that milk in the cool and come!"

Some young man friend? But there was no good to be got from puzzling. Mare poured the milk in the pan in the dark of the low house over the well, and as she came out, stooping, she saw a figure waiting for her, black in silhouette against the yellowing sky.

"Who are you?" she asked, a native timidity making her sound sulky.

" 'Amarantha!' " the fellow mused. "That's poetry." And she knew then that she did not know him.

She walked past, her arms straight down and her eyes front. Strangers always affected her with a kind of muscular terror simply by being strangers. So she gained the kitchen steps, aware by his tread that he followed. There, taking courage at the sight of her mother in the doorway, she turned on him, her eyes down at the level of his knees.

"Who are you and what d' y' want?"

He still mused. "Amarantha! Amarantha in Carolina! That makes me happy!"

Mare hazarded one upward look. She saw that he had red hair, brown eyes, and hollows under his cheekbones, and though the green sweater he wore on top of a gray overall was plainly not meant for him, sizes too large as far as girth went, yet he was built so long of limb that his wrists came inches out of the sleeves and made his big hands look even bigger.

Mrs. Doggett complained. "Why don't you introduce us, daughter?"

The girl opened her mouth and closed it again. Her mother, unaware that no sound had come out of it, smiled and nodded, evidently taking to the tall, homely fellow and tickled by the way he could not seem to get his eyes off her daughter. But the daughter saw none of it, all her attention centered upon the stranger's hands.

Restless, hard-fleshed, and chap-bitten, they were like a countryman's hands; but the fingers were longer than the ordinary, and slightly spatulate at their ends, and these ends were slowly and continuously at play among themselves.

The girl could not have explained how it came to her to be frightened and at the same time to be calm, for she was inept with words. It was simply that in an animal way she knew animals, knew them in health and ailing, and when they were ailing she knew by instinct, as her father had known, how to move so as not to fret them.

Her mother had gone in to light up; from beside the lampshelf she called back, "If he's aimin' to stay to supper you should've told me, Amarantha, though I guess there's plenty of the side-meat to go 'round, if you'll bring me in a few more turnips and potatoes, though it is late."

At the words the man's cheeks moved in and out. "I'm very hungry," he said.

Mare nodded deliberately. Deliberately, as if her mother could hear her, she said over her shoulder, "I'll go get the potatoes and turnips, Ma." While she spoke she was moving, slowly, softly, at first, toward the right of the yard, where the fence gave over into the field. Unluckily her mother spied her through the window.

"Amarantha, where *are* you goin'?"

"I'm goin' to get the potatoes and turnips." She neither raised her voice nor glanced back, but lengthened her stride. He won't hurt her, she said to herself. He won't hurt her; it's me, not her, she kept repeating, while she got over the fence and down into the shadow that lay more than ever like a fog on the field.

The desire to believe that it actually did hide her, the temptation to break from her rapid but orderly walk grew till she could no longer fight it. She saw the road willows only a dash ahead of her. She ran, her feet floundering among the furrows.

She neither heard nor saw him, but when she realized he was with her she knew he had been with her all the while. She stopped, and he stopped, and so they stood, with the dark open of the field all around. Glancing sidewise presently, she saw he was no longer looking at her with those strangely importunate brown eyes of his, but had raised them to the crest of the wooded ridge behind her.

By and by, "What does it make you think of?" he asked. And when she made no move to see, "Turn around and look!" he said, and though it was low and almost tender in its tone, she knew enough to turn.

A ray of the sunset hidden in the west struck through the tops of the topmost trees, far and small up there, a thin, bright hem.

"What does it make you think of, Amarantha? . . . Answer!"

"Fire," she made herself say.

"Or blood."

"Or blood, yeh. That's right, or blood." She had heard a Ford going up the road beyond the willows, and her attention was not on what she said.

The man soliloquized. "Fire and blood, both; spare one or the other, and where is beauty, the way the world is? It's an awful thing to have to carry, but Christ had it. Christ came with a sword. I love beauty, Amarantha. . . . I say, I love beauty!"

"Yeh, that's right, I hear." What she heard was the car stopping at the house.

"Not prettiness. Prettiness'll have to go with ugliness, because it's only ugliness trigged up. But beauty!" Now again he was looking at her. "Do you know how beautiful you are, Amarantha, Amarantha sweet and fair?" Of a sudden, reaching behind her, he began to un- ravel the meshes of her hair braid, the long, flat-tipped fingers at once impatient and infinitely gentle. "Braid no more that shining hair!"

Flat-faced Mare Doggett tried to see around those glowing eyes so near to hers, but wise in her instinct, did not try too hard. "Yeh," she temporized. "I mean, no, I mean."

"Amarantha, I've come a long, long way for you. Will you come away with me now?"

"Yeh — that is — in a minute I will, mister — yeh . . ."

"Because you want to, Amarantha? Because you love me as I love you? Answer!"

"Yeh — sure — uh . . . *Ruby!*"

The man tried to run, but there were six against him, coming up out of the dark that lay in the plowed ground. Mare stood where she was while they knocked him down and got a rope around him; after that she walked back toward the house with Ruby and Older Haskins, her father's cousin.

Ruby wiped his brow and felt of his muscles. "Gees, you're lucky we come, Mare. We're no more'n past the town, when they come hollerin' he'd broke over this way."

When they came to the fence the girl sat on the rail for a moment and rebraided her hair before she went into the house, where they were making her mother smell ammonia.

Lots of cars were coming. Judge North was coming, somebody said. When Mare heard this she went into her bedroom off the kitchen and got her shoes and put them on. They were brand-new two-dollar shoes with cloth tops, and she had only begun to break them in last Sunday; she wished afterwards she had put her stockings on too, for they would have eased the seams. Or else that she had put on the old button pair, even though the soles were worn through.

Judge North arrived. He thought first of taking the loony straight through to Dayville that night, but then decided to keep him in the lockup at the courthouse till morning and make the drive by day. Older Haskins stayed in, gentling Mrs. Doggett, while Ruby went out to help get the man into the Judge's sedan. Now that she had them on, Mare didn't like to take the shoes off till Older went; it might make him feel small, she thought.

Older Haskins had a lot of facts about the loony.

"His name's Humble Jewett," he told them. "They belong back in Breed County, all them Jewetts, and I don't reckon there's none of 'em that's not a mite unbalanced. He went to college though, worked his way, and he taught somethin' 'rother in some academy-school a spell, till he went off his head all of a sudden and took after folks with an axe. I remember it in the paper at the time. They give out one while how the Principal wasn't goin' to live, and there was others — there was a girl he tried to strangle. That was four-five year back."

Ruby came in guffawing. "Know the only thing they can get 'im to say, Mare? Only God thing he'll say is 'Amarantha, she's goin' with me.' . . . Mare!"

"Yeh, I know."

The cover of the kettle the girl was handling slid off the stove with a clatter. A sudden sick wave passed over her. She went out to the back, out into the air. It was not till now she knew how frightened she had been.

Ruby went home, but Older Haskins stayed to supper with them, and helped Mare do the dishes afterward; it was nearly nine when he left. The mother was already in bed, and Mare was about to sit down to get those shoes off her wretched feet at last, when she heard the cow carrying on up at the barn, lowing and kicking, and next minute the sow was in it with a horning note. It might be a fox passing by to get at the henhouse, or a weasel. Mare forgot her feet, took a broom handle they used in boiling clothes, opened the back door, and stepped out. Blinking the lamplight from her eyes, she peered up toward the outbuildings, and saw the gable end of the barn standing like a red arrow in the dark, and the top of a butternut tree beyond it drawn in skeleton traceries, and just then a cock crowed.

She went to the right corner of the house and saw where the light came from, ruddy above the woods down the valley. Returning into the house, she bent close to her mother's ear and shouted, "Somethin's a-fire down to the town, looks like," then went out again and up to the barn. "Soh! Soh!" she called in to the animals. She climbed up and stood on the top rail of the cow-pen fence, only to find she could not locate the flame even there.

Ten rods behind the buildings a mass of rock mounted higher than their ridgepoles, a chopped off buttress of the back ridge, covered with oak scrub and wild grapes and blackberries, whose thorny ropes the girl beat away from her skirt with the broom handle as she scrambled up in the wine-colored dark. Once at the top, and the brush held aside, she could see the tongue-tip of the conflagration half a mile away at the town. And she knew by the bearing of the two church steeples that it was the building where the lockup was that was burning.

There is a horror in knowing animals trapped in a fire, no matter what the animals.

"Oh, my God!" Mare said.

A car went down the road. Then there was a horse galloping. That would be Older Haskins probably. People were out at Ruby's father's farm; she could hear their voices raised. There must have been another car up from the other way, for lights wheeled and shouts were exchanged in the neighborhood of the bridge. Next thing she knew, Ruby was at the house below, looking for her probably.

He was telling her mother, Mrs. Doggett was not used to him, so he had to shout even louder than Mare had to.

"What y' reckon he done, the hellion! he broke the door and killed Lew Fyke and set the courthouse afire! . . . Where's Mare?"

Her mother would not know. Mare called. "Here, up the rock here."

She had better go down. Ruby would likely break his bones if he tried to climb the rock in the dark, not knowing the way. But the sight of the fire fascinated her simple spirit, the fearful element, more fearful than ever now, with the news. "Yes, I'm comin'," she called sulkily, hearing feet in the brush. "You wait; I'm comin'."

When she turned and saw it was Humble Jewett, right behind her among the branches, she opened her mouth to screech. She was not quick enough. Before a sound came out he got one hand over her face and the other around her body.

Mare had always thought she was strong, and the loony looked gangling, yet she was so easy for him that he need not hurt her. He made no haste and little noise as he carried her deeper into the undergrowth. Where the hill began to mount it was harder though. Presently he set her on her feet. He let the hand that had been over her mouth slip down to her throat, where the broad-tipped fingers wound, tender as yearning, weightless as caress.

"I was afraid you'd scream before you knew who 'twas, Amarantha. But I didn't want to hurt your lips, dear heart, your lovely, quiet lips."

It was so dark under the trees she could hardly see him, but she felt his breath on her mouth, near to. But then, instead of kissing her, he said, "No! No!" took from her throat for an instant the hand that had held her mouth, kissed its palm, and put it back softly against her skin.

"Now, my love, let's go before they come."

She stood stock-still. Her mother's voice was to be heard in the distance, strident and meaningless. More cars were on the road.

Nearer, around the rock, there were sounds of tramping and thrashing. Ruby fussed and cursed. He shouted, "Mare, dang you, where are you, Mare?" his voice harsh with uneasy anger. Now, if she aimed to do anything, was the time to do it. But there was neither breath nor power in her windpipe. It was as if those yearning fingers had paralyzed the muscles.

"Come!" The arm he put around her shivered against her shoulder blades. It was anger. "I hate killing. It's a dirty, ugly thing. It makes me sick." He gagged, judging by the sound. But then he ground his teeth. "Come away, my love!"

She found herself moving. Once when she broke a branch underfoot with an instinctive awkwardness he chided her. "Quiet, my heart, else they'll hear!" She made herself heavy. He thought she grew tired and bore more of her weight till he was breathing hard.

Men came up the hill. There must have been a dozen spread out, by the angle of their voices as they kept touch. Always Humble Jewett kept caressing Mare's throat with one hand; all she could do was hang back.

"You're tired and you're frightened," he said at last. "Get down here."

There were twigs in the dark, the overhang of a thicket of some sort. He thrust her in under this, and lay beside her on the bed of groundpine. The hand that was not in love with her throat reached across her; she felt the weight of its forearm on her shoulder and its fingers among the strands of her hair, eagerly, but tenderly, busy. Not once did he stop speaking, no louder than breathing, his lips to her ear.

"*Amarantha sweet and fair — Ah, braid no more that shining hair . . .*"

Mare had never heard of Lovelace, the poet; she thought the loony was just going on, hardly listened, got little sense. But the cadence of it added to the lethargy of all her flesh.

"*Like a dew of golden thread — Most excellently ravelled . . .*"

Voices loudened; feet came tramping; a pair went past not two rods away.

"*. . . Do not then wind up the light — In ribbands, and o'ercloud in night . . .*"

The search went on up the woods, men shouting to one another and beating the brush.

". . . *But shake your head and scatter day.* I've never loved, Amarantha. They've tried me with prettiness, but prettiness is too cheap, yes, it's too cheap."

Mare was cold, and the coldness made her lazy. All she knew was that he talked on.

"But dogwood blowing in the spring isn't cheap. The earth of a field isn't cheap. Lots of times I've lain down and kissed the earth of a field, Amarantha. That's beauty, and a kiss for beauty." His breath moved up her cheek. He trembled violently. "No, no, not yet!" He got to his knees and pulled her by an arm. "We can go now."

They went back down the slope, but at an angle, so that when they came to the level they passed two hundred yards to the north of the house, and crossed the road there. More and more her walking was like sleepwalking, the feet numb in their shoes. Even where he had to let go of her, crossing the creek on stones, she stepped where he stepped with an obtuse docility. The voices of the searchers on the back ridge were small in distance when they began to climb the fence of Coward Hill, on the opposite side of the valley.

There is an old farm on top of Coward Hill, big hayfields as flat as tables. It had been half-past nine when Mare stood on the rock above the barn; it was toward midnight when Humble Jewett put aside the last branches of the woods and let her out on the height, and a half a moon had risen. And a wind blew there, tossing the withered tops of last year's grasses, and mists ran with the wind, and ragged shadows with the mists, and mares'-tails of clear moonlight among the shadows, so that now the boles of birches on the forest's edge beyond the fences were but opal blurs and now cut alabaster. It struck so cold against the girl's cold flesh, this wind, that another wind of shivers blew through her, and she put her hands over her face and eyes. But the madman stood with his eyes open and his mouth open, drinking the moonlight and the wet wind.

His voice, when he spoke at last, was thick in his throat.

"Get down on your knees." He got down on his and pulled her after. "And pray!"

Once in England a poet sang four lines. Four hundred years have forgotten his name, but they have remembered his lines. The daft man knelt upright, his face raised to the wild scud, his long wrists hanging to the dead grass. He began simply:

O western wind, when wilt thou blow
That the small rain down can rain?

The Adam's apple was big in his bent throat. As simply he finished.

Christ, that my love were in my arms
And I in my bed again!

Mare got up and ran. She ran without aim or feeling in the power of the wind. She told herself again that the mists would hide her from him, as she had done at dusk. And again, seeing that he ran at her shoulder, she knew he had been there all the while, making a race of it, flailing the air with his long arms for joy of play in the cloud of spring, throwing his knees high, leaping the moon-blue waves of the brown grass, shaking his bright hair; and her own hair was a weight behind her, lying level on the wind. Once a shape went bounding ahead of them for instants; she did not realize it was a fox till it was gone.

She never thought of stopping; she never thought of anything, except once, Oh, my God, I wish I had my shoes off! And what would have been the good in stopping or in turning another way, when it was only play? The man's ecstasy magnified his strength. When a snake fence came at them he took the top rail in flight, like a college hurdler, and seeing the girl hesitate and half turn as if to flee, he would have releaped it without touching a hand. But then she got a loom of buildings, climbed over quickly, before he should jump, and ran along the lane that ran with the fence.

Mare had never been up there, but she knew that the farm and the house belonged to a man named Wyker, a kind of cousin of Ruby Herter's, a violent, bearded old fellow who lived by himself. She could not believe her luck. When she had run half the distance and Jewett had not grabbed her, doubt grabbed her instead. "Oh, my God, go careful!" she told herself. "Go slow!" she implored herself, and stopped running, to walk.

Here was a misgiving the deeper in that it touched her special knowledge. She had never known an animal so far gone that its instincts failed it; a starving rat will scent the trap sooner than a fed one. Yet, after one glance at the house they approached, Jewett paid it no further attention, but walked with his eyes to the right, where the cloud had blown away, and wooded ridges, like black waves rimed with silver, ran down away toward the Valley of Virginia.

"I've never lived!" In his single cry there were two things, beatitude and pain.

Between the bigness of the falling world and his eyes the flag of her hair blew. He reached out and let it whip between his fingers. Mare was afraid it would break the spell then, and he would stop looking away and look at the house again. So she did something incredible; she spoke.

"It's a pretty — I mean — a beautiful view down that-a-way."

"God Almighty beautiful, to take your breath away. I knew I'd never loved, Beloved —" He caught a foot under the long end of one of the boards that covered the well and went down heavily on his hands and knees. It seemed to make no difference. "But I never knew I'd never lived," he finished in the same tone of strong rapture, quadruped in the grass, while Mare ran for the door and grabbed the latch.

When the latch would not give, she lost what little sense she had. She pounded with her fists. She cried with all her might: "Oh — hey — in there — hey — in there!" Then Jewett came and took her gently between his hands and drew her away, and then, though she was free, she stood in something like an awful embarrassment while he tried shouting.

"Hey! Friend! whoever you are, wake up and let my love and me come in!"

"No!" wailed the girl.

He grew peremptory. "Hey, wake up!" He tried the latch. He passed to full fury in a wink's time; he cursed, he kicked, he beat the door till Mare thought he would break his hands. Withdrawing, he ran at it with his shoulder; it burst at the latch, went slamming in, and left a black emptiness. His anger dissolved in a big laugh. Turning in time to catch her by a wrist, he cried joyously, "Come, my Sweet One!"

"No! No! Please — aw — listen. There ain't nobody there. He ain't to home. It wouldn't be right to go in anybody's house if they wasn't to home, you know that."

His laugh was blither than ever. He caught her high in his arms.

"I'd do the same by his love and him if 'twas my house, I would." At the threshold he paused and thought. "That is, if she was the true love of his heart forever."

The room was the parlor. Moonlight slanted in at the door, and another shaft came through a window and fell across a sofa, its covering dilapidated, showing its wadding in places. The air was sour, but both of them were farm-bred.

"Don't, Amarantha!" His words were pleading in her ear. "Don't be so frightened."

He set her down on the sofa. As his hands let go of her they were shaking.

"But look, I'm frightened too." He knelt on the floor before her, reached out his hands, withdrew them. "See, I'm afraid to touch you." He mused, his eyes rounded. "Of all the ugly things there are, fear is the ugliest. And yet, see, it can be the very beautifulest. That's a strange queer thing."

The wind blew in and out of the room, bringing the thin, little bitter sweetness of new April at night. The moonlight that came across Mare's shoulders fell full upon his face, but hers it left dark, ringed by the aureole of her disordered hair.

"Why do you wear a halo, Love?" He thought about it. "Because you're an angel, is that why?" The swift, untempered logic of the mad led him to dismay. His hands came flying to hers, to make sure they were of earth; and he touched her breast, her shoulders, and her hair. Peace returned to his eyes as his fingers twined among the strands.

"*Thy hair is as a flock of goats that appear from Gilead . . .*" He spoke like a man dreaming. "*Thy temples are like a piece of pomegranate within thy locks.*"

Mare never knew that he could not see her for the moonlight.

"Do you remember, Love?"

She dared not shake her head under his hand. "Yeh, I reckon," she temporized.

"You remember how I sat at your feet, long ago, like this, and made up a song? And all the poets in all the world have never made one to touch it, have they, Love?"

"Ugh-ugh — never."

"*How beautiful are thy feet with shoes . . .* Remember?"

"Oh, my God, what's he sayin' now?" she wailed to herself.

*"How beautiful are thy feet with shoes, O prince's daughter! the joints of
thy thighs are like jewels, the work of the hands of a cunning workman.*

*Thy navel is like a round goblet, which wanteth not liquor; thy belly is like
an heap of wheat set about with lilies.*

Thy two breasts are like two young roes that are twins."

Mare had not been to church since she was a little girl, when her
mother's black dress wore out. "No, no!" she wailed under her breath.
"You're awful to say such awful things." She might have shouted it;
nothing could have shaken the man now, rapt in the immortal, passionate periods of Solomon's Song.

*". . . now also thy breasts shall be as clusters of the vine, and the smell of
thy nose like apples."*

Hotness touched Mare's face for the first time. "Aw, no, don't talk
so!"

*"And the roof of thy mouth like the best wine for my beloved . . . causing
the lips of them that are asleep to speak."*

He had ended. His expression changed. Ecstasy gave place to anger,
love to hate. And Mare felt the change in the weight of the fingers in
her hair.

"What do you mean, I mustn't say it like that?" But it was not to
her his fury spoke, for he answered himself straightway. "Like poetry,
Mr. Jewett; I won't have blasphemy around my school."

"Poetry. My God! If that isn't poetry — if that isn't music —" . . .
"It's Bible, Jewett. What you're paid to teach here is *literature.*"

"Doctor Ryeworth, you're the blasphemer and you're an ignorant
man." . . . "And you're principal. And I won't have you going around
reading sacred allegory like earthly love."

"Ryeworth, you're an old man, a dull man, a dirty man, and you'd
be better dead."

Jewett's hands had slid down from Mare's head. "Then I went to put
my fingers around his throat, so. But my stomach turned, and I didn't
do it. I went to my room. I laughed all the way to my room. I sat in my
room at my table and laughed. I laughed all afternoon and long after

dark came. And then, about ten, somebody came and stood beside me in my room."

" 'Wherefore dost thou laugh, son?'

"Then I knew who He was, He was Christ.

" 'I was laughing about that dirty, ignorant, crazy old fool, Lord.'

" 'Wherefore dost thou laugh?'

"I didn't laugh any more. He didn't say any more. I kneeled down, bowed my head.

" 'Thy will be done! Where is he, Lord?'

" 'Over at the girls' dormitory, waiting for Blossom Sinckley.'

"Brassy Blossom, dirty Blossom . . ."

It had come so suddenly it was nearly too late. Mare tore at his hands with hers, tried with all her strength to pull her neck away.

"Filthy Blossom! and him an old filthy man, Blossom! and you'll find him in Hell when you reach there, Blossom. . . ."

It was more the nearness of his face than the hurt of his hands that gave her power of fright to choke out three words.

"I — ain't — Blossom!"

Light ran in crooked veins. Through the veins she saw his face bewildered. His hands loosened. One fell down and hung; the other he lifted and put over his eyes, took it away again and looked at her.

"Amarantha!" His remorse was fearful to see. "What have I done!" His hands returned to hover over the hurts, ravening with pity, grief and tenderness. Tears fell down his cheeks. And with that, dammed desire broke its dam.

"Amarantha, my love, my dove, my beautiful love —"

"And I ain't Amarantha neither, I'm Mary! Mary, that's my name!"

She had no notion what she had done. He was like a crystal crucible that a chemist watches, changing hue in a wink with one adeptly added drop; but hers was not the chemist's eye. All she knew was that she felt light and free of him; all she could see of his face as he stood away above the moonlight were the whites of his eyes.

"Mary!" he muttered. A slight paroxysm shook his frame. So in the transparent crucible desire changed its hue. He retreated farther, stood in the dark by some tall piece of furniture. And still she could see the whites of his eyes.

"Mary! Mary Adorable!" A wonder was in him. "Mother of God." Mare held her breath. She eyed the door, but it was too far. And already he came back to go on his knees before her, his shoulders so bowed and his face so lifted that it must have cracked his neck, she thought; all she could see on the face was pain.

"Mary Mother, I'm sick to my death. I'm so tired."

She had seen a dog like that, one she had loosed from a trap after it had been there three days, its caught leg half gnawed free. Something about the eyes.

"Mary Mother, take me in your arms . . ."

Once again her muscles tightened. But he made no move.

". . . and give me sleep."

No, they were worse than the dog's eyes.

"Sleep, sleep! why won't they let me sleep? Haven't I done it all yet, Mother? Haven't I washed them yet of all their sins? I've drunk the cup that was given me; is there another? They've mocked me and reviled me, broken my brow with thorns and my hands with nails, and I've forgiven them, for they knew not what they did. Can't I go to sleep now, Mother?"

Mare could not have said why, but now she was more frightened than she had ever been. Her hands lay heavy on her knees, side by side, and she could not take them away when he bowed his head and rested his face upon them.

After a moment he said one thing more. "Take me down gently when you take me from the Tree."

Gradually the weight of his body came against her shins, and he slept.

The moon streak that entered by the eastern window crept north across the floor, thinner and thinner; the one that fell through the southern doorway traveled east and grew fat. For a while Mare's feet pained her terribly and her legs too. She dared not move them, though, and by and by they did not hurt so much.

A dozen times, moving her head slowly on her neck, she canvassed the shadows of the room for a weapon. Each time her eyes came back to a heavy earthenware pitcher on a stand some feet to the left of the sofa. It would have had flowers in it when Wyker's wife was alive; probably it had not been moved from its dust ring since she died. It would be a long grab, perhaps too long; still, it might be done if she had her hands.

To get her hands from under the sleeper's head was the task she set herself. She pulled first one, then the other, infinitesimally. She waited. Again she tugged a very, very little. The order of his breathing was not disturbed. But at the third trial he stirred.

"Gently! gently!" His own muttering waked him more. With some drowsy instinct of possession he threw one hand across her wrists, pinning them together between thumb and fingers. She kept dead quiet, shut her eyes, lengthened her breathing, as if she too slept.

There came a time when what was pretense grew a peril; strange as it was, she had to fight to keep her eyes open. She never knew whether or not she really napped. But something changed in the air, and she was wide awake again. The moonlight was fading on the doorsill, and the light that runs before dawn waxed in the window behind her head.

And then she heard a voice in the distance, lifted in maundering song. It was old man Wyker coming home after a night, and it was plain he had had some whiskey.

Now a new terror laid hold of Mare.

"Shut up, you fool you!" she wanted to shout. "Come quiet, quiet!" She might have chanced it now to throw the sleeper away from her and scramble and run, had his powers of strength and quickness not taken her simple imagination utterly in thrall.

Happily the singing stopped. What had occurred was that the farmer had espied the open door and, even befuddled as he was, wanted to know more about it quietly. He was so quiet that Mare had begun to fear he had gone away. He had the squirrel-hunter's foot, and the first she knew of him was when she looked and saw his head in the doorway, his hard, soiled, whiskery face half upside-down with craning.

He had been to the town. Between drinks he had wandered in and out of the night's excitement; had even gone a short distance with one search party himself. Now he took in the situation in the room. He used his forefinger. First he held it to his lips. Next he pointed it with a jabbing motion at the sleeper. Then he tapped his own forehead and described wheels. Lastly, with his whole hand, he made pushing gestures, for Mare to wait. Then he vanished as silently as he had appeared.

The minutes dragged. The light in the east strengthened and turned rosy. Once she thought she heard a board creaking in another part of the house, and looked down sharply to see if the loony stirred. All she could see of his face was a temple with freckles on it and the sharp ridge of a cheekbone, but even from so little she knew how deeply and peacefully he slept. The door darkened. Wyker was there again. In one hand he carried something heavy; with the other he beckoned.

"Come jumpin'!" he said out loud.

Mare went jumping, but her cramped legs threw her down halfway to the sill; the rest of the distance she rolled and crawled. Just as she tumbled through the door it seemed as if the world had come to an end above her; two barrels of a shotgun discharged into a room make a noise. Afterwards all she could hear in there was something twisting and bumping on the floor boards. She got up and ran.

Mare's mother had gone to pieces; neighbor women put her to bed when Mare came home. They wanted to put Mare to bed, but she would not let them. She sat on the edge of her bed in her lean-to bedroom off the kitchen, just as she was, her hair down all over her shoulders and her shoes on, and stared away from them, at a place in the wallpaper.

"Yeh, I'll go myself. Lea' me be!"

The women exchanged quick glances, thinned their lips, and left her be. "God knows," was all they would answer to the questionings of those that had not gone in, "but she's gettin' herself to bed."

When the doctor came through he found her sitting just as she had been, still dressed, her hair down on her shoulders and her shoes on.

"What d' y' want?" she muttered and stared at the place in the wallpaper.

How could Doc Paradise say, when he did not know himself?

"I didn't know if you might be — might be feeling very smart, Mary."

"I'm all right. Lea' me be."

It was a heavy responsibility. Doc shouldered it. "No, it's all right," he said to the men in the road. Ruby Herter stood a little apart, chewing sullenly and looking another way. Doc raised his voice to make certain it carried. "Nope, nothing."

Ruby's ears got red, and he clamped his jaws. He knew he ought to go in and see Mare, but he was not going to do it while everybody hung around waiting to see if he would. A mule tied near him reached out and mouthed his sleeve in idle innocence; he wheeled and banged a fist against the side of the animal's head.

"Well, what d' y' aim to do 'bout it?" he challenged its owner.

He looked at the sun then. It was ten in the morning. "Hell, I got work!" he flared, and set off down the road for home. Doc looked at Judge North, and the Judge started after Ruby. But Ruby shook his head angrily. "Lea' me be!" He went on, and the Judge came back.

It got to be eleven and then noon. People began to say, "Like enough she'd be as thankful if the whole neighborhood wasn't camped here." But none went away.

As a matter of fact they were no bother to the girl. She never saw them. The only move she made was to bend her ankles over and rest her feet on the edge; her shoes hurt terribly and her feet knew it, though she did not. She sat all the while staring at that one figure in the wallpaper, and she never saw the figure.

Strange as the night had been, this day was stranger. Fright and physical pain are perishable things once they are gone. But while pain merely dulls and telescopes in memory and remains diluted pain, terror looked back upon has nothing of terror left. A gambling chance taken, at no matter what odds, and won was a sure thing since the world's beginning; perils come through safely were never perilous. But what fright does do in retrospect is this — it heightens each sensuous recollection, like a hard, clear lacquer laid on wood, bringing out the color and grain of it vividly.

Last night Mare had lain stupid with fear on groundpine beneath a bush, loud footfalls and light whispers confused in her ear. Only now, in her room, did she smell the groundpine.

Only now did the conscious part of her brain begin to make words of the whispering.

Amarantha, she remembered, *Amarantha sweet and fair.* That was as far as she could go for the moment, except that the rhyme with "fair" was "hair." But then a puzzle, held in abeyance, brought other words. She wondered what "ravel Ed" could mean. *Most excellently ravell-ed.* It was left to her mother to bring the end.

They gave up trying to keep her mother out at last. The poor woman's prostration took the form of fussiness.

"Good gracious, daughter, you look a sight. Them new shoes, half ruined; ain't your feet *dead?* And look at your hair, all tangled like a wild one!"

She got a comb.

"Be quiet, daughter; what's ailin' you. Don't shake your head!"

"But shake your head and scatter day."

"What you say, Amarantha?" Mrs. Doggett held an ear down.

"Go 'way! Lea' me be!"

Her mother was hurt and left. And Mare ran, as she stared at the wallpaper.

Christ, that my love were in my arms . . .

Mare ran. She ran through a wind white with moonlight and wet with "the small rain." And the wind she ran through, it ran through her, and made her shiver as she ran. And the man beside her leaped high over the waves of the dead grasses and gathered the wind in his arms, and her hair was heavy and his was tossing, and a little fox ran before them across the top of the world. And the world spread down around in waves of black and silver, more immense than she had ever known the world could be, and more beautiful.

God Almighty beautiful, to take your breath away!

Mare wondered, and she was not used to wondering. "Is it only crazy folks ever run like that and talk that way?"

She no longer ran; she walked; for her breath was gone. And there was some other reason, some other reason. Oh, yes, it was because her feet were hurting her. So, at last, and roundabout, her shoes had made contact with her brain.

Bending over the side of the bed, she loosened one of them mechanically. She pulled it half off. But then she looked down at it sharply, and she pulled it on again.

How beautiful . . .

Color overspread her face in a slow wave.

How beautiful are thy feet with shoes . . .

"Is it only crazy folks ever say such things?"

O prince's daughter!

"Or call you that?"

By and by there was a knock at the door. It opened, and Ruby Herter came in.

"Hello, Mare old girl!" His face was red. He scowled and kicked at the floor. "I'd 'a' been over sooner, except we got a mule down sick."

He looked at his dumb betrothed. "Come on, cheer up, forget it! He won't scare you no more, not that boy, not what's left o' him. What you lookin' at, sourface? Ain't you glad to see me?"

Mare quit looking at the wallpaper and looked at the floor.

"Yeh," she said.

"That's more like it, babe." He came and sat beside her, reached down behind her and gave her a spank. "Come on, give us a kiss, babe!" He wiped his mouth on his jumper sleeve, a good farmer's sleeve, spotted with milking. He put his hands on her; he was used to handling animals. "Hey, you, warm up a little; reckon I'm goin' to do all the lovin'?"

"Ruby, lea' me be!"

"What!"

She was up, twisting. He was up, purple.

"What's ailin' of you, Mare? What you bawlin' about?"

"Nothin' — only go 'way!"

She pushed him to the door and through it with all her strength, and closed it in his face, and stood with her weight against it, crying, "Go 'way! Go 'way! Lea' me be!"

The Idyll of Miss Sarah Brown

by Damon Runyon

OF ALL THE HIGH PLAYERS this country ever sees, there is no doubt but that the guy they call The Sky is the highest. In fact, the reason he is called The Sky is because he goes so high when it comes to betting on any proposition whatever. He will bet all he has, and nobody can bet any more than this.

His right name is Obadiah Masterson, and he is originally out of a little town in southern Colorado where he learns to shoot craps, and play cards, and one thing and another, and where his old man is a very well-known citizen, and something of a sport himself. In fact, The Sky tells me that when he finally cleans up all the loose scratch around his home town and decides he needs more room, his old man has a little private talk with him and says to him like this:

"Son," the old guy says, "you are now going out into the wide, wide world to make your own way, and it is a very good thing to do, as there are no more opportunities for you in this burg. I am only sorry," he says, "that I am not able to bank-roll you to a very large start, but," he says, "not having any potatoes to give you, I am now going to stake you to some very valuable advice, which I personally collect in my years of experience around and about, and I hope and trust you will always bear this advice in mind.

"Son," the old guy says, "no matter how far you travel, or how smart you get, always remember this: Some day, somewhere," he says, "a guy is going to come to you and show you a nice brand-new deck of cards on which the seal is never broken, and this guy is going to offer to bet you that the jack of spades will jump out of this deck and squirt cider in your ear. But, son," the old guy says, "do not bet him, for as sure as you do you are going to get an ear full of cider."

Well, The Sky remembers what his old man says, and he is always very cautious about betting on such propositions as the jack of spades jumping out of a sealed deck of cards and squirting cider in his ear, and so he makes few mistakes as he goes along. In fact, the only real mistake The Sky makes is when he hits St. Louis after leaving his old home town, and loses all his potatoes betting a guy St. Louis is the biggest town in the world.

Now of course this is before The Sky ever sees any bigger towns, and he is never much of a hand for reading up on matters such as this. In fact, the only reading The Sky ever does as he goes along through life is in these Gideon Bibles such as he finds in the hotel rooms where he lives, for The Sky never lives anywhere else but in hotel rooms for years.

He tells me that he reads many items of great interest in these Gideon Bibles, and furthermore The Sky says that several times these Gideon Bibles keep him from getting out of line, such as the time he finds himself pretty much frozen-in over in Cincinnati, what with owing everybody in town except maybe the mayor from playing games of chance of one kind and another.

Well, The Sky says he sees no way of meeting these obligations and he is figuring the only thing he can do is to take a run-out powder, when he happens to read in one of these Gideon Bibles where it says like this:

"Better is it," the Gideon Bible says, "that thou shouldest not vow, than that thou shouldest vow and not pay."

Well, The Sky says he can see that there is no doubt whatever but that this means a guy shall not welsh, so he remains in Cincinnati until he manages to wiggle himself out of the situation, and from that day to this, The Sky never thinks of welshing.

He is maybe thirty years old, and is a tall guy with a round kisser, and big blue eyes, and he always looks as innocent as a little baby. But The Sky is by no means as innocent as he looks. In fact, The Sky is smarter than three Philadelphia lawyers, which makes him very smart, indeed, and he is well established as a high player in New Orleans, and Chicago, and Los Angeles, and wherever else there is any action in the way of card-playing, or crap-shooting, or horse-racing, or betting on the baseball games, for The Sky is always moving around the country following the action.

But while The Sky will bet on anything whatever, he is more of a short-card player and a crap shooter than anything else, and furthermore he is a great hand for propositions, such as are always coming up among citizens who follow games of chance for a living. Many citizens prefer betting on propositions to anything you can think of, because they figure a proposition gives them a chance to out-smart somebody, and in fact I know citizens who will sit up all night making up propositions to offer other citizens the next day.

A proposition may be only a problem in cards, such as what is the price against a guy getting aces back-to-back, or how often a pair of deuces will win a hand in stud, and then again it may be some very daffy proposition, indeed, although the daffier any proposition seems to be, the more some citizens like it. And no one ever sees The Sky when he does not have some proposition of his own.

The first time he ever shows up around this town, he goes to a baseball game at the Polo Grounds with several prominent citizens, and while he is at the ball game, he buys himself a sack of Harry Stevens' peanuts, which he dumps in a side pocket of his coat. He is eating these peanuts all through the game, and after the game is over and he is walking across the field with the citizens, he says to them like this:

"What price," The Sky says, "I cannot throw a peanut from second base to the home plate?"

Well, everybody knows that a peanut is too light for anybody to throw it this far, so Big Nig, the crap shooter, who always likes to have a little the best of it running for him, speaks as follows:

"You can have 3 to 1 from me, stranger," Big Nig says.

"Two C's against six," The Sky says, and then he stands on second base, and takes a peanut out of his pocket, and not only whips it to the home plate, but on into the lap of a fat guy who is still sitting in the grand stand putting the zing on Bill Terry for not taking Walker out of the box when Walker is getting a pasting from the other club.

Well, naturally, this is a most astonishing throw, indeed, but afterwards it comes out that The Sky throws a peanut loaded with lead, and of course it is not one of Harry Stevens' peanuts, either, as Harry is not selling peanuts full of lead at a dime a bag, with the price of lead what it is.

It is only a few nights after this that The Sky states another most unusual proposition to a group of citizens sitting in Mindy's restaurant when he offers to bet a C note that he can go down into Mindy's cellar and catch a live rat with his bare hands and everybody is greatly astonished when Mindy himself steps up and takes the bet, for ordinarily Mindy will not bet you a nickel he is alive.

But it seems that Mindy knows that The Sky plants a tame rat in the cellar, and this rat knows The Sky and loves him dearly, and will let him catch it any time he wishes, and it also seems that Mindy knows that one of his dish washers happens upon this rat, and not knowing it is tame, knocks it flatter than a pancake. So when The Sky goes down into the cellar and starts trying to catch a rat with his bare hands, he is greatly surprised how inhospitable the rat turns out to be, because it is one of Mindy's personal rats, and Mindy is around afterwards saying he will lay plenty of 7 to 5 against even Strangler Lewis being able to catch one of his rats with his bare hands, or with boxing gloves on.

I am only telling you all this to show you what a smart guy The Sky is, and I am only sorry I do not have time to tell you about many other very remarkable propositions that he thinks up outside of his regular business.

It is well-known to one and all that he is very honest in every respect, and that he hates and despises cheaters at cards, or dice, and furthermore The Sky never wishes to play with any the best of it himself, or anyway not much. He will never take the inside of any situation, as many gamblers love to do, such as owning a gambling house, and having the percentage run for him instead of against him, for always The Sky is strictly a player, because he says he will never care to settle down in one spot long enough to become the owner of anything.

In fact, in all the years The Sky is drifting around the country, nobody ever knows him to own anything except maybe a bank roll, and when he comes to Broadway the last time, which is the time I am now speaking of, he has a hundred G's in cash money, and an extra suit of clothes, and this is all he has in the world. He never owns such a thing as a house, or an automobile, or a piece of jewelry. He never owns a watch, because The Sky says time means nothing to him.

Of course some guys will figure a hundred G's comes under the head of owning something, but as far as The Sky is concerned, money is nothing but just something for him to play with and the dollars may as well be doughnuts as far as value goes with him. The only time The Sky ever thinks of money as money is when he is broke, and the only way he can tell he is broke is when he reaches into his pocket and finds nothing there but his fingers.

Then it is necessary for The Sky to go out and dig up some fresh scratch somewhere, and when it comes to digging up scratch, The Sky is practically supernatural. He can get more potatoes on the strength of a telegram to some place or other than John D. Rockefeller can get on collateral, for everybody knows The Sky's word is as good as wheat in the bin.

Now one Sunday evening The Sky is walking along Broadway, and at the corner of Forty-ninth Street he comes upon a little bunch of mission workers who are holding a religious meeting, such as mission workers love to do of a Sunday evening, the idea being that they may round up a few sinners here and there, although personally I always claim the mission workers come out too early to catch any sinners on this part of Broadway. At such an hour the sinners are still in bed resting up from their sinning of the night before, so they will be in good shape for more sinning a little later on.

There are only four of these mission workers, and two of them are old guys, and one is an old doll, while the other is a young doll who is tootling on a cornet. And after a couple of ganders at this young doll, The Sky is a goner, for this is one of the most beautiful young dolls anybody ever sees on Broadway, and especially as a mission worker. Her name is Miss Sarah Brown.

She is tall, and thin, and has a first-class shape, and her hair is a light brown, going on blond, and her eyes are like I do not know what, except that they are one-hundred-per-cent eyes in every respect. Furthermore, she is not a bad cornet player, if you like cornet players, although at this spot on Broadway she has to play against a scat band in a chop-suey joint near by, and this is tough competition, although at that many citizens believe Miss Sarah Brown will win by a large score if she only gets a little more support from one of the old guys with her who has a big bass drum, but does not pound it hearty enough.

Well, The Sky stands there listening to Miss Sarah Brown tootling on the cornet for quite a spell, and then he hears her make a speech in which she puts the blast on sin very good, and boosts religion quite some, and says if there are any souls around that need saving the owners of same may step forward at once. But no one steps forward, so The Sky comes over to Mindy's restaurant where many citizens are congregated, and starts telling us about Miss Sarah Brown. But of course we already know about Miss Sarah Brown, because she is so beautiful, and so good.

Furthermore, everybody feels somewhat sorry for Miss Sarah Brown, for while she is always tootling the cornet, and making speeches, and looking to save any souls that need saving, she never seems to find any souls to save, or at least her bunch of mission workers never gets any bigger. In fact, it gets smaller, as she starts out with a guy who plays a very fair sort of trombone, but this guy takes it on the lam one night with the trombone, which one and all consider a dirty trick.

Now from this time on, The Sky does not take any interest in anything but Miss Sarah Brown, and any night she is out on the corner with the other mission workers, you will see The Sky standing around looking at her, and naturally after a few weeks of this, Miss Sarah Brown must know The Sky is looking at her, or she is dumber than seems possible. And nobody ever figures Miss Sarah Brown dumb, as she is always on her toes, and seems plenty able to take care of herself, even on Broadway.

Sometimes after the street meeting is over, The Sky follows the mission workers to their headquarters in an old storeroom around in Forty-eighth Street where they generally hold an indoor session, and I hear The Sky drops many a large coarse note in the collection box while looking at Miss Sarah Brown, and there is no doubt these notes come in handy around the mission, as I hear business is by no means so good there.

It is called the Save-a-Soul Mission, and it is run mainly by Miss Sarah Brown's grandfather, an old guy with whiskers, by the name of Arvide Abernathy, but Miss Sarah Brown seems to do most of the work, including tootling the cornet, and visiting the poor people around and about, and all this and that, and many citizens claim it is a great shame that such a beautiful doll is wasting her time being good.

How The Sky ever becomes acquainted with Miss Sarah Brown is a very great mystery, but the next thing anybody knows, he is saying hello to her, and she is smiling at him out of her one-hundred-per-cent eyes, and one evening when I happen to be with The Sky we run into her walking along Forty-ninth Street, and The Sky hauls off and stops her, and says it is a nice evening, which it is, at that. Then The Sky says to Miss Sarah Brown like this:

"Well," The Sky says, "how is the mission dodge going these days? Are you saving any souls?" he says.

Well, it seems from what Miss Sarah Brown says the soul-saving is very slow, indeed, these days.

"In fact," Miss Sarah Brown says, "I worry greatly about how few souls we seem to save. Sometimes I wonder if we are lacking in grace."

She goes on up the street, and The Sky stands looking after her, and he says to me like this:

"I wish I can think of some way to help this little doll," he says, "especially," he says, "in saving a few souls to build up her mob at the mission. I must speak to her again, and see if I can figure something out."

But The Sky does not get to speak to Miss Sarah Brown again, because somebody weighs in the sacks on him by telling her he is nothing but a professional gambler, and that he is a very undesirable character, and that his only interest in hanging around the mission is because she is a good-looking doll. So all of a sudden Miss Sarah Brown plays plenty of chill for The Sky. Furthermore, she sends him word that she does not care to accept any more of his potatoes in the collection box, because his potatoes are nothing but ill-gotten gains.

Well, naturally, this hurts The Sky's feelings no little, so he quits standing around looking at Miss Sarah Brown, and going to the mission, and takes to mingling again with the citizens in Mindy's, and showing some interest in the affairs of the community, especially the crap games.

Of course the crap games that are going on at this time are nothing much, because practically everybody in the world is broke, but there is a head-and-head game run by Nathan Detroit over a garage in Fifty-second Street where there is occasionally some action, and who shows up at this crap game early one evening but The Sky, although it seems he shows up there more to find company than anything else.

In fact, he only stands around watching the play, and talking with other guys who are also standing around and watching, and many of these guys are very high shots during the gold rush, although most of them are now as clean as a jaybird, and maybe cleaner. One of these guys is a guy by the name of Brandy Bottle Bates, who is known from coast to coast as a high player when he has anything to play with, and who is called Brandy Bottle Bates because it seems that years ago he is a great hand for belting a brandy bottle around.

This Brandy Bottle Bates is a big, black-looking guy, with a large beezer, and a head shaped like a pear, and he is considered a very immoral and wicked character, but he is a pretty slick gambler, and a fast man with a dollar when he is in the money.

Well, finally The Sky asks Brandy Bottle why he is not playing and Brandy laughs, and states as follows:

"Why," he says, "in the first place I have no potatoes, and in the second place I doubt if it will do me much good if I do have any potatoes the way I am going the past year. Why," Brandy Bottle says, "I cannot win a bet to save my soul."

Now this crack seems to give The Sky an idea, as he stands looking at Brandy Bottle very strangely, and while he is looking, Big Nig, the crap shooter, picks up the dice and hits three times hand-running, bing, bing, bing. Then Big Nig comes out on a six and Brandy Bottle Bates speaks as follows:

"You see how my luck is," he says. "Here is Big Nig hotter than a stove, and here I am without a bob to follow him with, especially," Brandy says, "when he is looking for nothing but a six. Why," he says, "Nig can make sixes all night when he is hot. If he does not make this six, the way he is, I will be willing to turn square and quit gambling forever."

"Well, Brandy," The Sky says, "I will make you a proposition. I will lay you a G note Big Nig does not get his six. I will lay you a G note against nothing but your soul," he says. "I mean if Big Nig does not get his six, you are to turn square and join Miss Sarah Brown's mission for six months."

"Bet!" Brandy Bottle Bates says right away, meaning the proposition is on, although the chances are he does not quite understand the proposition. All Brandy understands is The Sky wishes to wager that Big Nig does not make his six, and Brandy Bottle Bates will be willing to bet his soul a couple of times over on Big Nig making his six, and figure he is getting the best of it, at that, as Brandy has great confidence in Nig.

Well, sure enough, Big Nig makes the six, so The Sky weeds Brandy Bottle Bates a G note, although everybody around is saying The Sky makes a terrible overlay of the natural price in giving Brandy Bottle a G against his soul. Furthermore, everybody around figures the chances are The Sky only wishes to give Brandy an opportunity to get in action, and nobody figures The Sky is on the level about trying to win Brandy Bottle Bates' soul, especially as The Sky does not seem to wish to go any further after paying the bet.

He only stands there looking on and seeming somewhat depressed as Brandy Bottle goes into action on his own account with the G note, fading other guys around the table with cash money. But Brandy Bottle Bates seems to figure what is in The Sky's mind pretty well, because Brandy Bottle is a crafty old guy.

It finally comes his turn to handle the dice, and he hits a couple of times, and then he comes out on a four, and anybody will tell you that a four is a very tough point to make, even with a lead pencil. Then Brandy Bottle turns to The Sky and speaks to him as follows:

"Well, Sky," he says, "I will take the odds off you on this one. I know you do not want my dough," he says. "I know you only want my soul for Miss Sarah Brown, and," he says, "without wishing to be fresh about it, I know why you want it for her. I am young once myself," Brandy Bottle says. "And you know if I lose to you, I will be over there in Forty-eighth Street in an hour pounding on the door, for Brandy always settles.

"But, Sky," he says, "now I am in the money, and my price goes up. Will you lay me ten G's against my soul I do not make this four?"

"Bet!" The Sky says, and right away Brandy Bottle hits with a four.

Well, when word goes around that The Sky is up at Nathan Detroit's crap game trying to win Brandy Bottle Bates' soul for Miss Sarah Brown, the excitement is practically intense. Somebody telephones Mindy's, where a large number of citizens are sitting around arguing about this and that, and telling one another how much they will bet in support of their arguments, if only they have something to bet, and Mindy himself is almost killed in the rush for the door.

One of the first guys out of Mindy's and up to the crap game is Regret, the horse player, and as he comes in Brandy Bottle is looking for a nine, and The Sky is laying him twelve G's against his soul that he does not make this nine, for it seems Brandy Bottle's soul keeps getting more and more expensive.

Well, Regret wishes to bet his soul against a G that Brandy Bottle gets his nine, and is greatly insulted when The Sky cannot figure his price any better than a double saw, but finally Regret accepts this price, and Brandy Bottle hits again.

Now many other citizens request a little action from The Sky, and if there is one thing The Sky cannot deny a citizen it is action, so he says he will lay them according to how he figures their word to join Miss Sarah Brown's mission if Brandy Bottle misses out, but about this time The Sky finds he has no more potatoes on him, being now around thirty-five G's loser, and he wishes to give markers.

But Brandy Bottle says that while ordinarily he will be pleased to extend The Sky this accommodation, he does not care to accept markers against his soul, so then The Sky has to leave the joint and go over to his hotel two or three blocks away, and get the night clerk to open his damper so The Sky can get the rest of his bank roll. In the meantime the crap game continues at Nathan Detroit's among the small operators, while the other citizens stand around and say that while they hear of many a daffy proposition in their time, this is the daffiest that ever comes to their attention, although Big Nig claims he hears of a daffier one, but cannot think what it is.

Big Nig claims that all gamblers are daffy anyway, and in fact he says if they are not daffy they will not be gamblers, and while he is arguing this matter back comes The Sky with fresh scratch, and Brandy Bottle Bates takes up where he leaves off, although Brandy says he is accepting the worst of it, as the dice have a chance to cool off.

Now the upshot of the whole business is that Brandy Bottle hits thirteen licks in a row, and the last lick he makes is on a ten, and it is for twenty G's against his soul, with about a dozen other citizens getting anywhere from one to five C's against their souls, and complaining bitterly of the price.

And as Brandy Bottle makes his ten, I happen to look at The Sky and I see him watching Brandy with a very peculiar expression on his face, and furthermore I see The Sky's right hand creeping inside his coat where I know he always packs a Betsy in a shoulder holster, so I can see something is wrong somewhere.

But before I can figure out what it is, there is quite a fuss at the door, and loud talking, and a doll's voice, and all of a sudden in bobs nobody else but Miss Sarah Brown. It is plain to be seen that she is all steamed up about something.

She marches right up to the crap table where Brandy Bottle Bates and The Sky and the other citizens are standing, and one and all are feeling sorry for Dobber, the doorman, thinking of what Nathan Detroit is bound to say to him for letting her in. The dice are still lying on the table showing Brandy Bottle Bates' last throw, which cleans The Sky and gives many citizens the first means they enjoy in several months.

Well, Miss Sarah Brown looks at The Sky, and The Sky looks at Miss Sarah Brown, and Miss Sarah Brown looks at the citizens around and about, and one and all are somewhat dumfounded, and nobody seems to be able to think of much to say, although The Sky finally speaks up as follows:

"Good evening," The Sky says. "It is a nice evening," he says. "I am trying to win a few souls for you around here, but," he says, "I seem to be about half out of luck."

"Well," Miss Sarah Brown says, looking at The Sky most severely out of her hundred-per-cent eyes, "you are taking too much upon yourself. I can win any souls I need myself. You better be thinking of your own soul. By the way," she says, "are you risking your own soul, or just your money?"

Well, of course up to this time The Sky is not risking anything but his potatoes, so he only shakes his head to Miss Sarah Brown's question, and looks somewhat disorganized.

"I know something about gambling," Miss Sarah Brown says, "especially about crap games. I ought to," she says. "It ruins my poor papa and my brother Joe. If you wish to gamble for souls, Mister Sky, gamble for your own soul."

Now Miss Sarah Brown opens a small black leather pocketbook she is carrying in one hand, and pulls out a two-dollar bill, and it is such a two-dollar bill as seems to have seen much service in its time, and holding up this deuce, Miss Sarah Brown speaks as follows:

"I will gamble with you, Mister Sky," she says. "I will gamble with you," she says, "on the same terms you gamble with these parties here. This two dollars against your soul, Mister Sky. It is all I have, but," she says, "it is more than your soul is worth."

Well, of course anybody can see that Miss Sarah Brown is doing this because she is very angry, and wishes to make The Sky look small, but right away The Sky's duke comes from inside his coat, and he picks up the dice and hands them to her and speaks as follows:

"Roll them," The Sky says, and Miss Sarah Brown snatches the dice out of his hand and gives them a quick sling on the table in such a way that anybody can see she is not a professional crap shooter, and not even an amateur crap shooter, for all amateur crap shooters first breathe on the dice, and rattle them good, and make remarks to them, such as "Come on, baby!"

In fact, there is some criticism of Miss Sarah Brown afterwards on account of her haste, as many citizens are eager to string with her to hit, while others are just as anxious to bet she misses, and she does not give them a chance to get down.

Well, Scranton Slim is the stick guy, and he takes a gander at the dice as they hit up against the side of the table and bounce back, and then Slim hollers, "Winner, winner, winner," as stick guys love to do, and what is showing on the dice as big as life, but a six and a five, which makes eleven, no matter how you figure, so The Sky's soul belongs to Miss Sarah Brown.

She turns at once and pushes through the citizens around the table without even waiting to pick up the deuce she lays down when she grabs the dice. Afterwards a most obnoxious character by the name of Red Nose Regan tries to claim the deuce as a sleeper and gets the heave-o from Nathan Detroit, who becomes very indignant about this, stating that Red Nose is trying to give his joint a wrong rap.

Naturally, The Sky follows Miss Brown, and Dobber, the doorman, tells me that as they are waiting for him to unlock the door and let them out, Miss Sarah Brown turns on The Sky and speaks to him as follows:

"You are a fool," Miss Sarah Brown says.

Well, at this Dobber figures The Sky is bound to let one go, as this seems to be most insulting language, but instead of letting one go, The Sky only smiles at Miss Sarah Brown and says to her like this:

"Why," The Sky says, "Paul says 'If any man among you seemeth to be wise in this world, let him become a fool, that he may be wise.' I love you, Miss Sarah Brown," The Sky says.

Well, now, Dobber has a pretty fair sort of memory, and he says that Miss Sarah Brown tells The Sky that since he seems to know so much about the Bible, maybe he remembers the second verse of the Song of Solomon, but the chances are Dobber muffs the number of the verse, because I look the matter up in one of these Gideon Bibles, and the verse seems a little too much for Miss Sarah Brown, although of course you never can tell.

Anyway, this is about all there is to the story, except that Brandy Bottle Bates slides out during the confusion so quietly even Dobber scarcely remembers letting him out, and he takes most of The Sky's potatoes with him, but he soon gets batted in against the faro bank out in Chicago, and the last anybody hears of him he gets religion all over again, and is preaching out in San Jose, so The Sky always claims he beats Brandy for his soul, at that.

I see The Sky the other night at Forty-ninth Street and Broadway, and he is with quite a raft of mission workers, including Mrs. Sky, for it seems that the soul-saving business picks up wonderfully, and The Sky is giving a big bass drum such a first-class whacking that the scat band in the chop-suey joint can scarcely be heard. Furthermore, The Sky is hollering between whacks, and I never see a guy look happier, especially when Mrs. Sky smiles at him out of her hundred-per-cent eyes. But I do not linger long, because The Sky gets a gander at me, and right away he begins hollering:

"I see before me a sinner of deepest dye," he hollers. "Oh, sinner, repent before it is too late. Join with us, sinner," he hollers, "and let us save your soul."

Naturally, this crack about me being a sinner embarrasses me no little, as it is by no means true, and it is a good thing for The Sky there is no copper in me, or I will go to Mrs. Sky, who is always bragging about how she wins The Sky's soul by outplaying him at his own game, and tell her the truth.

And the truth is that the dice with which she wins The Sky's soul, and which are the same dice with which Brandy Bottle Bates wins all his potatoes, are strictly phony, and that she gets into Nathan Detroit's just in time to keep The Sky from killing old Brandy Bottle.

Imagine Kissing Pete

by John O'Hara

1

To those who knew the bride and groom, the marriage of Bobbie
Hammersmith and Pete McCrea was the surprise of the year. As late
as April of '29 Bobbie was still engaged to a fellow who lived in
Greenwich, Connecticut, and she had told friends that the wedding
would take place in September. But the engagement was broken and
in a matter of weeks the invitations went out for her June wedding to
Pete. One of the most frequently uttered comments was that Bobbie
was not giving herself much opportunity to change her mind again.
The comment was doubly cruel, since it carried the implication that if
she gave herself time to think, Pete McCrea would not be her ideal
choice. It was not only that she was marrying Pete on the rebound; she
seemed to be going out of her way to find someone who was so unlike
her other beaus that the contrast was unavoidable. And it was.

I was working in New York and Pete wrote to ask me to be an usher.
Pete and I had grown up together, played together as children, and
gone to dancing school and to the same parties. But we had never
been close friends and when Pete and I went away to our separate prep
schools and, later, Pete to Princeton and I to work, we drifted into
that relationship of young men who had known each other all their
lives without creating anything that was enduring or warm. As a
matter of fact, I had never in my life received a written communication from Pete McCrea, and his handwriting on the envelope was new
to me, as mine in my reply was to him. He mentioned who the best
man and the other ushers would be — all Gibbsville boys — and this

somewhat pathetic commentary on his four years in prep school and four years in college made an appeal to home town and boyhood loyalty that I could not reject. I had some extra days coming to me at the office, and so I told Pete I would be honored to be one of his ushers. My next step was to talk to a Gibbsville girl who lived in New York, a friend of Bobbie Hammersmith's. I took her to dinner at an Italian speakeasy where my credit was good, and she gave me what information she had. She was to be a bridesmaid.

"Bobbie isn't saying a word," said Kitty Clark. "That is, nothing about the inner turmoil. Nothing *intime*. Whatever happened happened the last time she was in New York, four or five weeks ago. All she'd tell me was that Johnny White was impossible. Impossible. Well, he'd been very possible all last summer and fall."

"What kind of a guy was he?" I asked.

"Oh — *attractive*," she said. "Sort of wild, I guess, but not a roué. Maybe he is a roué, but I'd say more just wild. I honestly don't know a thing about it, but it wouldn't surprise me if Bobbie was ready to settle down, and he wasn't. She was probably more in love with him than he was with her."

"I doubt that. She wouldn't turn around and marry Pete if she were still in love with this White guy."

"Oh, *wouldn't* she? Oh, are you ever wrong there. If she wanted to thumb her nose at Johnny, I can't think of a better way. Poor Pete. You know *Pete*. Ichabod McCrea. Remember when Mrs. McCrea made us stop calling him Ichabod? Lord and Taylor! She went to see my mother and I guess all the other mothers and said it just had to stop. Bad enough calling her little Angus by such a common nickname as Pete. But calling a boy Ichabod. I don't suppose Pete ever knew his mother went around like that."

"Yes he did. It embarrassed him. It always embarrassed him when Mrs. McCrea did those things."

"Yes, she was uncanny. I can remember when I was going to have a party, practically before I'd made out the list Mrs. McCrea would call Mother to be sure Pete wasn't left out. Not that I ever would have left him out. We all always had the same kids to our parties. But Mrs. McCrea wasn't leaving anything to chance. I'm dying to hear what she has to say about this marriage. I'll bet she doesn't like it, but I'll bet she's in fear and trembling in case Bobbie changes her mind again.

Ichabod McCrea and Bobbie Hammersmith. Beauty and the beast. And actually he's not even a beast. It would be better if he were. She's the third of our old bunch to get married, but much as I hate to say it, I'll bet she'll be the first to get a divorce. Imagine *kissing* Pete, let alone any of the rest of it."

The wedding was on a Saturday afternoon; four o'clock in Trinity Church, and the reception at the country club. It had been two years since I last saw Bobbie Hammersmith and she was now twenty-two, but she could have passed for much more than that. She was the only girl in her crowd who had not bobbed her hair, which was jet-black and which she always wore with plaited buns over the ears. Except in the summer her skin was like Chinese white and it was always easy to pick her out first in group photographs; her eyes large dark dots, quite far apart, and her lips small but prominent in the whiteness of her face beneath the two small dots of her nose. In summer, with a tan, she reminded many non-operagoers of Carmen. She was a striking beauty, although it took two years' absence from her for me to realize it. In the theatre they have an expression, "walked through the part," which means that an actress played a role without giving it much of herself. Bobbie walked through the part of bride-to-be. A great deal of social activity was concentrated in the three days — Thursday, Friday, and Saturday — up to and including the wedding reception; but Bobbie walked through the part. Today, thirty years later, it would be assumed that she had been taking tranquilizers, but this was 1929.

Barbara Hammersmith had never been anything but a pretty child; if she had ever been homely it must have been when she was a small baby, when I was not bothering to look at her. We — Pete McCrea and the other boys — were two, three, four years older than Bobbie, but when she was fifteen or sixteen she began to pass among us, from boy to boy, trying one and then another, causing several fist fights, and half promising but never delivering anything more than the "soul kisses" that were all we really expected. By the time she was eighteen she had been in and out of love with all of us with the solitary exception of Pete McCrea. When she broke off with a boy, she would also make up with the girl he had temporarily deserted for Bobbie, and all the girls came to understand that every boy in the crowd had to go through a love affair with her. Consequently Bobbie was popular; the boys remembered her kisses, the girls forgave her because the boys had been returned virtually intact. We used the word hectic a lot in those days; Kitty Clark explained the short duration of Bobbie's love affairs by observing that being in love with Bobbie was too hectic for most boys. It was also true that it was not hectic enough. The boys agreed that Bobbie was a hot little number, but none of us could claim that she was not a virgin. At eighteen Bobbie entered a personal middle age, and for the big social occasions her beaus came from out-of-town. She was also busy at the college proms and football games, as far west as Ann Arbor, as far north as Brunswick, Maine. I was working on the Gibbsville paper during some of those years, the only boy in our crowd who was not away at college, and I remember Ann Arbor because Bobbie went there wearing a Delta Tau Delta pin and came back wearing the somewhat larger Psi U. "Now don't you say anything in front of Mother," she said. "She thinks they're both the same."

We played auction bridge, the social occupation in towns like ours, and Bobbie and I were assimilated into an older crowd: the younger married set and the youngest of the couples who were in their thirties. We played for prizes — flasks, cigarette lighters, vanity cases, cartons of cigarettes — and there was a party at someone's house every week. The hostess of the evening usually asked me to stop for Bobbie, and I saw her often. Her father and mother would be reading the evening paper and sewing when I arrived to pick up Bobbie. Philip Hammersmith was not a native of Gibbsville, but he had lived there long enough to have gone to the Mexican Border in 1916 with the Gibbsville company of mounted engineers, and he had gone to France with them, returning as a first lieutenant and with the Croix de Guerre with palm. He was one of the best golfers in the club, and everyone said he was making money hand-over-fist as an independent coal operator. He wore steel-rim glasses and he had almost completely gray hair, cut short. He inspired trust and confidence. He was slow-moving, taller than six feet, and always thought before speaking. His wife, a Gibbsville girl, was related, as she said, to half the town; a lively little woman who took her husband's arm even if they were walking only two doors away. I always used to feel that whatever he may have wanted out of life, yet unattained or unattainable, she had just what she wanted: a good husband, a nice home, and a pretty daughter who would not long remain unmarried. At home in the evening, and whenever I saw him on the street, Mr. Hammersmith was wearing a dark-gray worsted suit, cut loose and with a soft roll to the lapel; black knit four-in-hand necktie; white shirt; heavy gray woolen socks, and thick-soled brogues. This costume, completely un-adorned — he wore a wrist watch — was what he always wore except for formal occasions, and the year-to-year sameness of his attire con-stituted his only known eccentricity. He was on the board of the second most conservative bank, the trustees of Gibbsville Hospital, the armory board, the Y.M.C.A., and the Gibbsville and Lantenengo country clubs. Nevertheless I sensed that that was not all there was to Philip Hammersmith, that the care he put into the creation of the general picture of himself — hard work, quiet clothes, thoughtful manner, conventional associations — was done with a purpose that was not necessarily sinister but was extraordinarily private. It de-lighted me to discover, one night while waiting for Bobbie, that he knew more about what was going on than most of us suspected he would know. "Jimmy, you know Ed Charney, of course," he said.

I knew Ed Charney, the principal bootlegger in the area. "Yes, I know him pretty well," I said.

"Then do you happen to know if there's any truth to what I heard? I heard that his wife is threatening to divorce him."

"I doubt it. They're Catholics."

"Do you know her?"

"Yes. I went to Sisters' school with her."

"Oh, then maybe you can tell me something else. I've heard that she's the real brains of those two."

"She quit school after eighth grade, so I don't know about that. I don't remember her being particularly bright. She's about my age but she was two grades behind me."

"I see. And you think their religion will keep them from getting a divorce?"

"Yes, I do. I don't often see Ed at Mass, but I know he carries rosary beads. And she's at the eleven o'clock Mass every Sunday, all dolled up."

This conversation was explained when Repeal came and with it public knowledge that Ed Charney had been quietly buying bank stock, one of several moves he had made in the direction of respect-ability. But the chief interest to me at the time Mr. Hammersmith and I talked was in the fact that he knew anything at all about the Char-neys. It was so unlike him even to mention Ed Charney's name.

To get back to the weekend of Bobbie Hammersmith's wedding: it was throughout that weekend that I first saw Bobbie have what we called that faraway look, that another generation called Cloud 90. If you happened to catch her at the right moment, you would see her smiling up at Pete in a way that must have been reassuring to Mrs. McCrea and to Mrs. Hammersmith, but I also caught her at several wrong moments and I saw something I had never seen before: a resemblance to her father that was a subtler thing than the mere duplication of such features as mouth, nose, and set of the eyes. It was almost the same thing I have mentioned in describing Philip Hammersmith; the wish yet unattained or unattainable. However, the pre-nuptial parties and the wedding and reception went off without a hitch, or so I believed until the day after the wedding.

Kitty Clark and I were on the same train going back to New York and I made some comment about the exceptional sobriety of the ushers and how everything had gone according to plan. "Amazing, considering," said Kitty.

"Considering what?"

"That there was almost no wedding at all," she said. "You must promise word of honor, Jimmy, or I won't tell you."

"I promise. Word of honor."

"Well, after Mrs. McCrea's very-dull-I-must-say luncheon, when we all left to go to Bobbie's? A little after two o'clock?"

"Yes."

"Bobbie asked me if I'd go across the street to our house and put in a long distance call to Johnny White. I said I couldn't do that, and what on earth was she thinking of. And Bobbie said, 'You're my oldest and best friend. The least you can do is make this one last effort, to keep me from ruining my life.' So I gave in and I dashed over to our house and called Johnny. He was out and they didn't know where he could be reached or what time he was coming home. So I left my name. My name, not Bobbie's. Six o'clock, at the reception, I was dancing with — I was dancing with *you*."

"When the waiter said you were wanted on the phone."

"It was Johnny. He'd been sailing and just got in. I made up some story about why I'd called him, but he didn't swallow it. 'You didn't call me,' he said. 'Bobbie did.' Well of course I wouldn't admit that. By that time she was married, and if her life was already ruined it would be a darned sight more ruined if I let him talk to her. Which he wanted to do. Then he tried to pump me. Where were they going on their wedding trip? I said nobody knew, which was a barefaced lie. I knew they were going to Bermuda. Known it since Thursday. But I wouldn't tell Johnny . . . I don't like him a bit after yesterday. I'd thought he was attractive, and he *is*, but he's got a mean streak that I never knew before. Feature this, if you will. When he realized I wasn't going to get Bobbie to come to the phone, or give him any information, he said, 'Well, no use wasting a long-distance call. What are you doing next weekend? How about coming out here?' 'I'm not that hard up,' I said, and banged down the receiver. I hope I shattered his eardrum."

I saw Pete and Bobbie McCrea when I went home the following Christmas. They were living in a small house on Twin Oaks Road, a recent real-estate development that had been instantly successful with the sons and daughters of the big two- and three-servant mansions. They were not going to any of the holiday dances; Bobbie was expecting a baby in April or early May.

"You're not losing any time," I said.

"I don't want to lose any time," said Bobbie. "I want to have a lot of children. Pete's an only child and so am I, and we don't think it's fair, if you can afford to have more."

"If we can afford it. The way that stock market is going, we'll be lucky to pay for this one," said Pete.

"Oh, don't start on that, Pete. That's all Father talks about," said Bobbie. "My father *was* hit pretty hard, but I wish he didn't have to keep talking about it all the time. Everybody's in the same boat."

"No, they're not. *We're* on a *raft*."

"I asked you, please, Pete. Jimmy didn't come here to listen to our financial woes. Do you see much of Kitty? I've owed her a letter for ages."

"No, I haven't seen her since last summer, we went out a few times," I said.

"Kitty went to New York to try to rope in a millionaire. She isn't going to waste her time on Jim."

"That's not what she went to New York for at all. And as far as wasting her time on Jim, Jim may not want to waste his time on her." She smiled. "Have you got a girl, Jim?"

"Not really."

"Wise. Very wise," said Pete McCrea.

"I don't know how wise. It's just that I have a hell of a hard time supporting myself, without trying to support a wife, too," I said.

"Why I understood you were selling articles to magazines, and going around with all the big shots."

"I've had four jobs in two years, and the jobs didn't last very long. If things get any tougher I may have to come back here. At least I'll have a place to sleep and something to eat."

"But I see your name in magazines," said Pete. "I don't always read your articles, but they must pay you well."

"They don't. At least I can't live on the magazine pieces without a steady job. Excuse me, Bobbie. Now you're getting *my* financial woes."

"She'll listen to yours. It's mine she doesn't want to hear about."

"That's because I know about ours. I'm never allowed to forget them," said Bobbie. "Are you going to all the parties?"

"Yes, stag. I have to bum rides. I haven't got a car."

"We resigned from the club," said Pete.

"Well we didn't *have* to do that," said Bobbie. "Father was going to give it to us for a Christmas present. And you have your job."

"We'll see how much longer I have it. Is that the last of the gin?"

"Yes."

Pete rose. "I'll be back."

"Don't buy any more for me," I said.

"You flatter yourself," he said. "I wasn't only getting it for you." He put on his hat and coat. "No funny business while I'm gone. I remember you two."

He kept a silly grin on his face while saying the ugly things, but the grin was not genuine and the ugly things were.

"I don't know what's the matter with him," said Bobbie. "Oh, I do, but why talk about it?"

"He's only kidding."

"You know better than that. He says worse things, much worse, and I'm only hoping they don't get back to Father. Father has enough on his mind. I thought if I had this baby right away it would — you know — give Pete confidence. But it's had just the opposite effect. He says it isn't his child. *Isn't his child!* Oh, I married him out of spite. I'm sure Kitty must have told you that. But it *is* his child, I swear it, Jim. It couldn't be anybody else's."

"I guess it's the old inferiority complex," I said.

"The first month we were married — Pete was a virgin — and I admit it, I wasn't. I stayed with two boys before I was married. But I was certainly not pregnant when I married Pete, and the first few weeks he was loving and sweet, and grateful. But then something happened to him, and he made a pass at I-won't-say-who. It was more than a pass. It was quite a serious thing. I might as well tell you. It was Phyllis. We were all at a picnic at the Dam and several people got pretty tight, Pete among them. And there's no other word for it, he tried to rape Phyllis. Tore her bathing suit and slapped her and did other things. She got away from him and ran back to the cottage without anyone seeing her. Luckily Joe didn't see her or I'm sure he'd have killed Pete. You know, Joe's strong as an ox and terribly jealous. I found out about it from Phyllis herself. She came here the next day and told me. She said she wasn't going to say anything to Joe, but that we mustn't invite her to our house and she wasn't going to invite us to hers."

"I'm certainly glad Joe didn't hear about it. He would do something drastic," I said. "But didn't he notice that you two weren't going to his house, and they to yours? It's a pretty small group."

She looked at me steadily. "We haven't been going anywhere. My excuse is that I'm pregnant, but the truth is, we're not being asked. It didn't end with Phyllis, Jim. One night at a dinner party Mary Lander just slapped his face, in front of everybody. Everybody laughed and thought Pete must have said something, but it wasn't something he'd said. He'd taken her hand and put it — you know. This is *Pete! Ichabod!* Did you ever know any of this about him?"

"You mean have I heard any of this? No."

"No, I didn't mean that. I meant, did he go around making passes and I never happened to hear about it?"

"No. When we'd talk dirty he'd say, 'Why don't you fellows get your minds above your belts?'"

"I wish your father were still alive. I'd go see him and try to get some advice. I wouldn't think of going to Dr. English."

"Well, you're not the one that needs a doctor. Could you get Pete to go to one? He's a patient of Dr. English's, isn't he?"

"Yes, but so is Mrs. McCrea, and Pete would never confide in Dr. English."

"Or anyone else at this stage, I guess," I said. "I'm not much help, am I?"

"Oh, I didn't expect you to have a solution. You know, Jim, I wish you would come back to Gibbsville. Other girls in our crowd have often said it was nice to have you to talk to. Of course you were a very bad boy, too, but a lot of us miss you."

"That's nice to hear, Bobbie. Thank you. I may be back, if I don't soon make a go of it in New York. I won't have any choice."

During that Christmas visit I heard other stories about Pete McCrea. In general they were told as plain gossip, but two or three times there was a hint of a lack of sympathy for Bobbie. "She knew what she was doing . . . she made her bed . . ." And while there was no lack of righteous indignation over Pete's behavior, he had changed in six months from a semi-comic figure to an unpleasant man, but a man nevertheless. In half a year he had lost most of his old friends; they all said, "You've never seen such a change come over anybody in all your life," but when they remembered to call him Ichabod it was only to emphasize the change.

Bobbie's baby was born in April, but lived only a few weeks. "She was determined to have that baby," Kitty Clark told me. "She had to prove to Pete that it was anyway *conceived* after she married him. But it must have taken all her strength to hold on to it that long. All her strength *and* the baby's. Now would be a good time for her to divorce him. She can't go on like that."

But there was no divorce, and Bobbie was pregnant again when I saw her at Christmas, 1930. They no longer lived in the Twin Oaks Road house, and her father and mother had given up their house on Lantenengo Street. The Hammersmiths were living in an apartment on Market Street, and Bobbie and Pete were living with Mrs. McCrea. "Temporarily, till Pete decides whether to take this job in Tulsa, Oklahoma," said Bobbie.

"Who do you think you're kidding?" said Pete. "It isn't a question of me deciding. It's a cousin of mine deciding if he'll take me on. And why the hell should he?"

"Well, you've had several years' banking experience," she said.

"Yes. And if I was so good, why did the bank let me go? Jim knows all this. What else have you heard about us, Jim? Did you hear Bobbie was divorcing me?"

"It doesn't look that way from here," I said.

"You mean because she's pregnant? That's elementary biology, and God knows you're acquainted with the facts of life. But if you want to be polite, all right. Pretend you didn't hear she was getting a divorce. You might as well pretend Mr. and Mrs. Hammersmith are still living on Lantenengo Street. If they were, Bobbie'd have got her divorce."

"Everybody tells me what I *was* going to do or *am* going to do," said Bobbie. "Nobody ever consults me."

"I suppose that's a crack at my mother."

"Oh, for Christ's sake, Pete, lay off, at least while I'm here," I said.

"Why? You like to think of yourself as an old friend of the family, so you might as well get a true picture. When you get married, if you ever do, I'll come and see you, and maybe your wife will cry on my shoulder." He got up and left the house.

"Well, it's just like a year ago," said Bobbie. "When you came to call on us last Christmas?"

"Where will he go now?"

"Oh, there are several places where he can charge drinks. They all think Mrs. McCrea has plenty of money, but they're due for a rude awakening. She's living on capital, but she's not going to sell any bonds to pay his liquor bills."

"Then maybe *he's* due for a rude awakening."

"Any awakening would be better than the last three months, since the bank fired him. He sits here all day long, then after Mrs. McCrea goes to bed he goes to one of his speakeasies." She sat up straighter. "He has a lady friend. Or have you heard?"

"No."

"Yes. He graduated from making passes at all my friends. He had to. We were never invited anywhere. Yes, he has a girl friend. Do you remember Muriel Nierhaus?"

"The chiropractor's wife. Sure. Big fat Muriel Minzer till she married Nierhaus, then we used to say he gave her some adjustments. Where is Nierhaus?"

"Oh, he's opened several offices. Very prosperous. He divorced her but she gets alimony. She's Pete's girl friend. Muriel Minzer is *Angus McCrea's* girl friend."

"You don't seem too displeased," I said.

"Would you be, if you were in my position?"

"I guess I know what you mean. But — well, nothing."

"But why don't I get a divorce?" She shook her head. "A spite marriage is a terrible thing to do to anybody. If I hadn't deliberately selected Pete out of all the boys I knew, he'd have gone on till Mrs. McCrea picked out somebody for him, and it would almost have had to be the female counterpart of Pete. A girl like — oh — Florence. Florence Temple."

"Florence Temple, with her cello. Exactly right."

"But I did that awful thing to Pete, and the first few weeks of marriage were just too much for him. He went haywire. I'd slept with two boys before I was married, so it wasn't as much of a shock to me. But Pete almost wore me out. And such adoration, I can't tell you. Then when we came back from Bermuda he began to see all the other girls he'd known all his life, and he'd ask me about them. It was as though he'd never seen them before, in a way. In other ways, it was as though he'd just been waiting all his life to start ripping their clothes off. He was dangerous, Jim. He really was. I could almost tell who would be next by the questions he'd ask. Before we'd go to a party, he'd say 'Who's going to be there tonight?' And I'd say I thought the usual crowd. Then he'd rattle off the list of names of our friends, and leave out one name. That was supposed to fool me, but it didn't for long. The name he left out, that girl was almost sure to be in for a bad time."

"And now it's all concentrated on Muriel Minzer?"

"As far as I know."

"Well, that's a break for you, *and* the other girls. Did you ever talk to him about the passes he made at the others?"

"Oh, how could we avoid it? Whoever it was, she was always 'that little whore.' "

"Did he ever get anywhere with any of them?"

She nodded. "One, but I won't tell you who. There was one girl that didn't stop him, and when that happened he wanted me to sleep with her husband."

"Swap, eh?"

"Yes. But I said I wasn't interested. Pete wanted to know why not? Why wouldn't I? And I almost told him. The boy was one of the two boys I'd stayed with before I was married — oh, when I was seventeen. And he never told anybody and neither have I, or ever will."

"You mean one of our old crowd actually did get somewhere with you, Bobbie?"

"One did. But don't try to guess. It won't do you any good to guess, because I'd never, never tell."

"Well, whichever one it was, he's the best liar I ever knew. And I guess the nicest guy in our whole crowd. You know, Bobbie, the whole damn bunch are going to get credit now for being as honorable as one guy."

"You were all nice, even if you all did talk too much. If it had been you, you would have lied, too."

"No, I don't think I would have."

"You lied about Kitty. Ha ha ha. You didn't know I knew about you and Kitty. I knew it the next day. The very next day. If you don't believe me, I'll tell you where it happened and how it happened, and all about it. That was the great bond we had in common. You and Kitty, and I and this other boy."

"Then Kitty's a gentleman, because she never told me a word about you."

"I kissed every boy in our crowd except Pete, and I necked, heavy-necked two, as you well know, and stayed with one."

"The question is, did you stay with the other one that you heavy-necked with?"

"You'll never know, Jim, and please don't try to find out."

"I won't, but I won't be able to stop theorizing," I said.

We knew everything, everything there was to know. We were so far removed from the technical innocence of eighteen, sixteen, nineteen. I was a man of the world, and Bobbie was indeed a woman, who had borne a child and lived with a husband who had come the most recently to the knowledge we had acquired, but was already the most intricately involved in the complications of sex. We — Bobbie and I — could discuss him and still remain outside the problems of Pete McCrea. We could almost remain outside our own problems. We knew so much, and since what we knew seemed to be all there was to know, we were shockproof. We had come to our maturity and our knowledgeability during the long decade of cynicism that was usually dismissed as "a cynical disregard of the law of the land," but that was something else, something deeper. The law had been passed with a "noble" but nevertheless cynical disregard of men's right to drink. It was a law that had been imposed on some who took pleasure in drinking by some who did not. And when the law was an instant failure, it was not admitted to be a failure by those who had imposed it. They fought to retain the law in spite of its immediate failure and its proliferating corruption, and they fought as hard as they would have for a law that had been an immediate success. They gained no recruits to their own way; they had only deserters, who were not brave deserters but furtive ones; there was no honest mutiny but only grumbling and small disobediences. And we grew up listening to the grumbling, watching the small disobediences; laughing along when the grumbling was intentionally funny, imitating the small disobediences in other ways besides the customs of drinking. It was not only a cynical disregard for a law of the land; the law was eventually changed. Prohibition, the zealots' attempt to force total abstinence on a temperate nation, made liars of a hundred million men and cheats of their children; the West Point cadets who cheated in examinations, the basketball players who connived with gamblers, the thousands of uncaught cheats in the high schools and colleges. We had grown up and away from our earlier esteem of God and country and valor, and had matured at a moment when riches were vanishing for reasons that we could not understand. We were the losing, not the lost, generation. We could not blame Pete McCrea's troubles — and Bobbie's — on the Southern Baptists and the Northern Methodists. Since we knew everything, we knew that Pete's sudden release from twenty years of frustrations had turned him loose in a world filled with women. But Bobbie and I sat there in her mother-in-law's house, breaking several laws of possession, purchase, transportation and consumption of liquor, and with great calmness discussing the destruction of two lives — one of them hers — and the loss of her father's fortune, the depletion of her mother-in-law's, the allure of a chiropractor's divorcée, and our own promiscuity. We knew everything, but we were incapable of recognizing the meaning of our complacency.

I was wearing my dinner jacket, and someone was going to pick me up and take me to a dinner dance at the club. "Who's stopping for you?" said Bobbie.

"It depends. Either Joe or Frank. Depends on whether they go in Joe's car or in Frank's. I'm to be ready when they blow their horn."

"Do me a favor, Jim. Make them come in. Pretend you don't hear the horn."

"If it's Joe, he's liable to drive off without me. You know Joe if he's had a few too many."

In a few minutes there was a blast of a two-tone horn, repeated. "That's Joe's car," said Bobbie. "You'd better go." She went to the hall with me and I kissed her cheek. The front door swung open and it was Joe Whipple.

"Hello, Bobbie," he said.

"Hello, Joe. Won't you all come in? Haven't you got time for one drink?" She was trying not to sound suppliant, but Joe was not deceived.

"Just you and Jim here?" he said.

"Yes. Pete went out a little while ago."

"I'll see what the others say," said Joe. He left to speak to the three in the sedan, and obviously he was not immediately persuasive, but they came in with him. They would not let Bobbie take their coats, but they were nice to her and with the first sips of our drinks we were all six almost back in the days when Bobbie Hammersmith's house was where so many of our parties started from. Then we heard the front door thumping shut and Pete McCrea looked in.

There were sounds of hello, but he stared at us over his horn-rims and said to Bobbie: "You didn't have to invite me, but you could have told me." He turned and again the front door thumped.

"Get dressed and come with us," said Joe Whipple.

"I can't do that," said Bobbie.

"She can't, Joe," said Phyllis Whipple. "That would only make more trouble."

"What trouble? She's going to have to sit here alone till he comes home. She might as well be with us," said Joe.

"Anyway, I haven't got a dress that fits," said Bobbie. "But thanks for asking me."

"I won't have you sitting here —"

"Now don't make matters worse, Joe, for heaven's sake," said his wife.

"I could lend you a dress, Bobbie, but I think Phyllis is right," said Mary Lander. "Whatever *you* want to do."

"*Want* to do! That's not the question," said Bobbie. "Go on before I change my mind. Thanks, everybody. Frank, you haven't said a word."

"Nothing much for me to say," said Frank Lander. But as far as I was concerned he, and Bobbie herself, had said more than anyone else. I caught her looking at me quickly.

"Well, all right, then," said Joe. "I'm outnumbered. Or outpersuaded or something."

I was the last to say goodbye, and I whispered to Bobbie: "Frank, eh?"

"You're only guessing," she said. "Goodnight, Jim." Whatever they would be after we left, her eyes were brighter than they had been in years. She had very nearly gone to a party, and for a minute or two she had been part of it.

I sat in the back seat with Phyllis Whipple and Frank Lander. "If you'd had any sense you'd know there'd be a letdown," said Phyllis.

"Oh, drop it," said Joe.

"It might have been worth it, though, Phyllis," said Mary Lander. "How long is it since she's seen anybody but that old battle-ax, Mrs. McCrea? God, I hate to think what it must be like, living in that house with Mrs. McCrea."

"I'm sure it would have been a *lot* easier if Bobbie'd come with us," said Phyllis. "That would have fixed things just right with Mrs. McCrea. She's just the type that wants Bobbie to go out and have a good time. Especially without Pete. You forget how the old lady used to call up all the mothers as soon as she heard there was a party planned. What Joe did was cruel because it was so downright stupid. Thoughtless. Like getting her all excited and then leaving her hung up."

"You've had too much to drink," said Joe.

"*I* have?"

"Yes, you don't say things like that in front of a bachelor," said Joe.

"Who's — oh, Jim? It is to laugh. Did I shock you, Jim?"

"Not a bit. I didn't know what you meant. Did you say something risqué?"

"My husband thinks I did."

"Went right over my head," I said. "I'm innocent about such things."

"So's your old man," said Joe.

"Do you think she should have come with us, Frank?" I said.

"Why ask me? No. I'm with Phyllis. What's the percentage for Bobbie? You saw that son of a bitch in the doorway, and you know damn well when he gets home from Muriel Nierhaus's, he's going to raise hell with Bobbie."

"Then Bobbie had nothing to lose," said Joe. "If Pete's going to raise hell with her, anyway, she might as well have come with us."

"How does he raise hell with her?" I said.

No one said anything.

"Do you know, Phyllis?" I said.

"What?" said Phyllis.

"Oh, come on. You heard me," I said. "Mary?"

"I'm sure I don't know."

"Oh, nuts," I said.

"Go ahead, tell him," said Frank Lander.

"Nobody ever knew for sure," said Phyllis, quietly.

"That's not true. Caroline English, for one. She knew for sure."

Phyllis spoke: "A few weeks before Bobbie had her baby she rang Caroline's doorbell in the middle of the night and asked Caroline if she could stay there. Naturally Caroline said yes, and she saw that Bobbie had nothing but a coat over her nightgown and had bruises all over her arms and shoulders. Julian was away, a lucky break because he'd have gone over and had a fight with Pete. As it was, Caroline made Bobbie have Dr. English come out and have a look at her, and nothing more was said. I mean, it was kept secret from everybody, especially Mr. Hammersmith. But the story got out somehow. Not widespread, but we all heard about it."

"We don't want it to get back to Mr. Hammersmith," said Mary Lander.

"He knows," said Frank Lander.

"You keep saying that, but I don't believe he does," said Mary.

"I don't either," said Joe Whipple. "Pete wouldn't be alive today if Phil Hammersmith knew."

"That's where I think you're wrong," said Phyllis. "Mr. Hammersmith might want to kill Pete, but killing him is another matter. And what earthly good would it do? The Hammersmiths have lost every penny, so I'm told, and at least with Pete still alive, Mrs. McCrea supports Bobbie. Barely. But they have food and a roof over their heads."

"Phil Hammersmith knows the whole damn story, you can bet anything on that. And it's why he's an old man all of a sudden. Have you seen him this trip, Jim?" said Frank Lander.

"I haven't seen him since the wedding."

"Oh, well —" said Mary.

"You won't —" said Joe.

"You won't recognize him," said Frank Lander. "He's bent over —"

"They say he's had a stroke," said Phyllis Whipple.

"And on top of everything else he got a lot of people sore at him by selling his bank stock to Ed Charney," said Joe. "Well, not a lot of people, but some that could have helped him. My old man, to name one. And I don't think that was so hot. Phil Hammersmith was a carpetbagger himself, and damn lucky to be in the bank. Then to sell his stock to a lousy stinking bootlegger . . . You should hear Harry Reilly on the subject."

"I don't want to hear Harry Reilly on any subject," said Frank Lander. "Cheap Irish Mick."

"I don't like him any better than you do, Frank, but call him something else," I said.

"I'm sorry, Jim. I didn't mean that," said Frank Lander.

"No. It just slipped out," I said.

"I apologize," said Frank Lander.

"Oh, all right."

"Don't be sensitive, Jim," said Mary.

"Stay out of it, Mary," said Frank Lander.

"*Everybody* calm down," said Joe. "Everybody knows that Harry Reilly is a cheap Irish Mick, and nobody knows it better than Jim, an Irish Mick but not a cheap one. So shut the hell up, everybody."

"Another country heard from," said Phyllis.

"Now *you*, for Christ's sake," said Joe. "Who has the quart?"

"I have my quart," said Frank Lander.

"I have mine," I said.

"I asked who has mine. Phyllis?"

"When we get to the club, time enough," said Phyllis.

"Hand it over," said Joe.

"Three quarts of whiskey between five people. I'd like to know how we're going to get home tonight," said Mary Lander.

"Drunk as a monkey, if you really want to know," said Joe. "Tight as a nun's."

"Well, at least we're off the subject of Bobbie and Pete," said Phyllis.

"I'm not. I was coming back to it. Phyllis. The quart," said Joe.

"No," said Phyllis.

"Here," I said. "And remember where it came from." I handed him my bottle.

Joe took a swig in the corner of his mouth, swerving the car only slightly. "Thanks," he said, and returned the bottle. "Now, Mary, if you'll light me a cigarette like a dear little second cousin."

"Once removed," said Mary Lander.

"Once removed, and therefore related to Bobbie through her mother."

"No, *you* are but I'm not," said Mary Lander.

"Well, you're in it some way, through me. Now for the benefit of those who are not related to Bobbie or Mrs. Hammersmith, or Mary or me. Permit me to give you a little family history that will enlighten you on several points."

"Is this going to be about Mr. Hammersmith?" said Phyllis. "I don't think you'd better tell that."

"You're related only by marriage, so kindly keep your trap shut. If I want to tell it, I can."

"Everybody remember that I asked him not to," said Phyllis.

"Don't tell it, Joe, whatever it is," said Mary Lander.

"Yeah, what's the percentage?" said Frank Lander. "They have enough trouble without digging up past history."

"Oh, you're so noble, Lander," said Joe. "You fool nobody."

"If you're going to tell the story, go ahead, but stop insulting Frank," said Mary Lander.

"We'll be at the club before he gets started," said Phyllis.

"Then we'll sit there till I finish. Anyway, it doesn't take that long. So, to begin at the beginning. Phil Hammersmith. Phil Hammersmith came here before the war, just out of Lehigh."

"You're not even telling it right," said Phyllis.

"Phyllis is right. I'm screwing up my own story. Well, I'll begin again. Phil Hammersmith graduated from Lehigh, then a few years *later* he came to Gibbsville."

"That's better," said Phyllis.

"The local Lehigh contingent all knew him. He'd played lacrosse and he was a Sigma Nu around the time Mr. Chew was there. So he already had friends in Gibbsville."

"Now you're on the right track," said Phyllis.

"Thank you, love," said Joe.

"Where was he from originally?" I asked.

"Don't ask questions, Jim. It only throws me. He was from some place in New Jersey. So anyway he arrived in Gibbsville and got a job with the Coal & Iron Company. He was a civil engineer, and he had the job when he arrived. That is, he didn't come here looking for a job. He was hired before he got here."

"You've made that plain," said Phyllis.

"Well, it's important," said Joe.

"Yes, but you don't have to say the same thing over and over again," said Phyllis.

"Yes I do. Anyway, apparently the Coal & Iron people hired him on the strength of his record at Lehigh, plus asking a few questions of the local Lehigh contingent, that knew him, *plus* a very good recommendation he'd had from some firm in Bethlehem. Where he'd worked after getting out of college. But after he'd been here a while, and was getting along all right at the Coal & Iron, one day a construction engineer from New York arrived to talk business at the C. & I. Building. They took him down-cellar to the drafting-room and who should he see but Phil Hammersmith. But apparently Phil didn't see him. Well, the New York guy was a real wet smack, because he tattled on Phil.

"Old Mr. Duncan was general superintendent then and he sent for Phil. Was it true that Phil had once worked in South America, and if so, why hadn't he mentioned it when he applied for a job? Phil gave him the obvious answer. 'Because if I had, you wouldn't have hired me.' 'Not necessarily,' said Mr. Duncan. 'We might have accepted your explanation.' 'You say that now, but I tried telling the truth and I couldn't get a job.' 'Well, tell me the truth now,' said Mr. Duncan. 'All right,' said Phil. So he told Mr. Duncan what had happened.

"He was working in South America. Peru, I think. Or maybe Bolivia. In the jungle. And the one thing they didn't want the na-tives, the Indians, to get hold of was firearms. But one night he caught a native carrying an armful of rifles from the shanty, and when Phil yelled at him, the native ran, and Phil shot him. Killed him. The next day one of the other engineers was found with his throat cut. And the day after that the native chief came and called on the head man of the construction outfit. Either the Indians thought they'd killed the man that had killed their boy, or they didn't much care. But the chief told the white boss that the next time an Indian was killed, two white men would be killed. And not just killed. Tortured. Well, there were four or maybe five engineers, including Phil and the boss. The only white men in an area as big as Pennsylvania, and I guess they weighed their chances and being mathematicians, the odds didn't look so hot. So they quit. No hero stuff. They just quit. Except Phil. He was fired. The boss blamed Phil for everything and in his report to the New York office he put in a lot of stuff that just about fixed Phil for good. The boss, of course, was the same man that spotted Phil at the C. & I. drafting-room."

"You told it very well," said Phyllis.

"So any time you think of Phil Hammersmith killing Pete McCrea, it wouldn't be the first time," said Joe.

"And the war," I said. "He probably killed a few Germans."

"On the other hand, he never got over blaming himself for the other engineer's getting his throat cut," said Joe. "This is all the straight dope. Mr. Duncan to my old man."

We were used to engineers, their travels and adventures in far-off places, but engineers came and went and only a few became fixtures in our life. Phil Hammersmith's story was all new to Mary and Frank and me, and in the cold moonlight, as we sat in a heated automobile in a snow-covered parking area of a Pennsylvania country club, Joe Whip-ple had taken us to a dark South American jungle, given us a touch of fear, and in a few minutes covered Phil Hammersmith in mystery and then removed the mystery.

"Tell us more about Mr. Hammersmith," said Mary Lander.

Mary Lander. I had not had time to realize the inference that must accompany my guess that Frank Lander was the one boy in our crowd who had stayed with Bobbie. Mary Lander was the only girl who had

not fought off Pete McCrea. She was the last girl I would have suspected of staying with Pete, and yet the one that surprised me the
least. She had always been the girl our mothers liked us to take out, a
kind of mothers' ideal for their sons, and possibly even for themselves.
Mary Morgan Lander was the third generation of a family that had
always been in the grocery business, the only store in the county that
sold caviar and English biscuits and Sportsmen's Bracer chocolate, as
well as the most expensive domestic items of fruit, vegetables, and
tinned goods. Her brother Llewellyn Morgan still scooped out dried
prunes and operated the rotary ham slicer, but no one seriously believed that all the Morgan money came from the store. Lew Morgan
taught Sunday School in the Methodist Episcopal Church and played
basketball at the Y.M.C.A., but he had been to Blair Academy and
Princeton, and his father had owned one of the first Pierce-Arrows in
Gibbsville. Mary had been unfairly judged a teaser, in previous years.
She was not a teaser, but a girl who would kiss a boy and allow him
to wander all over her body so long as he did not touch bare skin.
Nothing surprised me about Mary. It was in character for her to have
slapped Pete McCrea at a dinner party, and then to have let him stay
with her and to have discussed with him a swap of husbands and
wives. No casual dirty remark ever passed unnoticed by Mary; when
someone made a slip we would all turn to see how Mary was taking it,
and without fail she had heard it, understood it, and taken a pious
attitude. But in our crowd she was the one person most conscious of
sex and scatology. She was the only one of whom I would say she had a
dirty mind, but I kept that observation to myself along with my theory
that she hated Frank Lander. My theory, based on no information
whatever, was that marriage and Frank Lander had not been enough
for her and that Pete McCrea had become attractive to her because he
was so awful.

"There's no more to tell," said Joe Whipple. We got out of the car
and Mary took Joe's arm, and her evening was predictable: fathers and
uncles and older brothers would cut in on her, and older women would
comment as they always did that Mary Lander was *such* a sensible girl,
so considerate of her elders, a *wonderful* wife to Frank. And we of her
own age would dance with her because under cover of the dancing
crowd Mary would wrap both legs around our right legs with a promise
that had fooled us for years. Quiet little Mary Lander, climbing up a

boy's leg but never forgetting to smile her Dr. Lyons smile at old Mrs. Ginyan and old Mr. Heff. And yet through some mental process that I did not take time to scrutinize, I was less annoyed with Mary than I had been since we were children. I was determined not to dance with her, and I did not, but my special knowledge about her and Pete McCrea reduced her power to allure. Bobbie had married Pete McCrea and she was still attractive in spite of it; but Mary's seductiveness vanished with the revelation that she had picked Pete as her lover, if only for once, twice, or how many times. I had never laughed at Mary before, but now she was the fool, not we, not I.

I got quite plastered at the dance, and so did a lot of other people. On the way home we sang a little — "Body and Soul" was the song, but Phyllis was the only one who could sing the middle part truly — and Frank Lander tried to tell about an incident in the smoking-room, where Julian English apparently had thrown a drink in Harry Reilly's face. It did not seem worth making a fuss about, and Frank never finished his story. Mary Lander attacked me: "You never danced with me, not once," she said.

"I didn't?"

"No, you didn't, and you know you didn't," she said. "And you always do."

"Well, this time I guess I didn't."

"Well, *why* didn't you?"

"Because he didn't want to," said Frank Lander. "You're making a fool of yourself. I should think you'd have more pride."

"Yeah, why don't you have more pride, Mary?" said Joe Whipple. "You'd think it was an honor to dance with this Malloy guy."

"It is," I said.

"That's it. You're getting so conceited," said Mary. "Well, I'm sure I didn't have to sit any out."

"Then why all the fuss?" said Frank Lander.

"Such popularity must be deserved," I said, quoting an advertising slogan.

"Whose? Mary's or yours?" said Phyllis.

"Well, I was thinking of Mary's, but now that you mention it . . ." I said.

"How many times did he dance with *you*, Phyllis?" said Joe.

"Three or four," said Phyllis.

"In that case, Frank, Jim has insulted your wife. I don't see any other way out of it. You have to at least slap his face. Shall I stop the car?"

"My little trouble-maker," said Phyllis.

"Come on, let's have a fight," said Joe. "Go ahead, Frank. Give him a punch in the nose."

"Yeah, like you did at the Dam, Frank," I said.

"Oh, God. I remember that awful night," said Phyllis. "What did you fight over?"

"Bobbie," I said.

"Bobbie was the cause of *more* fights," said Mary Lander.

"Well, we don't need her to fight over now. We have you," said Joe. "Your honor's been attacked and your husband wants to defend it. The same as I would if Malloy hadn't danced with *my* wife. It's a good thing you danced with Phyllis, Malloy, or you and I'd get out of this car and start slugging."

"Why did you fight over Bobbie? I don't remember that," said Mary.

"Because she came to the picnic with Jim and then went off necking with Frank," said Phyllis. "I remember the whole thing."

"Stop *talking* about fighting and let's *fight*," said Joe.

"All right, stop the car," I said.

"Now you're talking," said Joe.

"Don't be ridiculous," said Phyllis.

"Oh, shut up," said Joe. He pulled up on the side of the road. "I'll referee." He got out of the car, and so did Frank and I and Phyllis. "All right, put up your dukes." We did so, moved around a bit in the snow and slush. "Go on, mix it," said Joe, whereupon Frank rushed me and hit me on the left cheek. All blows were directed at the head, since all three of us were armored in coonskin coats. "That was a good one, Frank. Now go get him, Jim." I swung my right hand and caught Frank's left eye, and at that moment we were all splashed by slush, taken completely by surprise as Phyllis, whom we had forgotten, drove the car away.

"That bitch!" said Joe. He ran to the car and got hold of a door handle but she increased her speed and he fell in the snow. "God damn that bitch, I should have known she was up to something. Now what? Let's try to bum a ride." The fight, such as it was, was over, and we tried to flag down cars on their way home from the dance. We recognized many of them, but not one would stop.

"Well, thanks to you, we've got a nice three-mile walk to Swedish Haven," said Frank Lander.

"Oh, she'll be back," said Joe.

"I'll bet you five bucks she's not," I said.

"Well, I won't bet, but I'll be damned if I'm going to walk three miles. I'm just going to wait till we can bum a ride."

"If you don't keep moving you'll freeze," said Frank.

"We're nearer the club than we are Swedish Haven. Let's go back there," I said.

"And have my old man see me?" said Joe.

"Your old man went home hours ago," I said.

"Well, somebody'll see me," said Joe.

"Listen, half the club's seen you already, and they wouldn't even stop," I said.

"Who has a cigarette?" said Joe.

"Don't give him one," said Frank.

"I have no intention of giving him one," I said. "Let's go back to the club. My feet are soaking wet."

"So are mine," said Frank. We were wearing pumps, and our feet had been wet since we got out of the car.

"That damn Phyllis, she knows I just got over a cold," said Joe.

"Maybe that's why she did it," I said. "It'd serve you right if you got pneumonia."

We began to walk in the middle of the road, in the direction of the clubhouse, which we could see, warm and comfortable on top of a distant plateau. "That old place never looked so good," said Joe. "Let's spend the night there."

"The rooms are all taken. The orchestra's staying there," I said.

We walked about a mile, our feet getting sorer at every step, and the combination of exhaustion and the amount we had had to drink made even grumbling an effort. Then a Dodge touring car, becurtained, stopped about fifty yards from us and a spotlight was turned on each of our faces. A man in a short overcoat and fur-lined cap came toward us. He was a State Highway patrolman. "What happened to you fellows?" he said. "You have a wreck?"

"I married one," said Joe.

"Oh, a weisscrackah," said the patrolman, a Pennsylvania Dutchman. "Where's your car?"

"We got out to take a leak and my wife drove off with it," said Joe.

"You from the dance at the gulf club?"

"Yes," said Joe. "How about giving us a lift?"

"Let me see you' driwah's license," said the cop.

Joe took out his billfold and handed over the license. "So? From Lantenengo street yet? All right, get in. Whereabouts you want to go to?"

"The country club," said Joe.

"The hell with that," said Frank. "Let's go on to Gibbsville."

"This aint no taxi service," said the cop. "And I aint taking you to no Gippsfille. I'm on my way to my substation. Swedish Haven. You can phone there for a taxi. Privileged characters, you think you are. A bunch of drunks, you ask me."

I had to go back to New York on the morning train and the events of the next few days, so far as they concerned Joe and Phyllis Whipple and Frank and Mary Lander, were obscured by the suicide, a day or two later, of Julian English, the man who had thrown a drink at Harry Reilly. The domestic crisis of the Whipples and the Landers and even the McCreas seemed very unimportant. And yet when I heard about English, who had not been getting along with his wife, I wondered about my own friends, people my own age but not so very much younger than Julian and Caroline English. English had danced with Phyllis and Mary that night, and now he was dead. I knew very little about the causes of the difficulties between him and Caroline, but they could have been no worse than the problems that existed in Bobbie's marriage and that threatened the marriage of Frank and Mary Lander. I was shocked and saddened by the English suicide; he was an attractive man whose shortcomings seemed out of proportion to the magnitude of killing himself. He had not been a friend of mine, only an acquaintance with whom I had had many drinks and played some golf; but friends of mine, my closest friends in the world, boys-now-men like myself, were at the beginning of the same kind of life and doing the same kind of thing that for Julian English ended in a sealed-up garage with a motor running. I hated what I thought those next few days and weeks. There is nothing young about killing oneself, no matter when it happens, and I hated this being deprived of the sweetness of youth. And that was what it was, that was what was happening to us. I, and I think the others, had looked upon our squabbles as unpleasant incidents but belonging to our youth. Now they were plainly recognizable as symptoms of life without youth, without youth's excuses or youth's recoverability. I wanted to love someone, and during the next year or two I confused the desperate need for love with love itself. I had put a hopeless love out of my life; but that is not part of this story, except to state it and thus to show that I knew what I was looking for.

2

When you have grown up with someone it is much easier to fill in gaps of five years, ten years, in which you do not see him, than to supply those early years in the life of a friend you meet in maturity. I do not know why this is so, unless it is a mere matter of insufficient time. With the friends of later life you may exchange boyhood stories that seem worth telling, but boyhood is not all stories. It is mostly not stories, but day-to-day, unepisodic living. And most of us are too polite to burden our later-life friends with unexciting anecdotes about people they will never meet. (Likewise we hope they will not burden us.) But it is easy to bring old friends up to date in your mental dossiers by the addition of a few vital facts. Have they stayed married? Have they had many more children? Have they made money or lost it? Usually the basic facts will do, and then you tell yourself that Joe Whipple is still Joe Whipple, plus two sons, a new house, a hundred thousand dollars, forty pounds, bifocals, fat in the neck, and a new concern for the state of the nation.

Such additions I made to my friends' dossiers as I heard about them from time to time; by letters from them, conversations with my mother, an occasional newspaper clipping. I received these facts with joy for the happy news, sorrow for the sad, and immediately went about my business, which was far removed from any business of theirs. I seldom went back to Gibbsville during the Thirties — mine and the century's — and when I did I stayed only long enough to stand at a grave, to toast a bride, to spend a few minutes beside a sickbed. In my brief encounters with my old friends I got no information about Bobbie and Pete McCrea, and only after I had returned to New York or California would I remember that I had intended to inquire about them.

There is, of course, some significance in the fact that no one volunteered information about Bobbie and Pete. It was that they had disappeared. They continued to live in Gibbsville, but in parts of the town that were out of the way for their old friends. There is no town so small that that cannot happen, and Gibbsville, a third-class city, was large enough to have all the grades of poverty and wealth and the many half grades in between, in which $10 a month in the husband's income could make a difference in the kind and location of the house in which he lived. No one had volunteered any information about Bobbie and Pete, and I had not remembered to inquire. In five years I had had no new facts about them, none whatever, and their disappearance from my ken might have continued but for a broken shoelace.

I was in Gibbsville for a funeral, and the year was 1938. I had broken a shoelace, it was evening and the stores were closed, and I was about to drive back to New York. The only place open that might have shoelaces was a poolroom that in my youth had had a two-chair bootblack stand. The poolroom was in a shabby section near the railroad stations and a couple of cheap hotels, four or five saloons, an automobile tire agency, a barber shop, and a quick-lunch counter. I opened the poolroom door, saw that the bootblack's chairs were still there, and said to the man behind the cigar counter: "Have you got any shoelaces?"

"Sorry I can't help you, Jim," said the man. He was wearing an eyeshade, but as soon as he spoke I recognized Pete McCrea.

"Pete, for God's sake," I said. We shook hands.

"I thought you might be in town for the funeral," he said. "I should have gone, too, I guess, but I decided I wouldn't. It was nice of you to make the trip."

"Well, you know. He was a friend of my father's. Do you own this place?"

"I run it. I have a silent partner, Bill Charney. You remember Ed Charney? His younger brother. I don't know where to send you to get a shoelace."

"The hell with the shoelace. How's Bobbie?"

"Oh, Bobbie's fine. *You* know. A lot of changes, but this is better than nothing. Why don't you call her up? She'd love to hear from you. We're living out on Mill Street, but we have a phone. Call her up and say hello. The number is 3385-J. If you have time maybe you could go see her. I have to stay here till I close up at one o'clock, but she's home."

"What number on Mill Street? You call her up and tell her I'm coming? Is that all right?"

"Hell, yes."

Someone thumped the butt of a cue on the floor and called out: "Rack 'em up, Pete?"

"I have to be here. You go on out and I'll call her up," he said. "Keep your shirt on," he said to the pool player, then, to me: "It's 402 Mill Street, across from the open hearth, second house from the corner. I guess I won't see you again, but I'm glad we had a minute. You're looking very well." I could not force a comment on his appearance. His nose was red and larger, his eyes watery, the dewlaps sagging, and he was wearing a blue denim work shirt with a dirty leather bow tie.

"Think I could get in the Ivy Club if I went back to Princeton?" he said. "I didn't make it the first time around, but now I'm a big shot. So long, Jim. Nice to've seen you."

The open hearth had long since gone the way of all the mill equipment; the mill itself had been inactive for years, and as a residential area the mill section was only about a grade and a half above the poorest Negro slums. But in front of most of the houses in the McCreas' row there were cared-for plots; there always had been, even when the mill was running and the air was full of smoke and acid. It was an Irish and Polish neighborhood, but knowledge of that fact did not keep me from locking all the doors of my car. The residents of the neighborhood would not have touched my father's car, but this was not his car and I was not he.

The door of Number 402 opened as soon as I closed my car door. Bobbie waited for me to lock up and when I got to the porch, she said: "*Jim*. Jim, Jim, Jim. How nice. I'm so glad to see you." She quickly closed the door behind me and then kissed me. "Give me a real kiss and a real hug. I didn't dare while the door was open." I kissed her and held her for a moment and then she said: "Hey, I guess we'd better cut this out."

"Yes," I said. "It's nice, though."

"Haven't done that since we were — God!" She stood away and looked at me. "You could lose some weight, but you're not so bad. How about a bottle of beer? Or would you rather have some cheap whiskey?"

"What are you drinking?"

"Cheap whiskey, but I'm used to it," she said.

"Let's both have some cheap whiskey," I said.

"Straight? With water? Or how?"

"Oh, a small slug of whiskey and a large slug of water in it. I'm driving back to New York tonight."

She went to the kitchen and prepared the drinks. I recognized some of the furniture from the Hammersmith and McCrea houses. "Brought together by a shoestring," she said. "Here's to it. How do I look?"

"If you want my frank and candid opinion, good enough to go right upstairs and make up for the time we lost. Pete won't be home till one o'clock."

"If then," she said. "Don't think I wouldn't, but it's too soon after my baby. Didn't Pete tell you I finally produced a healthy son?"

"No."

"You'll hear him in a little while. We have a daughter, two years old, and now a son. Angus McCrea, Junior. Seven pounds two ounces at birth."

"Good for you," I said.

"Not so damn good for me, but it's over, and he's healthy."

"And what about your mother and father?" I said.

"Oh, poor Jim. You didn't know? Obviously you didn't, and you're going to be so sorry you asked. Daddy committed suicide two years ago. He shot himself. And Mother's in Swedish Haven." Swedish Haven was local lore for the insane asylum. "I'm sorry I had to tell you."

"God, why won't they lay off you?" I said.

"Who is they? Oh, you mean just — life?"

"Yes."

"I don't know, Jim," she said. "I've had about as much as I can stand, or so I keep telling myself. But I must be awfully tough, because there's always something else, and I go right on. Will you let me complain for just a minute, and then I'll stop? The only one of the old crowd I ever see is Phyllis. She comes out and never forgets to bring a bottle, so we get tight together. But some things we don't discuss, Phyllis and I. Pete is a closed subject."

"What's he up to?"

"Oh, he has his women. I don't even know who they are any more, and couldn't care less. Just as long as he doesn't catch a disease. I told him that, so he's been careful about it." She sat up straight. "I haven't been the soul of purity, either, but it's Pete's son. Both children are Pete's. But I haven't been withering on the vine."

"Why should you?"

"That's what *I* said. Why should I have nothing? Nothing? The children are mine, and I love them, but I need more than that, Jim. Children don't love you back. All they do is depend on you to feed them and wash them and all the rest of it. But after they're in bed for the night — I never know whether Pete will be home at two o'clock or not at all. So I've had two tawdry romances, I guess you'd call them. Not you, but Mrs. McCrea would."

"Where is dear Mrs. McCrea?"

"She's living in Jenkintown, with an old maid sister. Thank heaven they can't afford carfare, so I'm spared that."

"Who are your gentlemen friends?"

"Well, the first was when we were living on the East Side. A gentleman by the name of Bill Charney. Yes, Ed's brother and Pete's partner. I was crazy about him. Not for one single minute in love with him, but I never even thought about love with him. He wanted to marry me, too, but I was a nasty little snob. I *couldn't* marry Bill Charney, Jim. I just couldn't. So he married a nice little Irish girl and they're living on Lantenengo Street in the house that used to belong to old Mr. Duncan. And I'm holding court on Mill Street, thirty dollars a month rent."

"Do you want some money?"

"Will you give me two hundred dollars?"

"More than that, if you want it."

"No, I'd just like to have two hundred dollars to hide, to keep in case of emergency."

"In case of emergency, you can always send me a telegram in care of my publisher." I gave her $200.

"Thank you. Now I have some money. For the last five or six years I haven't had any money of my own. You don't care how I spend this, do you?"

"As long as you spend it on yourself."

"I've gotten so stingy I probably won't spend any of it. But this is wonderful. Now I can read the ads and say to myself I could have some expensive lingerie. I think I will get a permanent, next month."

"Is that when you'll be back in circulation again?"

"Good guess. Yes, about a month," she said. "But not the same man. I didn't tell you about the second one. You don't know him. He came here after you left Gibbsville. His name is McCormick and he went to Princeton with Pete. They sat next to each other in a lot of classes, McC, McC, and he was sent here to do some kind of an advertising survey and ran into Pete. They'd never been exactly what you'd call pals, but they *knew* each other and Mac took one look and sized up the situation and — well, I thought, why not? He wasn't as exciting as Mr. Charney, but at one time I would have married him. *If* he'd asked me. He doesn't live here any more."

"But you've got the next one picked out?"

"No, but I know there will be a next one. Why lie to myself? And why lie to you? I don't think I ever have."

"Do you ever see Frank?"

"Frank? Frank Lander? What made you think of him?"

"Bobbie," I said.

"Oh, of course. That was a guess of yours, a long time ago," she said. "No, I never see Frank." She was smoking a cigarette, and sitting erect with her elbow on the arm of her chair, holding the cigarette high and with style. If her next words had been "Jeeves, have the black Rolls brought round at four o'clock" she would not have been more naturally grand. But her next words were: "I haven't even thought about Frank. There was another boy, Johnny White, the one I was engaged to. *Engaged to.* That close to spending the rest of my life with him — or at least part of it. But because he wanted me to go away with him before we were married, I broke the engagement and married Pete."

"Is that all it was? That he wanted you to go away with him?"

"That's really all it was. I got huffy and said he couldn't really love me if he wanted to take that risk. Not that we hadn't been taking risks, but a pre-marital trip, that was something else again. My five men, Jim. Frank. Johnny. Bill and Mac. And Pete."

"Why didn't you and Frank ever get engaged?"

"I wonder. I *have* thought about *that,* so I was wrong when I said I never think of Frank. But Frank in the old days, not Frank now. What may have happened was that Frank was the only boy I'd gone all the way with, and then I got scared because I didn't want to give up the fun, popularity, good times. Jim, I have a confession to make. About you."

"Oh?"

"I told Frank I'd stayed with you. He wouldn't believe he was my first and he kept harping on it, so I really got rid of Frank by telling him you were the first."

"Why me?"

"Because the first time I ever stayed with Frank, or anybody, it was at a picnic at the Dam, and I'd gone to the picnic with you. So you were the logical one."

"Did you tell him that night?"

"No. Later. Days later. But you had a fight with him that night, and the fight made it all the more convincing."

"Well, thanks, little pal," I said.

"Oh, you don't care, do you?"

"No, not really."

"You had Kitty, after all," she said. "Do you ever see Kitty?"

"No. Kitty lives in Cedarhurst and they keep to themselves, Cedarhurst people."

"What was your wife like?"

"She was nice. Pretty. Wanted to be an actress. I still see her once in a while. I like her, and always will, but if ever there were two people that shouldn't have got married . . ."

"I can name two others," said Bobbie.

"You and Pete. But you've stuck to him."

"Don't be polite. I'm stuck with him. Can you imagine what Pete would be like if I left him?"

"Well, to be brutally frank, what's he like anyway? You don't have to go on paying for a dirty trick the rest of your life."

"It wasn't just a dirty trick. It would have been a dirty trick if I'd walked out on him the day we were getting married. But I went through with it, and that made it more than a dirty trick. I *should have* walked out on him, the day we got married. I even tried. And he'd have recovered — then. Don't forget, Pete McCrea was used to dirty tricks being played on him, and he might have got over it if I'd left him at the church. But once I'd married him, he became a different person, took himself much more seriously, and so did everyone else. They began to dislike him, but that was better than being laughed at." She sipped her drink.

"Well, who did it? I did. Your little pal," she said. "How about some more cheap whiskey?"

"No thanks, but you go ahead," I said.

"The first time I ever knew there *was* a Mill Street was the day we rented this house," she said, as she poured herself a drink. "I'd never been out this way before."

"You couldn't have lived here when the mill was operating. The noise and the smoke."

"I can live anywhere," she said. "So can anyone else. And don't be too surprised if you find us back on Lantenengo. Do you know the big thing nowadays? Slot machines and the numbers racket. Pete wants to get into The Numbers, but he hasn't decided how to go about it. Bill Charney is the kingpin in the county, although not the real head. It's run by a syndicate in Jersey City."

"Don't let him do it, Bobbie," I said. "Really don't."

"Why not? He's practically in it already. He has slot machines in the poolroom, and that's where people call up to find out what number won today. He might as well be in it."

"No."

"It's the only way Pete will ever have any money, and if he ever gets his hands on some money, maybe he'll divorce me. Then I could take the children and go away somewhere. California."

"That's a different story. If you're planning it that way. But stay out of The Numbers if you ever have any idea of remaining respectable. You can't just go in for a few years and then quit."

"Respectable? Do you think my son's going to be able to get into Princeton? His father is the proprietor of a poolroom, and they're going to know that when Angus gets older. Pete will never be anything else. He's found his niche. But if I took the children to California they might have a chance. And *I* might have a chance, before it's too late. It's our only hope, Jim. Phyllis agrees with me."

I realized that I would be arguing against a hope and a dream, and if she had that much left, and only that much, I had no right to argue. She very nearly followed my thinking. "It's what I live on, Jim," she said. "That — and this." She held up her glass. "And a little admiration. A little — admiration. Phyllis wants to give me a trip to New York. Would you take us to '21' and those places?"

"Sure."

"Could you get someone for Phyllis?"

"I think so. Sure. Joe wouldn't go on this trip?"

"And give up a chance to be with Mary Lander?"

"So now it's Joe and Mary?"

"Oh, that's old hat in Gibbsville. They don't even pretend otherwise."

"And Frank? What about him?"

"Frank is the forgotten man. If there were any justice he ought to pair off with Phyllis, but they don't like each other. Phyllis calls Frank a wishy-washy namby-pamby, and Frank calls Phyllis a drunken trouble-maker. We've all grown up, Jim. Oh, haven't we just? Joe doesn't like Phyllis to visit me because Mary says all we do is gossip. Although how she'd know *what* we do . . ."

"They were all at the funeral, and I thought what a dull, stuffy little group they've become," I said.

"But that's what they are," said Bobbie. "Very stuffy and very dull. What else is there for them to do? If I were still back there with them I'd be just as bad. Maybe worse. In a way, you know, Pete McCrea has turned out to be the most interesting man in our crowd, present company excepted. Joe was a very handsome young man and so was Frank, and their families had lots of money and all the rest of it. But you saw Joe and Frank today. I haven't seen them lately, but Joe looks like a professional wrestler and I remember how hairy he was, all over his chest and back and his arms and legs. And Frank just the opposite, skin like a girl's and slender, but now we could almost call *him* Ichabod. He looks like a cranky schoolteacher, and his glasses make him look like an owl. Mary, of course, beautifully dressed I'm sure, and not looking a day older."

"Several days older, but damn good-looking," I said.

A baby cried and Bobbie made no move. "That's my daughter. Teething. Now she'll wake up my son and you're in for a lot of howling." The son began to cry, and Bobbie excused herself. She came back in a few minutes with the infant in her arms. "It's against my rules to pick them up, but I wanted to show him to you. Isn't he an ugly little creature? The answer is yes." She took him away and returned with the daughter. "She's begun to have a face."

"Yes, I can see that. Your face, for which she can be thankful."

"Yes, I wouldn't want a girl to look like Pete. It doesn't matter so much with a boy." She took the girl away and when she rejoined me she refilled her glass.

"Are you sorry you didn't have children?" she said.

"Not the way it turned out, I'm not," I said.

"These two haven't had much of a start in life, the poor little things. They haven't even been christened. Do you know why? There was nobody we could ask to be their godfathers." Her eyes filled with tears. "That was when I really saw what we'd come to."

"Bobbie, I've got a four-hour drive ahead of me, so I think I'd better get started."

"Four hours to New York? In that car?"

"I'm going to stop and have a sandwich halfway."

"I could give you a sandwich and make some coffee."

"I don't want it now, thanks."

We looked at each other. "I'd like to show how much I appreciate your coming out to see me," she said. "But it's probably just as well I can't. But I'll be all right in New York, Jim. That is, if I ever get there. I won't believe that, either, till I'm on the train."

If she came to New York I did not know about it, and during the war years Bobbie and her problems receded from my interest. I heard that Pete was working in a defense plant, from which I inferred that he had not made the grade in the numbers racket. Frank Lander was in the Navy, Joe Whipple in the War Production Board, and by the time the war was over I discovered that so many other people and things had taken the place of Gibbsville in my thoughts that I had almost no active curiosity about the friends of my youth. I had even had a turnover in my New York friendships. I had married again, I was working hard, and most of my social life originated with my wife's friends. I was making, for me, quite a lot of money, and I was a middle-aged man whose physician had made some honest, un-equivocal remarks about my life expectancy. It took a little time and one illness to make me realize that if I wanted to see my child grow to maturity, I had to retire from night life. It was not nearly so difficult as I had always anticipated it would be.

After I became reconciled to middle age and the quieter life I made another discovery: that the sweetness of my early youth was a persis-tent and enduring thing, so long as I kept it at the distance of years. Moments would come back to me, of love and excitement and music and laughter that filled my breast as they had thirty years earlier. It was not nostalgia, which only means homesickness, nor was it a wish to be living that excitement again. It was a splendid contentment with the knowledge that once I had felt those things so deeply and well that the throbbing urging of George Gershwin's "Do It Again" could evoke the original sensation and the pictures that went with it: a tea dance at the club and a girl in a long black satin dress and my furious jealousy of a fellow who wore a yellow foulard tie. I wanted none of it ever again, but all I had I wanted to keep. I could remember precisely the tone in which her brother had said to her: "Are you coming or aren't you?" and the sounds of his galoshes after she said: "I'm going home with Mr. Malloy." They were the things I knew before we knew everything, and, I suppose, before we began to learn. There was always a girl, and nearly always there was music; if the Gershwin tune belonged to that girl, a Romberg tune belonged to another and "When Hearts Are Young" became a personal anthem, enduringly sweet and safe from all harm, among the protected memories. In middle age I was proud to have lived according to my emotions at the right time, and content to live that way vicariously and at a distance. I had missed almost nothing, escaped very little, and at fifty I had begun to devote my energy and time to the last, simple but big task of putting it all down as well as I knew how.

In the midst of putting it all down, as novels and short stories and plays, I would sometimes think of Bobbie McCrea and the dinginess of her history. But as the reader will presently learn, the "they" — life — that had once made me cry out in anger, were not through with her yet. (Of course "they" are never through with anyone while he still lives, and we are not concerned here with the laws of compensation that seem to test us, giving us just enough strength to carry us in another trial.) I like to think that Bobbie got enough pleasure out of a pair of nylons, a permanent wave, a bottle of Phyllis Whipple's whiskey, to recharge the brightness in her. As we again take up her story I promise the reader a happy ending, if only because I want it that way. It happens also to be the true ending. . . .

Pete McCrea did not lose his job at the end of the war. His Princeton degree helped there. He had gone into the plant, which specialized in aluminum extrusion, as a manual laborer, but his IBM card revealed that he had taken psychology courses in college, and he was transferred to Personnel. It seemed an odd choice, but it is not hard to imagine that Pete was better fitted by his experience as a poolroom proprietor than as a two-year student of psychology. At least he spoke both languages, he liked the work, and in 1945 he was not bumped by a returning veteran.

Fair Grounds, the town in which the plant was situated, was only three miles from Gibbsville. For nearly a hundred years it had been the trading center for the Pennsylvania Dutch farmers in the area, and its attractions had been Becker's general store, the Fair Grounds Bank, the freight office of the Reading Railway, the Fair Grounds Hotel, and five Protestant churches. Clerks at Becker's and at the bank and the Reading, and bartenders at the hotel and the pastors of the churches, all had to speak Pennsylvania Dutch. English was desirable but not a requirement. The town was kept scrubbed, dusted and painted, and until the erection of the aluminum plant, jobs and trades were kept in the same families. An engineman's son worked as waterboy until he was old enough to take the examinations for brakeman; a master mechanic would give his boy calipers for Christmas. There were men and women in Fair Grounds who visited Gibbsville only to serve on juries or to undergo surgery at the Gibbsville Hospital. There were some men and women who had never been to Gibbsville at all and regarded Gibbsville as some Gibbsville citizens regarded Paris, France. That was the pre-aluminum Fair Grounds.

To this town in 1941 went Pete and Bobbie McCrea. They rented a house no larger than the house on Mill Street but cleaner and in better repair. Their landlord and his wife went to live with his mother-in-law, and collected the $50 legally frozen monthly rent and $50 side payment for the use of the radio and the gas stove. But in spite of under-the-table and black-market prices Peter and Bobbie McCrea were financially better off than they had been since their marriage, and nylons at black-market prices were preferable to the no nylons she had on Mill Street. The job, and the fact that he continued to hold it, restored some respectability to Pete, and they discussed rejoining the club. "Don't try it, I warn you," said Phyllis Whipple. "The club isn't run by your friends any more. Now it's been taken over by people that couldn't have got in ten years ago."

"Well, we'd have needed all our old friends to go to bat for us, and I guess some would think twice about it," said Pete. "So we'll do our drinking at the Tavern."

The Dan Patch Tavern, which was a new name for the renovated Fair Grounds Hotel bar, was busy all day and all night, and it was one of the places where Pete could take pleasure in his revived respectability. It was also one of the places where Bobbie could count on getting that little admiration that she needed to live on. On the day of Pearl Harbor she was only thirty-four years old and at the time of the Japanese surrender she was only thirty-eight. She was accorded admiration in abundance. Some afternoons just before the shift changed she would walk the three blocks to the Tavern and wait for Pete. The bartender on duty would say "Hi, Bobbie," and bring her currently favorite drink to her booth. Sometimes there would be four men sitting with her when Pete arrived from the plant; she was never alone for long. If one man tried to persuade her to leave, and became annoyingly insistent, the bartenders came to her rescue. The bartenders and the proprietor knew that in her way Bobbie was as profitable as the juke box. She was an attraction. She was a good-looking broad who was not a whore or a falling-down lush, and all her drinks were paid for. She was the Tavern's favorite customer, male or female, and if she had given the matter any thought she could have been declared in. All she wanted in return was a steady supply of Camels and protection from being mauled. The owner of the Tavern, Rudy Schau, was the only one who was aware that Bobbie and Pete had once lived on Lantenengo Street in Gibbsville, but far from being impressed by their background, he had a German opinion of aristocrats who had lost standing. He was actively suspicious of Bobbie in the beginning, but in time he came to accept her as a wife whose independence he could not condone and a good-looking woman whose morals he had not been able to condemn. And she was good for business. Beer business was good, but at Bobbie's table nobody drank beer, and the real profit was in the hard stuff.

In the Fair Grounds of the pre-aluminum days Bobbie would have had few women friends. No decent woman would have gone to a saloon every day — or any day. She most likely would have received warnings from the Ku Klux Klan, which was concerned with personal conduct in a town that had only a dozen Catholic families, no Negroes and no Jews. But when the aluminum plant (which was called simply The Aluminum or The Loomy) went into war production the population of Fair Grounds immediately doubled and the solid Protestant character of the town was changed in a month. Eight hundred new people came to town and they lived in apartments in a town where there were no apartments: in rooms in private houses, in garages and old stables, in rented rooms and haylofts out in the farming area. The newcomers wasted no time with complaints of double-rent, inadequate heating, holes in the roof, insufficient sanitation. The town was no longer scrubbed, dusted or painted, and thousands of man-hours were lost while a new shift waited for the old to vacate parking space in the streets of the town. Bobbie and Pete were among the lucky early ones: they had a house. That fact of itself gave Bobbie some distinction. The house had two rooms and kitchen on the first floor, three rooms and bath on the second, and it had a cellar and an attic. In the identical houses on both sides there were a total of four families and six roomers. As a member of Personnel it was one of Pete's duties to find housing for workers, but Bobbie would have no roomers. "The money wouldn't do us much good, so let's live like human beings," she said.

"You mean there's nothing to buy with the money," said Pete. "But we could save it."

"If we had it, we'd spend it. You've never saved a cent in your life and neither have I. If you're thinking of the children's education, buy some more war bonds and have it taken out of your pay. But I'm not going to share my bathroom with a lot of dirty men. I'd have to do all the extra work, not you."

"You could make a lot of money doing their laundry. Fifty cents a shirt."

"Are you serious?"

"No."

"It's a good thing you're not, because I could tell you how else I could make a lot more money."

"Yes, a lot more," said Pete.

"Well, then, keep your ideas to yourself. I won't have boarders and I won't do laundry for fifty cents a shirt. That's final."

And so Bobbie had her house, she got the admiration she needed, and she achieved a moderate popularity among the women of her neighborhood by little friendly acts that came spontaneously out of her friendly nature. There was a dinginess to the new phase: the house was not much, the men who admired her and the women who welcomed her help were the ill-advantaged, the cheap, the vulgar, and sometimes the evil. But the next step down from Mill Street would have been hopeless degradation, and the next step up, Fair Grounds, was at least up. She was envied for her dingy house, and when Pete called her the Queen of the Klondike she was not altogether displeased. There was envy in the epithet, and in the envy was the first sign of respect he had shown her in ten years. He had never suspected her of an affair with Mac McCormick, and if he had suspected her during her infatuation with Bill Charney he had been afraid to make an accusation; afraid to anticipate his own feelings in the event that Charney would give him a job in The Numbers. When Charney brought in a Pole from Detroit for the job Pete had wanted, Pete accepted $1,000 for his share of the poolroom and felt only grateful relief. Charney did not always buy out his partners, and Pete refused to wonder if the money and the easy dissolution of the partnership had been paid for by Bobbie. It was not a question he wanted to raise, and when the war in Europe created jobs at Fair Grounds he believed that his luck had begun to change.

Whatever the state of Pete's luck, the pace of his marriage had begun to change. The pace of his marriage — and not his alone — was set by the time he spent at home and what he did during that time. For ten years he had spent little more time at home than was necessary for sleeping and eating. He could not sit still in the same room with Bobbie, and even after the children were born he did not like to have her present during the times he would play with them. He would arrive in a hurry to have his supper, and in a short time he would get out of the house, to be with a girl, to go back to work at the poolroom.

He was most conscious of time when he was near Bobbie; everywhere else he moved slowly, spoke deliberately, answered hesitantly. But after the move to Fair Grounds he spent more time in the house, with the children, with Bobbie. He would sit in the front room, doing paper work from the plant, while Bobbie sewed. At the Tavern he would say to Bobbie: "It's time we were getting home." He no longer darted in and out of the house and ate his meals rapidly and in silence.

He had a new girl. Martha — "Martie" — Klinger was a typist at the plant, a Fair Grounds woman whose husband was in the Coast Guard at Lewes, Delaware. She was Bobbie's age and likewise had two children. She retained a young prettiness in the now round face and her figure had not quite reached the stage of plumpness. Sometimes when she moved an arm the flesh of her breast seemed to go all the way up to her neckline, and she had been one of the inspirations for a plant memo to women employees, suggesting that tight sweaters and tight slacks were out of place in wartime industry. Pete brought her to the Tavern one day after work, and she never took her eyes off Bobbie. She looked up and down, up and down, with her mouth half open as though she were listening to Bobbie through her lips. She showed no animosity of a defensive nature and was not openly possessive of Pete, but Bobbie knew on sight that she was Pete's new girl. After several sessions at the Tavern Bobbie could tell which of the men had already slept with Martie and which of them were likely to again. It was impossible to be jealous of Martie, but it was just as impossible not to feel superior to her. Pete, the somewhat changed Pete, kept up the absurd pretense that Martie was just a girl from the plant whom he happened to bring along for a drink, and there was no unpleasantness until one evening Martie said: "Jesus, I gotta go or I won't get any supper."

"Come on back to our house and have supper with us," said Pete. "That's okay by you, isn't it, Bobbie?"

"No, it isn't," said Bobbie.

"Rudy'll give us a steak and we can cook it at home," said Pete.

"I said no," said Bobbie, and offered no explanation.

"I'll see you all tomorrow," said Martie. "Goodnight, people."

"Why wouldn't you let her come home with us? I could have got a steak from Rudy. And Martie's a hell of a good cook."

"When we can afford a cook I may hire her," said Bobbie.

"Oh, that's what it is. The old snob department."

"That's exactly what it is."

"We're not in any position —"

"*You're* not."

"*We're* not. If I can't have my friends to my house," he said, but did not know how to finish.

"It's funny that she's the first one you ever asked. Don't forget what I told you about having boarders, and fifty cents a shirt. You keep your damn Marties out of my house. If you don't, I'll get a job and you'll be just another boarder yourself."

"Oh, why are you making such a stink about Martie?"

"Come *off* it, Pete, for heaven's *sake.*"

The next statement, he knew, would have to be a stupidly transparent lie or an admission, so he made no statement. If there had to be a showdown he preferred to avert it until the woman in question was someone more entertaining than Martie Klinger. And he liked the status quo.

They both liked the status quo. They had hated each other, their house, the dinginess of their existence on Mill Street. When the fire whistle blew it was within the hearing of Mill Street and of Lantenengo Street; rain from the same shower fell on Mill Street and Lantenengo Street; Mill Street and Lantenengo Street read the same Gibbsville newspaper at the same time every evening. And the items of their proximity only made the nearness worse, the remoteness of Mill Street from Lantenengo more vexatious. But Fair Grounds was a new town, where they had gone knowing literally nobody. They had spending money, a desirable house, the respectability of a white-collar job, and the restored confidence in a superiority to their neighbors that they had not allowed themselves to feel on Mill Street. In the Dan Patch Tavern they would let things slip out that would have been meaningless on Mill Street, where their neighbors' daily concern was a loaf of bread and a bottle of milk. "Pete, did you know Jimmy Stewart, the movie actor?" "No, he was several classes behind me, but he was in my club." "Bobbie, what's it like on one of them yachts?" "I've only been on one, but it was fun while it lasted." They could talk now about past pleasures and luxuries without being contradicted by their surroundings, and their new friends at the Tavern had no knowledge of the decade of dinginess that lay between that past and this present.

If their new friends also guessed that Pete McCrea was carrying on with Martie Klinger, that very fact made Bobbie more credibly and genuinely the woman who had once cruised in a yacht. They would have approved Bobbie's reason for not wanting Martie Klinger as a guest at supper, as they would have fiercely resented Pete's reference to Bobbie as the Queen of the Klondike. Unintentionally they were creating a symbol of order that they wanted in their lives as much as Bobbie needed admiration, and if the symbol and the admiration were slightly ersatz, what, in war years, was not?

There was no one among the Tavern friends whom Bobbie desired to make love with. "I'd give a week's pay to get in bed with you, Bobbie," said one of them.

"Fifty-two weeks' pay, did you say?" said Bobbie.

"No dame is worth fifty-two weeks' pay," said the man, a foreman named Dick Hartenstein.

"Oh, I don't know. In fifty-two weeks you make what?"

"A little over nine thousand. Nine gees, about."

"A lot of women can get that, Dick. I've heard of women getting a diamond necklace for just one night, and they cost a lot more than nine thousand dollars."

"Well, I tell you, Bobbie, if I ever hit the crap game for nine gees I'd seriously consider it, but not a year's pay that I worked for."

"You're not romantic enough for me. Sorry."

"Supposing I did hit the crap game and put nine gees on the table in front of you? Would you and me go to bed?"

"No."

"No, I guess not. If I asked you a question would you give me a truthful answer? No. You wouldn't."

"Why should I?"

"Yeah, why should you? I was gonna ask you, what does it take to get you in bed with a guy?"

"I'm a married woman."

"I skipped all that part, Bobbie. You'd go, if it was the right guy."

"You could get to be an awful nuisance, Dick. You're not far from it right this minute."

"I apologize."

"In fact, why don't you take your drink and stand at the bar?"

"What are you sore at? You get propositioned all the time."

"Yes, but you're too persistent, and you're a bore. The others don't keep asking questions when I tell them no. Go on, now, or I'll tell Rudy to keep you out of here."

"You know what you are?"

"Rudy! Will you come here, please?" she called. "All right, Dick. What am I? Say it in front of Rudy."

Rudy Schau made his way around from the bar. "What can I do for you, Bobbie?"

"I think Dick is getting ready to call me a nasty name."

"He won't," said Rudy Schau. He had the build of a man who had handled beer kegs all his life and he was now ready to squeeze the wind out of Hartenstein. "Apolochise to Bobbie and get the hell outa my place. And don't forget you got a forty-dollar tab here. You won't get a drink nowheres else in tahn."

"I'll pay my God damn tab," said Hartenstein.

"That you owe me. Bobbie you owe an apolochy."

"I apologize," said Hartenstein. He was immediately clipped behind the ear, and sunk to the floor.

"I never like that son of a bitch," said Rudy Schau. He looked down at the unconscious Hartenstein and very deliberately kicked him in the ribs.

"Oh, *don't*, Rudy," said Bobbie. "*Please* don't."

Others in the bar, which was now half filled, stood waiting for Rudy's next kick, and some of them looked at each other and then at Rudy, and they were already to rush him. Bobbie stood up quickly. "Don't, Rudy," she said.

"All right. I learned him. Joe, throw the son of a bitch out," said Rudy. Then suddenly he wheeled and grabbed a man by the belt and lifted him off the floor, holding him tight against his body with one hand and making a hammer of his other hand. "You, you son of a bitch, you was gonna go after me, you was, yeah? Well, go ahead. Let's see you, you son of a bitch. You son of a bitch, I break you in pieces." He let go and the man retreated out of range of Rudy's fist. "Pay your bill and don't come back. Don't ever show your face in my place again. And any other son of a bitch was gonna gang me. You gonna gang Rudy, hey? I kill any two of you." Two of the men picked Hartenstein off the floor before the bartender got to him. "Them two, they paid up, Joe?"

"In the clear, Rudy," said the bartender.

"You two. Don't come back," said Rudy.

"Don't worry. We won't," they said.

Rudy stood at Bobbie's table. "Okay if I sit down with you, Bobbie?"

"Of course," said Bobbie.

"Joe, a beer, please, hey? Bobbie, you ready?"

"Not yet, thanks," she said.

Rudy mopped his forehead with a handkerchief. "You don't have to take it from these bums," said Rudy. "Any time any of them get fresh, you tell me. You're what keeps this place decent, Bobbie. I know. As soon as you go home it's a pigpen. I get sick of hearing them, some of the women as bad as the men. Draft-dotchers. Essengial industry! Draft-dotchers. A bunch of 4-F draft-dotchers. I like to hear what your Daddy would say about them."

"Did you know him, my father?"

"Know him? I was in his platoon. Second platoon, C Company. I went over with him and come back with him. Phil Hammersmith."

"I never knew that."

Rudy chuckled. "Sure. Some of these 4-F draft-dotchers from outa town, they think I'm a Nazi because I never learn to speak good English, but my Daddy didn't speak no English at all and he was born out in the Walley. My old woman says put my dischartch papers up over the back-bar. I say what for? So's to make the good impression on a bunch of draft-dotchers? Corporal Rudolph W. Schau. Your Daddy was a good man and a good soldier."

"Why didn't you ever tell me you knew him?"

"Oh, I don't know, Bobbie. I wasn't gonna tell you now, but I did. It don't pay to be a talker in my business. A listener, not a talker."

"You didn't approve of me, did you?"

"I'm a saloonkeeper. A person comes to my —"

"You didn't approve of me. Don't dodge the issue."

"Well, your Daddy wouldn't of liked you coming to a saloon that often. But times change, and you're better off here than the other joints."

"I hope you don't *mind* my coming here."

"Listen, you come here as much as you want."

"Try and stop me," she said, smiling.

Pete joined them. "What happened to Dick Hartenstein?" he said.
"The same as will happen to anybody gets fresh with your wife,"
said Rudy, and got up and left them.

"There could be a hell of a stink about this. Rudy could lose his
license if the Company wanted to press the point."

"Well, you just see that he doesn't," said Bobbie.

"Maybe it isn't such a good idea, your coming here so often."

"Maybe. On the other hand, maybe it's a wonderful idea. I happen
to think it's a wonderful idea, so I'm going to keep on coming. If *you*
want to go to one of the other places, that's all right. But I like Rudy's.
I like it better than ever, now."

No action was taken against Rudy Schau, and Bobbie visited the
Tavern as frequently as ever. Hartenstein was an unpopular foreman
and the women said he got what had been coming to him for a long
time. Bobbie's friends were pleased that their new symbol had such a
forthright defender. It was even said that Bobbie had saved Hartenstein from a worse beating, a rumor that added to the respect she was
given by the men and the women.

The McCrea children were not being brought up according to Lantenengo Street standards. On the three or four afternoons a week that
Bobbie went to the Tavern she would take her son and daughter to a
neighbor's yard. On the other afternoons the neighbors' children
would play in her yard. During bad weather and the worst of the
winter the McCreas' house was in more frequent service as a nursery,
since some of the neighbors were living in one- or two-room apartments. But none of the children, the McCreas' or the neighbors', had
individual supervision. Children who had learned to walk were separated from those who were still crawling, on the proven theory that
the crawling children were still defenseless against the whimsical
cruelties of the older ones. Otherwise there was no distinction, and all
the children were toughened early in life, as most of their parents had
been. "I guess it's all right," Pete once said to Bobbie. "But I hate to
think what they'll be like when they get older. Little gangsters."

"Well, that was never your trouble, God knows," said Bobbie.
"And I'm no shining example of having a nannie take care of me. Do
you remember my nannie?"

"Vaguely."

" 'Let's go and see the horsies,' she'd say. And we'd go to Mr.

Duncan's stable and I'd come home covered with scratches from the stable cat. And I guess Patrick was covered with scratches from my nannie. Affectionate scratches, of course. Do you remember Mr. Duncan's Patrick?"

"Sure."

"He must have been quite a man. Phyllis used to go there with her nannie, too. But the cat liked Phyllis."

"I'm not suggesting that we have a nannie."

"No. You're suggesting that I stay away from the Tavern."

"In the afternoon."

"The afternoon is the only time the mothers will watch each other's children, except in rare cases. Our kids are all right. I'm with them all day most of the time, and we're home every evening, seven nights a week."

"What else is there to do?"

"Well, for instance once a month we could go to a movie."

"Where? Gibbsville?"

"Yes. Two gallons of gas at the most."

"Are you getting the itch to move back to Gibbsville?"

"Not at all. Are you?"

"Hell, no."

"We could get some high school kid to watch the children. I'd just like to have a change once in a while."

"All right. The next time there's something good at the Globe."

Their first trip to the Globe was their last. They saw no one they knew in the theatre or in the bar of the John Gibb Hotel, and when they came home the high school kid was naked in bed with a man Pete recognized from the plant. "Get out of here," said Pete.

"Is she your kid, McCrea?"

"No, she's not my kid. But did you ever hear of statutory rape?"

"Rape? This kid? I had to wait downstairs, for God's sake. She took on three other guys tonight. Ten bucks a crack."

The girl put on her clothes in sullen silence. She never spoke except to say to the man: "Do you have a room some place?"

"Well," said Pete, when they had gone. "Where did you get her from? The Junior League?"

"If you'd stared at her any more you'd have had to pay ten dollars too."

"For sixteen she had quite a shape."

"She won't have it much longer."

"You got an eyeful, too, don't pretend you didn't."

"Well, at least she won't get pregnant that way. And she *will* get *rich*," said Bobbie.

Pete laughed. "It was really quite funny. Where *did* you get her?"

"If you want her name and telephone number, I have it downstairs. I got her through one of the neighbors. She certainly got the word around quickly enough, where she'd be. There's the doorbell. Another customer?"

Pete went downstairs and informed the stranger at the door that he had the wrong address.

"Another customer, and I think he had two guys with him in the car. Seventy dollars she was going to make tonight. I guess I'm supposed to report this at the plant. We have a sort of a V-D file of known prostitutes. We sic the law on them before they infect the whole outfit, and I'll bet this little character —"

"Good heavens, yes. I must burn everything. Bed linen. Towels. Why the little bitch. Now I'm getting sore." She collected the linen and took it downstairs and to the trash burner in the yard. When she returned Pete was in bed, staring at the ceiling. "I'm going to sleep in the other room," she said.

"What's the matter?"

"I didn't like that tonight. I don't want to sleep with you."

"Oh, all right then, go to hell," said Pete.

She made up one of the beds in the adjoining room. He came and sat on the edge of her bed in the dark. "Go away, Pete," she said.

"Why?"

"Oh, all right, I'll *tell* you why. Tonight made me think of the time you wanted to exchange with Mary and Frank. That's all I've been able to think of."

"That's all passed, Bobbie. I'm not like that any more."

"You would have got in bed with that girl. I saw you."

"Then I'll tell you something. You would have got in bed with that man. I saw you, too. You were excited."

"How could I help being excited, to suddenly come upon something like that. But I was disgusted, too. And still am. Please go away and let me try to get some sleep."

She did not sleep until first light, and when the alarm clock sounded she prepared his and the children's breakfasts. She was tired and nervous throughout the day. She could not go to the Tavern because it was her turn to watch neighbors' children, and Pete telephoned and said bluntly that he would not be home for supper, offering no excuse. He got home after eleven that night, slightly drunk and with lipstick on his neck.

"Who was it? Martie?" said Bobbie.

"What difference does it make who it was? I've been trying to give up other women, but you're no help."

"I have no patience with that kind of excuse. It's easy enough to blame me. Remember, Pete, I can pick up a man as easily as you can make a date with Martie."

"I know you can, and you probably will."

It was the last year of the war, and she had remained faithful to Pete throughout the life of their son Angus. A week later she resumed her affair with Bill Charney. "You never forgot me," he said. "I never forgot you, either, Bobbie. I heard about you and Pete living in Fair Grounds. You know a couple times I took my car and dro' past your house to see which one it was. I didn't know, maybe you'd be sitting out on the front porch and if you saw me, you know. Maybe we just say hello and pass the time of day. But I didn't think no such thing, to tell you the God's honest truth. I got nothing against my wife, only she makes me weary. The house and the kids, she got me going to Mass every Sunday, all like that. But I ain't built that way, Bobbie. I'm the next thing to a hood, and you got that side of you, too. I'll make you any price you say, the other jerks you slept with, they never saw that side of you. You know, you hear a lot about love, Bobbie, but I guess I came closer to it with you than any other woman I ever knew. I never forgot you any more than you ever forgot me. It's what they call a mutual attraction. Like you know one person has it for another person."

"I know."

"I don't see how we stood it as long as we did. Be honest, now, didn't you often wish it was me instead of some other guy?"

"Yes."

"All right, I'll be honest with you. Many's the time in bed with my wife I used to say to myself, 'Peggy, you oughta take lessons from Bobbie McCrea.' But who can give lessons, huh? If you don't have the mutual attraction, you're nothin'. How do you think I look?" He slapped his belly. "You know I weigh the same as I used to weigh? You look good. You put on a little. What? Maybe six pounds?"

"Seven or eight."

"But you got it distributed. In another year Peggy's gonna weigh a hundred and fifty pounds, and I told her, I said either she took some of that off or I'd get another girl. Her heighth, you know. She can't get away with that much weight. I eat everything, but I do a lot of walking and standing. I guess I use up a lot of excess energy. Feel them muscles. Punch me in the belly. I got no fat on me anywhere, Bobbie. For my age I'm a perfect physical specimen. I could get any amount of insurance if I got out of The Numbers. But nobody's gonna knock me off so why do I want insurance? I may even give up The Numbers one of these days. I got a couple of things lined up, strictly, strictly legitimate, and when my kids are ready to go away to school, I may just give up The Numbers. For a price, naturally."

"That brings up a point."

"You need money? How much do you want? It's yours. I *mean* like ten, fifteen gees."

"No, no money. But everybody knows you now. Where can we meet?"

"What's the matter with here? I told you, I own this hotel."

"But I can't just come and go. People know me, too. I have an idea, though."

"What?"

"Buy a motel."

"Buy a motel. You know, that thought crossed me a year ago, but you know what I found out? They don't make money. You'd think they would, but those that come out ahead, you be surprised how little they make."

"There's one near Swedish Haven. It's only about a mile from my house."

"We want a big bed, not them twin beds. I tell you what I could do. I could rent one of the units by the month and move my own furniture in. How would that suit you?"

"I'd like it better if you owned the place."

"Blackmail? Is that what you're thinking about? Who'd blackmail me, Bobbie? Or my girl? I'm still a hood in the eyes of some people."

There was no set arrangement for their meetings. Bill Charney postponed the purchase of the motel until she understood he had no intention of buying it or of making any other arrangement that implied permanence. At first she resented his procrastination, but she discovered that she preferred his way; he would telephone her, she would telephone him whenever desire became urgent, and sometimes they would be together within an hour of the telephone call. They spaced out their meetings so that each one produced novelty and excitement, and a year passed and another and Bobbie passed the afternoon of her fortieth birthday with him.

It was characteristic of their relationship that she did not tell him it was her birthday. He always spoke of his wife and children and his business enterprises, but he did not notice that she never spoke of her home life. He was a completely egocentric man, equally admiring of his star sapphire ring on his strong short-fingered hand and of her slender waist, which in his egocentricity became his possession. Inevitably, because of the nature of his businesses, he had a reputation for being closemouthed, but alone with Bobbie he talked freely. "You know, Bobbie, I laid a friend of yours?"

"Was it fun?"

"Aren't you gonna ask me who?"

"You'll tell me."

"At least I guess she's a friend of yours. Mary Lander."

"She used to be a friend of mine. I haven't seen her in years."

"Yeah. While her husband was in the service. Frank."

"You're so busy, with all your women."

"There's seven days in the week, honey, and it don't take up too much of your time. This didn't last very long, anyway. Five, maybe six times I slept with her. I took her to New York twice, that is I met her there. The other times in her house. You know, she's a neighbor of mine."

"And very neighborly."

"Yeah, that's how it started. She come to my house to collect for something, some war drive, and Peggy said I took care of all them things so when I got home I made out a cheque and took it over to the

Landers' and inside of fifteen minutes — less than that — we were necking all over the parlor. Hell, I knew the minute she opened the door —"

"One of those mutual attractions?"

"Yeah, sure. I gave her the cheque and she said, 'I don't know how to thank you,' and I said if she had a couple minutes I'd show her how. 'Oh, Mr. Charney,' but she didn't even tell me to get out, so I knew I was in."

"What ever broke up this romance?"

"Her. She had some guy in Washington, D.C., she was thinking of marrying, and when I finally got it out of her who the guy was, I powdered out. Joe Whipple. I gotta do business with Joe. We got a home-loan proposition that we're ready to go with any day, and this was three years ago when Joe and I were just talking about it, what they call the talking stage."

"So you're the one that broke it off, not Mary."

"If a guy's looking at you across a desk and thinking you're laying his girl, you stand to get a screwing from that guy. Not that I don't trust Joe, because I do."

"Do you trust Mary?"

"I wondered about that, if she'd blab to Joe. A dame like Mary Lander, is she gonna tell the guy she's thinking of marrying that she's been laying a hood like me? No. By the way, she's queer. She told me she'd go for a girl."

"I'm surprised she hasn't already."

"Maybe she has. I couldn't find out. I always try to find out."

"You never asked me."

"I knew you wouldn't. But a dame like Mary, as soon as she opened the door I knew I was in, but then the next thing is you find out what else she'll go for. In her case, the works, as long as it isn't gonna get around. I guess I always figured her right. I have to figure all angles, men *and* women. That's where my brother Ed was stupid. I used to say to him, find out what kind of a broad a guy goes for before you declare him in. Ed used to say all he had to do was play a game of cards with a guy. But according to my theory, everybody goes into a card game prepared. Both eyes open. But not a guy going after a broad. You find out more from broads, like take for instance Mary. Now I know Frank is married to a dame that is screwing his best friend, laid a hood like me, and will go for a girl. You think I'd ever depend on Frank Lander? No. And Joe Whipple. Married to a lush, and sleeping with his best friend's wife, Mary."

"Then you wouldn't depend on Joe, either?"

"Yes, I would. Women don't bother him. He don't care if his wife is a lush, he'll get his nooky from his best friend's wife, he *isn't* going to marry her because that was three-four years ago, and he's tough about everybody. His wife, his dame, his best friend, *and* the United States government. Because I tell you something, if we ever get going on the home-loan proposition, don't think Joe didn't use his job in Washington every chance he got. The partnership is gonna be me and Joe Whipple, because he's just as tough as I am. And one fine day he'll fall over dead from not taking care of himself, and I'll be the main guy. You know the only thing I don't like about you, Bobbie, is the booze. If you'd lay off the sauce for a year I'd get rid of Peggy, and you and I could get married. But booze is women's weakness like women are men's weakness."

"Men are women's weakness."

"No, you're wrong. Men don't make women talk, men don't make women lose their looks, and women can give up men for a hell of a long time, but a female lush is the worst kind of lush."

"Am I a lush?"

"You have a couple drinks every day, don't you?"

"Yes."

"Then you're on the way. Maybe you only take three-four drinks a day now, but five years from now three or four drinks will get you stewed, so you'll be stewed every day. That's a lush. Peggy eats like a God damn pig, but if she ever started drinking, I'd kick her out. Fortunately her old man died with the D.T.'s, so she's afraid of it."

"Would you mind getting me a nice double Scotch with a little water?"

"Why should I mind?" He grinned from back molar to back molar. "When you got a little load on, you forget home and mother." He got her the drink, she took it in her right hand and slowly poured it down his furry chest. He jumped when the icy drink touched him.

"Thank you so much," she said. "Been a very pleasant afternoon, but the party's over."

"You sore at me?"

"Yes, I am. I don't like being called a lush, and I certainly don't like you to think I'd make a good substitute for Peggy."

"You *are* sore."

"Yes."

The children did not know it was her birthday, but when Pete came home he handed her two parcels. "For me?" she said.

"Not very much imagination, but I didn't have a chance to go to Gibbsville," he said.

One package contained half a dozen nylons, the other a bottle of Chanel Number 5. "Thank you. Just what I wanted. I really did."

He suddenly began to cry, and rushed out of the room.

"Why is Daddy crying?" said their daughter.

"Because it's my birthday and he did a very sweet thing."

"Why should he cry?" said their son. He was nine years old, the daughter eleven.

"Because he's sentimental," said the daughter.

"And it's a very nice thing to be," said Bobbie.

"Aren't you going to go to him?"

"Not quite yet. In a minute. Angus, will you go down to the drug store and get a quart of ice cream? Here's a dollar, and you and your sister may keep the change, divided."

"What flavor?" said the boy.

"Vanilla and strawberry, or whatever else they have."

Pete returned. "Kids gone to bed?"

"I sent them for some ice cream."

"Did they see me bawling?"

"Yes, and I think it did them good. Marjorie understood it. Angus was a little mystified. But it was good for both of them."

"Marjorie understood it? Did you?"

"She said it was because you were sentimental."

He shook his head. "I don't know if you'd call it sentimental. I just couldn't help thinking you were forty years old. Forty. You forty. Bobbie Hammersmith. And all we've been through, and what I've done to you. I know why you married me, Bobbie, but why did you stick it out?"

"Because I married you."

"Yes. Because you married Ichabod. You know, I wasn't in love with you when we were first married. You thought I was, but I wasn't.

It was wonderful, being in bed with you and watching you walking around without any clothes on. Taking a bath. But it was too much for me and that's what started me making passes at everybody. And underneath it all I knew damn well why you married me and I hated you. You were making a fool of me and I kept waiting for you to say this farce was over. If you had, I'd have killed you."

"And I guess rightly."

"And all the later stuff. Running a poolroom and living on Mill Street. I blamed all of that on you. But things are better now since we moved here. Aren't they?"

"Yes, much better, as far as the way we live —"

"That's all I meant. If we didn't have Lantenengo Street and Princeton and those things to look back on, this wouldn't be a bad life for two ordinary people."

"It's not bad," she said.

"It's still pretty bad, but that's because we once had it better. Here's what I want to say. Any time you want to walk out on me, I won't make any fuss. You can have the children, and I won't fight about it. That's my birthday present to you, before it's too late. And I have no plans for myself. I'm not trying to get out of this marriage, but you're forty now and you're entitled to whatever is left."

"Thank you, Pete. I have nobody that wants to marry me."

"Well, maybe not. But you may have, sometime. I love you now, Bobbie, and I never used to. I guess you can't love anybody else while you have no self-respect. When the war was over I was sure I'd get the bounce at the plant, but they like me there, they've kept me on, and that one promotion. We'll never be back on Lantenengo Street, but I think I can count on a job here maybe the rest of my life. In a couple of years we can move to a nicer house."

"I'd rather buy this and fix it up a little. It's a better-built house than the ones they're putting up over on Fair Grounds Heights."

"Well, I'm glad you like it too," he said. "The other thing, that we hardly ever talk about. In fact never talk about. Only fight about sometimes. I'll try, Bobbie. I've been trying."

"I know you have."

"Well — how about you trying, too?"

"I did."

"But not lately. I'm not going to ask you who or when or any of that, but why is it you're faithful to me while I'm chasing after other women, and then when I'm faithful to you, you have somebody else? You're forty now and I'm forty-four. Let's see how long we can go without cheating?"

"You don't mean put a time limit on it, or put up a trophy, like an endurance contest? That's the way it sounds. We both have bad habits, Pete."

"Yes, and I'm the worst. But break it off, Bobbie, whoever it is. Will you please? If it's somebody you're not going to marry, and that's what you said, I've — well, it's a long time since I've cheated, and I like it much better this way. Will you stop seeing this other guy?"

"All right. As a matter of fact I *have* stopped, but don't ask me how long ago."

"I won't ask you anything. And if you fall in love with somebody and want to marry him —"

"And he wants to marry me."

"And he wants to marry you, I'll bow out." He leaned down and kissed her cheek. "I know you better than you think I do, Bobbie."

"That's an irritating statement to make to any woman."

"I guess it is, but not the way I meant it."

Now that is as far as I need go in the story of Pete and Bobbie McCrea. I promised a happy ending, which I shall come to in a moment. We have left Pete and Bobbie in 1947, on Bobbie's fortieth birthday. During the next thirteen years I saw them twice. On one occasion my wife and I spent the night with them in their house in Fair Grounds, which was painted, scrubbed and dusted like the Fair Grounds houses of old. My wife went to bed early, and Pete and Bobbie and I talked until past midnight, and then Pete retired and Bobbie and I continued our conversation until three in the morning. Twice she emptied our ash trays of cigarette butts, and we drank a drip-flask of coffee. It seemed to me that she was so thorough in her description of their life because she felt that the dinginess would vanish if she once succeeded in exposing it. But as we were leaving in the morning I was not so sure that it had vanished. My wife said to me: "Did she get it all out of her system?"

"Get what out of her system?"

"I don't know, but I don't think she did, entirely."

"That would be asking too much," I said. "But I guess she's happy."

"Content, but not happy," said my wife. "But the children are what interested me. The girl is going to be attractive in a few more years, but that boy! You didn't talk to him, but do you know about him? He's fourteen, and he's already passed his senior mathematics. He's *finished* the work that the high school seniors are supposed to be taking. The principal is trying to arrange correspondence courses for him. He's the brightest student they ever had in Fair Grounds High School, ever, and all the scientific men at the aluminum plant know about him. And he's a good-looking boy, too."

"Bobbie didn't tell me any of this."

"And I'll bet I know why. He's their future. With you she wanted to get rid of the past. She adores this boy, adores him. That part's almost terrifying."

"Not to me," I said. "It's the best thing that could have happened to her, and to Pete. The only thing that's terrifying is that they could have ruined it. And believe me, they could have."

In 1960, then, I saw Pete and Bobbie again. They invited me, of all their old friends, to go with them to the Princeton commencement. Angus McCrea, Junior, led his class, was awarded the mathematics prize, the physics prize, the Eubank Prize for scholarship, and some other honors that I am sure are listed in the program. I could not read the program because I was crying most of the time. Pete would lean forward in his chair, listening to the things that were being said about his son, but in an attitude that would have been more suitable to a man who was listening to a pronouncement of sentence. Bobbie sat erect and smiling, but every once in a while I could hear her whisper, "Oh, God. Oh, God."

There, I guess, is our happy ending.

If They Hang You (excerpt)

by Dashiell Hammett

The Maltese Falcon *is the well-known tale of some suave crooks in search of an ebony-colored bird and its priceless cache of jewels. Pitted against them as he investigates a series of murders is Sam Spade, a smart and tough detective, gifted with purity of sentiment. In the middle: Brigid O'Shaughnessy, Sam's client, another pursuer of the bird. This scene is from the novel's final chapter. All the murders have been solved but one: the killing of Miles Archer, Sam's partner. Sam and Brigid are alone in Spade's apartment. If love is greed for most of the story's characters — Gutman, Cairo, Jacobi, Thursby — for Spade, love is something else again. He puts down the phone after alerting the police to the whereabouts of the conspirators. What follows is not your ordinary lovers' quarrel. — L.R.*

HE TURNED and took three long swift steps into the living-room.

Brigid O'Shaughnessy, startled by the suddenness of his approach, let her breath out in a little laughing gasp.

Spade, face to face with her, very close to her, tall, big-boned and thick-muscled, coldly smiling, hard of jaw and eye, said: "They'll talk when they're nailed — about us. We're sitting on dynamite, and we've only got minutes to get set for the police. Give me all of it — fast. Gutman sent you and Cairo to Constantinople?"

She started to speak, hesitated, and bit her lip.

He put a hand on her shoulder. "God damn you, talk!" he said. "I'm in this with you and you're not going to gum it. Talk. He sent you to Constantinople?"

"Y-yes, he sent me. I met Joe there and — and asked him to help me. Then we —"

"Wait. You asked Cairo to help you get it from Kemidov?"

"Yes."

"For Gutman?"

She hesitated again, squirmed under the hard angry glare of his eyes, swallowed, and said: "No, not then. We thought we would get it for ourselves."

"All right. Then?"

"Oh, then I began to be afraid that Joe wouldn't play fair with me, so — so I asked Floyd Thursby to help me."

"And he did. Well?"

"Well, we got it and went to Hongkong."

"With Cairo? Or had you ditched him before that?"

"Yes. We left him in Constantinople, in jail — something about a check."

"Something you fixed up to hold him there?"

She looked shamefacedly at Spade and whispered: "Yes."

"Right. Now you and Thursby are in Hongkong with the bird."

"Yes, and then — I didn't know him very well — I didn't know whether I could trust him. I thought it would be safer — anyway, I met Captain Jacobi and I knew his boat was coming here, so I asked him to bring a package for me — and that was the bird. I wasn't sure I could trust Thursby, or that Joe or — or somebody working for Gutman might not be on the boat we came on — and that seemed the safest plan."

"All right. Then you and Thursby caught one of the fast boats over. Then what?"

"Then — then I was afraid of Gutman. I knew he had people — connections — everywhere, and he'd soon know what we had done. And I was afraid he'd have learned that we had left Hongkong for San Francisco. He was in New York and I knew if he heard that by cable he would have plenty of time to get here by the time we did, or before. He did. I didn't know that then, but I was afraid of it, and I had to wait here until Captain Jacobi's boat arrived. And I was afraid Gutman would find me — or find Floyd and buy him over. That's why I came to you and asked you to watch him for —"

"That's a lie," Spade said. "You had Thursby hooked and you knew it. He was a sucker for women. His record shows that — the only falls he took were over women. And once a chump, always a chump. Maybe you didn't know his record, but you'd know you had him safe."

She blushed and looked timidly at him.

He said: "You wanted to get him out of the way before Jacobi came with the loot. What was your scheme?"

"I — I knew he'd left the States with a gambler after some trouble. I didn't know what it was, but I thought that if it was anything serious and he saw a detective watching him he'd think it was on account of the old trouble, and would be frightened into going away. I didn't think —"

"You told him he was being shadowed," Spade said confidently. "Miles hadn't many brains, but he wasn't clumsy enough to be spotted the first night."

"I told him, yes. When we went out for a walk that night I pretended to discover Mr. Archer following us and pointed him out to Floyd." She sobbed. "But please believe, Sam, that I wouldn't have done it if I had thought Floyd would kill him. I thought he'd be frightened into leaving the city. I didn't for a minute think he'd shoot him like that."

Spade smiled wolfishly with his lips, but not at all with his eyes. He said: "If you thought he wouldn't you were right, angel."

The girl's upraised face held utter astonishment.

Spade said: "Thursby didn't shoot him."

Incredulity joined astonishment in the girl's face.

Spade said: "Miles hadn't many brains, but, Christ! he had too many years' experience as a detective to be caught like that by the man he was shadowing. Up a blind alley with his gun tucked away on his hip and his overcoat buttoned? Not a chance. He was as dumb as any man ought to be, but he wasn't quite that dumb. The only two ways out of the alley could be watched from the edge of Bush Street over the tunnel. You'd told us Thursby was a bad actor. He couldn't have tricked Miles into the alley like that, and he couldn't have driven him in. He was dumb, but not dumb enough for that."

He ran his tongue over the inside of his lips and smiled affectionately at the girl. He said: "But he'd've gone up there with you, angel, if he was sure nobody else was up there. You were his client, so he would have had no reason for not dropping the shadow on your say-so, and if you caught up with him and asked him to go up there he'd've gone. He was just dumb enough for that. He'd've looked you up and down and licked his lips and gone grinning from ear to ear — and then you could've stood as close to him as you liked in the dark and put a hole through him with the gun you had got from Thursby that evening."

Brigid O'Shaughnessy shrank back from him until the edge of the table stopped her. She looked at him with terrified eyes and cried: "Don't — don't talk to me like that, Sam! You know I didn't! You know —"

"Stop it." He looked at the watch on his wrist. "The police will be blowing in any minute now and we're sitting on dynamite. Talk!"

She put the back of a hand on her forehead. "Oh, why do you accuse me of such a terrible —?"

"Will you stop it?" he demanded in a low impatient voice. "This isn't the spot for the schoolgirl-act. Listen to me. The pair of us are sitting under the gallows." He took hold of her wrists and made her stand up straight in front of him. "Talk!"

"I — I — How did you know he — he licked his lips and looked —?"

Spade laughed harshly. "I knew Miles. But never mind that. Why did you shoot him?"

She twisted her wrists out of Spade's fingers and put her hands up around the back of his neck, pulling his head down until his mouth all but touched hers. Her body was flat against his from knees to chest. He put his arms around her, holding her tight to him. Her dark-lashed lids were half down over velvet eyes. Her voice was hushed, throbbing: "I didn't mean to, at first. I didn't, really. I meant what I told you, but when I saw Floyd couldn't be frightened I —"

Spade slapped her shoulder. He said: "That's a lie. You asked Miles and me to handle it ourselves. You wanted to be sure the shadower was somebody you knew and who knew you, so they'd go with you. You got the gun from Thursby that day — that night. You had already rented the apartment at the Coronet. You had trunks there and none at the hotel and when I looked the apartment over I found a rent-receipt dated five or six days before the time you told me you rented it."

She swallowed with difficulty and her voice was humble. "Yes, that's a lie, Sam. I did intend to if Floyd — I — I can't look at you and tell you this, Sam." She pulled his head farther down until her cheek was against his cheek, her mouth by his ear, and whispered: "I knew Floyd wouldn't be easily frightened, but I thought that if he knew somebody was shadowing him either he'd — Oh, I can't say it, Sam!" She clung to him, sobbing.

Spade said: "You thought Floyd would tackle him and one or the other of them would go down. If Thursby was the one then you were rid of him. If Miles was, then you could see that Floyd was caught and you'd be rid of him. That it?"

"S-something like that."

"And when you found that Thursby didn't mean to tackle him you borrowed the gun and did it yourself. Right?"

"Yes — though not exactly."

"But exact enough. And you had that plan up your sleeve from the first. You thought Floyd would be nailed for the killing."

"I — I thought they'd hold him at least until after Captain Jacobi had arrived with the falcon and —"

"And you didn't know then that Gutman was here hunting for you. You didn't suspect that or you wouldn't have shaken your gunman. You knew Gutman was here as soon as you heard Thursby had been shot. Then you knew you needed another protector, so you came back to me. Right?"

"Yes, but — oh, sweetheart! — it wasn't only that. I would have come back to you sooner or later. From the first instant I saw you I knew —"

Spade said tenderly: "You angel! Well, if you get a good break you'll be out of San Quentin in twenty years and you can come back to me then."

She took her cheek away from his, drawing her head far back to stare up without comprehension at him.

He was pale. He said tenderly: "I hope to Christ they don't hang you, precious, by that sweet neck." He slid his hands up to caress her throat.

In an instant she was out of his arms, back against the table, crouching, both hands spread over her throat. Her face was wild-eyed, haggard. Her dry mouth opened and closed. She said in a small parched voice: "You're not —" She could get no other words out.

Spade's face was yellow-white now. His mouth smiled and there were smile-wrinkles around his glittering eyes. His voice was soft, gentle. He said: "I'm going to send you over. The chances are you'll get off with life. That means you'll be out again in twenty years. You're an angel. I'll wait for you." He cleared his throat. "If they hang you I'll always remember you."

She dropped her hands and stood erect. Her face became smooth and untroubled except for the faintest of dubious glints in her eyes. She smiled back at him, gently. "Don't, Sam, don't say that even in fun. Oh, you frightened me for a moment! I really thought you — You know you do such wild and unpredictable things that —" She broke off. She thrust her face forward and stared deep into his eyes. Her cheeks and the flesh around her mouth shivered and fear came back into her eyes. "What —? Sam!" She put her hands to her throat again and lost her erectness.

Spade laughed. His yellow-white face was damp with sweat and though he held his smile he could not hold softness in his voice. He croaked: "Don't be silly. You're taking the fall. One of us has got to take it, after the talking those birds will do. They'd hang me sure. You're likely to get a better break. Well?"

"But — but, Sam, you can't! Not after what we've been to each other. You can't —"

"Like hell I can't."

She took a long trembling breath. "You've been playing with me? Only pretending you cared — to trap me like this? You didn't — care at all? You didn't — don't — l-love me?"

"I think I do," Spade said. "What of it?" The muscles holding his smile in place stood out like wales. "I'm not Thursby. I'm not Jacobi. I won't play the sap for you."

"That is not just," she cried. Tears came to her eyes. "It's unfair. It's contemptible of you. You know it was not that. You can't say that."

"Like hell I can't," Spade said. "You came into my bed to stop me asking questions. You led me out yesterday for Gutman with that phoney call for help. Last night you came here with them and waited outside for me and came in with me. You were in my arms when the trap was sprung — I couldn't have gone for a gun if I'd had one on me and couldn't have made a fight of it if I had wanted to. And if they didn't take you away with them it was only because Gutman's got too much sense to trust you except for short stretches when he has to and because he thought I'd play the sap for you and — not wanting to hurt you — wouldn't be able to hurt him."

Brigid O'Shaughnessy blinked her tears away. She took a step towards him and stood looking him in the eyes, straight and proud. "You called me a liar," she said. "Now you are lying. You're lying if you say you don't know down in your heart that, in spite of anything I've done, I love you."

Spade made a short abrupt bow. His eyes were becoming bloodshot, but there was no other change in his damp and yellowish fixedly smiling face. "Maybe I do," he said. "What of it? I should trust you? You who arranged that nice little trick for — for my predecessor, Thursby? You who knocked off Miles, a man you had nothing against, in cold blood, just like swatting a fly, for the sake of double-crossing Thursby? You who double-crossed Gutman, Cairo, Thursby — one, two, three? You who've never played square with me for half an hour at a stretch since I've known you? I should trust you? No, no, darling. I wouldn't do it even if I could. Why should I?"

Her eyes were steady under his and her hushed voice was steady when she replied: "Why should you? If you've been playing with me, if you do not love me, there is no answer to that. If you did, no answer would be needed."

Blood streaked Spade's eyeballs now and his long-held smile had become a frightful grimace. He cleared his throat huskily and said: "Making speeches is no damned good now." He put a hand on her shoulder. The hand shook and jerked. "I don't care who loves who I'm not going to play the sap for you. I won't walk in Thursby's and Christ knows who else's footsteps. You killed Miles and you're going over for it. I could have helped you by letting the others go and standing off the police the best way I could. It's too late for that now. I can't help you now. And I wouldn't if I could."

She put a hand on his hand on her shoulder. "Don't help me then," she whispered, "but don't hurt me. Let me go away now."

"No," he said. "I'm sunk if I haven't got you to hand over to the police when they come. That's the only thing that can keep me from going down with the others."

"You won't do that for me?"

"I won't play the sap for you."

"Don't say that, please." She took his hand from her shoulder and held it to her face. "Why must you do this to me, Sam? Surely Mr. Archer wasn't as much to you as —"

"Miles," Spade said hoarsely, "was a son of a bitch. I found that out the first week we were in business together and I meant to kick him out as soon as the year was up. You didn't do me a damned bit of harm by killing him."

"Then what?"

Spade pulled his hand out of hers. He no longer either smiled or grimaced. His wet yellow face was set hard and deeply lined. His eyes burned madly. He said: "Listen. This isn't a damned bit of good. You'll never understand me, but I'll try once more and then we'll give it up. Listen. When a man's partner is killed he's supposed to do something about it. It doesn't make any difference what you thought of him. He was your partner and you're supposed to do something about it. Then it happens we were in the detective business. Well, when one of your organization gets killed it's bad business to let the killer get away with it. It's bad all around — bad for that one organization, bad for every detective everywhere. Third, I'm a detective and expecting me to run criminals down and then let them go free is like asking a dog to catch a rabbit and let it go. It can be done, all right, and sometimes it is done, but it's not the natural thing. The only way I could have let you go was by letting Gutman and Cairo and the kid go. That's —"

"You're not serious," she said. "You don't expect me to think that these things you're saying are sufficient reason for sending me to the —"

"Wait till I'm through and then you can talk. Fourth, no matter what I wanted to do now it would be absolutely impossible for me to let you go without having myself dragged to the gallows with the others. Next, I've no reason in God's world to think I can trust you and if I did this and got away with it you'd have something on me that you could use whenever you happened to want to. That's five of them. The sixth would be that, since I've also got something on you, I couldn't be sure you wouldn't decide to shoot a hole in me some day. Seventh, I don't even like the idea of thinking that there might be one chance in a hundred that you'd played me for a sucker. And eighth — but that's enough. All those on one side. Maybe some of them are unimportant. I won't argue about that. But look at the number of them. Now on the other side we've got what? All we've got is the fact that maybe you love me and maybe I love you."

"You know," she whispered, "whether you do or not."

"I don't. It's easy enough to be nuts about you." He looked hungrily from her hair to her feet and up to her eyes again. "But I don't know what that amounts to. Does anybody ever? But suppose I do? What of it? Maybe next month I won't. I've been through it before — when it lasted that long. Then what? Then I'll think I played the sap. And if I did it and got sent over then I'd be sure I was the sap. Well, if I send you over I'll be sorry as hell — I'll have some rotten nights — but that'll pass. Listen." He took her by the shoulders and bent her back, leaning over her. "If that doesn't mean anything to you forget it and we'll make it this: I won't because all of me wants to — wants to say to hell with the consequences and do it — and because — God damn you — you've counted on that with me the same as you counted on that with the others." He took his hands from her shoulders and let them fall to his sides.

She put her hands up to his cheeks and drew his face down again. "Look at me," she said, "and tell me the truth. Would you have done this to me if the falcon had been real and you had been paid your money?"

"What difference does that make now? Don't be too sure I'm as crooked as I'm supposed to be. That kind of reputation might be good business — bringing in high-priced jobs and making it easier to deal with the enemy."

She looked at him, saying nothing.

He moved his shoulders a little and said: "Well, a lot of money would have been at least one more item on the other side of the scales."

She put her face up to his face. Her mouth was slightly open with lips a little thrust out. She whispered: "If you loved me you'd need nothing more on that side."

Spade set the edges of his teeth together and said through them: "I won't play the sap for you."

She put her mouth to his, slowly, her arms around him, and came into his arms. She was in his arms when the door-bell rang.

Spade, left arm around Brigid O'Shaughnessy, opened the corridor-door. Lieutenant Dundy, Detective-sergeant Tom Polhaus, and two other detectives were there.

Spade said: "Hello, Tom. Get them?"

Polhaus said: "Got them."

"Swell. Come in. Here's another one for you." Spade pressed the girl forward. "She killed Miles."

Lila the Werewolf

by Peter Beagle

LILA BRAUN had been living with Farrell for three weeks before he found out she was a werewolf. They had met at a party when the moon was a few nights past the full, and by the time it had withered to the shape of a lemon Lila had moved her suitcase, her guitar, and her Ewan MacColl records two blocks north and four blocks west to Farrell's apartment on Ninety-Eighth Street. Girls sometimes happened to Farrell like that.

One evening Lila wasn't in when Farrell came home from work at the bookstore. She had left a note on the table, under a can of tunafish. The note said that she had gone up to the Bronx to have dinner with her mother, and would probably be spending the night there. The cole slaw in the refrigerator should be finished up before it went bad.

Farrell ate the tunafish and gave the cole slaw to Grunewald. Grunewald was a half-grown Russian wolfhound, the color of sour milk. He looked like a goat, and had no outside interests except shoes. Farrell was taking care of him for a girl who was away in Europe for the summer. She sent Grunewald a tape recording of her voice every week.

Farrell went to a movie with a friend, and to the West End afterward for beer. Then he walked home alone under the full moon, which was red and yellow. He reheated the morning coffee, played a record, read through a week-old "News Of The Week In Review" section of the Sunday *Times*, and finally took Grunewald up to the roof for the night, as he always did. The dog had been accustomed to sleep in the same bed with his mistress, and the point was not negotiable. Grunewald mooed and scrabbled and butted all the way, but Farrell pushed him out among the looming chimneys and ventilators and slammed the door. Then he came back downstairs and went to bed.

He slept very badly. Grunewald's baying woke him twice; and there was something else that brought him half out of bed, thirsty and lonely, with his sinuses full and the night swaying like a curtain as the figures of his dream scurried offstage. Grunewald seemed to have gone off the air — perhaps it was the silence that had awakened him. Whatever the reason, he never really got back to sleep.

He was lying on his back, watching a chair with his clothes on it becoming a chair again, when the wolf came in through the open window. It landed lightly in the middle of the room and stood there for a moment, breathing quickly, with its ears back. There was blood on the wolf's teeth and tongue, and blood on its chest.

Farrell, whose true gift was for acceptance, especially in the morning, accepted the idea that there was a wolf in his bedroom and lay quite still, closing his eyes as the grim, black-lipped head swung toward him. Having once worked at a zoo, he was able to recognize the beast as a Central European subspecies: smaller and lighter-boned than the northern timber wolf variety, lacking the thick, ruffy mane at the shoulders and having a more pointed nose and ears. His own pedantry always delighted him, even at the worst moments.

Blunt claws clicking on the linoleum, then silent on the throw rug by the bed. Something warm and slow splashed down on his shoulder, but he never moved. The wild smell of the wolf was over him, and that did frighten him at last — to be in the same room with that smell and the Miró prints on the walls. Then he felt the sunlight on his eyelids, and at the same moment he heard the wolf moan softly and deeply. The sound was not repeated, but the breath on his face was suddenly sweet and smoky, dizzyingly familiar after the other. He opened his eyes and saw Lila. She was sitting naked on the edge of the bed, smiling, with her hair down.

"Hello, baby," she said. "Move over, baby. I came home."

Farrell's gift was for acceptance. He was perfectly willing to believe that he had dreamed the wolf; to believe Lila's story of boiled chicken and bitter arguments and sleeplessness on Tremont Avenue; and to forget that her first caress had been to bite him on the shoulder, hard enough so that the blood crusting there as he got up and made breakfast might very well be his own. But then he left the coffee perking and went up to the roof to get Grunewald. He found the dog sprawled in a grove of TV antennas, looking more like a goat than ever, with his throat torn out. Farrell had never actually seen an animal with its throat torn out.

The coffeepot was still chuckling when he came back into the apartment, which struck him as very odd. You could have either werewolves or Pyrex nine-cup percolators in the world, but not both, surely. He told Lila, watching her face. She was a small girl, not really pretty, but with good eyes and a lovely mouth, and with a curious sullen gracefulness that had been the first thing to speak to Farrell at the party. When he told her how Grunewald had looked, she shivered all over, once.

"Ugh!" she said, wrinkling her lips back from her neat white teeth. "Oh baby, how awful. Poor Grunewald. Oh, poor Barbara." Barbara was Grunewald's owner.

"Yeah," Farrell said. "Poor Barbara, making her little tapes in Saint-Tropez." He could not look away from Lila's face.

She said, "Wild dogs. Not really wild, I mean, but with owners. You hear about it sometimes, how a pack of them get together and attack children and things, running through the streets. Then they go home and eat their Dog Yummies. The scary thing is that they probably live right around here. Everybody on the block seems to have a dog. God, that's scary. Poor Grunewald."

"They didn't tear him up much," Farrell said. "It must have been just for the fun of it. And the blood. I didn't know dogs killed for the blood. He didn't have any blood left."

The tip of Lila's tongue appeared between her lips, in the unknowing reflex of a fondled cat. As evidence, it wouldn't have stood up even in old Salem; but Farrell knew the truth then, beyond laziness or rationalization, and went on buttering toast for Lila. Farrell had nothing against werewolves, and he had never liked Grunewald.

He told his friend Ben Kassoy about Lila when they met in the Automat for lunch. He had to shout it over the clicking and rattling all around them, but the people sitting six inches away on either hand never looked up. New Yorkers never eavesdrop. They hear only what they simply cannot help hearing.

Ben said, "I told you about Bronx girls. You better come stay at my place for a few days."

Farrell shook his head. "No, that's silly. I mean, it's only Lila. If she were going to hurt me, she could have done it last night. Besides, it won't happen again for a month. There has to be a full moon."

His friend stared at him. "So what? What's that got to do with anything? You going to go on home as though nothing had happened?"

"Not as though nothing had happened," Farrell said lamely. "The thing is, it's still only Lila, not Lon Chaney or somebody. Look, she goes to her psychiatrist three afternoons a week, and she's got her guitar lesson one night a week, and her pottery class one night, and she cooks eggplant maybe twice a week. She calls her mother every Friday night, and one night a month she turns into a wolf. You see what I'm getting at? It's still Lila, whatever she does, and I just can't get terribly shook about it. A little bit, sure, because what the hell. But I don't know. Anyway, there's no mad rush about it. I'll talk to her when the thing comes up in the conversation, just naturally. It's okay."

Ben said, "God damn. You see why nobody has any respect for liberals anymore? Farrell, I know you. You're just scared of hurting her feelings."

"Well, it's that too," Farrell agreed, a little embarrassed. "I hate confrontations. If I break up with her now, she'll think I'm doing it because she's a werewolf. It's awkward, it feels nasty and middle-class. I should have broken up with her the first time I met her mother, or the second time she served the eggplant. Her mother, boy, there's the real werewolf, there's somebody I'd wear wolfbane against, that woman. Damn, I wish I hadn't found out. I don't think I've ever found out anything about people that I was the better for knowing."

Ben walked all the way back to the bookstore with him, arguing. It touched Farrell, because Ben hated to walk. Before they parted, Ben suggested, "At least you could try some of that stuff you were talking about, the wolfbane. There's garlic, too — you put some in a little bag and wear it around your neck. Don't laugh, man. If there's such a thing as werewolves, the other stuff must be real too. Cold iron, silver, oak, running water —"

"I'm not laughing at you," Farrell said, but he was still grinning. "Lila's shrink says she has a rejection thing, very deep-seated, take us years to break through all that scar tissue. Now if I start walking around wearing amulets and mumbling in Latin every time she looks at me, who knows how far it'll set her back? Listen, I've done some things I'm not proud of, but I don't want to mess up anyone's analysis. That's the sin against God." He sighed and slapped Ben lightly on the arm. "Don't worry about it. We'll work it out, I'll talk to her."

But between that night and the next full moon, he found no good, casual way of bringing the subject up. Admittedly, he did not try as hard as he might have: it was true that he feared confrontations more than he feared werewolves, and he would have found it almost as difficult to talk to Lila about her guitar playing, or her pots, or the political arguments she got into at parties. "The thing is," he said to Ben, "it's sort of one more little weakness not to take advantage of. In a way."

They made love often that month. The smell of Lila flowered in the bedroom, where the smell of the wolf still lingered almost visibly, and both of them were wild, heavy zoo smells, warm and raw and fearful, the sweeter for being savage. Farrell held Lila in his arms and knew what she was, and he was always frightened; but he would not have let her go if she had turned into a wolf again as he held her. It was a relief to peer at her while she slept and see how stubby and childish her fingernails were, or that the skin around her mouth was rashy because she had been snacking on chocolate. She loved secret sweets, but they always betrayed her.

It's only Lila after all, he would think as he drowsed off. Her mother used to hide the candy, but Lila always found it. Now she's a big girl, neither married nor in a graduate school, but living in sin with an Irish musician, and she can have all the candy she wants. What kind of a werewolf is that. Poor Lila, practicing *Who killed Davey Moore? Why did he die? . . .*

The note said that she would be working late at the magazine, on layout, and might have to be there all night. Farrell put on about four feet of Telemann laced with Django Reinhardt, took down *The Golden*

Bough, and settled into a chair by the window. The moon shone in at him, bright and thin and sharp as the lid of a tin can, and it did not seem to move at all as he dozed and woke.

Lila's mother called several times during the night, which was interesting. Lila still picked up her mail and most messages at her old apartment, and her two roommates covered for her when necessary, but Farrell was absolutely certain that her mother knew she was living with him. Farrell was an expert on mothers. Mrs. Braun called him Joe each time she called and that made him wonder, for he knew she hated him. *Does she suspect that we share a secret? Ah, poor Lila.*

The last time the telephone woke him, it was still dark in the room, but the traffic lights no longer glittered through rings of mist, and the cars made a different sound on the warming pavement. A man was saying clearly in the street, "Well, *I'd* shoot'm. *I'd* shoot'm." Farrell let the telephone ring ten times before he picked it up.

"Let me talk to Lila," Mrs. Braun said.

"She isn't here." *What if the sun catches her, what if she turns back to herself in front of a cop, or a bus driver, or a couple of nuns going to early Mass?* "Lila isn't here, Mrs. Braun."

"I have reason to believe that's not true." The fretful, muscular voice had dropped all pretense of warmth. "I want to talk to Lila."

Farrell was suddenly dry-mouthed and shivering with fury. It was her choice of words that did it. "Well, I have reason to believe you're a suffocating old bitch and a bourgeois Stalinist. How do you like them apples, Mrs. B?" As though his anger had summoned her, the wolf was standing two feet away from him. Her coat was dark and lank with sweet, and yellow saliva was mixed with the blood that strung from her jaws. She looked at Farrell and growled far away in her throat.

"Just a minute," he said. He covered the receiver with his palm. "It's for you," he said to the wolf. "It's your mother."

The wolf made a pitiful sound, almost inaudible, and scuffed at the floor. She was plainly exhausted. Mrs. Braun pinged in Farrell's ear like a bug against a lighted window. "What, what? Hello, what is this? Listen, you put Lila on the phone right now. Hello? I want to talk to Lila. I know she's there."

Farrell hung up just as the sun touched a corner of the window. The wolf became Lila. As before, she only made one sound. The phone rang again, and she picked it up without a glance at Farrell. "Bernice?" Lila always called her mother by her first name. "Yes — no, no — yeah, I'm fine. I'm all right, I just forgot to call. No, I'm all right, will you listen? Bernice, there's no law that says you have to get hysterical. Yes, you are." She dropped down on the bed, groping under her pillow for cigarettes. Farrell got up and began to make coffee.

"Well, there was a little trouble," Lila was saying. "See, I went to the Zoo, because I couldn't find — Bernice, I know, I *know*, but that was, what, three months ago. The thing is, I didn't think they'd have their horns so soon. Bernice, I had to, that's all. There'd only been a couple of cats and a — well, sure they chased me, but I — well, Momma, Bernice, what did you want me to do? Just what did you want me to do? You're always so dramatic — why do I shout? I shout because I can't get you to listen to me any other way. You remember what Dr. Schechtman said — what? No, I told you, I just forgot to call. No, that is the reason, that's the real and only reason. Well, whose fault is that? What? Oh, Bernice. Jesus Christ, Bernice. All right, *how* is it Dad's fault?"

She didn't want the coffee, or any breakfast but she sat at the table in his bathrobe and drank milk greedily. It was the first time he had ever seen her drink milk. Her face was sandy-pale, and her eyes were red. Talking to her mother left her looking as though she had actually gone ten rounds with the woman. Farrell asked, "How long has it been happening?"

"Nine years," Lila said. "Since I hit puberty. First day, cramps; the second day, this. My introduction to womanhood." She snickered and spilled her milk. "I want some more," she said. "Got to get rid of that taste."

"Who knows about it?" he asked. "Pat and Janet?" They were the two girls she had been rooming with.

"God, no. I'd never tell them. I've never told a girl. Bernice knows, of course, and Dr. Schechtman — he's my head doctor. And you now. That's all." Farrell waited. She was a bad liar, and only did it to heighten the effect of the truth. "Well, there was Mickey," she said. "The guy I told you about the first night, you remember? It doesn't matter. He's an acidhead in Vancouver, of all the places. He'll never tell anybody."

He thought: I wonder if any girl has ever talked about me in that sort of voice. I doubt it, offhand. Lila said, "It wasn't too hard to keep it secret. I missed a lot of things. Like I never could go to the riding camp, and I still want to. And the senior play, when I was in high school. They picked me to play the girl in *Liliom*, but then they changed the evening, and I had to say I was sick. And the winter's bad, because the sun sets so early. But actually, it's been a lot less trouble than my god-damn allergies." She made a laugh, but Farrell did not respond.

"Dr. Schechtman says it's a sex thing," she offered. "He says it'll take years and years to cure it. Bernice thinks I should go to someone else, but I don't want to be one of those women who runs around changing shrinks like hair colors. Pat went through five of them in a month one time. Joe, I wish you'd say something. Or just go away."

"Is it only dogs?" he asked. Lila's face did not change, but her chair rattled, and the milk went over again. Farrell said, "Answer me. Do you only kill dogs, and cats, and zoo animals?"

The tears began to come, heavy and slow, bright as knives in the morning sunlight. She could not look at him; and when she tried to speak she could only make creaking, cartilaginous sounds in her throat. "*You* don't know," she whispered at last. "You don't have any idea what it's like."

"That's true," he answered. He was always very fair about that particular point.

He took her hand, and then she really began to cry. Her sobs were horrible to hear, much more frightening to Farrell than any wolf noises. When he held her, she rolled in his arms like a stranded ship with the waves slamming into her. I always get the criers, he thought sadly. My girls always cry, sooner or later. But never for me.

"Don't leave me!" she wept. "I don't know why I came to live with you — I knew it wouldn't work — but don't leave me! There's just Bernice and Dr. Schechtman, and it's so lonely. I want somebody else, I get so lonely. Don't leave me, Joe. I love you, Joe. I love you."

She was patting his face as though she were blind. Farrell stroked her hair and kneaded the back of her neck, wishing that her mother would call again. He felt skilled and weary, and without desire. I'm doing it again, he thought.

"I love you," Lila said. And he answered her, thinking, I'm doing it again. That's the great advantage of making the same mistake a lot of times. You come to know it, and you can study it and get inside it, really make it yours. It's the same good old mistake, except this time the girl's hangup is different. But it's the same thing. I'm doing it again.

The building superintendent was thirty or fifty: dark, thin, quick and shivering. A Lithuanian or a Latvian, he spoke very little English. He smelled of black friction tape and stale water, and he was strong in the twisting way that a small, lean animal is strong. His eyes were almost purple, and they bulged a little, straining out — the terrible eyes of a herald angel stricken dumb. He roamed in the basement all day, banging on pipes and taking the elevator apart.

The superintendent met Lila only a few hours after Farrell did; on that first night, when she came home with him. At the sight of her the little man jumped back, dropping the two-legged chair he was carrying. He promptly fell over it, and did not try to get up, but cowered there, clucking and gulping, trying to cross himself and make the sign of the horns at the same time. Farrell started to help him up, but he screamed. They could hardly hear the sound.

It would have been merely funny and embarrassing, except for the fact that Lila was equally as frightened of the superintendent, from that moment. She would not go down to the basement for any reason, nor would she enter or leave the house until she was satisfied that he was nowhere near. Farrell had thought then that she took the superintendent for a lunatic.

"I don't know how he knows," he said to Ben. "I guess if you believe in werewolves and vampires, you probably recognize them right away. I don't believe in them at all, and I live with one."

He lived with Lila all through the autumn and the winter. They went out together and came home, and her cooking improved slightly, and she gave up the guitar and got a kitten named Theodora. Sometimes she wept, but not often. She turned out not to be a real crier.

She told Dr. Schechtman about Farrell, and he said that it would probably be a very beneficial relationship for her. It wasn't, but it wasn't a particularly bad one either. Their love-making was usually good, though it bothered Farrell to suspect that it was the sense and smell of the Other that excited him. For the rest, they came near being friends. Farrell had known that he did not love Lila before he found out that she was a werewolf, and this made him feel a great deal easier about being bored with her.

"It'll break up by itself in the spring," he said, "like ice."

Ben asked, "What if it doesn't?" They were having lunch in the Automat again. "What'll you do if it just goes on?"

"It's not that easy." Farrell looked away from his friend and began to explore the mysterious, swampy innards of his beef pie. He said, "The trouble is that I know her. That was the real mistake. You shouldn't get to know people if you know you're not going to stay with them, one way or another. It's all right if you come and go in ignorance, but you shouldn't know them."

A week or so before the full moon, she would start to become nervous and strident, and this would continue until the day preceding her transformation. On that day, she was invariably loving, in the tender, desperate manner of someone who is going away; but the next day would see her silent, speaking only when she had to. She always had a cold on the last day, and looked gray and patchy and sick, but she usually went to work anyway.

Farrell was sure, though she never talked about it, that the change into wolf shape was actually peaceful for her, though the returning hurt. Just before moonrise she would take off her clothes and take the pins out of her hair, and stand waiting. Farrell never managed not to close his eyes when she dropped heavily down on all fours; but there was a moment before that when her face would grow a look that he never saw at any other time, except when they were making love. Each time he saw it, it struck him as a look of wondrous joy at not being Lila any more.

"See, I know her," he tried to explain to Ben. "She only likes to go to color movies, because wolves can't see color. She can't stand the Modern Jazz Quartet, but that's all she plays the first couple of days afterward. Stupid things like that. Never gets high at parties, because she's afraid she'll start talking. It's hard to walk away, that's all. Taking what I know with me."

Ben asked, "Is she still scared of the super?"

"Oh, God," Farrell said. "She got his dog last time. It was a Dalmatian — good-looking animal. She didn't know it was his. He doesn't hide when he sees her now, he just gives her a look like a stake through the heart. That man is a really classy hater, a natural. I'm scared of him myself." He stood up and began to pull on his overcoat. "I wish he'd get turned onto her mother. Get some practical use out of him. Did I tell you she wants me to call her Bernice?"

Ben said, "Farrell, if I were you, I'd leave the country. I would."

They went out into the February drizzle that sniffled back and forth between snow and rain. Farrell did not speak until they reached the corner where he turned toward the bookstore. Then he said very softly, "Damn, you have to be so careful. Who wants to know what people turn into?"

May came, and a night when Lila once again stood naked at the window, waiting for the moon. Farrell fussed with dishes and garbage bags, and fed the cat. These moments were always awkward. He had just asked her, "You want to save what's left of the rice?" when the telephone rang.

It was Lila's mother. She called two and three times a week now. "This is Bernice. How's my Irisher this evening?"

"I'm fine, Bernice," Farrell said. Lila suddenly threw back her head and drew a heavy, whining breath. The cat hissed silently and ran into the bathroom.

"I called to inveigle you two uptown this Friday," Mrs. Braun said. "A couple of old friends are coming over, and I know if I don't get some young people in we'll just sit around and talk about what went wrong with the Progressive party. The Old Left. So if you could sort of sweet-talk our girl into spending an evening in Squaresville —"

"I'll have to check with Lila." She's *doing* it, he thought, that terrible woman. Every time I talk to her, I sound married. I see what she's doing, but she goes right ahead anyway. He said, "I'll talk to her in the morning." Lila struggled in the moonlight, between dancing and drowning.

"Oh," Mrs. Braun said. "Yes, of course. Have her call me back." She sighed. "It's such a comfort to me to know you're there. Ask her if I should fix a fondue."

Lila made a handsome wolf: tall and broad-chested for a female, moving as easily as water sliding over stone. Her coat was dark brown, showing red in the proper light, and there were white places on her breast. She had pale green eyes, the color of the sky when a hurricane is coming.

Usually she was gone as soon as the changing was over, for she never cared for him to see her in her wolf form. But tonight she came slowly toward him, walking in a strange way, with her hindquarters almost dragging. She was making a high, soft sound, and her eyes were not focusing on him.

"What is it?" he asked foolishly. The wolf whined and skulked under the table, rubbing against the leg. Then she lay on her belly and rolled and as she did so the sound grew in her throat until it became an odd, sad, thin cry; not a hunting howl, but a shiver of longing turned into breath.

"Jesus, don't do that!" Farrell gasped. But she sat up and howled again, and a dog answered her from somewhere near the river. She wagged her tail and whimpered.

Farrell said, "The super'll be up here in two minutes flat. What's the matter with you?" He heard footsteps and low frightened voices in the apartment above them. Another dog howled, this one nearby, and the wolf wriggled a little way toward the window on her haunches, like a baby, scooting. She looked at him over her shoulder, shuddering violently. On an impulse, he picked up the phone and called her mother.

Watching the wolf as she rocked and slithered and moaned, he described her actions to Mrs. Braun. "I've never seen her like this," he said. "I don't know what's the matter with her."

"Oh, my God," Mrs. Braun whispered. She told him.

When he was silent, she began to speak very rapidly. "It hasn't happened for such a long time. Schechtman gives her pills, but she must have run out and forgotten — she's always been like that, since she was little. All the thermos bottles she used to leave on the school bus, and every week her piano music —"

"I wish you'd told me before," he said. He was edging very cautiously toward the open window. The pupils of the wolf's eyes were pulsing with her quick breaths.

"It isn't a thing you tell people!" Lila's mother wailed in his ears. "How do you think it was for me when she brought her first little boyfriend —" Farrell dropped the phone and sprang for the window. He had the inside track, and he might have made it, but she turned her head and snarled so wildly that he fell back. When he reached the window, she was already two fire-escape landings below, and there was eager yelping waiting for her in the street.

Dangling and turning just above the floor, Mrs. Braun heard Farrell's distant yell, followed immediately by a heavy thumping on the door. A strange, tattered voice was shouting unintelligibly beyond the knocking. Footsteps crashed by the receiver and the door opened.

"My dog, my dog!" the strange voice mourned. "My dog, my dog, my dog!"

"I'm sorry about your dog," Farrell said. "Look, please go away. I've got work to do."

"I got work," the voice said. "I know my work." It climbed and spilled into another language, out of which English words jutted like broken bones. "Where is she? Where is she? She kill my dog."

"She's not here." Farrell's own voice changed on the last word. It seemed a long time before he said, "You'd better put that away."

Mrs. Braun heard the howl as clearly as though the wolf were running beneath her own window: lonely and insatiable, with a kind of gasping laughter in it. The other voice began to scream. Mrs. Braun caught the phrase *silver bullet* several times. The door slammed; then opened and slammed again.

Farrell was the only man of his own acquaintance who was able to play back his dreams while he was having them: to stop them in mid-flight, no matter how fearful they might be — or how lovely — and run them over and over studying them in his sleep, until the most terrifying reel became at once utterly harmless and unbearably familiar. This night that he spent running after Lila was like that.

He would find them congregated under the marquee of an apartment house, or romping around the moonscape of a construction site: ten or fifteen males of all races, creeds, colors, and previous conditions of servitude; whining and yapping, pissing against tires, inhaling indiscriminately each other and the lean, grinning bitch they surrounded. She frightened them, for she growled more wickedly than coyness demanded, and where she snapped, even in play, bone showed. Still they tumbled on her and over her, biting her neck and ears in their turn; and she snarled but she did not run away.

Never, at least, until Farrell came charging upon them, shrieking like any cuckold, kicking at the snuffling lovers. Then she would turn and race off into the spring dark, with her thin, dreamy howl floating behind her like the train of a smoky gown. The dogs followed, and so did Farrell, calling and cursing. They always lost him quickly, that jubilant marriage procession, leaving him stumbling down rusty iron ladders into places where he fell over garbage cans. Yet he would come upon them as inevitably in time, loping along Broadway or trotting across Columbus Avenue toward the Park; he would hear them in the tennis courts near the river, breaking down the nets over Lila and her moment's Ares. There were dozens of them now, coming from all directions. They stank of their joy, and he threw stones at them and shouted, and they ran.

And the wolf ran at their head, on sidewalks and on wet grass; her tail waving contentedly, but her eyes still hungry, and her howl growing ever more warning than wistful. Farrell knew that she must have blood before sunrise, and that it was both useless and dangerous to follow her. But the night wound and unwound itself, and he knew the same things over and over, and ran down the same streets, and saw the same couples walk wide of him, thinking he was drunk.

Mrs. Braun kept leaping out of a taxi that pulled up next to him; usually at corners where the dogs had just piled by, knocking over the crates stacked in market doorways and spilling the newspapers at the subway kiosks. Standing in broccoli, in black taffeta, with a front like a ferryboat — yet as lean in the hips as her wolf-daughter — with her plum-colored hair all loose, one arm lifted, and her orange mouth pursed in a bellow, she was no longer Bernice but a wronged fertility goddess getting set to blast the harvest. "We've got to split up!" she would roar at Farrell, and each time it sounded like a sound idea. Yet he looked for her whenever he lost Lila's trail, because she never did.

The superintendent kept turning up too, darting after Farrell out of alleys or cellar entrances, or popping from the freight elevators that load through the sidewalk. Farrell would hear his numberless passkeys clicking on the flat piece of wood tucked into his belt.

"You see her? You see her, the wolf, kill my dog?" Under the fat, ugly moon, the Army .45 glittered and trembled like his own mad eyes.

"Mark with a cross." He would pat the barrel of the gun and shake it under Farrell's nose like a maracas. "Mark with a cross, bless by a priest. Three silver bullets. She kill my dog."

Lila's voice would come sailing to them then, from up in Harlem or away near Lincoln Center, and the little man would whirl and dash down into the earth, disappearing into the crack between two slabs of sidewalk. Farrell understood quite clearly that the superintendent was hunting Lila underground, using the keys that only superintendents have to take elevators down to the black sub-sub-basements, far below the bicycle rooms and the wet, shaking laundry rooms, and below the furnace rooms, below the passages walled with electricity meters and roofed with burly steam pipes; down to the realms where the great dim water mains roll like whales, and the gas lines hump and preen, down where the roots of the apartment houses fade together; and so along under the city, scrabbling through secret ways with silver bullets, and his keys rapping against the piece of wood. He never saw Lila, but he was never very far behind her.

Cutting across parking lots, pole-vaulting between locked bumpers, edging and dancing his way through fluorescent gaggles of haughty children; leaping uptown like a salmon against the current of the theater crowds; walking quickly past the random killing faces that floated down the night tide like unexploded mines, and especially avoiding the crazy faces that wanted to tell him what it was like to be crazy — so Farrell pursued Lila Braun, of Tremont Avenue and CCNY, in the city all night long. Nobody offered to help him, or tried to head off the dangerous-looking bitch bounding along with the delirious raggle of admirers streaming after her; but then, the dogs had to fight through the same clenched legs and vengeful bodies that Farrell did. The crowds slowed Lila down, but he felt relieved whenever she turned towards the emptier streets. *She must have blood soon, somewhere.*

Farrell's dreams eventually lost their clear edge after he played them back a certain number of times, and so it was with the night. The full moon skidded down the sky, thinning like a tatter of butter in a skillet, and remembered scenes began to fold sloppily into each other. The sound of Lila and the dogs grew fainter whichever way he followed. Mrs. Braun blinked on and off at longer intervals; and in dark doorways and under subway gratings, the superintendent burned like a corposant, making the barrel of his pistol run rainbow. At last he lost Lila for good, and with that it seemed that he woke.

It was still night, but not dark, and he was walking slowly home on

Riverside Drive through a cool, grainy fog. The moon had set, but the river was strangely bright: glittering gray as far up as the Bridge, where headlights left shiny, wet paths like snails. There was no one else on the street.

"Dumb broad," he said aloud. "The hell with it. She wants to mess around, let her mess around." He wondered whether werewolves could have cubs, and what sort of cubs they might be. Lila must have turned on the dogs by now, for the blood. Poor dogs, he thought. They were all so dirty and innocent and happy with her.

"A moral lesson for all of us," he announced sententiously. "Don't fool with strange, eager ladies, they'll kill you." He was a little hysterical. Then, two blocks ahead of him, he saw the gaunt shape in the gray light of the river; alone now, and hurrying. Farrell did not call to her, but as soon as he began to run, the wolf wheeled and faced him. Even at that distance, her eyes were stained and streaked and wild. She showed all the teeth on one side of her mouth, and she growled like fire.

Farrell trotted steadily toward her, crying, "Go home, go home! Lila, you dummy, get on home, it's morning!" She growled terribly, but when Farrell was less than a block away she turned again and dashed across the street, heading for West End Avenue. Farrell said, "Good girl, that's it," and limped after her.

In the hours before sunrise on West End Avenue, many people came out to walk their dogs. Farrell had done it often with poor Grunewald to know many of the dawn walkers by sight, and some to talk to. A fair number of them were whores and homosexuals, both of whom always seem to have dogs in New York. Quietly, almost always alone, they drifted up and down the Nineties, piloted by their small, fussy beasts, but moving in a kind of fugitive truce with the city and the night that was ending. Farrell sometimes fancied that they were all asleep, and that this hour was the only true rest they ever got.

He recognized Robie by his two dogs, Scone and Crumpet. Robie lived in the apartment directly below Farrell's, usually unhappily. The dogs were horrifying little homebrews of Chihuahua and Yorkshire terrier, but Robie loved them.

Crumpet, the male, saw Lila first. He gave a delighted yap of welcome and proposition (according to Robie, Scone bored him, and he liked big girls anyway) and sprang to meet her, yanking his leash through Robie's slack hand. The wolf was almost upon him before he realized his fatal misunderstanding and scuttled desperately in retreat, meowing with utter terror.

Robie wailed, and Farrell ran as fast as he could, but Lila knocked Crumpet off his feet and slashed his throat while he was still in the air. Then she crouched on the body, nuzzling it in a dreadful way.

Robie actually came within a step of leaping upon Lila and trying to drag her away from his dead dog. Instead, he turned on Farrell as he came panting up, and began hitting him with a good deal of strength and accuracy. "Damn you, damn you!" he sobbed. Little Scone ran away around the corner, screaming like a mandrake.

Farrell put up his arms and went with the punches, all the while yelling at Lila until his voice ripped. But the blood frenzy had her, and Farrell had never imagined what she must be like at those times. Somehow she had spared the dogs who had loved her all night, but she was nothing but thirst now. She pushed and kneaded Crumpet's body as though she were nursing.

All along the avenue, the morning dogs were barking like trumpets. Farrell ducked away from Robie's soft fists and saw them coming; tripping over their trailing leashes, running too fast for their stubby legs. They were small, spoiled beasts, most of them, overweight and shortwinded, and many were not young. Their owners cried unmanly pet names after them, but they waddled gallantly toward their deaths, barking promises far bigger than themselves, and none of them looked back.

She looked up with her muzzle red to the eyes. The dogs did falter then, for they knew murder when they smelled it, and even their silly, nearsighted eyes understood vaguely what creature faced them. But they knew the smell of love too, and they were all gentlemen.

She killed the first two to reach her — a spitz and a cocker spaniel — with two snaps of her jaws. But before she could settle down to her meal, three Pekes were scrambling up to her, though they would have had to stand on each others' shoulders. Lila whirled without a sound, and they fell away, rolling and yelling but unhurt. As soon as she turned, the Pekes were at her again, joined now by a couple of valiant poodles. Lila got one of the poodles when she turned again.

Robie had stopped beating on Farrell, and was leaning against a traffic light, being sick. But other people were running up now: a middle-aged black man, crying; a plump youth in a plastic car coat and bedroom slippers, who kept whimpering, "Oh God, she's eating them, look at her, she's really eating them!"; two lean, ageless girls in slacks, both with foamy beige hair. They all called wildly to their unheeding dogs, and they all grabbed at Farrell and shouted in his face. Cars began to stop.

The sky was thin and cool, rising pale gold, but Lila paid no attention to it. She was ramping under the swarm of little dogs; rearing and spinning in circles, snarling blood. The dogs were terrified and bewildered, but they never swerved from their labor. The smell of love told them that they were welcome, however ungraciously she seemed to receive them. Lila shook herself, and a pair of squealing dachshunds, hobbled in a double harness, tumbled across the sidewalk to end at Farrell's feet. They scrambled up and immediately towed themselves back into the maelstrom. Lila bit one of them almost in half, but the other dachshund went on trying to climb her hindquarters, dragging his ripped comrade with him. Farrell began to laugh.

The black man said, "You think it's funny?" and hit him. Farrell sat down, still laughing. The man stood over him, embarrassed, offering Farrell his handkerchief. "I'm sorry, I shouldn't have done that," he said. "But your dog killed my dog."

"She isn't my dog," Farrell said. He moved to let a man pass between them, and then saw that it was the superintendent, holding his pistol with both hands. Nobody noticed him until he fired; but Farrell pushed one of the foamy-haired girls, and she stumbled against the superintendent as the gun went off. The silver bullet broke a window in a parked car.

The superintendent fired again while the echoes of the first shot were still clapping back and forth between the houses. A Pomeranian screamed that time, and a woman cried out, "Oh, my God, he shot Borgy!" But the crowd was crumbling away, breaking into its individual components like pills on television. The watching cars had sped off at sight of the gun, and the faces that had been peering down from windows disappeared. Except for Farrell, the few people who remained were scattered halfway down the block. The sky was brightening swiftly now.

"For God's sake, don't let him!" the same woman called from the shelter of a doorway. But two men made shushing gestures at her, saying, "It's all right, he knows how to use that thing. Go ahead, buddy."

The shots had at last frightened the little dogs away from Lila. She crouched among the twitching splotches of fur, with her muzzle wrinkled back and her eyes more black than green. Farrell saw a plaid rag that had been a dog jacket protruding from under her body. The superintendent stooped and squinted over the gun barrel, aiming with grotesque care, while the men cried to him to shoot. He was too far from the werewolf for her to reach him before he fired the last silver bullet, thought he would surely die before she died. His lips were moving as he took aim.

Two long steps would have brought Farrell up behind the superintendent. Later he told himself that he had been afraid of the pistol, because that was easier than remembering how he had felt when he looked at Lila. Her tongue never stopped lapping around her dark jaws; and even as she set herself to spring, she lifted a bloody paw to her mouth. Farrell thought of her padding in the bedroom, breathing on his face. The superintendent grunted and Farrell closed his eyes. Yet even then he expected to find himself doing something.

Then he heard Mrs. Braun's unmistakable voice. *"Don't you dare!"* She was standing between Lila and the superintendent: one shoe gone, and the heel off the other one; her knit dress torn at the shoulder, and her face tired and smudgy. But she pointed a finger at the startled superintendent, and he stepped quickly back, as though she had a pistol too.

"Lady, that's a wolf," he protested nervously. "Lady, you please get, get out of the way. That's a wolf, I go shoot her now."

"I want to see your license for that gun." Mrs. Braun held out her hand. The superintendent blinked at her, muttering in despair. She said, "Do you know that you can be sent to prison for twenty years for carrying a concealed weapon in this state? Do you know what the fine is for having a gun without a license? The fine is Five. Thousand. Dollars." The men down the street were shouting at her, but she swung around to face the creature snarling among the little dead dogs.

"Come on, Lila," she said. "Come on home with Bernice. I'll make tea and we'll talk. It's been a long time since we've really talked, you know? We used to have nice long talks when you were little, but we don't anymore." The wolf had stopped growling, but she was crouching even lower, and her ears were still flat against her head. Mrs. Braun said, "Come on, baby. Listen, I know what — you'll call in sick at the office and stay for a few days. You'll get a good rest, and maybe we'll even look around a little for a new doctor, what do you say? Schechtman hasn't done a thing for you, I never liked him. Come on home, honey. Momma's here, Bernice knows." She took a step toward the silent wolf, holding out her hand.

The superintendent gave a desperate, wordless cry and pumped forward, clumsily shoving Mrs. Braun to one side. He leveled the pistol point-blank, wailing, "My dog, my dog!" Lila was in the air when the gun went off, and her shadow sprang after her, for the sun had risen. She crumpled down across a couple of dead Pekes. Their blood dabbled her breasts and her pale throat.

Mrs. Braun screamed like a lunch whistle. She knocked the superintendent into the street and sprawled over Lila, hiding her completely from Farrell's sight. "Lila, Lila," she keened her daughter, "poor baby, you never had a chance. He killed you because you were different, the way they kill everything different." Farrell approached her and stooped down, but she pushed him against a wall without looking up. "Lila, Lila, poor baby, poor darling, maybe it's better, maybe you're happy now. You never had a chance, poor Lila."

The dog owners were edging slowly back, and the surviving dogs were running to them. The superintendent squatted on the curb with his head in his arms. A weary, muffled voice said, "For God's sake, Bernice, would you get up off me? You don't have to stop yelling, just get off."

When she stood up, the cars began to stop in the street again. It made it very difficult for the police to get through.

Nobody pressed charges, because there was no one to lodge them against. The killer dog — or wolf, as some insisted — was gone; and if she had an owner, he could not be found. As for the people who had actually seen the wolf turn into a young girl when the sunlight touched her, most of them managed not to have seen it, though they never really forgot. There were a few who knew quite well what they had seen, and never forgot it either, but they never said anything. They did, however, chip in to pay the superintendent's fine for possessing an unlicensed handgun. Farrell gave what he could.

Lila vanished out of Farrell's life before sunset. She did not go uptown with her mother, but packed her things and went to stay with friends in the Village. Later he heard that she was living on Christopher Street; and later still, that she had moved to Berkeley and gone back to school. He never saw her again.

"It had to be like that," he told Ben once. "We got to know too much about each other. See, there's another side to knowing. She couldn't look at me."

"You mean because you saw her with all those dogs? Or because she knew you'd have let that little nut shoot her?" Farrell shook his head.

"It was that, I guess, but it was more something else, something I know. When she sprang, just as he shot at her that last time, she wasn't leaping at him. She was going straight for her mother. She'd have got her too, if it hadn't been sunrise."

Ben whistled softly. "I wonder if her old lady knows."

"Bernice knows everything about Lila," Farrell said.

Mrs. Braun called him nearly two years later to tell him that Lila was getting married. It must have cost her a good deal of money and ingenuity to find him (where Farrell was living then, the telephone line was open for four hours a day), but he knew by the spitefulness in the static that she considered it money well spent.

"He's at Stanford," she crackled. "A research psychologist. They're going to Japan for their honeymoon."

"That's fine," Farrell said. "I'm really happy for her, Bernice." He hesitated before he asked, "Does he know about Lila? I mean, about what happens —?"

"Does he know?" she cried. "He's proud of it — he thinks it's wonderful! It's his field!"

"That's great. That's fine. Goodbye, Bernice. I really am glad."

And he was glad, and a little wistful, thinking about it. The girl he was living with here had a really strange hangup.

No Place for You, My Love

by Eudora Welty

THEY WERE STRANGERS to each other, both fairly well strangers to the place, now seated side by side at luncheon — a party combined in a free-and-easy way when the friends he and she were with
recognized each other across Galatoire's. The time was a Sunday in
summer — those hours of afternoon that seem Time Out in New
Orleans.

The moment he saw her little blunt, fair face, he thought that here
was a woman who was having an affair. It was one of those odd
meetings when such an impact is felt that it has to be translated at
once into some sort of speculation.

With a married man, most likely, he supposed, slipping quickly into
a groove — he was long married — and feeling more conventional,
then, in his curiosity as she sat there, leaning her cheek on her hand,
looking no further before her than the flowers on the table, and
wearing that hat.

He did not like her hat, any more than he liked tropical flowers. It
was the wrong hat for her, thought this Eastern businessman who had
no interest whatever in women's clothes and no eye for them; he
thought the unaccustomed thing crossly.

It must stick out all over me, she thought, so people think they can
love me or hate me just by looking at me. How did it leave us — the
old, safe, slow way people used to know of learning how one another
feels, and the privilege that went with it of shying away if it seemed

best? People in love like me, I suppose, give away the short cuts to everybody's secrets.

Something, though, he decided, had been settled about her predicament — for the time being, anyway; the parties to it were all still alive, no doubt. Nevertheless, her predicament was the only one he felt so sure of here, like the only recognizable shadow in that restaurant, where mirrors and fans were busy agitating the light, as the very local talk drawled across and agitated the peace. The shadow lay between her fingers, between her little square hand and her cheek, like something always best carried about the person. Then suddenly, as she took her hand down, the secret fact was still there — it lighted her. It was a bold and full light, shot up under the brim of that hat, as close to them all as the flowers in the center of the table.

Did he dream of making her disloyal to that hopelessness that he saw very well she'd been cultivating down here? He knew very well that he did not. What they amounted to was two Northerners keeping each other company. She glanced up at the big gold clock on the wall and smiled. He didn't smile back. She had that naïve face that he associated, for no good reason, with the Middle West — because it said "Show me," perhaps. It was a serious, now-watch-out-everybody face, which orphaned her entirely in the company of these Southerners. He guessed her age, as he could not guess theirs: thirty-two. He himself was further along.

Of all human moods, deliberate imperviousness may be the most quickly communicated — it may be the most successful, most fatal signal of all. And two people can indulge in imperviousness as well as in anything else. "You're not very hungry either," he said.

The blades of fan shadows came down over their two heads, as he saw inadvertently in the mirror, with himself smiling at her now like a villain. His remark sounded dominant and rude enough for everybody present to listen back a moment; it even sounded like an answer to a question she might have just asked him. The other women glanced at him. The Southern look — Southern mask — of life-is-a-dream irony, which could turn to pure challenge at the drop of a hat, he could wish well away. He liked naïveté better.

"I find the heat down here depressing," she said, with the heart of Ohio in her voice.

"Well — I'm in somewhat of a temper about it, too," he said.

They looked with grateful dignity at each other.

"I have a car here, just down the street," he said to her as the luncheon party was rising to leave, all the others wanting to get back to their houses and sleep. "If it's all right with — Have you ever driven down south of here?"

Out on Bourbon Street, in the bath of July, she asked at his shoulder, "South of New Orleans? I didn't know there was any south to *here*. Does it just go on and on?" She laughed, and adjusted the exasperating hat to her head in a different way. It was more than frivolous, it was conspicuous, with some sort of glitter or flitter tied in a band around the straw and hanging down.

"That's what I'm going to show you."

"Oh — you've been there?"

"No!"

His voice rang out over the uneven, narrow sidewalk and dropped back from the walls. The flaked-off, colored houses were spotted like the hides of beasts faded and shy, and were hot as a wall of growth that seemed to breathe flower-like down onto them as they walked to the car parked there.

"It's just that it couldn't be any worse — we'll see."

"All right, then," she said. "We will."

So, their actions reduced to amiability, they settled into the car — a faded-red Ford convertible with a rather threadbare canvas top, which had been standing in the sun for all those lunch hours.

"It's rented," he explained. "I asked to have the top put down, and was told I'd lost my mind."

"It's out of this world. *Degrading* heat," she said and added, "Doesn't matter."

The stranger in New Orleans always sets out to leave it as though following the clue in a maze. They were threading through the narrow and one-way streets, past the pale-violet bloom of tired squares, the brown steeples and statues, the balcony with the live and probably famous black monkey dipping along the railing as over a ballroom floor, past the grillework and the lattice-work to all the iron swans painted flesh color on the front steps of bungalows outlying.

Driving, he spread his new map and put his finger down on it. At the intersection marked Arabi, where their road led out of the tangle and he took it, a small Negro seated beneath a black umbrella astride a box chalked "Shou Shine" lifted his pink-and-black hand and waved them languidly good-by. She didn't miss it, and waved back.

Below New Orleans there was a raging of insects from both sides of the concrete highway, not quite together, like the playing of separated marching bands. The river and the levee were still on her side, waste and jungle and some occasional settlements on his — poor houses. Families bigger than housefuls thronged the yards. His nodding, driving head would veer from side to side, looking and almost lowering. As time passed and the distance from New Orleans grew, girls ever darker and younger were disposing themselves over the porches and the porch steps, with jet-black hair pulled high, and ragged palm-leaf fans rising and falling like rafts of butterflies. The children running forth were nearly always naked ones.

She watched the road. Crayfish constantly crossed in front of the wheels, looking grim and bonneted, in a great hurry.

"How the Old Woman Got Home," she murmured to herself.

He pointed, as it flew by, at a saucepan full of cut zinnias which stood waiting on the open lid of a mailbox at the roadside, with a little note tied onto the handle.

They rode mostly in silence. The sun bore down. They met fishermen and other men bent on some local pursuits, some in sulphur-colored pants, walking and riding; met wagons, trucks, boats in trucks, autos, boats on top of autos — all coming to meet them, as though something of high moment were doing back where the car came from, and he and she were determined to miss it. There was nearly always a man lying with his shoes off in the bed of any truck otherwise empty — with the raw, red look of a man sleeping in the daytime, being jolted about as he slept. Then there was a sort of dead man's land, where nobody came. He loosened his collar and tie. By rushing through the heat at high speed, they brought themselves the effect of fans turned onto their cheeks. Clearing alternated with jungle and canebrake like something tried, tried again. Little shell roads led off on both sides; now and then a road of planks led into the yellow-green.

"Like a dance floor in there." She pointed.

He informed her, "In there's your oil, I think."

There were thousands, millions of mosquitoes and gnats — a universe of them, and on the increase.

A family of eight or nine people on foot strung along the road in the same direction the car was going, beating themselves with the wild palmettos. Heels, shoulders, knees, breasts, back of the heads, elbows, hands, were touched in turn — like some game, each playing it with himself.

He struck himself on the forehead, and increased their speed. (His wife would not be at her most charitable if he came bringing malaria home to the family.)

More and more crayfish and other shell creatures littered their path, scuttling or dragging. These little samples, little jokes of creation, persisted and sometimes perished, the more of them the deeper down the road went. Terrapins and turtles came up steadily over the horizons of the ditches.

Back there in the margins were worse — crawling hides you could not penetrate with bullets or quite believe, grins that had come down from the primeval mud.

"Wake up." Her Northern nudge was very timely on his arm. They had veered toward the side of the road. Still driving fast, he spread his map.

Like a misplaced sunrise, the light of the river flowed up; they were mounting the levee on a little shell road.

"Shall we cross here?" he asked politely.

He might have been keeping track over years and miles of how long they could keep that tiny ferry waiting. Now skidding down the levee's flank, they were the last-minute car, the last possible car that could squeeze on. Under the sparse shade of one willow tree, the small, amateurish-looking boat slapped the water, as, expertly, he wedged on board.

"Tell him we put him on hub cap!" shouted one of the numerous olive-skinned, dark-eyed young boys standing dressed up in bright shirts at the railing, hugging each other with delight that that last straw was on board. Another boy drew his affectionate initials in the dust of the door on her side.

She opened the door and stepped out, and, after only a moment's standing at bay, started up a little iron stairway. She appeared above the car, on the tiny bridge beneath the captain's window and the whistle.

From there, while the boat still delayed in what seemed a trance — as if it were too full to attempt the start — she could see the panlike deck below, separated by its rusty rim from the tilting, polished water.

The passengers walking and jostling about there appeared oddly amateurish, too — amateur travelers. They were having such a good time. They all knew each other. Beer was being passed around in cans, bets were being loudly settled and new bets made, about local and special subjects on which they all doted. One red-haired man in a burst of wildness even tried to give away his truckload of shrimp to a man on the other side of the boat — nearly all the trucks were full of shrimp — causing taunts and then protests of "They good! They good!" from the giver. The young boys leaned on each other thinking of what next, rolling their eyes absently.

A radio pricked the air behind her. Looking like a great tomcat just above her head, the captain was digesting the news of a fine stolen automobile.

At last a tremendous explosion burst — the whistle. Everything shuddered in outline from the sound, everybody said something — everybody else.

They started with no perceptible motion, but her hat blew off. It went spiraling to the deck below, where he, thank heaven, sprang out of the car and picked it up. Everybody looked frankly up at her now, holding her hands to her head.

The little willow tree receded as its shade was taken away. The heat was like something falling on her head. She held the hot rail before her. It was like riding a stove. Her shoulders dropping, her hair flying, her skirt buffeted by the sudden strong wind, she stood there, thinking they all must see that with her entire self all she did was wait. Her set hands, with the bag that hung from her wrist and rocked back and forth — all three seemed objects bleaching there, belonging to no one; she could not feel a thing in the skin of her face; perhaps she was crying, and not knowing it. She could look down and see him just below her, his black shadow, her hat, and his black hair. His hair in the wind looked unreasonably long and rippling. Little did he know that from here it had a red undergleam like an animal's. When she looked up and outward, a vortex of light drove through and over the brown waves like a star in the water.

He did after all bring the retrieved hat up the stairs to her. She took it back — useless — and held it to her skirt. What they were saying below was more polite than their searchlight faces.

"Where you think he come from, that man?"

"I bet he come from Lafitte."

"Lafitte? What you bet, eh?" — all crouched in the shade of trucks, squatting and laughing.

Now his shadow fell partly across her; the boat had jolted into some other strand of current. Her shaded arm and shaded hand felt pulled out from the blaze of light and water, and she hoped humbly for more shade for her head. It had seemed so natural to climb up and stand in the sun.

The boys had a surprise — an alligator on board. One of them pulled it by a chain around the deck, between the cars and trucks, like a toy — a hide that could walk. He thought, Well they had to catch one sometime. It's Sunday afternoon. So they have him on board now, riding him across the Mississippi River. . . . The playfulness of it beset everybody on the ferry. The hoarseness of the boat whistle, commenting briefly, seemed part of the general appreciation.

"Who want to rassle him? Who want to, eh?" two boys cried, looking up. A boy with shrimp-colored arms capered from side to side, pretending to have been bitten.

What was there so hilarious about jaws that could bite? And what danger was there once in this repulsiveness — so that the last worldly evidence of some old heroic horror of the dragon had to be paraded in capture before the eyes of country clowns?

He noticed that she looked at the alligator without flinching at all. Her distance was set — the number of feet and inches between herself and it mattered to her.

Perhaps her measuring coolness was to him what his bodily shade was to her, while they stood pat up there riding the river, which felt like the sea and looked like the earth under them — full of the red-brown earth, charged with it. Ahead of the boat it was like an exposed vein of ore. The river seemed to swell in the vast middle with the curve of the earth. The sun rolled under them. As if in memory of the size of things, uprooted trees were drawn across their path, sawing at the air and tumbling one over the other.

When they reached the other side, they felt that they had been racing around an arena in their chariot, among lions. The whistle took and shook the stairs as they went down. The young boys, looking taller, had taken out colored combs and were combing their wet hair back in solemn pompadour above their radiant foreheads. They had been bathing in the river themselves not long before.

The cars and trucks, then the foot passengers and the alligator, waddling like a child to school, all disembarked and wound up the weed-sprung levee.

Both respectable and merciful, their hides, she thought, forcing herself to dwell on the alligator as she looked back. Deliver us all from the naked in heart. (As she had been told.)

When they regained their paved road, he heard her give a little sigh and saw her turn her straw-colored head to look back once more. Now that she rode with her hat in her lap, her earrings were conspicuous too. A little metal ball set with small pale stones danced beside each square, faintly downy cheek.

Had she felt a wish for someone else to be riding with them? He thought it was more likely that she would wish for her husband if she had one (his wife's voice) than for the lover in whom he believed. Whatever people liked to think, situations (if not scenes) were usually three-way — there was somebody else always. The one who didn't — couldn't — understand the two made the formidable third.

He glanced down at the map flapping on the seat between them, up at his wristwatch, out at the road. Out there was the incredible brightness of four o'clock.

On this side of the river, the road ran beneath the brow of the levee and followed it. Here was a heat that ran deeper and brighter and more intense than all the rest — its nerve. The road grew one with the heat as it was one with the unseen river. Dead snakes stretched across the concrete like markers — inlaid mosaic bands, dry as feathers, which their tires licked at intervals that began to seem clocklike.

No, the heat faced them — it was ahead. They could see it waving at them, shaken in the air above the white of the road, always at a certain distance ahead, shimmering finely as a cloth, with running edges of green and gold, fire and azure.

"It's never anything like this in Syracuse," he said.

"Or in Toledo, either," she replied with dry lips.

They were driving through greater waste down here, through fewer and even more insignificant towns. There was water under everything. Even where a screen of jungle had been left to stand, splashes could be heard from under the trees. In the vast open, sometimes boats moved inch by inch through what appeared endless meadows of rubbery flowers.

Her eyes overcome with brightness and size, she felt a panic rise, as sudden as nausea. Just how far below questions and answers, concealment and revelation, they were running now — that was still a new question, with a power of its own, waiting. How dear — how costly — could this ride be?

"It looks to me like your road can't go much further," she remarked cheerfully. "Just over there, it's all water."

"Time out," he said, and with that he turned the car into a sudden road of white shells that rushed at them narrowly out of the left.

They bolted over a cattle guard, where some rayed and crested purple flowers burst out of the vines in the ditch, and rolled onto a long, narrow, green, mowed clearing: a churchyard. A paved track ran between two short rows of raised tombs, all neatly white-washed and now brilliant as faces against the vast flushed sky.

The track was the width of the car with a few inches to spare. He passed between the tombs slowly but in the manner of a feat. Names took their places on the walls slowly at a level with the eye, names as near as the eyes of a person stopping in conversation, and as far away in origin, and in all their music and dead longing, as Spain. At intervals were set packed bouquets of zinnias, oleanders, and some kind of purple flowers, all quite fresh, in fruit jars, like nice welcomes on bureaus.

They moved on into an open plot beyond, of violent-green grass, spread before the green-and-white frame church with worked flower beds around it, flowerless poinsettias growing up to the windowsills. Beyond was a house, and left on the doorstep of the house a fresh-caught catfish the size of a baby — a fish wearing whiskers and bleeding. On a clothesline in the yard, a priest's black gown on a hanger hung airing, swaying at man's height, in a vague, trainlike, ladylike sweep along an evening breath that might otherwise have seemed imaginary from the unseen, felt river.

With the motor cut off, with the raging of the insects about them, they sat looking out at the green and white and black and red and pink as they leaned against the sides of the car.

"What is your wife like?" she asked. His right hand came up and spread — iron, wooden, manicured. She lifted her eyes to his face. He looked at her like that hand.

Then he lit a cigarette, and the portrait, and the right-hand testimonial it made, were blown away. She smiled, herself as unaffected as by some stage performance; and he was annoyed in the cemetery. They did not risk going on to her husband — if she had one.

Under the supporting posts of the priest's house, where a boat was, solid ground ended and palmettos and water hyacinths could not wait to begin; suddenly the rays of the sun, from behind the car, reached that lowness and struck the flowers. The priest came out onto the porch in his underwear, stared at the car a moment as if he wondered what time it was, then collected his robe off the line and his fish off the doorstep and returned inside. Vespers was next, for him.

After backing out between the tombs he drove on still south, in the sunset. They caught up with an old man walking in a sprightly way in their direction, all by himself, wearing a clean bright shirt printed with a pair of palm trees fanning green over his chest. It might better be a big colored woman's shirt, but she didn't have it. He flagged the car with gestures like hoops.

"You're coming to the end of the road," the old man told them. He pointed ahead, tipped his hat to the lady, and pointed again. "End of the road." They didn't understand that he meant, "Take me."

They drove on. "If we do go any further, it'll have to be by water — is that it?" he asked her, hesitating at this odd point.

"You know better than I do," she replied politely.

The road had for some time ceased to be paved; it was made of shells. It was leading into a small, sparse settlement like the others a few miles back, but with even more of the camp about it. On the lip of the clearing, directly before a green willow blaze with the sunset gone behind it, the row of houses and shacks faced out on broad, colored, moving water that stretched to reach the horizon and looked like an arm of the sea. The houses on their shaggy posts, patchily built, some with plank runways instead of steps, were flimsy and alike, and not much bigger than the boats tied up at the landing.

"Venice," she heard him announce, and he dropped the crackling map in her lap.

They coasted down the brief remainder. The end of the road — she could not remember ever seeing a road simply end — was a spoon shape, with a tree stump in the bowl to turn around by.

Around it, he stopped the car, and they stepped out, feeling put down in the midst of a sudden vast pause or subduement that was like a yawn. They made their way on foot toward the water, where at an idle-looking landing men in twos and threes stood with their backs to them.

The nearness of darkness, the still uncut trees, bright water partly under a sheet of flowers, shacks, silence, dark shapes of boats tied up, then the first sounds of people just on the other side of thin walls — all this reached them. Mounds of shells like day-old snow, pink-tinted, lay around a central shack with a beer sign on it. An old man up on the porch there sat holding an open newspaper, with a fat white goose sitting opposite him on the floor. Below, in the now shadowless and sunless open, another old man, with a colored pencil bright under his hat brim, was late mending a sail.

When she looked clear around, thinking they had a fire burning somewhere now, out of the heat had risen the full moon. Just beyond the trees, enormous, tangerine-colored, it was going solidly up. Other lights just striking into view, looking farther distant, showed moss shapes hanging, or slipped and broke matchlike on the water that so encroached upon the rim of ground they were standing on.

There was a touch at her arm — his, accidental.

"We're at the jumping-off place," he said.

She laughed, having thought his hand was a bat, while her eyes rushed downward toward a great pale drift of water hyacinths — still partly open, flushed and yet moonlit, level with her feet — through which paths of water for the boats had been hacked. She drew her hands up to her face under the brim of her hat; her own cheeks felt like the hyacinths to her, all her skin still full of too much light and sky, exposed. The harsh vesper bell was ringing.

"I believe there must be something wrong with me, that I came on this excursion to begin with," she said, as if he had already said this and she were merely in hopeful, willing, maddening agreement with him.

He took hold of her arm, and said, "Oh, come on — I see we can get something to drink here, at least."

But there was a beating, muffled sound from over the darkening water. One more boat was coming in, making its way through the tenacious, tough, dark flower traps, by the shaken light of what first appeared to be torches. He and she waited for the boat, as if on each other's patience. As if borne in on a mist of twilight or a breath, a horde of mosquitoes and gnats came singing and striking at them first. The boat bumped, men laughed. Somebody was offering somebody else some shrimp.

Then he might have cocked his dark city head down at her; she did not look up at him, only turned when he did. Now the shell mounds, like the shacks and trees, were solid purple. Lights had appeared in the not-quite-true window squares. A narrow neon sign, the lone sign, had come out in bright blush on the beer shack's roof: "Baba's Place." A light was on on the porch.

The barnlike interior was brightly lit and unpainted, looking not quite finished, with a partition dividing this room from what lay behind. One of the four cardplayers at a table in the middle of the floor was the newspaper reader; the paper was in his pants pocket. Midway along the partition was a bar, in the form of a pass-through to the other room, with a varnished, second-hand fretwork overhang. They crossed the floor and sat, alone there, on wooden stools. An eruption of humorous signs, newspaper cutouts and cartoons, razor-blade cards, and personal messages of significance to the owner or his friends decorated the overhang, framing where Baba should have been but wasn't.

Through there came a smell of garlic and cloves and red pepper, a blast of hot cloud escaped from a cauldron they could see now on a stove at the back of the other room. A massive back, presumably female, with a twist of gray hair on top, stood with a ladle akimbo. A young man joined her and with his fingers stole something out of the pot and ate it. At Baba's they were boiling shrimp.

When he got ready to wait on them, Baba strolled out to the counter, young, black-headed, and in very good humor.

"Coldest beer you've got. And food — What will you have?"

"Nothing for me, thank you," she said. "I'm not sure I could eat, after all."

"Well, I could," he said, shoving his jaw out. Baba smiled. "I want a good solid ham sandwich."

"I could have asked him for some water," she said, after he had gone.

While they sat waiting, it seemed very quiet. The bubbling of the shrimp, the distant laughing of Baba, and the slap of cards, like the beating of moths on the screens, seemed to come in fits and starts. The steady breathing they heard came from a big rough dog asleep in the corner. But it was bright. Electric lights were strung riotously over the room from a kind of spider web of old wires in the rafters. One of the written messages tacked before them read, "Joe! At the boyy!!" It looked very yellow, older than Baba's Place. Outside, the world was pure dark.

Two little boys, almost alike, almost the same size, and just cleaned up, dived into the room with a double bang of the screen door, and circled around the card game. They ran their hands into the men's pockets.

"Nickel for some pop!"

"Nickel for some pop!"

"Go 'way and let me play, you!"

They circled around and shrieked at the dog, ran under the lid of the counter and raced through the kitchen and back, and hung over the stools at the bar. One child had a live lizard on his shirt, clinging like a breast pin — like lapis lazuli.

Bringing in a strong odor of geranium talcum, some men had come in now — all in bright shirts. They drew near the counter, or stood and watched the game.

When Baba came out bringing the beer and sandwich, "Could I have some water?" she greeted him.

Baba laughed at everybody. She decided the woman back there must be Baba's mother.

Beside her, he was drinking his beer and eating his sandwich — ham, cheese, tomato, pickle, and mustard. Before he finished, one of the men who had come in beckoned from across the room. It was the old man in the palm-tree shirt.

She lifted her head to watch him leave her, and was looked at, from all over the room. As a minute passed, no cards were laid down. In a far-off way, like accepting the light from Arcturus, she accepted it that she was more beautiful or perhaps more fragile than the women they saw every day of their lives. It was just this thought coming into a woman's face, and at this hour, that seemed familiar to them.

Baba was smiling. He had set an opened, frosted brown bottle before her on the counter, and a thick sandwich, and stood looking at her. Baba made her eat some supper, for what she was.

"What the old fellow wanted," said he when he came back at last, "was to have a friend of his apologize. Seems church is just out. Seems the friend made a remark coming in just now. His pals told him there was a lady present."

"I see you bought him a beer," she said.

"Well, the old man looked like he wanted *something.*"

All at once the juke box interrupted from back in the corner, with the same old song as anywhere. The half-dozen slot machines along the wall were suddenly all run to like Maypoles, and thrown into action — taken over by further battalions of little boys.

There were three little boys to each slot machine. The local custom appeared to be that one pulled the lever for the friend he was holding up to put the nickel in, while the third covered the pictures with the flat of his hand as they fell into place, so as to surprise them all if anything happened.

The dog lay sleeping on in front of the raging juke box, his ribs working fast as a concertina's. At the side of the room a man with a cap on his white thatch was trying his best to open a side screen door, but it was stuck fast. It was he who had come in with the remark considered ribald; now he was trying to get out the other way. Moths as thick as ingots were trying to get in. The cardplayers broke into shouts of derision, then joy, then tired derision among themselves; they might have been here all afternoon — they were the only ones not cleaned up and shaved. The original pair of little boys ran in once more, with the hyphenated bang. They got nickels this time, then were brushed away from the table like mosquitoes, and they rushed under the counter and on to the cauldron behind, clinging to Baba's mother there. The evening was at the threshold.

They were quite unnoticed now. He was eating another sandwich, and she, having finished part of hers, was fanning her face with her hat. Baba had lifted the flap of the counter and come out into the room. Behind his head there was a sign lettered in orange crayon: "Shrimp Dance Sun. PM." That was tonight, still to be.

And suddenly she made a move to slide down from her stool, maybe wishing to walk out into that nowhere down the front steps to be cool a moment. But he had hold of her hand. He got down from his stool, and, patiently, reversing her hand in his own — just as she had had the look of being about to give up, faint — began moving her, leading her. They were dancing.

"I get to thinking this is what we get — what you and I deserve," she whispered, looking past his shoulder into the room. "And all the time, it's real. It's a real place — away off down here. . . ."

They danced gratefully, formally, to some song carried on in what must be the local patois, while no one paid any attention as long as they were together, and the children poured the family nickels steadily into the slot machines, walloping the handles down with regular crashes and troubling nobody with winning.

She said rapidly, as they began moving together too well, "One of those clippings was an account of a shooting right here. I guess they're proud of it. And that awful knife Baba was carrying . . . I wonder what he called me," she whispered in his ear.

"Who?"

"The one who apologized to you."

If they had ever been going to overstep themselves, it would be now as he held her closer and turned her, when she became aware that he could not help but see the bruise at her temple. It would not be six inches from his eyes. She felt it come out like an evil star. (Let it pay him back, then, for the hand he had stuck in her face when she'd tried once to be sympathetic, when she'd asked about his wife.) They danced on still as the record changed, after standing wordless and motionless, linked together in the middle of the room, for the moment between.

Then, they were like a matched team — like professional, Spanish dancers wearing masks — while the slow piece was playing.

Surely even those immune from the world, for the time being, need the touch of one another, or all is lost. Their arms encircling each other, their bodies circling the odorous, just-nailed-down floor, they were, at last, imperviousness in motion. They had found it, and had almost missed it: they had had to dance. They were what their separate hearts desired that day, for themselves and each other.

They were so good together that once she looked up and half smiled. "For whose benefit did we have to show off?"

Like people in love, they had a superstition about themselves almost as soon as they came out on the floor, and dared not think the words "happy" or "unhappy," which might strike them, one or the other, like lightning.

In the thickening heat they danced on while Baba himself sang with the mosquito-voiced singer in the chorus of "*Moi pas l'aimez ça,*" enumerating the *ça's* with a hot shrimp between his fingers. He was counting over the platters the old woman now set out on the counter, each heaped with shrimp in their shells boiled to iridescence, like mounds of honeysuckle flowers.

The goose wandered in from the back room under the lid of the counter and hitched itself around the floor among the table legs and people's legs, never seeing that it was neatly avoided by two dancers — who nevertheless vaguely thought of this goose as learned, having earlier heard an old man read to it. The children called it Mimi, and lured it away. The old thatched man was again drunkenly trying to get out by the stuck side door; now he gave it a kick, but was prevailed on to remain. The sleeping dog shuddered and snored.

It was left up to the dancers to provide nickels for the juke box; Baba kept a drawerful for every use. They had grown fond of all the selections by now. This was the music you heard out of the distance at night — out of the roadside taverns you fled past, around the late corners in cities half asleep, drifting up from the carnival over the hill, with one odd little strain always managing to repeat itself. This seemed a homey place.

Bathed in sweat, and feeling the false coolness that brings, they stood finally on the porch in the lapping night air for a moment before leaving. The first arrivals of the girls were coming up the steps under the porch light — all flowered fronts, their black pompadours giving out breathlike feelers from sheer abundance. Where they'd resprinkled it since church, the talcum shone like mica on their downy arms. Smelling solidly of geranium, they filed across the porch with short steps and fingers joined, just timed to turn their smiles loose inside the room. He held the door open for them.

"Ready to go?" he asked her.

Going back, the ride was wordless, quiet except for the motor and the insects driving themselves against the car. The windshield was soon blinded. The headlights pulled in two other spinning storms, cones of flying things that, it seemed, might ignite at the last minute. He stopped the car and got out to clean the windshield thoroughly with his brisk, angry motions of driving. Dust lay thick and cratered on the roadside scrub. Under the now ash-white moon, the world traveled through very faint stars — very many slow stars, very high, very low.

It was a strange land, amphibious — and whether water-covered or grown with jungle or robbed entirely of water and trees, as now, it had the same loneliness. He regarded the great sweep — like steppes, like moors, like deserts (all of which were imaginary to him); but more than it was like any likeness, it was South. The vast, thin, wide-thrown, pale, unfocused star-sky, with its veils of lightning adrift, hung over this land as it hung over the open sea. Standing out in the night alone, he was struck as powerfully with recognition of the extremity of this place as if all other bearings had vanished — as if snow had suddenly started to fall.

He climbed back inside and drove. When he moved to slap furiously at his shirtsleeves, she shivered in the hot, licking night wind that their speed was making. Once the car lights picked out two people — a Negro couple, sitting on two facing chairs in the yard outside their lonely cabin — half undressed, each battling for self against the hot night, with long white rags in endless, scarflike motions.

In peopleless open places there were lakes of dust, smudge fires burning at their hearts. Cows stood in untended rings around them, motionless in the heat, in the night — their horns standing up sharp against that glow.

At length, he stopped the car again, and this time he put his arm under her shoulder and kissed her — not knowing ever whether gently or harshly. It was the loss of that distinction that told him this was now. Then their faces touched unkissing, unmoving, dark, for a length of time. The heat came inside the car and wrapped them still, and the mosquitoes had begun to coat their arms and even their eyelids.

Later, crossing a large open distance, he saw at the same time two fires. He had the feeling that they had been riding for a long time across a face — great, wide, and upturned. In its eyes and open mouth were those fires they had had glimpses of, where the cattle had drawn together: a face, a head, far down here in the South — south of South, below it. A whole giant body sprawled downward then, on and on, always, constant as a constellation or an angel. Flaming and perhaps falling, he thought.

She appeared to be sound asleep, lying back flat as a child, with her hat in her lap. He drove on with her profile beside his, behind his, for he bent forward to drive faster. The earrings she wore twinkled with their rushing motion in an almost regular beat. They might have spoken like tongues. He looked straight before him and drove on, at a speed that, for the rented, overheated, not at all new Ford car, was demoniac.

It seemed often now that a barnlike shape flashed by, roof and all outlined in lonely neon — a movie house at a crossroads. The long white flat road itself, since they had followed it to the end and turned around to come back, seemed able, this far up, to pull them home.

A thing is incredible, if ever, only after it is told — returned to the world it came out of. For their different reasons, he thought, neither of them would tell this (unless something was dragged out of them): that, strangers, they had ridden down into a strange land together and were getting safely back — by a slight margin, perhaps, but margin enough. Over the levee wall now, like an aurora borealis, the sky of New Orleans, across the river, was flickering gently. This time they crossed by bridge, high above everything, merging into a long light-stream of cars turned cityward.

For a time afterward he was lost in the streets, turning almost at random with the noisy traffic until he found his bearings. When he stopped the car at the next sign and leaned forward frowning to make it out, she sat up straight on her side. It was Arabi. He turned the car right around.

"We're all right now," he muttered, allowing himself a cigarette.

Something that must have been with them all along suddenly, then, was not. In a moment, tall as panic, it rose, cried like a human, and dropped back.

"I never got my water," she said.

She gave him the name of her hotel, he drove her there, and he said good night on the sidewalk. They shook hands.

"Forgive . . ." For, just in time, he saw she expected it of him.

And that was just what she did, forgive him. Indeed, had she waked in time from a deep sleep, she would have told him her story. She disappeared through the revolving door, with a gesture of smoothing her hair, and he thought a figure in the lobby strolled to meet her. He got back in the car and sat there.

He was not leaving for Syracuse until early in the morning. At length, he recalled the reason; his wife had recommended that he stay where he was this extra day so that she could entertain some old, unmarried college friends without him underfoot.

As he started up the car, he recognized in the smell of exhausted, body-warm air in the streets, in which the flow of drink was an inextricable part, the signal that the New Orleans evening was just beginning. In Dickie Grogan's, as he passed, the well-known Josefina at her organ was charging up and down with "*Clair de Lune.*" As he drove the little Ford safely to its garage, he remembered for the first time in years when he was young and brash, a student in New York, and the shriek and horror and unholy smother of the subway had its original meaning for him as the lilt and expectation of love.

The Magic Barrel

by Bernard Malamud

NOT LONG AGO there lived in uptown New York, in a small, almost meager room, though crowded with books, Leo Finkle, a rabbinical student in the Yeshivah University. Finkle, after six years of study, was to be ordained in June and had been advised by an acquaintance that he might find it easier to win himself a congregation if he were married. Since he had no present prospects of marriage, after two tormented days of turning it over in his mind, he called in Pinye Salzman, a marriage broker, whose two-line advertisement he had read in the *Forward*.

The matchmaker appeared one night out of the dark fourth-floor hallway of the graystone rooming house, grasping a black, strapped portfolio that had been worn thin with use. Salzman, who had been long in the business, was of slight but dignified build, wearing an old hat and an overcoat too short and tight for him. He smelled frankly of fish, which he loved to eat, and although he was missing a few teeth, his presence was not displeasing, because of an amiable manner curiously contrasted by mournful eyes. His voice, his lips, his wisp of beard, his bony fingers were animated, but give him a moment of repose and his mild blue eyes soon revealed a depth of sadness, a characteristic that put Leo a little at ease although the situation, for him, was inherently tense.

He at once informed Salzman why he had asked him to come, explaining that his home was in Cleveland, and that but for his parents, who had married comparatively late in life, he was alone in the world. He had for six years devoted himself entirely to his studies, as a result of which, quite understandably, he had found himself without time for a social life and the company of young women. Therefore he thought it the better part of trial and error — of embarrassing fumbling — to call in an experienced person to advise him in these matters. He remarked in passing that the function of the marriage broker was ancient and honorable, highly approved in the Jewish community, because it made practical the necessary without hindering joy. Moreover, his own parents had been brought together by a matchmaker. They had made, if not a financially profitable marriage — since neither had possessed any worldly goods to speak of — at least a successful one in the sense of their everlasting devotion to one another. Salzman listened in embarrassed surprise, sensing a sort of apology. Later, however, he experienced a glow of pride in his work, an emotion that had left him years ago, and he heartily approved of Finkle.

The two men went to their business. Leo had led Salzman to the only clear place in the room, a table near a window that overlooked the lamplit city. He seated himself at the matchmaker's side but facing him, attempting by an act of will to suppress the unpleasant tickle in his throat. Salzman eagerly unstrapped his portfolio and removed a loose rubber band from a thin packet of much handled cards. As he flipped through them, a gesture and sound that physically hurt Leo, the student pretended not to see and gazed steadfastly out the window. Although it was still February, winter was on its last legs, signs of which he had for the first time in years begun to notice. He now observed the round white moon, moving high in the sky through a cloud menagerie, and watched with half-open mouth as it penetrated a huge hen, and dropped out of her like an egg laying itself. Salzman, though pretending through eyeglasses he had just slipped on to be engaged in scanning the writing on the cards, stole occasional glances at the young man's distinguished face, noting with pleasure the long, severe scholar's nose, brown eyes heavy with learning, sensitive yet ascetic lips, and a certain almost hollow quality of the dark cheeks. He gazed around at shelves upon shelves of books and let out a soft but happy sigh.

When Leo's eyes fell upon the cards, he counted six spread out in Salzman's hand.

"So few?" he said in disappointment.

"You wouldn't believe me how much cards I got in my office," Salzman replied. "The drawers are already filled to the top, so I keep them now in a barrel, but is every girl good for a new rabbi?"

Leo blushed at this, regretting all he had revealed of himself in a curriculum vitae he had sent to Salzman. He had thought it best to acquaint him with his strict standards and specifications, but in having done so now felt he had told the marriage broker more than was absolutely necessary.

He hesitantly inquired, "Do you keep photographs of your clients on file?"

"First comes family, amount of dowry, also what kind promises," Salzman replied, unbuttoning his tight coat and settling himself in the chair. "After comes pictures, rabbi."

"Call me Mr. Finkle. I'm not a rabbi yet."

Salzman said he would, but instead called him doctor, which he changed to rabbi when Leo was not listening too attentively.

Salzman adjusted his horn-rimmed spectacles, gently cleared his throat and read in an eager voice the contents of the top card:

"Sophie P. Twenty-four years. Widow for one year. No children. Educated high school and two years college. Father promises eight thousand dollars. Has wonderful wholesale business. Also real estate. On the mother's side comes teachers, also one actor. Well known on Second Avenue."

Leo gazed up in surprise. "Did you say a widow?"

"A widow don't mean spoiled, rabbi. She lived with her husband maybe four months. He was a sick boy, she made a mistake to marry him."

"Marrying a widow has never entered my mind."

"This is because you have no experience. A widow, specially if she is young and healthy like this girl, is a wonderful person to marry. She will be thankful to you the rest of her life. Believe me, if I was looking now for a bride, I would marry a widow."

Leo reflected, then shook his head.

Salzman hunched his shoulders in an almost imperceptible gesture of disappointment. He placed the card down on the wooden table and began to read another:

"Lily H. High school teacher. Regular. Not a substitute. Has savings and new Dodge car. Lived in Paris one year. Father is successful dentist thirty-five years. Interested in professional man. Well Americanized family. Wonderful opportunity.

"I know her personally," said Salzman. "I wish you could see this girl. She is a doll. Also very intelligent. All day you could talk to her about books and theyater and what not. She also knows current events."

"I don't believe you mentioned her age?"

"Her age?" Salzman said, raising his brows in surprise. "Her age is thirty-two years."

Leo said after a while, "I'm afraid that seems a little too old."

Salzman let out a laugh. "So how old are you, rabbi?"

"Twenty-seven."

"So what is the difference, tell me, between twenty-seven and thirty-two? My own wife is seven years older than me. So what did I suffer? — Nothing. If Rothschild's a daughter wants to marry you, would you say on account her age, no?"

"Yes," Leo said dryly.

Salzman shook off the no in the yes. "Five years don't mean a thing. I give you my word that when you will live with her for one week you will forget her age. What does it mean five years — that she lived more and knows more than somebody who is younger? On this girl, God bless her, years are not wasted. Each one that it comes makes better the bargain."

"What subject does she teach in high school?"

"Languages. If you heard the way she reads French, you will think it is music. I am in the business twenty-five years, and I recommend her with my whole heart. Believe me, I know what I'm talking, rabbi."

"What's on the next card?" Leo said abruptly.

Salzman reluctantly turned up the third card:

"Ruth K. Nineteen years. Honor student. Father offers thirteen thousand dollars cash to the right bridegroom. He is a medical doctor. Stomach specialist with marvelous practice. Brother-in-law owns own garment business. Particular people."

Salzman looked up as if he had read his trump card.

"Did you say nineteen?" Leo asked with interest.

"On the dot."

"Is she attractive?" He blushed. "Pretty?"

Salzman kissed his fingertips. "A little doll. On this I give you my word. Let me call the father tonight and you will see what means pretty."

But Leo was troubled. "You're sure she's that young?"

"This I am positive. The father will show you the birth certificate."

"Are you positive there isn't something wrong with her?" Leo insisted.

"Who says there is wrong?"

"I don't understand why an American girl her age should go to a marriage broker."

A smile spread over Salzman's face.

"So for the same reason you went, she comes."

Leo flushed. "I am pressed for time."

Salzman, realizing he had been tactless, quickly explained. "The father came, not her. He wants she should have the best, so he looks around himself. When we will locate the right boy he will introduce him and encourage. This makes a better marriage than if a young girl without experience takes for herself. I don't have to tell you this."

"But don't you think this young girl believes in love?" Leo spoke uneasily.

Salzman was about to guffaw but caught himself and said soberly, "Love comes with the right person, not before."

Leo parted dry lips but did not speak. Noticing that Salzman had snatched a quick glance at the next card, he cleverly asked, "How is her health?"

"Perfect," Salzman said, breathing with difficulty. "Of course, she is a little lame on her right foot from an auto accident that it happened to her when she was twelve years, but nobody notices on account she is so brilliant and also beautiful."

Leo got up heavily and went to the window. He felt curiously bitter and upbraided himself for having called in the marriage broker. Finally, he shook his head.

"Why not?" Salzman persisted, the pitch of his voice rising.

"Because I hate stomach specialists."

"So what do you care what is his business? After you marry her, do you need him? Who says he must come every Friday night to your house?"

Ashamed of the way the talk was going, Leo dismissed Salzman, who went home with melancholy eyes.

Though he had felt only relief at the marriage broker's departure, Leo was in low spirits the next day. He explained it as arising from Salzman's failure to produce a suitable bride for him. He did not care for his type of clientele. But when Leo found himself hesitating over whether to seek out another matchmaker, one more polished than Pinye, he wondered if it could be — his protestations to the contrary, and although he honored his father and mother — that he did not, in essence, care for the matchmaking institution. This thought he quickly put out of mind yet found himself still upset. All day he ran around in a fog — missed an important appointment, forgot to give out his laundry, walked out of a Broadway cafeteria without paying and had to run back with the ticket in his hand; had even not recognized his landlady in the street when she passed with a friend and courteously called out, "A good evening to you, Doctor Finkle." By nightfall, however, he had regained sufficient calm to sink his nose into a book and there found peace from his thoughts.

Almost at once there came a knock on the door. Before Leo could say enter, Salzman, commercial cupid, was standing in the room. His face was gray and meager, his expression hungry, and he looked as if he would expire on his feet. Yet the marriage broker managed, by some trick of the muscles, to display a broad smile.

"So good evening. I am invited?"

Leo nodded, disturbed to see him again, yet unwilling to ask him to leave.

Beaming still, Salzman laid his portfolio on the table. "Rabbi, I got for you tonight good news."

"I've asked you not to call me rabbi. I'm still a student."

"Your worries are finished. I have for you a first-class bride."

"Leave me in peace concerning this subject." Leo pretended lack of interest.

"The world will dance at your wedding."

"Please, Mr. Salzman, no more."

"But first must come back my strength," Salzman said weakly. He fumbled with the portfolio straps and took out of the leather case an oily paper bag, from which he extracted a hard seeded roll and a small smoked whitefish. With one motion of his hand he stripped the fish out of its skin and began ravenously to chew. "All day in a rush," he muttered.

Leo watched him eat.

"A sliced tomato you have maybe?" Salzman hesitantly inquired.

"No."

The marriage broker shut his eyes and ate. When he had finished he carefully cleaned up the crumbs and rolled up the remains of the fish in the paper bag. His spectacled eyes roamed the room until he discovered, amid some piles of books, a one-burner gas stove. Lifting his hat he humbly asked, "A glass tea you got, rabbi?"

Conscience-stricken, Leo rose and brewed the tea. He served it with a chunk of lemon and two cubes of lump sugar, delighting Salzman.

After he had drunk his tea, Salzman's strength and good spirits were restored.

"So tell me, rabbi," he said amiably, "you considered any more the three clients I mentioned yesterday?"

"There was no need to consider."

"Why not?"

"None of them suits me."

"What, then, suits you?"

Leo let it pass because he could give only a confused answer.

Without waiting for a reply, Salzman asked, "You remember this girl I talked to you — the high school teacher?"

"Age thirty-two?"

But, surprisingly, Salzman's face lit in a smile. "Age twenty-nine."

Leo shot him a look. "Reduced from thirty-two?"

"A mistake," Salzman avowed. "I talked today with the dentist. He took me to his safety deposit box and showed me the birth certificate. She was twenty-nine years last August. They made her a party in the mountains where she went for her vacation. When her father spoke to me the first time I forgot to write the age and I told you thirty-two, but now I remember this was a different client, a widow."

"The same one you told me about? I thought she was twenty-four?"

"A different. Am I responsible that the world is filled with widows?"

"No, but I'm not interested in them, nor for that matter, in school-teachers."

Salzman passionately pulled his clasped hands to his breast. Looking at the ceiling he exclaimed, "Jewish children, what can I say to somebody that he is not interested in high school teachers? So what then you are interested?"

Leo flushed but controlled himself.

"In who else you will be interested," Salzman went on, "if you not interested in this fine girl that she speaks four languages and has personally in the bank ten thousand dollars? Also her father guarantees further twelve thousand. Also she has a new car, wonderful clothes, talks on all subjects, and she will give you a first-class home and children. How near do we come in our life to paradise?"

"If she's so wonderful, why wasn't she married ten years ago?"

"Why?" said Salzman with a heavy laugh "— Why? Because she is *partikler*. This is why. She wants only the *best*."

Leo was silent, amused at how he had trapped himself. But Salzman had aroused his interest in Lily H., and he began seriously to consider calling on her. When the marriage broker observed how intently Leo's mind was at work on the facts he had supplied, he felt positive they would soon come to an agreement.

Late Saturday afternoon, conscious of Salzman, Leo Finkle walked with Lily Hirschorn along Riverside Drive. He walked briskly and erectly, wearing with distinction the black fedora he had that morning taken with trepidation out of the dusty hatbox on his closet shelf, and the heavy black Saturday coat he had thoroughly whisked clean. Leo also owned a walking stick, a present from a distant relative, but had decided not to use it. Lily, petite and not unpretty, had on something signifying the approach of spring. She was *au courant*, animatedly, with all subjects, and he weighed her words and found her surprisingly sound — score another for Salzman, whom he uneasily sensed to be somewhere around, hiding perhaps high in a tree along the street, flashing the lady signals; or perhaps a cloven-hoofed Pan, piping nuptial ditties as he danced his invisible way before them, strewing wild buds on the walk and purple summer grapes in their path, symbolizing fruit of a union, of which there was yet none.

Lily startled Leo by remarking, "I was thinking of Mr. Salzman, a curious figure, wouldn't you say?"

Not certain what to answer, he nodded.

She bravely went on, blushing, "I for one am grateful for his introducing us. Aren't you?"

He courteously replied, "I am."

"I mean," she said with a little laugh — and it was all in good taste, or at least gave the effect of being not in bad — "do you mind that we came together so?"

He was not afraid of her honesty, recognizing that she meant to set the relationship aright, and understanding that it took a certain amount of experience in life, and courage, to want to do it quite that way. One had to have some sort of past to make that kind of beginning.

He said that he did not mind. Salzman's function was traditional and honorable — valuable for what it might achieve, which he pointed out was frequently nothing.

Lily agreed with a sigh. They walked on for a while and she said after a long silence, again with a nervous laugh, "Would you mind if I asked you something a little bit personal? Frankly, I find the subject fascinating." Although Leo shrugged, she went on half embarrassedly, "How was it that you came to your calling? I mean was it a sudden passionate inspiration?"

Leo, after a time, slowly replied, "I was always interested in the Law."

"You saw revealed in it the presence of the Highest?"

He nodded and changed the subject. "I understand you spent a little time in Paris, Miss Hirschorn?"

"Oh, did Mr. Salzman tell you, Rabbi Finkle?" Leo winced but she went on, "It was ages and ages ago and almost forgotten. I remember I had to return for my sister's wedding."

But Lily would not be put off. "When," she asked in a trembly voice, "did you become enamored of God?"

He stared at her. Then it came to him that she was talking not about Leo Finkle, but a total stranger, some mystical figure, perhaps even passionate prophet that Salzman had conjured up for her — no relation to the living or dead. Leo trembled with rage and weakness. The trickster had obviously sold her a bill of goods, just as he had him, who'd expected to become acquainted with a young lady of twenty-nine, only to behold, the moment he laid eyes upon her strained and anxious face, a woman past thirty-five and aging very rapidly. Only his self-control, he thought, had kept him this long in her presence.

"I am not," he said gravely, "a talented religious person," and in seeking words to go on, found himself possessed by fear and shame. "I think," he said in a strained manner, "that I came to God not because I loved him, but because I did not."

This confession he spoke harshly because its unexpectedness shook him.

Lily wilted. Leo saw a profusion of loaves of bread sailing like ducks high over his head, not unlike the loaves by which he had counted himself to sleep last night. Mercifully, then, it snowed, which he would not put past Salzman's machinations.

He was infuriated with the marriage broker and swore he would throw him out of the room the moment he reappeared. But Salzman did not come that night, and when Leo's anger had subsided, an unaccountable despair grew in its place. At first he thought this was caused by his disappointment in Lily, but before long it became evident that he had involved himself with Salzman without a true knowledge of his own intent. He gradually realized — with an emptiness that seized him with six hands — that he had called in the broker to find him a bride because he was incapable of doing it himself. This terrifying insight he had derived as a result of his meeting and conversation with Lily Hirschorn. Her probing questions had somehow irritated him into revealing — to himself more than her — the true nature of his relationship with God, and from that it had come upon him, with shocking force, that apart from his parents, he had never loved anyone. Or perhaps it went the other way, that he did not love God so well as he might, because he had not loved man. It seemed to Leo that his whole life stood starkly revealed and he saw himself, for the first time, as he truly was — unloved and loveless. This bitter but somehow not fully unexpected revelation brought him to a point of panic controlled only by extraordinary effort. He covered his face with his hands and wept.

The week that followed was the worst of his life. He did not eat, and lost weight. His beard darkened and grew ragged. He stopped attending lectures and seminars and almost never opened a book. He seriously considered leaving the Yeshivah, although he was deeply troubled at the thought of the loss of all his years of study — saw them like pages from a book strewn over the city — and at the devastating effect of this decision upon his parents. But he had lived without knowledge of himself, and never in the Five Books and all the Commentaries — mea culpa — had the truth been revealed to him. He did not know where to turn, and in all this desolating loneliness there was no *to whom*, although he often thought of Lily but not once could bring himself to go downstairs and make the call. He became touchy and irritable, especially with his landlady, who asked him all manner of questions; on the other hand, sensing his own disagreeableness, he waylaid her on the stairs and apologized abjectly, until, mortified, she ran from him. Out of this, however, he drew the consolation that he was yet a Jew and that a Jew suffered. But gradually, as the long and terrible week drew to a close, he regained his composure and some idea of purpose in life: to go on as planned. Although he was imperfect, the ideal was not. As for his quest of a bride, the thought of continuing afflicted him with anxiety and heartburn, yet perhaps with this new knowledge of himself he would be more successful than in the past. Perhaps love would now come to him and a bride to that love. And for this sanctified seeking who needed a Salzman?

The marriage broker, a skeleton with haunted eyes, returned that very night. He looked, withal, the picture of frustrated expectancy — as if he had steadfastly waited the week at Miss Lily Hirschorn's side for a telephone call that never came.

Casually coughing, Salzman came immediately to the point: "So how did you like her?"

Leo's anger rose and he could not refrain from chiding the matchmaker: "Why did you lie to me, Salzman?"

Salzman's pale face went dead white, as if the world had snowed on him.

"Did you not state that she was twenty-nine?" Leo insisted.

"I give you my word —"

"She was thirty-five. *At least* thirty-five."

"Of this I would not be too sure. Her father told me —"

"Never mind. The worst of it was that you lied to her."

"How did I lie to her, tell me?"

"You told her things about me that weren't true. You made me out to be more, consequently less than I am. She had in mind a totally different person, a sort of semi-mystical Wonder Rabbi."

"All I said, you was a religious man."

"I can imagine."

Salzman sighed. "This is my weakness that I have," he confessed.

"My wife says to me I shouldn't be a salesman, but when I have two fine people that they would be wonderful to be married, I am so happy that I talk too much." He smiled wanly. "This is why Salzman is a poor man."

Leo's anger went. "Well, Salzman, I'm afraid that's all."

The marriage broker fastened hungry eyes on him.

"You don't want any more a bride?"

"I do," said Leo, "but I have decided to seek her in a different way. I am no longer interested in an arranged marriage. To be frank, I now admit the necessity of premarital love. That is, I want to be in love with the one I marry."

"Love?" said Salzman, astounded. After a moment he said, "For us, our love is our life, not for the ladies. In the ghetto they —"

"I know, I know," said Leo. "I've thought of it often. Love, I have said to myself, should be a by-product of living and worship rather than its own end. Yet for myself I find it necessary to establish the level of my need and to fulfill it."

Salzman shrugged but answered, "Listen, rabbi, if you want love, this I can find for you also. I have such beautiful clients that you will love them the minute your eyes will see them."

Leo smiled unhappily. "I'm afraid you don't understand."

But Salzman hastily unstrapped his portfolio and withdrew a manila packet from it.

"Pictures," he said, quickly laying the envelope on the table.

Leo called after him to take the pictures away, but as if on the wings of the wind, Salzman had disappeared.

March came. Leo had returned to his regular routine. Although he felt not quite himself yet — lacked energy — he was making plans for a more active social life. Of course it would cost something, but he was an expert in cutting corners; and when there were no corners left he could make circles rounder. All the while Salzman's pictures had lain on the table, gathering dust. Occasionally as Leo sat studying, or enjoying a cup of tea, his eyes fell on the manila envelope, but he never opened it.

The days went by and no social life to speak of developed with a member of the opposite sex — it was difficult, given the circumstances of his situation. One morning Leo toiled up the stairs to his room and stared out the window at the city. Although the day was bright his view of it was dark. For some time he watched the people in the street below hurrying along and then turned with a heavy heart to his little room. On the table was the packet. With a sudden relentless gesture he tore it open. For a half-hour he stood there, in a state of excitement, examining the photographs of the ladies Salzman had included. Finally, with a deep sigh he put them down. There were six, of varying degrees of attractiveness, but look at them long enough and they all became Lily Hirschorn: all past their prime, all starved behind bright smiles, not a true personality in the lot. Life, despite their anguished struggles and frantic yoohooings, had passed them by; they were photographs in a briefcase that stank of fish. After a while, however, as Leo attempted to return the pictures into the envelope, he found another in it, a small snapshot of the type taken by a machine for a quarter. He gazed at it a moment and let out a cry.

Her face deeply moved him. Why, he could at first not say. It gave him the impression of youth — all spring flowers, yet age — a sense of having been used to the bone, wasted; this all came from the eyes, which were hauntingly familiar, yet absolutely strange. He had a strong impression that he had met her before, but try as he might he could not place her, although he could almost recall her name, as if he had read it written in her own handwriting. No, this couldn't be; he would have remembered her. It was not, he affirmed, that she had an extraordinary beauty — no, although her face was attractive enough; it was that *something* about her moved him. Feature for feature, even some of the ladies of the photographs could do better; but she leaped forth to the heart — had lived, or wanted to — more than just wanted, perhaps regretted it — had somehow deeply suffered: it could be seen in the depths of those reluctant eyes, and from the way the light enclosed and shone from her, and within her, opening whole realms of possibility: this was her own. Her he desired. His head ached and eyes narrowed with the intensity of his gazing, then, as if a black fog had blown up in the mind, he experienced fear of her and was aware that he had received an impression, somehow, of filth. He shuddered, saying softly, it is thus with us all. Leo brewed some tea in a small pot and sat sipping it, without sugar, to calm himself. But before he had finished drinking, again with excitement he examined the face and found it good: good for him. Only such a one could truly understand Leo Finkle and help him to seek whatever he was seeking. How she had come to be among the discards in Salzman's barrel he could never guess, but he knew he must urgently go find her.

Leo rushed downstairs, grabbed up the Bronx telephone book, and searched for Salzman's home address. He was not listed, nor was his office. Neither was he in the Manhattan book. But Leo remembered having written down the address on a slip of paper after he had read Salzman's advertisement in the "personals" column of the *Forward*. He ran up to his room and tore through his papers, without luck. It was exasperating. Just when he needed the matchmaker he was nowhere to be found. Fortunately Leo remembered to look in his wallet. There on a card he found his name written and a Bronx address. No phone number was listed, which, Leo now recalled, was the reason he had originally communicated with Salzman by letter. He got on his coat, put a hat on over his skull cap and hurried to the subway station. All the way to the far end of the Bronx he sat on the edge of the seat. He was more than once tempted to take out the picture and see if the girl's face was as he remembered it, but he refrained, allowing the snapshot to remain in his inside coat pocket, content to have her so close. When the train pulled into the station he was waiting at the door and bolted out. He quickly located the street Salzman had advertised.

The building he sought was less than a block from the subway, but it was not an office building, nor even a loft, nor a store in which one could rent office space. It was an old and grimy tenement. Leo found Salzman's name in pencil on a soiled tag under the bell and climbed three dark flights to his apartment. When he knocked, the door was opened by a thin, asthmatic, gray-haired woman, in felt slippers.

"Yes?" she said, expecting nothing. She listened without listening. He could have sworn he had seen her somewhere before but knew it was illusion.

"Salzman — does he live here? Pinye Salzman," he said, "the matchmaker?"

She stared at him a long time. "Of course."

He felt embarrassed. "Is he in?"

"No." Her mouth was open, but she offered nothing more.

"This is urgent. Can you tell me where his office is?"

"In the air." She pointed upward.

"You mean he has no office?" Leo said.

"In his socks."

He peered into the apartment. It was sunless and dingy, one large room divided by a half-open curtain, beyond which he could see a sagging metal bed. The near side of the room was crowded with rickety chairs, old bureaus, a three-legged table, racks of cooking utensils, and all the apparatus of a kitchen. But there was no sign of Salzman or his magic barrel, probably also a figment of his imagination. An odor of frying fish made Leo weak to the knees.

"Where is he?" he insisted. "I've got to see your husband."

At length she answered, "So who knows where he is? Every time he thinks a new thought he runs to a different place. Go home, he will find you."

"Tell him Leo Finkle."

She gave no sign that she had heard.

He went downstairs, deeply depressed.

But Salzman, breathless, stood waiting at his door.

Leo was overjoyed and astounded. "How did you get here before me?"

"I rushed."

"Come inside."

They entered. Leo fixed tea and a sardine sandwich for Salzman.

As they were drinking he reached behind him for the packet of pictures and handed them to the marriage broker.

Salzman put down his glass and said expectantly, "You found maybe somebody you like?"

"Not among these."

The marriage broker turned sad eyes away.

"Here's the one I like." Leo held forth the snapshot.

Salzman slipped on his glasses and took the picture into his trembling hand. He turned ghastly and let out a miserable groan.

"What's the matter?" cried Leo.

"Excuse me. Was an accident this picture. She is not for you."

Salzman frantically shoved the manila packet into his portfolio. He thrust the snapshot into his pocket and fled down the stairs.

Leo, after momentary paralysis, gave chase and cornered the marriage broker in the vestibule. The landlady made hysterical outcries but neither of them listened.

"Give me back the picture, Salzman."

"No." The pain in his eyes was terrible.

"Tell me who she is then."

"This I can't tell you. Excuse me."

He made to depart, but Leo, forgetting himself, seized the matchmaker by his tight coat and shook him frenziedly.

"Please," sighed Salzman. "*Please*."

Leo ashamedly let him go. "Tell me who she is," he begged. "It's very important for me to know."

"She is not for you. She is a wild one — wild, without shame. This is not a bride for a rabbi."

"What do you mean wild?"

"Like an animal. Like a dog. For her to be poor was a sin. This is why she is dead now."

"In God's name, what do you mean?"

"Her I can't introduce to you," Salzman cried.

"Why are you so excited?"

"Why he asks," Salzman said, bursting into tears. "This is my baby, my Stella, she should burn in hell."

Leo hurried up to bed and hid under the covers. Under the covers he thought his whole life through. Although he soon fell asleep he could not sleep her out of his mind. He woke, beating his breast. Though he prayed to be rid of her, his prayers went unanswered. Through days of torment he struggled endlessly not to love her; fearing success, he escaped it. He then concluded to convert her to goodness, himself to God. The idea alternately nauseated and exalted him.

He perhaps did not know that he had come to a final decision until he encountered Salzman in a Broadway cafeteria. He was sitting alone at a rear table, sucking the bony remains of a fish. The marriage broker appeared haggard, and transparent to the point of vanishing.

Salzman looked up at first without recognizing him. Leo had grown a pointed beard and his eyes were weighted with wisdom.

"Salzman," he said, "love has at last come to my heart."

"Who can love from a picture?" mocked the marriage broker.

"It is not impossible."

"If you can love her, then you can love anybody. Let me show you some new clients that they just sent me their photographs. One is a little doll."

"Just her I want," Leo murmured.

"Don't be a fool, doctor. Don't bother with her."

"Put me in touch with her, Salzman," Leo said humbly. "Perhaps I can do her a service."

Salzman had stopped chewing, and Leo understood with emotion that it was now arranged.

Leaving the cafeteria, he was, however, afflicted by a tormenting suspicion that Salzman had planned it all to happen this way.

Leo was informed by letter that she would meet him on a certain corner, and she was there one spring night, waiting under a street lamp. He appeared, carrying a small bouquet of violets and rosebuds. Stella stood by the lamppost, smoking. She wore white with red shoes, which fitted his expectations, although in a troubled moment he had imagined the dress red, and only the shoes white. She waited uneasily and shyly. From afar he saw that her eyes — clearly her father's — were filled with desperate innocence. He pictured, in hers, his own redemption. Violins and lit candles revolved in the sky. Leo ran forward with the flowers outthrust.

Around the corner, Salzman, leaning against a wall, chanted prayers for the dead.

The Pot of Gold

by John Cheever

 ƆOU COULD NOT SAY FAIRLY of Ralph and Laura Whittemore that they had the failings and the characteristics of incorrigible treasure hunters, but you could say truthfully of them that the shimmer and the smell, the peculiar force of money, the promise of it, had an untoward influence on their lives. They were always at the threshold of fortune; they always seemed to have something on the fire. Ralph was a fair young man with a tireless commercial imagination and an evangelical credence in the romance and sorcery of business success, and although he held an obscure job with a clothing manufacturer, this never seemed to him anything more than a point of departure.

The Whittemores were not importunate or overbearing people, and they had an uncompromising loyalty to the gentle manners of the middle class. Laura was a pleasant girl of no particular beauty who had come to New York from Wisconsin at about the same time that Ralph had reached the city from Illinois, but it had taken two years of comings and goings before they had been brought together, late one afternoon, in the lobby of a lower Fifth Avenue office building. So true was Ralph's heart, so well did it serve him then, that the moment he saw Laura's light hair and her pretty and sullen face he was enraptured. He followed her out of the lobby, pushing his way through the crowd, and since she had dropped nothing, since there was no legitimate excuse to speak to her, he shouted after her, *"Louise! Louise!*

Louise!" and the urgency in his voice made her stop. He said he'd made a mistake. He said he was sorry. He said she looked just like a girl named Louise Hatcher. It was a January night and the dark air tasted of smoke, and because she was a sensible and a lonely girl, she let him buy her a drink.

This was in the thirties, and their courtship was hasty. They were married three months later. Laura moved her belongings into a walk-up on Madison Avenue, above a pants presser's and a florist's, where Ralph was living. She worked as a secretary, and her salary, added to what he brought home from the clothing business, was little more than enough to keep them going, but they never seemed touched by the monotony of a saving and gainless life. They ate dinners in drug-stores. She hung a reproduction of van Gogh's "Sunflowers" above the sofa she had bought with some of the small sum of money her parents had left her. When their aunts and uncles came to town — their parents were dead — they had dinner at the Ritz and went to the theatre. She sewed curtains and shined his shoes, and on Sundays they stayed in bed until noon. They seemed to be standing at the threshold of plenty; and Laura often told people that she was terribly excited because of this wonderful job that Ralph had lined up.

In the first year of their marriage, Ralph worked nights on a plan that promised him a well-paying job in Texas, but through no fault of his own this promise was never realized. There was an opening in Syracuse a year later, but an older man was decided upon. There were many other profitable but elusive openings and projects between these two. In the third year of their marriage, a firm that was almost identi-cal in size and character with the firm Ralph worked for underwent a change of ownership, and Ralph was approached and asked if he would be interested in joining the overhauled firm. His own job prom-ised only meager security after a series of slow promotions and he was glad of the chance to escape. He met the new owners, and their enthusiasm for him seemed intense. They were prepared to put him in charge of a department and pay him twice what he was getting then. The arrangement was to remain tacit for a month or two, until the new owners had secured their position, but they shook hands warmly and had a drink on the deal, and that night Ralph took Laura out to dinner at an expensive restaurant.

They decided, across the table, to look for a larger apartment, to have a child, and to buy a secondhand car. They faced their good fortune with perfect calm, for it was what they had expected all along. The city seemed to them a generous place, where people were rewarded either by a sudden and deserved development like this or by the capricious bounty of lawsuits, eccentric and peripheral business ventures, unexpected legacies, and other windfalls. After dinner, they walked in Central Park in the moonlight while Ralph smoked a cigar. Later, when Laura had fallen asleep, he sat in the open bedroom window in his pajamas.

The peculiar excitement with which the air of the city seems charged after midnight, when its life falls into the hands of watchmen and drunks, had always pleased him. He knew intimately the sounds of the night street: the bus brakes, the remote sirens, and the sound of water turning high in the air — the sound of water turning a mill wheel — the sum, he supposed, of many echoes, although, often as he had heard the sound, he had never decided on its source. Now he heard all this more keenly because the night seemed to him portentous.

He was twenty-eight years old; poverty and youth were inseparable in his experience, and one was ending with the other. The life they were about to leave had not been hard, and he thought with sentiment of the soiled tablecloth in the Italian restaurant where they usually went for their celebrations, and the high spirits with which Laura on a wet night ran from the subway to the bus stop. But they were drawing away from all this. Shirt sales in department-store basements, lines at meat counters, weak drinks, the roses he brought her up from the subway in the spring, when roses were cheap — these were all unmistakably the souvenirs of the poor, and while they seemed to him good and gentle, he was glad that they would soon be memories.

Laura resigned from her job when she got pregnant. The reorganization and Ralph's new position hung fire, but the Whittemores talked about it freely when they were with friends. "We're *terribly* pleased with the way things are going," Laura would say. "All we need is patience." There were many delays and postponements, and they waited with the patience of people expecting justice. The time came when they both needed clothes, and one evening Ralph suggested that they spend some of the money they had put aside. Laura refused. When he brought up the subject, she didn't answer him and seemed not to hear him. He raised his voice and lost his temper. He shouted. She cried. He thought of all the other girls he could have married — the dark blonde, the worshipful Cuban, the rich and pretty one with a cast in her right eye. All his desires seemed to lie outside the small apartment Laura had arranged. They were still not speaking in the morning, and in order to strengthen his position he telephoned his potential employers. Their secretary told him they were both out. This made him apprehensive. He called several times from the telephone booth in the lobby of the building he worked in and was told that they were busy, they were out, they were in conference with lawyers, or they were talking long-distance. This variety of excuses frightened him. He said nothing to Laura that evening and tried to call them the next day. Late in the afternoon, after many tries, one of them came to the phone. "We gave the job to somebody else, sonny," he said. Like a saddened father, he spoke to Ralph in a hoarse and gentle voice. "Don't try and get us on the telephone any more. We've got other things to do besides answer the telephone. This other fellow seemed better suited, sonny. That's all I can tell you, and don't try to get me on the telephone any more."

Ralph walked the miles from his office to his apartment that night, hoping to free himself in this way from some of the weight of his disappointment. He was so unprepared for the shock that it affected him like vertigo, and he walked with an old, high step, as if the paving were quicksand. He stood downstairs in front of the building he lived in, trying to decide how to describe the disaster to Laura, but when he went in, he told her bluntly. "Oh, I'm sorry, darling," she said softly and kissed him. "I'm terribly sorry." She wandered away from him and began to straighten the sofa cushions. His frustration was so ardent, he was such a prisoner of his schemes and expectations, that he was astonished at the serenity with which she regarded the failure. There was nothing to worry about, she said. She still had a few hundred dollars in the bank, from the money her parents had left her. There was nothing to worry about.

When the child, a girl, was born, they named her Rachel, and a week after the delivery Laura returned to the Madison Avenue walk-up. She took all the care of the baby and continued to do the cooking and the housework.

Ralph's imagination remained resilient and fertile, but he couldn't seem to hit on a scheme that would fit into his lack of time and capital. He and Laura, like the hosts of the poor everywhere, lived a simple life. They still went to the theatre with visiting relatives and occasionally they went to parties, but Laura's only continuous contact with the bright lights that surrounded them was vicarious and came to her through a friend she made in Central Park.

She spent many afternoons on a park bench during the first years of Rachel's life. It was a tyranny and a pleasure. She resented her en-chainment but enjoyed the open sky and the air. One winter after-noon, she recognized a woman she had met at a party, and a little before dark, as Laura and the other mothers were gathering their stuffed animals and preparing their children for the cold journey home, the woman came across the playground and spoke to her. She was Alice Holinshed, she said. They had met at the Galvins'. She was pretty and friendly, and walked with Laura to the edge of the Park. She had a boy of about Rachel's age. The two women met again the following day. They became friends.

Mrs. Holinshed was older than Laura, but she had a more youthful and precise beauty. Her hair and her eyes were black, her pale and perfectly oval face was delicately colored, and her voice was pure. She lighted her cigarettes with Stork Club matches and spoke of the in-convenience of living with a child in a hotel. If Laura had any regrets about her life, they were expressed in her friendship for this pretty woman, who moved so freely through expensive stores and restau-rants.

It was a friendship circumscribed, with the exception of the Gal-vins', by the sorry and touching countryside of Central Park. The women talked principally about their husbands, and this was a game that Laura could play with an empty purse. Vaguely, boastfully, the two women discussed the irons their men had in the fire. They sat together with their children through the sooty twilights, when the city to the south burns like a Bessemer furnace, and the air smells of coal, and the wet boulders shine like slag, and the Park itself seems like a strip of woods on the edge of a coal town. Then Mrs. Holinshed would remember that she was late — she was always late for something mysterious and splendid — and the two women would walk together to the edge of the woods. This vicarious contact with comfort pleased Laura, and the pleasure would stay with her as she pushed the baby carriage over to Madison Avenue and then began to cook supper, hearing the thump of the steam iron and smelling the cleaning fluid from the pants presser's below.

One night, when Rachel was about two years old, the frustration of Ralph's search for the goat track that would let him lead his family to a realm of reasonable contentment kept him awake. He needed sleep urgently, and when this blessing eluded him, he got out of bed and sat in the dark. The charm and excitement of the street after midnight escaped him. The explosive brakes of a Madison Avenue bus made him jump. He shut the window, but the noise of traffic continued to pass through it. It seemed to him that the penetrating voice of the city had a mortal effect on the precious lives of the city's inhabitants and that it should be muffled.

He thought of a Venetian blind whose outer surfaces would be treated with a substance that would deflect or absorb sound waves. With such a blind, friends paying a call on a spring evening would not have to shout to be heard above the noise of trucks in the street below. Bedrooms could be silenced that way — bedrooms, above all, for it seemed to him then that sleep was what everyone in the city sought and only half captured. All the harried faces on the streets at dusk, when even the pretty girls talk to themselves, were looking for sleep. Night-club singers and their amiable customers, the people waiting for taxis in front of the Waldorf on a wet night, policemen, cashiers, window washers — sleep eluded them all.

He talked over this Venetian blind with Laura the following night, and the idea seemed sensible to her. He bought a blind that would fit their bedroom window, and experimented with various paint mixtures. At last he stumbled on one that dried to the consistency of felt and was porous. The paint had a sickening smell, which filled their apartment during the four days it took him to coat and recoat the outer surface of the slats. When the paint had dried, he hung the blind, and they opened the window for a test. Silence — a relative silence — charmed their ears. He wrote down his formula, and took it during his lunch hour to a patent attorney. It took the lawyer several weeks to discover that a similar formula had been patented some years earlier. The patent owner — a man named Fellows — had a New York address, and the lawyer suggested that Ralph get in touch with him and try to reach some agreement.

The search for Mr. Fellows began one evening when Ralph had finished work, and took him first to the attic of a Hudson Street rooming house, where the landlady showed Ralph a pair of socks that Mr. Fellows had left behind when he moved out. Ralph went south from there to another rooming house and then west to the neighborhood of ship chandlers and marine boarding houses. The nocturnal search went on for a week. He followed the thread of Mr. Fellows' goings south to the Bowery and then to the upper West Side. He climbed stairs past the open doors of rooms where lessons in Spanish dancing were going on, past whores, past women practicing the "Emperor" Concerto, and one evening he found Mr. Fellows sitting on the edge of his bed in an attic room, rubbing the spots out of his necktie with a rag soaked in gasoline.

Mr. Fellows was greedy. He wanted a hundred dollars in cash and fifty per cent of the royalties. Ralph got him to agree to twenty per cent of the royalties, but he could not get him to reduce the initial payment. The lawyer drew up a paper defining Ralph's and Mr. Fellows' interests, and a few nights later Ralph went over to Brooklyn and got to a Venetian-blind factory after its doors had closed but while the lights of the office were still burning. The manager agreed to manufacture some blinds to Ralph's specifications, but he would not take an order of less than a hundred dollars. Ralph agreed to this and to furnish the compound for the outer surface of the slats. These expenditures had taken more than three-fourths of the Whittemores' capital, and now the problem of money was joined by the element of time. They put a small advertisement in the paper for a housewares salesman, and for a week Ralph interviewed candidates in the living room after supper. He chose a young man who was leaving at the end of the week for the Midwest. He wanted a fifty-dollar advance, and pointed out to them that Pittsburgh and Chicago were just as noisy as New York. A department-store collection agency was threatening to bring them into the small-claims court at this time, and they had come to a place where any illness, any fall, any damage to themselves or to the few clothes they owned would be critical. Their salesman promised to write them from Chicago at the end of the week, and they counted on good news, but there was no news from Chicago at all. Ralph wired the salesman twice, and the wires must have been forwarded, for he replied to them from Pittsburgh: "Can't merchandise blinds. Returning samples express." They put another advertisement for a salesman in the paper and took the first one who rang their bell, an old gentleman with a cornflower in his buttonhole. He had a number of other lines — mirror wastebaskets, orange-juicers — and he said that he knew all the Manhattan housewares buyers intimately. He was garrulous, and when he was unable to sell the blinds, he came to the Whittemores' apartment and discussed their product at length, and with a blend of criticism and charity that we usually reserve for human beings.

Ralph was to borrow money, but neither his salary nor his patent was considered adequate collateral for a loan at anything but ruinous rates, and one day, at his office, he was served a summons by the department-store collection agency. He went out to Brooklyn and offered to sell the Venetian blinds back to the manufacturer. The man gave him sixty dollars for what had cost a hundred, and Ralph was able to pay the collection agency. They hung the samples in their windows and tried to put the venture out of their minds.

Now they were poorer than ever, and they ate lentils for dinner every Monday and sometimes again on Tuesday. Laura washed the dishes after dinner while Ralph read to Rachel. When the girl had fallen asleep, he would go to his desk in the living room and work on one of his projects. There was always something coming. There was a job in Dallas and a job in Peru. There were the plastic arch preserver, the automatic closing device for icebox doors, and the scheme to pirate marine specifications and undersell Jane's. For a month, he was going to buy some fallow acreage in upstate New York and plant Christmas trees on it, and then, with one of his friends, he projected a luxury mail-order business, for which they could never get backing. When the Whittemores met Uncle George and Aunt Helen at the Ritz, they seemed delighted with the way things were going. They were terribly excited, Laura said, about a sales agency in Paris that had been offered to Ralph but that they had decided against, because of the threat of war.

The Whittemores were apart for two years during the war. Laura took a job. She walked Rachel to school in the morning and met her at the end of the day. Working and saving, Laura was able to buy herself and Rachel some clothes. When Ralph returned at the end of the war, their affairs were in good order. The experience seemed to have refreshed him, and while he took up his old job as an anchor to windward, as an ace in the hole, there had never been more talk about jobs — jobs in Venezuela and jobs in Iran. They resumed all their old habits and economies. They remained poor.

Laura gave up her job and returned to the afternoons with Rachel in Central Park. Alice Holinshed was there. The talk was the same. The Holinsheds were living in a hotel. Mr. Holinshed was vice-president of a new firm manufacturing a soft drink, but the dress that Mrs. Holinshed wore day after day was one that Laura recognized from before the war. Her son was thin and bad-tempered. He was dressed in serge, like an English schoolboy, but his serge, like his mother's dress, looked worn and outgrown. One afternoon when Mrs. Holinshed and her son came into the Park, the boy was crying. "I've done a dreadful thing," Mrs. Holinshed told Laura. "We've been to the doctor's and I forgot to bring any money, and I wonder if you could lend me a few dollars, so I can take a taxi back to the hotel." Laura said she would be glad to. She had only a five-dollar bill with her, and she gave Mrs. Holinshed this. The boy continued to cry, and his mother dragged him off toward Fifth Avenue. Laura never saw them in the Park again.

Ralph's life was, as it had always been, dominated by anticipation. In the years directly after the war, the city appeared to be immensely rich. There seemed to be money everywhere, and the Whittemores, who slept under their worn overcoats in the winter to keep themselves warm, seemed separated from their enjoyment of this prosperity by only a little patience, resourcefulness, and luck. On Sunday, when the weather was fine, they walked with the prosperous crowds on upper Fifth Avenue. It seemed to Ralph that it might only be another month, at the most another year, before he found the key to the prosperity they deserved. They would walk on Fifth Avenue until the afternoon was ended and then go home and eat a can of beans for dinner and, in order to balance the meal, an apple for dessert.

They were returning from such a walk one Sunday when, as they climbed the stairs to their apartment, the telephone began to ring. Ralph went on ahead and answered it.

He heard the voice of his Uncle George, a man of the generation that remains conscious of distance, who spoke into the telephone as if he were calling from shore to a passing boat. "This is Uncle George, Ralphie!" he shouted, and Ralph supposed that he and Aunt Helen were paying a surprise visit to the city, until he realized that his uncle was calling from Illinois. "Can you hear me?" Uncle George shouted. "Can you hear me, Ralphie? . . . I'm calling you about a job, Ralphie. Just in case you're looking for a job. Paul Hadaam came through — can you hear me, Ralphie? — Paul Hadaam came through here on his way East last week and he stopped off to pay me a visit. He's got a lot of money, Ralphie — he's rich — and he's starting this business out in the West to manufacture synthetic wool. Can you hear me, Ralphie? . . . I told him about you, and he's staying at the Waldorf, so you go and see him. I saved his life once. I pulled him out of Lake Erie. You go and see him tomorrow at the Waldorf, Ralphie. You know where that is? The Waldorf Hotel. . . . Wait a minute, here's Aunt Helen. She wants to talk with you."

Now the voice was a woman's, and it came to him faintly. All his cousins had been there for dinner, she told him. They had had a turkey for dinner. All the grandchildren were there and they behaved very well. George took them all for a walk after dinner. It was hot, but they sat on the porch, so they didn't feel the heat. She was interrupted in her account of Sunday by her husband, who must have seized the instrument from her to continue his refrain about going to see Mr. Hadaam at the Waldorf. "You go see him tomorrow, Ralphie — the nineteenth — at the Waldorf. He's expecting you. Can you hear me? . . . The Waldorf Hotel. He's a millionaire. I'll say goodbye now."

Mr. Hadaam had a parlor and a bedroom in the Waldorf Towers, and when Ralph went to see him, late the next afternoon, on his way home from work, Mr. Hadaam was alone. He seemed to Ralph a very old man, but an obdurate one, and in the way he shook hands, pulled at his earlobes, stretched himself, and padded around the parlor on his bandy legs Ralph recognized a spirit that was unimpaired, independent, and canine. He poured Ralph a strong drink and himself a weak one. He was undertaking the manufacture of synthetic wool on the West Coast, he explained, and had come East to find men who were experienced in merchandising wool. George had given him Ralph's name, and he wanted a man with Ralph's experience. He would find the Whittemores a suitable house, arrange for their transportation, and begin Ralph at a salary of fifteen thousand. It was the size of the salary that made Ralph realize that the proposition was an oblique attempt to repay his uncle for having saved Mr. Hadaam's life, and the old man seemed to sense what he was feeling. "This hasn't got anything to do with your uncle's saving my life," he said roughly. "I'm grateful to him — who wouldn't be? — but this hasn't got anything to do with your uncle, if that's what you're thinking. When you get to be as old and as rich as I am, it's hard to meet people. All my old friends are dead — all of them but George. I'm surrounded by a cordon of associates and relatives that's damned near impenetrable, and if it wasn't for George giving me a name now and then, I'd never get to see a new face. Last year, I got into an automobile accident. It was my fault. I'm a terrible driver. I hit this young fellow's car and I got right out and went over to him and introduced myself. We had to wait about twenty minutes for the wreckers and we got to talking. Well, he's working for me today and he's one of the best friends I've got, and if I hadn't run into him, I'd never have met him. When you get to be as old as me, that's the only way you can meet people — automobile accidents, fires, things like that."

He straightened up against the back of his chair and tasted his drink. His rooms were well above the noise of traffic and it was quiet there. Mr. Hadaam's breath was loud and steady, and it sounded, in a pause, like the heavy breath of someone sleeping. "Well, I don't want to rush you into this," he said. "I'm going back to the Coast the day after tomorrow. You think it over and I'll telephone you." He took out an engagement book and wrote down Ralph's name and telephone number. "I'll call you on Tuesday evening, the twenty-seventh, about nine o'clock — nine o'clock your time. George tells me you've got a nice wife, but I haven't got time to meet her now. I'll see her on the Coast." He started talking about baseball and then brought the conversation back to Uncle George. "He saved my life. My damned boat capsized and then righted herself and sunk right from underneath me. I can still feel her going down under my feet. I couldn't swim. Can't swim today. Well, goodbye." They shook hands, and as soon as the door closed, Ralph heard Mr. Hadaam begin to cough. It was the profane, hammering cough of an old man, full of bitter complaints and distempers, and it hit him pitilessly for all the time that Ralph was waiting in the hallway for the elevator to take him down.

On the walk home, Ralph felt that this might be it, that this preposterous chain of contingencies that had begun with his uncle's pulling a friend out of Lake Erie might be the one that would save them. Nothing in his experience made it seem unlikely. He recognized that the proposition was the vagary of an old man and that it originated in the indebtedness Mr. Hadaam felt to his uncle — an indebtedness that age seemed to have deepened. He gave Laura the details of the interview when he came in, and his own views on Mr. Hadaam's conduct, and, to his mild surprise, Laura said that it looked to her like the bonanza. They were both remarkably calm, considering the change that confronted them. There was no talk of celebrating, and he helped her wash the dishes. He looked up the site of Mr. Hadaam's factory in an atlas, and the Spanish place name on the coast north of San Francisco gave them a glimpse of a life of reasonable contentment.

Eight days lay between Ralph's interview and the telephone call, and he realized that nothing would be definite until Tuesday, and that there was a possibility that old Mr. Hadaam, while crossing the country, might, under the subtle influence of travel, suffer a change of heart. He might be poisoned by a fish sandwich and be taken off the train in Chicago, to die in a nursing home there. Among the people meeting him in San Francisco might be his lawyer, with the news that he was ruined or that his wife had run away. But eventually Ralph was unable to invent any new disasters or to believe in the ones he had invented.

This inability to persevere in doubting his luck showed some weakening of character. There had hardly been a day when he had not been made to feel the power of money, but he found that the force of money was most irresistible when it took the guise of a promise, and that years of resolute self-denial, instead of rewarding him with reserves of fortitude, had left him more than ordinarily susceptible to temptation. Since the change in their lives still depended upon a telephone call, he refrained from talking — from thinking, so far as possible — about the life they might have in California. He would go so far as to say that he would like some white shirts, but he would not go beyond this deliberately contrite wish, and here, where he thought he was exercising restraint and intelligence, he was, instead, beginning to respect the bulk of superstition that is supposed to attend good fortune, and when he wished for white shirts, it was not a genuinely modest wish so much as it was a memory — he could not have put it into words himself — that the gods of fortune are jealous and easily deceived by false modesty. He had never been a superstitious man, but on Tuesday he scooped the money off his coffee table and was elated when he saw a ladybug on the bathroom window sill. He could not remember when he had heard money and this insect associated, but neither could he have explained any of the other portents that he had begun to let govern his movements.

Laura watched this subtle change that anticipation worked on her husband, but there was nothing she could say. He did not mention Mr. Hadaam or California. He was quiet; he was gentle with Rachel; he actually grew pale. He had his hair cut on Wednesday. He wore his best suit. On Saturday, he had his hair cut again and his nails manicured. He took two baths a day, put on a fresh shirt for dinner, and frequently went into the bathroom to wash his hands, brush his teeth, and wet down his cowlick. The preternatural care he gave his body and his appearance reminded her of an adolescent surprised by early love.

The Whittemores were invited to a party for Monday night and Laura insisted that they go. The guests at the party were the survivors of a group that had coalesced ten years before, and if anyone had called the roll of the earliest parties in the same room, like the retreat ceremony of a breached and decimated regiment, "Missing. . . . Missing. . . . Missing" would have been answered for the squad that had gone into Westchester; "Missing. . . . Missing. . . . Missing" would have been spoken for the platoon that divorce, drink, nervous disorders, and adversity had slain or wounded. Because Laura had gone to the party in indifferent spirits, she was conscious of the missing.

She had been at the party less than an hour when she heard some people coming in, and, looking over her shoulder, saw Alice Holinshed and her husband. The room was crowded and she put off speaking to Alice until later. Much later in the evening, Laura went into the toilet, and when she came out of it into the bedroom, she found Alice sitting on the bed. She seemed to be waiting for Laura. Laura sat down at the dressing table to straighten her hair. She looked at the image of her friend in the glass.

"I hear you're going to California," Alice said.

"We hope to. We'll know tomorrow."

"Is it true that Ralph's uncle saved his life?"

"That's true."

"You're lucky."

"I suppose we are."

"You're lucky, all right." Alice got up from the bed and crossed the room and closed the door, and came back across the room again and sat on the bed. Laura watched her in the glass, but she was not watching Laura. She was stooped. She seemed nervous. "You're lucky," she said. "You're so lucky. Do you know how lucky you are? Let me tell you about this cake of soap," she said. "I have this cake of soap. I mean I had this cake of soap. Somebody gave it to me when I was married, fifteen years ago. I don't know who. Some maid, some music teacher — somebody like that. It was good soap, good English soap, the kind I like, and I decided to save it for the big day when Larry made a killing, when he took me to Bermuda. First, I was going to use it when he got the job in Bound Brook. Then I thought I could use it when we were going to Boston, and then Washington, and then when he got this new job, I thought maybe this is it, maybe *this* is the time when I get to take the boy out of that rotten school and pay the bills and move out of those bum hotels we've been living in. For fifteen years I've been planning to use this cake of soap. Well, last week I was looking through my bureau drawers and I saw this cake of soap. It was all cracked. I threw it out. I threw it out because I knew I was never going to have a chance to use it. Do you realize what that means? Do you know what that feels like? To live for fifteen years on promises and expectations and loans and credits in hotels that aren't fit to live in, never for a single day to be out of debt, and yet to pretend, to feel that every year, every winter, every job, every meeting is going to be the one. To live like this for fifteen years and then to realize that it's never going to end. Do you know what that feels like?" She got up and went over to the dressing table and stood in front of Laura. Tears had risen into her large eyes, and her voice was harsh and loud. "I'm never going to get to Bermuda," she said. "I'm never even going to get to Florida. I'm never going to get out of hock, ever, ever, *ever*. I know that I'm never going to have a decent home and that everything I own that is worn and torn and no good is going to stay that way. I know that for the rest of my life, for the rest of my life, I'm going to wear ragged slips and torn nightgowns and torn underclothes and shoes that hurt me. I know that for the rest of my life nobody is going to come up to me and tell me that I've got on a pretty dress, because I'm not going to be able to afford that kind of a dress. I know that for the rest of my life every taxi driver and doorman and head-waiter in this town is going to know in a minute that I haven't got five bucks in that black imitation-suede purse that I've been brushing and brushing and brushing and carrying around for ten years. How do you get it? How do you rate it? What's so wonderful about you that you get a break like this?" She ran her fingers down Laura's bare arm. The dress she was wearing smelled of benzine. "Can I rub it off you? Will that make me lucky? I swear to Jesus I'd murder somebody if I thought it would bring us in any money. I'd wring somebody's neck — yours, anybody's — I swear to Jesus I would —"

Someone began knocking on the door. Alice strode to the door, opened it, and went out. A woman came in, a stranger looking for the toilet. Laura lighted a cigarette and waited in the bedroom for about ten minutes before she went back to the party. The Holinsheds had gone. She got a drink and sat down and tried to talk, but she couldn't keep her mind on what she was saying.

The hunt, the search for money that had seemed to her natural, amiable, and fair when they first committed themselves to it, now seemed like a hazardous and piratical voyage. She had thought, earlier in the evening, of the missing. She thought now of the missing again. Adversity and failure accounted for more than half of them, as if beneath the amenities in the pretty room a keen race were in progress, in which the loser's forfeits were extreme. Laura felt cold. She picked the ice out of her drink with her fingers and put it in a flower vase, but the whiskey didn't warm her. She asked Ralph to take her home.

After dinner on Tuesday, Laura washed the dishes and Ralph dried them. He read the paper and she took up some sewing. At a quarter after eight, the telephone, in the bedroom, rang, and he went to it calmly. It was someone with two theatre tickets for a show that was closing. The telephone didn't ring again, and at half past nine he told Laura that he was going to call California. It didn't take long for the connection be be made, and the fresh voice of a young woman spoke to him from Mr. Hadaam's number. "Oh, yes, Mr. Whittemore," she said. "We tried to get you earlier in the evening but your line was busy."

"Could I speak to Mr. Hadaam?"

"No, Mr. Whittemore. This is Mr. Hadaam's secretary. I know he meant to call you, because he had entered this in his engagement book. Mrs. Hadaam has asked me to disappoint as few people as possible, and I've tried to take care of all the calls and appointments in his engagement book. Mr. Hadaam had a stroke on Sunday. We don't expect him to recover. I imagine he made you some kind of promise, but I'm afraid he won't be able to keep it."

"I'm very sorry," Ralph said. He hung up.

Laura had come into the bedroom while the secretary was talking. "Oh, darling!" she said. She put her sewing basket on the bureau and went toward the closet. Then she went back and looked for something in the sewing basket and left the basket on her dressing table. Then she took off her shoes, treed them, slipped her dress over her head and hung it up neatly. Then she went to the bureau, looking for her sewing basket, found it on the dressing table, and took it into the closet, where she put it on a shelf. Then she took her brush and comb into the bathroom and began to run the water for a bath.

The lash of frustration was laid on and the pain stunned Ralph. He sat by the telephone for he did not know how long. He heard Laura come out of the bathroom. He turned when he heard her speak.

"I feel dreadfully about old Mr. Hadaam," she said. "I wish there were something we could do." She was in her nightgown, and she sat down at the dressing table like a skillful and patient woman establishing herself in front of a loom, and she picked up and put down pins and bottles and combs and brushes with the thoughtless dexterity of an experienced weaver, as if the time she spent there were all part of a continuous operation. "It did look like the treasure . . ."

The word surprised him, and for a moment he saw the chimera, the pot of gold, the fleece, the treasure buried in the faint lights of a rainbow, and the primitivism of his hunt struck him. Armed with a sharp spade and a homemade divining rod, he had climbed over hill and dale, through droughts and rain squalls, digging wherever the maps he had drawn himself promised gold. Six paces east of the dead pine, five panels in from the library door, underneath the creaking step, in the roots of the pear tree, beneath the grape arbor lay the bean pot full of doubloons and bullion.

She turned on the stool and held her thin arms toward him, as she had done more than a thousand times. She was no longer young, and more wan, thinner than she might have been if he had found the doubloons to save her anxiety and unremitting work. Her smile, her naked shoulders had begun to trouble the indecipherable shapes and symbols that are the touchstones of desire, and the light from the lamp seemed to brighten and give off heat and shed that unaccountable complacency, that benevolence, that the spring sunlight brings to all kinds of fatigue and despair. Desire for her delighted and confused him. Here it was, here it all was, and the shine of the gold seemed to him then to be all around her arms.

Here Come the Maples

by John Updike

THEY HAD ALWAYS been a lucky couple, and it was just their luck that, as they at last decided to part, the Puritan Commonwealth in which they lived passed a no-fault amendment to its creaking, overworked body of divorce law. By its provisions a joint affidavit had to be filed. It went, "Now come Richard F. and Joan R. Maple and swear under the penalties of perjury that an irretrievable breakdown of the marriage exists." For Richard, reading a copy of the document in his Boston apartment, the wording conjured up a vision of himself and Joan breezing into a party hand in hand while a liveried doorman trumpeted their names and a snow of confetti and champagne bubbles exploded in the room. In the many years of their marriage, they had gone together to a lot of parties, and always with a touch of excitement, a little hope, a little expectation of something lucky happening.

With the affidavit were enclosed various frightening financial forms and a request for a copy of their marriage license. Though they had lived in New York and London, on islands and farms and for one summer even in a log cabin, they had been married a few subway stops from where Richard now stood, reading his mail. He had not been in the Cambridge City Hall since the morning he had been granted the license, the morning of their wedding. His parents had driven him up from the Connecticut motel where they had all spent the night, on their way from West Virginia; they had risen at six, to get there on time, and for much of the journey he had had his coat over his head, hoping to get back to sleep. He seemed in memory now a sea creature, boneless beneath the jellyfish bell of his own coat, rising helplessly along the coast as the air grew hotter and hotter. It was June, and steamy. When, toward noon, they got to Cambridge, and dragged their bodies and boxes of wedding clothes up the four flights to Joan's apartment, on Avon Street, the bride was taking a bath. Who else was in the apartment Richard could not remember; his recollection of the day was spotty — legible patches on a damp gray blotter. The day had no sky and no clouds, just a fog of shadowless sunlight enveloping the bricks on Brattle Street, and the white spires of Harvard, and the fat cars baking in the tarry streets. He was twenty-one, and Eisenhower was President, and the bride was behind the door, shouting that he mustn't come in, it would be bad luck for him to see her. Someone was in there with her, giggling and splashing. Who? Her sister? Her mother? Richard leaned against the bathroom door, and heard his parents heaving themselves up the stairs behind him, panting but still chattering, and pictured Joan as she was when in the bath, her toes pink, her neck tendrils flattened, her breasts floating and soapy and slick. Then the memory dried up, and the next blot showed her and him side by side, driving together into the shimmering noontime traffic jam of Central Square. She wore a summer dress of sun-faded cotton; he kept his eyes on the traffic, to minimize the bad luck of seeing her before the ceremony. Other couples, he thought at the time, must have arranged to have their papers in order more than two hours before the wedding. But then, no doubt, other grooms didn't travel to the ceremony with their coats over their heads like children hiding from a thunderstorm. Hand in hand, smaller than Hänsel and Gretel in his mind's eye, they ran up the long flight of stairs into a gingerbread-brown archway and disappeared.

Cambridge City Hall, in a changed world, was unchanged. The rounded Richardsonian castle, red sandstone and pink granite, loomed as a gentle giant in its crass neighborhood. Its interior was varnished oak, pale and gleaming. Richard seemed to remember receiving the license at a grated window downstairs with a brass plate, but an arrow on cardboard directed him upward. His knees trembled and his stomach churned at the enormity of what he was doing. He turned a corner. A grandmotherly woman reigned within a spacious, idle territory of green-topped desks and great ledgers in steel racks. "Could I get a c-copy of a marriage license?" he asked her.

"Year?"

"Beg pardon?"

"What is the year of the marriage license, sir?"

"1954." Enunciated, the year seemed distant as a star, yet here he was again, feeling not a minute older, and sweating in the same summer heat. Nevertheless, the lady, having taken down the names and the date, had to leave him and go to another chamber of the archives, so far away in truth was the event he wished to undo.

She returned with a limp he hadn't noticed before. The ledger she carried was three feet wide when opened, a sorcerer's tome. She turned the vast pages carefully, as if the chasm of lost life and forsaken time they represented might at a slip leap up and swallow them both. She must once have been a flaming redhead, but her hair had dulled to apricot and had stiffened to permanent curls, lifeless as dried paper. She smiled, a crimpy little smile. "Yes," she said. "Here we are."

And Richard could read, upside down, on a single long red line, Joan's maiden name and his own. Her profession was listed as "Teacher" (she had been an apprentice art teacher; he had forgotten her spattered blue smock, the clayey smell of her fingers, the way she would bicycle to work on even the coldest days) and his own, inferiorly, as "Student." And their given addresses surprised him, in being different — the foyer on Avon Street, the entryway in Lowell House, forgotten doors opening on the corridor of shared addresses that stretched from then to now. Their signatures — He could not bear to study their signatures, even upside down. At a glance, Joan's seemed firmer, and bluer. "You want one or more copies?"

"One should be enough."

As fussily as if she had not done this thousands of times before, the former redhead, smoothing the paper and repeatedly dipping her antique pen, copied the information onto a standard form.

What else survived of that wedding day? There were a few slides, Richard remembered. A cousin of Joan's had posed the main members of the wedding on the sidewalk outside the church, all gathered around a parking meter. The meter, a slim silvery representative of the municipality, occupies the place of honor in the grouping, with his narrow head and scarlet tongue. Like the meter, the groom is very thin. He blinked simultaneously with the shutter, so the suggestion of a death mask hovers about his face. The dimpled bride's pose, tense and graceful both, has something dancerlike about it, the feet pointed outward on the hot bricks; she might be about to pick up the organdie skirt of her bridal gown and vault herself into a tour jeté. The four parents, not yet transmogrified into grandparents, seem dim in the slide, half lost in the fog of light, benevolent and lumpy like the stones of the building in which Richard was shelling out the three-dollar fee for his copy, his anti-license.

Another image was captured by Richard's college roommate, who drove them to their honeymoon cottage in a seaside town an hour south of Cambridge. A croquet set had been left on the porch, and Richard, in one of those stunts he had developed to mask unease, picked up three of the balls and began to juggle. The roommate, perhaps also uneasy, snapped the moment up; the red ball hangs there forever, blurred, in the amber slant of the dying light, while the yellow and green glint in Richard's hands and his face concentrates upward in a slack-jawed ecstasy.

"I have another problem," he told the grandmotherly clerk as she shut the vast ledger and prepared to shoulder it.

"What would that be?" she asked.

"I have an affidavit that should be notarized."

"That wouldn't be my department, sir. First floor, to the left when you get off the elevator, to the right if you use the stairs. The stairs are quicker, if you ask me."

He followed her directions and found a young black woman at a steel desk bristling with gold-framed images of fidelity and solidarity and stability, of children and parents, of a somber brown boy in a brown military uniform, of a family laughing by a lakeside; there was even a photograph of a house — an ordinary little ranch house somewhere, with a green lawn. She read Richard's affidavit without comment. He suppressed his urge to beg her pardon. She asked to see his driver's license and compared its face with his. She handed him a pen and set a seal of irrevocability beside his signature. The red ball still hung in the air, somewhere in a box of slides he would never see again, and the luminous hush of the cottage when they were left alone in it still traveled, a capsule of silence, outward to the stars; but what grieved Richard more, wincing as he stepped from the brown archway into the summer glare, was a suspended detail of the wedding. In his daze, his sleepiness, in his wonder at the white creature trembling beside him at the altar, on the edge of his awareness like a rainbow in a fog, he had forgotten to seal the vows with a kiss. Joan had glanced over at him, smiling, expectant; he had smiled back, not remembering. The moment passed, and they hurried down the aisle as now he hurried, ashamed, down the City Hall stairs to the street and the tunnel of the subway.

As the subway racketed through darkness, he read about the forces of nature. A scholarly extract had come in the mail, in the same mail as the affidavit. Before he lived alone, he would have thrown it away without a second look, but now, as he slowly took on the careful habits of a Boston codger, he read every scrap he was sent, and even stooped in the alleys to pick up a muddy fragment of newspaper and scan it for a message. *Thus*, he read, *it was already known in 1935 that the natural world was governed by four kinds of force: in order of increasing strength, they are the gravitational, the weak, the electromagnetic, and the strong.* Reading, he found himself rooting for the weak forces; he identified with them. Gravitation, though negligible at the microcosmic level, *begins to predominate with objects on the order of magnitude of a hundred kilometers, like large asteroids; it holds together the moon, the earth, the solar system, the stars, clusters of stars within galaxies, and the galaxies themselves.* To Richard it was as if a fainthearted team overpowered at the start of the game was surging to triumph in the last, macrocosmic quarter; he inwardly cheered. The subway lurched to a stop at Kendall, and he remembered how, a few days after their wedding, he and Joan took a train north through New Hampshire, to summer jobs they had contracted for, as a couple. The train, long since discontinued, had wound its way north along the busy rivers sullied by sawmills and into evergreen mountains where ski lifts stood rusting. The seats had been purple plush, and the train incessantly, gently swayed. Her arms, pale against the plush, showed a pink shadowing of sunburn. Uncertain of how to have a honeymoon, yet certain that they must create memories to last till death did them part, they had played croquet naked, in the little yard that, amid the trees, seemed an eye of grass gazing upward at the sky. She beat him, every game. *The weak force,* Richard read, *does not appreciably affect the structure of the nucleus before the decay occurs; it is like a flaw in a bell of cast metal which has no effect on the ringing of the bell until it finally causes the bell to fall into pieces.*

The subway car climbed into light, to cross the Charles. Sailboats tilted on the glitter below. Across the river, Boston's smoke-colored skyscrapers hung like paralyzed fountains. The train had leaned around a bay of a lake and halted at The Weirs, a gritty summer place of ice cream dripped on asphalt, of a candy-apple scent wafted from the edge of childhood. After a wait of hours, they caught the mail boat to their island where they would work. The island was on the far side of Lake Winnipesaukee, with many other islands intervening, and many mail drops necessary. Before each docking, the boat blew its whistle — an immense noise. The Maples had sat on the prow, for the sun and scenery; once there, directly under the whistle, they felt they had to stay. The islands, the water, the mountains beyond the shore did an adagio of shifting perspectives around them and then — each time, astoundingly — the blast of the whistle would flatten their hearts and crush the landscape into a wad of noise; these blows assaulted their young marriage. He both blamed her and wished to beg her forgiveness for what neither of them could control. After each blast, the engine would be cut, the boat would sidle to a rickety dock, and from the dappled soft paths of this or that evergreen island tan children and counselors in bathing trunks and moccasins would spill forth to receive their mail, their shouts ringing strangely in the deafened ears of the newlyweds. By the time they reached their own island, the Maples were exhausted.

Quantum mechanics and relativity, taken together, are extraordinarily restrictive and they, therefore, provide us with a great logical engine. Richard returned the pamphlet to his pocket and got off at Charles. He walked across the overpass toward the hospital, to see his arthritis man. His bones ached at night. He had friends who were dying, who were dead; it no longer seemed incredible that he would follow them. The first time he had visited this hospital, it had been to court Joan. He had climbed this same ramp to the glass doors and inquired within, stammering, for the whereabouts, in this grand maze of unhealth, of the girl who had sat, with a rubber band around her ponytail, in the front row of English 162b: "The English Epic Tradition, Spenser to

Tennyson." He had admired the tilt of the back of her head for three hours a week all winter. He gathered up courage to talk in exam period as, together at a library table, they were mulling over murky photostats of Blake's illustrations to *Paradise Lost*. They agreed to meet after the exam and have a beer. She didn't show. In that amphitheater of desperately thinking heads, hers was absent. And, having put *The Faerie Queene* and *The Idylls of the King* to rest together, he called her dorm and learned that Joan had been taken to the hospital. A force of nature drove him to brave the long corridors and the wrong turns and the crowd of aunts and other suitors at the foot of the bed; he found Joan in white, between white sheets, her hair loose about her shoulders and a plastic tube feeding something transparent into the underside of her arm. In later visits, he achieved the right to hold her hand, trussed though it was with splints and tapes. Platelet deficiency had been the diagnosis. The complaint had been she couldn't stop bleeding. Blushing, she told him how the doctors and internes had asked her when she had last had intercourse, and how embarrassing it had been to confess, in the face of their polite disbelief, never.

The doctor removed the blood-pressure tourniquet from Richard's arm and smiled. "Have you been under any stress lately?"

"I've been getting a divorce."

"Arthritis, as you may know, belongs to a family of complaints with a psychosomatic component."

"All I know is that I wake up at four in the morning and it's very depressing to think I'll never get over this, this pain'll be inside my shoulder for the rest of my life."

"You will. It won't."

"When?"

"When your brain stops sending out punishing signals."

Her hand, in its little cradle of healing apparatus, its warmth unresisting and noncommittal as he held it at her bedside, rested high, nearly at the level of his eyes. On the island, the beds in the log cabin set aside for them were of different heights, and though Joan tried to make them into a double bed, there was a ledge where the mattresses met which either he or she had to cross, amid a discomfort of sheets pulling loose. But the cabin was in the woods and powerful moist scents of pine and fern swept through the screens with the morning chirrup of birds and the evening rustle of animals. There was a rumor there were deer on the island; they crossed the ice in the winter and were trapped when it melted in the spring. Though no one, neither camper nor counselor, ever saw the deer, the rumor persisted that they were there.

Why then has no one ever seen a quark? As he walked along Charles Street toward his apartment, Richard vaguely remembered some such sentence, and fished in his pockets for the pamphlet on the forces of nature, and came up instead with a new prescription for painkiller, a copy of his marriage license, and the signed affidavit. *Now come . . .* The pamphlet had got folded into it. He couldn't find the sentence, and instead read, *The theory that the strong force becomes stronger as the quarks are pulled apart is somewhat speculative; but its complement, the idea that the force gets weaker as the quarks are pushed closer to each other, is better established.* Yes, he thought, that had happened. In life there are four forces: love, habit, time, and boredom. Love and habit at short range are immensely powerful, but time, lacking a minus charge, accumulates inexorably, and with its brother boredom levels all. He was dying; that made him cruel. His heart flattened in horror at what he had just done. How could he tell Joan what he had just done to their marriage license? The very quarks in the telephone circuits would rebel.

In the forest, there had been a green clearing, an eye of grass, a meadow starred with microcosmic white flowers, and here one dusk the deer had come, the female slightly in advance, the male larger and darker, his rump still in shadow as his mate nosed out the day's last sun, the silhouettes of both haloed by the same light that gilded the meadow grass. A fleet of blank-faced motorcyclists roared by, a rummy waved to Richard from a laundromat doorway, a girl in a seductive halter gave him a cold eye, the light changed from red to green, and he could not remember if he needed orange juice or bread, doubly annoyed because he could not remember if they had ever really seen the deer, or if he had imagined the memory, conjured it from the longing that it be so.

"I don't remember," Joan said over the phone. "I don't think we did, we just talked about it."

"Wasn't there a kind of clearing beyond the cabin, if you followed the path?"

"We never went that way, it was too buggy."

"A stag and a doe, just as it was getting dark. Don't you remember anything?"

"No. I honestly don't, Richard. How guilty do you want me to feel?"

"Not at all, if it didn't happen. Speaking of nostalgia —"

"Yes?"

"I went up to Cambridge City Hall this afternoon and got a copy of our marriage license."

"Oh dear. How was it?"

"It wasn't bad. The place is remarkably the same. Did we get the license upstairs or downstairs?"

"Downstairs, to the left of the elevator as you go in."

"That's where I got our affidavit notarized. You'll be getting a copy soon; it's a shocking document."

"I did get it, yesterday. What was shocking about it? I thought it was funny, the way it was worded. Here we come, there we go."

"Darley, you're so tough and brave."

"I assume I must be. No?"

"Yes."

Not for the first time in these two years did he feel an eggshell thinness behind which he crouched and which Joan needed only to raise her voice to break. But she declined to break it, either out of ignorance of how thin the shell was, or because she was hatching on its other side, just as, on the other side of that bathroom door, she had been drawing near to marriage at the same rate as he, and with the same regressive impulses. "What I don't understand," she was saying, "are we both supposed to sign the same statement, or do we each sign one, or what? And which one? My lawyer keeps sending me three of everything, and some of them are in blue covers. Are these the important ones or the unimportant ones that I can keep?"

In truth, the lawyers, so adroit in their accustomed adversary world of blame, of suit and countersuit, did seem confused by the no-fault provision. On the very morning of the divorce, Richard's greeted him on the courthouse steps with the possibility that he as plaintiff might be asked to specify what in the marriage had persuaded him of its irretrievable breakdown. "But that's the whole point of no-fault," Joan interposed, "that you don't have to say anything." She had climbed the courthouse steps beside Richard; indeed, they had come in the same car, because one of their children had taken her Volvo.

The proceeding was scheduled for early in the day. Picking her up at a quarter after seven, he had found her standing barefoot on the lawn in the circle of their driveway, up to her ankles in mist and dew. She was holding her high-heeled shoes in her hand. The sight made him laugh. Opening the car door, he said, "So there *are* deer on the island!"

She was too preoccupied to make sense of his allusion. She asked him, "Do you think the judge will mind if I don't wear stockings?"

"Keep your legs behind his bench," he said. He was feeling fluttery, light-headed. He had scarcely slept, though his shoulder had not hurt, for a change. She got into the car, bringing with her her shoes and the moist smell of dawn. She had always been an early riser, and he a late one. "Thanks for doing this," she said, of the ride, adding, "I guess."

"My pleasure," Richard said. As they drove to court, discussing their cars and their children, he marveled at how light Joan had become; she sat on the side of his vision as light as a feather, her voice tickling his ear, her familiar intonations and emphases thoroughly musical and half unheard, like the patterns of a concerto that sets us to daydreaming. He no longer blamed her: that was the reason for the lightness. All those years, he had blamed her for everything — for the traffic jam in Central Square, for the blasts of noise on the mail boat, for the difference in the levels of their beds. No longer: he had set her adrift from omnipotence. He had set her free, free from fault. She was to him as Gretel to Hänsel, a kindred creature moving beside him down a path while birds behind them ate the bread crumbs.

Richard's lawyer eyed Joan lugubriously. "I understand that, Mrs. Maple," he said. "But perhaps I should have a word in private with my client."

The lawyers they had chosen were oddly different. Richard's was a big rumpled Irishman, his beige summer suit baggy and his belly straining his shirt, a melancholic and comforting father-type. Joan's was small, natty, and flip; he dressed in checks and talked from the side of his mouth, like a racing tout. Twinkling, chipper even at this sleepy hour, he emerged from behind a pillar in the marble temple of justice and led Joan away. Her head, slightly higher than his, tilted to give him her ear; she dimpled, docile. Richard wondered in amazement, Could this sort of man have been, all these years, the secret type of her desire? His own lawyer, breathing heavily, asked him, "If the judge does ask for a specific cause of the breakdown — and I don't say he will, we're all sailing uncharted waters here — what will you say?"

"I don't know," Richard said. He studied the swirl of marble, like a tiny wave breaking, between his shoe tips. "We had political differences. She used to make me go on peace marches."

"Any physical violence?"

"Not much. Not enough, maybe. You really think he'll ask this sort of thing? Is this no-fault or not?"

"No-fault is a *tabula rasa* in this state. At this point, Dick, it's what we make of it. I don't know what he'll do. We should be prepared."

"Well — aside from the politics, we didn't get along that well sexually."

The air between them thickened; with his own father, too, sex had been a painful topic. His lawyer's breathing became grievously audible. "So you'd be prepared to say there was personal and emotional incompatibility?"

It seemed profoundly untrue, but Richard nodded. "If I have to."

"Good enough." The lawyer put his big hand on Richard's arm and squeezed. His closeness, his breathiness, his air of restless urgency and forced cheer, his old-fashioned suit and the folder of papers tucked under his arm like roster sheets all came into focus: he was a coach, and Richard was about to kick the winning field goal, do the high-difficulty dive, strike out the heart of the batting order with the bases already loaded. Go.

They entered the courtroom two by two. The chamber was chaste and empty; the carved trim was painted forest green. The windows gave on an ancient river blackened by industry. Dead judges gazed down from above. The two lawyers conferred, leaving Richard and Joan to stand awkwardly apart. He made his "What now?" face at her. She made her "Beats me" face back. "Oyez, oyez," a disembodied voice chanted, and the judge hurried in, smiling, his robes swinging. He was a little sharp-featured man with a polished pink face; his face declared that he was altogether good, and would never die. He stood and nodded at them. He seated himself. The lawyers went forward to confer in whispers. Richard inertly gravitated toward Joan, the only animate object in the room that did not repel him. "It's a Daumier," she whispered, of the tableau being enacted before them. The lawyers parted. The judge beckoned. He was so clean his smile squeaked. He showed Richard a piece of paper; it was the affidavit. "Is this your signature?" he asked him.

"It is," Richard said.

"And do you believe, as this paper states, that your marriage has suffered an irretrievable breakdown?"

"I do."

The judge turned his face toward Joan. His voice softened a notch. "Is this *your* signature?"

"It is." Her voice was a healing spray, full of tiny rainbows, in the corner of Richard's eye.

"And do you believe that your marriage has suffered an irretrievable breakdown?"

A pause. She did not believe that, Richard knew. She said, "I do."

The judge smiled and wished them both good luck. The lawyers sagged with relief, and a torrent of merry legal chitchat — speculations about the future of no-fault, reminiscences of the old days of Alabama quickies — excluded the Maples. Obsolete at their own ceremony, Joan and Richard stepped back from the bench in unison and stood side by side, uncertain of how to turn, until Richard at last remembered what to do; he kissed her.

The Spinoza of Market Street

by Isaac Bashevis Singer

1

Dr. Nahum Fischelson paced back and forth in his garret room in Market Street, Warsaw. Dr. Fischelson was a short, hunched man with a grayish beard, and was quite bald except for a few wisps of hair remaining at the nape of the neck. His nose was as crooked as a beak and his eyes were large, dark, and fluttering like those of some huge bird. It was a hot summer evening, but Dr. Fischelson wore a black coat which reached to his knees, and he had on a stiff collar and a bow tie. From the door he paced slowly to the dormer window set high in the slanting room and back again. One had to mount several steps to look out. A candle in a brass holder was burning on the table and a variety of insects buzzed around the flame. Now and again one of the creatures would fly too close to the fire and sear its wings, or one would ignite and glow on the wick for an instant. At such moments Dr. Fischelson grimaced. His wrinkled face would twitch and beneath his disheveled mustache he would bite his lips. Finally he took a handkerchief from his pocket and waved it at the insects.

"Away from there, fools and imbeciles," he scolded. "You won't get warm here; you'll only burn yourself."

The insects scattered but a second later returned and once more circled the trembling flame. Dr. Fischelson wiped the sweat from his wrinkled forehead and sighed, "Like men they desire nothing but the pleasure of the moment." On the table lay an open book written in Latin, and on its broad-margined pages were notes and comments printed in small letters by Dr. Fischelson. The book was Spinoza's *Ethics* and Dr. Fischelson had been studying it for the last thirty years. He knew every proposition, every proof, every corollary, every note by heart. When he wanted to find a particular passage, he generally opened to the place immediately without having to search for it. But, nevertheless, he continued to study the *Ethics* for hours every day with a magnifying glass in his bony hand, murmuring and nodding his head in agreement. The truth was that the more Dr. Fischelson studied, the more puzzling sentences, unclear passages, and cryptic remarks he found. Each sentence contained hints unfathomed by any of the students of Spinoza. Actually the philosopher had anticipated all of the criticisms of pure reason made by Kant and his followers. Dr. Fischelson was writing a commentary on the *Ethics*. He had drawers full of notes and drafts, but it didn't seem that he would ever be able to complete his work. The stomach ailment which had plagued him for years was growing worse from day to day. Now he would get pains in his stomach after only a few mouthfuls of oatmeal. "God in Heaven, it's difficult, very difficult," he would say to himself using the same intonation as had his father, the late Rabbi of Tishevitz. "It's very, very hard."

Dr. Fischelson was not afraid of dying. To begin with, he was no longer a young man. Secondly, it is stated in the fourth part of the *Ethics* that "a free man thinks of nothing less than of death and his wisdom is a meditation not of death, but of life." Thirdly, it is also said that "the human mind cannot be absolutely destroyed with the human body but there is some part of it that remains eternal." And yet Dr. Fischelson's ulcer (or perhaps it was a cancer) continued to bother him. His tongue was always coated. He belched frequently and emitted a different foul-smelling gas each time. He suffered from heartburn and cramps. At times he felt like vomiting and at other times he was hungry for garlic, onions, and fried foods. He had long ago discarded the medicines prescribed for him by the doctors and had sought his own remedies. He found it beneficial to take grated radish after meals and lie on his bed, belly down, with his head hanging over the side. But these home remedies offered only temporary relief. Some of the doctors he consulted insisted there was nothing the matter with him. "It's just nerves," they told him. "You could live to be a hundred."

But on this particular hot summer night, Dr. Fischelson felt his strength ebbing. His knees were shaky, his pulse weak. He sat down to read and his vision blurred. The letters on the page turned from green to gold. The lines became waved and jumped over each other, leaving white gaps as if the text had disappeared in some mysterious way. The heat was unbearable, flowing down directly from the tin roof; Dr. Fischelson felt he was inside of an oven. Several times he climbed the four steps to the window and thrust his head out into the cool of the evening breeze. He would remain in that position for so long his knees would become wobbly. "Oh it's a fine breeze," he would murmur, "really delightful," and he would recall that according to Spinoza, morality and happiness were identical, and that the most moral deed a man could perform was to indulge in some pleasure which was not contrary to reason.

2

Dr. Fischelson, standing on the top step at the window and looking out, could see into two worlds. Above him were the heavens, thickly strewn with stars. Dr. Fischelson had never seriously studied astronomy but he could differentiate between the planets, those bodies which like the earth, revolve around the sun, and the fixed stars, themselves distant suns, whose light reaches us a hundred or even a thousand years later. He recognized the constellations which mark the path of the earth in space and that nebulous sash, the Milky Way. Dr. Fischelson owned a small telescope he had bought in Switzerland where he had studied and he particularly enjoyed looking at the moon through it. He could clearly make out on the moon's surface the volcanoes bathed in sunlight and the dark, shadowy craters. He never wearied of gazing at these cracks and crevasses. To him they seemed both near and distant, both substantial and insubstantial. Now and then he would see a shooting star trace a wide arc across the sky and disappear, leaving a fiery trail behind it. Dr. Fischelson would know then that a meteorite had reached our atmosphere, and perhaps some unburned fragment of it had fallen into the ocean or had landed in the desert or perhaps even in some inhabited region. Slowly the stars which had appeared from behind Dr. Fischelson's roof rose until they were shining above the house across the street. Yes, when Dr. Fischelson looked up into the heavens, he became aware of that infinite extension which is, according to Spinoza, one of God's attributes. It comforted Dr. Fischelson to think that although he was only a weak, puny man, a changing mode of the absolutely infinite Substance, he was nevertheless a part of the cosmos, made of the same matter as the celestial bodies; to the extent that he was a part of the Godhead, he knew he could not be destroyed. In such moments, Dr. Fischelson experienced the *Amor dei Intellectualis* which is, according to the philosopher of Amsterdam, the highest perfection of the mind. Dr. Fischelson breathed deeply, lifted his head as high as his stiff collar permitted and actually felt he was whirling in company with the earth, the sun, the stars of the Milky Way, and the infinite host of galaxies known only to infinite thought. His legs became light and weightless and he grasped the window frame with both hands as if afraid he would lose his footing and fly out into eternity.

When Dr. Fischelson tired of observing the sky, his glance dropped to Market Street below. He could see a long strip extending from Yanash's market to Iron Street with the gas lamps lining it merged into a string of fiery dots. Smoke was issuing from the chimneys on the black, tin roofs; the bakers were heating their ovens, and here and there sparks mingled with the black smoke. The street never looked so noisy and crowded as on a summer evening. Thieves, prostitutes, gamblers, and fences loafed in the square which looked from above like a pretzel covered with poppy seeds. The young men laughed coarsely and the girls shrieked. A peddler with a keg of lemonade on his back pierced the general din with his intermittent cries. A watermelon vendor shouted in a savage voice, and the long knife which he used for cutting the fruit dripped with the blood-like juice. Now and again the street became even more agitated. Fire engines, their heavy wheels clanging, sped by; they were drawn by sturdy black horses which had to be tightly curbed to prevent them from running wild. Next came an ambulance, its siren screaming. Then some thugs had a fight among themselves and the police had to be called. A passerby was robbed and ran about shouting for help. Some wagons loaded with firewood sought to get through into the courtyards where the bakeries were located but the horses could not lift the wheels over the steep curbs and the drivers berated the animals and lashed them with their whips. Sparks rose from the clanging hoofs. It was now long after seven, which was the prescribed closing time for stores, but actually business had only begun. Customers were led in stealthily through back doors. The Russian policemen on the street, having been paid off, noticing nothing of this. Merchants continued to hawk their wares, each seeking to outshout the others.

"Gold, gold, gold," a woman who dealt in rotten oranges shrieked.

"Sugar, sugar, sugar," croaked a dealer of overripe plums.

"Heads, heads, heads," a boy who sold fishheads roared.

Through the window of a Hasidic study house across the way, Dr. Fischelson could see boys with long sidelocks swaying over holy volumes, grimacing and studying aloud in sing-song voices. Butchers, porters, and fruit dealers were drinking beer in the tavern below. Vapor drifted from the tavern's open door like steam from a bathhouse, and there was the sound of loud music. Outside of the tavern, streetwalkers snatched at drunken soldiers and at workers on their way home from the factories. Some of the men carried bundles of wood on their shoulders, reminding Dr. Fischelson of the wicked who are condemned to kindle their own fires in Hell. Husky record players poured out their raspings through open windows. The liturgy of the high holidays alternated with vulgar vaudeville songs.

Dr. Fischelson peered into the half-lit bedlam and cocked his ears. He knew that the behavior of this rabble was the very antithesis of reason. These people were immersed in the vainest of passions, were drunk with emotions, and, according to Spinoza, emotion was never good. Instead of the pleasure they ran after, all they succeeded in obtaining was disease and prison, shame and the suffering that resulted from ignorance. Even the cats which loitered on the roofs here seemed more savage and passionate than those in other parts of the town. They caterwauled with the voices of women in labor, and like demons scampered up walls and leaped onto eaves and balconies. One of the toms paused at Dr. Fischelson's window and let out a howl which made Dr. Fischelson shudder. The doctor stepped from the window and, picking up a broom, brandished it in front of the black beast's glowing, green eyes. "Scat, begone, you ignorant savage!" — and he rapped the broom handle against the roof until the tom ran off.

3

When Dr. Fischelson had returned to Warsaw from Zurich, where he had studied philosophy, a great future had been predicted for him. His friends had known that he was writing an important book on Spinoza. A Jewish Polish journal had invited him to be a contributor; he had been a frequent guest at several wealthy households and he had been made head librarian at the Warsaw synagogue. Although even then he had been considered an old bachelor, the matchmakers had proposed several rich girls for him. But Dr. Fischelson had not taken advantage of these opportunities. He had wanted to be as independent as Spinoza himself. And he had been. But because of his heretical ideas he had come into conflict with the rabbi and had had to resign his post as librarian. For years after that, he had supported himself by giving private lessons in Hebrew and German. Then, when he had become sick, the Berlin Jewish community had voted him a subsidy of five hundred marks a year. This had been made possible through the intervention of the famous Dr. Hildesheimer with whom he corresponded about philosophy. In order to get by on so small a pension, Dr. Fischelson had moved into the attic room and had begun cooking his own meals on a kerosene stove. He had a cupboard which had many drawers, and each drawer was labeled with the food it contained — buckwheat, rice, barley, onions, carrots, potatoes, mushrooms. Once a week Dr. Fischelson put on his wide-brimmed black hat, took a basket in one hand and Spinoza's *Ethics* in the other, and went off to the market for his provisions. While he was waiting to be served, he would open the *Ethics*. The merchants knew him and would motion him to their stalls.

"A fine piece of cheese, Doctor — just melts in your mouth."

"Fresh mushrooms, Doctor, straight from the woods."

"Make way for the doctor, ladies," the butcher would shout. "Please don't block the entrance."

During the early years of his sickness, Dr. Fischelson had still gone in the evening to a café which was frequented by Hebrew teachers and other intellectuals. It had been his habit to sit there and play chess while drinking a half a glass of black coffee. Sometimes he would stop at the bookstores on Holy Cross Street where all sorts of old books and magazines could be purchased cheap. On one occasion a former pupil of his had arranged to meet him at a restaurant one evening. When Dr. Fischelson arrived, he had been surprised to find a group of friends and admirers who forced him to sit at the head of the table while they made speeches about him. But these were things that had happened long ago. Now people were no longer interested in him. He had isolated himself completely and had become a forgotten man. The events of 1905 when the boys of Market Street had begun to organize strikes, throw bombs at police stations, and shoot strike breakers so that the stores were closed even on weekdays had greatly increased his isolation. He began to despise everything associated with the modern Jew — Zionism, socialism, anarchism. The young men in question seemed to him nothing but an ignorant rabble intent on destroying society, society without which no reasonable existence was possible. He still read a Hebrew magazine occasionally, but he felt contempt for modern Hebrew, which had no roots in the Bible or the Mishnah. The spelling of Polish words had changed also. Dr. Fischelson concluded that even the so-called spiritual men had abandoned reason and were doing their utmost to pander to the mob. Now and again he still visited a library and browsed through some of the modern histories of philosophy, but he found that the professors did not understand Spinoza, quoted him incorrectly, attributed their own muddled ideas to the philosopher. Although Dr. Fischelson was well aware that anger was an emotion unworthy of those who walk the path of reason, he would become furious, and would quickly close the book and push it from him. "Idiots," he would mutter, "asses, upstarts." And he would vow never again to look at modern philosophy.

4

Every three months a special mailman who only delivered money orders brought Dr. Fischelson eighty rubles. He expected his quarterly allotment at the beginning of July but as day after day passed and the tall man with the blond mustache and the shiny buttons did not appear, the doctor grew anxious. He had scarcely a groschen left. Who knows — possibly the Berlin community had rescinded his subsidy; perhaps Dr. Hildesheimer had died, God forbid; the post office might have made a mistake. Every event has its cause, Dr. Fischelson knew. All was determined, all necessary, and a man of reason had no right to worry. Nevertheless, worry invaded his brain, and buzzed about like the flies. If the worst came to the worst, it occurred to him, he could commit suicide, but then he remembered that Spinoza did not approve of suicide and compared those who took their own lives to the insane.

One day when Dr. Fischelson went out to a store to purchase a composition book, he heard people talking about war. In Serbia somewhere, an Austrian prince had been shot and the Austrians had delivered an ultimatum to the Serbs. The owner of the store, a young man with a yellow beard and shifty yellow eyes, announced, "We are about to have a small war," and he advised Dr. Fischelson to store up food because in the near future there was likely to be a shortage.

Everything happened so quickly. Dr. Fischelson had not even decided whether it was worthwhile to spend four groschen on a newspaper, and already posters had been hung up announcing mobilization. Men were to be seen walking on the street with round, metal tags on their lapels, a sign that they were being drafted. They were followed by their crying wives. One Monday when Dr. Fischelson descended to the street to buy some food with his last kopecks, he found the stores closed. The owners and their wives stood outside and explained that merchandise was unobtainable. But certain special customers were pulled to one side and let in through back doors. On the street all was confusion. Policemen with swords unsheathed could be seen riding on horseback. A large crowd had gathered around the tavern where, at the command of the czar, the tavern's stock of whiskey was being poured into the gutter.

Dr. Fischelson went to his old café. Perhaps he would find some acquaintances there who would advise him. But he did not come across a single person he knew. He decided, then, to visit the rabbi of the synagogue where he had once been librarian, but the sexton with the six-sided skull cap informed him that the rabbi and his family had gone off to the spas. Dr. Fischelson had other old friends in town but he found no one at home. His feet ached from so much walking; black and green spots appeared before his eyes and he felt faint. He stopped and waited for the giddiness to pass. The passers-by jostled him. A dark-eyed high-school girl tried to give him a coin. Although the war had just started, soldiers eight abreast were marching in full battle dress — the men were covered with dust and were sunburnt. Canteens were strapped to their sides and they wore rows of bullets across their chests. The bayonets on their rifles gleamed with a cold, green light. They sang with mournful voices. Along with the men came cannons, each pulled by eight horses; their blind muzzles breathed gloomy terror. Dr. Fischelson felt nauseous. His stomach ached; his intestines seemed about to turn themselves inside out. Cold sweat appeared on his face.

"I'm dying," he thought. "This is the end." Nevertheless, he did manage to drag himself home where he lay down on the iron cot and remained, panting and gasping. He must have dozed off because he imagined that he was in his home town, Tishevitz. He had a sore throat and his mother was busy wrapping a stocking stuffed with hot salt around his neck. He could hear talk going on in the house; something about a candle and about how a frog had bitten him. He wanted to go out into the street but they wouldn't let him because a Catholic procession was passing by. Men in long robes, holding double-edged axes in their hands, were intoning in Latin as they sprinkled holy water. Crosses gleamed; sacred pictures waved in the air. There was an odor of incense and corpses. Suddenly the sky turned a burning red and the whole world started to burn. Bells were ringing; people rushed madly about. Flocks of birds flew overhead, screeching. Dr. Fischelson awoke with a start. His body was covered with sweat and his throat was now actually sore. He tried to meditate about his extraordinary dream, to find its rational connection with what was happening to him and to comprehend it *sub specie eternitatis*, but none of it made sense. "Alas, the brain is a receptacle for nonsense," Dr. Fischelson thought. "This earth belongs to the mad."

And he once more closed his eyes; once more he dozed; once more he dreamed.

5

The eternal laws, apparently, had not yet ordained Dr. Fischelson's end.

There was a door to the left of Dr. Fischelson's attic room which opened off a dark corridor, cluttered with boxes and baskets, in which the odor of fried onions and laundry soap was always present. Behind this door lived a spinster whom the neighbors called Black Dobbe. Dobbe was tall and lean, and as black as a baker's shovel. She had a broken nose and there was a mustache on her upper lip. She spoke with the hoarse voice of a man and she wore men's shoes. For years Black Dobbe had sold breads, rolls, and bagels which she had bought from the baker at the gate of the house. But one day she and the baker had quarreled and she had moved her business to the marketplace and now she dealt in what were called "wrinklers," which was a synonym for cracked eggs. Black Dobbe had no luck with men. Twice she had been engaged to bakers' apprentices but in both instances they had returned the engagement contract to her. Some time afterwards she had received an engagement contract from an old man, a glazier who claimed that he was divorced, but it had later come to light that he still had a wife. Black Dobbe had a cousin in America, a shoemaker, and repeatedly she boasted that this cousin was sending her passage, but she remained in Warsaw. She was constantly being teased by the women who would say, "There's no hope for you, Dobbe. You're fated to die an old maid." Dobbe always answered, "I don't intend to be a slave for any man. Let them all rot."

That afternoon Dobbe received a letter from America. Generally she would go to Leizer the tailor and have him read it to her. However, that day Leizer was out and so Dobbe thought of Dr. Fischelson, whom the other tenants considered a convert since he never went to prayer. She knocked on the door of the doctor's room but there was no answer. "The heretic is probably out," Dobbe thought but, nevertheless, she knocked once more, and this time the door moved slightly. She pushed her way in and stood there frightened. Dr. Fischelson lay fully clothed on his bed; his face was as yellow as wax; his Adam's apple stuck out prominently; his beard pointed upward. Dobbe screamed; she was certain that he was dead, but — no — his body moved. Dobbe picked up a glass which stood on the table, ran into the corridor, filled the glass with water from the faucet, hurried back, and threw the water into the face of the unconscious man. Dr. Fischelson shook his head and opened his eyes.

"What's wrong with you?" Dobbe asked. "Are you sick?"

"Thank you very much. No."

"Have you a family? I'll call them."

"No family," Dr. Fischelson said.

Dobbe wanted to fetch the barber from across the street but Dr. Fischelson signified that he didn't wish the barber's assistance. Since Dobbe was not going to the market that day, no "wrinklers" being available, she decided to do a good deed. She assisted the sick man to get off the bed and smoothed down the blanket. Then she undressed Dr. Fischelson and prepared some soup for him on the kerosene stove.

The sun never entered Dobbe's room, but here squares of sunlight shimmered on the faded walls. The floor was painted red. Over the bed hung a picture of a man who was wearing a broad frill around his neck and had long hair. "Such an old fellow and yet he keeps his place so nice and clean," Dobbe thought approvingly. Dr. Fischelson asked for the *Ethics,* and she gave it to him disapprovingly. She was certain it was a gentile prayer book. Then she began bustling about, brought in a pail of water, swept the floor. Dr. Fischelson ate; after he had finished, he was much stronger and Dobbe asked him to read her the letter.

He read it slowly, the paper trembling in his hands. It came from New York, from Dobbe's cousin. Once more he wrote that he was about to send her a "really important letter" and a ticket to America. By now, Dobbe knew the story by heart and she helped the old man decipher her cousin's scrawl. "He's lying," Dobbe said. "He forgot about me a long time ago." In the evening, Dobbe came again. A candle in a brass holder was burning on the chair next to the bed. Reddish shadows trembled on the walls and ceiling. Dr. Fischelson sat propped up in bed, reading a book. The candle threw a golden light on his forehead which seemed as if cleft in two. A bird had flown in through the window and was perched on the table. For a moment Dobbe was frightened. This man made her think of witches, of black mirrors and corpses wandering around at night and terrifying women. Nevertheless, she took a few steps toward him and inquired, "How are you? Any better?"

"A little, thank you."

"Are you really a convert?" she asked although she wasn't quite sure what the word meant.

"Me, a convert? No, I'm a Jew like any other Jew," Dr. Fischelson answered.

The doctor's assurances made Dobbe feel more at home. She found the bottle of kerosene and lit the stove, and after that she fetched a glass of milk from her room and began cooking kasha. Dr. Fischelson continued to study the *Ethics,* but that evening he could make no sense of the theorems and proofs with their many references to axioms and definitions and other theorems. With trembling hand he raised the book to his eyes and read, "The idea of each modification of the human body does not involve adequate knowledge of the human body itself. . . . The idea of the idea of each modification of the human mind does not involve adequate knowledge of the human mind."

6

Dr. Fischelson was certain he would die any day now. He made out his will, leaving all of his books and manuscripts to the synagogue library. His clothing and furniture would go to Dobbe since she had taken care of him. But death did not come. Rather his health improved. Dobbe returned to her business in the market, but she visited the old man several times a day, prepared soup for him, left him a glass of tea, and told him news of the war. The Germans had occupied Kalish, Bendin, and Cestechow, and they were marching on Warsaw. People said that on a quiet morning one could hear the rumblings of the cannon. Dobbe reported that the casualties were heavy. "They're falling like flies," she said. "What a terrible misfortune for the women."

She couldn't explain why, but the old man's attic room attracted her. She liked to remove the gold-rimmed books from the bookcase, dust them, and then air them on the windowsill. She would climb the few steps to the window and look out through the telescope. She also enjoyed talking to Dr. Fischelson. He told her about Switzerland, where he had studied, of the great cities he had passed through, of the high mountains that were covered with snow even in the summer. His father had been a rabbi, he said, and before he, Dr. Fischelson, had become a student, he had attended a yeshiva. She asked him how many languages he knew and it turned out that he could speak and write Hebrew, Russian, German, and French, in addition to Yiddish. He also knew Latin. Dobbe was astonished that such an educated man should live in an attic room on Market Street. But what amazed her most of all was that although he had the title "Doctor," he couldn't write prescriptions. "Why don't you become a real doctor?" she would ask him. "I am a doctor," he would answer. "I'm just not a physician." "What kind of a doctor?" "A doctor of philosophy." Although she had no idea of what this meant, she felt it must be very important. "Oh, my blessed mother," she would say, "where did you get such a brain?"

Then one evening after Dobbe had given him his crackers and his glass of tea with milk, he began questioning her about where she came from, who her parents were, and why she had not married. Dobbe was surprised. No one had ever asked her such questions. She told him her story in a quiet voice and stayed until eleven o'clock. Her father had been a porter at the kosher butcher shops. Her mother had plucked chickens in the slaughterhouse. The family had lived in a cellar at No. 19 Market Street. When she had been ten, she had become a maid. The man she had worked for had been a fence who bought stolen goods from thieves on the square. Dobbe had had a brother who had gone into the Russian army and had never returned. Her sister had married a coachman in Praga and had died in childbirth. Dobbe told of the battles between the underworld and the revolutionaries in 1905, of blind Itche and his gang and how they collected protection money from the stores, of the thugs who attacked young boys and girls out on Saturday afternoon strolls if they were not paid money for security. She also spoke of the pimps who drove about in carriages and abducted women to be sold in Buenos Aires. Dobbe swore that some men had even sought to inveigle her into a brothel, but that she had run away. She complained of a thousand evils done to her. She had been robbed; her boy friend had been stolen; a competitor had once poured a pint of kerosene into her basket of bagels; her own cousin, the shoemaker, had cheated her out of a hundred rubles before he had left for America. Dr. Fischelson listened to her attentively. He asked her questions, shook his head, and grunted.

"Well, do you believe in God?" he finally asked her.

"I don't know," she answered. "Do you?"

"Yes, I believe."

"Then why don't you go to synagogue?" she asked.

"God is everywhere," he replied. "In the synagogue. In the market-place. In this very room. We ourselves are parts of God."

"Don't say such things," Dobbe said. "You frighten me."

She left the room and Dr. Fischelson was certain she had gone to bed. But he wondered why she had not said good night. "I probably drove her away with my philosophy," he thought. The very next moment he heard her footsteps. She came in carrying a pile of clothing like a peddler.

"I wanted to show you these," she said. "They're my trousseau." And she began to spread out, on the chair, dresses — woolen, silk, velvet. Taking each dress up in turn, she held it to her body. She gave him an account of every item in her trousseau — underwear, shoes, stockings.

"I'm not wasteful," she said. "I'm a saver. I have enough money to go to America."

Then she was silent and her face turned brick-red. She looked at Dr. Fischelson out of the corner of her eyes, timidly, inquisitively. Dr. Fischelson's body suddenly began to shake as if he had the chills. He said, "Very nice, beautiful things." His brow furrowed and he pulled at his beard with two fingers. A sad smile appeared on his toothless mouth and his large fluttering eyes, gazing into the distance through the attic window, also smiled sadly.

7

The day that Black Dobbe came to the rabbi's chambers and announced that she was to marry Dr. Fischelson, the rabbi's wife thought she had gone mad. But the news had already reached Leizer the tailor, and had spread to the bakery, as well as to other shops. There were those who thought that the "old maid" was very lucky; the doctor, they said, had a vast hoard of money. But there were others who took the view that he was a run-down degenerate who would give her syphilis. Although Dr. Fischelson had insisted that the wedding be a small, quiet one, a host of guests assembled in the rabbi's rooms. The bakers' apprentices who generally went about barefoot, and in their underwear, with paper bags on the tops of their heads, now put on light-colored suits, straw hats, yellow shoes, gaudy ties, and they brought with them huge cakes and pans filled with cookies. They had even managed to find a bottle of vodka although liquor was forbidden in wartime. When the bride and groom entered the rabbi's chamber, a murmur arose from the crowd. The women could not believe their eyes. The woman that they saw was not the one they had known. Dobbe wore a wide-brimmed hat which was amply adorned with cherries, grapes, and plumes, and the dress that she had on was of white silk and was equipped with a train; on her feet were high-heeled shoes, gold in color, and from her thin neck hung a string of imitation pearls. Nor was this all: her fingers sparkled with rings and glittering stones. Her face was veiled. She looked almost like one of those rich brides who were married in the Vienna Hall. The bakers' apprentices whistled mockingly. As for Dr. Fischelson, he was wearing his black coat and broad-toed shoes. He was scarcely able to walk; he was leaning on Dobbe. When he saw the crowd from the doorway, he became frightened and began to retreat, but Dobbe's former employer approached him saying, "Come in, come in, bridegroom. Don't be bashful. We are all brethren now."

The ceremony proceeded according to the law. The rabbi, in a worn satin gaberdine, wrote the marriage contract and then had the bride and groom touch his handkerchief as a token of agreement; the rabbi wiped the point of the pen on his skullcap. Several porters who had been called from the street to make up the quorum supported the canopy. Dr. Fischelson put on a white robe as a reminder of the day of his death and Dobbe walked around him seven times as custom required. The light from the braided candles flickered on the walls. The shadows wavered. Having poured wine into a goblet, the rabbi chanted the benedictions in a sad melody. Dobbe uttered only a single cry. As for the other women, they took out their lace handkerchiefs and stood with them in their hands, grimacing. When the bakers' boys began to whisper wisecracks to each other, the rabbi put a finger to his lips and murmured, "Eh nu oh," as a sign that talking was forbidden. The moment came to slip the wedding ring on the bride's finger, but the bridegroom's hand started to tremble and he had trouble locating Dobbe's index finger. The next thing, according to custom, was the smashing of the glass, but though Dr. Fischelson kicked the goblet several times, it remained unbroken. The girls lowered their heads, pinched each other gleefully, and giggled. Finally one of the apprentices struck the goblet with his heel and it shattered. Even the rabbi could not restrain a smile. After the ceremony the guests drank vodka and ate cookies. Dobbe's former employer came up to Dr. Fischelson and said, "Mazel tov, bridegroom. Your luck should be as good as your wife." "Thank you, thank you," Dr. Fischelson murmured, "but I don't look forward to any luck." He was anxious to return as quickly as possible to his attic room. He felt a pressure in his stomach and his chest ached. His face had become greenish. Dobbe had suddenly become angry. She pulled back her veil and called out to the crowd, "What are you laughing at? This isn't a show." And without picking up the cushion-cover in which the gifts were wrapped, she returned with her husband to their rooms on the fifth floor.

Dr. Fischelson lay down on the freshly made bed in his room and began reading the *Ethics*. Dobbe had gone back to her own room. The doctor had explained to her that he was an old man, that he was sick and without strength. He had promised her nothing. Nevertheless she returned wearing a silk nightgown, slippers with pompoms, and with her hair hanging down over her shoulders. There was a smile on her face, and she was bashful and hesitant. Dr. Fischelson trembled and the *Ethics* dropped from his hands. The candle went out. Dobbe groped for Dr. Fischelson in the dark and kissed his mouth. "My dear husband," she whispered to him, "*Mazel tov.*"

What happened that night could be called a miracle. If Dr. Fischelson hadn't been convinced that every occurrence is in accordance with the laws of nature, he would have thought that Black Dobbe had bewitched him. Powers long dormant awakened in him. Although he had had only a sip of the benediction wine, he was as if intoxicated. He kissed Dobbe and spoke to her of love. Long-forgotten quotations from Klopstock, Lessing, Goethe, rose to his lips. The pressures and aches stopped. He embraced Dobbe, pressed her to himself, was again a man as in his youth. Dobbe was faint with delight; crying, she murmured things to him in a Warsaw slang which he did not understand. Later, Dr. Fischelson slipped off into the deep sleep young men know. He dreamed that he was in Switzerland and that he was climbing mountains — running, falling, flying. At dawn he opened his eyes; it seemed to him that someone had blown into his ears. Dobbe was snoring. Dr. Fischelson quietly got out of bed. In his long nightshirt he approached the window, walked up the steps and looked out in wonder. Market Street was asleep, breathing with a deep stillness. The gas lamps were flickering. The black shutters on the stores were fastened with iron bars. A cool breeze was blowing. Dr. Fischelson looked up at the sky. The black arch was thickly sown with stars — there were green, red, yellow, blue stars; there were large ones and small ones, winking and steady ones. There were those that were clustered in dense groups and those that were alone. In the higher sphere, apparently, little notice was taken of the fact that a certain Dr. Fischelson had in his declining days married someone called Black

Dobbe. Seen from above even the Great War was nothing but a temporary play of the modes. The myriads of fixed stars continued to travel their destined courses in unbounded space. The comets, planets, satellites, asteroids kept circling these shining centers. Worlds were born and died in cosmic upheavals. In the chaos of nebulae, primeval matter was being formed. Now and again a star tore loose, and swept across the sky, leaving behind it a fiery streak. It was the month of August when there are showers of meteors. Yes, the divine substance was extended and had neither beginning nor end; it was absolute, indivisible, eternal, without duration, infinite in its attributes. Its waves and bubbles danced in the universal cauldron, seething with change, following the unbroken chain of causes and effects, and he, Dr. Fischelson, with his unavoidable fate, was part of this. The doctor closed his eyelids and allowed the breeze to cool the sweat on his forehead and stir the hair of his beard. He breathed deeply of the midnight air, supported his shaky hands on the window-sill and murmured, "Divine Spinoza, forgive me. I have become a fool."

The Ballad of the Sad Café

by Carson McCullers

THE TOWN ITSELF is dreary; not much is there except the cotton mill, the two-room houses where the workers live, a few peach trees, a church with two colored windows, and a miserable main street only a hundred yards long. On Saturdays the tenants from the near-by farms come in for a day of talk and trade. Otherwise the town is lonesome, sad, and like a place that is far off and estranged from all other places in the world. The nearest train stop is Society City, and the Greyhound and White Bus Lines use the Forks Falls Road which is three miles away. The winters here are short and raw, the summers white with glare and fiery hot.

If you walk along the main street on an August afternoon there is nothing whatsoever to do. The largest building, in the very center of the town, is boarded up completely and leans so far to the right that it seems bound to collapse at any minute. The house is very old. There is about it a curious, cracked look that is very puzzling until you suddenly realize that at one time, and long ago, the right side of the front porch had been painted, and part of the wall — but the painting was left unfinished and one portion of the house is darker and dingier than the other. The building looks completely deserted. Nevertheless, on the second floor there is one window which is not boarded; sometimes in the late afternoon when the heat is at its worst a hand will slowly open the shutter and a face will look down on the town. It is a face like the terrible dim faces known in dreams — sexless and white, with two gray crossed eyes which are turned inward so sharply that they seem to be exchanging with each other one long and secret gaze of grief. The face lingers at the window for an hour or so, then the shutters are closed once more, and as likely as not there will not be another soul to be seen along the main street. These August afternoons — when your shift is finished there is absolutely nothing to do; you might as well walk down to the Forks Falls Road and listen to the chain gang.

However, here in this very town there was once a café. And this old boarded-up house was unlike any other place for many miles around. There were tables with cloths and paper napkins, colored streamers from the electric fans, great gatherings on Saturday nights. The owner of the place was Miss Amelia Evans. But the person most responsible for the success and gaiety of the place was a hunchback called Cousin Lymon. One other person had a part in the story of this café — he was the former husband of Miss Amelia, a terrible character who returned to the town after a long term in the penitentiary, caused ruin, and then went on his way again. The café has long since been closed, but it is still remembered.

The place was not always a café. Miss Amelia inherited the building from her father, and it was a store that carried mostly feed, guano, and staples such as meal and snuff. Miss Amelia was rich. In addition to the store she operated a still three miles back in the swamp, and ran out the best liquor in the county. She was a dark, tall woman with bones and muscles like a man. Her hair was cut short and brushed back from the forehead, and there was about her sunburned face a tense, haggard quality. She might have been a handsome woman if, even then, she was not slightly cross-eyed. There were those who would have courted her, but Miss Amelia cared nothing for the love of men and was a solitary person. Her marriage had been unlike any other marriage ever contracted in this county — it was a strange and dangerous marriage, lasting only for ten days, that left the whole town wondering and shocked. Except for this queer marriage, Miss Amelia had lived her life alone. Often she spent whole nights back in her shed in the swamp, dressed in overalls and gum boots, silently guarding the low fire of the still.

With all things which could be made by the hands Miss Amelia prospered. She sold chitterlins and sausage in the town near-by. On fine autumn days, she ground sorghum, and the syrup from her vats was dark golden and delicately flavored. She built the brick privy behind her store in only two weeks and was skilled in carpentering. It was only with people that Miss Amelia was not at ease. People, unless they are nilly-willy or very sick, cannot be taken into the hands and changed overnight to something more worthwhile and profitable. So that the only use that Miss Amelia had for other people was to make money out of them. And in this she succeeded. Mortgages on crops and property, a sawmill, money in the bank — she was the richest woman for miles around. She would have been rich as a congressman if it were not for her one great failing, and that was her passion for lawsuits and the courts. She would involve herself in long and bitter litigation over just a trifle. It was said that if Miss Amelia so much as stumbled over a rock in the road she would glance around instinctively as though looking for something to sue about it. Aside from these lawsuits she lived a steady life and every day was very much like the day that had gone before. With the exception of her ten-day marriage, nothing happened to change this until the spring of the year that Miss Amelia was thirty years old.

It was toward midnight on a soft quiet evening in April. The sky was the color of a blue swamp iris, the moon clear and bright. The crops that spring promised well and in the past weeks the mill had run a night shift. Down by the creek the square brick factory was yellow with light, and there was the faint, steady hum of the looms. It was such a night when it is good to hear from faraway, across the dark fields, the slow song of a Negro on his way to make love. Or when it is pleasant to sit quietly and pick a guitar, or simply to rest alone and think of nothing at all. The street that evening was deserted, but Miss Amelia's store was lighted and on the porch outside there were five people. One of these was Stumpy MacPhail, a foreman with a red face and dainty, purplish hands. On the top step were two boys in overalls, the Rainey twins — both of them lanky and slow, with white hair and sleepy green eyes. The other man was Henry Macy, a shy and timid person with gentle manners and nervous ways, who sat on the edge of the bottom step. Miss Amelia herself stood leaning against the side of the open door, her feet crossed in their big swamp boots, patiently untying knots in a rope she had come across. They had not talked for a long time.

One of the twins, who had been looking down the empty road, was the first to speak. 'I see something coming,' he said.

'A calf got loose,' said his brother.

The approaching figure was still too distant to be clearly seen. The moon made dim, twisted shadows of the blossoming peach trees along the side of the road. In the air the odor of blossoms and sweet spring grass mingled with the warm, sour smell of the near-by lagoon.

'No. It's somebody's youngun,' said Stumpy MacPhail.

Miss Amelia watched the road in silence. She had put down her rope and was fingering the straps of her overalls with her brown bony hand. She scowled, and a dark lock of hair fell down on her forehead. While they were waiting there, a dog from one of the houses down the road began a wild, hoarse howl that continued until a voice called out and hushed him. It was not until the figure was quite close, within the range of the yellow light from the porch, that they saw clearly what had come.

The man was a stranger, and it is rare that a stranger enters the town on foot at that hour. Besides, the man was a hunchback. He was scarcely more than four feet tall and he wore a ragged, dusty coat that reached only to his knees. His crooked little legs seemed too thin to carry the weight of his great warped chest and the hump that sat on his shoulders. He had a very large head, with deep-set blue eyes and a sharp little mouth. His face was both soft and sassy — at the moment his pale skin was yellowed by dust and there were lavender shadows beneath his eyes. He carried a lopsided old suitcase which was tied with a rope.

'Evening,' said the hunchback, and he was out of breath.

Miss Amelia and the men on the porch neither answered his greeting nor spoke. They only looked at him.

'I am hunting for Miss Amelia Evans.'

Miss Amelia pushed back her hair from her forehead and raised her chin. 'How come?'

'Because I am kin to her,' the hunchback said.

The twins and Stumpy MacPhail looked up at Miss Amelia.

'That's me,' she said. 'How do you mean "kin"?'

'Because ——' the hunchback began. He looked uneasy, almost as though he was about to cry. He rested the suitcase on the bottom step, but did not take his hand from the handle. 'My mother was Fanny Jesup and she come from Cheehaw. She left Cheehaw some thirty years ago when she married her first husband. I remember hearing her tell how she had a half-sister named Martha. And back in Cheehaw today they tell me that was your mother.'

Miss Amelia listened with her head turned slightly aside. She ate her Sunday dinners by herself; her place was never crowded with a flock of relatives, and she claimed kin with no one. She had had a great-aunt who owned the livery stable in Cheehaw, but that aunt was now dead. Aside from her there was only one double first cousin who lived in a town twenty miles away, but this cousin and Miss Amelia did not get on so well, and when they chanced to pass each other they spat on the side of the road. Other people had tried very hard, from time to time, to work out some kind of far-fetched connection with Miss Amelia, but with absolutely no success.

The hunchback went into a long rigmarole, mentioning names and places that were unknown to the listeners on the porch and seemed to have nothing to do with the subject. 'So Fanny and Martha Jesup were half-sisters. And I am the son of Fanny's third husband. So that would make you and I ——' He bent down and began to unfasten his suit-case. His hands were like dirty sparrow claws and they were trembling. The bag was full of all manner of junk — ragged clothes and odd rubbish that looked like parts out of a sewing machine, or something just as worthless. The hunchback scrambled among these belongings and brought out an old photograph. 'This is a picture of my mother and her half-sister.'

Miss Amelia did not speak. She was moving her jaw slowly from side to side, and you could tell from her face what she was thinking about. Stumpy MacPhail took the photograph and held it out toward the light. It was a picture of two pale, withered-up little children of about two and three years of age. The faces were tiny white blurs, and it might have been an old picture in anyone's album.

Stumpy MacPhail handed it back with no comment. 'Where you come from?' he asked.

The hunchback's voice was uncertain. 'I was traveling.'

Still Miss Amelia did not speak. She just stood leaning against the side of the door, and looked down at the hunchback. Henry Macy winked nervously and rubbed his hands together. Then quietly he left the bottom step and disappeared. He is a good soul, and the hunchback's situation had touched his heart. Therefore he did not want to wait and watch Miss Amelia chase this newcomer off her property and run him out of town. The hunchback stood with his bag open on the bottom step; he sniffled his nose, and his mouth quivered. Perhaps he began to feel his dismal predicament. Maybe he realized what a miserable thing it was to be a stranger in the town with a suitcase full of junk, and claiming kin with Miss Amelia. At any rate he sat down on the steps and suddenly began to cry.

It was not a common thing to have an unknown hunchback walk to the store at midnight and then sit down and cry. Miss Amelia rubbed back her hair from her forehead and the men looked at each other uncomfortably. All around the town was very quiet.

At last one of the twins said: 'I'll be damned if he ain't a regular Morris Finestein.'

Everyone nodded and agreed, for that is an expression having a certain special meaning. But the hunchback cried louder because he could not know what they were talking about. Morris Finestein was a person who had lived in the town years before. He was only a quick, skipping little Jew who cried if you called him Christ-killer, and ate light bread and canned salmon every day. A calamity had come over him and he had moved away to Society City. But since then if a man were prissy in any way, or if a man ever wept, he was known as a Morris Finestein.

'Well, he is afflicted,' said Stumpy MacPhail. 'There is some cause.'

Miss Amelia crossed the porch with two slow, gangling strides. She went down the steps and stood looking thoughtfully at the stranger. Gingerly, with one long brown forefinger, she touched the hump on his back. The hunchback still wept, but he was quieter now. The night was silent and the moon still shone with a soft, clear light — it was getting colder. Then Miss Amelia did a rare thing; she pulled out a bottle from her hip pocket and after polishing off the top with the palm of her hand she handed it to the hunchback to drink. Miss Amelia could seldom be persuaded to sell her liquor on credit, and for her to give so much as a drop away free was almost unknown.

'Drink,' she said. 'It will liven your gizzard.'

The hunchback stopped crying, neatly licked the tears from around his mouth, and did as he was told. When he was finished, Miss Amelia took a slow swallow, warmed and washed her mouth with it, and spat. Then she also drank. The twins and the foreman had their own bottle they had paid for.

'It is smooth liquor,' Stumpy MacPhail said. 'Miss Amelia, I have never known you to fail.'

The whiskey they drank that evening (two big bottles of it) is important. Otherwise, it would be hard to account for what followed. Perhaps without it there would never have been a café. For the liquor of Miss Amelia has a special quality of its own. It is clean and sharp on the tongue, but once down a man it glows inside him for a long time afterward. And that is not all. It is known that if a message is written with lemon juice on a clean sheet of paper there will be no sign of it. But if the paper is held for a moment to the fire then the letters turn brown and the meaning becomes clear. Imagine that the whiskey is the fire and that the message is that which is known only in the soul of a man — then the worth of Miss Amelia's liquor can be understood. Things that have gone unnoticed, thoughts that have been harbored far back in the dark mind, are suddenly recognized and comprehended. A spinner who has thought only of the loom, the dinner pail, the bed, and then the loom again — this spinner might drink some on a Sunday and come across a marsh lily. And in his palm he might hold this flower, examining the golden dainty cup, and in him suddenly might come a sweetness keen as pain. A weaver might look up suddenly and see for the first time the cold, weird radiance of midnight January sky, and a deep fright at his own smallness stop his heart. Such things as these, then, happen when a man has drunk Miss Amelia's liquor. He may suffer, or he may be spent with joy — but the experience has shown the truth; he has warmed his soul and seen the message hidden there.

They drank until it was past midnight, and the moon was clouded over so that the night was cold and dark. The hunchback still sat on the bottom steps, bent over miserably with his forehead resting on his knee. Miss Amelia stood with her hands in her pockets, one foot resting on the second step of the stairs. She had been silent for a long time. Her face had the expression often seen in slightly cross-eyed persons who are thinking deeply, a look that appears to be both very wise and very crazy. At last she said: 'I don't know your name.'

'I'm Lymon Willis,' said the hunchback.

'Well, come on in,' she said. 'Some supper was left in the stove and you can eat.'

Only a few times in her life had Miss Amelia invited anyone to eat with her, unless she were planning to trick them in some way, or make money out of them. So the men on the porch felt there was something wrong. Later, they said among themselves that she must have been drinking back in the swamp the better part of the afternoon. At any rate she left the porch, and Stumpy MacPhail and the twins went on off home. She bolted the front door and looked all around to see that her goods were in order. Then she went to the kitchen, which was at the back of the store. The hunchback followed her, dragging his suit-case, sniffing and wiping his nose on the sleeve of his dirty coat.

'Sit down,' said Miss Amelia. 'I'll just warm up what's here.'

It was a good meal they had together on that night. Miss Amelia was rich and she did not grudge herself food. There was fried chicken (the breast of which the hunchback took on his own plate), mashed rootabeggars, collard greens, and hot, pale golden, sweet potatoes. Miss Amelia ate slowly and with the relish of a farm hand. She sat with both elbows on the table, bent over the plate, her knees spread wide apart and her feet braced on the rungs of the chair. As for the hunchback, he gulped down his supper as though he had not smelled food in months. During the meal one tear crept down his dingy cheek — but it was just a little leftover tear and meant nothing at all. The lamp on the table was well-trimmed, burning blue at the edges of the wick, and casting a cheerful light in the kitchen. When Miss Amelia had eaten her supper she wiped her plate carefully with a slice of light bread, and then poured her own clear, sweet syrup over the bread. The hunchback did likewise — except that he was more finicky and asked for a new plate. Having finished, Miss Amelia tilted back her chair, tightened her fist, and felt the hard, supple muscles of her right arm beneath the clean, blue cloth of her shirtsleeves — an uncon-scious habit with her, at the close of a meal. Then she took the lamp from the table and jerked her head toward the staircase as an invita-tion for the hunchback to follow after her.

Above the store there were the three rooms where Miss Amelia had lived during all her life — two bedrooms with a large parlor in be-tween. Few people had even seen these rooms, but it was generally known that they were well-furnished and extremely clean. And now Miss Amelia was taking up with her a dirty little hunchbacked stranger, come from God knows where. Miss Amelia walked slowly, two steps at a time, holding the lamp high. The hunchback hovered so close behind her that the swinging light made on the staircase wall one great, twisted shadow of the two of them. Soon the premises above the store were dark as the rest of the town.

The next morning was serene, with a sunrise of warm purple mixed with rose. In the fields around the town the furrows were newly plowed, and very early the tenants were at work setting out the young, deep green tobacco plants. The wild crows flew down close to the fields, making swift blue shadows on the earth. In town the people set out early with their dinner pails, and the windows of the mill were blinding gold in the sun. The air was fresh and the peach trees light as March clouds with their blossoms.

Miss Amelia came down at about dawn, as usual. She washed her head at the pump and very shortly set about her business. Later in the morning she saddled her mule and went to see about her property, planted with cotton, up near the Forks Falls Road. By noon, of course, everybody had heard about the hunchback who had come to the store in the middle of the night. But no one as yet had seen him. The day soon grew hot and the sky was a rich, midday blue. Still no one had laid an eye on this strange guest. A few people remembered that Miss Amelia's mother had had a half-sister — but there was some difference of opinion as to whether she had died or had run off with a tobacco stringer. As for the hunchback's claim, everyone thought it was a trumped-up business. And the town, knowing Miss Amelia, decided that surely she had put him out of the house after feeding him. But toward evening, when the sky had whitened, and the shift was done, a woman claimed to have seen a crooked face at the window of one of the rooms up over the store. Miss Amelia herself said nothing. She clerked in the store for a while, argued for an hour with a farmer over a plow shaft, mended some chicken wire, locked up near sundown, and went to her rooms. The town was left puzzled and talkative.

The next day Miss Amelia did not open the store, but stayed locked up inside her premises and saw no one. Now this was the day that the rumor started — the rumor so terrible that the town and all the country about were stunned by it. The rumor was started by a weaver called Merlie Ryan. He is a man of not much account — sallow, shambling, and with no teeth in his head. He has the three-day malaria, which means that every third day the fever comes on him. So on two days he is dull and cross, but on the third day he livens up and sometimes has an idea or two, most of which are foolish. It was while Merlie Ryan was in his fever that he turned suddenly and said:

'I know what Miss Amelia done. She murdered that man for something in that suitcase.'

He said this in a calm voice, as a statement of fact. And within an hour the news had swept through the town. It was a fierce and sickly tale the town built up that day. In it were all the things which cause the heart to shiver — a hunchback, a midnight burial in the swamp, the dragging of Miss Amelia through the streets of the town on the way to prison, the squabbles over what would happen to her property — all told in hushed voices and repeated with some fresh and weird detail. It rained and women forgot to bring in the washing from the lines. One or two mortals, who were in debt to Miss Amelia, even put on Sunday clothes as though it were a holiday. People clustered together on the main street, talking and watching the store.

It would be untrue to say that all the town took part in this evil festival. There were a few sensible men who reasoned that Miss Amelia, being rich, would not go out of her way to murder a vagabond for a few trifles of junk. In the town there were even three good people, and they did not want this crime, not even for the sake of the interest and the great commotion it would entail; it gave them no pleasure to think of Miss Amelia holding to the bars of the penitentiary and being electrocuted in Atlanta. These good people judged Miss Amelia in a different way from what the others judged her. When a person is as contrary in every single respect as she was and when the sins of a person have amounted to such a point that they can hardly be remembered all at once — then this person plainly requires a special judgment. They remembered that Miss Amelia had been born dark and somewhat queer of face, raised motherless by her father who was a solitary man, that early in youth she had grown to be six feet two inches tall which in itself is not natural for a woman, and that her ways and habits of life were too peculiar ever to reason about. Above all, they remembered her puzzling marriage, which was the most unreasonable scandal ever to happen in this town.

So these good people felt toward her something near to pity. And when she was out on her wild business, such as rushing in a house to drag forth a sewing machine in payment for a debt, or getting herself worked up over some matter concerning the law — they had toward her a feeling which was a mixture of exasperation, a ridiculous little inside tickle, and a deep, unnamable sadness. But enough of the good people, for there were only three of them; the rest of the town was making a holiday of this fancied crime the whole of the afternoon.

Miss Amelia herself, for some strange reason, seemed unaware of all this. She spent most of her day upstairs. When down in the store, she prowled around peacefully, her hands deep in the pockets of her overalls and head bent so low that her chin was tucked inside the collar of her shirt. There was no bloodstain on her anywhere. Often she stopped and just stood somberly looking down at the cracks in the floor, twisting a lock of her short-cropped hair, and whispering something to herself. But most of the day was spent upstairs.

Dark came on. The rain that afternoon had chilled the air, so that the evening was bleak and gloomy as in wintertime. There were no stars in the sky, and a light, icy drizzle had set in. The lamps in the houses made mournful, wavering flickers when watched from the street. A wind had come up, not from the swamp side of the town but from the cold black pinewoods to the north.

The clocks in the town struck eight. Still nothing had happened. The bleak night, after the gruesome talk of the day, put a fear in some people, and they stayed home close to the fire. Others were gathered in groups together. Some eight or ten men had convened on the porch of Miss Amelia's store. They were silent and were indeed just waiting about. They themselves did not know what they were waiting for, but it was this: in times of tension, when some great action is impending, men gather and wait in this way. And after a time there will come a moment when all together they will act in unison, not from thought or from the will of any one man, but as though their instincts had merged together so that the decision belongs to no single one of them, but to the group as a whole. At such a time, no individual hesitates. And whether the matter will be settled peaceably, or whether the joint action will result in ransacking, violence, and crime, depends on destiny. So the men waited soberly on the porch of Miss Amelia's store, not one of them realizing what they would do, but knowing inwardly that they must wait, and that the time had almost come.

Now the door to the store was open. Inside it was bright and natural-looking. To the left was the counter where slabs of white meat, rock candy, and tobacco were kept. Behind this were shelves of salted white meat and meal. The right side of the store was mostly filled with farm implements and such. At the back of the store, to the left, was the door leading up the stairs, and it was open. And at the far right of the store there was another door which led to a little room that Miss Amelia called her office. This door was also open. And at eight o'clock that evening Miss Amelia could be seen there sitting before her rolltop desk, figuring with a fountain pen and some pieces of paper.

The office was cheerfully lighted, and Miss Amelia did not seem to notice the delegation on the porch. Everything around her was in great order, as usual. This office was a room well-known, in a dreadful way, throughout the country. It was there Miss Amelia transacted all business. On the desk was a carefully covered typewriter which she knew how to run, but used only for the most important documents. In the drawers were literally thousands of papers, all filed according to the alphabet. This office was also the place where Miss Amelia received sick people, for she enjoyed doctoring and did a great deal of it. Two whole shelves were crowded with bottles and various paraphernalia. Against the wall was a bench where the patients sat. She could sew up a wound with a burnt needle so that it would not turn green. For burns she had a cool, sweet syrup. For unlocated sickness there were any number of different medicines which she had brewed herself from unknown recipes. They wrenched loose the bowels very well, but they could not be given to small children, as they caused bad convulsions; for them she had an entirely separate draught, gentler and sweet-flavored. Yes, all in all, she was considered a good doctor. Her hands, though very large and bony, had a light touch about them. She possessed great imagination and used hundreds of different cures. In the face of the most dangerous and extraordinary treatment she did not hesitate, and no disease was so terrible but what she would undertake to cure it. In this there was one exception. If a patient came with a female complaint she could do nothing. Indeed at the mere mention of the words her face would slowly darken with shame, and she would stand their craning her neck against the collar of her shirt, or rubbing her swamp boots together, for all the world like a great, shamed, dumb-tongued child. But in other matters people trusted her. She charged no fees whatsoever and always had a raft of patients.

On this evening, Miss Amelia wrote with her fountain pen a good deal. But even so she could not be forever unaware of the group waiting out there on the dark porch, and watching her. From time to time she looked up and regarded them steadily. But she did not holler out to them to demand why they were loafing around her property like a sorry bunch of gabbies. Her face was proud and stern, as it always was when she sat at the desk of her office. After a time their peering in like that seemed to annoy her. She wiped her cheek with a red handkerchief, got up, and closed the office door.

Now to the group on the porch this gesture acted as a signal. The time had come. They had stood for a long while with the night raw and gloomy in the street behind them. They had waited long and just at that moment the instinct to act came on them. All at once, as though moved by one will, they walked into the store. At that moment the eight men looked very much alike — all wearing blue overalls, most of them with whitish hair, all pale of face, and all with a set, dreaming look in the eye. What they would have done next no one knows. But at that instant there was a noise at the head of the staircase. The men looked up and then stood dumb with shock. It was the hunchback, whom they had already murdered in their minds. Also, the creature was not at all as had been pictured to them — not a pitiful and dirty little chatterer, alone and beggared in this world. Indeed, he was like nothing any man among them had ever beheld until that time. The room was still as death.

The hunchback came down slowly with the proudness of one who owns every plank of the floor beneath his feet. In the past days he had greatly changed. For one thing he was clean beyond words. He still wore his little coat, but it was brushed off and neatly mended. Beneath this was a fresh red and black checkered shirt belonging to Miss Amelia. He did not wear trousers such as ordinary men are meant to wear, but a pair of tight-fitting little knee-length breeches. On his skinny legs he wore black stockings, and his shoes were of a special kind, being queerly shaped, laced up over the ankles, and newly cleaned and polished with wax. Around his neck, so that his large, pale ears were almost completely covered, he wore a shawl of lime-green wool, the fringes of which almost touched the floor.

The hunchback walked down the store with his stiff little strut and then stood in the center of the group that had come inside. They cleared a space about him and stood looking with hands loose at their sides and eyes wide open. The hunchback himself got his bearings in an odd manner. He regarded each person steadily at his own eye-level, which was about belt line for an ordinary man. Then with shrewd deliberation he examined each man's lower regions — from the waist to the sole of the shoe. When he had satisfied himself he closed his eyes for a moment and shook his head, as though in his opinion what he had seen did not amount to much. Then with assurance, only to confirm himself, he tilted back his head and took in the halo of faces around him with one long, circling stare. There was a half-filled sack of guano on the left side of the store, and when he had found his bearings in this way, the hunchback sat down upon it. Cozily settled, with his little legs crossed, he took from his coat pocket a certain object.

Now it took some moments for the men in the store to regain their ease. Merlie Ryan, he of the three-day fever who had started the rumor that day, was the first to speak. He looked at the object which the hunchback was fondling, and said in a hushed voice:

'What is it you have there?'

Each man knew well what it was the hunchback was handling. For it was the snuffbox which had belonged to Miss Amelia's father. The snuffbox was of blue enamel with a dainty embellishment of wrought gold on the lid. The group knew it well and marveled. They glanced warily at the closed office door, and heard the low sound of Miss Amelia whistling to herself.

'Yes, what is it, Peanut?'

The hunchback looked up quickly and sharpened his mouth to speak. 'Why, this is a lay-low to catch meddlers.'

The hunchback reached in the box with his scrambly little fingers and ate something, but he offered no one around him a taste. It was not even proper snuff which he was taking, but a mixture of sugar and cocoa. This he took, though, as snuff, pocketing a little wad of it beneath his lower lip and licking down neatly into this with a flick of his tongue which made a frequent grimace come over his face.

'The very teeth in my head have always tasted sour to me,' he said in explanation. 'That is the reason why I take this kind of sweet snuff.'

The group still clustered around, feeling somewhat gawky and bewildered. This sensation never quite wore off, but it was soon tempered by another feeling — an air of intimacy in the room and a vague festivity. Now the names of the men of the group there on that evening were as follows: Hasty Malone, Robert Calvert Hale, Merlie Ryan, Reverend T. M. Willin, Rosser Cline, Rip Wellborn, Henry Ford Crimp, and Horace Wells. Except for Reverend Willin, they are all alike in many ways as has been said — all having taken pleasure from something or other, all having wept and suffered in some way, most of them tractable unless exasperated. Each of them worked in the mill, and lived with others in a two- or three-room house for which the rent was ten dollars or twelve dollars a month. All had been paid that afternoon, for it was Saturday. So, for the present, think of them as a whole.

The hunchback, however, was already sorting them out in his mind. Once comfortably settled he began to chat with everyone, asking questions such as if a man was married, how old he was, how much his wages came to in an average week, et cetera — picking his way along to inquiries which were downright intimate. Soon the group was joined by others in the town, Henry Macy, idlers who had sensed something extraordinary, women come to fetch their men who lingered on, and even one loose, towhead child who tiptoed into the store, stole a box of animal crackers, and made off very quietly. So the premises of Miss Amelia were soon crowded, and she herself had not yet opened her office door.

There is a type of person who has a quality about him that sets him apart from other and more ordinary human beings. Such a person has an instinct which is usually found only in small children, an instinct to establish immediate and vital contact between himself and all things in the world. Certainly the hunchback was of this type. He had only been in the store half an hour before an immediate contact had been established between him and each other individual. It was as though he had lived in the town for years, was a well-known character, and had been sitting and talking there on that guano sack for countless evenings. This, together with the fact that it was Saturday night, could account for the air of freedom and illicit gladness in the store. There was a tension, also, partly because of the oddity of the situation and because Miss Amelia was still closed off in her office and had not yet made her appearance.

She came out that evening at ten o'clock. And those who were expecting some drama at her entrance were disappointed. She opened the door and walked in with her slow, gangling swagger. There was a streak of ink on one side of her nose, and she had knotted the red handkerchief about her neck. She seemed to notice nothing unusual. Her gray, crossed eyes glanced over to the place where the hunchback was sitting, and for a moment lingered there. The rest of the crowd in her store she regarded with only a peaceable surprise.

'Does anyone want waiting on?' she asked quietly.

There were a number of customers, because it was Saturday night, and they all wanted liquor. Now Miss Amelia had dug up an aged barrel only three days past and had siphoned it into bottles back by the still. This night she took the money from the customers and counted it beneath the bright light. Such was the ordinary procedure. But after this what happened was not ordinary. Always before, it was necessary to go around to the dark back yard, and there she would hand out your bottle through the kitchen door. There was no feeling of joy in the transaction. After getting his liquor the customer walked off into the night. Or, if his wife would not have it in the home, he was allowed to come back around to the front porch of the store and guzzle there or in the street. Now, both the porch and the street before it were the property of Miss Amelia, and no mistake about it — but she did not regard them as her premises; the premises began at the front door and took in the entire inside of the building. There she had never allowed liquor to be opened or drunk by anyone but herself. Now for the first time she broke this rule. She went to the kitchen, with the hunchback close at her heels, and she brought back the bottles into the warm, bright store. More than that she furnished some glasses and opened two boxes of crackers so that they were there hospitably in a platter on the counter and anyone who wished could take one free.

She spoke to no one but the hunchback, and she only asked him in a somewhat harsh and husky voice: 'Cousin Lymon, will you have yours straight, or warmed in a pan with water on the stove?'

'If you please, Amelia,' the hunchback said. (And since what time had anyone presumed to address Miss Amelia by her bare name, without a title of respect? — Certainly not her bridegroom and her husband of ten days. In fact, not since the death of her father, who for some reason had always called her Little, had anyone dared to address her in such a familiar way.) 'If you please, I'll have it warmed.'

Now, this was the beginning of the café. It was as simple as that. Recall that the night was gloomy as in wintertime, and to have sat around the property outside would have made a sorry celebration. But inside there was company and a genial warmth. Someone had rattled up the stove in the rear, and those who bought bottles shared their liquor with friends. Several women were there and they had twists of licorice, a Nehi, or even a swallow of the whiskey. The hunchback was still a novelty and his presence amused everyone. The bench in the office was brought in, together with several extra chairs. Other people leaned against the counter or made themselves comfortable on barrels and sacks. Nor did the opening of liquor on the premises cause any rambunctiousness, indecent giggles, or misbehavior whatsoever. On the contrary the company was polite even to the point of a certain timidness. For people in this town were then unused to gathering together for the sake of pleasure. They met to work in the mill. Or on Sunday there would be an all-day camp meeting — and though that is a pleasure, the intention of the whole affair is to sharpen your view of Hell and put into you a keen fear of the Lord Almighty. But the spirit of a café is altogether different. Even the richest, greediest old rascal will behave himself, insulting no one in a proper café. And poor people look about them gratefully and pinch up the salt in a dainty and modest manner. For the atmosphere of a proper café implies these qualities: fellowship, the satisfactions of the belly, and a certain gaiety and grace of behavior. This had never been told to the gathering in Miss Amelia's store that night. But they knew it of themselves, although never, of course, until that time had there been a café in the town.

Now, the cause of all this, Miss Amelia, stood most of the evening in the doorway leading to the kitchen. Outwardly she did not seem changed at all. But there were many who noticed her face. She watched all that went on, but most of the time her eyes were fastened lonesomely on the hunchback. He strutted about the store, eating from his snuffbox, and being at once sour and agreeable. Where Miss Amelia stood, the light from the chinks of the stove cast a glow, so that her brown, long face was somewhat brightened. She seemed to be looking inward. There was in her expression pain, perplexity, and uncertain joy. Her lips were not so firmly set as usual, and she swallowed often. Her skin had paled and her large empty hands were sweating. Her look that night, then, was the lonesome look of the lover.

This opening of the café came to an end at midnight. Everyone said good-bye to everyone else in a friendly fashion. Miss Amelia shut the front door of her premises, but forgot to bolt it. Soon everything — the main street with its three stores, the mill, the houses — all the town, in fact — was dark and silent. And so ended three days and nights in which had come an arrival of a stranger, an unholy holiday, and the start of the café.

Now time must pass. For the next four years are much alike. There are great changes, but these changes are brought about bit by bit, in simple steps which in themselves do not appear to be important. The hunchback continued to live with Miss Amelia. The café expanded in a gradual way. Miss Amelia began to sell her liquor by the drink, and some tables were brought into the store. There were customers every evening, and on Saturday a great crowd. Miss Amelia began to serve fried catfish suppers at fifteen cents a plate. The hunchback cajoled her into buying a fine mechanical piano. Within two years the place was a store no longer, but had been converted into a proper café, open every evening from six until twelve o'clock.

Each night the hunchback came down the stairs with the air of one who has a grand opinion of himself. He always smelled slightly of turnip greens, as Miss Amelia rubbed him night and morning with pot liquor to give him strength. She spoiled him to a point beyond reason, but nothing seemed to strengthen him; food only made his hump and his head grow larger while the rest of him remained weakly and deformed. Miss Amelia was the same in appearance. During the week she still wore swamp boots and overalls, but on Sunday she put on a dark red dress that hung on her in a most peculiar fashion. Her manners, however, and her way of life were greatly changed. She still loved a fierce lawsuit, but she was not so quick to cheat her fellow man and to exact cruel payments. Because the hunchback was so extremely sociable, she even went about a little — to revivals, to funerals, and so forth. Her doctoring was as successful as ever, her liquor even finer than before, if that were possible. The café itself proved profitable and was the only place of pleasure for many miles around.

So for the moment regard these years from random and disjointed views. See the hunchback marching in Miss Amelia's footsteps when on a red winter morning they set out for the pinewoods to hunt. See them working on her properties — with Cousin Lymon standing by and doing absolutely nothing, but quick to point out any laziness among the hands. On autumn afternoons they sat on the back steps chopping sugar cane. The glaring summer days they spent back in the swamp where the water cypress is a deep black green, where beneath the tangled swamp trees there is a drowsy gloom. When the path leads through a bog or a stretch of blackened water see Miss Amelia bend down to let Cousin Lymon scramble on her back — and see her wading forward with the hunchback settled on her shoulders, clinging to her ears or to her broad forehead. Occasionally Miss Amelia cranked up the Ford which she had bought and treated Cousin Lymon to a picture-show in Cheehaw, or to some distant fair or cockfight; the hunchback took a passionate delight in spectacles. Of course, they were in their café every morning, they would often sit for hours together by the fireplace in the parlor upstairs. For the hunchback was sickly at night and dreaded to lie looking into the dark. He had a deep fear of death. And Miss Amelia would not leave him by himself to suffer with this fright. It may even be reasoned that the growth of the café came about mainly on this account; it was a thing that brought him company and pleasure and that helped him through the night. So compose from such flashes an image of these years as a whole. And for a moment let it rest.

Now some explanation is due for all this behavior. The time has come to speak about love. For Miss Amelia loved Cousin Lymon. So much was clear to everyone. They lived in the same house together and were never seen apart. Therefore, according to Mrs. MacPhail, a warty-nosed old busybody who is continually moving her sticks of furniture from one part of the front room to another; according to her and to certain others, these two were living in sin. If they were related, they were only a cross between first and second cousins, and even that could in no way be proved. Now, of course, Miss Amelia was a powerful blunderbuss of a person, more than six feet tall — and Cousin Lymon a weakly little hunchback reaching only to her waist. But so much the better for Mrs. Stumpy MacPhail and her cronies, for they and their kind glory in conjunctions which are ill-matched and pitiful. So let them be. The good people thought that if those two had found some satisfaction of the flesh between themselves, then it was a matter concerning them and God alone. All sensible people agreed in their opinion about this conjecture — and their answer was a plain, flat top. What sort of thing, then, was this love?

First of all, love is a joint experience between two persons — but the fact that it is a joint experience does not mean that it is a similar experience to the two people involved. There are the lover and the beloved, but these two come from different countries. Often the beloved is only a stimulus for all the stored-up love which has lain quiet within the lover for a long time hitherto. And somehow every lover knows this. He feels in his soul that his love is a solitary thing. He comes to know a new, strange loneliness and it is this knowledge which makes him suffer. So there is only one thing for the lover to do. He must house his love within himself as best he can; he must create for himself a whole new inward world — a world intense and strange, complete in himself. Let it be added here that this lover about whom we speak need not necessarily be a young man saving for a wedding ring — this lover can be man, woman, child, or indeed any human creature on this earth.

Now, the beloved can also be of any description. The most outlandish people can be the stimulus for love. A man may be a doddering great-grandfather and still love only a strange girl he saw in the streets of Cheehaw one afternoon two decades past. The preacher may love a fallen woman. The beloved may be treacherous, greasy-headed, and given to evil habits. Yes, and the lover may see this as clearly as anyone else — but that does not affect the evolution of his love one whit. A most mediocre person can be the object of a love which is wild, extravagant, and beautiful as the poison lilies of the swamp. A good man may be the stimulus for a love both violent and debased, or a jabbering madman may bring about in the soul of someone a tender and simple idyll. Therefore, the value and quality of any love is determined solely by the lover himself.

It is for this reason that most of us would rather love than be loved. Almost everyone wants to be the lover. And the curt truth is that, in a deep secret way, the state of being beloved is intolerable to many. The beloved fears and hates the lover, and with the best of reasons. For the lover is forever trying to strip bare his beloved. The lover craves any possible relation with the beloved, even if this experience can cause him only pain.

It has been mentioned before that Miss Amelia was once married. And this curious episode might as well be accounted for at this point. Remember that it all happened long ago, and that it was Miss Amelia's only personal contact, before the hunchback came to her, with this phenomenon — love.

The town then was the same as it is now, except there were two stores instead of three and the peach trees along the street were more crooked and smaller than they are now. Miss Amelia was nineteen years old at the time, and her father had been dead many months. There was in the town at that time a loom-fixer named Marvin Macy. He was the brother of Henry Macy, although to know them you would never guess that those two could be kin. For Marvin Macy was the handsomest man in this region — being six feet one inch tall, hard-muscled, and with slow gray eyes and curly hair. He was well off, made good wages, and had a gold watch which opened in the back to a picture of a waterfall. From the outward and worldly point of view Marvin Macy was a fortunate fellow; he needed to bow and scrape to no one and always got just what he wanted. But from a more serious and thoughtful viewpoint Marvin Macy was not a person to be envied, for he was an evil character. His reputation was as bad, if not worse, than that of any young man in the county. For years, when he was a boy, he had carried about with him the dried and salted ear of a man he had killed in a razor fight. He had chopped off the tails of squirrels in the pinewoods just to please his fancy, and in his left hip pocket he carried forbidden marijuana weed to tempt those who were dis-couraged and drawn toward death. Yet in spite of his well-known reputation he was the beloved of many females in this region — and there were at the time several young girls who were clean-haired and soft-eyed, with tender sweet little buttocks and charming ways. These gentle young girls he degraded and shamed. Then finally, at the age of twenty-two, this Marvin Macy chose Miss Amelia. That solitary, gangling, queer-eyed girl was the one he longed for. Nor did he want her because of her money, but solely out of love.

And love changed Marvin Macy. Before the time when he loved Miss Amelia it could be questioned if such a person had within him a heart and soul. Yet there is some explanation for the ugliness of his character, for Marvin Macy had had a hard beginning in this world. He was one of seven unwanted children whose parents could hardly be called parents at all; these parents were wild younguns who liked to fish and roam around the swamp. Their own children, and there was a new one almost every year, were only a nuisance to them. At night when they came home from the mill they would look at the children as though they did not know wherever they had come from. If the children cried they were beaten, and the first thing they learned in this world was to seek the darkest corner of the room and try to hide themselves as best they could. They were as thin as little whitehaired ghosts, and they did not speak, not even to each other. Finally, they were abandoned by their parents altogether and left to the mercies of the town. It was a hard winter, with the mill closed down almost three months, and much misery everywhere. But this is not a town to let white orphans perish in the road before your eyes. So here is what came about: the eldest child, who was eight years old, walked into Cheehaw and disappeared — perhaps he took a freight train somewhere and went out into the world, nobody knows. Three other children were boarded out amongst the town, being sent around from one kitchen to another, and as they were delicate they died before Easter time. The last two children were Marvin Macy and Henry Macy, and they were taken into a home. There was a good woman in the town named Mrs. Mary Hale, and she took Marvin Macy and Henry Macy and loved them as her own. They were raised in her household and treated well.

But the hearts of small children are delicate organs. A cruel beginning in this world can twist them into curious shapes. The heart of a hurt child can shrink so that forever afterward it is hard and pitted as the seed of a peach. Or again, the heart of such a child may fester and swell until it is a misery to carry within the body, easily chafed and hurt by the most ordinary things. This last is what happened to Henry Macy, who is so opposite to his brother, is the kindest and gentlest man in town. He lends his wages to those who are unfortunate, and in the old days he used to care for the children whose parents were at the café on Saturday night. But he is a shy man, and he has the look of one who has a swollen heart and suffers. Marvin Macy, however, grew to be bold and fearless and cruel. His heart turned tough as the horns of Satan, and until the time when he loved Miss Amelia he brought to his brother and the good woman who raised him nothing but shame and trouble.

But love reversed the character of Marvin Macy. For two years he loved Miss Amelia, but he did not declare himself. He would stand near the door of her premises, his cap in his hand, his eyes meek and longing and misty gray. He reformed himself completely. He was good to his brother and foster mother, and he saved his wages and learned thrift. Moreover, he reached out toward God. No longer did he lie around on the floor of the front porch all day Sunday, singing and playing his guitar; he attended church services and was present at all religious meetings. He learned good manners: he trained himself to rise and give his chair to a lady, and he quit swearing and fighting and using holy names in vain. So for two years he passed through this transformation and improved his character in every way. Then at the end of the two years he went one evening to Miss Amelia, carrying a bunch of swamp flowers, a sack of chitterlins, and a silver ring — that night Marvin Macy declared himself.

And Miss Amelia married him. Later everyone wondered why. Some said it was because she wanted to get herself some wedding presents. Others believed it came about through the nagging of Miss Amelia's great-aunt in Cheehaw, who was a terrible old woman. Anyway, she strode with great steps down the aisle of the church wearing her dead mother's bridal gown, which was of yellow satin and at least twelve inches too short for her. It was a winter afternoon and the clear sun shone through the ruby windows of the church and put a curious glow on the pair before the altar. As the marriage lines were read Miss Amelia kept making an odd gesture — she would rub the palm of her right hand down the side of her satin wedding gown. She was reaching for the pocket of her overalls, and being unable to find it her face became impatient, bored, and exasperated. At last when the lines were spoken and the marriage prayer was done Miss Amelia hurried out of the church, not taking the arm of her husband, but walking at least two paces ahead of him.

The church is no distance from the store so the bride and groom walked home. It is said that on the way Miss Amelia began to talk about some deal she had worked up with a farmer over a load of kindling wood. In fact, she treated her groom in exactly the same manner she would have used with some customer who had come into the store to buy a pint from her. But so far all had gone decently enough; the town was gratified, as people had seen what this love had done to Marvin Macy and hoped that it might also reform his bride. At least, they counted on the marriage to tone down Miss Amelia's temper, to put a bit of bride-fat on her, and to change her at last into a calculable woman.

They were wrong. The young boys who watched through the window on that night said that this is what actually happened: The bride and groom ate a grand supper prepared by Jeff, the old Negro who cooked for Miss Amelia. The bride took second servings of everything, but the groom picked with his food. Then the bride went about her ordinary business — reading the newspaper, finishing an inventory of the stock in the store, and so forth. The groom hung about in the doorway with a loose, foolish, blissful face and was not noticed. At eleven o'clock the bride took a lamp and went upstairs. The groom followed close behind her. So far all had gone decently enough, but what followed after was unholy.

Within half an hour Miss Amelia had stomped down the stairs in breeches and a khaki jacket. Her face had darkened so that it looked quite black. She slammed the kitchen door and gave it an ugly kick. Then she controlled herself. She poked up the fire, sat down, and put her feet up on the kitchen stove. She read the Farmer's Almanac, drank coffee, and had a smoke with her father's pipe. Her face was hard, stern, and had now whitened to its natural color. Sometimes she paused to jot down some information from the Almanac on a piece of paper. Toward dawn she went into her office and uncovered her typewriter, which she had recently bought and was only just learning how to run. That was the way in which she spent the whole of her wedding night. At daylight she went out to her yard as though nothing whatsoever had occurred and did some carpentering on a rabbit hutch which she had begun the week before and intended to sell somewhere.

A groom is in a sorry fix when he is unable to bring his well-beloved bride to bed with him, and the whole town knows it. Marvin Macy came down that day still in his wedding finery, and with a sick face. God knows how he had spent the night. He moped about the yard, watching Miss Amelia, but keeping some distance away from her. Then toward noon an idea came to him and he went off in the direction of Society City. He returned with presents — an opal ring, a pink enamel doreen of the sort which was then in fashion, a silver bracelet with two hearts on it, and a box of candy which had cost two dollars and a half. Miss Amelia looked over these fine gifts and opened the box of candy, for she was hungry. The rest of the presents she judged shrewdly for a moment to sum up their value — then she put them in the counter out for sale. The night was spent in much the same manner as the preceding one — except that Miss Amelia brought her feather mattress to make a pallet by the kitchen stove, and she slept fairly well.

Things went on like this for three days. Miss Amelia went about her business as usual, and took great interest in some rumor that a bridge was to be built some ten miles down the road. Marvin Macy still followed her about around the premises, and it was plain from his face how he suffered. Then on the fourth day he did an extremely simple-minded thing: he went to Cheehaw and came back with a lawyer. Then in Miss Amelia's office he signed over to her the whole of his worldly goods, which was ten acres of timberland which he had bought with the money he had saved. She studied the paper sternly to make sure there was no possibility of a trick and filed it soberly in the drawer of her desk. That afternoon Marvin Macy took a quart bottle of whiskey and went with it alone out in the swamp while the sun was still shining. Toward evening he came in drunk, went up to Miss Amelia with wet wide eyes, and put his hand on her shoulder. He was trying to tell her something, but before he could open his mouth she had swung once with her fist and hit his face so hard that he was thrown back against the wall and one of his front teeth was broken.

The rest of this affair can only be mentioned in bare outline. After this first blow Miss Amelia hit him whenever he came within arm's reach of her, and whenever he was drunk. At last she turned him off the premises altogether, and he was forced to suffer publicly. During the day he hung around just outside the boundary line of Miss Amelia's property and sometimes with a drawn crazy look he would fetch his rifle and sit there cleaning it, peering at Miss Amelia steadily. If she was afraid she did not show it, but her face was sterner than ever, and often she spat on the ground. His last foolish effort was to climb in the window of her store one night and to sit there in the dark, for no purpose whatsoever, until she came down the stairs next morning. For this Miss Amelia set off immediately to the courthouse in Cheehaw with some notion that she could get him locked in the penitentiary for trespassing. Marvin Macy left the town that day, and no one saw him go, or knew just where he went. On leaving he put a long curious letter, partly written in pencil and partly with ink, beneath Miss Amelia's door. It was a wild love letter — but in it were also included threats, and he swore that in his life he would get even with her. His marriage had lasted for ten days. And the town felt the special satisfaction that people feel when someone has been thoroughly done in by some scandalous and terrible means.

Miss Amelia was left with everything that Marvin Macy had ever owned — his timberwood, his gilt watch, every one of his possessions. But she seemed to attach little value to them and that spring she cut up his Klansman's robe to cover her tobacco plants. So all that he had ever done was to make her richer and to bring her love. But, strange to say, she never spoke of him but with a terrible and spiteful bitterness. She never once referred to him by name but always mentioned him scornfully as 'that loom-fixer I was married to.'

And later, when horrifying rumors concerning Marvin Macy reached the town, Miss Amelia was very pleased. For the true character of Marvin Macy finally revealed itself, once he had freed himself of his love. He became a criminal whose picture and whose name were in all the papers in the state. He robbed three filling stations and held up the A & P store of Society City with a sawed-off gun. He was suspected of the murder of Slit-Eye Sam who was a noted highjacker. All these crimes were connected with the name of Marvin Macy, so that his evil became famous through many countries. Then finally the law captured him, drunk, on the floor of a tourist cabin, his guitar by his side, and fifty-seven dollars in his right shoe. He was tried, sentenced, and sent off to the penitentiary near Atlanta. Miss Amelia was deeply gratified.

Well, all this happened a long time ago, and it is the story of Miss Amelia's marriage. The town laughed a long time over this grotesque affair. But though the outward facts of this love are indeed sad and ridiculous, it must be remembered that the real story was that which took place in the soul of the lover himself. So who but God can be the final judge of this or any other love? On the very first night of the café there were several who suddenly thought of this broken bridegroom, locked in the gloomy penitentiary, many miles away. And in the years that followed, Marvin Macy was not altogether forgotten in the town. His name was never mentioned in the presence of Miss Amelia or the hunchback. But the memory of his passion and his crimes, and the thought of him trapped in his cell in the penitentiary, was like a troubling undertone beneath the happy love of Miss Amelia and the gaiety of the café. So do not forget this Marvin Macy, as he is to act a terrible part in the story which is yet to come.

During the four years in which the store became a café the rooms upstairs were not changed. This part of the premises remained exactly as it had been all of Miss Amelia's life, as it was in the time of her father, and most likely his father before him. The three rooms, it is already known, were immaculately clean. The smallest object had its exact place, and everything was wiped and dusted by Jeff, the servant of Miss Amelia, each morning. The front room belonged to Cousin Lymon — it was the room where Marvin Macy had stayed during the few nights he was allowed on the premises, and before that it was the bedroom of Miss Amelia's father. The room was furnished with a large chifforobe, a bureau covered with a stiff white linen cloth crocheted at the edges, and a marble-topped table. The bed was immense, an old fourposter made of carved, dark rosewood. On it were two feather mattresses, bolsters, and a number of handmade comforts. The bed was so high that beneath it were two wooden steps — no occupant had ever used these steps before, but Cousin Lymon drew them out each night and walked up in state. Beside the steps, but pushed modestly out of view, there was a china chamber-pot painted with pink roses. No rug covered the dark, polished floor and the curtains were of some white stuff, also crocheted at the edges.

On the other side of the parlor was Miss Amelia's bedroom, and it was smaller and very simple. The bed was narrow and made of pine. There was a bureau for her breeches, shirts, and Sunday dress, and she had hammered two nails in the closet wall on which to hang her swamp boots. There were no curtains, rugs, or ornaments of any kind.

The large middle room, the parlor, was elaborate. The rosewood sofa, upholstered in threadbare green silk, was before the fireplace. Marble-topped tables, two Singer sewing machines, a big vase of pampas grass — everything was rich and grand. The most important piece of furniture in the parlor was a big, glassed-doored cabinet in which was kept a number of treasures and curios. Miss Amelia had added two objects to this collection — one was a large acorn from a water oak, the other a little velvet box holding two small, grayish stones. Sometimes when she had nothing much to do, Miss Amelia would take out this velvet box and stand by the window with the stones in the palm of her hand, looking down at them with a mixture of fascination, dubious respect, and fear. They were the kidney stones of Miss Amelia herself, and had been taken from her by the doctor in Cheehaw some years ago. It had been a terrible experience, from the first minute to the last, and all she had got out of it were those two little stones; she was bound to set great store by them, or else admit to a mighty sorry bargain. So she kept them and in the second year of Cousin Lymon's stay with her she had them set as ornaments in a watch chain which she gave to him. The other object she had added to the collection, the large acorn, was precious to her — but when she looked at it her face was always saddened and perplexed.

'Amelia, what does it signify?' Cousin Lymon asked her.

'Why, it's just an acorn,' she answered. 'Just an acorn I picked up on the afternoon Big Papa died.'

'How do you mean?' Cousin Lymon insisted.

'I mean it's just an acorn I spied on the ground that day. I picked it up and put it in my pocket. But I don't know why.'

'What a peculiar reason to keep it,' Cousin Lymon said.

The talks of Miss Amelia and Cousin Lymon in the rooms upstairs, usually in the first few hours of the morning when the hunchback could not sleep, were many. As a rule, Miss Amelia was a silent woman, not letting her tongue run wild on any subject that happened to pop into her head. There were certain topics of conversation, however, in which she took pleasure. All these subjects had one point in common — they were interminable. She liked to contemplate problems which could be worked over for decades and still remain insoluble. Cousin Lymon, on the other hand, enjoyed talking on any subject whatsoever, as he was a great chatterer. Their approach to any conversation was altogether different. Miss Amelia always kept to the broad, rambling generalities of the matter, going on endlessly in a low, thoughtful voice and getting nowhere — while Cousin Lymon would interrupt her suddenly to pick up, magpie fashion, some detail which, even if unimportant, was at least concrete and bearing on some practical facet close at hand. Some of the favorite subjects of Miss Amelia were: the stars, the reason why Negroes are black, the best treatment for cancer, and so forth. Her father was also an interminable subject which was dear to her.

'Why, Law,' she would say to Lymon. 'Those days I slept. I'd go to bed just as the lamp was turned on and sleep — why, I'd sleep like I was drowned in warm axle grease. Then come daybreak Big Papa would walk in and put his hand down on my shoulder. "Get stirring, Little," he would say. Then later he would holler up the stairs from the kitchen when the stove was hot. "Fried grits," he would holler. "White meat and gravy. Ham and eggs." And I'd run down the stairs and dress by the hot stove while he was out washing at the pump. Then off we'd go to the still or maybe ——'

'The grits we had this morning was poor,' Cousin Lymon said. 'Fried too quick so that the inside never heated.'

'And when Big Papa would run off the liquor in those days ——' The conversation would go on endlessly, with Miss Amelia's long legs stretched out before the hearth; for winter or summer there was always a fire in the grate, as Lymon was cold-natured. He sat in a low chair across from her, his feet not quite touching the floor and his torso usually well-wrapped in a blanket or the green wool shawl. Miss Amelia never mentioned her father to anyone else except Cousin Lymon.

That was one of the ways in which she showed her love for him. He had her confidence in the most delicate and vital matters. He alone knew where she kept the chart that showed where certain barrels of whiskey were buried on a piece of property near by. He alone had access to her bankbook and the key to the cabinet of curios. He took money from the cash register, whole handfuls of it, and appreciated the loud jingle it made inside his pockets. He owned almost everything on the premises, for when he was cross Miss Amelia would prowl about and find him some present — so that now there was hardly anything left close at hand to give him. The only part of her life that she did not want Cousin Lymon to share with her was the memory of her ten-day marriage. Marvin Macy was the one subject that was never, at any time, discussed between the two of them.

So let the slow years pass and come to a Saturday evening six years after the time when Cousin Lymon came first to the town. It was August and the sky had burned above the town like a sheet of flame all day. Now the green twilight was near and there was a feeling of repose. The street was coated an inch deep with dry golden dust and the little children ran about half-naked, sneezed often, sweated, and were fretful. The mill had closed down at noon. People in the houses along the main street sat resting on their steps and the women had palmetto fans. At Miss Amelia's there was a sign at the front of the premises saying CAFE. The back porch was cool with latticed shadows and there Cousin Lymon sat turning the ice-cream freezer — often he unpacked the salt and ice and removed the dasher to lick a bit and see how the work was coming on. Jeff cooked in the kitchen. Early that morning Miss Amelia had put a notice on the wall of the front porch reading: Chicken Dinner — Twenty Cents Tonite. The café was already open and Miss Amelia had just finished a period of work in her office. All the eight tables were occupied and from the mechanical piano came a jingling tune.

In a corner, near the door and sitting at a table with a child, was Henry Macy. He was drinking a glass of liquor, which was unusual for him, as liquor went easily to his head and made him cry or sing. His face was very pale and his left eye worked constantly in a nervous tic, as it was apt to do when he was agitated. He had come into the café sidewise and silent, and when he was greeted he did not speak. The child next to him belonged to Horace Wells, and he had been left at Miss Amelia's that morning to be doctored.

Miss Amelia came out from her office in good spirits. She attended to a few details in the kitchen and entered the café with the pope's nose of a hen between her fingers, as that was her favorite piece. She looked about the room, saw that in general all was well, and went over to the corner table by Henry Macy. She turned the chair around and sat straddling the back, as she only wanted to pass the time of day and was not yet ready for her supper. There was a bottle of Kroup Kure in the hip pocket of her overalls — a medicine made from whiskey, rock candy, and a secret ingredient. Miss Amelia uncorked the bottle and put it to the mouth of the child. Then she turned to Henry Macy and, seeing the nervous winking of his left eye, she asked:

'What ails you?'

Henry Macy seemed on the point of saying something difficult, but, after a long look into the eyes of Miss Amelia, he swallowed and did not speak.

So Miss Amelia returned to her patient. Only the child's head showed above the table top. His face was very red, with the eyelids half-closed and the mouth partly open. He had a large, hard, swollen boil on his thigh, and had been brought to Miss Amelia so that it could be opened. But Miss Amelia used a special method with children; she did not like to see them hurt, struggling, and terrified. So she had kept the child around the premises all day, giving him licorice and frequent doses of the Kroup Kure, and toward evening she tied a napkin around his neck and let him eat his fill of the dinner. Now as he sat at the table his head wobbled slowly from side to side and sometimes as he breathed there came from him a little worn-out grunt.

There was a stir in the café and Miss Amelia looked around quickly. Cousin Lymon had come in. The hunchback strutted into the café as he did every night, and when he reached the exact center of the room he stopped short and looked shrewdly around him, summing up the people and making a quick pattern of the emotional material at hand that night. The hunchback was a great mischief-maker. He enjoyed any kind of to-do, and without saying a word he could set people at each other in a way that was miraculous. It was due to him that the Rainey twins had quarreled over a jackknife two years past, and had not spoken one word to each other since. He was present at the big fight between Rip Wellborn and Robert Calvert Hale, and every other fight for that matter since he had come into the town. He nosed around everywhere, knew the intimate business of everybody, and trespassed every waking hour. Yet, queerly enough, in spite of this it was the hunchback who was most responsible for the great popularity of the café. Things were never so gay as when he was around. When he walked into the room there was always a quick feeling of tension, because with this busybody about there was never any telling what might descend on you, or what might suddenly be brought to happen in the room. People are never so free with themselves and so recklessly glad as when there is some possibility of commotion or calamity ahead. So when the hunchback marched into the café everyone looked around at him and there was a quick outburst of talking and a drawing of corks.

Lymon waved his hand to Stumpy MacPhail who was sitting with Merlie Ryan and Henry Ford Crimp. 'I walked to Rotten Lake today to fish,' he said. 'And on the way I stepped over what appeared at first to be a big fallen tree. But then as I stepped over I felt something stir and I taken this second look and there I was straddling this here alligator long as from the front door to the kitchen and thicker than a hog.'

The hunchback chattered on. Everyone looked at him from time to time, and some kept track of his chattering and others did not. There were times when every word he said was nothing but lying and bragging. Nothing he said tonight was true. He had lain in bed with a summer quinsy all day long, and had only got up in the late afternoon in order to turn the ice-cream freezer. Everybody knew this, yet he stood there in the middle of the café and held forth with such lies and boasting that it was enough to shrivel the ears.

Miss Amelia watched him with her hands in her pockets and her head turned to one side. There was a softness about her gray, queer eyes and she was smiling gently to herself. Occasionally she glanced from the hunchback to the other people in the café — and then her look was proud, and there was in it the hint of a threat, as though daring anyone to try to hold him to account for all his foolery. Jeff was bringing in the suppers, already served on the plates, and the new electric fans in the café made a pleasant stir of coolness in the air.

'The little youngun is asleep,' said Henry Macy finally.

Miss Amelia looked down at the patient beside her, and composed her face for the matter in hand. The child's chin was resting on the table edge and a trickle of spit or Kroup Kure had bubbled from the corner of his mouth. His eyes were quite closed, and a little family of gnats had clustered peacefully in the corners. Miss Amelia put her hand on his head and shook it roughly, but the patient did not awake.

So Miss Amelia lifted the child from the table, being careful not to touch the sore part of his leg, and went into the office. Henry Macy followed after her and they closed the office door.

Cousin Lymon was bored that evening. There was not much going on, and in spite of the heat the customers in the café were good-humored. Henry Ford Crimp and Horace Wells sat at the middle table with their arms around each other, sniggering over some long joke — but when he approached them he could make nothing of it as he had missed the beginning of the story. The moonlight brightened the dusty road, and the dwarfed peach trees were black and motionless: there was no breeze. The drowsy buzz of swamp mosquitoes was like an echo of the silent night. The town seemed dark, except far down the road to the right there was the flicker of a lamp. Somewhere in the darkness a woman sang in a high wild voice and the tune had no start and no finish and was made up of only three notes which went on and on and on. The hunchback stood leaning against the banister of the porch, looking down the empty road as though hoping that someone would come along.

There were footsteps behind him, then a voice: 'Cousin Lymon, your dinner is set out upon the table.'

'My appetite is poor tonight,' said the hunchback, who had been eating sweet snuff all the day. 'There is a sourness in my mouth.'

'Just a pick,' said Miss Amelia. 'The breast, the liver, and the heart.'

Together they went back into the bright café, and sat down with Henry Macy. Their table was the largest one in the café, and on it there was a bouquet of swamp lilies in a Coca Cola bottle. Miss Amelia had finished with her patient and was satisfied with herself. From behind the closed office door there had come only a few sleepy whimpers, and before the patient could wake up and become terrified it was all over. The child was now slung across the shoulder of his father, sleeping deeply, his little arms dangling loose along his father's back and his puffed-up face very red — they were leaving the café to go home.

Henry Macy was still silent. He ate carefully, making no noise when he swallowed, and was not a third as greedy as Cousin Lymon who had claimed to have no appetite and was now putting down helping after helping of the dinner. Occasionally Henry Macy looked across at Miss Amelia and again held his peace.

It was a typical Saturday night. An old couple who had come in from the country hesitated for a moment at the doorway, holding each other's hand, and finally decided to come inside. They had lived together so long, this old country couple, that they looked as similar as twins. They were brown, shriveled, and like two little walking peanuts. They left early, and by midnight most of the other customers were gone. Rosser Cline and Merlie Ryan still played checkers, and Stumpy MacPhail sat with a liquor bottle on his table (his wife would not allow it in the home) and carried on peaceable conversations with himself. Henry Macy had not yet gone away, and this was unusual, as he almost always went to bed soon after nightfall. Miss Amelia yawned sleepily, but Lymon was restless and she did not suggest that they close up for the night.

Finally, at one o'clock, Henry Macy looked up at the corner of the ceiling and said quietly to Miss Amelia: 'I got a letter today.'

Miss Amelia was not one to be impressed by this, because all sorts of business letters and catalogues came addressed to her.

'I got a letter from my brother,' said Henry Macy.

The hunchback, who had been goose-stepping about the café with his hands clasped behind his head, stopped suddenly. He was quick to sense any change in the atmosphere of a gathering. He glanced at each face in the room and waited.

Miss Amelia scowled and hardened her right fist. 'You are welcome to it,' she said.

'He is on parole. He is out of the penitentiary.'

The face of Miss Amelia was very dark, and she shivered although the night was warm. Stumpy MacPhail and Merlie Ryan pushed aside their checker game. The café was very quiet.

'Who?' asked Cousin Lymon. His large, pale ears seemed to grow on his head and stiffen. 'What?'

Miss Amelia slapped her hands palm down on the table. 'Because Marvin Macy is a ———' But her voice hoarsened and after a few moments she only said: 'He belongs to be in that penitentiary the balance of his life.'

'What did he do?' asked Cousin Lymon.

There was a long pause, as no one knew exactly how to answer this. 'He robbed three filling stations,' said Stumpy MacPhail. But his words did not sound complete and there was a feeling of sins left unmentioned.

The hunchback was impatient. He could not bear to be left out of anything, even a great misery. The name Marvin Macy was unknown to him, but it tantalized him as did any mention of subjects which others knew about and of which he was ignorant — such as any reference to the old sawmill that had been torn down before he came, or a chance word about poor Morris Finestein, or the recollection of any event that had occurred before his time. Aside from this inborn curiosity, the hunchback took a great interest in robbers and crimes of all varieties. As he strutted around the table he was muttering the words 'released on parole' and 'penitentiary' to himself. But although he questioned insistently, he was unable to find anything, as nobody would dare to talk about Marvin Macy before Miss Amelia in the café.

'The letter did not say very much,' said Henry Macy. 'He did not say where he was going.'

'Humph!' said Miss Amelia, and her face was still hardened and very dark. 'He will never set his split hoof on my premises.'

She pushed back her chair from the table, and made ready to close the café. Thinking about Marvin Macy may have set her to brooding, for she hauled the cash register back to the kitchen and put it in a private place. Henry Macy went off down the dark road. But Henry Ford Crimp and Merlie Ryan lingered for a time on the front porch. Later Merlie Ryan was to make certain claims, to swear that on that night he had a vision of what was to come. But the town paid no attention, for that was just the sort of thing that Merlie Ryan would claim. Miss Amelia and Cousin Lymon talked for a time in the parlor. And when at last the hunchback thought that he could sleep he arranged the mosquito netting over his bed and waited until he had finished with his prayers. Then she put on her long nightgown, smoked two pipes, and only after a long time went to sleep.

That autumn was a happy time. The crops around the countryside were good, and over at the Forks Falls market the price of tobacco held firm that year. After the long hot summer the first cool days had a clean bright sweetness. Goldenrod grew along the dusty roads, and the sugar cane was ripe and purple. The bus came each day from Cheehaw to carry off a few of the younger children to the consolidated school to get an education. Boys hunted foxes in the pinewoods, winter quilts were aired out on the wash lines, and sweet potatoes bedded in the ground with straw against the colder months to come. In the evening, delicate shreds of smoke rose from the chimneys, and the moon was round and orange in the autumn sky. There is no stillness like the quiet of the first cold nights in the fall. Sometimes, late in the night when there was no wind, there could be heard in the town the thin wild whistle of the train that goes through Society City on its way far off to the North.

For Miss Amelia Evans this was a time of great activity. She was at work from dawn until sundown. She made a new and bigger condenser for her still, and in one week ran off enough liquor to souse the whole county. Her old mule was dizzy from grinding so much sorghum, and she scalded her Mason jars and put away pear preserves. She was looking forward greatly to the first frost, because she had traded for three tremendous hogs, and intended to make much barbecue, chitterlins, and sausage.

During these weeks there was a quality about Miss Amelia that many people noticed. She laughed often, with a deep ringing laugh, and her whistling had a sassy, tuneful trickery. She was forever trying out her strength, lifting up heavy objects, or poking her tough biceps with her finger. One day she sat down to her typewriter and wrote a story — a story in which there were foreigners, trap doors, and millions of dollars. Cousin Lymon was with her always, traipsing along behind her coat-tails, and when she watched him her face had a bright, soft look, and when she spoke his name there lingered in her voice the undertone of love.

The first cold spell came at last. When Miss Amelia awoke one morning there were frost flowers on the windowpanes, and rime had silvered the patches of grass in the yard. Miss Amelia built a roaring fire in the kitchen stove, then went out of doors to judge the day. The air was cold and sharp, the sky pale green and cloudless. Very shortly people began to come in from the country to find out what Miss Amelia thought of the weather; she decided to kill the biggest hog, and word got round the countryside. The hog was slaughtered and a low oak fire started in the barbecue pit. There was the warm smell of pig blood and smoke in the back yard, the stamp of footsteps, the ring of voices in the winter air. Miss Amelia walked around giving orders and soon most of the work was done.

She had some particular business to do in Cheehaw that day, so after making sure that all was going well, she cranked up her car and got ready to leave. She asked Cousin Lymon to come with her, in fact, she asked him seven times, but he was loath to leave the commotion and wanted to remain. This seemed to trouble Miss Amelia, as she always liked to have him near to her, and was prone to be terribly homesick when she had to go any distance away. But after asking him seven times, she did not urge him any further. Before leaving she found a stick and drew a heavy line all around the barbecue pit, about two feet back from the edge, and told him not to trespass beyond that boundary. She left after dinner and intended to be back before dark.

Now, it is not so rare to have a truck or an automobile pass along the road and through the town on the way from Cheehaw to somewhere else. Every year the tax collector comes to argue with rich people such as Miss Amelia. And if somebody in the town, such as Merlie Ryan, takes a notion that he can connive to get a car on credit, or to pay down three dollars and have a fine electric icebox such as they advertise in the store windows of Cheehaw, then a city man will come out asking meddlesome questions, finding out all his troubles, and ruining his chances of buying anything on the installment plan. Sometimes, especially since they are working on the Forks Falls highway, the cars hauling the chain gang come through the town. And frequently people in automobiles get lost and stop to inquire how they can find the right road again. So, late that afternoon it was nothing unusual to have a truck pass the mill and stop in the middle of the road near the café of Miss Amelia. A man jumped down from the back of the truck, and the truck went on its way.

The man stood in the middle of the road and looked about him. He was a tall man, with brown curly hair, and slow-moving, deep-blue eyes. His lips were red and he smiled the lazy, half-mouthed smile of the braggart. The man wore a red shirt, and a wide belt of tooled leather; he carried a tin suitcase and a guitar. The first person in the town to see this newcomer was Cousin Lymon, who had heard the shifting gears and come around to investigate. The hunchback stuck his head around the corner of the porch, but did not step out altogether into full view. He and the man stared at each other, and it was not the look of two strangers meeting for the first time and swiftly summing up each other. It was a peculiar stare they exchanged between them, like the look of two criminals who recognize each other. Then the man in the red shirt shrugged his left shoulder and turned away. The face of the hunchback was very pale as he watched the man go down the road, and after a few moments he began to follow along carefully, keeping many paces away.

It was immediately known throughout the town that Marvin Macy had come back again. First, he went to the mill, propped his elbows lazily on a window sill and looked inside. He liked to watch others hard at work, as do all born loafers. The mill was thrown into a sort of numb confusion. The dyers left the hot vats, the spinners and weavers forgot about their machines, and even Stumpy MacPhail, who was foreman, did not know exactly what to do. Marvin Macy still smiled his wet half-mouthed smiles, and when he saw his brother, his bragging expression did not change. After looking over the mill Marvin Macy went down the road to the house where he had been raised, and left his suitcase and guitar on the front porch. Then he walked around the millpond, looked over the church, the three stores, and the rest of the town. The hunchback trudged along quietly at some distance behind him, his hands in his pockets, and his little face still very pale.

It had grown late. The red winter sun was setting, and to the west the sky was deep gold and crimson. Ragged chimney swifts flew to their nests; lamps were lighted. Now and then there was the smell of smoke, and the warm rich odor of the barbecue slowly cooking in the pit behind the café. After making the rounds of the town Marvin Macy stopped before Miss Amelia's premises and read the sign above the porch. Then, not hesitating to trespass, he walked through the side yard. The mill whistle blew a thin, lonesome blast, and the day's shift was done. Soon there were others in Miss Amelia's back yard beside Marvin Macy — Henry Ford Crimp, Merlie Ryan, Stumpy MacPhail, and any number of children and people who stood around the edges of the property and looked on. Very little was said. Marvin Macy stood by himself on one side of the pit, and the rest of the people clustered together on the other side. Cousin Lymon stood somewhat apart from everyone, and he did not take his eyes from the face of Marvin Macy.

'Did you have a good time in the penitentiary?' asked Merlie Ryan, with a silly giggle.

Marvin Macy did not answer. He took from his hip pocket a large knife, opened it slowly, and honed the blade on the seat of his pants. Merlie Ryan grew suddenly very quiet and went to stand directly behind the broad back of Stumpy MacPhail.

Miss Amelia did not come home until almost dark. They heard the rattle of her automobile while she was still a long distance away, then the slam of the door and a bumping noise as though she were hauling something up the front steps of her premises. The sun had already set, and in the air there was the blue smoky glow of early winter evenings. Miss Amelia came down the back steps slowly, and the group in her yard waited very quietly. Few people in this world could stand up to Miss Amelia, and against Marvin Macy she had this special and bitter hate. Everyone waited to see her burst into a terrible holler, snatch up some dangerous object, and chase him altogether out of town. At first she did not see Marvin Macy, and her face had the relieved and dreamy expression that was natural to her when she reached home after having gone some distance away.

Miss Amelia must have seen Marvin Macy and Cousin Lymon at the same instant. She looked from one to the other, but it was not the wastrel from the penitentiary on whom she finally fixed her gaze of sick amazement. She, and everyone else, was looking at Cousin Lymon, and he was a sight to see.

The hunchback stood at the end of the pit, his pale face lighted by the soft glow from the smoldering oak fire. Cousin Lymon had a very peculiar accomplishment, which he used whenever he wished to ingratiate himself with someone. He would stand very still, and with just a little concentration, he could wiggle his large pale ears with marvelous quickness and ease. This trick he always used when he wanted to get something special out of Miss Amelia, and to her it was irresistible. Now as he stood there the hunchback's ears were wiggling furiously on his head, but it was not Miss Amelia at whom he was looking this time. The hunchback was smiling at Marvin Macy with an entreaty that was near to desperation. At first Marvin Macy paid no attention to him, and when he did finally glance at the hunchback it was without any appreciation whatsoever.

'What ails this Brokeback?' he asked with a rough jerk of his thumb.

No one answered. And Cousin Lymon, seeing that his accomplishment was getting him nowhere, added new efforts of persuasion. He fluttered his eyelids, so that they were like pale, trapped moths in his sockets. He scraped his feet around on the ground, waved his hands about, and finally began doing a little trotlike dance. In the last gloomy light of the winter afternoon he resembled the child of a swamphaunt.

Marvin Macy, alone of all the people in the yard, was unimpressed.

'Is the runt throwing a fit?' he asked, and when no one answered he stepped forward and gave Cousin Lymon a cuff on the side of his head. The hunchback staggered, then fell back on the ground. He sat where he had fallen, still looking up at Marvin Macy, and with great effort his ears managed one last forlorn little flap.

Now everyone turned to Miss Amelia to see what she would do. In all these years no one had so much as touched a hair of Cousin Lymon's head, although many had had the itch to do so. If anyone even spoke crossly to the hunchback, Miss Amelia would cut off this rash mortal's credit and find ways of making things go hard for him a long time afterward. So now if Miss Amelia had split open Marvin Macy's head with the ax on the back porch no one would have been surprised. But she did nothing of the kind.

There were times when Miss Amelia seemed to go into a sort of trance. And the cause of these trances was usually known and understood. For Miss Amelia was a fine doctor, and did not grind up swamp roots and other untried ingredients and give them to the first patient who came along; whenever she invented a new medicine she always tried it out first on herself. She would swallow an enormous dose and spend the following day walking thoughtfully back and forth from the café to the brick privy. Often, when there was a sudden keen gripe, she would stand quite still, her queer eyes staring down at the ground and her fists clenched; she was trying to decide which organ was being worked upon, and what misery the new medicine might be most likely to cure. And now as she watched the hunchback and Marvin Macy, her face wore this same expression, tense with reckoning some inward pain, although she had taken no new medicine that day.

'That will learn you, Brokeback,' said Marvin Macy.

Henry Macy pushed back his limp whitish hair from his forehead and coughed nervously. Stumpy MacPhail and Merlie Ryan shuffled their feet, and the children and black people on the outskirts of the property made not a sound. Marvin Macy folded the knife he had been honing, and after looking about him fearlessly he swaggered out of the yard. The embers in the pit were turning to gray feathery ashes and it was now quite dark.

That was the way Marvin Macy came back from the penitentiary. Not a living soul in all the town was glad to see him. Even Mrs. Mary Hale, who was a good woman and had raised him with love and care — at the first sight of him even this old foster mother dropped the skillet she was holding and burst into tears. But nothing could faze that Marvin Macy. He sat on the back steps of the Hale house, lazily picking his guitar, and when the supper was ready, he pushed the children of the household out of the way and served himself a big meal, although there had been barely enough hoecakes and white meat to go round. After eating he settled himself in the best and warmest sleeping place in the front room and was untroubled by dreams.

Miss Amelia did not open the café that night. She locked the doors and all the windows very carefully, nothing was seen of her and Cousin Lymon, and a lamp burned in her room all the night long.

Marvin Macy brought with him bad fortune, right from the first, as could be expected. The next day the weather turned suddenly, and it became hot. Even in the early morning there was a sticky sultriness in the atmosphere, the wind carried the rotten smell of the swamp, and delicate shrill mosquitoes webbed the green millpond. It was unseasonable, worst than August, and much damage was done. For nearly everyone in the county who owned a hog had copied Miss Amelia and slaughtered the day before. And what sausage could keep in such weather as this? After a few days there was everywhere the smell of slowly spoiling meat, and an atmosphere of dreary waste. Worse yet, a family reunion near the Forks Falls highway ate pork roast and died, every one of them. It was plain that their hog had been infected — and who could tell whether the rest of the meat was safe or not? People were torn between the longing for the good taste of pork, and the fear of death. It was a time of waste and confusion.

The cause of all this, Marvin Macy, had no shame in him. He was seen everywhere. During work hours he loafed about the mill, looking in at the windows, and on Sundays he dressed in his red shirt and paraded up and down the road with his guitar. He was still handsome — with his brown hair, his red lips, and his broad strong shoulders; but the evil in him was now too famous for his good looks to get him anywhere. And this evil was not measured only by the actual sins he had committed. True, he had robbed those filling stations. And before that he had ruined the tenderest girls in the county, and laughed about it. Any number of wicked things could be listed against him, but quite apart from these crimes there was about him a secret meanness that clung to him almost like a smell. Another thing — he never sweated, not even in August, and that surely is a sign worth pondering over.

Now it seemed to the town that he was more dangerous than he had ever been before, as in the penitentiary in Atlanta he must have learned the method of laying charms. Otherwise how could his effect on Cousin Lymon be explained? For since first setting eyes on Marvin Macy the hunchback was possessed by an unnatural spirit. Every minute he wanted to be following along behind this jailbird, and he was full of silly schemes to attract attention to himself. Still Marvin Macy either treated him hatefully or failed to notice him at all. Sometimes the hunchback would give up, perch himself on the banister of the front porch much as a sick bird huddles on a telephone wire, and grieve publicly.

'But why?' Miss Amelia would ask, staring at him with her crossed, gray eyes, and her fists closed tight.

'Oh, Marvin Macy,' groaned the hunchback, and the sound of the name was enough to upset the rhythm of his sobs so that he hiccuped. 'He has been to Atlanta.'

Miss Amelia would shake her head and her face was dark and hardened. To begin with she had no patience with any traveling; those who had made the trip to Atlanta or traveled fifty miles from home to see the ocean — those restless people she despised. 'Going to Atlanta does no credit to him.'

'He has been to the penitentiary,' said the hunchback, miserable with longing.

How are you going to argue against such envies as these? In her perplexity Miss Amelia did not herself sound any too sure of what she was saying. 'Been to the penitentiary, Cousin Lymon? Why, a trip like that is no travel to brag about.'

During these weeks Miss Amelia was closely watched by everyone. She went about absent-mindedly, her face remote as though she had lapsed into one of her gripe trances. For some reason, after the day of Marvin Macy's arrival, she put aside her overalls and wore always the red dress she had before this time reserved for Sundays, funerals, and sessions of the court. Then as the weeks passed she began to take some steps to clear up the situation. But her efforts were hard to understand. If it hurt her to see Cousin Lymon follow Marvin Macy about the town, why did she not make the issues clear once and for all, and tell the hunchback that if he had dealings with Marvin Macy she would turn him off the premises? That would have been simple, and Cousin Lymon would have had to submit to her, or else face the sorry business of finding himself loose in the world. But Miss Amelia seemed to have lost her will; for the first time in her life she hesitated as to just what course to pursue. And, like most people in such a position of uncertainty, she did the worst thing possible — she began following several courses at once, all of them contrary to each other.

The café was opened every night as usual, and, strangely enough, when Marvin Macy came swaggering through the door, with the hunchback at his heels, she did not turn him out. She even gave him free drinks and smiled at him in a wild, crooked way. At the same time she set a terrible trap for him out in the swamp that surely would have killed him if he had got caught. She let Cousin Lymon invite him to Sunday dinner, and then tried to trip him up as he went down the steps. She began a great campaign of pleasure for Cousin Lymon — making exhausting trips to various spectacles being held in distant places, driving the automobile thirty miles to a Chautauqua, taking him to Forks Falls to watch a parade. All in all it was a distracting time for Miss Amelia. In the opinion of most people she was well on her way in the climb up fools' hill, and everyone waited to see how it would all turn out.

The weather turned cold again, the winter was upon the town, and night came before the last shift in the mill was done. Children kept on all their garments when they slept, and women raised the backs of their skirts to toast themselves dreamily at the fire. After it rained, the mud in the road made hard frozen ruts, there were faint flickers of lamplight from the windows of the houses, the peach trees were scrawny and bare. In the dark, silent nights of wintertime the café was the warm center point of the town, the lights shining so brightly that they could be seen a quarter of a mile away. The great iron stove at the back of the room roared, crackled, and turned red. Miss Amelia had made red curtains for the windows, and from a salesman who passed through the town she bought a great bunch of paper roses that looked very real.

But it was not only the warmth, the decorations, and the brightness, that made the café what it was. There is a deeper reason why the café was so precious to this town. And this deeper reason has to do with a certain pride that had not hitherto been known in these parts. To understand this new pride the cheapness of human life must be kept in mind. There were always plenty of people clustered around a mill — but it was seldom that every family had enough meal, garments, and fat back to go the rounds. Life could become one long dim scramble just to get the things needed to keep alive. And the confusing point is this: All useful things have a price, and are bought only with money, as that is the way the world is run. You know without having to reason about it the price of a bale of cotton, or a quart of molasses. But no value has been put on human life; it is given to us free and taken without being paid for. What is it worth? If you look around, at times the value may seem to be little or nothing at all. Often after you have sweated and tried and things are not better for you, there comes a feeling deep down in the soul that you are not worth much.

But the new pride that the café brought to this town had an effect on almost everyone, even the children. For in order to come to the café you did not have to buy the dinner, or a portion of liquor. There were cold bottled drinks for a nickel. And if you could not even afford that, Miss Amelia had a drink called Cherry Juice which sold for a penny a glass, and was pink-colored and very sweet. Almost everyone, with the exception of Reverend T. M. Willin, came to the café at least once during the week. Children love to sleep in houses other than their own, and to eat at a neighbor's table; on such occasions they behave themselves decently and are proud. The people in the town were likewise proud when sitting at the tables in the café. They washed before coming to Miss Amelia's, and scraped their feet very politely on the threshold as they entered the café. There, for a few hours at least, the deep bitter knowing that you are not worth much in this world could be laid low.

The café was a special benefit to bachelors, unfortunate people, and consumptives. And here it may be mentioned that there was some reason to suspect that Cousin Lymon was consumptive. The brightness of his gray eyes, his insistence, his talkativeness, and his cough — these were all signs. Besides, there is generally supposed to be some connection between a hunched spine and consumption. But whenever this subject had been mentioned to Miss Amelia she had become furious; she denied these symptoms with bitter vehemence, but on the sly she treated Cousin Lymon with hot chest platters, Kroup Kure, and such. Now this winter the hunchback's cough was worse, and sometimes even on cold days he would break out in a heavy sweat. But this did not prevent him from following along after Marvin Macy.

Early every morning he left the premises and went to the back door of Mrs. Hale's house, and waited and waited — as Marvin Macy was a lazy sleeper. He would stand there and call out softly. His voice was just like the voices of children who squat patiently over those tiny little holes in the ground where doodlebugs are thought to live, poking the hole with a broom straw, and calling plaintively: 'Doodlebug, Doodlebug — fly away home. Mrs. Doodlebug, Mrs. Doodlebug. Come out, come out. Your house is on fire and all your children are burning up.' In just such a voice — at once sad, luring, and resigned — would the hunchback call Marvin Macy's name each morning. Then when Marvin Macy came out for the day, he would trail him about the town, and sometimes they would be gone for hours together out in the swamp.

And Miss Amelia continued to do the worst thing possible: that is, to try to follow several courses at once. When Cousin Lymon left the house she did not call him back, but only stood in the middle of the road and watched lonesomely until he was out of sight. Nearly every day Marvin Macy turned up with Cousin Lymon at dinnertime, and ate at her table. Miss Amelia opened the pear preserves, and the table was well-set with ham or chicken, great bowls of hominy grits, and winter peas. It is true that on one occasion Miss Amelia tried to poison Marvin Macy — but there was a mistake, the plates were confused, and it was she herself who got the poisoned dish. This she quickly realized by the slight bitterness of the food, and that day she ate no dinner. She sat tilted back in her chair, feeling her muscle, and looking at Marvin Macy.

Every night Marvin Macy came to the café and settled himself at the best and largest table, the one in the center of the room. Cousin Lymon brought him liquor, for which he did not pay a cent. Marvin Macy brushed the hunchback aside as if he were a swamp mosquito, and not only did he show no gratitude for these favors, but if the hunchback got in his way he would cuff him with the back of his hand, or say: 'Out of my way, Brokeback — I'll snatch you bald-headed.' When this happened Miss Amelia would come out from behind her counter and approach Marvin Macy very slowly, her fists clenched, her peculiar red dress hanging awkwardly around her bony knees. Marvin Macy would also clench his fists and they would walk slowly and meaningfully around each other. But, although everyone watched breathlessly, nothing ever came of it. The time for the fight was not yet ready.

There is one particular reason why this winter is remembered and still talked about. A great thing happened. People woke up on the second of January and found the whole world about them altogether changed. Little ignorant children looked out of the windows, and they were so puzzled that they began to cry. Old people harked back and could remember nothing in these parts to equal the phenomenon. For in the night it had snowed. In the dark hours after midnight the dim flakes started falling softly on the town. By dawn the ground was covered, and the strange snow banked the ruby windows of the church, and whitened the roofs of the houses. The snow gave the town a drawn, bleak look. The two-room houses near the mill were dirty, crooked, and seemed about to collapse, and somehow everything was dark and shrunken. But the snow itself — there was a beauty about it few people around here had ever known before. The snow was not white, as Northerners had pictured it to be; in the snow there were soft colors of blue and silver, the sky was a gentle shining gray. And the dreamy quietness of falling snow — when had the town been so silent?

People reacted to the snowfall in various ways. Miss Amelia, on looking out of her window, thoughtfully wiggled the toes of her bare feet, gathered close to her neck the collar of her nightgown. She stood there for some time, then commenced to draw the shutters and lock every window on the premises. She closed the place completely, lighted the lamps, and sat solemnly over her bowl of grits. The reason for this was not that Miss Amelia feared the snowfall. It was simply that she was unable to form an immediate opinion of this new event, and unless she knew exactly and definitely what she thought of a matter (which was nearly always the case) she preferred to ignore it. Snow had never fallen in this county in her lifetime, and she had never thought about it one way or the other. But if she admitted this snowfall she would have to come to some decision, and in those days there was enough distraction in her life as it was already. So she poked about the gloomy, lamp-lighted house and pretended that nothing had happened. Cousin Lymon, on the contrary, chased around in the wildest excitement, and when Miss Amelia turned her back to dish him some breakfast he slipped out of the door.

Marvin Macy laid claim to the snowfall. He said that he knew snow, had seen it in Atlanta, and from the way he walked about the town that day it was as though he owned every flake. He sneered at the little children who crept timidly out of the houses and scooped up handfuls of snow to taste. Reverend Willin hurried down the road with a furious face, as he was thinking deeply and trying to weave the snow into his Sunday sermon. Most people were humble and glad about this marvel; they spoke in hushed voices and said 'thank you' and 'please' more than was necessary. A few weak characters, of course, were demoralized and got drunk — but they were not numerous. To everyone this was an occasion and many counted their money and planned to go to the café that night.

Cousin Lymon followed Marvin Macy about all day, seconding his claim to the snow. He marveled that snow did not fall as does rain, and stared up at the dreamy, gently falling flakes until he stumbled from dizziness. And the pride he took on himself, basking in the glory of Marvin Macy — it was such that many people could not resist calling out to him: ' "Oho," said the fly on the chariot wheel. "What a dust we do raise." '

Miss Amelia did not intend to serve dinner. But when, at six o'clock, there was the sound of footsteps on the porch she opened the front door cautiously. It was Henry Ford Crimp, and though there was no food, she let him sit at a table and served him a drink. Others came. The evening was blue, bitter, and though the snow fell no longer there was a wind from the pine trees that swept up delicate flurries from the ground. Cousin Lymon did not come until after dark, with him Marvin Macy, and he carried his tin suitcase and his guitar.

'So you mean to travel?' said Miss Amelia quickly.

Marvin Macy warmed himself at the stove. Then he settled down at his table and carefully sharpened a little stick. He picked his teeth, frequently taking the stick out of his mouth to look at the end and wipe it on the sleeve of his coat. He did not bother to answer.

The hunchback looked at Miss Amelia, who was behind the counter. His face was not in the least beseeching; he seemed quite sure of himself. He folded his hands behind his back and perked up his ears confidently. His cheeks were red, his eyes shining, and his clothes were soggy wet. 'Marvin Macy is going to visit a spell with us,' he said.

Miss Amelia made no protest. She only came out from behind the counter and hovered over the stove, as though the news had made her suddenly cold. She did not warm her backside modestly, lifting her skirt only an inch or so, as do most women when in public. There was not a grain of modesty about Miss Amelia, and she frequently seemed to forget altogether that there were men in the room. Now as she stood warming herself, her red dress was pulled up quite high in the back so that a piece of her strong, hairy thigh could be seen by anyone who cared to look at it. Her head was turned to one side, and she had begun talking with herself, nodding and wrinkling her forehead, and there was the tone of accusation and reproach in her voice although the words were not plain. Meanwhile, the hunchback and Marvin Macy had gone upstairs — up to the parlor with the pampas grass and the two sewing machines, to the private rooms where Miss Amelia had lived the whole of her life. Down in the café you could hear them bumping around, unpacking Marvin Macy, and getting him settled.

That is the way Marvin Macy crowded into Miss Amelia's home. At first Cousin Lymon, who had given Marvin Macy his own room, slept on the sofa in the parlor. But the snowfall had a bad effect on him; he caught a cold that turned into a winter quinsy, so Miss Amelia gave up her bed to him. The sofa in the parlor was much too short for her, her feet lapped over the edges, and often she rolled off onto the floor. Perhaps it was this lack of sleep that clouded her wits; everything she tried to do against Marvin Macy rebounded on herself. She got caught in her own tricks, and found herself in many pitiful positions. But still she did not put Marvin Macy off the premises, as she was afraid that she would be left alone. Once you have lived with another, it is a great torture to have to live alone. The silence of a firelit room when suddenly the clock stops ticking, the nervous shadows in an empty house — it is better to take in your mortal enemy than face the terror of living alone.

The snow did not last. The sun came out and within two days the town was just as it had always been before. Miss Amelia did not open her house until every flake had melted. Then she had a big house cleaning and aired everything out in the sun. But before that, the very first thing she did on going out again into her yard, was to tie a rope to the largest branch of the chinaberry tree. At the end of the rope she tied a crocus sack tightly stuffed with sand. This was the punching bag she made for herself and from that day on she would box with it out in her yard every morning. Already she was a fine fighter — a little heavy on her feet, but knowing all manner of mean holds and squeezes to make up for this.

Miss Amelia, as has been mentioned, measured six feet two inches in height. Marvin Macy was one inch shorter. In weight they were about even — both of them weighing close to a hundred and sixty pounds. Marvin Macy had the advantage in slyness of movement, and in toughness of chest. In fact from the outward point of view the odds were altogether in his favor. Yet almost everybody in the town was betting on Miss Amelia; scarcely a person would put up money on Marvin Macy. The town remembered the great fight between Miss Amelia and a Forks Falls lawyer who had tried to cheat her. He had been a huge strapping fellow, but he was left three-quarters dead when she had finished with him. And it was not only her talent as a boxer that had impressed everyone — she could demoralize her enemy by making terrifying faces and fierce noises, so that even the spectators were sometimes cowed. She was brave, she practiced faithfully with her punching bag, and in this case she was clearly in the right. So people had confidence in her, and they waited. Of course there was no set date for this fight. There were just the signs that were too plain to be overlooked.

During these times the hunchback strutted around with a pleased little pinched-up face. In many delicate and clever ways he stirred up trouble between them. He was constantly plucking at Marvin Macy's trouser leg to draw attention to himself. Sometimes he followed in Miss Amelia's footsteps — but these days it was only in order to imitate her awkward long-legged walk; he crossed his eyes and aped her gestures in a way that made her appear to be a freak. There was something so terrible about this that even the silliest customers of the café, such as Merlie Ryan, did not laugh. Only Marvin Macy drew up the left corner of his mouth and chuckled. Miss Amelia, when this happened, would be divided between two emotions. She would look at the hunchback with a lost, dismal reproach — then turn toward Marvin Macy with her teeth clamped.

'Bust a gut!' she would say bitterly.

And Marvin Macy, most likely, would pick up the guitar from the floor beside his chair. His voice was wet and slimy, as he always had too much spit in his mouth. And the tunes he sang glided slowly from his throat like eels. His strong fingers picked the strings with dainty skill, and everything he sang both lured and exasperated. This was usually more than Miss Amelia could stand.

'Bust a gut!' she would repeat, in a shout.

But always Marvin Macy had the answer ready for her. He would cover the strings to silence the quivering leftover tones, and reply with slow, sure insolence.

'Everything you holler at me bounces back on yourself. Yah! Yah!'

Miss Amelia would have to stand there helpless, as no one has ever invented a way out of this trap. She could not shout out abuse that would bounce back on herself. He had the best of her, there was nothing she could do.

So things went on like this. What happened between the three of them during the nights in the rooms upstairs nobody knows. But the café became more and more crowded every night. A new table had to be brought in. Even the Hermit, the crazy man named Rainer Smith, who took to the swamps years ago, heard something of the situation and came one night to look in at the window and brood over the gathering in the bright café. And the climax each evening was the time when Miss Amelia and Marvin Macy doubled their fists, squared up, and glared at each other. Usually this did not happen after any especial argument, but it seemed to come about mysteriously, by means of some instinct on the part of both of them. At these times the café would become so quiet that you could hear the bouquet of paper roses rustling in the draft. And each night they held this fighting stance a little longer than the night before.

The fight took place on Ground Hog Day, which is the second of February. The weather was favorable, being neither rainy nor sunny, and with a neutral temperature. There were several signs that this was the appointed day, and by ten o'clock the news spread all over the county. Early in the morning Miss Amelia went out and cut down her punching bag. Marvin Macy sat on the back step with a tin can of hog fat between his knees and carefully greased his arms and his legs. A hawk with a bloody breast flew over the town and circled twice around the property of Miss Amelia. The tables in the café were moved out to the back porch, so that the whole big room was cleared for the fight. There was every sign. Both Miss Amelia and Marvin Macy ate four helpings of half-raw roast for dinner, and then lay down in the afternoon to store up strength. Marvin Macy rested in the big room upstairs, while Miss Amelia stretched herself out on the bench in her office. It was plain from her white stiff face what a torment it was for her to be lying still and doing nothing, but she lay there quiet as a corpse with her eyes closed and her hands crossed on her chest.

Cousin Lymon had a restless day, and his little face was drawn and tightened with excitement. He put himself up a lunch, and set out to find the ground hog — within an hour he returned, the lunch eaten, and said that the ground hog had seen his shadow and there was to be bad weather ahead. Then, as Miss Amelia and Marvin Macy were both resting to gather strength, and he was left to himself, it occurred to him that he might as well paint the front porch. The house had not been painted for years — in fact, God knows if it had ever been painted at all. Cousin Lymon scrambled around, and soon he had painted half the floor of the porch a gay bright green. It was a loblolly job, and he smeared himself all over. Typically enough he did not even finish the floor, but changed over to the walls, painting as high as he could reach and then standing on a crate to get up a foot higher. When the paint ran out, the right side of the floor was bright green and there was a jagged portion of wall that had been painted. Cousin Lymon left it at that.

There was something childish about his satisfaction with his painting. And in this respect a curious fact should be mentioned. No one in the town, not even Miss Amelia, had any idea how old the hunchback was. Some maintained that when he came to town he was about twelve years old, still a child — others were certain that he was well past forty. His eyes were blue and steady as a child's but there were lavender crêpy shadows beneath these blue eyes that hinted of age. It was impossible to guess his age by his hunched queer body. And even his teeth gave no clue — they were all still in his head (two were broken from cracking a pecan), but he had stained them with so much sweet snuff that it was impossible to decide whether they were old teeth or young teeth. When questioned directly about his age the hunchback professed to know absolutely nothing — he had no idea how long he had been on the earth, whether for ten years or a hundred! So his age remained a puzzle.

Cousin Lymon finished his painting at five-thirty o'clock in the afternoon. The day had turned colder and there was a wet taste in the air. The wind came up from the pinewoods, rattling windows, blowing an old newspaper down the road until at last it caught upon a thorn tree. People began to come in from the country; packed automobiles that bristled with the poked-out heads of children, wagons drawn by old mules who seemed to smile in a weary, sour way and plodded along with their tired eyes half-closed. Three young boys came from Society City. All three of them wore yellow rayon shirts and caps put on backward — they were as much alike as triplets, and could always be seen at cock fights and camp meetings. At six o'clock the mill whistle sounded the end of the day's shift and the crowd was complete. Naturally, among the newcomers there were some riffraff, unknown characters, and so forth — but even so the gathering was quiet. A hush was on the town and the faces of people were strange in the fading light. Darkness hovered softly; for a moment the sky was a pale clear yellow against which the gables of the church stood out in dark and bare outline, then the sky died slowly and the darkness gathered into night.

Seven is a popular number, and especially it was a favorite with Miss Amelia. Seven swallows of water for hiccups, seven runs around the millpond for cricks in the neck, seven doses of Amelia Miracle Mover as a worm cure — her treatment nearly always hinged on this number. It is a number of mingled possibilities, and all who love mystery and charms set store by it. So the fight was to take place at seven o'clock. This was known to everyone, not by announcement or words, but understood in the unquestioning way that rain is understood, or an evil odor from the swamp. So before seven o'clock everyone gathered gravely around the property of Miss Amelia. The cleverest got into the café itself and stood lining the walls of the room. Others crowded onto the front porch, or took a stand in the yard.

Miss Amelia and Marvin Macy had not yet shown themselves. Miss Amelia, after resting all afternoon on the office bench, had gone upstairs. On the other hand Cousin Lymon was at your elbow every minute, threading his way through the crowd, snapping his fingers nervously, and batting his eyes. At one minute to seven o'clock he squirmed his way into the café and climbed up on the counter. All was very quiet.

It must have been arranged in some manner beforehand. For just at the stroke of seven Miss Amelia showed herself at the head of the stairs. At the same instant Marvin Macy appeared in front of the café and the crowd made way for him silently. They walked toward each other with no haste, their fists already gripped, and their eyes like the eyes of dreamers. Miss Amelia had changed her red dress for her old overalls, and they were rolled up to the knees. She was barefooted and she had an iron strengthband around her right wrist. Marvin Macy had also rolled his trouser legs — he was naked to the waist and heavily greased; he wore the heavy shoes that had been issued him when he left the penitentiary. Stumpy MacPhail stepped forward from the crowd and slapped their hip pockets with the palm of his right hand to make sure there would be no sudden knives. Then they were alone in the cleared center of the bright café.

There was no signal, but they both struck out simultaneously. Both blows landed on the chin, so that the heads of Miss Amelia and Marvin Macy bobbed back and they were left a little groggy. For a few seconds after the first blows they merely shuffled their feet around on the bare floor, experimenting with various positions, and making mock fists. Then, like wildcats, they were suddenly on each other. There was the sound of knocks, panting, and thumpings on the floor. They were so fast that it was hard to take in what was going on — but once Miss Amelia was hurled backward so that she staggered and almost fell, and another time Marvin Macy caught a knock on the shoulder that spun him around like a top. So the fight went on in this wild violent way with no sign of weakening on either side.

During a struggle like this, when the enemies are as quick and strong as these two, it is worth-while to turn from the confusion of the fight itself and observe the spectators. The people had flattened back as close as possible against the walls. Stumpy MacPhail was in a corner, crouched over and with his fists tight in sympathy, making strange noises. Poor Merlie Ryan had his mouth so wide open that a fly buzzed into it, and was swallowed before Merlie realized what had happened. And Cousin Lymon — he was worth watching. The hunchback still stood on the counter, so that he was raised up above everyone else in the café. He had his hands on his hips, his big head thrust forward, and his little legs bent so that the knees jutted outward. The excitement had made him break out in a rash, and his pale mouth shivered.

Perhaps it was half an hour before the course of the fight shifted. Hundreds of blows had been exchanged, and there was still a deadlock. Then suddenly Marvin Macy managed to catch hold of Miss Amelia's left arm and pinion it behind her back. She struggled and got a grasp around his waist; the real fight was now begun. Wrestling is the natural way of fighting in this county — as boxing is too quick and requires much thinking and concentration. And now that Miss Amelia and Marvin were locked in a hold together the crowd came out of its daze and pressed in closer. For a while the fighters grappled muscle to muscle, their hipbones braced against each other. Backward and forward, from side to side, they swayed in this way. Marvin Macy still had not sweated, but Miss Amelia's overalls were drenched and so much sweat had trickled down her legs that she left wet footprints on the floor. Now the test had come, and in these moments of terrible effort, it was Miss Amelia who was the stronger. Marvin Macy was greased and slippery, tricky to grasp, but she was stronger. Gradually she bent him over backward, and inch by inch she forced him to the floor. It was a terrible thing to watch and their deep hoarse breaths were the only sound in the café. At last she had him down, and straddled; her strong big hands were on his throat.

But at that instant, just as the fight was won, a cry sounded in the café that caused a shrill bright shiver to run down the spine. And what took place has been a mystery ever since. The whole town was there to testify what happened, but there were those who doubted their own eyesight. For the counter on which Cousin Lymon stood was at least twelve feet from the fighters in the center of the café. Yet at the instant Miss Amelia grasped the throat of Marvin Macy the hunch-back sprang forward and sailed through the air as though he had grown hawk wings. He landed on the broad strong back of Miss Amelia and clutched at her neck with his clawed little fingers.

The rest is confusion. Miss Amelia was beaten before the crowd could come to their senses. Because of the hunchback the fight was won by Marvin Macy, and at the end Miss Amelia lay sprawled on the floor, her arms flung outward and motionless. Marvin Macy stood over her, his face somewhat popeyed, but smiling his old half-mouthed smile. And the hunchback, he had suddenly disappeared. Perhaps he was frightened about what he had done, or maybe he was so de-lighted that he wanted to glory with himself alone — at any rate he slipped out of the café and crawled under the back steps. Someone poured water on Miss Amelia, and after a time she got up slowly and dragged herself into her office. Through the open door the crowd could see her sitting at her desk, her head in the crook of her arm, and she was sobbing with the last of her grating, winded breath. Once she gathered her right fist together and knocked it three times on the top of her office desk, then her hand opened feebly and lay palm upward and still. Stumpy MacPhail stepped forward and closed the door.

The crowd was quiet, and one by one the people left the café. Mules were waked up and untied, automobiles cranked, and the three boys from Society City roamed off down the road on foot. This was not a fight to hash over and talk about afterward; people went home and pulled the covers up over their heads. The town was dark, except for the premises of Miss Amelia, but every room was lighted there the whole night long.

Marvin Macy and the hunchback must have left the town an hour or so before daylight. And before they went away this is what they did:

They unlocked the private cabinet of curios and took everything in it.

They broke the mechanical piano.

They carved terrible words on the café tables.

They found the watch that opened in the back to show a picture of a waterfall and took that also.

They poured a gallon of sorghum syrup all over the kitchen floor and smashed the jars of preserves.

They went out in the swamp and completely wrecked the still, ruining the big new condenser and the cooler, and setting fire to the shack itself.

They fixed a dish of Miss Amelia's favorite food, grits with sausage, seasoned it with enough poison to kill off the county, and placed this dish temptingly on the café counter.

They did everything ruinous they could think of without actually breaking into the office where Miss Amelia stayed the night. Then they went off together, the two of them.

That was how Miss Amelia was left alone in the town. The people would have helped her if they had known how, as people in this town will as often as not be kindly if they have a chance. Several housewives nosed around with brooms and offered to clear up the wreck. But Miss Amelia only looked at them with lost crossed eyes and shook her head. Stumpy MacPhail came in on the third day to buy a plug of Queenie tobacco, and Miss Amelia said the price was one dollar. Everything in the café had suddenly risen in price to be worth one dollar. And what sort of a café is that? Also, she changed very queerly as a doctor. In all the years before she had been much more popular than the Cheehaw doctor. She had never monkeyed with a patient's soul, taking away from him such real necessities as liquor, tobacco, and so forth. Once in a great while she might carefully warn a patient never to eat fried watermelon or some such dish it had never occurred to a person to want in the first place. Now all this wise doctoring was over. She told one-half of her patients that they were going to die outright, and to the remaining half she recommended cures so far-fetched and agonizing that no one in his right mind would consider them for a moment.

Miss Amelia let her hair grow ragged, and it was turning gray. Her face lengthened, and the great muscles of her body shrank until she

was thin as old maids are thin when they go crazy. And those gray eyes
— slowly day by day they were more crossed, and it was as though they
sought each other out to exchange a little glance of grief and lonely
recognition. She was not pleasant to listen to; her tongue had sharpened terribly.

When anyone mentioned the hunchback she would say only this:
'Ho! if I could lay hand to him I would rip out his gizzard and throw it
to the cat!' But it was not so much the words that were terrible, but
the voice in which they were said. Her voice had lost its old vigor;
there was none of the ring of vengeance it used to have when she
would mention 'that loom-fixer I was married to,' or some other enemy. Her voice was broken, soft, and sad as the wheezy whine of the
church pump-organ.

For three years she sat out on the front steps every night, alone and
silent, looking down the road and waiting. But the hunchback never
returned. There were rumors that Marvin Macy used him to climb
into windows and steal, and other rumors that Marvin Macy had sold
him into a side show. But both these reports were traced back to
Merlie Ryan. Nothing true was ever heard of him. It was in the fourth
year that Miss Amelia hired a Cheehaw carpenter and had him board
up the premises, and there in those closed rooms she has remained
ever since.

Yes, the town is dreary. On August afternoons the road is empty,
white with dust, and the sky above is bright as glass. Nothing moves
— there are no children's voices, only the hum of the mill. The peach
trees seem to grow more crooked every summer, and the leaves are dull
gray and of a sickly delicacy. The house of Miss Amelia leans so much
to the right that it is now only a question of time when it will collapse
completely, and people are careful not to walk around the yard. There
is no good liquor to be bought in the town; the nearest still is eight
miles away, and the liquor is such that those who drink it grow warts
on their livers the size of goobers, and dream themselves into a dangerous inward world. There is absolutely nothing to do in the town. Walk
around the millpond, stand kicking at a rotten stump, figure out what
you can do with the old wagon wheel by the side of the road near the
church. The soul rots with boredom. You might as well go down to the
Forks Falls highway and listen to the chain gang.

THE TWELVE MORTAL MEN

The Forks Falls highway is three miles from the town, and it is here the chain gang has been working. The road is of macadam, and the county decided to patch up the rough places and widen it at a certain dangerous place. The gang is made up of twelve men, all wearing black and white striped prison suits, and chained at the ankles. There is a guard, with a gun, his eyes drawn to red slits by the glare. The gang works all the day long, arriving huddled in the prison cart soon after daybreak, and being driven off again in the gray August twilight. All day there is the sound of the picks striking into the clay earth, hard sunlight, the smell of sweat. And every day there is music. One dark voice will start a phrase, half-sung, and like a question. And after a moment another voice will join in, soon the whole gang will be singing. The voices are dark in the golden glare, the music intricately blended, both somber and joyful. The music will swell until at last it seems that the sound does not come from the twelve men on the gang, but from the earth itself, or the wide sky. It is music that causes the heart to broaden and the listener to grow cold with ectasy and fright. Then slowly the music will sink down until at last there remains one lonely voice, then a great hoarse breath, the sun, the sound of the picks in the silence.

And what kind of gang is this that can make such music? Just twelve mortal men, seven of them black and five of them white boys from this county. Just twelve mortal men who are together.

Texasville (excerpt)

by Larry McMurtry

The "Texasville" of Larry McMurtry's novel is a town that never happened. Would-be founders and other interested parties tried to make it happen, but it never got beyond one building — a combination saloon, post office, and general store ("three rooms," it is pointed out, "didn't make a town"). The characters who people this novel — among them, Duane Moore; Karla, his wife; Suzie Nolan; Junior, her husband; and G. G. Rawley, the preacher — seem to live in the shadow of that original nonhappening. Though their town, Thalia, did sink roots and even flourish during the oil boom, it has again fallen on hard days. It is a measure of Larry McMurtry's talent that he has turned this bleakness into a rich-grained ribaldry.

In the scene just concluded, a meeting of the committee planning the centennial celebration, Duane has tangled with G. G. Rawley and Suzie has challenged Rawley's right to be there at all. Her anger kindles Duane's interest and that — plus his recent, heady discovery of new oil — leads him, in a unilateral and otherwise unparliamentary act, to adjourn the meeting. Other improprieties naturally follow. In the passage appearing below, love can be taken as comical, comforting, wholly absurd — and fun. As it opens, the adjournment has just taken place, to everyone's surprise, including Duane's own. — L.R.

HE MEANT IT. The meeting was silly, he was getting no help from anyone, the whole centennial was silly, he missed his family and he had had enough.

"You can't adjourn us, we just got here," Jenny said. "We have a lot of important things to discuss."

"No we don't," Duane said. "None of this is important."

He got up and walked out, leaving a roomful of stunned people behind him. He went to his pickup, drove it around the block and parked behind the post office. Then he hurried back to the courthouse and peeked around a corner to watch the committee take its leave. . . .

The last people out, as Duane had hoped, were Suzie Nolan and Old Man Balt, whose faithful daughter, Beulah, was waiting for him as usual. Suzie helped the old man down the sidewalk, waiting while he emptied his Crisco can onto the courthouse lawn. The minute he was in the car Beulah whisked him off to whatever TV show was about to come on.

Duane could not tell if Suzie was still angry, but she was obviously in no hurry. She slipped her shoes off before getting into her car. Driving in shoes, or even wearing them, didn't appeal to her.

Seeing her take her shoes off gave Duane an idea. He looked around and saw not a soul in sight except Suzie. The square and the town seemed deserted, the reason being that two crucial Little League games were being played that night on the local diamond. His son Jack was pitching in one of them, his daughter Julie playing shortstop in another. He meant to go, but had developed more immediate plans.

He quickly slipped off his boots and his pants. It generally took Suzie three or four minutes to find her car keys, comb her hair and get started. He watched her do all those things, his pants and boots in his hand. When she started the car he tiptoed over and hid behind a cedar tree on one corner of the lawn.

The traffic light had no traffic to stop, but it was still doing its job of turning red and then green anyway. Suzie had to pass through it. She had started the car, but hadn't backed away from the curb. She was lazily combing her hair. The light changed to red. Duane felt annoyed. If she had only stopped combing her hair and backed out, she would have immediately caught the light. But she was still combing. He waited, remembering how much he had wanted her that night in the hospital parking lot. The light turned to green and his heart sank, for Suzie had finally begun to back out. She would undoubtedly drive through it, leaving him with his old want and his new. Of course he could follow her home, but that was not exactly what he desired.

Then Suzie dropped something — her comb, an earring? — and bent over to retrieve it from the floorboard. She found it, and just as she did the light changed to red again. Suzie eased up to it. By the time she was fully stopped Duane was at the window on the driver's side. Suzie looked up. She didn't seem in the least surprised to see him standing under the traffic light in the very center of downtown Thalia with his boots and pants in his hand.

"Hi, you rat," she said, and put her car in park. Duane stuffed his boots and pants in the back seat and kissed her. Her kisses were as quick and eager as they had been at the hospital. He considered trying to go through the window, which would have made things perfect, but he decided to be mature and settle for 98 percent. The streets were totally empty. He opened the door, still not sure how things were going to work. He was every bit as aroused as he had been the first time, but felt a momentary faltering of confidence. Cars did pose logistical problems.

Suzie had lost none of her confidence, though — in such matters she seemed to experience no doubt.

"Sit in the seat, dummy," she said, with a grin. "We don't have to do it like we was married."

She slid as far from the steering wheel as she could. Duane got in, his legs stretched toward the far door. They were long legs, and the far door not really very far, but Suzie immediately straddled him. Passion, which rendered so many people awkward, brought her a heightened grace.

"This way I can watch the road," she said, easing him into place.

"We might have to hurry," Duane said. "We might have to set an all-time speed record." He felt as if he easily could, though he was also highly aware of what a bizarre thing they were doing. The town looked more brightly lit than it had when he was hiding in the darkness by the courthouse.

Suzie smiled. She opened his shirt. Then she leaned back and touched her breasts.

"We don't have to do any such thing," she said. "We can just take our time. There's not a soul in sight."

Events proved Suzie right. Traffic flow through downtown Thalia obligingly lapsed for five minutes, more time than Duane needed and then some. Suzie rose and sank with an authority that quickly proved irresistible.

Though, as she said, not a soul was in sight, the fact that he was involved in a deeply exciting sex act practically beneath the red light in the epicenter of Thalia may have hastened matters too. Seconds after enjoying a fine orgasm, Duane began to wonder why he hadn't asked her to pull around in the darkness behind the post office. That would have been an excellent site, he decided too late. Suzie soon came too, but that didn't mean she was through. The first orgasm often merely served to heighten her interest — if she paused at all it was merely to consider what kind of little game she might enjoy next. She liked to make a leisurely selection, to rummage through the possibilities for a while, perhaps choosing one game only to stop it after a bit in favor of another. Caution played no part in her choice, or her life — she seemed to feel that whatever time was needed was hers by right. She had no intention of hurrying from one pleasure to the next.

Duane found such leisure understandable when they were in bed, but less so when they were parked under bright street lights at a public intersection.

"Let's drive around behind the post office, where it's dark," he said.

"No," Suzie said. She was seated rather firmly on his legs, and gave him a squeeze with her inner muscles to emphasize her point.

"Why not?" he asked. "Then we don't have to worry about traffic."

"What traffic?" she asked. "There's not a car in sight."

"I know, but somebody'll come along sooner or later," he said.

"I like to see you," Suzie said. "The street lights make your body look different — sort of like a ghost. It's real interesting."

"Yeah, and it'll be real interesting to anybody who drives by," Duane said. "And I *will* be a ghost if Karla drives by."

Suzie was unimpressed. "It might just be strangers," she said. "People passing through. They won't even know us. Didn't you ever want to know how it would feel if people were looking?"

"No," Duane said truthfully. "It wouldn't feel at all, if people were looking, because I'd be too embarrassed to do anything."

Then he saw lights, far behind them — truck lights, he guessed.

"Here comes somebody," he said. "We gotta move."

He attempted to squirm out from under her, but Suzie gripped him more firmly with her inner muscles. She smiled and teased her nipples.

"It feels sexy, just knowing they're coming, don't it?" she said.

"No," Duane insisted. "It feels embarrassing. I can't appreciate sexy feelings when I'm embarrassed."

"Maybe you could learn to," Suzie suggested.

"I don't think I can learn to before that truck gets here," he said.

"You could try," Suzie pointed out. "Men don't ever want to try anything different."

The truck, by that time, was only a quarter of a mile away. Duane managed to reach under the steering wheel and turn on the hazard lights. If the truck rear-ended and killed them in the position they were in, the town would receive a rude shock. They themselves would be dead, and the credibility of the Centennial Committee destroyed forever.

Suzie continued to squeeze. The roar of the approaching truck aroused her even as it chilled Duane. His erection was shrinking so fast that even Suzie's squeezing failed to hold him in.

The truck, seeing the hazard lights, cut smoothly to the right of them. The driver tapped his brakes for a second at the light, glanced east and west, and roared on toward Wichita Falls. He didn't look at the occupants of the car at all, though one of the occupants came just as the other ceased to occupy her.

The fact that an orgasm occurred at a moment of exit didn't seem to diminish Suzie's pleasure at all. She grabbed his hand and stuffed it underneath her, leaning far back in ecstasy.

The streets were empty again. Duane relaxed a little. Suzie was an unusual woman, he had to admit. Though not entirely at ease in the situation, he wouldn't have wanted to miss her.

She straightened up, draping an arm across the seat. She scooted back down his legs, stroked his stomach lightly and fingered his equipment.

"Sorry," he said, assuming still more was expected.

"Why?" Suzie asked. "It's cute when it's floppy."

She scooted farther back down his legs, until her back was against the far door. Then she squatted on her haunches.

"Put your toe in me," she said.

"No," Duane said, horrified. He had just spotted another set of approaching headlights.

"I'm real wet," Suzie said. "Put your toe in."

"Another truck's coming," he said.

"I know," Suzie said. "I like that sound they make when they come roaring through town."

Duane decided she was interesting but crazy. He kept his feet to himself.

"I got my socks on," he said. "It won't work."

Suzie immediately reached down and peeled the sock off one foot. "Now what's your excuse?" she said.

"Why would you want me to do that with my old smelly foot?" Duane asked, as the truck roared nearer.

"To see if it feels interesting," Suzie said. "Stop asking dumb questions."

"I don't think I can. My foot's gone to sleep," Duane said, grasping at straws.

"Dickie does it," Suzie said. "Dickie's not afraid. He's the only one in this town with any imagination."

"I'm glad to hear it," Duane said, "but I'd rather be hearing it on the back side of the post office. What if that trucker saw me with my toe in you and lost his mind? He might run right through the hardware store, and then what would we do for lawn-mower parts?"

Suzie was still squatting on her haunches, more or less over his feet, when the truck arrived. This time the truck driver braked carefully at the light. The big motor throbbed beside them for several seconds, then the truck went on. The second driver showed no more interest in the car or its occupants than the first one had.

"If I let you drive around behind the post office will you try it?" Suzie asked.

"I don't know," Duane said. "It's a possibility. I don't want to commit myself."

"What do you think I'll do, make your stupid toe rot off?" Suzie asked. She seemed to be becoming irritated.

"No, of course not," Duane said.

"You put your finger in me," Suzie said. "You put your dick in me. Why not your toe?"

"Let's see what life's like around behind the post office," Duane said. He got his feet free and slipped under the wheel. He waited for Suzie to sit down, but she didn't sit down. She continued to squat.

"It's not very far to the post office," she pointed out.

Duane started the car.

In the comfortable darkness behind the post office Duane gingerly indulged in a number of games. Suzie made it clear that she regarded him as a coward, but she didn't let his cowardice prevent her from pursuing her interests.

When she was content, he asked her if G. G. Rawley had ever participated in any of her games.

"You bet," she said. "He was the first man I was ever unfaithful to Junior with. It happened in the Sunday-school room. He got me up there pretending he wanted me to help him tune that old piano they use in Sunday school."

"Is that why you're mad at him?" Duane asked.

"I'm mad at him because he wouldn't do it anywhere except in the Sunday-school room," Suzie said. "He could have come to my house, or we could have gone to a motel. I got tired of trying to get comfortable on a piano bench."

"There's the floor," Duane observed. Now that he was in the dark, he enjoyed talking to Suzie about sex.

"G.G.'s got arthritis," Suzie said. "It's all he can do to stoop over.

"It was good, though," she added. "I yelled so loud I scared him to death a couple of times. Doing it with a preacher's real exciting, I guess because they're not supposed to be doing it with you. It sure beats doing it with your husband."

"Couldn't get old Junior to play too many games, huh?" Duane said.

Suzie looked out the window. Her face changed — it looked for a moment as if she might cry.

"No," she said. "Junior gets scared if you even mention a game."

Duane saw that he had touched a raw nerve. He felt sorry he had asked.

"That was the sadness of our marriage," Suzie said. "I could have made him very happy if he'd let me. But he just never would let me."

She sighed and came back into his arms.

"We got nice kids," she said. "They win everything, everything. I think we would have had a real nice marriage if Junior hadn't been so scared. It seems such a waste. I don't think he wanted to be happy. Why would anybody not want to be happy, Duane?"

"I don't know," Duane said. He thought of Sonny, who had never been happy. Though he himself had often been sad, he had also been keenly happy. Sonny hadn't. He had concentrated on holding some middle space between victory and defeat. Now, despite a life of good planning, defeat was staring him in the face anyway.

"Junior's mother was never happy," Suzie said. "She had a real hard life. I guess it made Junior feel guilty to think of being happy when his mother never got to be.

"I'll tell you who's happy, and that's Dickie," she said. "You ought to be proud of yourself for raising such a nice kid. It just lifts my spirits the minute I see him coming. That's a great gift, to be able to lift people's spirits just by showing up."

Duane knew she had paid his son a fine compliment. But he was remembering Junior, her husband, nervously asking the question about whether women wanted sex more than men, at the Dairy Queen a few weeks earlier. It seemed sad. Junior had struggled hard and become wealthy. He had done all that he had been taught to do: work hard, save, get ahead. Then the economy had turned out from under him and he had lost his wealth. And all the while, for rich or for poor, he was being overmatched at home by a nice woman who just happened to have a much richer sexuality than he had.

"What are you thinking about?" Suzie asked.

"I just can't help feeling sorry for Junior," he said.

"Oh, well," Suzie said, "Junior enjoys feeling sorry for himself. Maybe all you men enjoy feeling sorry for yourselves. I'm hanging on to Dickie while I can. He don't feel sorry for himself. Dickie likes to live.

"I gotta go," she said. "The kids will be getting home from their swim meet any time."

Duane got into his pickup and followed her around the courthouse. They both caught the red light beneath which they had had such an interesting ten minutes. Duane felt a little sad. He — they — would never do that again, not in that place, that way. A short but exciting part of life was behind him.

Suzie had recovered her spirits. She wasn't sad at all. She grinned and blew him a kiss.

"I sure hope your toe don't rot off, Duane," she said, as the light changed.

St. George

by Gail Godwin

UNTIL TONIGHT, Silas had been working out perfectly. Lusty, uncomplex, the archetypal man of few words, he had hooked onto Gwen's well-ordered life like a charm. He had served as her antidote against Love, the disease that had felled all her friends in the midst of whatever they were pursuing and left them handicapped forever after, trapped in mortgaged homes with rather ordinary men, all their grand possibilities extinguished.

But tonight, as Silas stood over her bed, buttoning up his shirt, his usual blond, untroubled countenance clouded over and he said, "This isn't much of a relationship, is it?"

"Of course it's not!" exclaimed Gwen. Imagine Silas using a word like "relationship." "It's not supposed to be one. Relationships take too much libido and right now mine's all booked up." She was getting her master's degree in English next June. Then she could go out and make her demands on the world. Then she could begin to look for someone, her equal or better, with whom to fall in love. Silas was her Now man. She had picked him up in an all-night coffee shop. Having cleared her life of bearded graduate students who wanted to latch onto her psyche like leeches or lie in bed afterward discussing D. H. Lawrence, she had been on the prowl for a simple man, a truck driver perhaps, a non-soul-sharer she couldn't get serious about, but who would stand between her and loneliness in this impersonal city. Lonely people, she knew, were the most susceptible to the Disease of Love. "I thought we understood each other, Silas," she added, a little sadly, from her pillows.

"I understand," he said in his unruffled monotone. "I'm just feeling a little cold. Never mind." He gave her rump a friendly little pat. "If you're lucky, maybe I'll see you later in the week."

He always said this. She, in return, said, "That would be nice!" It was part of their unspoken ritual, never to plan ahead or "promise" anything, though in fact he came almost regularly every Tuesday, Thursday, and Saturday, subwaying to her place at ten, ravishing her by eleven, and departing at twelve for his all-night job in some plant. She could not get much information out of him, so most of the time she talked about herself. He had heard her opinions on everything, most of all concerning the Disease. He would scratch his blond curly hair and lie beside her, a remote smile on his big bland face, and listen to her go on and on about why she loved medieval literature the best ("It's full of saints having visions and great perfect love affairs and knights slaying monsters to win the love of their ladies"), and how utterly, hopelessly dull her married friends had become ("They got the fever and attached it to the first thing in pants that came along and now look at them"), and once in a while he would nod, or murmur "Mmm," or ask a question. She was never sure what he was thinking or how much he understood, but he was so warm and comfortable and always left at twelve. It was working out so well!

"You're not mad at me, Silas," she said, flirting a little to make up for her "libido" speech.

"Nope," he replied pleasantly. He let himself out of her apartment with a neat click of the lock and there he went, light-footing it down the stairs, headlong into a December's starry cold.

She got up at once, put on a Bach cantata, ran herself a hot bath, and while it was running flicked open the little white compact and punched out Tuesday's pill, being careful to lick up all the crumbly parts round the edge. Then she climbed into her bath, letting solitude fold warmly around her with the water. "Oh, Silas, don't you dare spoil things," she said aloud. After which she gave herself up to the pure, ethereal Bach, uncluttered by human emotions, and soaked for a while in daydreams of possible futures.

Silas did not come on Thursday. Gwen frowned but was not unduly worried. She listened to some Brandenburgs, made herself a radish-and-bacon sandwich, and translated thirty lines of *Beowulf*.

He didn't come on Saturday, either. Her weekend stretched endlessly ahead. Classes had let out for the long Christmas break. "That's all right, I have plenty to do," she said to herself. She made out a rigorous schedule: nine books to read for course work, two papers to write, and a volume of *lais* to translate from Old French. For several days she did not leave her comfortable little apartment on the top floor of a made-over warehouse near the river. How lovely, to be answerable to nobody but yourself, to sleep in the afternoons if you wished, and stay up all night reading Boethius, underlining passages of strength and beauty. Tuesday evening, she went to an early movie, hurrying home past the lighted windows of others to be there when Silas came.

But ten o'clock passed, and then eleven, and no Silas. "Perhaps he's sick, maybe I should call him." But she didn't have his number. She didn't know where he lived. She didn't even know his last name! Just for the hell of it, she put in a long-distance call to her parents, whom she'd outgrown years ago, but their phone rang and rang. "They must have gone to the movies." Then she just sat for a while, listening to the boats on the river, the night sounds. A strange thought crossed her mind: "If nobody in the world knows I am sitting here in this chair at this moment, how can I be sure I exist?" Enough of that. She translated some more of an Old French *lai*, about a knight who goes to a strange land locked in the thrall of a monster-king. About midnight she got hungry and wished for an omelet, whole-wheat toast with soft butter, strawberry preserves, and black coffee, and being free and alone to follow such whims whenever they arose went at once to her kitchen to satisfy these.

She got everything out, broke the first egg in the bowl, broke the second, and something dark came out with a *plop*. It moved beneath the sticky yolk in which it was entrapped. God, could an embryo chicken get through all that modern dairy apparatus alive? It was too horrible. She lost all appetite, made ready to dump the whole mess down the sink, turn on the hot water, and hope it died. But she hesitated. What would it look like? With a kind of morbid curiosity, she ran some tepid water into the bowl, loosening the yolk's stickiness and freeing the thing. It was a reddish color and began paddling slowly round the bowl. It had little legs and a tail which flicked drops of egg water in her face. "Ugg!" she cried, turning away, then had to look back at it. It was some sort of tiny lizard trying to blink open its eyes, which were stuck together with egg.

She ran to get her magnifying glass.

For some moments, she peered through it at the creature in the bowl and tried to get her bearings. In her mixing bowl swam a tiny but perfectly formed dragon. And she knew one when she saw one. She was, after all, a medieval-lit. scholar, and the thing that came out of her egg was an exact miniature of the dragon on the cover of her *Beowulf* book. Although it was scarcely an inch long from snout to tail, it was equipped with all its legendary parts. No bigger than inverted commas, its tiny nostrils flared. It had stand-up ears so straight they might have passed for horns. The birdlike talons had minuscule toenails, and a mane of fiery points ran like rickrack from the crest of his flat reptilian skull down to the tip of his very active barbed tail. Now he had got his eyes unstuck. They were comically large in proportion to the rest of him and regarded her sharply, with just a hint of coyness.

"God," she said aloud. "I am not insane, I'm not. He is down there in that bowl." How did she know he was a he? Gently she eased him onto a spoon, took a matchstick and probed at the soft red underbelly, trying to discern a hint of gender. The hackles sprang up all along its back, its tail stopped dead still and it plunged like a dart from the spoon into the bowl. She could see its shadow underwater, swimming round and round in a huff.

"Oh, dear, I've offended you. I'm sorry, I'm very sorry, really I am. We'll assume you're a man. O.K.?"

The shadow slowed down, as though considering. The whole thing was too much. She was overcome by a violent moment of disbelief. Taking down a clean Pyrex bowl from the shelf, she heard her own voice bribing him with some clean water. "And I'll even make you a small island," she coaxed, inverting a dessert dish into the bigger clean bowl which she filled almost to the top with water. "You're going to love this!" she said. The shadow paddled on, submerged in the eggy water, but some of the fury had gone out of him now. With just a hint of a shudder, she spooned him into his new kingdom. He seemed to enjoy the greater freedom but would neither look at her nor come up on his island.

Next morning when she went rather queasily into the kitchen, he was languishing on his dessert-bowl island. He wagged his tail several times, very listlessly, and appealed to her with the oversized eyes. He was undoubtedly hungry, but what did he eat? She offered him graham-cracker crumbs, bacon shreds, and slivers of lettuce. From all of these, he turned away sadly. Groaning, she knelt beneath the sink where a family of ants insisted on living and murdered one quickly between paper-toweled fingers. She thought she was going to vomit. The dragon refused the dead ant and wedged his head between his two front feet. The eyes rolled up at her imploringly.

"What can I *do!*" Gwen cried. "*I* don't know what you eat. Oh, why couldn't you have stayed in your egg!"

He was too weak to dive like a dart into the water. He stood up wearily and did a half-turn round the dessert bowl and lay down again with his back to her.

Gwen went out reluctantly into the city. Her palms were sweating and her heart beat loudly. The people she passed seemed to be wearing masks. The watery winter sun shimmered like lemon water on the streets. Everything seemed unreal. She went into a pet shop and asked the man what lizards ate. He sold her a box of turtle food. In a sort of automatic trance, she took the crosstown bus to the main library and went to the encyclopedias to look up "dragon." The *Americana* had but one paragraph on the creature and was careful to put the word in quotes. *Collier's* left it out altogether. *Britannica* gave the etymology of the word (Gk. for "sharpsighted") and went on to show its Oxbridge education by name-dropping Sigmund, Beowulf, Arthur, and Tristan, all of whom had bouts with the creatures. *New Catholic Encyclopedia* was *slightly* more helpful. Dragons could be found on land or in air, it said, but their most natural habitat was water. Gwen was proud of her dessert-bowl-in-Pyrex-bowl innovation. After paying tribute to St. George and a St. Margaret of Antioch, who had confronted dragons unflinchingly, this liberal source quoted Posidonius' story of a dragon covering an acre of land who swallowed a full-grown knight as though he were a mere pill. St. George's dragon ate two sheep a day until sheep ran short and then he decided he would eat the king's daughter.

Not a word about what very small dragons ate.

She checked out all the books on dragons and took the bus back across the unreal city where she didn't know a soul — except Silas, who seemed to have vanished. She was rather interested to see whether the little dragon would take the turtle food.

Dumping the books on the nearest chair, she hurried to the

kitchen, calling "Don't give up! Help is coming!" But he was not in his bowl. She got down on her hands and knees and searched the floor. Could he have tumbled down the drain? She shone a flashlight down it and saw nothing but a nasty coating of grease. Sadly, she ran a fast slosh of cool water from the tap, to speed him on his way in case he was stuck halfway down. The unopened box of turtle food lay abandoned on the sink counter.

Feeling very empty, Gwen sat down in a chair and surveyed her four walls, which were white. Deliberately, she had hung no pictures. She loathed the graduate-student style of sticking posters and unframed prints up everywhere, just to cover the emptiness. Until she could afford good originals, she would have nothing. But in her present isolation, the bare white walls appeared sinister — like an asylum or an anteroom between this world and the next.

The thought of the papers she could be writing for her courses nagged but did not spur her. She wished there was a pill she could take that would put her to sleep until Christmas vacation was over and classes started. She played a little Bach and went to sleep on the couch and when she woke up it was dark. Fumbling into her bedroom, she undressed, dropping her clothes on the floor.

"There's nothing wrong with me, Silas," she said reproachfully. The tall wraithlike girl leered at her from the mirror with rather hysterical eyes, and for a minute Gwen thought it was someone else. Shaken, she paused in front of her dresser and deposited her watch into her open jewelry box.

The little dragon leaped up with a start and she screamed.

He had been sleeping in the golden embrace of a pearl-studded bracelet which had belonged to her grandmother. His nostrils expanded and contracted exactly above the space where two pearls had formerly lodged. He seemed bigger. He wagged his tail ecstatically and costume jewelry clanked beneath his red belly. He was all attention, waiting to see what she'd do. After a long pause, she said aloud, "Well, *somebody's* glad to see me."

He leaped out of the jewelry box and scuttled across the dresser to hide behind a Shalimar bottle.

"Oh, you want to play, do you?" The tail thumped wildly to one side of the bottle. She tried to corral him with the pearl-studded bracelet, wondering where she'd lost those two pearls, when he caught hold of it like a baby will grab a finger, aimed a tiny flame from his mouth round the prongs of another pearl, and gulped it down with a wide grin.

"No, you idiot, that's an heirloom!" she cried, unclenching him from the bracelet. In doing so, she touched him for the first time. He was warm and dry; he throbbed slightly. She thought she was going to faint. When she didn't, she was so grateful she stroked him again and said, "I'll name you St. George."

Later that night, after St. George was asleep on his island, worn out from chasing round the dresser (he had knocked over the Shalimar, finally, and was the sweetest-smelling dragon ever), Gwen lay in bed, books lining the crack of her bedroom door, and read the dragon books. According to Grafton Elliot Smith (*The Evolution of the Dragon*, Manchester, 1919), "the dragon dines on precious gems and is partial to pearls. . . ."

She went into the kitchen and woke him up. He slept rather quaintly, with his tail curled round over his eyes, to keep out light.

"Look here, St. George," said Gwen, "I hope you're no gourmand. Because tomorrow and tomorrow and all the days after, you're getting the Woolworth's special." He wagged his tail happily and regarded her with the big sleepy eyes. There was no doubt about it, St. George *was* getting bigger. He covered almost the entire surface of the inverted dessert bowl.

Next morning she forced herself to make the trip downtown. The people on the streets seemed another species from herself, their faces grimly set toward a destination she could not see. "And not one of them will speak to me," she said aloud. An old woman, who looked like she'd been run through a strainer, turned to glare at her. Gwen looked at her reflection in a store window and saw she'd come out without combing her hair. Raking it down with her fingers, she went to Woolworth's jewelry counter. They sold a fairly long strand of imitation pearls for $1.99. She picked up one and, under the curious stare of the salesgirl, counted the pearls: forty-two. That should be enough. No, better get a couple of them.

"I'll take these," she told the girl. How croaky her own voice sounded. When was the last time she had talked to anybody? Time seemed to be stretching out of shape. Usually her life was neatly marked off by class schedules and Silas' three-times-a-week nocturnal visits.

By the end of the week, St. George was the size of a Chihuahua. He had eaten seventy-nine of the pearls by Saturday night, and the stores were shut on Sunday.

"You'll have to take potluck from my jewelry box when you run through your other five," Gwen told him. They were curled up on the sofa, the little dragon in her lap, watching the Saturday-night movie, which was a bore. But St. George loved it as he loved all TV programs. His tail lashed delightfully from side to side, snagging her best wool skirt and tearing the stuffing from the upholstery. A great silent chuckle seemed to be in progress inside him as he watched human beings going about their business on the screen. "But please remember, the diamonds and the turquoises are no-no's." St. George had cunningly pried open the box and eaten a diamond earring and several turquoises out of a favorite ring. He was ingenious and energetic as a naughty child, or a kitten. Gwen had never owned a pet. She was amazed at the destruction one could wreak in a simple act of play. Already, with one swipe of his barbed tail he had irrevocably scarred her Queen Anne writing desk, the most superior piece of furniture she had. He could not control his fiery tongue: Every time he got excited, out it came, and when the smoke had cleared there was another scorched tablecloth, towel, or book. Gallumphing tirelessly across her rooms, his razor-sharp toenails cut into the finish of her hardwood floors. As he no longer fit into his bowl, she'd given him the plugged-up kitchen sink, but he crawled out at night to roam wet-footed about the dark apartment. She would wake to hear him scratching at her bedroom door, which she kept locked, or playing by himself in the living room. On one of these late-night romps, her Dresden Satan came crashing to the floor, losing a foot, an arm, and a horn.

"Where does it all go?" asked Gwen, referring to the pearls and other jewels he'd gobbled down in the course of the week. But it was merely a rhetorical question. She spent half her time now creeping round with paper towel in hand, searching out his indiscriminately placed droppings. What St. George ate went *in* diamonds and pearls, but there the uniqueness stopped.

At that moment, an Alka-Seltzer ad came on and St. George

snorted with excitement. Gwen's skirt caught on fire and she rushed to pour water on herself. On her way back to the sofa, she saw that the electric clock read close to ten. She wondered what she would do with St. George if Silas called.

But they watched News and Weather and Johnny Carson and the late movie, and Silas did not call, and she wondered what she would do without St. George. He was, after all, company. Absorbing herself in his erratic behavior — he was enormous fun to watch — she had less chance to sit listening to the hollow river sounds and the buzz of the electric clock and wonder whether or not she *did* exist.

On Monday morning, she went back to Woolworth's. "Forty-two, eighty-four, a hundred and twenty-six, that ought to hold him," she muttered, counting pearls. The salesgirl looked at her as though she were mad. Hurrying along the decorated streets to the tune of Salvation Army Santa Clauses ringing their bells, Gwen caught the Christmas spirit. She had someone to buy presents for! She bought a small tree, some shiny ornaments, a bunch of silly toys, and psychedelic wrapping paper.

That night, after they played an exhausting game of hide-and-seek followed by a game of ball made from a yard or so of scrunched-up aluminum foil, Gwen crept to the kitchen to make sure St. George was asleep. Sometimes, he slept curled on a dish towel folded on the sink counter; other times, when he was feeling secure, beneath the water. Tonight he was submerged. A straight line of peaceful bubbles ascended from his nostrils to the surface of the water. Gwen hurried back to her room, locked the door, and wrapped all his presents in the psychedelic paper. She hung the little tree with colored balls and tinsel. The latter, she put in the living room. She left his presents in her suitcase, fearing they'd never make it till Christmas otherwise.

By Christmas morning, St. George was the size of a beagle puppy. He went berserk over all his wonderful presents and accidentally set the tree on fire. He frolicked in the bucketfuls of water as Gwen doused the flames. For his dinner, she placed the final turquoises from her ring, the ones he hadn't got, atop his Yuletide dish of imitation pearls. She was a little dismayed at how quickly it all disappeared. If he kept growing, with an appetite to match, she would soon be bankrupt.

About seven o'clock in the evening, the telephone rang. St.

George scuttled in terror beneath the Queen Anne writing desk. He had never heard the sound before. Silas!

It was only Gwen's mother and father, calling to wish her a Merry Christmas. Gwen said yes, her work was going very well and, yes, she had made some friends. "I'm going out to a party later this evening," she lied. The dragon's yellow eyes danced at her from the gloom beneath the desk. Her mother sounded relieved. "There's no need to be so *ruthless* about things," she said. "Enjoy life. You're young."

"Yes, Mother."

After Gwen hung up, she played her one Beatles record for St. George — he loathed Bach — and gave him a bubble bath. He loved to duck beneath the suds and come up spouting bubbles which he would blow carefully into the air with his hot breath before shooting them down in flames. She dried him in a thick Turkish towel, for the sake of her floors, and carried him to the kitchen.

"You're getting too big for the sink, aren't you?" she said, worried. "Well, give it another night's try and we'll put you in the tub tomorrow." He wagged his tail delightedly and knocked over a canister of flour. Before Gwen could fetch the sponge mop, he had found a new pastime, rolling in the flour.

"Damn you, I'm tired!" she cried. "I've just bathed you and I haven't the energy to bathe you again." A powdered dragon rolled comic-tragic eyes at her. He wagged his tail, stirring up more flour, and made her sneeze. Sighing, Gwen picked up the white, wriggly bundle. Back to the bathtub they went. "No bubbles this time, my friend." He shimmied delightedly at her feet. She felt exhausted as she gave him a second bath. Afterward, she deposited him on her bed and went to mop the kitchen. When she returned, he was curled up at the foot of her bed, snoring gently.

"Oh, what the hell," she said, climbing beneath the sheet. "If you set us on fire, we'll ascend together in glorious smoke. Nobody will miss us." The dragon moaned in his sleep. The red rickrack along his back rose and fell. She closed her eyes and saw unwelcome visions of her next bank statement. St. George's food bill was growing along with him, by leaps and bounds. Her scholarship did not make allowances for keeping dragons in pearls — even Woolworth ones.

By New Year's Eve he was the size of a St. Bernard. The floors shook when he rollicked and romped. Gwen had sold three of her favorite art books to a secondhand bookstore and pawned her watch to feed him. Over the past week, a dark and desperate plan had gradually worked its way into her conscious mind. She was going to have to kill St. George. Aside from the fact she could not afford even one more round of imitation pearls, he was too risky to leave alone in the apartment while she attended classes. He seldom got through the day without setting a fire and as he grew bigger, so did the fires. She doubted if a zoo would take him. There was probably a state law against the harboring of mythical animals. Since Christmas, she had taken to leafing stealthily through the dragon books, collecting bits of information on their disposal, while St. George lay beside her, singeing the sofa with every other breath as he ogled the TV commercials. "In China," she read, "the emperor ordered his men to beat the drums in order to attract the Dragon King. When he came out of his cave, the men riddled him with arrows until the ocean became red with dragon blood. Some weeks later, however, the emperor died in a dream." In ancient Guatemala, two crafty brothers, Hunahpu and Xbalanque, visited a dragon's house and pretended to be dentists because the dragon had a terrible toothache. When he let them in, they pulled out all his teeth, put out his eyes, and slew him. Upon reading this, Gwen winced so violently she frightened St. George off the sofa. Madly, he raced about the room. With a flick of his tail, which was now several yards long, he scattered a stack of thesis note-cards like a flurry of snow. God, how cruel. She could never do it the Guatemalan way.

Once again, Mr. Grafton Elliot Smith (*op. cit.*, p. 135) came to her rescue. The most humane way of killing the creature, he explained, was to get him drunk on beer (the beer of Osiris, if possible) and clout him on the head with something made of iron. An alchemical connection was made between beer and iron and the dragon was snuffed out painlessly.

At sunset, on New Year's Eve, Gwen opened the first of four six-packs. She turned on the stereo and unsheathed a brand-new Beatles album, a sort of going-away present for St. George, though he would never know. "Come here, Georgie!" she called, trying to keep the sadness from her voice. He lumbered into the kitchen, thrusting his funny face expectantly up to hers. He came to her waist now. She hoped four six-packs would be enough, and she would have to have a little for herself, to get up courage.

"Try a little of this." She gave him half a canful in a plastic dish. Oh, God, what if he didn't like beer?

But he lapped it up and rolled his eyes for more.

She poured him a bowlful and a glass for herself. She had no such ugly courage of a Margaret of Antioch. They drank to side one of the Beatles' new record, then side two; then side one again, and after that it didn't matter what was playing. St. George grew gayer. He wanted to play hide-and-seek. But he was too big for most of his favorite hiding places. Gwen lurched about the apartment, pretending not to see three-fourths of his tail hanging from the linen closet.

"I wonder where St. George is!" she cried drunkenly. The tail wagged violently. There were tears in her eyes. He thudded gaily to the floor, bringing half the linen closet with him. "There you are! How 'bout another drink?"

St. George eagerly lapped up another bowlful while Gwen got down the steam iron and set it in an easy-to-reach spot on the kitchen table. She remembered how St. George, when he was smaller, had learned the knack of perching beside her book, on the table, and turning the pages for her with his tail, so that she could read and eat. She burst into a flood of maudlin tears. St. George looked up at her, his head cocked to one side. His eyes had gone rather crossed. Then he wobbled drunkenly into the living room, tried to go beneath her desk, bumped his head on the too-low underpass, and dropped to the floor with a snuffly snore.

Still weeping, Gwen went to get the steam iron, decided to go to the bathroom first, and passed out on the return trip.

She woke, chilled and weak, to hear a terrible retching coming from the bathroom. She hurried in and found St. George being violently ill. He hardly recognized her, he was choking and spluttering so. His talons scraped wildly at the tile floor. His scarlet rickrack trembled like tissue paper in a storm. He looked up at her, helplessly, very apologetic, and vomited again and again. Then he collapsed at the foot of the toilet, wrapped his barbed tail listlessly round its base, and passed out from sheer exhaustion.

She was sponging up the beery vomit, weeping incoherently — he had looked up at her so *trustingly* just before he'd passed out! — when the phone rang. She stumbled through the dark apartment and groped for the phone.

"Hello?"

"Silas here," came the laconic voice. "How've you been?"

"Silas! Where in God's name are you?"

"Home. You O.K.? You sound a little hysterical. Did you miss me?"

"Miss you! I almost went out of my mind! I thought I was never going to see you again! I was all alone, except for — oh, God, I'm too drunk to make sense."

"You alone now? I thought we might get in a little New Year's celebration."

"Oh, please, Silas, come over quick. Yes, I'm alone except for — look, there's someone desperately sick here, not someone, I mean, something — a poor helpless animal — you wouldn't believe me if I told you what —"

"I'll be there as soon as I can," Silas said.

Gwen went back to the bathroom and lay beside St. George, who was still out cold. "Help is coming," she crooned. "Silas is a big, capable guy. You'll feel better the minute he comes." She sponged his nostrils, his slack jaws, his mane, which had gone soft as overcooked spaghetti. She covered him with a blanket and dozed with her arms around him.

The doorbell rang. At last! Gwen ran to open it and threw herself at six-foot-three of reassuring bulk. Silas was suntanned and smiling puzzledly. After she had mauled him for a few moments, he said: "Where's the sick animal? Did you get yourself a cat?"

"Listen, Silas, let me explain before we go in. . . ." She listened to her own voice, pouring out details of St. George. Silas listened with no more expression in his face than usual. They were still standing just inside the doorway. Once he scratched his mop of dry blond hair. ". . . but now I realize I can't possibly kill him," she concluded. "I've gotten attached to him. I think I'd stand by him if he grew big enough to swallow the world. Silas, you have to help me save poor George." She grabbed his fingers and tugged him to her bathroom. "There. Look at him. Who could murder a helpless dragon. You should have seen him when he was littler. He was so cute. He was vomiting his heart out, just before you called. We drank almost four six-packs between us."

Silas stood in the doorway of the bathroom. He reached a hand inside his jacket and into the top of his shirt and gave his chest a thoughtful scratch.

"Poor little guy," he said. "What he needs is some fresh air. That's obvious."

"Oh, he's never been out. And he's much too big to carry."

"I can manage," said Silas. He stooped down and gently collected the creature in his arms.

"Watch out for his tail, it's hooked around the toilet bowl," Gwen warned.

"Oh, yes." Silas stood up, carrying St. George easily.

"Thank God you're a big man," Gwen breathed. "Where will you take him?"

"Down by the river. There's a good wind blowing. He'll be all right. You look pretty bad, though. Go to bed."

"Will you come back?"

"Of course I'll come back. As soon as this dragon gets his air."

Some time later, Gwen woke. The bedroom was dark. From the living room came the sound of TV, turned down low: noises of the nation celebrating the New Year. She heard someone opening a beer can, then the soft gurgle into the glass, then a pause and a deep male sigh. "Silas?" she called. A strange lassitude had attached itself to her; she couldn't move. She felt like an invalid who had been very, very ill.

"You slept," he said, sitting down beside her in the dark.

"What happened? What did you do with St. George?"

"Ah," he began, stroking the back of her neck with his big fingers. "You aren't going to like this. I took him down to the river and sat beside it — so he could get the breeze — and all of a sudden he woke up and jumped right into the river and went swimming away. I never saw anything swim so fast. Not even the river police could have caught him. Don't cry. Look: On the way back, I was thinking how I could tell you. And I decided that now he's much better off. He has the whole river to himself. If he keeps growing at the rate you said, he'll need the ocean, and that's available, too. What could you offer him here?"

"A bathtub," she sobbed. "And you're right. He was getting too big for that. But I'll miss him. He's all I had for two weeks. At least, this way, he can stay alive. Where did you go? You've been on a holiday in the sun and didn't even send me a card."

"No, I was working. I had to cover an international scientists' meeting in Miami. The married reporters don't like going away over Christmas. So I volunteered."

Gwen sat up in bed. "But you said you worked in a plant!"

"A newspaper plant."

"But you're not a factory worker, then."

"I never said I was," came the bland reply in the dark.

"But you let me *think* you were. You had hundreds of opportunities to correct me. You knew I thought —"

"I would much rather have gone on listening to you," he said, rubbing her neck some more.

"That feels good. Oh, yes, I'll bet you were enjoying my grand speeches, weren't you? Did you even miss me, in Miami?"

"Yes." The hand went on rubbing.

"Then why didn't you call me, or write, or something?"

"I wanted to worry you," came the noncommittal voice. How she wished she could see his face. From the TV came sounds of tipsy America howling "Auld Lang Syne" to the tune of paper horns. Somewhere a gong began ringing in the New Year.

Innocence

by Harold Brodkey

1. ORRA AT HARVARD

Orra Perkins was a senior. Her looks were like a force that struck you. Truly, people on first meeting her often involuntarily lifted their arms as if about to fend off the brightness of the apparition. She was a somewhat scrawny, tulip-like girl of middling height. To see her in sunlight was to see Marxism die. I'm not the only one who said that. It was because seeing someone in actuality who has such a high immediate worth meant you had to decide whether such personal distinction had a right to exist or if she belonged to the state and ought to be shadowed in, reduced in scale, made lesser, laughed at.

Also, it was the case that you had to be rich and famous to get your hands on her; she could not fail to be a trophy and the question was whether the trophy had to be awarded on economic and political grounds or whether chance could enter in.

I was a senior too, and ironic. I had no money. I was without lineage. It seemed to me Orra was proof that life was a terrifying phenomenon of surface immediacy. She made any idea I had of psychological normalcy or of justice absurd since normalcy was not as admirable or as desirable as Orra; or rather she was normalcy and everything else was a falling off, a falling below; and justice was inconceivable if she, or someone equivalent to her if there was an equivalent once you had seen her, would not sleep with you. I used to create general hilarity in my room by shouting her name at my friends and then breaking up into laughter, gasping out, "God, we're so small time." It was grim that she existed and I had not had her. One could still prefer a more ordinary girl but not for simple reasons.

A great many people avoided her, ran away from her. She was, in part, more knowing than the rest of us because the experiences offered her had been so extreme, and she had been so extreme in response — scenes in Harvard Square with an English marquess, slapping a son of a billionaire so hard he fell over backwards at a party in Lowell House, her saying then and subsequently, "I never sleep with anyone who has a fat ass." Extreme in the humiliations endured and meted out, in the crassness of the publicity, of her life defined as those adventures, extreme in the dangers survived or not entirely survived, the cheapness undergone so that she was on a kind of frightening eminence, an eminence of her experiences and of her being different from everyone else. She'd dealt in intrigues, major and minor, in the dramas of political families, in passions, deceptions, folly on a large, expensive scale, promises, violence, the genuine pain of defeat when defeat is to some extent the result of your qualities and not of your defects, and she knew the rottenness of victories that hadn't been final. She was crass and impaired by beauty. She was like a giant bird, she was as odd as an ostrich walking around the Yard, in her absurd gorgeousness, she was so different from us in kind, so capable of a different sort of progress through the yielding medium of the air, through the strange rooms of our minutes on this earth, through the gloomy circumstances of our lives in those years.

People said it was worth it to do this or that just in order to see her — seeing her offered some kind of encouragement, was some kind of testimony that life was interesting. But not many people cared as much about knowing her. Most people preferred to keep their distance. I don't know what her having made herself into what she was had done for her. She could have been ordinary if she'd wished.

She had unnoticeable hair, a far from arresting forehead, and extraordinary eyes, deep-set, longing, hopeful, angrily bored behind smooth, heavy lids that fluttered when she was interested and when she was not interested at all. She had a great desire not to trouble or be troubled by supernumeraries and strangers. She has a proud, too large nose that gives her a noble, stubborn dog's look. Her mouth has a disconcertingly lovely set to it — it is more immediately expressive than her eyes and it shows her implacability: it is the implacability of her knowledge of life in her. People always stared at her. Some giggled nervously. *Do you like me, Orra? Do you like me at all?* They stared at the great hands of the Aztec priest opening them to feelings and to awe, exposing their hearts, the dread cautiousness of their lives. They stared at the incredible symmetries of her sometimes anguishedly passionate face, the erratic pain for her in being beautiful that showed on it, the occasional plunging gaiety she felt because she was beautiful. I like beautiful people. The symmetries of her face were often thwarted by her attempts at expressiveness — beauty was a stone she struggled free of. A ludicrous beauty. A cruel clown of a girl. Sometimes her face was absolutely impassive as if masked in dullness and she was trying to move among us incognito. I was aware that each of her downfalls made her more possible for me. I never doubted that she was privately a pedestrian shitting-peeing person. Whenever I had a chance to observe her for any length of time, in a classroom for instance, I would think, *I understand her.* Whenever I approached her, she responded up to a point and then even as I stood talking to her I would fade as a personage, as a sexual presence, as someone present and important to her into greater and greater invisibility. That was when she was a freshman, a sophomore, and a junior. When we were seniors, by then I'd learned how to avoid being invisible even to Orra. Orra was, I realized, hardly more than a terrific college girl, much vaunted, no more than that yet. But my god, my god, in one's eyes, in one's thoughts, she strode like a *Nike,* she entered like a blast of light, the thought of her was as vast as a desert. Sometimes in an early winter twilight in the Yard, I would see her in her coat, unbuttoned even in cold weather as if she burned slightly always, see her move clumsily along a walk looking like a scrawny field hockey player, a great athlete of a girl half-stumbling, uncoordinated off the playing field, yet with reserves of strength, do you know? and her face, as she walked along, might twitch like a dog's when the dog is asleep, twitching with whatever dialogue or adventure or daydream she was having in her head. Or she might in the early darkness stride along, cold-faced, haughty, angry, all the worst refusals one would ever receive bound up in one ridiculously beautiful girl. One always said, *I wonder what will become of her.* Her ignoring me marked me as a sexual nonentity. She was proof of a level of sexual adventure I had not yet with my best efforts reached: that level existed because Orra existed.

What is it worth to be in love in this way?

2. ORRA WITH ME

I distrust summaries, any kind of gliding through time, any too great a claim that one is in control of what one recounts; I think someone who claims to understand but who is obviously calm, someone who claims to write with emotion recollected in tranquillity, is a fool and a liar. To understand is to tremble. To recollect is to reenter and be riven. An acrobat after spinning through the air in a mockery of flight stands erect on his perch and mockingly takes his bow as if what he is being applauded for was easy for him and cost him nothing, although meanwhile he is covered with sweat and his smile is edged with a relief chilling to think about; he is indulging in a show business style; he is pretending to be superhuman. I am bored with that and with where it has brought us. I admire the authority of being on one's knees in front of the event.

In the last spring of our being undergraduates, I finally got her. We had agreed to meet for dinner in my room, to get a little drunk cheaply before going out to dinner. I left the door unlatched; and I lay naked on my bed under a sheet. When she knocked on the door, I said, "Come in," and she did. She began to chatter right away, to complain that I was still in bed; she seemed to think I'd been taking a nap and had forgotten to wake up in time to get ready for her arrival. I said, "I'm naked, Orra, under this sheet. I've been waiting for you. I haven't been asleep."

Her face went empty. She said, "Damn you — why couldn't you wait?" But even while she was saying that, she was taking off her blouse.

I was amazed that she was so docile; and then I saw that it was maybe partly that she didn't want to risk saying no to me — she didn't want me to be hurt and difficult, she didn't want me to explode; she had a kind of hope of making me happy so that I'd then appreciate her and be happy with her and let her know me: I'm putting it badly. But her not being able to say no protected me from having so great a fear of sexual failure that I would not have been able to be worried about her pleasure, or to be concerned about her in bed. She was very amateur-ish and uninformed in bed, which touched me. It was really sort of poor sex; she didn't come or even feel much that I could see. After-wards, lying beside her, I thought of her eight or ten or fifteen lovers being afraid of her, afraid to tell her anything about sex in case they might be wrong. I had an image of them protecting their own egos, holding their arms around their egos and not letting her near them. It seemed a kindness embedded in the event that she was, in quite an obvious way, with a little critical interpretation, a virgin. And im-paired, or crippled by having been beautiful, just as I'd thought. I said to myself that it was a matter of course that I might be deluding myself. But what I did for the rest of that night — we stayed up all night; we talked, we quarreled for a while, we confessed various things, we argued about sex, we fucked again (the second one was a little better) — I treated her with the justice with which I'd treat a boy my age, a young man, and with a rather exact or measured patience and tolerance, as if she was a paraplegic and had spent her life in a wheelchair and was tired of sentiment. I showed her no sentiment at all. I figured she'd been asphyxiated by the sentiments and sentimen-tality of people impressed by her looks. She was beautiful and fright-ened and empty and shy and alone and wounded and invulnerable (like a cripple: what more can you do to a cripple?). She was Caesar and ruler of the known world and not Caesar and no one as well.

It was a fairly complicated, partly witty thing to do. It meant I could not respond to her beauty but had to ignore it. She was a curious sort of girl; she had a great deal of isolation in her, isolation as a woman. It meant that when she said something on the order of "You're very defensive," I had to be a debater, her equal, take her seriously, and say, "How do you mean that?" and then talk about it, and alternately deliver a blow ("You can't judge defensiveness, you have the silly irresponsibility of women, the silly disconnectedness: I *have* to be defensive.") and defer to her: "You have a point: you think very clearly. All right, I'll adopt that as a premise." Of course, much of what we said was incoherent and nonsensical on examination but we worked out in conversation what we meant or thought we meant. I didn't react to her in any emotional way. She wasn't really a girl, not really quite human: how could she be? She was a position, a specific glory, a trophy, our local upper-middle-class pseudo Cleopatra. Or not pseudo. I could revel in my luck or be unself-consciously vain. I could not strut horizontally or loll as if on clouds, a demi-god with a goddess, although it was clear we were deeply fortunate, in spite of everything, the poor sex, the difference in attitude which were all we seemed to share, the tensions and the blundering. If I enjoyed her more than she enjoyed me, if I lost consciousness of her even for a moment, she would be closed into her isolation again. I couldn't love her and have her too. I could love her and have her if I didn't show love or the symptoms of having had her. It was like lying in a very lordly way, opening her to the possibility of feeling by making her comfortable inside the calm lies of my behavior, my inscribing the minutes with false messages. It was like meeting a requirement in Greek myth, like not looking back at Eurydice. The night crept on, swept on, late minutes, powdered with darkness, in the middle of a sleeping city, spring crawling like a plague of green snakes, bits of warmth in the air, at four A.M. smells of leaves when the stink of automobiles died down. Dawn came, so pink, so pastel, so silly: we were talking about the possibility of innate grammatical structures; I said it was an unlikely notion, that Jews really were God-haunted (the idea had been broached by a Jew), and the great difficulty was to invent a just God, that if God appeared at a moment of time or relied on prophets, there had to be degrees in the possibility of knowing him so that he was by definition unjust; the only just God would be one who consisted of what had always been known by everyone; and that you could always identify a basically Messianic, a hugely religious, fraudulent thinker by how much he tried to anchor his doctrine to having always been true, to be innate even in savage man; whereas an honest thinker, a non-liar, was caught in the grip of the truth of process and change and the profound absence of justice except as an invention, an attempt by the will to live with someone, or with many others without consuming them. At that moment Orra said, "I think we're falling in love."

I figured I had kept her from being too depressed after fucking — it's hard for a girl with any force in her and any brains to accept the whole thing of fucking, of being fucked without trying to turn it on its end, so that she does some fucking, or some fucking up; I mean the mere power of arousing the man so he wants to fuck isn't enough: she wants him to be willing to die in order to fuck. There's a kind of strain or intensity women are bred for, as beasts, for childbearing when childbearing might kill them, and childrearing when the child might die at any moment: it's in women to live under that danger, with that risk, that close to tragedy, with that constant taut or casual courage. They need death and nobility near. To be fucked when there's no drama inherent in it, when you're not going to rise to a level of nobility and courage forever denied the male, is to be cut off from what is inherently female, bestially speaking. I wanted to be halfway decent company for her. I don't know that it was natural to me. I am psychologically, profoundly, a transient. A form of trash. I am incapable of any continuing loyalty and silence; I am an informer. But I did all right with her. It was dawn, as I said. We stood naked by the window silently watching the light change. Finally she said, "Are you hungry? Do you want breakfast?"

"Sure. Let's get dressed and go —"

She cut me off; she said with a funny kind of firmness, "No! Let me go and get us something to eat."

"Orra, don't wait on me. Why are you doing this? Don't be like this."

But she was in a terrible hurry to be in love. After those few hours, after that short a time.

She said, "I'm not as smart as you, Wiley. Let me wait on you. Then things will be even."

"Things are even, Orra."

"No. I'm boring and stale. You just think I'm not because you're in love with me. Let me go."

I blinked. After a while, I said, "All right."

She dressed and went out and came back. While we ate, she was silent; I said things but she had no comment to make; she ate very little; she folded her hands and smiled mildly like some nineteenth-century portrait of a handsome young mother. Every time I looked at her, when she saw I was looking at her, she changed the expression on her face to one of absolute and undeviating welcome to me and to anything I might say.

So, it had begun.

3. ORRA

She hadn't come. She said she had never come with anyone at any time. She said it didn't matter.

After our first time, she complained. "You went twitch, twitch, twitch — just like a grasshopper." So she had wanted to have more pleasure than she'd had. But after the second fuck and after the dawn, she never complained again — unless I tried to make her come, and then she complained of that. She showed during sex no dislike for any of my sexual mannerisms or for the rhythms and postures I fell into when I fucked. But I was not pleased or satisfied; it bothered me that she didn't come. I was not pleased or satisfied on my own account either. I thought the reason for that was she attracted me more than she could satisfy me, maybe more than fucking could ever satisfy me, that the more you cared, the more undertow there was, so that the sexual thing drowned — I mean the sharpest sensations, and yet the dullest, are when you masturbate — but when you're vilely attached to somebody, there are noises, distractions that drown out the sensations of fucking. For a long time, her wanting to fuck, her getting undressed, and the soft horizontal bobble of her breasts as she lay there, and the soft wavering, the kind of sinewlessness of her legs and lower body with which she more or less showed me she was ready, that was more moving, was more immensely important to me than any mere ejaculation later, any putt-putt-putt in her darkness, any hurling of future generations into the clenched universe, the strict mitten inside her: I clung to her and grunted and anchored myself to the most temporary imaginable relief of the desire I felt for her; I would be hungry again and anxious to fuck again in another twenty minutes; it was pitiable, this sexual disarray. It seemed to me that in the vast spaces of the excitement of being welcomed by each other, we could only sightlessly and at best half-organize our bodies. But so what? We would probably die in these underground caverns; a part of our lives would die; a certain innocence and hope would never survive this: we were too open, too clumsy, and we were the wrong people: so what did a fuck matter? I didn't mind if the sex was always a little rasping, something of a failure, if it was just preparation for more sex in half an hour, if coming was just more foreplay. If this was all that was in store for us, fine. But I thought she was getting gypped in that she felt so much about me, she was dependent, and she was generous, and she didn't come when we fucked.

She said she had never come, not once in her life, and that she didn't need to. And that I mustn't think about whether she came or not. "I'm a sexual tigress," she explained, "and I like to screw but I'm too sexual to come: I haven't that kind of daintiness. I'm not selfish *that* way."

I could see that she had prowled around in a sense and searched out men and asked them to be lovers as she had me rather than wait for them or plot to capture their attention in some subtle way; and in bed she was sexually eager and a bit more forward and less afraid than most girls; but only in an upper-middle-class frame of reference was she *a sexual tigress.*

It seemed to me — my whole self was focused on this — that her not coming said something about what we had, that her not coming was an undeniable fact, a measure of the limits of what we had. I did not think we should think we were great lovers when we weren't.

Orra said we were, that I had no idea how lousy the sex was other people had. I told her that hadn't been my experience. We were, it seemed to me, two twenty-one-year-olds, overeducated, irrevocably shy beneath our glaze of sexual determination and of sexual appetite, and psychologically somewhat slashed up and only capable of being partly useful to each other. We weren't the king and queen of Cock-andcuntdom yet.

Orra said coming was a minor part of sex for a woman and was a demeaning measure of sexuality. She said it was imposed as a measure by people who knew nothing about sex and judged women childishly.

It seemed to me she was turning a factual thing, coming, into a public relations thing. But girls were under fearful public pressures in these matters.

When she spoke about them, these matters, she had a little, superior inpuckered look, a don't-make-me-make-mincemeat-of-you-in-argument look — I thought of it as her Orra-as-Orra look, Orra alone, Orra-without-Wiley, without me, Orra isolated and depressed, a terrific girl, an Orra who hated cowing men.

She referred to novels, to novels by women writers, to specific scenes and remarks about sex and coming for women, but I'd read some of those books, out of curiosity, and none of them were litera-ture, and the heroines in them invariably were innocent in every relation; but very strong and very knowing and with terrifically good judgment; and the men they loved were described in such a way they appeared to be examples of the woman's sexual reach, or of her intellectual value, rather than sexual companions or sexual objects; the women had sex generously with men who apparently bored them physically; I had thought the books and their writers and characters sexually naïve.

Very few women, it seemed to me, had much grasp of physical reality. Still, very strange things were often true, and a man's notion of orgasm was necessarily specialized.

When I did anything in bed to excite her with an eye to making her come, she asked me not to, and that irritated the hell out of me. But no matter what she said, it must be bad for her after six years of fucking around not to get to a climax. It had to be that it was a run on her neural patience. How strong could she be?

I thought about how women coming were at such a pitch of uncontrol they might prefer a dumb, careless lover, someone very unlike me: I had often played at being a strong, silent dunce. Some girls became fawning and doglike after they came, even toward dunces. Others jumped up and became immediately tough, proud of themselves as if the coming was *all* to their credit, and I ought to be flattered. God, it was a peculiar world. Brainy girls tended to control their comes, doling out one to a fuck, just like a man; and often they would try to keep that one under control, they would limit it to a single nozzle-contracted squirt of excitement. Even that sometimes racked and emptied them and made them curiously weak and brittle and embarrassed and delicate and lazy. Or they would act bold and say, "God, I needed that."

I wondered how Orra would look, in what way she would do it, a girl like that going off, how she'd hold herself, her eyes, how she'd act toward me when it was over.

To get her to talk about sex at all, I argued that analyzing something destroyed it, of course, but leaves rotted on the ground and prepared the way for what would grow next. So she talked.

She said I was wrong in what I told her I saw and that there was no difference in her between mental and physical excitement, that it wasn't true her mind was excited quickly, and her body slowly, if at all. I couldn't be certain I was right, but when I referred to a moment when there had seemed to be deep physical feeling in her, she sometimes agreed that had been a good moment in her terms; but sometimes she said, no, it had only been a little irritating then, like a peculiarly unpleasant tickle. In spite of her liking my mind, she gave me no authority for what I knew — I mean when it turned out I was right. She kept the authority for her reactions in her own hands. Her self-abnegation was her own doing. I liked that: some people just give you themselves, and it is too much to keep in your hands: your abilities aren't good enough. I decided to stick with what I observed and to think her somewhat mistaken and not to talk to her about sex any more.

I watched her in bed; her body was doubting, grudging, tardy, intolerant — and intolerably hungry — I thought. In her pride and self-consciousness and ignorance she hated all that in herself. She preferred to think of herself as quick, to have pleasure as she willed rather than as she actually had it, to have it on her own volition, to her own prescription, and almost out of politeness, so it seemed to me, to give herself to me, to give me pleasure, to ignore herself, to be a nice girl because she was in love. She insisted on that but that was too sentimental and she also insisted she was, she persuaded herself, she passed herself off as dashing.

In a way, sexually, she was a compulsive liar.

I set myself to remove every iota of misconception I had about Orra in bed, any romanticism, any pleasurable hope. It seemed to me what had happened to her with other boys was that she was distrustful to start with and they had overrated her, and they'd been overwrought and off-balance and uneasy about her judgment of them, and they'd taken their pleasure and run.

And then she had in her determination to have sex become more and more of a sexual fool. (I was all kinds of fool: I didn't mind her being a sexual fool.) The first time I'd gone to bed with her, she'd screamed and thrown herself around, a good two or three feet to one side or another, as she thought a sexual tigress would, I supposed. I'd argued with her afterwards that no one was that excited especially without coming; she said she had come, sort of. She said she was too sexual for most men. She said her reactions weren't fake but represented a real sexuality, a real truth. That proud, stubborn, stupid girl.

But I told her that if she and a man were in sexual congress, and she heaved herself around and threw herself a large number of inches to either the left or the right or even straight up, the man was going to be startled; and if there was no regular pattern or predictability, it was easy to lose an erection; that if she threw herself to the side, there was a good chance she would interrupt the congress entirely unless the man was very quick and scrambled after her, and scrambling after her was not likely to be sexual for him: it would be more like playing tag. The man would have to fuck while in a state of siege; not knowing what she'd do next, he'd fuck and hurry to get it over and to get out.

Orra had said on that first occasion, "That sounds reasonable. No one ever explained that to me before, no one ever made it clear. I'll try it your way for a while."

After that, she had been mostly shy and honest, and honestly lecherous in bed but helpless to excite herself or to do more to me than she did just by being there and welcoming me. As if her hands were webbed and her mind was glued, as if I didn't deserve more, or as if she was such a novice and so shy she could not begin to do anything *sexual*. I did not understand: I'd always found that anyone who *wanted* to give pleasure, could: it didn't take skill, just the desire to please and a kind of, I-don't-know, a sightless ability to feel one's way to some extent in the lightless maze of pleasure. But upper-middle-class girls might be more fearful of tying men to them by bands of excessive pleasure; such girls were careful and shy.

I set myself for her being rude and difficult although she hadn't been rude and difficult to me for a long time but those traits were in her like a shadow giving her the dimensionality that made her valuable to me, that gave point to her kindness toward me. She had the sloppiest and most uncertain and silliest and yet bravest and most generous ego of anyone I'd ever known; and her manners were the most stupid imaginable alternation between the distinguished, the sensitive, the intelligent, with a rueful, firm, almost snotty delicacy and kindness and protectiveness toward you, and the really selfish and bruising. The important thing was to prevent her from responding falsely, as if in a movie, or in some imitation of the movies she'd seen and the books she'd read — she had a curious faith in movies and in books; she admired anything that made her feel and that did not require responsibility from her because then she produced happiness like silk for herself and others. She liked really obscure philosophers, like Hegel, where she could admire the thought but where the thought didn't demand anything from her. Still, she was a realist, and she would probably learn what I knew and would surpass me. She had great possibilities. But she was also merely a good-looking, pseudo-rich girl, a paranoid, a Perkins. On the other hand she was a fairly marvelous girl a lot of the time, brave, eye-shattering, who could split my heart open with one slightly shaky approving-of-me brainy romantic heroine's smile. The romantic splendor of her face. So far in her life she had disappointed everyone. I had to keep all this in mind, I figured. She was fantastically alive and eerily dead at the same time. I wanted for my various reasons to raise her from the dead.

4. Orra: The Same World, a Different Time Scale

One afternoon, things went well for us. We went for a walk, the air was plangent, there was the amazed and polite pleasure we had some-times merely at being together. Orra adjusted her pace now and then to mine; and I kept mine adjusted to her most of the time. When we looked at each other, there would be small soft puffs of feeling as of toy explosions or sparrows bathing in the dust. Her willed softness, her inner seriousness or earnestness, her strength, her beauty muted and careful now in her anxiety not to lose me yet, made the pleasure of being with her noble, contrapuntal, and difficult in that one had to live up to it and understand it and protect it, against my clumsiness and Orra's falsity, kind as that falsity was; or the day would become simply an exploitation of a strong girl who would see through that sooner or later and avenge it. But things went well; and inside that careless and careful goodness, we went home; we screwed; I came — to get my excitement out of the way; she didn't know I was doing that; she was stupendously polite; taut; and very admiring. "How pretty you are," she said. Her eyes were blurred with half-tears. I'd screwed without any fripperies, coolly, in order to leave in us a large residue of sexual restlessness but with the burr of immediate physical restlessness in me removed: I still wanted her; I always wanted Orra; and the coming had been dull; but my body was not very assertive, was more like a glove for my mind, for my will, for my love for her, for my wanting to make her feel more.

She was slightly tearful, as I said, and gentle, and she held me in her arms after I came, and I said something like, "Don't relax. I want to come again," and she partly laughed, partly sighed, and was flattered, and said, "Again? That's nice." We had a terrific closeness, almost like a man and a secretary — I was free and powerful, and she was devoted: there was little chance Orra would ever be a secretary: she'd been offered executive jobs already for when she finished college, but to play at being a secretary who had no life of her own was a romantic thing for Orra. I felt some apprehension, as before a game of tennis that I wanted to win, or as before stealing something off a counter in a store: there was a dragging enervation, a fear and silence, and there was a lifting, a preparation, a willed and then unwilled, self-contained fixity of purpose; it was a settled thing; it would happen.

After about ten minutes or so, perhaps it was twenty, I moved in her: I should say that while I'd rested, I'd stayed in her (and she'd held on to me). As I'd expected — and with satisfaction and pride that everything was working, my endowments were cooperating — I felt my prick come up; it came up at once with comic promptness but it was sore — Jesus, was it sore. It, its head, ached like hell, with a dry, burning, reddish pain.

The pain made me chary and prevented me from being excited except in an abstract way; my mind was clear; I was idly smiling as I began, moving very slowly, just barely moving, sort of pressing on her inside her, moving around, lollygagging around, feeling out the reaches in there, arranging the space inside her, as if to put the inner soft-oiled shadows in her in order; or like stretching out your hand in the dark and pressing a curve of a blanket into familiarity or to locate yourself when you're half-asleep, when your eyes are closed. In fact, I did close my eyes and listened carefully to her breathing, concentrating on her but trying not to let her see I was doing that because it would make her self-conscious.

Her reaction was so minimal that I lost faith in fucking for getting her started, and I thought I'd better go down on her; I pulled out of her, which wasn't too smart, but I wasn't thinking all that consequentially; she'd told me on other occasions she didn't like "all that foreign la-di-dah," that it didn't excite her, but I'd always thought it was only that she was ashamed of not coming and that made being gone down on hard for her. I started in on it; she protested; and I pooh-poohed her objections and did it anyway; I was raw with nerves, with stifled amusement because of the lying and the tension, so much of it. I remarked to her that I was going down on her for my own pleasure; I was jolted by touching her with my tongue there when I was so raw-nerved but I hid that. It seemed to me physical unhappiness and readiness were apparent in her skin — my lips and tongue carried the currents of a jagged unhappiness and readiness in her into me; echoes of her stiffness and dissatisfaction sounded in my mouth, my head, my feet, my entire tired body was a stethoscope. I was entirely a stethoscope; I listened to her with my *bones;* the glimmers of excitement in her traveled to my *spine;* I felt her grinding sexual haltedness, like a car's broken starter motor grinding away in her, in my *stomach,* in my *knees.* Every part of me listened to her; every goddamned twinge of muscular contraction she had that I noticed or that she should have had because I was licking her clitoris and she didn't have, every testimony of excitement or of no-excitement in her, I listened for so hard it was amazing it didn't drive her out of bed with self-consciousness; but she probably couldn't tell what I was doing, since I was out of her line of sight, was down in the shadows, in the basement of her field of vision, in the basement with her sexual feelings where they lay, strewn about.

When she said, "No . . . No, Wiley . . . Please don't. No . . ." and wiggled, although it wasn't the usual pointless protest that some girls might make — it was real, she wanted me to stop — I didn't listen because I could feel she responded to my tongue more than she had to the fucking a moment before. I could feel beads sliding and whispering and being strung together rustlingly in her; the disorder, the scattered or strewn sexual bits, to a very small extent, were being put in order. She shuddered. With discomfort. She produced, was subjected to, her erratic responses. And she made odd, small cries, protests mostly, uttered little exclamations that mysteriously were protests although they were not protests too, cries that somehow suggested the ground of protest kept changing for her.

I tried to string a number of those cries together, to cause them to occur in a mounting sequence. It was a peculiar attempt: it seemed we moved, I moved with her, on dark water, between two lines of buoys, dark on one side, there was nothingness there, and on the other, lights, red and green, the lights of the body advancing on sexual heat, the signs of it anyway, nipples like scored pebbles, legs lightly thrashing, little *ohs;* nothing important, a body thing; you go on: you proceed.

When we strayed too far, there was nothingness, or only a distant flicker, only the faintest guidance. Sometimes we were surrounded by the lights of her responses, widely spaced, bobbing unevenly, on some darkness, some ignorance we both had, Orra and I, of what were the responses of her body. To the physical things I did and to the atmosphere of the way I did them, to the authority, the argument I made that this was sexual for her, that the way I touched her and concentrated on her, on the partly dream-laden dark water or underwater thing, she responded; she rested on that, rolled heavily on that. Everything I did was speech, was hieroglyphics, pictures on her nerves; it was what masculine authority was for, was what bravery and a firm manner and musculature were supposed to indicate that a man could bring to bed. Or skill at dancing; or musicianliness; or a sad knowingness. Licking her, holding her belly, stroking her belly pretty much with unthought-out movements — sometimes just moving my fingers closer together and spreading them again to show my pleasure, to show how rewarded I felt, not touching her breasts or doing anything so intensely that it would make her suspect me of being out to make her come — I did those things but it seemed like I left her alone and was private with my own pleasures. She felt unobserved with her sensations, she had them without responsibility, she clutched at them as something round and slippery in the water, and she would fall off them, occasionally gasping at the loss of her balance, the loss of her self-possession too.

I'd flick, idly almost, at her little spaghetti-ending with my tongue, then twice more idly, then three or four or five times in sequence, then settle down to rub it or bounce it between lip and tongue in a steadily more earnest way until my head, my consciousness, my lips and tongue were buried in the dark of an ascending and concentrated rhythm, in the way a stoned dancer lets a movement catch him and wrap him around and become all of him, become his voyage and not a collection of repetitions at all.

Then some boring stringy thing, a sinew at the base of my tongue, would begin to ache, and I'd break off that movement, and sleepily lick her, or if the tongue was too uncomfortable, I'd worry her clit, I'd nuzzle it with my pursed lips until the muscles that held my lips pursed grew tired in their turn; and I'd go back and flick at her tiny clitoris with my tongue, and go on as before, until the darkness came; she sensed the darkness, the privacy for her, and she seemed like someone in a hallway, unobserved, moving her arms, letting her mind stroke itself, taking a step in that dark.

But whatever she felt was brief and halting; and when she seemed to halt or to be dead or jagged, I authoritatively, gesturally accepted that as part of what was pleasurable to me and did not let it stand as hint or foretaste of failure; I produced sighs of pleasure, even gasps, not all of them false, warm nuzzlings, and caresses that indicated I was rewarded — I produced rewarded strokings; I made elements of sexual pleasure out of moments that were unsexual and that could be taken as the collapse of sexuality.

And she couldn't contradict me because she thought I was working on my own coming, and she loved me and meant to be cooperative.

What I did took nerve because it gave her a tremendous ultimate power to laugh at me, although what the courtship up until now had been for was to show that she was not an enemy, that she could control the hysteria of fear or jealousy in her or the cold judgments in her of me that would lead her to say or do things that would make me hate or fear her; what was at stake included the risk that I would look foolish in my own eyes — and might then attack her for failing to come — and then she would be unable to resist the inward conviction I was a fool. Any attempted act confers vulnerability on you but an act devoted to her pleasure represented doubled vulnerability since only she could judge it; and I was safe only if I was immune or insensitive to her; but if I was immune or insensitive I could not hope to help her come; by making myself vulnerable to her, I was in a way being a sissy or a creep because Orra wasn't organized or trained or prepared to accept responsibility for how I felt about myself: she was a woman who wanted to be left alone; she was paranoid about the inroads on her life men in their egos tried to make: there was dangerous masochism, dangerous hubris, dangerous hopefulness, and a form of love in my doing what I did: I nuzzled nakedly at the crotch of the sexual tigress; any weakness in her ego or her judgment and she would lash out at *me*; and the line was very frail between what I was doing as love and as intrusion, exploitation, and stupid boastfulness. There was no way for me even to begin to imagine the mental pain — or the physical pain — for her if I should fail, and, then to add to that, if I should withdraw from her emotionally too, because of my failure and hers and our pain.

Or merely because the failure might make me so uncomfortable I couldn't go on unless she nursed my ego, and she couldn't nurse my ego, she didn't know how to do it, and probably was inhibited about doing it.

Sometimes my hands, my fingers, not just the tips, but all of their inside surface and the palms, held her thighs, or cupped her little belly, or my fingers moved around the lips, the labia or whatever, or even poked a little into her, or with the nails or tips lightly nudged her clitoris, always within a fictional frame of my absolute sexual pleasure, of my admiration for this sex, of there being no danger in it for us. No tongues or brains handy to speak unkindly, I meant. My God, I felt exposed and noble. This was a great effort to make for her.

Perhaps that only indicates the extent of my selfishness. I didn't mind being feminized except for the feeling that Orra would not ever understand what I was doing but would ascribe it to the power of my or our sexuality. I minded being this self-conscious and so conscious of her; I was separated from my own sexuality, from any real sexuality; a poor sexual experience, even one based on love, would diminish the ease of my virility with her at least for a while; and she wouldn't understand. Maybe she would become much subtler and shrewder sexually and know how to handle me but that wasn't likely. And if I apologized or complained or explained in that problematic future why I was sexually a little slow or reluctant with her, she would then blame my having tried to give her orgasm, she would insist I must not be bored again, so I would in that problematic future, if I wanted her to come, have to lie and say I was having more excitement than I felt, and that too might diminish my pleasure. I would be deprived even of the chance for honesty: I would be further feminized in that regard. I thought all this while I went down on her. I didn't put it in words but thought in great misty blocks of something known or sensed. I felt an inner weariness I kept working in spite of. This ignoring myself gave me an odd, starved feeling, a mixture of agony and helplessness. I didn't want to feel like that. I suddenly wondered why in the Theory of Relativity the speed of light is given as a constant: was that more Jewish absolutism? Surely in a universe as changeable and as odd as this one, the speed of light, considering the variety of experiences, must vary; there must be a place where one could see a beam of light struggle to move. I felt silly and selfish; it couldn't be avoided that I felt like that — I mean it couldn't be avoided by *me*.

Whatever she did when I licked her, if she moved at all, if a muscle twitched in her thigh, a muscle twitched in mine, my body imitated hers as if to measure what she felt or perhaps for no reason but only because the sympathy was so intense. The same things happened to each of us but in amazingly different contexts as if we stood at opposite ends of the room and reached out to touch each other and to receive identical messages which then diverged as they entered two such widely separated sensibilities and two such divergent and incomplete ecstasies. The movie we watched was of her discovering how her sexual responses worked: we were seated far apart. My tongue pushed at her erasure, her wronged and heretofore hardly existent sexual powers. I stirred her with varieties of kisses far from her face. A strange river moved slowly, bearing us along, reeds hid the banks, willows braided and unbraided themselves, moaned and whispered, raveled and faintly clicked. Orra groaned, sighed, shuddered, shuddered harshly or liquidly; sometimes she jumped when I changed the pressure or posture of my hands on her or when I rested for a second and then resumed. Her body jumped and contracted interestingly but not at any length or in any pattern that I could understand. My mind grew tired. There is a limit to invention, to mine anyway: I saw myself (stupidly) as a Roman trireme, my tongue as the prow, *bronze,* pushing at her; she was the Mediterranean. Tiers of slaves, my god, the helplessness of them, pulled oars, long stalks that metaphorically and rhythmically bloomed with flowing clusters of short-lived lilies at the water's surface. The pompous and out-of-proportion boat, all of me hunched over Orra's small sea — not actually hunched: what I was, was lying flat, the foot of the bed was at my waist or near there, my legs were out, my feet were propped distantly on the floor, all of me was concentrated on the soft, shivery, furry delicacies of Orra's twat, the pompous boat advanced lickingly, leaving a trickling, gurgling wake of half-response, the ebbing of my will and activity into that fluster subsiding into the dark water of this girl's passivity, taut storminess, and self-ignorance.

The whitish bubbling, the splash of her discontinuous physical response: those waves, ah, that wake rose, curled outward, bubbled, and fell. Rose, curled outward, bubbled, and fell. The white fell of a naiad. In the vast spreading darkness and silence of the sea. There was nothing but that wake. The darkness of my senses when the rhythm absorbed me (so that I vanished from my awareness, so that I was blotted up and was a stain, a squid hidden, stroking Orra) made it twilight or night for me; and my listening for her pleasure, for our track on that markless ocean, gave me the sense that where we were was in a lit-up, great, ill-defined oval of night air and sea and opalescent fog, rainbowed where the lights from the portholes of an immense ship were altered prismatically by droplets of mist — as in some 1930's movie, as in some dream. Often I was out of breath; I saw spots, colors, ocean depths. And her protests, her doubts! My God, her doubts! Her *No don't, Wiley's* and her *I don't want to do this's* and her *Wiley, don't's* and *Wiley, I can't come — don't do this — I don't like this's.* Mostly I ignored her. Sometimes I silenced her by leaning my cheek on her belly and watching my hand stroke her belly and saying to her in a sex-thickened voice, "Orra, I like this — this is for me."

Then I went down on her again with unexpectedly vivid, real pleasure, as if merely thinking about my own pleasure excited and refreshed me, and there was yet more pleasure, when she — reassured or strengthened by my putative selfishness, by the conviction that this was all for me, that nothing was expected of her — cried out. Then a second later she *grunted.* Her whole body rippled. Jesus, I loved it when she reacted to me. It was like causing an entire continent to convulse, Asia, South America. I felt huge and tireless.

In her excitement, she threw herself into the air; but my hands happened to be on her belly; and I fastened her down, I held that part of her comparatively still with her twat fastened to my mouth, and I licked her while she was in mid-heave; and she yelled; I kept my mouth there as if I were drinking from her; I stayed like that until her upper body fell back on the bed and bounced, she made the whole bed bounce; then my head bounced away from her; but I still held her down with my hands; and I fastened myself, my mouth, on her twat again; and she yelled in a deep voice, "*Wiley, what are you doing!*"

Her voice was deep, as if her impulses at that moment were masculine, not out of neurosis but in generosity, in an attempt to improve on the sickliness she accused women of; she wanted to meet me halfway, to share; to share my masculinity: she thought men were beautiful: she cried out, "*I don't want you to do things to me! I want you to have a good fuck!*"

Her voice was deep and despairing, maybe with the despair that goes with surges of sexuality, but then maybe she thought I would make her pay for this. I said, "Orra, I like this stuff, this stuff is what gets me excited." She resisted, just barely, for some infinitesimal fragment of a second, and then her body began to vibrate; it twittered as if in it were the strings of a musical instrument set jangling; she said foolishly — but sweetly — "Wiley, I'm embarrassed, Wiley, this embarrasses *me* . . . Please stop . . . No . . . No . . . No . . . Oh . . . Oh . . . Oh . . . I'm very sexual, I'm too sexual to have orgasms, Wiley, stop, please . . . Oh . . . Oh . . . Oh . . ." And then a deeper shudder ran through her; she gasped; then there was a silence; then she gasped again; she cried out in an extraordinary voice, "*I FEEL SOME-THING!*" The hair stood up on the back of my neck; I couldn't stop; I hurried on; I heard a dim moaning come from her. What had she felt before? I licked hurriedly. How unpleasant for her, how unreal and twitchy had the feelings been that I'd given her? In what way was this different? I wondered if there was in her a sudden swarming along her nerves, a warm conviction of the reality of sexual pleasure. She heaved like a whale — no: not so much as that. But it was as if half an ocean rolled off her young flanks; some element of darkness vanished from the room; some slight color of physical happiness tinctured her body and its thin coating of sweat; I felt it all through me; she rolled on the surface of a pale blue, a pink and blue sea; she was dark and gleaming, and immense and wet. And warm.

She cried, "*Wiley, I feel a lot!*"

God, she was happy.

I said, "Why not?" I wanted to lower the drama quotient; I thought the excess of drama was a mistake, would overburden her. But also I wanted her to defer to me, I wanted authority over her body now, I wanted to make her come.

But she didn't get any more excited than that: she was rigid, almost boardlike after a few seconds. I licked at her thing as best I could but the sea was dry; the board collapsed. I faked it that I was very excited; actually I was so caught up in being sure of myself, I didn't know what I really felt. I thought, as if I was much younger than I was, Boy, if this doesn't work, is my name mud. Then to build up the risk, out of sheer hellish braggadocio, instead of just acting out that I was confident — and in sex, everything unsaid that is portrayed in gestures instead, is twice as powerful — when she said, because the feeling was less for her now, the feeling she liked having gone away, "Wiley, I can't — this is silly —" I said, "Shut up, Orra, I know what I'm doing . . ." But I didn't know.

And I didn't like that tone for sexual interplay either, except as a joke, or as role-playing, because pure authority involves pure submission, and people don't survive pure submission except by being slavishly, possessively, vindictively in love; when they are in love like that, they can *give* you nothing but rebellion and submission, bitchiness and submission; it's a general rottenness: you get no part of them out of bed that has any value; and in bed, you get a grudging submission, because what the slave requires is your total attention, or she starts paying you back; I suppose the model is childhood, that slavery. Anyway I don't like it. But I played at it, then, with Orra, as a gamble.

Everything was a gamble. I didn't know what I was doing; I figured it out as I went along; and how much time did I have for figuring things out just then? I felt strained as at poker or roulette, sweaty and a little stupid, placing bets — with my tongue — and waiting to see what the wheel did, risking my money when no one forced me to, hoping things would go my way, and I wouldn't turn out to have been stupid when this was over.

Also, there were sudden fugitive convulsions of lust now, in sympathy with her larger but scattered responses, a sort of immediate and automatic sexuality — I was at the disposal, inwardly, of the sexuality in her and could not help myself, could not hold it back and avoid the disappointments, and physical impatience, the impatience in my skin and prick, of the huge desire that unmistakably accompanies love, of a primitive longing for what seemed her happiness, for closeness to her as to something I had studied and was studying and had found more and more of value in — what was of value was the way she valued me, a deep, and no doubt limited (but in the sexual moment it seemed illimitable) permissiveness toward me, a risk she took, an allowance she made as if she'd let me damage her and use her badly.

Partly what kept me going was stubbornness because I'd made up my mind before we started that I wouldn't give up; and partly what it was

was the feeling she aroused in me, a feeling that was, to be honest, made up of tenderness and concern and a kind of mere affection, a brotherliness, as if she was my brother, not different from me at all.

Actually this was brought on by an increasing failure, as the sex went on, of one kind of sophistication — of worldly sophistication — and by the increase in me of another kind, of a childish sophistication, a growth of innocence: Orra said, or exclaimed, in a half-harried, half-amazed voice, in a hugely admiring, gratuitous way, as she clutched at me in approval, "Wiley, I never had feelings like these before!"

And to be the first to have caused them, you know? It's like being a collector, finding something of great value, where it had been unsuspected and disguised, or like earning any honor; this partial success, this encouragement gave rise to this pride, this inward innocence.

Of course that lessened the risk for this occasion; I could fail now and still say, *It was worth it,* and she would agree; but it lengthened the slightly longer-term risk; because I might feel trebly a fool someday. Also it meant we might spend months making love in this fashion — I'd get impotent, maybe not in terms of erection, but I wouldn't look forward to sex — still, that was beautiful to me in a way too and exciting. I really didn't know what I was thinking: whatever I thought was part of the sex.

I went on, I wanted to hit the jackpot now. Then Orra shouted, "It's *there!* It's *THERE!*" I halted, thinking she meant it was in some specific locale, in some specific motion I'd just made with my tired tongue and jaw; I lifted my head — but couldn't speak: in a way, the sexuality pressed on me too hard for me to speak; anyway I didn't have to; she had lifted her head with a kind of overt twinship and she was looking at me down the length of her body; her face was askew and boyish — every feature was wrinkled; she looked angry and yet naïve and swindleable; she said angrily, naïvely, *"Wiley, it's there!"*

But even before she spoke that time, I knew she'd meant it was in her; the fox had been startled from its covert again; she had seen it, had felt it run in her again. She had been persuaded that it was in her for good.

I started manipulating her delicately with my hand; and in my own excitement, and thinking she was ready, I sort of scrambled up and covering her with myself, and playing with her with one hand, guided my other self, my lower consciousness, into her. My God, she was warm and restless inside; it was heated in there and smooth, insanely smooth, and oiled, and full of movements. But I knew at once I'd made a mistake: I should have gone on licking her; there were no regular contractions; she was anxious for the prick, she rose around it, closed around it, but in a rigid, dumb, far-away way; and her twitchings played on it, ran through it, through the walls of it and into me; and they were uncontrolled and not exciting, but empty; she didn't know what to do, how to be fucked and come. I couldn't pull out of her, I didn't want to, I couldn't pull out; but if there were no contractions for me to respond to, how in hell would I find the rhythm for her? I started slowly with what seemed infinite suggestiveness to me, with great dirtiness, a really grownup sort of fucking — just in case she was far along — and she let out a huge, shuddering hour-long sigh and cried out my name and then in a sobbing, exhausted voice, said, "I lost it . . . Oh Wiley, I lost it . . . Let's stop . . ." My face was above hers; her face was wet with tears; why was she crying like that? She had changed her mind; now she wanted to come; she turned her head back and forth; she said, "I'm no good . . . I'm no good . . . Don't worry about me . . . You come . . ."

No matter what I mumbled, "Hush," and "Don't be silly," and in a whisper, "Orra, I love you," she kept on saying those things until I slapped her lightly and said, *Shut up, Orra.*"

Then she was silent again.

The thing was, apparently, that she was arhythmic: at least that's what I thought; and that meant there weren't going to be regular contractions; any rhythm for me to follow; and, any rhythm I set up as I fucked, she broke with her movements: so that it was that when she moved, she made her excitement go away: it would be best if she moved very smally: but I was afraid to tell her that, or even to try to hold her hips firmly, and guide them, to instruct her in that way for fear she'd get self-conscious and lose what momentum she'd won. And also I was ashamed that I'd stopped going down on her. I experimented — doggedly, sweatily, to make up for what I'd done — with fucking in different ways, and I fantasized about us being in Mexico, some place warm and lushly colored where we made love easily and filthily and graphically. The fantasy kept me going. That is, it kept me hard. I kept acting out an atmosphere of sexual pleasure — I mean of my sexual pleasure — for her to rest on, so she could count on that. I discovered that a not very slow sort of one-one-one stroke, or fuck-fuck-fuck-Orra-now-now-now really got to her; her feelings would grow heated; and she could shift up from that with me into a one-two, one-two, one-two, her excitement rising; but if she or I then tried to shift up farther to one-two-three, one-two-three, one-two-three, she'd lose it all. That was too complicated for her: my own true love, my white American. But her feelings when they were present were very strong, they came in gusts, huge squalls of heat as if from a furnace with a carelessly banging door, and they excited and allured both of us. That excitement and the dit-dit-ditting got to her; she began to be generally, continuingly sexual. It's almost standard to compare sexual excitement to holiness; well, after a while, holiness seized her; she spoke with tongues, she testified. She was shaking all over; she was saved temporarily and sporadically; that is, she kept lapsing out of that excitement too. But it would recur. Her hands would flutter; her face would be pale and then red, then very, very red; her eyes would stare at nothing; she'd call my name. I'd plug on one-one-one, then one-two, one-two, then I'd go back to one-one-one: I could see as before — in the deep pleasure I felt even in the midst of the labor — why a man might kill her in order to stimulate in her (although he might not know this was why he did it) these signs of pleasure. The familiar Orra had vanished; she said, "GodohGodohGod"; it was sin and redemption and holiness and visions time. Her throbs were very direct, easily comprehensible, but without any pattern; they weren't in any regular sequence; still, they were exciting to me, maybe all the more exciting because of the piteousness of her not being able to regulate them, of their being like blows delivered inside her by an enemy whom she couldn't even half-domesticate or make friendly to herself or speak to. She was the most out-of-control girl I ever screwed. She would at times start to thrust like a woman who had her sexuality readied and well-understood at last and I'd start to distend with anticipation and a pride and relief as large as a house; but after two thrusts — or four, or six — she'd have gotten too excited, she'd be shaking, she'd thrust crookedly and out of tempo, the movement would collapse; or she'd suddenly jerk in mid-movement without warning and crash around with so great and so meaningless a violence that she'd lose her thing; and she'd start to cry. She'd whisper wetly, "I lost it"; so I'd say, "No you didn't," and I'd go on or start over, one-one-one; and of course, the excitement would come back; sometimes it came back at once; but she was increasingly afraid of herself, afraid to move her lower body; she would try to hold still and just *receive* the excitement; she would let it pool up in her; but then too she'd begin to shake more and more; she'd leak over into spasmodic and oddly sad, too large movements; and she'd whimper, knowing, I suppose, that those movements were breaking the tempo in herself; again and again, tears streamed down her cheeks; she said in a not quite hoarse, in a sweet, almost hoarse whisper, "I don't want to come, Wiley, you go ahead and come."

My mind had pretty much shut off; it had become exhausted; and I didn't see how we were going to make this work; she said, "Wiley, it's all right — please, it's all right — I don't want to come."

I wondered if I should say something and try to trigger some fantasy in her; but I didn't want to risk saying something she'd find unpleasant or think was a reproach or a hint for her to be sexier. I thought if I just kept on dit-dit-ditting, sooner or later, she'd find it in herself, the trick of riding on her feelings, and getting them to rear up, crest, and topple. I held her tightly, in sympathy and pity, and maybe fear, and admiration: she was so unhysterical; she hadn't yelled at me or broken anything; she hadn't ordered me around: she was simply alone and shaking in the middle of a neural storm in her that she seemed to have no gift for handling. I said, "Orra, it's OK: I really prefer long fucks," and I went on, dit-dit-dit-dit, then I'd shift up to dit-dot, dit-dot, dit-dot, dit-dot . . . My back hurt, my legs were going; if sweat was sperm, we would have looked like liquefied snow fields.

Orra made noises, more and more quickly, and louder and louder; then the noises she made slackened off. Then, step by step, with shorter and shorter strokes, then out of control and clumsy, simply reestablishing myself inside the new approach, I settled down, fucked slowly. The prick was embedded far in her; I barely stirred; the drama of sexual movement died away, the curtains were stilled; there was only sensation on the stage.

I bumped against the stone blocks and hidden hooks that nipped and bruised me into the soft rottenness, the strange, glowing, breakable hardness of coming, of the sensations at the approaches to coming.

I panted and half-rolled and pushed and edged it in, and slid it back, sweatily — I was semi-expert, aimed, intent: sex can be like a wilderness that imprisons you: the daimons of the locality claim you: I was achingly nagged by sensations; my prick had been somewhat softened before and now it swelled with a sore-headed, but fine distention; Orra shuddered and held me cooperatively; I began to forget her.

I thought she was making herself come on the slow fucking, on the prick which, when it was seated in her like this, when I hardly moved it, seemed to belong to her as much as to me; the prick seemed to *enter* me too; we both seemed to be sliding on it, the sensation was like that; but there was the moment when I became suddenly aware of her again, of the flesh and blood and bone in my arms, beneath me. I had a feeling of grating on her, and of her grating on me. I didn't recognize the unpleasantness at first. I don't know how long it went on before I felt it as a withdrawal in her, a withdrawal that she had made, a patient and restrained horror in her, and impatience in me: our arrival at sexual shambles.

My heart filled suddenly — filled; and then all feeling ran out of it — it emptied itself.

I continued to move in her slowly, numbly, in a shabby hubbub of faceless shudderings and shufflings of the mid-section and half-thrusts, half-twitches; we went on holding each other, in silence, without slackening the intensity with which we held each other; our movements, that flopping in place, that grinding against each other, went on; neither of us protested in any way. Bad sex can be sometimes stronger and more moving than good sex. She made sobbing noises — and held on to me. After a while sex seemed very ordinary and familiar and unromantic. I started going dit-dit-dit again.

Her hips jerked up half a dozen times before it occurred to me again that she liked to thrust like a boy, that she wanted to thrust, and then it occurred to me she wanted me to thrust.

I maneuvered my ass slightly and tentatively delivered a shove, or rather, delivered an authoritative shove, but not one of great length, one that was exploratory; Orra sighed, with relief it seemed to me; and jerked, encouragingly, too late, as I was pulling back. When I delivered a second thrust, a somewhat more obvious one, more amused, almost boyish, I was like a boy whipping a fairly fast ball in a game, at a first baseman — she jerked almost wolfishly, gobbling up the extravagant power of the gesture, of the thrust; with an odd shudder of pleasure, of irresponsibility, of boyishness, I suddenly realized how physically strong Orra was, how well-knit, how well put together her body was, how great the power in it, the power of endurance in it; and a phrase — absurd and demeaning but exciting just then — came into my head: *to throw a fuck*; and I settled myself atop her, braced my toes and knees and elbows and hands on the bed and half-scramblingly worked *it* — *it* was clearly mine; but I was Orra's — worked *it* into a passionate shove, a curving stroke about a third as long as a full stroke; but amateur and gentle, that is, tentative still; and Orra screamed then; how she screamed; she made known her readiness: then the next time, she grunted: "Uhnnnnahhhhhh . . ." a sound thick at the beginning but that trailed into refinement, into sweetness, a lingering sweetness.

It seemed to me I really wanted to fuck like this, that *I* had been waiting for this all my life. But it wasn't really my taste, that kind of fuck: I liked to throw a fuck with less force and more gradations and implications of force rather than with the actual thing; and with more immediate contact between the two sets of pleasures and with more admissions of defeat and triumph; my pleasure was a thing of me reflecting her; her spirit entering me; or perhaps it was merely a mistake, my thinking that; but it seemed shameful and automatic, naïve and animal: to throw the prick into her like that.

She took the thrust: she convulsed a little; she fluttered all over; her skin fluttered; things twitched in her, in the disorder surrounding the phallic blow in her. After two thrusts, she collapsed, went flaccid, then toughened and readied herself again, rose a bit from the bed, aimed the flattened, mysteriously funnel-like container of her lower end at me, too high, so that I had to pull her down with my hands on her butt or on her hips; and her face, when I glanced at her beneath my lids, was fantastically pleasing, set, concentrated, busy, harassed; her body was strong, was stone, smooth stone and wet-satin paper bags and snaky webs, thin and alive, made of woven snakes that lived, thrown over the stone; she held the great, writhing-skinned stone construction toward me, the bony marvel, the half-dish of bone with its secretive, gluey-smooth entrance, *the place where I was* — it was undefined, except for that: *the place where I was*: she took and met each thrust — and shuddered and collapsed and rose again: she seemed to rise to the act of taking it; I thought she was partly mistaken, childish, to think that the center of sex was to meet and take

the prick thrown into her as hard as it could be thrown, now that she
was excited; but there was a weird wildness, a wild freedom, like children cavorting, uncontrolled, set free, but not hysterical merely without restraint; the odd, thickened, knobbed pole springing back and
forth as if mounted on a web of wide rubber bands; it was a naïve
and a complete release. I whomped it in and she went, "UHNNN!"
and a half-iota of a second later, I was seated all the way in her, I
jerked a minim of an inch deeper in her, and went "UHNNN!" too.
Her whole body shook. She would go, "UHN!" And I would go,
"UHN!"

Then when it seemed from her strengthening noises and her more
rapid and jerkier movements that she was near the edge of coming, I'd
start to place whomps, in neater and firmer arrangements, more obviously in a rhythm, more businesslike, more teasing with pauses at each
end of a thrust; and that would excite her up to a point; but then her
excitement would level off, and not go over the brink. So I would
speed up: I'd thrust harder, then harder yet, then harder and faster;
she made her noises and half-thrust back. She bit her lower lip; she set
her teeth in her lower lip; blood appeared. I fucked still faster, but on a
shorter stroke, almost thrumming on her, and angling my abdomen
hopefully to drum on her clitoris; sometimes her body would go limp;
but her cries would speed up, bird after bird flew out of her mouth
while she lay limp as if I were a boxer and had destroyed her ability to
move; then when the cries did not go past a certain point, when she
didn't come, I'd slow and start again. I wished I'd been a great athlete,
a master of movement, a woman, a lesbian, a man with a gigantic
prick that would explode her into coming. I moved my hands to the
corners of the mattress; and spread my legs; I braced myself with my
hands and feet; and braced like that, free-handed in a way, drove into
her; and the new posture, the feeling she must have had of being
covered; and perhaps the difference in the thrust got to her; but Orra's
body began to set up a babble, a babble of response then — I think the
posture played on her mind.

But she did not come.

I moved my hands and held the dish of her hips so that she couldn't
wiggle or deflect the thrust or pull away: she began to "Uhn" again but
interspersed with small screams: we were like kids playing catch (her
poor brutalized clitoris), playing hard hand: this was what she thought

sex was; it was sexual, as throwing a ball hard is sexual; in a way, too, we were like acrobats hurling ourselves at each other, to meet in mid-air, and fall entangled to the net. It was like that.

Her mouth came open, her eyes had rolled to one side and stayed there — it felt like twilight to me — I knew where she was sexually, or thought I did. She pushed, she egged us on. She wasn't breakable this way. Orra. I wondered if she knew, it made me like her how naïve this was, this American fuck, this kids-playing-at-twilight-on-the-neighborhood-street fuck. After I seated it and wriggled a bit in her and moozed on her clitoris with my abdomen, I would draw it out not in a straight line but at some curve so that it would press against the walls of her cunt and she could keep track of where it was; and I would pause fractionally just before starting to thrust, so she could brace herself and expect it; I whomped it in and understood her with an absurd and probably unfounded sense of my sexual virtuosity; and she became silent suddenly, then she began to breathe loudly, then something in her toppled; or broke, then all at once she shuddered in a different way. It really was as if she lay on a bed of wings, as if she had a half-dozen wings folded under her, six huge wings, large, veined, throbbing, alive wings, real ones, with fleshy edges from which glittering feathers spring backwards; and they all stirred under her.

She half-rose; and I'd hold her so she didn't fling herself around and lose her footing, or her airborneness, on the uneasy glass mountain she'd begun to ascend, the frail transparency beneath her, that was forming and growing beneath her, that seemed to me to foam with light and darkness, as if we were rising above a landscape of hedges and moonlight and shadows: a mountain, a sea that formed and grew; it grew and grew; and she said "OH!" and "OHHHH!" almost with vertigo, as if she was airborne but unsteady on the vans of her wings, and as if I was there without wings but by some magic dispensation and by some grace of familiarity; I thunked on and on, and she looked down and was frightened; the tension in her body grew vast; and suddenly a great, a really massive violence ran through her but now it was as if, in fear at her height or out of some automatism, the first of her three pairs of wings began to beat, great fans winnowingly, great wings of flesh out of which feathers grew, catching at the air, stabilizing and yet lifting her: she whistled and rustled so; she was at once so still and so violent; the great wings engendered, their movement engendered in her, patterns of flexed and crossed muscles: her arms and legs and breasts echoed or carried out the strain, or strained to move the weight of those winnowing, moving wings. Her breaths were wild but not loud and slanted every which way, irregular and new to this particular dream, and very much as if she looked down on great spaces of air; she grabbed at me, at my shoulders, but she had forgotten how to work her hands, her hands just made the gestures of grabbing, the gestures of a well-meaning, dark but beginning to be luminous, mad, amnesiac angel. She called out, "Wiley, Wiley!" but she called it out in a *whisper*, the whisper of someone floating across a night sky, of someone crazily ascending, someone who was going crazy, who was taking on the mad purity and temper of angels, someone who was tormented unendurably by this, who was unendurably frightened, whose pleasure was enormous, half-human, mad. Then she screamed in rebuke, "Wiley!" She screamed my name: "*Wiley!*" — she did it hoarsely and insanely, asking for help, but blaming me, and merely as exclamation; it was a gutter sound in part, and ugly; the ugliness, when it destroyed nothing, or maybe it had an impetus of its own, but it whisked away another covering, a membrane of ordinariness — I don't know — and her second pair of wings began to beat; her whole body was aflutter on the bed. I was as wet as — as some fish, thonking away, sweatily. Grinding away. I said, "It's OK, Orra. It's OK." And poked on. In mid-air. She shouted, "*What is this!*" She shouted it in the way a tremendously large person who can defend herself might shout at someone who was unwisely beating her up. She shouted — angrily, as an announcement of anger, it seemed — "*Oh my God!*" Like: *Who broke this cup?* I plugged on. She raised her torso, her head, she looked me clearly in the eye, her eyes were enormous, were bulging, and she said "*Wiley, it's happening!*" Then she lay down again and screamed for a couple of seconds. I said a little dully, grinding on, "It's OK, Orra, It's OK," I didn't want to say *Let go* or to say anything lucid because I didn't know a damn thing about female orgasm after all, and I didn't want to give her any advice and wreck things; and also I didn't want to commit myself in case this turned out to be a false alarm; and we had to go on. I pushed in, lingered, pulled back, went in, only half on beat, one-thonk-one-thonk, then one-one-one, saying, "This is sexy, this is good for me, Orra, this is very good for me," and then, "Good Orra," and she trembled in a new way at that, "*Good* Orra," I said, "Good . . . Orra," and then all at once, it happened. Something pulled her over; and something gave in; and all three pairs of wings began to beat: she was the center and the source and the victim of a storm of wing beats; we were at the top of the world; the huge bird of God's body in us hovered; the great miracle pounded on her back, pounded around us; she was straining and agonized and distraught, estranged within this corporeal-incorporeal thing, this angelic other avatar, this other substance of herself: the wings were outspread; they thundered and gaspily galloped with her; they half broke her; and she screamed, "Wiley!" and "Mygodmygod" and "IT'S NOT STOPPING, WILEY, IT'S NOT STOPPING!" She was pale and red; her hair was everywhere; her body was wet, and thrashing. It was as if something unbelievably strange and fierce — like the holy temper — lifted her to where she could not breathe or walk: she choked in the ether, a scrambling seraph, tumbling, and aflame and alien, powerful beyond belief, hideous and frightening and beautiful beyond the reach of the human. A screaming child, an angel howling in the Godly sphere: she churned without delicacy, as wild as an angel bearing threats; her body lifted from the sheets, fell back, lifted again; her hands beat on the bed; she made very loud hoarse tearing noises — I was frightened for her: this was her first time after six years of playing around with her body. It hurt her; her face looked like something made of stone, a monstrous carving; only her body was alive; her arms and legs were outspread and tensed and they beat or they were weak and fluttering. She was an angel as brilliant as a beautiful insect infinitely enlarged and irrevocably foreign: she was unlike me: she was a girl making rattling, astonished, uncontrolled, unhappy noises, a girl looking shocked and intent and harassed by the variety and viciousness of the sensations, including relief, that attacked her. I sat up on my knees and moved a little in her and stroked her breasts, with smooth sideways, winglike strokes. And she screamed, "Wiley, I'm coming!" and with a certain idiocy entered on her second orgasm or perhaps her third since she'd started to come a few minutes before; and we should have gone on for hours but she said, "It hurts, Wiley, I hurt, make it stop . . ." So I didn't move; I just held her thighs with my hands; and her things began to trail off, to trickle down, into little shiverings; the stoniness left her face; she calmed into moderated shudders, and then she said, she started to speak with wonder but then it became an exclamation and ended on a kind of a hollow note, the prelude to a small scream: she said "I *came* . . ." Or "I ca-a-a-ammmmmmmme . . ." What happened was that she had another orgasm at the thought that she'd had her first.

That one was more like three little ones, diminishing in strength. When she was quieter, she was gasping, she said, "Oh you *love* me . . ."

That too excited her. When that died down, she said — angrily — "I always knew they were doing it wrong, I always knew there was nothing wrong with me . . ." And that triggered a little set of ripples. Some time earlier, without knowing it, I'd begun to cry. My tears fell on her thighs, her belly, her breasts, as I moved up, along her body, above her, to lie atop her. I wanted to hold her, my face next to hers; I wanted to hold her. I slid my arms in and under her, and she said, "Oh, Wiley," and she tried to lift her arms, but she started to shake again; then trembling anyway, she lifted her arms and hugged me with a shuddering sternness that was unmistakable; then she began to cry too.

Lust

by Susan Minot

LEO WAS from a long time ago, the first one I ever saw nude. In the spring before the Hellmans filled their pool, we'd go down there in the deep end, with baby oil, and like that. I met him the first month away at boarding school. He had a halo from the campus light behind him. I flipped.

Roger was fast. In his illegal car, we drove to the reservoir, the radio blaring, talking fast, fast, fast. He was always going for my zipper. He got kicked out sophomore year.

By the time the band got around to playing "Wild Horses," I had tasted Bruce's tongue. We were clicking in the shadows on the other side of the amplifier, out of Mrs. Donovan's line of vision. It tasted like salt, with my neck bent back, because we had been dancing so hard before.

Tim's line: "I'd like to see you in a bathing suit." I knew it was his line when he said the exact same thing to Annie Hines.

You'd go on walks to get off campus. It was raining like hell, my sweater as sopped as a wet sheep. Tim pinned me to a tree, the woods light brown and dark brown, a white house half-hidden with the lights already on. The water was as loud as a crowd hissing. He made certain comments about my forehead, about my cheeks.

We started off sitting at one end of the couch and then our feet were squished against the armrest and then he went over to turn off the TV and came back after he had taken off his shirt and then we slid onto the floor and he got up again to close the door, then came back to me, a body waiting on the rug.

You'd try to wipe off the table or to do the dishes and Willie would untuck your shirt and get his hands up under in front, standing behind you, making puffy noises in your ear.

He likes it when I wash my hair. He covers his face with it and if I start to say something, he goes, "Shush."

For a long time, I had Philip on the brain. The less they noticed you, the more you got them on the brain.

My parents had no idea. Parents never really know what's going on, especially when you're away at school most of the time. If she met them, my mother might say, "Oliver seems nice" or "I like that one" without much of an opinion. If she didn't like them, "He's a funny fellow, isn't he?" or "Johnny's perfectly nice but a drink of water." My father was too shy to talk to them at all, unless they played sports and he'd ask them about that.

The sand was almost cold underneath because the sun was long gone. Eben piled a mound over my feet, patting around my ankles, the ghostly surf rumbling behind him in the dark. He was the first person I ever knew who died, later that summer, in a car crash. I thought about it for a long time.

"Come here," he says on the porch.

I go over to the hammock and he takes my wrist with two fingers. "What?"

He kisses my palm then directs my hand to his fly.

Songs went with whichever boy it was. "Sugar Magnolia" was Tim, with the line "Rolling in the rushes/down by the riverside." With "Darkness Darkness," I'd picture Philip with his long hair. Hearing "Under My Thumb" there'd be the smell of Jamie's suede jacket.

We hid in the listening rooms during study hall. With a record cover over the door's window, the teacher on duty couldn't look in. I came out flushed and heady and back at the dorm was surprised how red my lips were in the mirror.

One weekend at Simon's brother's, we stayed inside all day with the shades down, in bed, then went out to Store 24 to get some ice cream. He stood at the magazine rack and read through *MAD* while I got butterscotch sauce, craving something sweet.

I could do some things well. Some things I was good at, like math or painting or even sports, but the second a boy put his arm around me, I forgot about wanting to do anything else, which felt like a relief at first until it became like sinking into a muck.

It was different for a girl.

When we were little, the brothers next door tied up our ankles. They held the door of the goat house and wouldn't let us out till we showed them our underpants. Then they'd forget about being after us and when we played whiffle ball, I'd be just as good as them.

Then it got to be different. Just because you have on a short skirt, they yell from the cars, slowing down for a while and if you don't look, they screech off and call you a bitch.

"What's the matter with me?" they say, point-blank.

Or else, "Why won't you go out with me? I'm not asking you to get married," about to get mad.

Or it'd be, trying to be reasonable, in a regular voice, "Listen, I just want to have a good time."

So I'd go because I couldn't think of something to say back that wouldn't be obvious, and if you go out with them, you sort of have to do something.

I sat between Mack and Eddie in the front seat of the pickup. They were having a fight about something. I've a feeling about me.

Certain nights you'd feel a certain surrender, maybe if you'd had wine. The surrender would be forgetting yourself and you'd put your nose to his neck and feel like a squirrel, safe, at rest, in a restful dream. But then you'd start to slip from that and the dark would come in and there'd be a cave. You make out the dim shape of the windows and feel yourself become a cave, filled absolutely with air, or with a sadness that wouldn't stop.

Teenage years. You know just what you're doing and don't see the things that start to get in the way.

Lots of boys, but never two at the same time. One was plenty to keep you in a state. You'd start to see a boy and something would rush over you like a fast storm cloud and you couldn't possibly think of anyone else. Boys took it differently. Their eyes perked up at any little number that walked by. You'd act like you weren't noticing.

The joke was that the school doctor gave out the pill like aspirin. He didn't ask you anything. I was fifteen. We had a picture of him in assembly, holding up an IUD shaped like a T. Most girls were on the pill, if anything, because they couldn't handle a diaphragm. I kept the dial in my top drawer like my mother and thought of her each time I tipped out the yellow tablets in the morning before chapel.

If they were too shy, I'd be more so. Andrew was nervous. We stayed up with his family album, sharing a pack of Old Golds. Before it got light, we turned on the TV. A man was explaining how to plant seedlings. His mouth jerked to the side in a tic. Andrew thought it was a riot and kept imitating him. I laughed to be polite. When we finally dozed off, he dared to put his arm around me but that was it.

You wait till they come to you. With half fright, half swagger, they stand one step down. They dare to touch the button on your coat then lose their nerve and quickly drop their hand so you — you'd do anything for them. You touch their cheek.

The girls sit around in the common room and talk about boys, smoking their heads off.

"What are you complaining about?" says Jill to me when we talk about problems.

"Yeah," says Giddy. "You always have a boyfriend."

I look at them and think, As if.

I thought the worst thing anyone could call you was a cockteaser. So, if you flirted, you had to be prepared to go through with it. Sleeping with someone was perfectly normal once you had done it. You didn't really worry about it. But there were other problems. The problems had to do with something else entirely.

Mack was during the hottest summer ever recorded. We were renting a house on an island with all sorts of other people. No one slept during the heat wave, walking around the house with nothing on which we were used to because of the nude beach. In the living room, Eddie lay on top of a coffee table to cool off. Mack and I, with the bedroom door open for air, sweated and sweated all night.

"I can't take this," he said at 3 A.M. "I'm going for a swim." He and some guys down the hall went to the beach. The heat put me on edge. I sat on a cracked chest by the open window and smoked and smoked till I felt even worse, waiting for something — I guess for him to get back.

One was on a camping trip in Colorado. We zipped our sleeping bags together, the coyotes' hysterical chatter far away. Other couples murmured in other tents. Paul was up before sunrise, starting a fire for breakfast. He wasn't much of a talker in the daytime. At night, his hand leafed about in the hair at my neck.

There'd be times when you overdid it. You'd get carried away. All the next day, you'd be in a total fog, delirious, absent-minded, crossing the street and nearly getting run over.

The more girls a boy has, the better. He has a bright look, having reaped fruits, blooming. He stalks around, sure-shouldered, and you have the feeling he's got more in him, a fatter heart, more stories to tell. For a girl, with each boy it's like a petal gets plucked each time.

Then you start to get tired. You begin to feel diluted, like watered-down stew.

Oliver came skiing with us. We lolled by the fire after everyone had gone to bed. Each creak you'd think was someone coming downstairs. The silver-loop bracelet he gave me had been a present from his girlfriend before.

On vacations, we went skiing, or you'd go south if someone invited you. Some people had apartments in New York that their families hardly ever used. Or summer houses, or older sisters. We always managed to find someplace to go.

We made the plan at coffee hour. Simon snuck out and met me at Main Gate after lights-out. We crept to the chapel and spent the night in the balcony. He tasted like onions from a submarine sandwich.

The boys are one of two ways: either they can't sit still or they don't move. In front of the TV, they won't budge. On weekends they play touch football while we sit on the sidelines, picking blades of grass to chew on, and watch. We're always watching them run around. We shiver in the stands, knocking our boots together to keep our toes warm and they whizz across the ice, chopping their sticks around the puck. When they're in the rink, they refuse to look at you, only eyeing each other beneath low helmets. You cheer for them but they don't look up, even if it's a face-off when nothing's happening, even if they're doing drills before any game has started at all.

Dancing under the pink tent, he bent down and whispered in my ear. We slipped away to the lawn on the other side of the hedge. Much later, as he was leaving the buffet with two plates of eggs and sausage, I saw the grass stains on the knees of his white pants.

Tim's was shaped like a banana, with a graceful curve to it. They're all different. Willie's like a bunch of walnuts when nothing was happening, another's as thin as a thin hot dog. But it's like faces; you're never really surprised.

Still, you're not sure what to expect.

I look into his face and he looks back. I look into his eyes and they look back at mine. Then they look down at my mouth so I look at his mouth, then back to his eyes, backing up, at his whole face. I think, Who? Who are you? His head tilts to one side.

I say, "Who are you?"

"What do you mean?"

"Nothing."

I look at his eyes again, deeper. Can't tell who he is, what he thinks.

"What?" he says. I look at his mouth.

"I'm just wondering," I say and go wandering across his face. Study the chin line. It's shaped like a persimmon.

"Who are you? What are you thinking?"

He says, "What the hell are you talking about?"

Then they get mad after when you say enough is enough. After, when it's easier to explain that you don't want to. You wouldn't dream of saying that maybe you weren't really ready to in the first place.

Gentle Eddie. We waded into the sea, the waves round and plowing in, buffalo-headed, slapping our thighs. I put my arms around his freckled shoulders and he held me up, buoyed by the water, and rocked me like a seashell.

I had no idea whose party it was, the apartment jam-packed, stepping over people in the hallway. The room with the music was practically empty, the bare floor, me in red shoes. This fellow slides onto one knee and takes me around the waist and we rock to jazzy tunes, with my toes pointing heavenward, and waltz and spin and dip to "Smoke Gets in Your Eyes" or "I'll Love You Just for Now." He puts his head to my chest, runs a sweeping hand down my inside thigh and we go loose-limbed and sultry and as smooth as silk and I stamp my red heels and he takes me into a swoon. I never saw him again after that but I thought, I could have loved that one.

You wonder how long you can keep it up. You begin to feel like you're showing through, like a bathroom window that only lets in gray light, the kind you can't see out of.

They keep coming around. Johnny drives up at Easter vacation from Baltimore and I let him in the kitchen with everyone sound asleep. He has friends waiting in the car.

"What are you crazy? It's pouring out there," I say.

"It's okay," he says. "They understand."

So he gets some long kisses from me, against the refrigerator, before he goes because I hate those girls who push away a boy's face as if she were made out of Ivory soap, as if she's that much greater than he is.

The note on my cubby told me to see the headmaster. I had no idea for what. He had received complaints about my amorous displays on the town green. It was Willie that spring. The headmaster told me he didn't care what I did but that Casey Academy had a reputation to uphold in the town. He lowered his glasses on his nose. "We've got twenty acres of woods on this campus," he said. "If you want to smooch with your boyfriend, there are twenty acres for you to do it out of the public eye. You read me?"

Everybody'd get weekend permissions for different places then we'd all go to someone's house whose parents were away. Usually there'd be more boys than girls. We raided the liquor closet and smoked pot at the kitchen table and you'd never know who would end up where, or with whom. There were always disasters. Ceci got bombed and cracked her head open on the banister and needed stitches. Then there was the time Wendel Blair walked through the picture window at the Lowe's and got slashed to ribbons.

He scared me. In bed, I didn't dare look at him. I lay back with my eyes closed, luxuriating because he knew all sorts of expert angles, his hands never fumbling, going over my whole body, pressing the hair up and off the back of my head, giving an extra hip shove, as if to say *There.* I parted my eyes slightly, keeping the screen of my lashes low because it was too much to look at him, his mouth loose and pink and parted, his eyes looking through my forehead, or kneeling up, looking through my throat. I was ashamed but couldn't look him in the eye.

You wonder about things feeling a little off-kilter. You begin to feel like a piece of pounded veal.

At boarding school, everyone gets depressed. We go in and see the housemother, Mrs. Gunther. She got married when she was eighteen. Mr. Gunther was her high-school sweetheart, the only boyfriend she ever had.

"And you knew you wanted to marry him right off?" we ask her. She smiles and says, "Yes."

"They always want something from you," says Jill, complaining about her boyfriend.

"Yeah," says Giddy. "You always feel like you have to deliver something."

"You do," says Mrs. Gunther. "Babies."

After sex, you curl up like a shrimp, something deep inside you ruined, slammed in a place that sickens at slamming, and slowly you fill up with an overwhelming sadness, an elusive gaping worry. You don't try to explain it, filled with the knowledge that it's nothing after all, everything filling up finally and absolutely with death. After the briskness of loving, loving stops. And you roll over with death stretched out alongside you like a feather boa, or a snake, light as air, and you . . . you don't even ask for anything or try to say something to him because it's obviously your own damn fault. You haven't been able to — to what? To open your heart. You open your legs but can't, or don't dare anymore, to open your heart.

It starts this way:

You stare into their eyes. They flash like all the stars are out. They look at you seriously, their eyes at a low burn and their hands no matter what starting off shy and with such a gentle touch that the only thing you can do is take that tenderness and let yourself be swept away. When, with one attentive finger they tuck the hair behind your ear, you —

You do everything they want.

Then comes after. After when they don't look at you. They scratch their balls, stare at the ceiling. Or if they do turn, their gaze is altogether changed. They are surprised. They turn casually to look at you, distracted, and get a mild distracted surprise. You're gone. Their blank look tells you that the girl they were fucking is not there anymore. You seem to have disappeared.

The Pacific

by Mark Helprin

THIS WAS PROBABLY the last place in the world for a factory. There were pine-covered hills and windy bluffs stopped still in a wavelike roll down to the Pacific, groves of fragrant trees with clay-red trunks and soft greenery that made a white sound in the wind, and a chain of boiling, fuming coves and bays in which the water — when it was not rocketing foam — was a miracle of glassy curves in cold blue or opalescent turquoise, depending upon the season, and depending upon the light.

A dirt road went through the town and followed the sea from point to point as if it had been made for the naturalists who had come before the war to watch the seals, sea otters, and fleets of whales passing offshore. It took three or four opportunities to travel into the hills and run through long valleys onto a series of flat mesas as large as battlefields, which for a hundred years had been a perfect place for raising horses. And horses still pressed up against the fences or stood in family groupings in golden pastures as if there were no such thing as time, and as if many of the boys who had ridden them had never grown up and had never left. At least a dozen fishing boats had once bobbed at the pier and ridden the horizon, but they had been turned into minesweepers and sent to Pearl Harbor, San Diego, and the Aleutians.

The factory itself, a long low building in which more than five hundred women and several hundred men made aircraft instruments, had been built in two months, along with a forty-mile railroad spur that had been laid down to connect it to the Union Pacific main line.

In this part of the state the railroad had been used heavily only during the harvests and was usually rusty for the rest of the year. Now even the spur was gleaming and weedless, and small steam engines pulling several freight cars shuttled back and forth, their hammerlike exhalations silencing the cicadas, breaking up perfect afternoons, and shattering perfect nights.

The main halls and outbuildings were only a mile from the sea but were placed in such a way, taking up almost all of the level ground on the floor of a wide ravine, that they were out of the line of fire of naval guns. And because they were situated in a narrow trench between hills, they were protected from bombing.

"But what about landings?" a woman had asked an Army officer who had been brought very early one morning to urge the night shift to maintain the blackout and keep silent about their work. Just after dawn the entire shift had finished up and gathered on the railroad siding.

"Who's speaking, please?" the officer had asked, unable to see in the dim light who was putting the question.

"Do you want my name?" she asked back in surprise. She had not intended to say anything, and now everyone was listening to her.

Nor had the officer intended to ask her name. "Sure," he answered. "You're from the South."

"That's right," she said. "South Carolina. My name is Paulette Ferry."

"What do you do?"

"I'm a precision welder."

That she should have the word *precision* in her title seemed just. She was neat, handsome, and delicate. Every gesture seemed well considered. Her hands were small — hardly welder's hands, even those of a precision welder.

"You don't have to worry about troop landings," the officer said. "It's too far for the Japanese to come in a ship small enough to slip through our seaward defenses, and it's too far for airplanes, too."

He put his hands up to shield his eyes. The sun was rising, and as its rays found bright paths between the firs, he was blinded. "The only danger here is sabotage. Three or four men could hike in with a few satchels of explosive and do a lot of damage. But the sea is clear. Japanese submarines just don't have the range, and the Navy's out there, though you seldom see it. If you lived in San Francisco or

San Diego, believe me, you'd see it. The harbors are choked with warships."

Then the meeting dissolved, because the officer was eager to move on. He had to drive to Bakersfield and speak at two more factories, both of which were more vulnerable and more important than this one. And this place was so out of the way and so beautiful that it seemed to have nothing to do with the war.

Before her husband left for the South Pacific, he and Paulette had found a place for her to live, a small house above the ocean, on a cliff, looking out, where it seemed that nothing would be between them but the air over the water.

Though warships were not visible off the coast, she could see from her windows the freighters that moved silently within the naval cordon. Sometimes one of these ships would defy the blackout and become a castle of lights that glided on the horizon like a skater with a torch.

"Paulette," he had said, when he was still in training at Parris Island, "after the war's over, everything's going to be different. When I get back — if I get back," he added, because he knew that not all Marine lieutenants were going to make it home — "I want to go to California. The light there is supposed to be extraordinary. I've heard that because of the light, living there is like living in a dream. I want to be in a place like that — not so much as a reward for seeing it through, but because we will already have been so disconnected from everything we know. Do you understand?"

She had understood, and she had come quickly to a passionate agreement about California, swept into it not only by the logic and the hope but by the way he had looked at her when he had said "— if I get back." For he thought truly nothing was as beautiful as Paulette in a storm, riding above it smoothly, just about to break, quivering, but never breaking.

When he was shifted from South Carolina to the Marine base at Twentynine Palms, they had their chance to go to California, and she rode out with him on the train. Rather than have them suffer the whole trip in a Pullman with stiff green curtains, her parents had paid for a compartment. Ever since Lee had been inducted, both sets of parents had fallen into a steady devotion. It seemed as if they would not be satisfied until they had given all their attention and everything they had to their children. Packages arrived almost daily for Paulette. War bonds accumulated for the baby that did not yet exist. Paulette's father, a schoolteacher, was a good carpenter, and he had vowed that when Lee got back, if they wanted him to, he would come out to California to help with his own hands in building them a house. Their parents were getting old. They moved and talked slowly now, but they were ferociously determined to protect their children, and though they could do little more than book railway compartments and buy war bonds, they did whatever they could, hoping that it would some- how keep Lee alive and prevent Paulette from becoming a widow at the age of twenty-six.

For three nearly speechless days in early September, the Marine lieutenant and his young wife stared out the open window of their compartment as they crossed the country in perfect weather and north light. Magnificent thunderstorms would close on the train like Indian riders and then withdraw in favor of the clear. Oceans of wheat, the deserts, and the sky were gold, white, and infinitely blue, blue. And at night, as the train charged across the empty prairie, its spotlight flashing against the tracks that lay far ahead of it straight and true, the stars hung close and bright. Stunned by the beauty of all this, Paulette and Lee were intent upon remembering, because they wanted what they saw to give them strength, and because they knew that should things not turn out the way they wanted, this would have to have been enough.

Distant whirlwinds and dust storms, mountain rivers leaping coolly against the sides of their courses, four-hundred-mile straightaways, fifty-mile bends, massive canyons and defiles, still forests, and glowing lakes calmed them and set them up for their first view of the Pacific's easy waves rolling onto the deserted beaches south of Los Angeles.

Paulette lived in a small white cottage that was next to an orange grove, and worked for six months on instrumentation for P-38s. The factory was a mile away, and to get to it, she had to go through the ranks of trees. Lee thought that this might be dangerous, until one morning he accompanied her and was amazed to see several thousand women walking silently through the orange grove on their way to and from factories that worked around the clock.

Though Lee had more leave than he would have had as an enlisted man, he didn't have much, and the occasional weekends, odd days, and one or two weeks when he came home during the half year at

Twentynine Palms were as tightly packed as stage plays. At the beginning of each furlough the many hours ahead (they always broke the time into hours) seemed like great riches. But as the hours passed and only a few remained, Lee no less than Paulette would feel that they would soon be parting as if never to be reunited. He was stationed only a few hours away and they knew that he would try to be back in two weeks, but they knew as well that someday he would leave for the Pacific.

When his orders finally came, he had ten days before he went overseas, and when Paulette came home from work the evening of the first day and saw him sitting on the porch, she was able to tell just by looking at him that he was going. She cried for half an hour, but then he was able to comfort her by saying that though it did not seem right or natural that they should be put to this kind of test in their middle twenties, everyone in the world had to face death and separation sometime, and it was finally what they would have to endure anyway.

On his last leave they took the train north and then hitchhiked forty miles to the coast to look at a town and a new factory to which Lockheed was shifting employees from its plants in Los Angeles. At first Paulette had refused to move there, despite an offer of more money and a housing allowance, because it was too far from Twentynine Palms. But now that Lee was on his way overseas, it seemed perfect. Here she would wait, she would dream of his return, and she would work so hard that, indirectly, she might help to bring him back.

This town, isolated at the foot of hills that fronted the sea, this out-of-the-way group of houses with its factory that would vanish when the war was over, seemed like the proper place for her to hold her ground in full view of the abyss. After he had been gone for two or three weeks, she packed her belongings and moved up there, and though she was sad to give up her twice-daily walks through the orange groves with the thousands of other women, who appeared among the trees as if by magic, she wanted to be in the little house that overlooked the Pacific, so that nothing would be between them but the air over the water.

To withstand gravitational forces as fighter planes rose, banked, and dived, and to remain intact over the vibrations of 2,000-horsepower engines, buffeting crosswinds, rapid-fire cannon, and rough landings, aircraft instruments had spot welds wherever possible rather than screws or rivets. Each instrument might require as many as several hundred welds, and the factory was in full production of a dozen different mechanisms: altimeters, air-speed indicators, fuel gauges, attitude indicators, counters, timers, compasses, gyroscopes — all those things that would measure and confine objective forces and put them, like weapons, in the hands of the fighter pilots who attacked fortified islands and fought high over empty seas.

On fifteen production lines, depending upon the instrument in manufacture, the course of construction was interspersed with anywhere from twenty to forty welders. Amidst the welders were machine-tool operators, inspectors, assemblers, and supervisors. Because each man or woman had to have a lot of room in which to keep parts, tools, and the work itself as it came down the line, and because the ravine and, therefore, the building were narrow, the lines stretched for a quarter of a mile.

Welders' light is almost pure. Despite the spectral differences between the various techniques, the flash of any one of them gives rise to illusions of depth and dimension. No gaudy showers of dancing sparks fall as with a cutting torch, and no beams break through the darkness to carry the eye on a wave of blue. One sees only points of light so faithful and pure that they seem to race into themselves. The silvery whiteness is like the imagined birth of stars or souls. Though each flash is beautiful and stretches out time, it seldom lasts long. For despite the magnetizing brightness, or perhaps because of it, the flash is born to fade. Still, the sharp burst of light is a brave and wonderful thing that makes observers count the seconds and cheer it on.

From her station on the altimeter line, Paulette could see over gray steel tables down the length of the shed. Of the four hundred electric-arc or gas-welding torches in operation, the number lighted varied at any one time from twenty or thirty to almost all of them. As each welder pulled down her mask, bent over as if in a dive, and squeezed the lever on her torch, the pattern of the lights emerged, and it was never the same twice. Through the dark glass of the face plate the flames in the distance were like a spectacular convocation of fireflies on a hot, moonless night. With the mask up, the plane of the work tables looked like the floor of the universe, the smoky place where stars were born. All the lights, even those that were distant, commanded attention and assaulted the senses — by the score, by the hundreds.

Directly across from Paulette was a woman whose job was to make oxyacetylene welds on the outer cases of the altimeters. The cases were finished, and then carried by trolley to the end of the line, where they would be hooded over the instruments themselves. Paulette, who worked with an electric arc, never tired of watching this woman adjust her torch. When she lit it, the flame was white inside but surrounded by a yellow envelope that sent up twisting columns of smoke. Then she changed the mixture and a plug of intense white appeared at the end of the torch, in the center of a small orange flare. When finally she got her neutral flame — with a tighter white plug, a colorless core, and a sapphire-blue casing — she lowered her mask and bent over the work.

Paulette had many things to do on one altimeter. She had to attach all the brass, copper, and aluminum alloy parts to the steel superstructure of the instrument. She had to use several kinds of flux; she had to assemble and brace the components; and she had to jump from one operation to the other in just the right order, because if she did not, pieces due for insertion would be blocked or bent.

She had such a complicated routine only because she was doing the work of two. The woman who had been next to her got sick one day, and Paulette had taken on her tasks. Everyone assumed that the line would slow down. But Paulette doubled her speed and kept up the pace.

"I don't know how you do it, Paulette," her supervisor had said, as she worked with seemingly effortless intensity.

"I'm going twice as fast, Mr. Hannon," she replied.

"Can you keep it up?"

"I sure can," she answered. "In fact, when Lindy comes back, you can put her down the line and give her work to me." Whereas Lindy always talked about clothes and shoes, Paulette preferred to concentrate on the instrument that she was fashioning. She was granted her wish. Among other things, Hannon and just about everyone else on the line wanted to see how long she could continue the pace before she broke. But she knew this, and she didn't break. She got better, and she got faster.

When Paulette got home in the morning, the sea was illuminated as the sun came up behind her. The open and fluid light of the Pacific was as entrancing as the light of the Carolinas in springtime. At times the sea looked just like the wind-blue mottled waters of the Albemarle, and the enormous clouds that rose in huge columns far out over the ocean were like the aromatic pine smoke that ascended undisturbed from a farmer's clearing fire toward a flawless blue sky.

She was elated in the morning. Joy and relief came not only from the light on the waves but also from having passed the great test of the day, which was to open the mailbox and check the area near the front door. The mailman, who served as the telegraph messenger, thought that he was obliged to wedge telegrams tightly in the doorway. One of the women, a lathe operator who had had to go back to her family in Chicago, had found her telegram actually nailed down. The mailman had feared that it might blow into the sea, and that then she would find out in some shocking, incidental manner that her husband had been killed. At the factory were fifty women whose husbands, like Lee, had passed through Twentynine Palms into the Second Marine Division. They had been deeply distressed when their men were thrown into the fighting on Guadalcanal, but, miraculously, of the fifty Marines whose wives were gathered in this one place only a few had been wounded and none had been killed.

When her work was done, knowing that she had made the best part of thirty altimeters that would go into thirty fighters, and that each of these fighters would do a great deal to protect the ships on which the Marines sailed, and pummel the beaches on which they had to fight, Paulette felt deserving of sleep. She would change into a nightgown, turn down the covers, and then sit in a chair next to the bed, staring at the Pacific as the light got stronger, trying to master the fatigue and stay awake. Sometimes she would listen to the wind for an hour, nod asleep, and force herself to open her eyes, until she fell into bed and slept until two in the afternoon.

Lee had returned from his training at Parris Island with little respect for what he once had thought were human limitations. His company had marched for three days, day and night, without stopping. Some recruits, young men, had died of heart attacks.

"How can you walk for three whole days without stopping?" she had asked. "It seems impossible."

"We had forty-pound packs, rifles, and ammunition," he answered. "We had to carry mortars, bazookas, stretchers, and other equipment, some of it very heavy, that was passed from shoulder to shoulder."

"For three days?"

"For three days. And when we finally stopped, I was picked as a sentinel. I had to stand guard for two hours while everyone else slept. And you know what happens if you fall asleep, God help you, on sentry duty?"

She shook her head, but did know.

"Article eighty-six of the Articles of War: 'Misbehavior of a sentinel.' " He recited it from memory. " 'Any sentinel who is found drunk or sleeping upon his post, or leaves it before he is regularly relieved, shall, if the offense is committed in time of war, suffer death or such other punishment as a court-martial may direct.'

"I was so tired . . . My eyelids weighed ten thousand pounds apiece. But I stayed up, even though the only enemies we had were officers and mosquitoes. They were always coming around to check."

"Who?" she asked. "Mosquitoes?"

"Yeah," Lee replied. "And as you know, officers are hatched in stagnant pools."

So when Paulette returned from her ten-hour shifts, she sat in a chair and tried not to sleep, staring over the Pacific like a sentinel.

She had the privilege of awakening at two in the afternoon, when the day was strongest, and not having to be ashamed of having slept through the morning. In the six hours before the shift began, she would rise, bathe, eat lunch, and gather her garden tools. Then she walked a few miles down the winding coast road — the rake, hoe, and shovel resting painfully upon her shoulders — to her garden. No shed was anywhere near it, and had one been there she probably would have carried the tools anyway.

Because she shared the garden with an old man who came in the morning and two factory women who were on the second day shift, she was almost always alone there. Usually she worked in the strong sun until five-thirty. To allow herself this much hard labor she did her shopping and eating at a brisk pace. The hours in the garden made her strong and fit. She was perpetually sunburned, and her hair became lighter. She had never been so beautiful, and when people looked at her, they kept on looking. Seeing her speed through the various and difficult chores of cultivation, no one ever would have guessed that she might shoulder her tools, walk home as fast as she could, and then set off for ten hours on a production line.

"Don't write about the garden anymore," he had written from a place undisclosed. "Don't write about the goddamned altimeters. Don't write about what we're going to do when the war is over. Just tell me about you. They have altimeters here, they even have gardens. Tell me what you're thinking. Describe yourself as if we had never met. Tell me in detail exactly how you take your bath. Do you sing to yourself? What do the sheets on the bed look like — I mean do they have a pattern or are they a color? I never saw them. Take pictures, and send them. Send me your barrette. (I don't want to wear it myself, I want to keep it in my pocket.) I care so much about you, Paulette. I love you. And I'm doing my best to stay alive. You should see me when it gets tight. I don't throw myself up front, but I don't hold my breath either. I run around like hell, alert and listening every second. My aim is sure and I don't let off shots when I don't have to. You'd never know me, Paulette, and I don't know if there's anything left of me. But I'm going to come home."

Although she didn't write about the garden anymore, she tilled it deep. The rows were straight, and not a single weed was to be seen, and when she walked home with the tools on her shoulders, she welcomed their weight.

They exchanged postscripts for two months in letters that were late in coming and always crossed. "P.S. What do you eat?" he wrote.

"P.S. What do you mean, what do I eat? Why do you want to know? What do you eat?"

"P.S. I want to know because I'm hungry. I eat crud. It all comes from a can, it's very salty, and it has a lot of what seems to be pork fat. Some local vegetables haven't been bombed, or crushed by heavy vehicles, but if you eat them you can wave good-bye to your intestines. Sometimes we have cakes that are baked in pans four feet by five feet. The bottom is cinder and the top is raw dough. What happened to steak? No one has it here, and I haven't seen one in a year. Where are they keeping it? Is there going to be a big barbecue after the war?"

"P.S. You're right, we have no beef around here and practically no sugar or butter, either. I thought maybe you were getting it. I eat a lot of fresh vegetables, rice, fish that I get in exchange for the stuff in my garden, and chicken now and then. I've lost some weight, but I look real good. I drink my tea black, and I mean black, because at the plant they have a huge samovar thing where it boils for hours. What with your pay mounting up in one account, my pay mounting up in another, and what the parents have been sending us lately, when the war is over we're going to have a lot of money. We have almost four thousand dollars now. We'll have the biggest barbecue you've ever seen."

As long as she did her work and as long as he stayed alive, she sensed some sort of justice and equilibrium. She enjoyed the feminine triumph in the factory, where the women, doing men's work, sometimes broke into song that was as tentative and beautiful as only women's voices can be. They did not sing often. The beauty and the power embarrassed them, for they had their independence only because their men were at risk and the world was at war. But sometimes they couldn't help it, and a song would rise above the production lines, lighter than the ascending smoke, more luminous than the blue and white arcs.

The Pacific and California's golden hills caught the clear sunshine but made it seem like a dream in which sight was confused and the dreamer giddy. The sea, with its cold colors and foaming cauldrons in which seals were cradle-rocked, was the northern part of the same ocean that held ten thousand tropical islands. All these things, these reversals, paradoxes, and contradictions, were burned in day by day until they seemed to make sense, until it appeared as if some great thing were being accomplished, greater than perhaps they knew. For they felt tremendous velocity in the way they worked, the way they lived, and even in the way they sang.

On the twentieth of November, 1943, five thousand men of the Second Marine Division landed on the beaches of Tarawa. The action of war, the noise, smoke, and intense labor of battle, seemed frozen when it reached home, especially for those whose husbands or sons were engaged in the fighting. A battle from afar is only a thing of silence, of souls ascending as if drawn up in slow motion by malevolent angels floating above the fray. Tarawa, a battle afar, seemed no more real than a painting. Paulette and the others had no chance to act. They were forced to listen fitfully to the silence and stare faithfully into the dark.

Now, when the line broke into song, the women did not sing the energetic popular music that could stoke production until it glowed. Nor did they sing the graceful ballads that had kept them on the line when they would otherwise have faltered. Now the songs were from the hymnal, and they were sung not in a spirit of patriotism or of production but in prayer.

As the battle was fought in Tarawa, two women fell from the line. One had been called from her position and summoned to what they knew as the office, which was a maze of wavy-glass partitions beyond which other people did the paperwork, and she, like the lathe operator from Chicago, simply dropped away. Another had been given a telegram as she worked; no one really knew how to tell anyone such a thing. But with so many women working, the absence of two did not slow their industry. Two had been beaten. Five hundred were not, and the lights still flickered down the line.

Paulette had known from the first that Lee was on the beach. She wondered which was more difficult, being aware that he might be in any battle, or knowing for sure that he was in one. The first thing she did when she got the newspaper was to scan the casualty lists, dropping immediately to the *F*s. It did not matter that they sent telegrams; telegrams sometimes blew into the sea. Next she raced through reports of the fighting, tracing is she could the progress of his unit and looking for any mention of him. Only then would she read the narrative so as to judge the progress of the offensive and the chances of victory, though she cared not so much for victory as for what it meant to the men in the field who were still alive.

The line was hypnotic and it swallowed up time. If she wanted to do good work, she couldn't think about anything except what was directly in front of her, especially since she was doing the work of two. But when she was free she now dreamed almost continually of her young husband, as if the landings in Tarawa, across the Pacific, had been designed to make her imagine him.

During these days the garden needed little attention, so she did whatever she could and then went down to a sheltered cove by the sea, where she lay on the sand, in the sun, half asleep. For as long as her eyes were closed and the sea seemed to pound everything but dreams into meaningless foam and air, she lay with him, tightly, a slight smile on her face, listening to him breathe. She would awake from this half sleep to find that she was holding her hands and arms in such a way that had he been there she would have been embracing him.

She often spoke to him under her breath, informing him, as if he could hear her, of everything she thought and did — of the fact that she was turning off the flame under the kettle, of the sunrise and its golden-red light flooding against the pines, of how the ocean looked when it was joyously misbehaving.

These were the things she could do, the powers to which she was limited, in the town on the Pacific that was probably the last place in the world for a factory or the working of transcendent miracles too difficult to explain or name. But she felt that somehow her devotion and her sharp attention would have repercussions, that, just as in a concert hall, where music could only truly rise within the hearts of its listeners, she could forge a connection over the thin air. When a good wave rolled against the rocks of the cove, it sent up rockets of foam that hung in the sun, motionlessly and — if one could look at them hard enough to make them stand still — forever. To make them a target, to sight them with concentration as absolute as a burning weld, to draw a bead, to hold them in place with the eye, was to change the world.

The factory was her place for this, for precision, devotion, and concentration. Here the repercussions might begin. Here, in the darkness, the light that was so white it was almost blue — sapphire-colored — flashed continually, like muzzle bursts, and steel was set to steel as if swords were being made. Here she could push herself, drive herself, and work until she could hardly stand — all for him.

As the battle of Tarawa became more and more difficult, and men fell, Paulette doubled and redoubled her efforts. Every weld was true. She built the instruments with the disciplined ferocity that comes only from love. For the rhythm of the work seemed to signify something far greater than the work itself. The timing of her welds, the blinking of the arc, the light touch that held two parts together and was then withdrawn, the patience and the quickness, the generation of blinding flares and small pencil-shots of smoke: these acts, qualities, and their progress, like the repetitions in the hymns that the women sang on the line, made a kind of quiet thunder that rolled through all things, and that, in Paulette's deepest wishes, shot across the Pacific in performance of a miracle she dared not even name — though that miracle was not to be hers.

Elena, Unfaithful

by Gloria Kurian Broder

ALEXEI SAZEVITCH leapt out of the barber's chair and looked
into the mirror after his haircut, and when he saw that he was excep-
tionally handsome for his age, he decided to retire. From his office he
placed a call to his childhood friend, André, who lived in Paris, and
said, "I'm stopping this nonsense, André. From now on I intend to
spend all my time with Elena.

"She's getting younger and prettier," he told André, though in fact
he thought she was getting older and homelier. After that, he descended a long flight of stairs to the office of a man he knew only
slightly, but who was also a Russian by birth and an engineer, and
leaning on the man's desk with the palms of his hands, he confided,
"Rothkovitch . . . Rothkovitch . . . I have four children — Arianne,
Eva, Ilya, and Katya. They are all grown and out of the house now,
thank God, and my wife is not growing any younger or thinner; she's
not like you and me" — he punched Rothkovitch in the stomach and
planted a cigar in Rothkovitch's pocket — "so I've decided to stop all
this and retire."

Finally, Alexei gave his secretary a silk scarf, a scarf unusual for
being so long. After she had unwound it and wound it up again,
Alexei noisily kissed her on the mouth and tossed her in the direction
of the radiator. Forcefully he grasped and shook the hands of the rest
of his staff and at last went down in the elevator carrying his framed
diplomas; a silver plaque for designing the Elgar Bridge; two brass cups
for jumping overboard and saving lives at the scene of that bridge; a

wedding picture of his mother and father; and a large, embossed, half-eaten box of Ghiradelli chocolates. He put all of these in the back seat of his Bentley and drove through Detroit, cruising one-handedly through streets arched over with dust-laden trees and factory-filtered sunlight, past tight rows of brick-faced houses offering their ancient, cracked, cement porches, out into the raw, bleak avenues of tire and automotive supply stores, and finally beyond, to his own neighborhood of wide and utterly isolated lawns.

"Elena, Elena," he shouted at the front door. And when his wife appeared, he greeted her: "From this moment on, my darling girl, I will spend each and every moment at home with you!"

At these words it seemed to him that Elena's eyes started up and that she turned peculiarly pale. But he was altogether unprepared when, two days later, she took ill and died. The entire family went to the funeral and the priest read a eulogy.

Alexei could not believe anything like this had happened. He caught a cold and felt numb. All the same, grief — which he did not like, which he had always hid from — threatened to visit him, while terrible questions pushed their way into his clogged mind, such as, had he, during his and Elena's forty-five years together, treated her well enough for a European husband of average morality who was the head of his house and irresistible to women? On her last birthday, had he written a large enough check to Products for the Blind? And why had he gone fishing with his friend, Vassily, and their redheaded, then their brunette, mistresses on the very day that his second daughter, Eva, was born? the following year when Ilya was born? two mornings after the premature arrival of Katya, and exactly one week later, on the Fourth of July?

Alexei blamed his naïveté most of all. He had thought, initially, that his children would somehow look better. But no, in the early years he had always seemed to come upon them sitting on the linoleum in the pantry in wet snowsuits, holding out their swathed and dripping arms. "Papa, Papa," they would urge, while he would take a few steps back and as a young father observe that they had features he had not wholly counted on, mannerisms he was not prepared for. From the very beginning, Arianne was too awkward, Eva too mean, Ilya too pulling, and Katya unaccountably squashy and low to the ground.

"Think of the poor," Elena sang to them in their cradles, training them for good deeds. "Think of the poor," she warned them, each time he took off for a weekend. Busily, she sent forth baskets of fruit and new shoes, mailed out letters to the city council, and steadily brought in painting after painting of hefty-looking fruit, which she bought from starving artists. Nor was he, Alexei, exempt either, for each time he headed for the door, carrying suitcases, Elena would unlock his fingers, take hold of both of his hands, gaze into his eyes and say, "Alexei Mihailovitch, think once more about the poor." On these occasions he understood she spoke about herself.

Had it been all his fault then, he wondered. Was there time to start anew? His cold got better, his head cleared, and for a brief time he faced the fact that Elena had died; but he was a man who had always hid from unhappiness, who now grew aware that a terrible horizon of pain waited in the distance for him like a bank of fog. Massing together, it thickened and inexorably moved closer. In his sleep he moaned; he called out for Elena, and awoke each day feeling drugged and dizzy. Then in the middle of one night Birdie, the old housekeeper, brought him ice water, and after drinking it he fell asleep and dreamed of love, of youth, of bands of handsome, free, unfettered people moving along the banks of a rich, green river. Violets and poppies embroidered the meadows and a scent of lilac inundated the air while he — only he could not be certain it was he — and Elena danced, wandering amidst it all. In the morning he woke up feeling sensual, played upon, vulnerable to desire; and with the idea that something miraculous had happened, he got out of bed, crossed the carpeted bedroom, thrust open the windows, and, looking lightheartedly out onto Elena's garden, understood in the sweet, wild, and pungent summer air that Elena Petrovna had not died after all: she had simply run off with another man — very likely with a man who still worked — and she was happy.

Tears of gratitude glistened in Alexei's eyes. A photograph of Elena stood on the dresser. "Look at you!" he exclaimed, pressing the cardboard between his fingers. "Fifty pounds overweight, hair in braids like my great-grandmother, bags under your eyes, forever taking your shoes off and leaving them where I can trip — unable to wear a pair of shoes comfortably for more than five minutes — talking on and on about

Congress, the war, the poor — and yet . . . yet I've misjudged you, I've never fully known what you are!"

He kissed the photograph, leaving wet marks, put it down, opened Elena's closet and looked in. Except for a strange umbrella and a folding chair, it was empty. She had taken all of her clothes, he thought, which was just as well since she did not own very many. His own wardrobe exceeded hers by ten times.

Alexei went to the phone. He wanted to ring up people and tell them his news. He would say to Vassily, "Vassily, just think of it — Elena's going off like that. Isn't it unusual, isn't it ironic!" But as luck would have it, he had recently kicked Vassily out of his house. And then, he debated, if he placed a call to André, there was a good chance André might misjudge his marriage — after all, they had not seen each other in thirty years. As for his children, they doted and depended on their mother much too much: finally he did not wish to cause them any pain.

His hand still on the phone, for a moment Alexei considered telling the lady in the bakery whose blue, fractured eyes already held the knowledge of hundreds, perhaps even thousands, of different lives. Unfortunately, he thought, he did not know that lady. He took the umbrella from Elena's closet and went downstairs, still wearing his robe. Through the double glass doors that led into the living room he saw Birdie dusting the furniture with a feather duster, her hand moving like a pendulum as she mechanically turned here and there, touching the worn, rose-colored satin settee and couches, the samovar on the coffee table, the mended china lamps and clocks. He opened the glass doors and stepped in, then stepped out as a smell of stale oranges and apples rushed at him from the framed pictures of fruit on all the walls. Stepping in again, he shut the glass doors behind him.

"Birdie," he said, thinking perhaps she should be the first to know. After all, she had helped diaper and she had stuck pins, he conjectured, into all four of his children. For that alone she deserved something: should he clap her on the back and shout into her good ear, "Birdie, you old vixen, you demon! Just guess what your mistress has gone and done!"

He decided not. She would not believe him; worse still, she might say nothing at all. "Birdie, whose umbrella is this?"

She took it from him and looked at it for a long time. "It's Arianne's. She left it here last week, when it rained." Then she walked past him with the umbrella, which she put in a closet in the front hall.

"Arianne!" he exclaimed; Arianne, he thought. Why hadn't he singled her out from the others? She was his eldest daughter, the only one at whose birth he'd been present, the only child who had grown up as tall as he, with shoulders practically as broad; who beat him at badminton, who was more of a son to him than his other daughters or his son, and who could match him drink for drink at family gatherings until late in the night, when they would smile at one another, clasp their arms about each other's powerful shoulders, and loudly chorus "Auld Lang Syne."

He rushed to the phone in the den, and when she answered in the familiar, hearty voice that cracked in between syllables due to hoarseness and the headlong intensity of her goodwill, he leaned way back in the swivel chair behind the desk, stretched out his legs, and to the ceiling trilled out, "A..ri..anne, A..ri..anne!"

"Papa, I'm glad you called. I was just about to call and ask you how things are."

"They're wonderful."

"I'm glad to hear that."

"Yes, they're perfect," he offered again, happy with such an exchange. Arianne, he thought, smiling broadly, was always cheerful. Unfortunately this virtue had also become her failing and he conceded that it even showed on her, physically — for although up to the neck she stood as proudly as a colt or soldier, her head with its close-cropped, curly, dark hair tended to droop, and on her gaunt and pleasant face loomed the resigned and tragic expression of one who can never publicly come up with any but jovial things to say.

"How are your husband and children?" he asked her.

"We're all first rate."

"Excellent. How is the dog?"

"Getting much better. Thank you very much for asking."

"How is the cat?"

"Papa, uh . . . we don't have a cat."

"Never mind then; forget that I asked you." He leaned into the phone. "Arianne, I have something to tell you." A surge of anticipation welled up inside of him. "Your mother's gone . . . she's gone . . .

shopping." His heart sank; he felt that he had failed. He let out his breath.

There was silence for a few moments and then Arianne shouted with no crack in her voice this time, "Papa, what did you say?"

"I said she's gone shopping." The statement sounded plausible enough to him except, of course, that everyone knew Elena never went shopping: it was always he who spent his spare time riding escalators in search of the latest, most elegant accessory from Italy or France.

"Papa, what did you say?"

"She's gone . . ." unsuccessfully, he tried again, "she's gone shopping."

"Listen, Papa, don't think about it. You have a point. Don't think about it and I'll come see you at two this afternoon. You have a point. There are good sales all over town. There are excellent sales in all the shopping centers." She hung up.

Downcast, Alexei remained seated at the desk, thinking that if only he had been able to tell Arianne the truth about her mother, he might have been able to tell her more — such as the differences between some of his competitors' work on bridges, and his own work; and how Vassily, after marrying a dreadful woman too late in his life, had forgotten the names of all their mistresses. Subsequently he and Vassily had had nothing to talk about; they'd quarreled over cards; at last Alexei threw him out of the door.

Brooding stonily in the swivel chair, Alexei turned prey to old irritations. Why, he wondered — as he had often wondered — why had Arianne, on the morning before her marriage, jumped into her mother's lap and remained there for half an hour when she was twice the size of Elena and might just as easily have jumped into his? Rehearsing these tales, Alexei's eyes began to flicker, his fingers to touch and move an ashtray, a letter opener on the desk, until all at once he grew impatient, jumped up and ran into the front hall.

"Breakfast, Birdie," he called, "right after my shower." He climbed the stairs, turned on the water in the bathroom, went into the bedroom and slid open the doors of his wall-to-wall, beloved closet. At this instant, the phone rang.

"Father?"

"Eva?"

"I hear that mother's gone shopping."

Eva's voice, suspicious and complaining at best, now snapped and accused. Alexei held the receiver a distance from his ear and inured himself by gazing at the orderly array of suits, trousers, jackets, vests, and coats that hung from wall to wall, harmoniously arranged by color. It was a sight he found soothing and peaceful, but which angered Eva, for whenever she visited the house, after she had eaten up all the scraps in the icebox, opened and searched in every drawer for childhood mementos, stormed abstractly through the basement and sniffed into the attic, she invariably ended up by confronting his clothes.

"Fifty-one suits," she would declare, pointing to them with a long, ink-stained, crooked finger. "It's disgusting! Give some to the poor!"

"But they're not for the poor," Alexei would inform her, very simply, "they're for me."

Sometimes Katya would follow her sister to Alexei's closet. Katya was the baby. She was plump, with chubby upper arms Alexei liked to pinch. She had a small, cupid's face with hair planted on top of her head like a robin's nest; she had short legs and wore long dresses with uneven hems; and instead of becoming a ballet dancer, as Alexei had hoped, she had gone petulantly, yet unhesitatingly, into social work. Hair pins fell from her head, and like Eva, she said, "Give some to the poor."

And on occasion Ilya would wander in and, standing with his nose comfortably inside Alexei's closet with his hands on his hips, would inquire with a show of great kindness and concern, "Papa, what are you trying to prove? Why do you have so many clothes?" Alexei would answer, "Why do you have a moustache? Why, in these ecologically troubled times, do you have nine children? Why do you always only act in plays by Gorki?" — to which Ilya would raise his head high and, with heartfelt sincerity and the voice projection of an actor, solemnly intone, "At least I don't have so many clothes."

"What," Eva now pursued, as she liked her facts to fit, "what did mother go shopping for?"

Alexei frowned into the phone. *"For?"* An expression of pride —

self-loving and stubborn — chiseled itself onto Alexei's face. He lifted his chin and reflected. "For shoes. Stockings. A dress. A purse." He paused. He leaned against the bedroom wall and crossed his ankles. "A hat. Some gloves. A bottle of perfume. You ought to go shopping yourself." He referred, as he knew she understood quite well, to the fact that she always wore an old serape and sandals and drove a camper truck with a broken muffler, and beyond that to the greater facts: that she taught in a ghetto school with hungry, angry dedication; that she stared glassily at him through thick lenses while clutching an enormous guitar; that she was bowlegged, vast-hipped, militant about women's rights, middle-aged, and had never married; and that more than any of the others, she had been influenced by her mother, but did not have her mother's grace.

Yet the tone of her voice suddenly softened. "Listen, Papa, tell me something. Have you been feeling yourself? How have you been feeling? Father . . . Papa, I think I'll come sleep home tonight. Tell Birdie to put out fresh sheets."

"No, no, no, no!"

"Why not?"

"No, no!"

"I'd like to."

"I think . . . it occurs to me," he recovered from her offer, "there's no need to." He smiled and murmured gallantly into the phone, "After all, my dear, you have your own apartment, your own little kitty cats, your guitar . . ."

"What I think," Eva said, "is that I'll pick Ilya up at the airport at one. That's when his plane comes in."

"Ilya?" For an instant he panicked. "Where's Ilya been?"

"Chicago. Don't you remember? In a play. He's been there for two weeks."

Alexei felt both relief and annoyance. "Gorki again. Why does Ilya only act in plays by old Russians? Why doesn't he act in something modern, up-to-date?"

"Right after that," Eva went on, ignoring him, "I'll stop by for Katya at her work and we'll come to you around two."

"All of you?" Alexei objected.

"All of us," Eva confirmed, and added before hanging up, "Arianne said she'd drive over at the same time."

This plan depressed Alexei. He showered and dressed, thinking that his children were coming to see him. What could he do with them? He came down the stairs, shouting, "Breakfast, Birdie, breakfast!" and went into the living room to wait. Opening the double glass doors, he stepped on figured rugs that lay on top of the heavy carpet. He glanced about. Pictures of glossy fruit — one of peaches and pears, one of plums and pears, one of plums and apples, and one simply of bananas — painted by artists, each one more poor, he guessed, than the others — hung on three thick, ivory walls, while at the windows heavy drapes kept out the light, the air. He had never liked this room. He had often told his family it was too old-fashioned, too Russian, and they had answered that they were Russian. Each time he came home from an illicit weekend, he had wanted to tear out walls, put in a bold expanse of vinyl floor and a sleek, white, modern couch. But Elena pleaded that he had his office and his outings and that this was her room. She began to go out less and less. She grew heavier, closer to life, less willing to keep on her shoes. Neighbors, teachers, other Europeans, and her own four children came to see her — brought her their troubles — as she sat on the worn, rose-colored satin settee, listening through long winter afternoons, her shoes paired next to her and two bunions on her toes. While she listened, her fingers peeled and divided an orange, and he remembered that her lips would first purse together as if they could taste each trouble and then grow round as if they were labeling and judging the trouble as "pretty good" or "pretty bad." After that, her manner changed. She gave advice. Handing around sections of the fruit, she tossed her head, her black eyes gleamed like a girl's amidst their bed of wrinkles, a high color rose to her flat cheeks, and even her chins — her grand and battered chins — jumped about with a certain ebullience and style.

Watching her in those last few years, Alexei's throat had closed; he had wanted those bursts of animation for himself. At the same time he eyed her audience, wondering if her opinions had come to be more respected than his own. How could that be? He, after all, had built fifteen bridges and designed six exhibits in the 1939 New York World's Fair where, whenever he turned around, one hundred beautiful women seemed to be concentrating raptly on him. And yet just this past spring, unable to make his presence felt, he had shouted into a group of acquaintances and strangers, "Let me talk, let me talk!" and then, overcome with shame, with chagrin, had quit the room, fled up the stairs, and placed a call — for no good reason — to André in Paris.

Alexei gazed at the rose-colored settee. It was empty; Elena was not there; and yet he seemed to hear her say, "Alexei, let's not eat cake; let's eat bread." She said it liltingly, with humor and in the voice of her youth, the same voice that had promised him a sweet, unjudging, shrewd frivolity forever — and then betrayed him.

At breakfast, Alexei ate in the dining room, alone, his eyes fixed on the buffet opposite him. Lifting his spoon, he reflected that inside those carved and massive drawers, both his and Elena's family silver was stored and lay together, rested side by side — a fact that struck him as so peculiarly intimate and fitting that briefly he faced the idea that Elena had died. But he got up at once and went into the den. Like the other rooms in the downstairs of the house, the den was dark and heavily carpeted. Drapes and venetian blinds hung at the windows. Two brown leather couches, a charcoal drawing of mangoes, and a desk lined the walls. In the center of the desk stood an immense world globe, its roundness and airiness, its light-blue color, and the fact that it so easily revolved making it a focal point in the room. Spinning the globe, Alexei's fingers caught at Rome, St. Tropez, at Venice, and impulsively, as though he were proposing some marvelous vacation by the sea, he urged out loud, "Elena, let's be young again!" The sound of his voice shocked him and he retreated up the stairs.

There, looking out the window over Elena's garden, he again smelled honeysuckle, saw fresh primroses, orchids, and daisies, and was once more reassured that Elena had run off with another man and was happy. He phoned the bakery and requested that they send up a cake. Then he lay down on the bed and fell deeply asleep.

When he awoke, he remembered that his children were coming to see him, and he felt pleased. He changed his shirt and brushed his hair. On the landing he met Birdie as she inched her way up for an afternoon nap, her bald head ringed round with ancient markings. They exchanged awareness of each other but no words and Alexei continued down, saw in the kitchen that his cake had arrived and transferred it to a crystal platter.

At two o'clock, he stood outside the front door and heard Eva's broken muffler in the distance. Presently the camper came into view and Eva maneuvered the vehicle up the driveway, her head craned out one window of the cab, Ilya's head protruding out the other window, and Katya in between them, staring straight ahead. A few houses down, Arianne parked her VW by the curb and ran at a gallop until she joined the others. The four of them headed up the path. They called, "Papa . . . Papa."

Eva confronted him first. Clasping her guitar with one hand, she removed her glasses with the other and lunged at him, timing her kiss so that it landed in the air. At this she looked wounded and angry, as if it were somehow all his fault. He gazed closely at her, struck as always by the beauty, not of her features, which were coarse, but of her translucent, pearly skin. She had, if nothing else, inherited his grandmother's complexion. He said to her, "Try again."

Surprised, Eva obeyed and then stepped back, tripping on her guitar. Katya took her place. She, too, appeared surprised by Alexei's order. Katya stood on tiptoe. Delicately she bestowed on her father a sweet and prissy peck, then turned her head away. As she was still his baby, this greeting — ambiguous though it was — pleased and undid him a bit. "Katya," he said. "But why are you so thin?"

"I've lost weight."

"Ah, Katya," he mourned, wondering if her husband beat her. He felt in his pocket for a piece of candy and at the same time noticed that her hair had turned entirely gray. "Ah, Katya, you've lost too much weight. You look like a cobweb."

"I've lost," she corrected him, proud and plaintive at once, "the right amount."

"Then never mind," he told her, comforting them both and dismissing her, for behind Katya, Ilya pushed for his turn, and behind Ilya he saw his tall and self-effacing Arianne, a brown paper bag in her hand — doubtless it contained brandy — who registered his awareness of her by signaling above the heads of the others in a voice that croaked like a frog's, "It's a most beautiful day. Papa — it's a most beautiful day in summer!"

"Arianne . . . Ilya . . . Katya . . . Eva . . . I'm so happy to see all of you!"

"And we're so happy to see you," said Ilya, stepping forward. He took both of his father's hands in his and stared intently into his father's eyes as if trying to glean from them something vital and unknown. His moustache quivered.

Uncertain as to what Ilya wanted, Alexei said, "Your mother isn't home."

"We understand," said Ilya.

"She'll be back quite late. But what I have for you is . . ."

"We understand," Ilya said. "She's gone shopping."

"She's gone shopping," said Katya.

"She's gone shopping," Arianne confirmed.

Alexei felt uncomfortable, but overcame it. "Come in, come in," he said, holding the door open. "What I have for you is . . . I have some very excellent cake. Birdie didn't make it. Your mother didn't make it either. I got this exceptional cake by ordering it from the bakery." He led them through the front hall, the dining room, turned to face them by the kitchen. "As you will see, it is chocolate and has icing out of spun sugar and flowers and other such decorations." Flutelike, his fingers gestured in the air to convey the ambience of such a cake: its roses, its sugared avenues and lanes, the possibility of castles. "Now who will help me? Katya, put on coffee. Eva, bring out cups and plates. What else do we need? Napkins. Did I forget napkins? Ilya, see if you can find some napkins."

Alexei carried the cake into the living room, carefully set it down on the dark wood of the inlaid coffee table and sat down in the center of the rose-colored satin settee in what had always been Elena's place. He bent down to remove his shoes, but straightened up again, feeling foolish. His children arranged themselves in a semicircle around him and appeared fascinated. They had an air of being welcome strangers. Conscious of their mood, Alexei sliced the first piece of cake and meticulously placed it in the perfect center of a plate. He sliced a second, third, and fourth piece and handed these around. He had, he supposed, never served his children before and yet now, in Elena's absence, it seemed absolutely proper and what he wanted.

He watched as they began to eat: Eva avidly gobbled, Katya licked, Arianne chewed awkwardly, getting crumbs caught between her teeth and claiming she had never tasted anything better. As for Ilya, his cake went into his mouth and simply disappeared. Alexei smiled. A sense of satisfaction and fulfillment swept subtly over him. He decided he would call in his children's spouses, even all his grandchildren, despite their bad manners and unkempt hair.

To pave the way, he said, "I think . . . it occurs to me . . . I have something to tell you. Your mother's run off . . . with a lover."

"Oh, Papa!" all of them scolded at once and Katya added, "Stop it!"

"Don't worry, Katya. It will be a nice change for her; it will do her good."

Arianne objected, "Papa, she wouldn't do such a thing."

Ilya said, "I thought you told us she went shopping."

Katya cried out indignantly, "Listen to that! Have you ever heard such a thing! It's too much! I can't bear it!"

Through thick glasses Eva eyed him steadily and warned, "You'd better be careful, Father. You'd better stay off that track. Go back to shopping."

"But I don't understand," Alexei told them, shrugging, "you act as if your mother isn't capable of having a lover when, after all, she's like everyone else in this world; she's as capable of carrying on . . . of enjoying herself . . . as you and me."

"No more, no more!" Katya wailed. She stamped her foot. "One more word and I'll scream."

But Alexei could not stop himself. "Most likely this is not her first lover. Indeed, there is good reason to think," he went on, lifting a speculative finger into the air, "that your mother has had many different lovers in the past. Perhaps some of them were social workers, community workers, teachers, even psychologists — yet they were lovers all the same." But even as he said this — even as he recognized its hollow sound — he knew he had gone too far.

Ilya stood up and faced his father. A sound of muffled choking issued from his throat. From his moustache came a whistle like a train's. Yet all he could utter was, "Cad!" A few minutes later he managed, "Bounder!" Katya fell out of her chair, sideways, and began to sob. Dragging her guitar behind her, Eva started to pace, agitatedly marching up and down the length of the room and in a cold, even voice summing up: "You never deserved her. You never thought of anyone but yourself."

Of the four, only Arianne approached her father. She put a long, large-boned arm around him and tried to chuckle. "You're mistaken, Papa. She wouldn't do that, you know. She *couldn't* do that." But then, as if suddenly overcome, she moved off to a corner behind the fireplace, dropped into an armchair and covered her face with her hands.

Eva continued pacing and narrating, "You never tried to understand her. She was a saint, a free spirit." From the floor, Katya sent up sharp yelps. Eva stepped over her and went on, "You never cared enough for her . . . or for us. You were always too vain, too arrogant, too unfeeling." Ilya, who had remained rooted to the same spot, his face pale, his neck livid, now grabbed hold of the cake knife, brandished it in the air, gnashed his teeth violently, and cut himself another piece of cake. He then left the room and went into the den to phone his wife. Katya crawled after him; she phoned her office.

Reentering the living room together, the two of them looked about, preparing to resume their angry postures. But in that dim, enclosed room — crowded with the clocks and china of their childhood, the pictures, upholstery, and samovars of their lives — they could not bear the violence of the fury and the anguish that they felt, so that, with a shriek, Katya opened the double glass doors and tumbled through the back hallway. One by one the others followed after her, squeezing through the narrow door and catapulting out into Elena's garden. And there, surrounded by the green spread of lawn, and under the splendor of the sky, they seemed more easily able to breathe. They said, "Ahhhh . . . ahhhh."

Ilya stretched out on a chaise, lifting his face to the sun. Eva uncovered an old guitar behind a rose bush, and gently administered to it. On her hands and knees, Katya picked herself a bouquet of small flowers, and Arianne, her mighty shoulders bent, emerged from the garage with the lawnmower. At once she sent the tall weeds flying.

Alexei isolated himself from them. Pulling a chaise a good distance away, to the other side of the cement path, he lay down and shut his eyes, his head also seeking the summer sun. Instead, in his mind's eye, he saw the brown, chill winter before snow. He stood on the frozen lawn while his small children ran toward him from the candy store, clasping white paper bags and sticks of licorice in their hands; calling him, while he, aloof and detached, held off, waited until the last minute when they reached him before embracing and claiming them for his own.

Now it was all over, he thought. They could have nothing more to do with one another; he had waited too long. For the first time he wondered whom Elena had run off with, and where they'd gone. A powerful jealousy invaded him, and almost vengefully he decided he would phone Vassily and say, "Vassily, do you remember those wig models we met in New York City, in that restaurant on 57th Street? They were eating cannelloni and had ribbons in their hair?" Vassily's memory, he knew, was worth nothing these days, but he would prod it, stir it up. "Remember, you had veal parmigian and I had saltimbocca and those girls were done up just like gift packages? Vassily, my friend, let's go to New York and look for them. I'll take the taller of the two and since you're so very much shorter . . ."

But he did not feel like going on. He let his hand drop over the edge of the chaise and plucked a blade of grass, which he put to his mouth. Once, at the beginning of his marriage, he had lain in a field with Elena and tasted one of her toes. He had never done that again, not having particularly liked it; yet the memory came back to him in the deep, bitter taste of the grass, this time telling him that what he wanted, more than anything else, was to take Elena from her lover and bring her back — beautiful and black-haired — for himself.

Quickly he went into the house and up the stairs, pulled out two suitcases from a closet and opened them on his bed. He chose underwear, shirts, handkerchiefs, and socks. On the way he planned that he would run into a shop and buy Elena a necklace, a new wedding ring. He would buy himself a tie. From down the corridor he heard a banging and Eva's voice that said, "Wake up, Birdie, wake up. There are a lot of things to do. We're taking inventory, and Ilya wants to see you." Alexei glanced at his watch, thinking that Birdie had slept long enough. He went on packing, elaborately folding his clothes, taking fresh pleasure in his skill.

But when he descended the stairs half an hour later, he found his way to the front door barred by a carton of books, a samovar, the world globe from the den, and Arianne's umbrella. Behind these, three large paintings stood lined up against a wall. Setting down his suitcases, he followed voices to the dining room.

There, Katya and Eva leaned over the open drawers of the buffet,

Katya with a pad and pencil in her hand. They were counting silver. Above them, where a picture of avocados always hung, was an empty space. Everything, Alexei thought, seemed odd. He sensed something — some strange current in the air, some bewildering change that he could not identify. Fear and suspicion seized him. His pulse began to pound.

"Twelve spoons," Katya said, "leaf pattern."

"No, ten," said Eva.

His two daughters stopped when they noticed him. But Ilya and Birdie, who were playing cards at the dining-room table, did not look up even after he had entered and demanded, "What's going on? What's going on?" His fear grew stronger, became a kind of panic. Then suddenly he thought he understood: he had been duped. His children had been in on Elena's plan from the very beginning; all along they'd known where she'd gone off to, and with whom.

A false smile stretched across Alexei's face — a wheedling, over-intimate expression so alien to him it cut his cheeks. "You might as well tell me. There's no point to hiding it. Where has Elena gone?"

Eva strode over to him. It was then that he started to feel the other fear, the other terror. Eva lifted her face close to his and, looking down at her, he knew what she was going to say. More than ever before, he was aware of her extraordinary complexion, inherited from his own family. And indeed the skin on her face appeared so milky-white, so translucent, that for a moment he believed in the possibility of seeing right through her to some preferable object — such as bridges, even trees — but was stopped by the stubborn, owl-like challenge of her nearsighted eyes, by her brooding nose, by her chin as she said, "Mama has not run away. She is dead. She died six weeks ago."

Even as Alexei's head cleared, his mouth opened in a cry of pain. "A . . . ri . . . anne!"

Eva told him, "Arianne's busy drinking. She's drinking because, on top of other things, the house is too big. It's too big for you alone. We're closing it up."

He found Arianne in the den, sitting in the dim room with a bottle of Scotch, a bottle of bourbon, and an ice bucket at her side. Still disoriented and with no exact motive in mind, he tried out his grotesquely unconnected smile on her, but was relieved when she did not see it in the dark. She said, "Come sit down next to me, Papa, and have a drink. I'm way ahead of you. I've finished the bourbon. It was wonderful bourbon. First rate, really. Let me fix you a Scotch."

He drank from the glass she handed him, taking comfort from it and from her hoarse, warm, cracking voice. "Do you remember, Papa," she asked him, "all those games of badminton we used to play? Do you remember all those nights we ended up drinking brandy in the garden at two o'clock in the morning and singing 'O Tannenbaum' and 'Auld Lang Syne'? Those are first-rate songs. I love those songs." She poured them each another drink.

But he would not touch his. Something was stuck in his mind, in his heart. He fought both to locate and to control it, and presently he said, "Arianne, I think . . . it occurs to me . . . your mother died."

Through the slats in the venetian blinds he could see Eva carrying one of the large paintings down the front path. She loaded it into the cab of her camper. Alexei waited for Arianne to answer. But Arianne, as always unable to think of any but jovial things to say, stared straight ahead in her sorrow.

The Consolation of Philosophy

by Nicholas Delbanco

WHEN HE HEARD his first lover was getting divorced, Robert Lewin panicked. He had not seen her in ten years; they had not been together for fifteen. They had few friends in common; her world was not his world. She was an actress of sufficient fame for her private life to seem public; she smiled at him from newsstands or in the supermarket checkout display. He read about her husband's drinking problem, her near-fatal car crash in Topanga Canyon and their second son's kidney malfunction. The photographs in gossip magazines had captions like "Sally Smiles to Hide the Tears," or "Tragedy Offstage!"

Robert disapproved. But in a way that was not casual he had loved her all his life; he dreamed that they grew old together, laughing in their sixties at the passion they shared when eighteen. He was thirty-eight years old, an architect; he, his wife and daughter lived on the Connecticut and Massachusetts border. Sally would purchase a house near their village. Knowing that he lived there, she would hire him to remodel her country retreat. She would want the silo to have two bedrooms and a bathroom, and the barn to be a studio. She would dam the stream and have him build a sauna and a free-form swimming pool. All this would be accomplished at long distance, and via intermediaries. She would buy the property sight unseen, and with all its furniture; Samantha, his wife, would not know. One bright autumn morning, Sally would fly in from the Coast to check on her dream's progress. He would receive her smiling, wearing dark glasses, not old.

She would fold herself into his arms. She would say nothing, since nothing could improve the silence they shared.

At other times he gave her lines. "I never loved another man," she said. "Not the way that I loved you. It never does happen again."

"I know."

"It happens differently," she said, "I won't pretend I didn't love Bill. Our marriage was — well, workable. But no other man in my life . . ."

"We don't have to discuss it."

"We do. No other man in my life was ever quite as — what shall I call it, *protective* as you were. Considerate. You *did* take me under your wing."

Her diction had grown formal. "Is this a performance?" he asked.

"No. You took care of me. You helped with my homework, remember?"

At this point inventiveness stopped. Robert pictured them in bed but using their twenty-year-previous bodies; he had not seen her in the flesh to judge how flesh had changed. His own had thickened, some; his hair had thinned. Her consorts were the beautiful people, and he would not fit. His clothes were out of date. He passed for fashionable in the Berkshires, still, but felt less and less at ease in cities or with the gaudy young. He designed doctors' offices and banks. His clients all distrusted what they called the avant-garde. They wanted renovation work and, where possible, restoration. They wanted contemporary styling with a Colonial theme.

He worked alone. He had a large, illuminated globe on a teak stand by his desk. When drinking coffee, or in the intervals when concentration failed, his habit was to spin the globe and shut his eyes and stop its spinning with his finger. There, where the rotation ceased, he would embark on a new life. He landed in Afghanistan and northern Italy and the Atlantic Ocean and near Singapore. With disconcerting frequency, he landed on the Yucatán peninsula; once he pinpointed Mérida four times in a row.

The phone rang. "Are you coming home for lunch?" Samantha asked.

"I wasn't planning to."

"All right."

"Has something happened?"

"No. It's just I've got some errands, and you said you might come home this morning. And I wanted to be here if you did."

"If you're coming into town," he offered, "we could meet."

"No, darling, really. I've got forty things to do and might as well start doing them."

"I'll work right through," said Robert. "And I'll be home by five. Five-thirty at the latest."

"See you then."

Something in her manner troubled him, as if she called to know his plans rather than meet him for lunch. He lifted the receiver in order to return the call, to find her at the house and tell her he was coming home; his plans had changed. It was eleven o'clock. He did not dial. The prospect of a day without appointments was satisfying, nearly; he shut his eyes and spun and landed in Zagreb.

As the years passed, his years with Sally grew abstract; they both had been beginners, he would say. He forgot the reasons why they grew apart, the bitterness and boredom, and remembered only love. His memory was made up of amorous scenes. He remembered singing with her on a moonlit night in Tanglewood, standing by their blanket in the intermission, drinking rum from his initialed flask and harmonizing on the chorus of "Old Devil Moon." It was 1963; they both played the guitar. Their parents approved. She told him her last boyfriend drove a Thunderbird and wanted to be an astronaut; he probably would be, she said, he understood machines and thought the human body was just another machine. He didn't understand the finer things, spiritual things; by comparison with her last boyfriend — by comparison with everybody — Robert was a prince. Each night when he left her she whispered, " 'Good night, sweet prince.' " He said, " 'And flights of angels sing thee to thy rest.' " She said, "Drive carefully," and he walked backward to the car so as not to lose the imprint of her face. She blinked the house lights three times in farewell; he flashed his car lights also and, for her sake, did drive carefully.

Sally wore her dark hair long. She had a Roman nose and large brown eyes. He called her "almond-eyes" and "beauty" and "love."

They took each other's virginity. He remembered how she came to him in her parents' house in Weston, wearing a white negligee and carrying a towel. They spent their college weekends together; he attended Amherst and she, Smith. They embraced in pine lots and in barns and on the rear seat of his Impala and, later, in hotels. They intended to marry as soon as he got his degree. A hollowed-out tree trunk, he said, with a view of the sky would be plenty; it doesn't matter what we do so long as we do it together.

While Robert studied architecture, she applied to and was accepted by the Yale Drama School. They shared an apartment in New Haven, but her schedule and his schedule did not coincide. She performed when he came home from class, and he could not rouse her in the mornings. She dressed in black. They struggled with fidelity; she said she was attracted to Mercutio in her scene-study class. He did not confess to it but slept with a girl in Design; their afternoon encounters increased his passion for Sally at night. When she discovered his affair, she broke their stoneware plates and slammed the cutting board so hard against the counter that it broke.

He could remember how he watched her in rehearsal and saw a gifted stranger. Even then she had the quality of apartness, that silent holding-back the critics came to praise. Her first reviews were raves. They called it "presence," "power in reserve," and when she went to Hollywood, they said that Broadway lost a rising star. Robert lost control. All that fall he called her nightly, running up a telephone bill he had to borrow to pay. He drank too much and worked too little and flew round trip to Los Angeles just to have a cup of coffee with her at the airport. She was living with another man, she said, and would not take him home.

He completed architecture school and elected to practice in Stockbridge, not Manhattan. At twenty-six he married a girl from Springfield; they bought property southwest of town. He modernized the farmhouse and converted the barns. Samantha played the violin and formed a local string quartet; on their sixth anniversary, Helen, their daughter, was born. He prospered; they spent summers on the Cape.

He could have been an actor, people said; his voice was so mellifluous. He could have been associated with such men as I. M. Pei or Edward Larrabee Barnes. Once a friend had said to him, "Don't sweat the small stuff. I see you with a beggar's cup. Saffron robes. That's the kind of change you ought to contemplate, that's the way to get in touch with universal flux. I *see* it. . . ." Robert failed to, but he had been flattered. He carried with him, always, a sense of alternative possibility; his dreams were of escape.

"What's wrong?" Samantha asked.

"Nothing. Why?"

"You're sure?"

He had been splitting wood. He brought in an armload of logs. "It's cold out there," he said. "It feels like snow."

"Is something bothering you?"

"No."

"Do you want to talk about it?"

"I told you," Robert said. "It's only I'm restless. That's all."

"Would you rather I take her?"

"No."

Helen studied ballet. She was plump and unenthusiastic; he had promised to drive her, that afternoon, to see *The Nutcracker* in Springfield. Helen had wanted to go with a friend. "Why can't we take Jessie?" she asked.

"There aren't any seats left."

"How do you know?"

"It's sold out," he said. "I heard it on the radio."

"Jessie's busy anyhow," Samantha said. "Her grandparents are visiting."

"Would *you* come, Mommy?"

Samantha looked at Robert, and he shook his head. He would have liked nothing better than an afternoon of silence, but he had committed himself. He showered and shaved; the forecast was for flurries, so he took the Jeep. "Be careful," said Samantha.

"Yes."

He called her Sam. They were happily married, he said; she had the kind of resilience he lacked. She lived in the present, he said; if she had an emotion she showed it. If she was angry she expressed it, and the anger disappeared; when she was happy she sang. Helen slept beside him, her seat belt cinching her coat. Beleaguered by desire, he watched the women in the cars he passed, and in oncoming cars. He was, he told himself, just facing middle age, the loss of prowess and mobility that torments every man. This did not help.

He had last seen Sally at a party in Hyannis Port. They had been eating baked stuffed clams and drinking spritzers; his host was saying that he never ate an uncooked clam these days. There had been a hepatitis scare. "It's not as if," his host admitted, "cooking makes a difference. But I feel safer, understand, as if the odds are better when it's cooked." He offered Robert the tray. "It's a kind of roulette we play with our bellies," he said. "It's the bourgeois way of risking things." He discoursed on the difference between littlenecks and cherrystones and quahogs; they were standing on a lawn that sloped down to the shore. "Littlenecks grow up to be cherrystones," said his host. "You understand that, I suppose. And cherrystones to quahogs; it's just a question of when you harvest them. As Marx observes, a sufficient change in quantity means a qualitative change." He lit a pipe. "I always ask myself at what point such change is enforced."

"Enforced?"

"Yes. Decided on. Agreed on, if you'd prefer. When does someone somewhere say, 'Enough. Thou shalt be no more Mr. Littleneck. I dub thee Cherrystone'?" His host laughed and flourished the pipe. "The trial by fire. Sir Clam."

Sally approached. She was wearing white. He felt his stomach tighten and release. "Ah," said his host. "The guest of honor. How *are* you, my darling? Do you know each other? This is Robert . . ."

"Lewin," Robert said. "Yes. We've met."

She had been as shocked as he, she confessed, but had seen him from the patio. She had been in the area for summer stock, a one-week stint, and was leaving; why is it always like this, she asked, why do we have to go just when we want to remain? He was looking wonderful; his beard made him look like a badger. Was his marriage working out; was his wife at the party?

They made their way to the beach. A rowboat and a Sunfish were pulled up past the tide line, and she settled in the rowboat. He also sat, facing her, facing the house.

"I miss you," Sally said.

"Yes."

"It doesn't change, does it?"

"Not really. No."

"This is horrible," she said. "I wish you wouldn't look like that. I wish I'd come here by myself."

"Who's with you?"

"Everybody. I hide it better, that's all. You should have seen your face — oh, Robert, when that man said, 'Do you know each other?' How *are* you, anyway?"

He scanned the lawn, then patio, then porch.

"All right."

"You mean it?"

He nodded.

"We've wrecked each other's lives, you know."

"No."

"Yes."

"That's overstating it."

With one of those reversals that had made her, always, his equal adversary, Sally said, "Of course. I know I'm overstating it. I'm being theatrical, darling. That's what I do best."

"Other things also," he said.

"But I'm not lying. You lied. You said you were all right."

She shifted weight in the boat. In a movement he could picture clearly, ten years thereafter, she stripped off her white tights. It was a practiced motion, neither suggestive nor coy; she crossed her long, bare legs. She leaned back on her seat. He asked himself — and would, repeatedly — if she were proposing sex or getting ready to walk on the sand. Her clothing was intact, her sandals and her tights placed neatly by her side. He looked away. Samantha appeared on the porch. Men stood with her, gesticulating. He could hear her laughter. "I hate this," Robert said. He rose; the rowboat rocked. He put one foot over the gunwale. "I want what's best for you," he lied. "And that was never me."

"I'll stay here, thanks," she said. "Goodnight."

"How did it go?" Samantha asked, when he and Helen returned. He hung up his coat. He kicked off his boots. "Terrific," Robert said. "Twenty dollars so she gets to see the bottom of the chair. The part you look at from the floor."

"I closed my eyes, Mommy," she said.

"But what about the Christmas tree? The celebration?"

"I liked *that* part," said Helen.

"And the dance of the Sugar Plum Fairy?"

"He was horrible," she said. "He had big teeth and this enormous tail and his sword was all bloody. He looked like a *rat*."

"The Nutcracker kills him," Robert said. "You should have watched that part."

"I *told* you," she said, stamping. She turned from him.

"Well, maybe next year," offered Samantha. "Maybe this year was too early for you."

"Let's have a drink," Robert said. "Two vodka Martinis and one hot chocolate for our famous ballerina here."

"All right."

"You do the hot chocolate," he said. "And I'll do the vodka."

They entered the kitchen. Light from the kitchen fireplace played off the copper pots. "Next year," Helen asserted, "I'll be the Sugar Plum Fairy. I will be. You'll see."

Outside, the first snow continued. He had spotlights in the tamarack and maple trees; he turned them on. The garden appeared to leap forward and the kitchen's cage recede. He watched with genuine attention while the fall increased. The grass above the septic tank retained a warmth that melted snow, making a rectangle of bare land on the lawn; it looked like a lap rug thrown over a sheet.

"I don't know what you want from me," Samantha said. "It feels like it's never enough. No matter how much I give, it feels like there's always this one thing left over — this way that we fail you."

"What is it now?" Robert asked.

"She's scared of the Mouse King." Helen was drinking her cocoa in the television room. "So you make it seem *my* fault . . ."

"It isn't your fault."

"I'm not saying that. I'm saying you *think* so; I'm saying you've blamed me all day. As if no child of yours could ever hide under a chair." Samantha exhaled. "As if her sensitivity is something we should apologize for — as if there's something, oh, shameful in a child who has feelings."

"It isn't shameful," he said. He set himself to placate her; he poured another drink. "Control yourself" had been his mother's injunction. Whenever he was greedy, loud or frightened, she would say, "Control yourself. A gentleman has self-control. He doesn't make a fuss about the things he doesn't understand. And if he understands them, there's no need to fuss."

"I love you," Sally said again. She would have purchased Sevenoaks Farm; they would be forty-five. "These barns, that view of the mountains."

"And I love you," he said.

"What have you been up to, baby?" She lit a cigarette. She offered him one; he declined.

"I didn't know you smoked," he said.

"Only when I'm happy. This house makes me happy. And how's your family?"

"They're good," he said. "We live a quiet life."

"You have a daughter, don't you?"

"Helen. Yes."

Sally examined the bay window. "Will you move in with me?" she asked.

"Right now?"

"No. Tomorrow," she said.

His most recent client had been a family therapy center. They had wanted picture windows in the waiting rooms. This had violated Robert's sense of decorum. He said so; they disagreed. There was a village graveyard in the adjoining lot, and he situated the pentagonal structure so the picture windows overlooked the graveyard. "It's tempting," Robert said.

"Be tempted."

"You're serious?"

"Yes. Never more so."

"We've got twenty years," he said. "With luck. Twenty good years, anyhow."

"I'm ready to quit," Sally said. She was emphatic. "I've done enough acting."

"You'll miss it."

"No way. Not for a minute."

He knew enough to know this was not likely. "It's a hard habit to kick," Robert said. "I'm sure it must be difficult. All that applause."

"Those flowers," she would tease him. "Those parties at Sardi's, those feet in Grauman's Theater. Baby, it's nothing like that. It's sons of bitches, ego trips and cameos from here on in."

"You're sure?"

"I'm sure. I've never been more certain in my life."

They would sit in peaceable silence; there were no telephones. They would not bicker as they'd bickered when young; they understood the value of a gentle reticence. The sunset would be doubled by the clear reflecting mirror in the pond and, beneath it, the pool. He dreamed of this in winter while he sluiced down his own pond and scraped it for skating; he dreamed of it that early spring while the ice cracked and thawed. He filled the pool in May. Brian Dennis, after his annual checkup and the lab results, pronounced Robert fit. He redesigned the railroad station, making it a restaurant. Samantha started to jog. She was a natural athlete and soon attained four miles a day. She looked radiant; he wondered what she pictured as she ran.

Their village had a harpsichord maker. He had a shop in West Street, with a sign saying "Master Craftsman" in the window and a harpsichord-in-progress on display. There were marble steps and lintels in the shop, and ornamental hand-carved treble clefs on the door. Samantha knew him, apparently; she mentioned him in passing as a person Robert might enjoy, an adequate instrument maker. He sometimes joined their string quartet to add a piano part. The shop had an apartment on the second floor. Robert, walking to the bank or on his way from lunch or driving home from work, would slow down at the door. He was prepared to ask the price of harpsichords and, perhaps, to commission a lute. The door was never open. There were signs of life, however — fresh piles of sawdust at the workbench, or coffee mugs, or a wastepaper basket filled with what he recognized as that week's Sunday *Times*.

The upstairs apartment, too, seemed untenanted. One day Robert noticed its windows were open, and a woman with her back to him was brushing her brown hair. He stopped. He stood on the opposite side of the street, staring up. There were white lace curtains that obscured his view. He half crouched by a pickup truck; he put his feet on the bumper, one after the other, and pretended to adjust the laces of his boots. He felt exposed, aroused, but could not leave. Her body was supple. She wore a white brassiere that emphasized the pallor of her back. The light was on. She brushed her hair with metronomic regularity, stopping to shift angles every twenty strokes. She was looking at a mirror; he could not see her face. He wondered, was there someone in the room? Her attitude suggested readiness, a knowledge that she might be watched, a sense of self-display. She was familiar, somehow, yet he thought he did not know her: the mistress of the man who made the harpsichords. Her arms were lean. Robert shook his head to clear it, and in that unfocused instant the woman in the window disappeared. Yet he thought he heard her voice. He waited for some minutes, then continued home. Samantha was not there.

He turned thirty-nine in March, and they invited friends for dinner. There were jokes about Jack Benny and the wheelchair he would get next year. "If you think *this* one was bad," said Brian Dennis, "wait till you're forty." Richard Beale had been studying Baba Ram Dass. " 'Doing your own being,' " he said. "That's what it's all about, really. Just being here in the here and now. Your health, amigo," he said. "May you be here with joy."

Samantha served poached salmon, and then a rack of lamb. This repeated the menu they shared on their first night as man and wife; Robert was touched. "It's better now," he told her. "You're a better cook than those restaurant chefs."

"You're paying more attention to your food these days."

"All right. I meant it as a compliment."

"I take it that way."

"I'm grateful," he said. "When I said things were better, I didn't mean only the food."

"Happy birthday. Many happy returns of the day."

" 'After forty,' " Ellen Dennis said, " 'I hold a man's face against him.' Who said that, anyway? I think it was Abraham Lincoln."

"Winston Churchill," Brian said. "It must have been Churchill, not Lincoln."

So they argued over eloquence, and whether Lincoln or Churchill had been the better native speaker, more in touch with the language and times. Jim and Patty Rosenfield had just returned from England, from his sabbatical semester; they contended that the English had a greater native eloquence. "The problem is, however," Jim said, "they all speak so well that you never know who's *saying* something. And who's just making sentences. Even the dumb ones sound smart."

"Another thing," said Patty. "Inflation. You can't imagine how bad it is over there. How expensive everything has gotten. We entertained a little less. Maybe we ate out more often. But at the end of every week we filled two garbage cans."

Richard drank. "What does all this have to do with Lincoln or with Churchill?"

"Waste," she said. "That's what I'm discussing. We throw away more food than all Australia eats."

"I'll drink to that," Robert said. He shut his eyes. The image of Sally assailed him again — some taste or word or smell or sight inciting memory. They were near a sandbar in a saltwater inlet, making love. He lay on his back in the warm shallows, and she sat on top of him. There was a thick fog. Sailors glided in the distance; he propped himself up on his elbows so as not to swallow salt. It was the start of the fall. The cranberries were purple already, and the beach-heather was brown. Gulls watched, incurious. She bounced and settled on him, smiling, her eyes wide. They rented a bungalow called Peony; it stood in a strip of bungalows named after flowers; their neighbors were Tulip and Rose. The fog felt palpable. He saw himself the sailor now, seeing from the channel how the complicated obscure shape of youth is jointed at the waist; he watched how fleetingly they fused and broke apart. He toasted his guests and his wife.

They kept in touch, but distantly; a friend of friends said, "Sally sends regards." Her telephone number was unlisted; she sent it to him in April and wrote, "Hope to hear from you." By the time he did call, from his office, a recorded voice pronounced, "We're sorry. We cannot complete your call as dialed." He was not sorry, he decided, he would not have known what to say. Panic is the fear engendered by the great god Pan. He comes to the party unannounced and overturns the chairs and spills his drink on the rug. He will attempt his magic trick with the tablecloth. He scratches his beard, paws the floor.

Promising the cutlery and plate and crystal will remain in place, he whisks the white linen away. He is clumsy, however; things crash and tumble all over. The girl at the head of the table gets wine on her jumpsuit. She scrambles to her feet and scampers down the hall. He follows her, apologetic. There are remedies. They huddle together. There are dry cleaners, other parties, prospects of the sea. There is time.

Wind rattled at the pantry door when she opened the door to the mud room. She settled her handbag and two paper bags on the bench.

"You're having an affair," he said.

Samantha took off her gloves. She placed them on the shelf. "Was that a question?"

"No."

"Good." She shrugged out of her coat. "It didn't sound like a question."

"Are you having an affair?"

"In any case" — she selected a hook — "I don't think I'll bother to answer."

"His harpsichord. How quickly can he build one?"

"That depends," she said.

"He's careful?"

"Yes."

"Attentive?"

"Very."

"A master craftsman," Robert said.

"I've been downtown, master. Shopping." She opened the mudroom door again. "In case you're curious."

"Yes."

"Be careful with the eggs," she said. "They're in the bag in the Jeep."

In June the local ballet school offered a performance. It ran for three successive nights, and each was sold out in advance; the children came home from rehearsal with their allocated tickets. Helen was in the school's youngest class, but there were students all the way through high school. The program was immense. Its theme was that of "The Magic Garden," and children were divided, according to age and experience, into several units: there were butterflies and inchworms, bumblebees and bunny rabbits, a group of birds and flowers and scarecrows. The soloists were labeled Spring, Summer, Autumn, Winter; there were twelve such soloists, with four to perform on each night. The owner of the ballet school was, as she put it, *bouleversée*; she made a speech before the performance and said she was just so excitable because of these wonderful wonderful students that *bouleversée* was her only expression; we are enraptured to see you all here.

Helen was a Black-Eyed Susan; she wore a bright green tutu and brown leotard and fitted orange cap. There were twenty other Black-

Eyed Susans, and they skipped onstage, then curtsied and circled and whirled. Helen did so by herself. Then they all joined hands and did what looked like the Virginia Reel; fathers filled the aisles and, using flash attachments, photographed their girls. Robert had not brought his camera. He had had a long afternoon. He had come directly from the office to the auditorium; there were problems with the railroad ties he'd used for decorative beams.

During intermission, he could not find Samantha in the sea of women and daughters waiting in the hall. He pushed through swinging doors to what would be backstage; the Rhododendrons and the Owls were doing warm-ups by the barre. There were belly dancers also, waiting for their turn in "The Magic Garden"; they wore veils and diaphanous skirts. Mothers were removing rouge and lipstick from their daughters' upturned faces. Helen said, "Hi, Daddy."

He looked for her.

"Hi. Here we are."

Samantha closed her makeup kit. She stood.

"Well, look at you," said Robert. "You look beautiful."

"Thank you, Daddy." Helen pursed her lips, demure.

"Doesn't she?" Samantha said. "How do you like these sequins?"

"Very much," he said.

"The ponytail?" asked Helen.

"Yes. You'll be a star."

All around him, Robert knew, fathers were thinking the same of their daughters; all around him the girls were transformed. She was, he said, his precious ballerina, his precocious soloist. A belly dancer brushed past. "Do you want to watch the second half?" he asked.

"I'm tired, Daddy."

"You?" he asked Samantha.

"I'll tell the Cartwrights we're leaving. We got a ride down here with them, so we could all go home together."

She was, he told Samantha, wonderful. Helen wore eyeliner and mascara and had not smudged her lipstick or her rouge. Samantha turned and, bending, began to scrub at the upturned face. "Leave it," he said to his ladies. Helen wore her tutu to the car.

Bluebeard's Second Wife

by Susan Fromberg Schaeffer

*W*HEN HE FIRST APPEARED in our village, I thought nothing of him. He came from the great world, which had nothing to do with mine. Our village was so small that when people from the great world wanted to express boredom, they would ask one another, "So, what's doing in Plonsk?" I, however, liked Plonsk. It had harsh winters, and something in my blood responded to the snow. Whenever anyone wanted to know about the weather (Should they or shouldn't they start out on a trip to Minsk? If they did, would they later be found with their horses, frozen stiff as statues, blue among blue-white drifts of snow?), they would come to me because they said I could read the sky like the back of my hand. That was in the beginning, before my mother acquired her reputation first for magic, and then as a witch. Later, they said the sky *was* the back of my hand. Still later, they said that in the palm of my hand was a small window and through it, I could see the sky as it was hundreds of miles away, the weather coming closer. All this was, of course, nonsense. I had been brought up in Plonsk. I loved the snow, I waited for it in the way most young girls wait for lovers. I could tell by looking up at the sky, by feeling how the wind blew or didn't blow against my skin, if it was going to snow. And since I was never wrong, the villagers concluded I had powers. At first, I tried to deny it, but my mother said, "Why deny what no one will believe? And besides, look at where my powers have gotten us."

Her powers were undeniable. She could cure people by touching them, although afterwards the people she ministered to had to tend to the ten burns on their flesh, the imprint of my mother's curing hands. There were days when she knew she would not cure, when no fire would light in our house and we would be sent to neighbors to keep warm, and when she would lie under bearskins cold and still and blue as dead ice. When the villagers saw our chimney cold and smokeless, they would stay inside, telling one another today was a day for catastrophes. Whatever happened was sure to be irrevocable. The witch was cold and had no fire in her; better in that case to stay inside around one's own stove where all one had to fear was the falling in of one's own roof. There were other days, too, when they might want to hide, when my mother's hair blazed like fire from her scalp and seemed to rise like roots into the sky above her, when her eyes glistened in the daylight as wolves' eyes are said to glisten by the light of the moon. On these days, she put curses upon people. No matter how they begged and cried, she would never lift the curse. The truth was, as my mother told me when I was old enough to know about these things, that she did not know how to lift one of her own curses. Once she had tried; she had applied her own hot hands to a peasant's shoulder again and again. He had died of the burns before the curse had a chance to work. "That," she said, "is the only cure for a curse I know."

Did I say our town was poor? It was very poor, made of brown wooden houses, the wood unpainted, left to take its color from the onslaughts of the weather. Some houses were already giving in to the elements; people lived in them, but one could see, if one looked, the sharp teeth of the light chewing through the walls. Our streets were of slatted wood; in the winter, they grew porous under the heavy snow. In the spring, mud bubbled up from beneath and covered them. In the summer, the mud dried and gave off clouds of dust beneath even bare feet. It was a small town, in flat, brown country, far from the mountains — the usual square with the usual fountain (ours did not have running water, although from the stains at its base, we believed it once did) and the usual drunken loungers lay against it. So we were surprised when the rich man came to town and when he insisted on living in the largest dwelling on the east side of the square. He was, he said, looking for a wife.

He came in winter, wearing a heavy bearskin coat, and every few minutes his heavy, thickly veined hand would extract a heavy gold watch. He liked to know the precise time. He was amused by how well the children could tell the time simply by looking at the shadows they cast on the snow. "But you can't tell time in the dark," he said to them; "I can tell time in the dark." At night, the children would sneak off to meet him, and he would hold his watch up to the stars and tell them the exact time. "Without shadows! Without shadows!" they said. And so we came to call him the man without shadows.

This was a man who wanted life more precise than God had made it, more predictable, more measurable, so it was no surprise when we saw his carriage pull up in front of our house. My mother immediately knew what had happened: someone had told him how accurately I could predict weather. He did not come into our house alone; he came in with servants carrying covered silver trays and a steaming, golden samovar. Every day he arrived with his feast and every day he would test me about the coming weather. The villagers laughed at my mother, who was taking these ceremonial visits seriously. They said as soon as she makes a mistake, he will stop coming. But my mother did not listen to them; she brought down her marriage trunk and took out a bolt of scarlet Indian silk threaded with gold and proceeded to sew me a dress fit for an Indian princess. She did this under his eyes and the eyes of his servants, and he observed from under lids hooded like an eagle's. He saw all this without surprise, as if he took her public sewing of my dowry as a matter of course, a tribute due him, who had not yet proposed, who had not hinted at any such intention.

In this way we were fed for weeks, for months. I never made a mistake. My mother sewed more and more dresses. We were too well fed and sleepy to ask her where she found the cloth. I never made a mistake, and then spring began, the snows were gone, and the rains came. "Can you predict rain?" he asked me, and I laughed. Rain was simply another form of snow. And so he tested me until the high, dry days of summer, and then he announced that he wanted to possess me in marriage.

"And will you keep me as close to you as you keep that gold watch?" I asked. I heard my own voice, my laugh, hard and sinister. I was not surprised, but I thought he should be. He thought I was a young country girl, sweet and innocent. Closer. He said he would hold me closer. He said he was sorry I was not made of metal and cogs because then I would last forever, and he laughed, and in his laugh I heard the metallic, coglike cruelty of wheels turning, locking into one another, forcing one another in circles absolutely predictable, absolutely regular, a round, circular world in which there was no margin for error. I would preside, he told me, over great things. I would have a great ring of keys. "Never trust a man without keys," said my mother; "a man with only one key has only one door to his heart and he keeps it locked. He alone has the key to it." He turned and looked hard at my mother but her head was bent over the next of my dresses. "I know she will not need so many," said my mother; "you will buy her the only dress she needs." I thought my mother was talking about my wedding dress, and I shuddered. I had seen wedding dresses and I had seen shrouds; to me, they looked the same.

Arrangements were made for the wedding and the bridal trip. He wavered only once, when a villager told him of my mother's ability to cast spells that she could not undo. "But," he muttered to himself, "she will be far from our castle." He had no idea how far. The night before my wedding, my mother took me aside. She said once I was married, I must not look back, because there would be no one to look back for. It would be her fate, she said, to die two days after my wedding. Then, I said, I would not marry. No, she said, fate was itself a spell. Once cast, it could not be undone. I cried, but she had little sympathy for my tears. On the eve of my wedding, she came into my room, already guarded by two of the rich man's servants. "This is my book," she said, giving it to me. "In it are spells. You can make the dead move and talk. You can cure. You can curse but you cannot recall the curse. You may, if you have the ability to heat the tips of your fingers and toes, foretell the future. Do not let your husband know you have this book."

"And how will I prevent him?" I asked her.

"By covering it with this," she said, and under my eyes, she took the cover she had removed from her cookery book and glued it patiently and neatly over her book of spells. With sadness, I watched the odd pentangle and star vanish, in its place the copper cauldron and ladle. Into the front of the book and the back, she glued recipes, one after another. "Now he will not want to see it. Do not hide it," she said. "Keep it always in plain sight."

"I fear getting caught in the cogs of a wheel," I said. I expected her to tell me that all brides feared this, that I would not be a bride if I did not. Instead, she said, "A cog can give as good as it gets." Her smile was strange.

"And will you really die?" I asked her.

"I will."

"And is there nothing in this book that can prevent it?" I asked her.

"Nothing," she said; "but there is a great deal in the book all the same."

I will spare you the details of our wedding, which, for once, gave an answer to the proverbial, "So what's doing in Plonsk?" I will spare you the sight of our brown, varnished carriage, its fittings solid gold, setting out in back of scarlet-clad livery, followed by ten more liveried men in identical costumes. It is pleasant to think of the Prince and Cinderella when one still thinks one may be chosen to live in the palace; it is a bitter thing to watch the princess drive off, leaving you in her cloud of dust. I did not want to see bitter faces. I did not want my mother to see them and absentmindedly put a curse upon them that she could not remove. That was my last glimpse of Plonsk, the people staring bitterly and silently after us — with the exception of one girl, who wept hopelessly as I left. "Ah," I thought, "that one has a heart of gold." I saw the faces of my own sisters, bitter and set, and my mother, her face blue and white, her blue-white hand over her heart.

"Did you see the girl weeping?" I asked my husband. "She weeps out of happiness."

"No one weeps out of happiness," he said. I felt cold, as my mother at that moment felt cold. "Here," he said, taking a plump bag of gold from the deep pocket of his black greatcoat. "Call the rider from the window and tell him to take this back to the girl."

"Her name is Agnes," I said. So he was kind, perhaps sentimental. As the carriage rolled on, into the silence, punctuated only by the ticking of the great gold watch when my husband drew it from deep within his coat and brought it into the light, I thought how little I knew about marriage. I had married in order to send for my sisters, to bring them to a house (although my husband was said to live in a castle) where it was always warm enough and where there were enough books to keep their minds eagerly ticking, as did my husband's carnivorous watch. I had once described his watch to him in this way: his carnivorous watch. He laughed. He laughed and stroked his watch as if it were a tiny, wild beast that must be mollified, as if it were a mad, wild rat that must be petted and tamed or it would gnaw a hole through his chest, into his heart, and would not stop until it had tired itself grinding its teeth against his spinal cord. Things I said amused him. I thought about the suede purses of gold coins in the bottom of all his deep coat pockets, like mouths of tunnels, deep and dark, but the ore already mined, purified, minted by the touch of his hand. Money had a life of its own; it moved from one person to another as if by magic. It accomplished what it wanted as sorcerers did. I had also married because I wanted to know about the secret life of money. On our wedding trip, I dreamed incessantly of money. When I was awake, I saw the gold wheels of his watch, turning, the cogs and the wheels, and this too was a vision of money. Once when I slept, I heard the clank of his keys deep in an as yet undiscovered pocket, and that, too, was the sound of money. It was a long trip, but outside, the scenery moved magically, puffing up as the carriage moved through the hills, until we were traveling through mountains, and as the domed lids of the gold trays were lifted, I felt once more the touch of coming snow against my skin, the smell of it, which overpowered even the steaming, curried odors of our wedding dishes.

The castle. You know all about the castle, its stones bluish gray in the twilight, its tall turrets penetrating the heavens, surrounded by clustering stars, its cathedral windows, its stained-glass murals of boar hunts, of marriages in deep woods, of gibbeted criminals, of ships setting forth for distant destinations. Who does not know of the tapestries with their scenes of Sodom and Gomorrah, of the Tower of Babel, so exquisite it took one weaver two years to complete one square foot? Who has not heard of the Persian carpets so deep one feels one is not walking on them, but on deep grass just bent under a heavy rain? Everyone knows the castle; the castle has always been there, as has been the lord of the castle. But perhaps you do not know about the wolves who live in the wood around the castle, who my lord and husband has made his particular creatures, huge gray wolves, almost as large as a man, larger perhaps (I never could bear looking at them long), whose eyes stared out at you as if they were not the wolves' eyes, but the eyes of souls imprisoned within those sleek skins of fur.

Did you know they would come when my husband whistled, obedient as any dog? That when they came, he threw them pastries, which they adored even more than meat, and that their favorite treats were huge chocolate rum balls whose surfaces were covered with shavings of milk chocolate? Thus he had corrupted them. There were rumors — of course I heard them, how could I not have? — that on certain nights he threw other morsels, bloody and dripping, to the wolves, morsels from bodies that ought to have received proper burial. But by then I was his wife, the castle was his, as was the land around it, the housekeeper in it was dismissed every night before dusk, and my mother was dead (two days after my arrival, a blackbird came with the news of her death, the bird, I presume, under the last of her spells). He was — my husband, my lord — the only other human being left in the world. Do not ask how it feels to live in a castle, seeing no one but one's husband and the wolves and an occasional blackbird. Ask instead what it would be like to have things any other way. This was my world, and in time, it became precious.

We would hunt, we would eat our meals, they were not meals but feasts, he would show me his watch, I would supervise the clock winders who came to wind the many, many long-throated clocks, and occasionally I read the recipes in my mother's book. The time passed and seemed full. When it was warm, I went out into the garden and came in laden with flowers, covered with their dew. In time, I thought, I would have a child and then the castle would come alive; its blue-gray stones would flush with blood, rose-hued, although, on certain days when the sun set, they already seemed suffused with blood. But it was not my blood. So I waited, and was happy. And why should I not have been happy? The absence of suffering can produce happiness, or at least one can mistake it for happiness. Who knows the truth about these things? Not I. I was only sixteen when I married.

Eventually, my husband decided to take a trip. He took from his pocket the huge ring of keys and solemnly laid it on the dining-room table, a table big enough to hold twelve sleeping princesses. "What shall I do with all these keys?" I asked, playfully throwing them into the air. "Whatever you like," he said, "with *these*. But this small one opens a chamber at the end of the hall behind the kitchen. You must not, for any reason, open that door." I wanted to know why not. Was I not, as he always told me, mistress of what I surveyed? "If you open that door," he said, his tones mournful as a tolling bell, "you will cause us both great pain." He should not have said that. Immediately I saw that all my days here amidst the mythic tapestries and the splendid rugs, amidst the wild hunts on the windows, had been without pain, or suffering, or joy or drama. I could barely contain my impatience. I wanted him to leave. I wanted to open that door. But he was not finished with me yet. He had, he said, a small egg that I was to carry with me wherever I went. The egg was the source of our well-being, even our lives; the very rocks of the castle rested upon it.

Of course, you think you know what happened next. My husband went off in a great flurry, but before he got into his coach, he consulted his watch and told me he would be back in precisely three weeks. At this exact moment, in three weeks time, I could expect him. He was hardly out of sight before I had the little key in my hand and was flying down the narrow, dark passage behind the kitchen, to the door with the little room, where, kneeling against the damp, almost slimy cobblestones, I fitted the little key to the little keyhole of the tiny door. I remember having to half-stoop and half-crawl to go through it. I expected to find myself in a room that belonged in a doll's house, but when I was finally through the door, I found myself in a two-story-high chamber, whose walls were adorned only with bits and pieces of machinery. Then I looked closer. From what looked like a giant clockwork wheel, the body of a young woman was suspended by the neck. She hung against the stone wall as if she were a dress suspended carelessly from a hook on a closet. On the floor beneath her was a puddle of blood, and as I watched, another drop of blood wended its way down the gray stones and pooled beneath her feet. To tell the truth, I was not surprised. To tell the truth, I had always believed that any child of mine and the man I had married would be a child of blood — blood and flesh, nothing more, dead from the start. I felt the air against my skin. It would snow and it was going to snow. No one could come to the castle; no one could leave it. Even my husband could not come back before three weeks had passed. I advanced boldly upon the dead woman, holding the egg in my hand. The egg jumped forward as if it had frog's legs. It flew up toward the woman's shoulder, as if it had wings, and perched there. When I found a small stool in the corner, I climbed up and took it down and found it stained with blood. "Now he will know I have been here," I thought, "and I too will hang from this wall." But the thought did not frighten me. Instead, I sat down some distance from the young woman's feet (they were encased in red felt slippers, identical to the ones I wore) and took out my mother's book, which I always carried in my skirt's deepest pocket, but until that minute had not opened. At least I had not yet proceeded past the recipes to the spells. I began to read them. They were complicated and each spell was accompanied by warnings: one could not make a mistake. The consequences of mistakes were dreadful. I decided to take my time. After all, I had three weeks.

I left the bloody egg on the floor of the little room and went into the sitting room, lit a fire, and began studying the spells. The first one taught how to speak to the recently dead. I returned to the little room, threw my herbs in the air, made my circles on the ground with a wooden stick, pricked my own finger, and stirred five drops of blood into a cupful of dust. The woman stirred on the wall.

"Were you his wife?" I asked. She nodded. "Do you hang there because you entered this room?" She nodded again. Another drop of her blood splashed against the damp stones. "He will do the same to me, of course," I said. She nodded once more. "Then you and I must see to the safety of the one who comes after us," I said. I told her she must start to smile; when he came into the room and held up the bloody egg in his hand, she must laugh and continue laughing until the wolves came in. She nodded. (Did she have any will of her own, or was she animated only by the magic spell? I never knew.) When I left the room, she was smiling. In the sitting room, I went on to *curses*. These were of two kinds, the recallable and the irrevocable, but I remembered my mother's words and picked the irrevocable. Before I studied the spells, I had to decide on an appropriate curse. I thought about my husband's heavy gold watch, as heavy as a woman's head, and I knew.

I went back into the little room. I had brought what I needed. With a burner and a small, rounded glass vase, I fashioned a crystal globe. In it, I conjured up the young woman hanging on the wall. In it, I imprisoned the room. To the room and the young woman, I added myself, hanging beside her from a hook on the wall. To this vision, I added my husband and a third woman, one whose hair was black like mine and whose eyes were green, as the eyes of the woman hanging from the hook. Her slippers, too, were green, and in the globe, I drew her unwillingly through the doorway. I conjured up my husband, trying to hold her back, trying to stop her, but against his will, his hand pressed the key into hers, closed over her hand, forced her to turn the key in the lock. Then, when I had it all in the glass globe — room, woman on the wall, myself on the wall next to her, my husband and his third wife in green slippers staring in horror at the wall, I smiled. I looked up at the wall, and his first wife hung there, smiling too. Then I added the sound of all the clocks in the castle, chiming, striking, and tolling. It was exactly the time my husband had left the castle, exactly the time he had promised to return. I left the room.

But I was not finished. I had two more weeks. I learned the spells that allowed me to speak to animals; I learned the spells that allowed me to control them, and when I was finished, I went out through the french doors of my bedroom and onto the battlements, and whistled as my husband did. The wolves appeared but I had nothing for them. I asked them if they preferred chocolate or blood; they said blood. I promised them blood if they were willing to wait a long time for it. They watched me with unblinking eyes; already they understood. They promised to wait forever if necessary. We howled together at the moon, sealing our pact. I told them I would vanish, but my eyes would not. I would be able to see them from a crystal globe, and my husband could do nothing about it because he would not be able to find it. In winter, the globe would turn to snow and fall around the castle. He would never be able to gather up all the flakes and join them together. In summer, the globe would travel the world in droplets. In winter, when the earth gave up its rain, when the rain formed back into clouds, when the clouds began their long journey through the sky, the globe would return. For an instant they would recognize it as a tiny full moon, and then it would disappear and reappear as snow. They would always know the time of the first snowfall because in front of the green moons of their eyes a light, white snow would fall, and they were to howl whenever they saw this. Even if another magician were to come and give them voices with which to speak, they were not to tell of this. They howled their agreement at the moon.

In the small room, I completed my preparations. I put a spell on the crystal globe, one to keep it impregnable on my husband's desk for ten days after his arrival, another to make it travel with the snow. "Who taught you this?" asked a voice from the wall. So she could speak on her own!

"My mother, who gave me this book," I said.

"Your mother," said the voice; "I knew her well." I turned, and saw she was watching me. "You do not believe I knew her," she said, "yet I too am from Plonsk." She told me this story. When she was a young girl, she complained about her mother who was unpredictable and moody. Her mother threatened to put a spell on her, but she laughed at her mother. Her mother said if she wanted predictability, she could have it, and upon her cast the spell of unalterable events. Frightened by her mother, she ran away. It was snowing, and four miles outside of Plonsk, a man in a great coach stopped for her, took her in, and wrapped her in his bearskin coat. He showed her his watch. The watch fascinated her. At the time she ran away, she said, her mother was pregnant. Her mother knew, she said, she was going to have a girl. I looked at my sister on the wall.

"From now on," I said, "he will only meet young women in the snow. He will have to take them in and he will have to take them here. Eventually, he will throw himself from the battlement and the wolves will eat him." She started to laugh. For all I know she is laughing yet.

My husband returned. He found the bloodstained egg, and asked me how I wanted to die. I said I wanted to be thrown to the wolves. He threw me from the battlement, but the wolves would not touch me. He looked at me in a new way, his eyes full of dread. Because I was injured by the fall and could not walk, he carried me back to the little room. Did I want to be hung? he asked me, and I said no. Hanging ruined one's features. On the wall, my sister began laughing. His hand shook when he put the cup of silver, its poisoned, aromatic wine, to my lips. I, too, began laughing. I had forgotten that laughter, like fate and revenge, is contagious.

The poison was slow to take effect. "Here is your egg," I said, throwing it to him. He caught it, looked at the bloodstain on it, and the whites of his eyes absorbed the blood; now his eyes were bloody, like a setting sun. "Look in the glass globe," I said, and threw it to him. He paled. I don't think he understood. The poison was moving through my veins. I stretched out like a cat on the floor. My husband was puzzled by my great content, my evident happiness. On the wall my sister was still laughing. I would have laughed too, had I the strength. When I closed my eyes, the eye in the glass globe opened. I know that for ten days after I began to hang on the wall, my husband looked into the glass globe constantly. Every hour, he took out his watch, looked at the globe, and saw the same thing. He threw the globe on the floor, but it would not break. He put the egg into a chocolate rum ball and gave it to the wolves, but they would not eat it, and the next morning, when he threw back his fur rug from his great bed, the glass globe sat on his desk. On the tenth day, it was gone.

I come and go now with the snow. Yesterday, he found a young girl in a thin dress half-frozen in the snowdrifts near Pinsk. I knew her before he did; her name was Agnes. He stopped for her; he bent over her; he breathed life into her. I watched him as he inhaled her soul. I saw him learning to love. I saw him bring her back to the castle and put her green felt slippers on her long, narrow feet still blue with cold. I saw him do this with his own hands. I saw him take his ring of keys and hide them in the hollow of a bronze eagle. I saw her eyes follow him from behind a drapery, where she had concealed herself. I saw her get up in the dark of night, in the howling of the wolves, to look for the keys. I saw her start down the corridor with the small key, which seemed to be speaking to her, telling her what to do. I saw him run down the corridor after her, mad as a bull in a maze. I saw his face when his hand closed, without will, over hers, forcing her to open the door, pulling her into the room, where my laughter and my sister's poured over them. Reader, I saw this drama repeated many times, so many times the walls of the room became crowded as a butcher's wall is crowded with sides of meat.

Near the end of one winter, on a night when the sky was the color of milk glass and the snow fell continuously like a living waterfall of light, I saw him stand on the battlements and whistle for the wolves. In his hands, he had no chocolates, no bits of flesh. He stood there without clothing, naked to the weather. I saw a tiny moon appear in the sky and then it was gone, as was I.

Reader, if you find that castle, if you hear the voice of many women laughing, do not go in. Look for the wolves. It has been a long time since they tasted chocolate or rum. They are once again what they were. Their hearts are simple. They will protect you and show you the way back. If you know a simple spell, you will know how to free them. You may not need to know the spell. The wolves have already freed themselves. They are only waiting for a reason to come out of their fur.

Dating Your Mom

by Ian Frazier

IN TODAY'S fast-moving, transient, rootless society, where people meet and make love and part without ever really touching, the relationship every guy already has with his own mother is too valuable to ignore. Here is a grown, experienced, loving woman — one you do not have to go to a party or a singles bar to meet, one you do not have to go to great lengths to get to know. There are hundreds of times when you and your mother are thrown together naturally, without the tension that usually accompanies courtship — just the two of you, alone. All you need is a little presence of mind to take advantage of these situations. Say your mom is driving you downtown in the car to buy you a new pair of slacks. First, find a nice station on the car radio, one that she likes. Get into the pleasant lull of freeway driving — tires humming along the pavement, air-conditioner on max. Then turn to look at her across the front seat and say something like, "You know, you've really kept your shape, Mom, and don't think I haven't noticed." Or suppose she comes into your room to bring you some clean socks. Take her by the wrist, pull her close, and say, "Mom, you're the most fascinating woman I've ever met." Probably she'll tell you to cut out the foolishness, but I can guarantee you one thing: she will never tell your dad. Possibly she would find it hard to say, "Dear, Piper just made a pass at me," or possibly she is secretly flattered, but, whatever the reason, she will keep it to herself until the day comes when she is no longer ashamed to tell the world of your love.

Dating your mother seriously might seem difficult at first, but once you try it I'll bet you'll be surprised at how easy it is. Facing up to your intention is the main thing: you have to want it bad enough. One problem is that lots of people get hung up on feelings of guilt about their dad. They think, Oh, here's this kindly old guy who taught me how to hunt and whittle and dynamite fish — I can't let him go on into his twilight years alone. Well, there are two reasons you can dismiss those thoughts from your mind. First, *every* woman, I don't care who she is, prefers her son to her husband. That is a simple fact; ask any woman who has a son, and she'll admit it. And why shouldn't she prefer someone who is so much like herself, who represents nine months of special concern and love and intense physical closeness — someone whom she actually created? As more women begin to express the need to have something all their own in the world, more women are going to start being honest about this preference. When you and your mom begin going together, you will simply become part of a natural and inevitable historical trend.

Second, you must remember this about your dad: you have your mother, he has his! Let him go put the moves on his own mother and stop messing with yours. If his mother is dead or too old to be much fun anymore, that's not your fault, is it? It's not your fault that he didn't realize his mom for the woman she was, before it was too late. Probably he's going to try a lot of emotional blackmail on you just because you had a good idea and he never did. Don't buy it. Comfort yourself with the thought that your dad belongs to the last generation of guys who will let their moms slip away from them like that.

Once your dad is out of the picture — once he has taken up fly-tying, joined the Single Again Club, moved to Russia, whatever — and your mom has been wooed and won, if you're anything like me you're going to start having so much fun that the good times you had with your mother when you were little will seem tame by comparison. For a while, Mom and I went along living a contented, quiet life, just happy to be with each other. But after several months we started getting into some different things, like the big motorized stroller. The thrill I felt the first time Mom steered me down the street! On the tray, in addition to my Big Jim doll and the wire with the colored wooden beads, I have my desk blotter, my typewriter, an in-out basket, and my name plate. I get a lot of work done, plus I get a great chance to people-watch. Then there's my big, adult-sized highchair, where I sit in the evening as Mom and I watch the news and discuss current events, while I paddle in my food and throw my dishes on the floor. When Mom reaches to wipe off my chin and I take her hand, and we fall to the floor in a heap — me, Mom, highchair, and all — well, those are the best times, those are the very best times.

It is true that occasionally I find myself longing for even more — for things I know I cannot have, like the feel of a firm, strong, gentle hand at the small of my back lifting me out of bed into the air, or someone who could walk me around and burp me after I've watched all the bowl games and had about nine beers. Ideally, I would like a mom about nineteen or twenty feet tall, and although I considered for a while asking my mom to start working out with weights and drinking Nutrament, I finally figured, Why put her through it? After all, she is not only my woman, she is my best friend. I have to take her as she is, and the way she is is plenty good enough for me.

Residents and Transients

by Bobbie Ann Mason

SINCE MY HUSBAND went away to work in Louisville, I have, to my surprise, taken a lover. Stephen went ahead to start his new job and find us a suitable house. I'm to follow later. He works for one of those companies that require frequent transfers, and I agreed to that arrangement in the beginning, but now I do not want to go to Louisville. I do not want to go anywhere.

Larry is our dentist. When I saw him in the post office earlier in the summer, I didn't recognize him at first, without his smock and drills. But then we exchanged words — "Hot enough for you?" or something like that — and afterward I started to notice his blue Ford Ranger XII passing on the road beyond the fields. We are about the same age, and he grew up in this area, just as I did, but I was away for eight years, pursuing higher learning. I came back to Kentucky three years ago because my parents were in poor health. Now they have moved to Florida, but I have stayed here, wondering why I ever went away.

Soon after I returned, I met Stephen, and we were married within a year. He is one of those Yankees who are moving into this region with increasing frequency, a fact which disturbs the native residents. I would not have called Stephen a Yankee. I'm very much an outsider myself, though I've tried to fit in since I've been back. I only say this because I overhear the skeptical and desperate remarks, as though the town were being invaded. The schoolchildren are saying "you guys" now and smoking dope. I can image a classroom of bashful country hicks, listening to some new kid blithely talking in a Northern brogue about his year in Europe. Such influences are making people jittery. Most people around here would rather die than leave town, but there are a few here who think Churchill Downs in Louisville would be the grandest place in the world to be. They are dreamers, I could tell them.

"I can't imagine living on a *street* again," I said to my husband. I complained for weeks about living with *houses* within view. I need cornfields. When my parents left for Florida, Stephen and I moved into their old farmhouse, to take care of it for them. I love its stateliness, the way it rises up from the fields like a patch of mutant jimsonweeds. I'm fond of the old white wood siding, the sagging outbuildings. But the house will be sold this winter, after the corn is picked, and by then I will have to go to Louisville. I promised my parents I would handle the household auction because I knew my mother could not bear to be involved. She told me many times about a widow who had sold off her belongings and afterward stayed alone in the empty house until she had to be dragged away. Within a year, she died of cancer. Mother said to me, "Heartbreak brings on cancer." She went away to Florida, leaving everything the way it was, as though she had only gone shopping.

The cats came with the farm. When Stephen and I appeared, the cats gradually moved from the barn to the house. They seem to be my responsibility, like some sins I have committed, like illegitimate children. The cats are Pete, Donald, Roger, Mike, Judy, Brenda, Ellen, and Patsy. Reciting their names for Larry, my lover of three weeks, I feel foolish. Larry had asked, "Can you remember all their names?"

"What kind of question is that?" I ask, reminded of my husband's new job. Stephen travels to cities throughout the South, demonstrating word-processing machines, fancy typewriters that cost thousands of dollars and can remember what you type. It doesn't take a brain like that to remember eight cats.

"No two are alike," I say to Larry helplessly.

We are in the canning kitchen, an airy back porch which I use for the cats. It has a sink where I wash their bowls and cabinets where I keep their food. The canning kitchen was my mother's pride. There, she processed her green beans twenty minutes in a pressure canner, and her tomato juice fifteen minutes in a water bath. Now my mother lives in a mobile home. In her letters she tells me all the prices of the foods she buys.

From the canning kitchen, Larry and I have a good view of the cornfields. A cross-breeze makes this the coolest and most pleasant place to be. The house is in the center of the cornfields, and a dirt lane leads out to the road, about half a mile away. The cats wander down the fence rows, patroling the borders. I feed them Friskies and vacuum their pillows. I ignore the rabbits they bring me. Larry strokes a cat with one hand and my hair with the other. He says he has never known anyone like me. He calls me Mary Sue instead of Mary. No one has called me Mary Sue since I was a kid.

Larry started coming out to the house soon after I had a six-month checkup. I can't remember what signals passed between us, but it was suddenly appropriate that he drop by. When I saw his truck out on the road that day, I knew it would turn up my lane. The truck has a chrome streak on it that makes it look like a rocket, and on the doors is has flames painted.

"I brought you some ice cream," he said.

"I didn't know dentists made house calls. What kind of ice cream is it?"

"I thought you'd like choc-o-mint."

"You're right."

"I know you have a sweet tooth."

"You're just trying to give me cavities, so you can charge me thirty dollars a tooth."

I opened the screen door to get dishes. One cat went in and another went out. The changing of the guard. Larry and I sat on the porch and ate ice cream and watched crows in the corn. The corn had shot up after a recent rain.

"You shouldn't go to Louisville," said Larry. "This part of Kentucky is the prettiest. I wouldn't trade it for anything."

"I never used to think that. Boy, I couldn't wait to get out!" The ice cream was thrillingly cold. I wondered if Larry envied me. Compared to him, I was a world traveler. I had lived in a commune in Aspen, backpacked through the Rockies, and worked on the National Limited as one of the first female porters. When Larry was in high school, he was known as a hell-raiser, so the whole town was amazed when he became a dentist, married, and settled down. Now he was divorced.

Larry and I sat on the porch for an interminable time on that sultry day, each waiting for some external sign — a sudden shift in the weather, a sound, an event of some kind — to bring our bodies together. Finally, it was something I said about my new filling. He leaped up to look in my mouth.

"You should have let me take X-rays," he said.

"I told you I don't believe in all that radiation."

"The amount is teensy," said Larry, holding my jaw. A mouth is a word processor, I thought suddenly, as I tried to speak.

"Besides," he said, "I always use the lead apron to catch any fragmentation."

"What are you talking about?" I cried, jerking loose. I imagined splintering X-rays zinging around the room. Larry patted me on the knee.

"I should put on some music," I said. He followed me inside.

Stephen is on the phone. It is 3:00 P.M. and I am eating supper — pork and beans, cottage cheese and dill pickles. My routines are cockeyed since he left.

"I found us a house!" he says excitedly. His voice is so familiar I can almost see him, and I realize that I miss him. "I want you to come up here this weekend and take a look at it," he says.

"Do I have to?" My mouth is full of pork and beans.

"I can't buy it unless you see it first."

"I don't care what it looks like."

"Sure you do. But you'll like it. It's a three-bedroom brick with a two-car garage, finished basement, dining alcove, patio —"

"Does it have a canning kitchen?" I want to know.

Stephen laughs. "No, but it has a rec room."

I quake at the thought of a rec room. I tell Stephen, "I know this is crazy, but I think we'll have to set up a kennel in back for the cats, to keep them out of traffic."

I tell Stephen about the New Jersey veterinarian I saw on a talk show who keeps an African lioness, an ocelot, and three margays in his yard in the suburbs. They all have the run of his house. "Cats aren't that hard to get along with," the vet said.

"Aren't you carrying this a little far?" Stephen asks, sounding worried. He doesn't suspect how far I might be carrying things. I have managed to swallow the last trace of the food, as if it were guilt.

"What do *you* think?" I ask abruptly.

"I don't know what to think," he says.

I fall silent. I am holding Ellen, the cat who had a vaginal infection not long ago. The vet X-rayed her and found she was pregnant. She lost the kittens, because of the X-ray, but the miscarriage was incomplete, and she developed a rare infection called pyometra and had to be spayed. I wrote every detail of this to my parents, thinking they would care, but they did not mention it in their letters. Their minds are on the condominium they are planning to buy when this farm is sold. Now Stephen is talking about out investments and telling me things to do at the bank. When we buy a house, we will have to get a complicated mortgage.

"The thing about owning real estate outright," he says, "is that one's assets aren't liquid."

"Daddy always taught me to avoid debt."

"That's not the way it works anymore."

"He's going to pay cash for his condo."

"That's ridiculous."

Not long ago, Stephen and I sat before an investment counselor, who told us, without cracking a smile, "You want to select an investment posture that will maximize your potential." I had him confused with a marriage counselor, some kind of weird sex therapist. Now I think of water streaming in the dentist's bowl. When I was a child, the water in a dentist's bowl ran continuously. Larry's bowl has a shut-off button to save water. Stephen is talking about flexibility and fluid assets. It occurs to me that wordprocessing, all one word, is also a runny sound. How many billion words a day could one of Stephen's machines process without forgetting? How many pecks of pickled peppers can Peter Piper pick? You don't *pick* pickled peppers, I want to say to Stephen defiantly, as if he has asked this question. Peppers can't be pickled till *after* they're picked, I want to say, as if I have a point to make.

Larry is here almost daily. He comes over after he finishes overhauling mouths for the day. I tease him about this peculiarity of his profession. Sometimes I pretend to be afraid of him. I won't let him near my mouth. I clamp my teeth shut and grin widely, fighting off imaginary drills. Larry is gap-toothed. He should have had braces, I say. Too late now, he says. Cats march up and down the bed purring while we are in it. Larry does not seem to notice. I'm accustomed to the cats. Cats, I'm aware, like to be involved in anything that's going on. Pete has a hobby of chasing butterflies. When he loses sight of one, he searches the air, wailing pathetically, as though abandoned. Brenda plays with paper clips. She likes the way she can hook a paper clip so simply with one claw. She attacks spiders in the same way. Their legs draw up and she drops them.

I see Larry watching the cats, but he rarely comments on them. Today he notices Brenda's odd eyes. One is blue and one is yellow. I show him her paper clip trick. We are in the canning kitchen and the daylight is fading.

"Do you want another drink?" asks Larry.

"No."

"You're getting one anyway."

We are drinking Bloody Marys, made with my mother's canned tomato juice. There are rows of jars in the basement. She would be mortified to know what I am doing, in her house, with her tomato juice.

Larry brings me a drink and a soggy grilled cheese sandwich.

"You'd think a dentist would make something dainty and precise," I say. "Jello molds, maybe, the way you make false teeth."

We laugh. He thinks I am being funny.

The other day he took me up in a single-engine Cessna. We circled west Kentucky, looking at the land, and when we flew over the farm I felt I was in a creaky hay wagon, skimming just above the fields. I thought of the Dylan Thomas poem with the dream of birds flying along with the stacks of hay. I could see eighty acres of corn and pasture, neat green squares. I am nearly thirty years old. I have two men, eight cats, no cavities. One day I was counting the cats and I absentmindedly counted myself.

Larry and I are playing Monopoly in the parlor, which is full of doilies and trinkets on whatnots. Every day I notice something that I must save for my mother. I'm sure Larry wishes we were at his house, a modern brick home in a good section of town, five doors down from a U.S. congressman. Larry gets up from the card table and mixes another Bloody Mary for me. I've been buying hotels left and right, against the advice of my investment counselor. I own all the utilities. I shuffle my paper money and it feels like dried corn shucks. I wonder if there is a new board game involving money market funds.

"When my grandmother was alive, my father used to bury her savings in the yard, in order to avoid inheritance taxes," I say as Larry hands me the drink.

He laughs. He always laughs, whatever I say. His lips are like parentheses, enclosing compliments.

"In the last ten years of her life she saved ten thousand dollars from her social security checks."

"That's incredible." He looks doubtful, as though I have made up a story to amuse him. "Maybe there's still money buried in your yard."

"Maybe. My grandmother was very frugal. She wouldn't let go of *anything.*"

"Some people are like that."

Larry wears a cloudy expression of love. Everything about me that I find dreary he finds intriguing. He moves his silvery token (a flatiron) around the board so carefully, like a child learning to cross the street. Outside, a cat is yowling. I do not recognize it as one of mine. There is nothing so mournful as the yowling of a homeless cat. When a stray appears, the cats sit around, fascinated, while it eats, and then later, just when it starts to feel secure, they gang up on it and chase it away.

"This place is full of junk that no one could throw away," I say distractedly. I have just been sent to jail. I'm thinking of the boxes in the attic, the rusted tools in the barn. In a cabinet in the canning kitchen I found some Bag Balm, antiseptic salve to soften cows' udders. Once I used teat extenders to feed a sick kitten. The cows are gone, but I feel their presence like ghosts. "I've been reading up on cats," I say suddenly. The vodka is making me plunge into something I know I cannot explain. "I don't want you to think I'm this crazy cat freak with a mattress full of money."

"Of course I don't." Larry lands on Virginia Avenue and proceeds to negotiate a complicated transaction.

"In the wild, there are two kinds of cat populations," I tell him when he finishes his move. "Residents and transients. Some stay put, in their fixed home ranges, and others are on the move. They don't have real homes. Everybody always thought that the ones who establish the territories are the most successful — like the capitalists who get ahold of Park Place." (I'm eyeing my opportunities on the board.) "They are the strongest, while the transients are the bums, the losers."

"Is that right? I didn't know that." Larry looks genuinely surprised. I think he is surprised at how far the subject itself extends. He is such a specialist. Teeth.

I continue bravely. "The thing is — this is what the scientists are wondering about now — it may be that the transients are the superior ones after all, with the greatest curiosity and most intelligence. They can't decide."

"That's interesting." The Bloody Marys are making Larry seem very satisfied. He is the most relaxed man I've ever known. "None of that is true of domestic cats," Larry is saying. "They're all screwed up."

"I bet somewhere there are some who are footloose and fancy free," I say, not believing it. I buy two hotels on Park Place and almost go broke. I think of living in Louisville. Stephen said the house he wants to buy is not far from Iroquois Park. I'm reminded of Indians. When certain Indians got tired of living in a place — when they used up the soil, or the garbage pile got too high — they moved on to the next place.

It is a hot summer night, and Larry and I are driving back from Paducah. We went out to eat and then we saw a movie. We are rather careless about being seen together in public. Before we left the house, I brushed my teeth twice and used dental floss. On the way, Larry told me of a patient who was a hemophiliac and couldn't floss. Working on his teeth was very risky.

We ate at a place where you choose your food from pictures on a wall, then wait at a numbered table for the food to appear. On another wall was a framed arrangement of farm tools against red felt. Other objects — saw handles, scythes, pulleys — were mounted on wood like fish trophies. I could hardly eat for looking at the tools. I was wondering what my father's old tit-cups and dehorning shears would look like on the wall of a restaurant. Larry was unusually quiet during the meal. His reticence exaggerated his customary gentleness. He even ate french fries cautiously.

On the way home, the air is rushing through the truck. My elbow is propped in the window, feeling the cooling air like water. I think of the pickup truck as a train, swishing through the night.

Larry says then, "Do you want me to stop coming out to see you?"

"What makes you ask that?"

"I don't have to be an Einstein to tell that you're bored with me."

"I don't know. I still don't want to go to Louisville, though."

"I don't want you to go. I wish you would just stay here and we would be together."

"I wish it could be that way," I say, trembling slightly. "I wish that was right."

We round a curve. The night is black. The yellow line in the road is faded. In the other lane I suddenly see a rabbit move. It is hopping in place, the way runners will run in place. Its forelegs are frantically working, but its rear end has been smashed and it cannot get out of the road.

By the time we reach home I have become hysterical. Larry has his arms around me, trying to soothe me, but I cannot speak intelligibly and I push him away. In my mind, the rabbit is a tape loop that crowds out everything else.

Inside the house, the phone rings and Larry answers. I can tell from his expression that it is Stephen calling. It was crazy to let Larry answer the phone. I was not thinking. I will have to swear on a stack of cats that nothing is going on. When Larry hands me the phone I am incoherent. Stephen is saying something nonchalant, with a sly question in his voice. Sitting on the floor, I'm rubbing my feet vigorously. "Listen," I say in a tone of great urgency. "I'm coming to Louisville — to see that house. There's this guy here who'll give me a ride in his truck —"

Stephen is annoyed with me. He seems not to have heard what I said, for he is launching into a speech about my anxiety.

"Those attachments to a place are so provincial," he says.

"People live all their lives in one place," I argue frantically. "What's wrong with that?"

"You've got to be flexible," he says breezily. "That kind of romantic emotion is just like flag-waving. It leads to nationalism, fascism — you name it; the very worst kinds of instincts. Listen, Mary, you've got to be more open to the way things are."

Stephen is processing words. He makes me think of liquidity, investment postures. I see him floppy as a Raggedy Andy, loose as a goose. I see what I am shredding in my hand as I listen. It is Monopoly money.

After I hang up, I rush outside. Larry is discreetly staying behind. Standing in the porch light, I listen to katydids announce the harvest. It is the kind of night, mellow and languid, when you can hear corn growing. I see a cat's flaming eyes coming up the lane to the house. One eye is green and one is red, like a traffic light. It is Brenda, my odd-eyed cat. Her blue eye shines red and her yellow eye shines green. In a moment I realize that I am waiting for the light to change.

His Own Where

by June Jordan

THE FIRST PAGE

You be different from the dead. All them tombstones tearing up the ground, look like a little city, like a small Manhattan, not exactly. Here is not the same.

Here, you be bigger than the buildings, bigger than the little city. You be really different from the rest, the resting other ones.

Moved in his arms, she make him feel like smiling. Him, his head an Afro-bush spread free beside the stones, headstones thinning in the heavy air. Him, a ready father, public lover, privately at last alone with her, with Angela, a half an hour walk from the hallway where they start out to hold themselves together in the noisy darkness, kissing, kissed him, kissed her, kissing.

Cemetery let them lie there belly close, their shoulders now undressed down to the color of the heat they feel, in lying close, their legs a strong disturbing of the dust. His own where, own place for loving made for making love, the cemetery where nobody guard the dead.

ONE

First time they come, he simply say, "Come on." He tell her they are going not too far away. She go along not worrying about the heelstrap pinching at her skin, but worrying about the conversation. Long walks take some talking. Otherwise it be embarrassing just side by side embarrassing.

Buddy stay quiet, walking pretty fast, but every step right next to her. They trip together like a natural sliding down the street.

Block after block after block begin to bother her. Nothing familiar is left. The neighborhood is changing. Strangers watch them from the windows.

Angela looking at Buddy, look at his shoes and wish for summertime and beaches when his body, ankle, toes will shock the ocean, yelling loud and laughing hard and wasting no sand.

Buddy think about time and the slowspeed of her eyes that leave him hungry, nervous, big and quick. Slide by the closedup drugstore, cross under the train, run the redlight, circle past two women leaning on two wire carts, and reach the avenue of showrooms. Green, blue, yellow, orange cars driving through, cars at the curb, cars behind the glass, cars where houses used to stand, cars where people standing now, and tree to tree electric lights.

"Play the radio?"

Buddy turn it with his thumb. The plastic handle strings around his wrist.

> *No moon no more*
> *No moon no more*
> *I want to see what I seen before.*
>
> *Please no surprise*
> *Please no surprise*
> *I just want to see your lovin eyes.*

Holding her hand in his is large and hers almost loose inside it. She feel visitor-stiff, but the music make a difference, and his hand.

Cars make Buddy mad. Right now his father lying in the hospital from what they call A Accident. And was no accident about it, Buddy realize. The street set up that way so cars can clip the people easy kill them even. Easy.

"What you say?" she ask him.

"Damn," he answer her. "Another one. Another corner. Street-crossing-time again."

"You crazy, Buddy? What you mean?"

"I hate them. Corners. They really be a dumb way try to split the people from the cars. Don't even work. Look how a car come up and almost kill my father, minding his own business, on the corner. Corners good for nothing." Buddy frown so bad that Angela start laughing. Buddy swing around her waist.

"Show you what I mean."

He jump back behind her. Walk forward like a flatfoot counting steps: Left-foot-right-foot-left-foot-one-two.

"Here come the corner!"

Down. Buddy buckle at the knee for *down.* When he really reach the corner then he drop to one knee. Seem like a commando on the corner. Wild looking left then right. Arms like a rifle in rotation: Covering the danger east and west. Buddy standing on his two feet urgent. Put his face an inch from her: "Watch now. Here. It's here." He roll the radio dial to loud yell over it. "Not clear! Not clear at the crossing. On your mark" (whispering in her ear), "get set." Buddy stop. "Green. Where's the green? You seen it, Angela?" He fold his arms and spread his legs and hold everything right there. "Well my Lookout Man is out to lunch." Buddy sitting on the curb, to wait.

Angela feel a question, but the radio so loud she would have to scream. With him, she rather not be screaming.

Angela not laughing and no smile. Buddy sitting on the curb and she beside him, so he roll the dial to soft.

"You see them signs. The curb-your-dog signs. But the people be like slaves. Don't need no signs. Just do it. Curb-the-People. Step right up, then down, then up. Then out. Into it. Into the traffic, baby. You be crucify like Jesus at the crossing. Traffic like a 4-way nail the joker on his feet. It be strictly D.O.A. for corners. Danger on Arrival. D.O.A. Even dogs can smell that danger, smell it just as good as looking at the lights. You tired?"

"No." She is. But nothing they can do about that. No bench. No sidewalk, walkway tables, benches. Only fences fixed outfront.

"Buddy, this no place to stop."

Rises from the curb, his arm around her, moving on together, slower walking easy on the edge. The sidewalk is a concrete edge.

The lined-up traffic multiplies. The fenders blur. Windshield swiping windshield chrome and autocolors. Hold her close, his side comes long and close beside her.

At the intersection they will cross together. Intersection circus stunt for everyday.

"Angela, look out."

She hear his shaking inner sound. She listen to him. Coordination is together trial.

Matched to her to him out in the middle of the mess machinery. He be strong enough and she be fast enough to swerve it safely through, across, around, ahead. Landed on the other edge, the sidewalk opposite. She smell intoxicating leather jacket, how he wears it, how he smells to her.

He slowly flaming from the small size of her neck, its naked expectation.

"Buddy, this is a cemetery. Let's go back."

"No. Let's go on."

"I don't like it here."

"Why not?"

"You know why."

"Angela, where can we go beside the cemetery. What else is there?"

"We can go home."

"Home." The idea, the memories, the fact of home straightens him away from her, from what she probably mean.

"Just trust me five more minutes. Trust me." They step ahead, single file. She following him. He leading them, both of them. Trees like a skinny curtain start appearing. What they can see are cemetery furnishings. Somebody leave a potted plant. The flabby petals from the $4.95 racketeer store close to the scene of the absolutely dead.

They notice the one-by-one increasing trees. She watch Buddy how he walk ahead of her, how he seems a bit ahead of her. They come to a silent place. The only sounds, the engine highway sounds.

They climb up sidesoil to a fence that stretches high above their heads and out beyond armstretching.

Angela be blinded by the light wiggles blinding in the silent waterfills her eyes. They say nothing, just look and feel full. It be like a big open box, sides of sloping stone, moss covered rainy dark and, behind them, a little to the left, there be a small brick tower room, a locked-up house where no one ever live.

Buddy say, "This is the reservoir." Angela be thinking *water* and, over by the furthest rim of it, they see the roof of streets and houses that they know. Nobody close to them. Buddy and Angela begin to make believe about the house next to the reservoir. They see how they would open it up, how they would live inside, what they would do with only the birds, the water and the skylight fallen blinding into it.

"What they saving the water for? Who suppose to use it."

"Saving it for birds. This a bathroom for the birds."

They laugh about the pretty water bathroom for the birds.

"Be nice if we can swim here."

"They not hardly let you swim in it. Unless you be a bird."

Go over to the doorsill of the house, sit down for talking.

"Why you bring me here?"

"You don't like it?"

"So quiet. I don't know."

"How come you always want some sound?"

"Real quiet bother me. But then again, when I go to like the super-market they be playing loony tunes and you be looking at a can of soup, or pork chops, but you have to hear dah-dah-blah-blah and violins and mustard and potatoes dah-dah-blah-blah-violins, it can make you feel really weird."

"So what you want to hear with mustard and potatoes?"

"Well, could be somebody like that kind of music, but I don't. I rather be hearing other things. Like if you play the radio and we decide what we want to hear I mean at this very moment."

"What you want?"

"You talk to me, Buddy. Tell me what you thinking."

They have to leave soon. Reservoir growing dim. They have to walk back.

"What you doing tonight?"

"Study, can you stop by after you see your father?"

"I don't know. Might be really too late."

"Is he better?"

"No. My relatives rap strong about insurance and inheritance. I say he be dying, but not dead. And at the hospital they be fooling with him. Half the time I go, can't see him. They exploring this or that, testing him for what not. The other half, he be sleeping, from the pills they give him. The dude that knock him down, you know that dumbhead driver? Last week he actually come by, call himself paying some respects. I tell him that respect don't make him better, but I say well let him come. Don't make no difference. My father dying lonely and I figure that respect don't hurt a lonely man."

Call it accidental but to him, to Buddy, was no accident. Things set up like that. You cross the street you taking chances. Odds against you. Knock his father down, down from the sidewalk stop, down from the curb, down bleeding bad, ribs crushed. The lungs be puncture, and his father living slow inside a tent.

TWO

The hospital seem nice. Nothing too loud or filthy, beds adjustable, regular food. Different people, men and women, asking how you are, how you feel. Friends drop around. Privacy. Whole attitude all allright. You suppose to heal, be well, stay well in the hospital.

Don't let no rumbly trucks rock through the streets. Floors be clean enough to eat on. Buddy sure the whole city should be like a hospital and everybody taking turns to heal the people. People turning doctor, patient, nurse. Whole city asking asking everybody how you are, how you feel, what can I do for you, how can I help.

Fantastic if the city turn into a hospital the city fill with a million people asking a million other people how you feeling, how's everything, what you need. Dig, policeman move up to this Momma, ask her do she sleep well.

She say no. Explaining how the heat turn off at midnight. Policeman make a note. Act like a nurse.

That was how he meet her, Angela. Inside the hospital. Father dying in a semiprivate room more private than the room he share so many years ago, with Buddy's mother. Semiprivate room for dying seem all right. Who want to be alone, completely. Seem all right for living too; a semiprivate room for keep alive. Buddy by the bed, sitting still. His mind remembering home.

Brownstone and cigar smoke. Women pocketbooks and peppermint. Shined shoes. His father sharpening the Sunday razor slap the leather slap the blade to silver sharp. In the bureau drawer blue enamel cufflinks, brassy bullets from the war. Few photographs. His mother prim-sarcastic posing straight ahead. Old box of contraceptives. Blow them up. Bounceback old-timer tricks from when.

When his mother and his father in the double-softbed underneath the walnut crucifix cost not so much as you might think. It be so heavy hanging there above the doubledecker pillows too clean for anybody use them. But they use them when they use to be asleep around the morning after Buddy father do his downtown nightwatch. And before when Buddy mother leave without him, Buddy. Disappear his father say without no reason.

But Buddy remember how his mother use to stay gaze on the ground around the neighborhood. She brokenhearted in the brokenland of Brooklyn small-scale brokenland. She cry the day they rip one tree right out the concrete ground in front of the dining-room windows. Tree already attacked by lightning on a rainy afternoon when Buddy watch the men their caps firm to the eyebrows walking to the corners, carrying a paper bag of lunch. And when he watch the women breasted motherly and crooked walking with a Horn and Hardart/ Bargaintown/Macy's Christmas shopping bag. The dining room, where she cry that day, on other days unusual with celery and olives.

Sweet port wine and soda, flower wineglasses, crochet lacy tablecloth, and two red candles definitely lit. The greens and ham the rice and peas and cheese and crackers and tomato juice standing in small glasses on small glassy plates. The perspiration smell of toilet water. Buddy, helping carve, he feel the swarm of aunts and uncles cousins. Feel them sweaty near, amazing and predictable. And rhinestones and the wellmade gray-plaid special suit. The hugging and the jokes. The sudden ashtrays and his mother in a brandnew apron serving. Serving and remote. Retreating to the kitchen sink excuse from laughter where the family relax drink rum to celebrate another year survival.

His mother serving her way out of the loosely loving festival of food and thankyou to the Lord.

His father when he help to dry the dishes silverware pots cup and saucers try to bring her into the ordinary comfort of his arms and she collapse in them unhappy. "We need another cabinet," she tell his father. She continuous in putaway and polish: sort and starch. "This is our own house," she would repeat. "We sacrifice, we save and borrow for this house. At least it is our own. Or will be." And then she say, "I know it is not beautiful, but it is clean."

She leave it, finally. When she leave them then his father turn to him, to Buddy and the house. The house become a house of men strip to the basic structure truth of it, the four rooms gradual like one that spreads around the actions of a day. His mother hungering for order among things themselves, for space she could admire, simply hungering and gone. Where did she go, and Buddy wondering about this last disorder she did not repair. This disordering of life of marriage of her motherhood. Strange lovely woman warm and hungering and gone.

Buddy father clean the house down to the linoleum. Remove the moldings. Take away the window drapes and teach him, Buddy, how to calculate essentials how to calculate one table and two chairs, four plates, two mugs. Together they build shelves and stain them. Throw out the cabinets and bureaus opening and closing like a bank. His father teach him hammering and saws and measuring and workshop science. House be like a workshop where men live creating how they live. Throw out the lamps and build lights into the ceiling. Indirect direct white/lavender. Buddy working with wires and pliers rush from school to work beside his father on the house.

On duty in the night his father dream and draw the next plan for the next day, working the house into a dream they can manage with their hands. Years like this working on the way they live with open shelves and changing furniture from store to slowly made in wood they pick up awkward.

Buddy see him sleeping and unconscious. Bandages a brace a cast a bruise black swollen on the brown skin of his face. His father face asleep, unshaven. Thick lips promising to speak to smile again. Eyes closed. No intimation of their waking focus gentle calculating inches

and diameter or grain. A short man, Buddy's father, short and powerful and maybe handsome. Buddy not sure what handsome mean, in
general, but to him, to Buddy, this man, his father, is a lonely,
handsome man, powerful and short.

THREE

From the other side of the other bed the nurse was speaking to him,
that longago first time.

"Don't you have no mother, boy?"

Buddy stare back sullen.

"You don't have to answer me. A woman my age know who has a
mother and who don't. You don't. You don't have no mother. Night
after night, from afternoon you come sit by your father. Very nice, and
what you should be doing. But how old you getting to be and what
they call you?" Buddy stir himself, feeling most of all surprise. The
woman talk like a knife try to butter but cuts the bread.

"Sixteen."

"I knew you was sixteen. Or seventeen. Who's taking care of you
and what's you name?"

"Buddy. Buddy Rivers."

"Well, that's all right too, but who is taking care of you, when you
leave the hospital, Buddy Rivers?"

"Everything's okay. We got things under control."

"That's how all you young people answer me. Everything is mind
your own business, am I right?"

Buddy be annoy by now. The woman is a private nurse for the
patient in the next bed. Be bad to make an enemy have to see an
enemy in the same room where his father dying. And her question
bother him. His relatives ask the same thing and discuss where he
should move. Assume that he should move out of the house he and his
father put together like their lives until now. Move! He will not move
among the doilies, wallpaper, headboard beds, and extra extra chairs
that scatter through the houses of his relatives. The gold-thread sofa-
beds. The monstrous glossy large television console. The wobbling
bright installment furniture and Woolworth bric-a-brac that make it
dangerous to stretch your legs straight out or swing your arms around.

He will not move. It is a home they made. Not very clean in the usual way. But beautiful and full of what they absolutely need for everyday. Full and free from stuff just lying and lying around.

"I'm sure your father would expect you to show respect when people speak to you," the nurse was saying. That was the whole nagging way she came on on the first night that she talk to him, to Buddy.

Buddy could never get over this difference between women and their daughters. Like this nurse, this obnoxious, nosy woman who spoke to him like that when they were strangers, she was the mother of his Angela. She was the mother of the girl Buddy felt guilty to be so aware of there right where his father lay, his face asleep, his life dying. But he was. He was even waiting for her. Weeks before they even spoke, he would feel himself waiting for the girl whose name he didn't know.

Every evening around eight, just before the end of visiting hours, she would come and get her orders from headquarters. Her mother jangling with coins and keys and inquiries and orders: who ate what for dinner, who was where, and so forth. Angela was pretty. And she was pretty cool. He could tell she was embarrass by his witness to the nightly scene. But she keep cool. Keep her voice down low, releasing monosyllables as brief as possible:

"Yes. Okay. You said that. I won't. I did it."

She was pretty. And he like the coolness. The splash tongue of her mother inhibit both of them. Neither said hello.

Buddy always remember how the woman sizzle with suspicion even before Angela and him really start to talking with each other.

Then one time when Angela come by, wearing jeans and looking comfortable, her mother run through a tirade so tough that Buddy try to help out Angela and introduce himself and walk her home. The tirade start because of the bluejeans:

"Angela! Did you forget something?"

"Don't think so."

"Did you forget you were coming here to see me in the hospital?"

"What's the matter?"

"What's the matter? You see how you dress and you askin me what is the matter. Are you a hippy? You think a hospital is a hippy hangout? This is a hospital and I am a professional woman. And I am your mother. Look at you."

Angela try to walk out. The woman seize Angela by the arm and snarl upclose.

"You wait right there. I'm not finish talking to you. Do you hear me?"

Buddy want to interfere.

"And you, Mr. Rivers, you can sit right down again. What you standing for?"

"I think you should let go of Angela."

"Angela, you saying. Angela. What other names you call each other, I would like to know. You pretending not to know each other all this time and what's the truth behind it?"

"I hear you call her Angela, that's all," Buddy say, still standing.

Angela be trembling furious. The woman whirl and scream at her. "On top of everything, you better not let me see you evil lip."

"I be as evil as I want to be."

"All right. You said it."

"I say what? Let me go, Ma."

The woman smack Angela in the face.

"You finish, Ma? You finish now?"

"No. I'm not finish. I'm just starting with you. Come back here."

Angela break through the doorway, knowing her mother probably will not leave the patient by himself to follow her. Buddy follow Angela.

"What you want?" Angela be crying but no streaming tears.

"Let me walk you home." Buddy catch up to her, walking along, worrying about her face. Thinking, feeling about Angela, he almost forget his father.

On the street they walk separated.

"Why the two of you go on like that?"

Angela feel stung: "the two of you." She like the solid look of Buddy dark out the corner of her eyes upon her mother every night. Him, Buddy sitting there sly don't miss a minute of the interaction. Still he say, "the two of you." What did he mean? They walk separated. She not answering the question, hurt.

Streets turning off except for candystores, and liquor stores and iron grates dull interlocking over glass. Except for the bars the people party high, knees and feet poke rapid sharp toward an indoor kitchen, bedroom. People hurry calmly from the nighttime start to glittering like oil.

"My mother picking on me, picking, picking on me. I wish she would just kick me out."

"You must be the oldest."

"I am. Three brothers younger than me, and then a baby sister. My mother work and scream. My daddy work and both of them work nights. The problem is they think I'm working nighttime too — They think I'm maybe running the streets."

"What your father do?"

"Driving a cab. So I take care of all the cooking. Baby-sit. But I try to study anyhow."

"Where you go to school?"

"Lane."

"Didn't know people studying at Lane. Thought you people just fight and then just fight some more."

"Oh, come on! Only thing we did was try to raise the flag of liberation. Now you know how folks react to liberation. But I been hearing about you. At Boys' High. I even know your name."

She don't tell him how she hear how he suppose to be so fine and really B A D and have the teachers shook and shaking. Buddy have a lot of friends hanging out with him at school. They stick together pretty tight, and he have a reputation everybody say the same about him so she hear things all the time.

When they reach her building Buddy see chalk scribbling on the granite and the outside stairs curve interesting worn.

Angela ask him inside.

Two of her brothers, Ronald, three, and Edwin, eleven, in front of the TV, wearing undershirts and BVDs. The third brother, eight-year-old Tyrone wearing the same, in the bathroom floating a TV dinner tray in the bathtub. Angela take Buddy to her room where the baby, Debby, is sleeping. A doll carriage holding Debby asleep. Angela have a cot and ironing on top of it, she have to iron. Over by the radiator a scratch formica table and chair Angela use for studying. An overhead three-socket fixture, one bulb screw into it. Long nails in the wall hold clothing, hangers, dresses, skirts and jackets hung on them.

Buddy feel depression in the clutter-stricken room. Feel like a carpenter hands tied. Want to toss out everything and start the room from scratch. Keep it bare enough so Angela feel free.

"Your parents think you pretty wild." Buddy not quite leaning on the edge of the table desk. "Are you?"

Angela answer, giggling. "You believe it. After I cook dinner, feed my baby sister, I drag over hear my mother, come back, wash or iron, study, worry about my father when he come home will he be shaking me awake and want to carry on, complain, and like that, I am pretty wild. Just like my mother say, a freak for parties."

Buddy dig on the fantastic stack of 45's piling from the floor. "Don't you have no phonograph?"

Angela say no and she explain why she don't play her records in the parlor where her father turn hysterical and call the music sinful. Call her when she dance and sing "a whore."

Buddy like this girl, this Angela. He hate the room she have. Make even Angela seem clumsy. Make him feel himself like overgrown from Mars. He hate the whole apartment skimpy on the people-space. Rooms crush small by stuffed-up piece of furniture huge sofa and huge matching lamps huge things that squeeze the family mix into a quarrel just to move around a little. But all he say, that first night when he look at how she live at home is that he see her in the hospital, tomorrow.

FOUR

His life form into habits following his love. Angela and the hospital and his father all roll into hours that he spend with them. Now every night he be walking Angela home from the hospital and then he go back there and stay there at the hospital watching his father/the body of his father on the hospital bed until they make him leave.

Sometimes Buddy wishing he could bring Angela to the house sanded and hammered into a home by him and his father. The house of things eliminated. The house made simple into home where Buddy waiting to know his father again alive in action taking a wall apart or building a low wall like a window ledge between two rooms.

Angela parents carry on so strict and wild that Buddy can only see her every day. Walking home. And for half a minute visits when her father may be sure to be out working. Or a few times managing the walk into the cemetery on a weekend afternoon. And one time at a party. And sometimes at the store.

Buddy and Angela keep track of daytime just by figuring out the last and then the next time they will come together for how long alone. They become the heated habit of each other.

FIVE

Another evening and Angela mother rip into the love between them. Say she cannot sleep for worrying about her daughter and "that poor man, your father" and his son, Buddy.

Buddy ask the woman why she worrying and what about. The woman sob and shriek and curse at Angela and call her nogood lowdown. Angela feel humiliated and refuse to answer back.

Again her mother smack her in her face and Angela break away running. That night after Buddy walk Angela home he does not go back to see his father at the hospital. His head feel heavy and his feet.

Instead, Buddy slide into the darkness, thinking and feeling about Angela, and find himself walking to his father house. Buddy takes the sidewalk broom from inside and come out to the cold night, sweeping the stoop, the stairs, the yard, the sidewalk. Sweeping under the night. Ragged and shrill in the ragged shrubbery three or four male cats howl close to the female magnet listening calm.

Buddy consider bothering the cats but change his mind.

Back into the house, the workshop of his father and his life and wanders heavily and tall inside the easy space.

Saying her name, Angela. Pretending she is here to dance with him here where nothing but himself will move.

The phonograph lies low along one wall on a board shelf where the parts in factory packages remind him of the work to do the wires to organize attach. Work interrupted by the accident that snatch his father. Buddy start to fool with parts and try to concentrate on diagrams of wiring and speaker placement. But he be thinking Angela.

In the kitchen, absentminded opening a can of soup, stirring with a wooden spoon. Into the basement opening with a screwdriver a can of black lacquer paint, stirring with a wooden spatula. Back upstairs to relocate the (parts of the) phonograph packages. Buddy abandon the phonograph project. Next he remove a long piece of lumber from its wall hinge supports. Clean it, start to paint it.

Lacquer shining smoothly. Black black like a glisten polishing the lumber plank he handle easily. The black the lacquer black glistening lumber invitation to his touch and finger press he better not. Too soon to touch still wet. Too soon to touch like Angela. Too soon to really touch her.

SIX

When Angela father come home drunk that night the phone ring and he hear his wife telling him that Angela defy disgrace them in the hospital calling her a loudmouth woman.

Angela father smile at this but still his wife continue: "She left here with a boy. Were you there when they came home?"

"What boy?"

Angela mother explain how Angela run out on her because she wouldn't hardly leave the bedside of her patient. She describe how the boy, Buddy, follow after her, Angela, and how the boy, whose father be dying in the hospital bed, how the boy never come back to the bedside of his father, that night. Is he, the boy, in that house with Angela? What did the devil daughter do with the boy? That devil daughter can't be trust no way. She making it impossible for decent people try to earn a living to go out with easy mind and earn they bread.

Angela father say he will take care of it, find out what is going on behind they back. Hang up the phone. A spare, goodlooking man. Slip into the room where Angela in bed, turn a flashlight on her face.

"Angela, get up," he shout at her.

"Angela!"

Rubbing her eyes from sleep she see him stepping on the clothes she have iron and stack by her bed.

"Move, Daddy —"

That's as much as she can say. His fist come down her face, her cheek. She scream aloud. His knuckle slap her head around, and pound her punching through to ribs. Angela struggle her hand under the pillow where to protect herself she hide a kitchen knife not to be beaten like she is. Seize the handle, whip the knife into his view and tell him "Leave me alone."

"You little prostitute."

He kick the cot over and she fall to the floor face down and lose the knife. He leap beside her beating her across her back.

"You get out of this house, get out of this house, get out."

Angela pass out. Her father pause, then drop his arm and leave the room. After a while Angela come to. Her mouth taste ugly. She wince to move. She listen if she hear him near, awake. Hear nothing. Tears come from the pain of putting her coat around her. She struggle down into the street. It be almost morning. Angela staggering, bolt and collapse along the street toward Buddy house. Some men in a old Cadillac try to pick her up (thinking she drunk) until one of them come close enough to see her swollen face and bloody.

Angela use all her strength to ring the bell. Buddy look through the dining-room window where his mother watch the tree rip from the concrete and he see his girl fallen down small against the first floor window bars.

Angela. He bring her inside into the house the home of his life where he imagine her, but never, not this way, so fallen small she only seem a small girl. Buddy try to see how bad it is. He feel like vomiting. The loneliness is gone but in place of loneliness, this stranger Angela, so small.

Look at her, afraid. Wrap her warm and carry her to his father car. Drive to the hospital.

The attendant in the Emergency Room act very suspicious. "You beat up your girlfriend. Then you want us to patch her up for you, so you can beat her up some more."

He look at Angela.

"She just a baby. You should be ashame."

He look at Buddy.

"You just a kid yourself. What's her name?"

"Angela."

Man call the police.

Angela unconscious so she can't answer any of the questions that you have to if you want the hospital to treat you. Police come and question him, Buddy, and he tell them the street, house, and apartment of her parents. The police tell him stay there until they return.

Buddy leaning on the rear wall of the Emergency Room. His body tight, fearing for Angela untended as the time continues to count by. Aides have taken her away from the waiting-room area, put her on a rolling steel-strong stretcher, cover lightly by a single sheet. Buddy leaning tired and horrify at the back of the gigantic room. Rows of churchly hardback wooden pews. Fat women slow tears from they eyes, they waiting. Girls, with babies on they knees, they waiting. Old men, floppy trousers, scar-tissue skin, they waiting. Younger men, often mumbling to they self, they waiting too.

Buddy leaning on the wall be thinking that the whole city of his people like a all-night emergency room. People mostly suffering, uncomfortable, and waiting.

Police reach the building where Angela live. Find the apartment Buddy describe to them and knock on the door. Does he, Mr. Figueroa, have a daughter name of Angela?

"Yes."

"She home?"

"No."

"Where is she?"

Angela father say he don't know. "She sneak out, din't leave no note."

"Has your daughter done this before?"

"No."

"Anything unusual happen tonight?"

"I tell her show some more respect."

"Where's your wife?"

"Sleeping."

"Don't you want to know what has happened to your daughter, why we're here?"

"No. Maybe one of her boyfriends beat her."

The police demand to talk to Angela mother. They take her back with them to the hospital. Before they leave, Angela mother put on her uniform.

At the hospital, Angela mother approach the stretcher, like a professional.

"Yes, that's Angela."

"Do you know what happened to her?"

"No. Maybe one of her boyfriends beat her."

"She have a boyfriend name Buddy?"

Mrs. Figueroa start to accuse Buddy, but she think of Buddy father, change her mind.

"Mrs. Figueroa, we need you to answer some questions and give permission for the hospital to treat your daughter. She's in serious condition. Will you do that?"

Angela mother shrug her agreement and go into the Administration Office with the police.

The desk attendant keep his eye on Buddy leaning like stone at the back of the Emergency Room. Buddy almost frozen there and barely blink his eyes. The attendant feel sorry for him, and after making some inquiries, he go back and tell Buddy the word:

"Your girlfriend's in shock. They take her to the X-ray. Check out if she have a fracture. She lose a lot of blood, you know."

The attendant keep halting. Expect Buddy to say something. Buddy say nothing, just look away.

"That must have been some terrible beating. You listening to me? Boy, what's the matter?"

Buddy roll his eyes towards the man face, slowly, see a kindly looking guy, brown skin with a clip mustache.

Buddy tell him, "Well, you betta watch your language."

The kindly guy feel better because Buddy have answer him at last.

"Hey, man, why don't you take a load off the floor? Sit down someplace. You not helping nobody standing up there. It's gone be a while."

"Okay."

Buddy move towards a open space, take a seat. Everywhere around him people into pain. Or asthma. Or just plain cold. They using the long wait as a kind of rescue from the street. Buddy thinking and feeling about Angela. Buddy thinking and feeling about his father. The life of the only two people, his father and his girl, inside this hospital.

Buddy jump a little bit. Is he praying?

Buddy don't believe in God, but he catch himself inside his head like he be praying Angela, my father, Angela, my father. Help me. Somebody. Help.

Both the two lives may be dying now, and nothing he can do. Buddy look around him, feel ridiculous, deserted, lonely, sitting there. Consider how much money do he have. Dollar seventy-five. And all at once his pockets swell with cash.

Him, Buddy, up and down the aisle of the Emergency Room.

Ask the lady "want some coffee?" Ask the man "you want a taste?" Pass out chewing gum and Hershey bars and Bali Hai and hot chocolate and hot coffee, lotsa cream. Got the sugar in his hand. Drop the sugar, one lump, two. Pass out pillows, airplane blankets. Taking towels to the men's room, roll up carts of toilet paper, two-ply tissue, soft, oval sweetly scented soap. Strap himself to a outside window belt and wash the windows. Jump down afterwards and rush and grab a broom and sweep and mop, then wring the mop. Bop into his father room. Close the curtains, lower the bed, take a shower, shake his head. Rush out find a florist, buy some flowers, tulips look to him like Angela.

For his father buy some seeds, and haul some open land into the hospital.

Buddy sitting still where he has sat.

SEVEN

They call it child abuse. They mean when Angela get beat so bad the hospital have to treat her.

But why Angela parents have to work so hard and long and why they have to live so crowded up they saying nothing. Point no finger. Take no action. Still the consequences standing pretty terrible and clear. The beating Angela have suffer come through pretty terrible and clear. The Family Court hold Angela in custody. Send Angela to what the Court call "shelter," in Manhattan.

Angela brothers and sister be parcel out among the relatives until police will finish the investigation. When Angela seem well to leave the hospital a large policewoman bring her to the "shelter" in Manhattan. The shelter cross up between a penitentiary and school.

Look like a regular old school look like a prison. Shelter girls forbidden to see boys. Buddy measuring the place from outside only. Out across the street from where his Angela be force to stay among too many girls women girls, no men. No boys. Only lonely miserable girls kept lonely.

Buddy starving for the sight of Angela.

The sound of her.

Dictionary tell him shelter keep you safe from danger. He be worrying about a "shelter" separating her from him. He be worrying about old people when they think that love be dangerous.

EIGHT

A couple weeks go by. Buddy father slipping into worse condition. Doctors tell him, anyday. Buddy go to school and blank out in the classroom chair. Thinking and feeling about Angela. Think about her face. Think about how small she seem. Think about her breasts. Think about her room.

In Phys. Ed. Buddy organize his friends. They make it plain they don't want no phony one-two exercising. They want real live physical education: sex education. Want straight films on sex. Want to learn anatomy. Buddy want to know what Angela look like inside. That where the giggle come from. They want contraceptives. They want sex free and healthy like they feel it. Buddy want his Angela.

The principal say no. So Buddy organize his friends. His friends organize their friends. They organize some more. All come together in the gym. Confront the principal.

"What do we want?"

"Sex!"

"When do we want it?"

"Now!"

"What do we want?"

"Sex!"

"When do we want it?"

"Now!"

Principal be very annoy. Principal, a balding son of somebody, send for the A. V. teacher. Ask him bring a tape recorder and a microphone. Buddy and his friends raise the chant:

"What do we want?"
"What do we need?"
"When do we need it?"
"When do we want it?"
The A. V. man arrive carrying a tape recorder and a microphone. The principal trying to bring the gym to order. Fifteen hundred boys calling out:
"Now!"
"Sex!"
"Now!"
"Sex!"
Principal say, "Boys! Boys!"
They lower the chant into a growling consultation among themselves. Come up with a new cry:
"Girls! Girls!"
"Two-four-six-eight-why don't you coeducate?"
"Girls! Girls!"
"Two-four-six-eight-coeducate-coeducate!"
"When do we want it?"
"Now!"
"Wow! Now! Girls! Girls!"

The principal call out: "I am willing to negotiate, send me your leader."
Tremendous roar of laughter break loose from the boys.
They rush forward as one man, Buddy at the front. Present the principal with their demands. Talk back and forth. The principal agree to order films immediately. But he want to negotiate the contraceptives.
The boys appoint a committee who will meet with the principal, settle the details, settle the details. Design a contraceptive clinic. Buddy shove a clipboard underneath the principal nose. Tell him he will write down the particulars of the agreement. Sign it on the spot.
The principal capitulate. Anyway, what can he argue? Do he want more unwed mothers? Tense unhappy students in the classroom? Rape around the corner? Streets too dangerous for his wife to walk down them alone? Mr. Hickey sign the paper.

Buddy handspring somersault high hysterical and happy flying down the lunchroom. Want to eat some food.

He reach the lunchroom. Smell the starchy cheese smell. Slide by the dry steam succotash. The superpeel potato. Stale whole wheat bread. The jerkoff corny butter squares.

Buddy say "God-damn!"

His friend ask, "What you mean?"

Buddy say, "Today. From now. No more. No more eating garbage. And no more this rig-the-lunchroom garbage meaning that we have to squeeze uptight against the walls."

Buddy look around. Tell his lieutenant, "Get the biggest baddest phonograph and get it down here quick." Tell his right-hand man, "Go find some sides. Don't care where you get them. Get them. And bring them here."

Spot the lunchroom supervisor. Give out the word. The boys fall in behind him, close and ready. Buddy move slow to the supervisor Mr. Jenkins. Loudly put his question.

"Mr. Jenkins, why you scrunch up all the tables one side of the lunchroom?"

"Listen here, Rivers. What you trying to do?"

"No, man, answer me. Why we got to sit in all these tables jam up to the side like that?"

Mr. Jenkins reach out to hold on Buddy arm.

"Don't you touch me, Brother Jenkins."

"Rivers, I can explain this to you privately."

"I don't wanna hear no *privately*."

"You can understand, it's a lot easier."

"Don't you tell me what I understand. You tell me what you have to say, then I'll tell *you* what I understand."

"Only two of us patrol the lunchroom, Rivers. You know that." Jenkins talking quickly, nervous now about the boys surrounding him. "Make it easier to control the situation."

"Control!" Buddy mimicking. "Control. You pack us in like animals, and then you say, they act like nothing more than animals. To hell with your control." Buddy start to snap his fingers, rhythmic. Snap. Snap.

Get it together!

Snap. Snap. Snap. Snap.
Get it together.
Snap. Snap. Snap. Snap.
Other students pick it up. Snap. Snap. Snap. Snap.
Get it together.
Buddy say, "Shit. Must be some women in this lunchroom. Find the women!"
Snap. Snap. Snap. Snap.
Buddy dash. Buddy dash over to the counter. Jump the counter. Run over, hold a woman.
"Hey, sweetheart, I know you *got* to be somebody's mother! Am I right or wrong?"

The woman try to be angry with him, but she laugh.
Buddy say, "Come on, big Momma, dance with me!"
Buddy urge the woman out. The other boys be imitating what he do. Find all them women in the lunchroom. Bring them out, and proud. Buddy yell, "Some music, jim, some music!"
First lieutenant plug the phonograph and wail the volume to the limit. The music start. The boys push drag and shove the tables out the way. Furore in the lunchroom. Big Mommas in the middle, like church sisters taking care a ceremony. Dignified, and happy. Rocking to the beat.
The boys be jumping on the tables. Snatch some silverware. Beat the furniture to drums. Beat and stamp and clap and dance, and listen to the music. Moving to the music. Making up the music. In the middle, all the Mommas jiggle and they wiggle, dip and strut, break and shake. Take the handkerchief from out the pocket of they uniform. Wipe they forehead. Rock around the floor. Rock. Rock. Rock. Snap, snap. Stamp, stamp. Turn the lunchroom on.

Seven hundred young Black men and four big Mommas doing a dance, in the Boys High lunchroom.
They having so much fun, they hardly hear the sirens racing to the school. The police rush in at the four doors to the lunchroom. Stand there stupefied. Try to figure out what's happening.
Some of the students leap right over, friendly style, ask, "Any women with you?"

Police uncertain what to do. Suddenly the music stop. Mr. Hickey cross the lunchroom, hurriedly on the diagonal. "Arrest him! Arrest him! Where is Rivers? Arrest him!"

The dancing stop.

Buddy come right over to Hickey. Ask him, "Are you looking for me?"

"There he is. Book the troublemaker. Get him out of my school."

Sergeant look around, see all the boys friendly and relax. He see the big Mommas smiling hope to dance some more.

"What's the charge?"

"Disorderly conduct, idiot!"

"Who are you calling 'idiot'? Mr. ——?"

"Hickey. I'm the principal here."

Sergeant look at the floor and say, "Disorderly conduct. You got a printed rule prohibit dancing in the lunchroom, Mr. Hickey?"

"Printed?! You know the rules, Sergeant. You can see for yourself what has happened here!" Exasperated, he shouts, "Jenkins! Where are you?"

Jenkins stroll slowly over to the principal. Jenkins looking at the four big Mommas. Think about his own. He say, "Mr. Hickey, we —"

Hickey interrupt him. "We!?"

"Well, I — I mean — the fellas — you know — and I — just have some music going on. You know, break the monotony, change from the routine."

So the talk goes. The sergeant shake his head and leave the lunchroom, laughing. Ask the Mommas, "How you doing? How's everything?"

They tell him everything be fine.

But Buddy be suspended.

And beside the principal tell Buddy that he can't come back to school unless he bring a parent with him. Buddy think about how dumb the idea is: his parents. Would have to mean a uncle or a aunt come up explaining and polite. Buddy rather wait until his father maybe leave the hospital and come to school: his father be right there to deal with the principal. So Buddy have to stay suspended.

NINE

Time and time and day and night Buddy be alone. At the hospital, he watch his father, hanging on, unconscious. Live on sugar, flow down from a bottle through a tube into a vein of his muscular and idle arm.

Buddy try for small talk with Mrs. Figueroa. But she give him the glaring of her ugly eye. Angela be transfer from the shelter to a Catholic Home for Girls, outside the city, call St. Margaret.

Buddy be practicing to drive his father's car the long way up to Angela in Middlebrook. He have been around the local corners some before but never no long practice drive to get him ready for the big trip.

Tuesday he decide to practice right around the city where the traffic bars the river from the people. Buddy off into a territory takes it thirty-five miles per at midday in-between what folks call heavy. Thirty-five miles per.

The car run like two tons of filthy thick and deeply spotted oil down Halsey Street between the Blackwood Keep-Your-Neighborhood-Clean placards tilted up strict in the flowerless front yards of redand-yellow grayandbrown brownstones. Then the street merge into Fulton Street and subway stops. The workclothes clothingstores. Novelty shops. Goodwill centers. Secondhand refrigerators icebox bedspring coffeepercolator shoes and dresses trouserpants and earmuffs. Fish and barbecue and Jesus Saves Me tabernacles. Drug and beautybarbershops. A stonewhite Virgin Mary statue and a place where Flats Be Fixed and Records Sold at Bargain Prices. Fulton Street.

One time Buddy want to buy a present for Angela so he walk Reid Avenue past all the short thin younger kids who live half in the hallway half on the avenue. Go walk on up to Fulton Street and bop into one shop after another. Find nothing but the smell of old cheese and old fat men with dirty smiles. Or else the smell of old yellow cheese and heavy dust covered crap nobody ever want under Easter egg sloppycolor cellophane.

Nothing good enough for Angela. And you know the price be twice as high as downtown.

Buddy drive down Fulton Street and onto Flatbush Avenue between the blank big office buildings mostly vacant on each side. And then he reach the bridge go over it and cross Canal Street. Make a right turn. Take the West Side Highway north.

The highway like a Funny House. You don't know when something will open at you let you off or what. Drive north past the storybook apartment houses. People dress up for the movies. Dress down to walk the dog. Drive by below the marble bullshit memory of Prez Grant.

Drive by these Bronxlike Mountainside apartments. Look like high-rise outhouse and no door. No tree. Drive across the narrow northern edge of the Manhattan secret-island (people use it like the island part's a secret part). Under a tunnel under eight different intersecting streets under skyscraping (more) apartments on top of George Washington Bridge and curve onto the East Side Drive. The really river drive by Harlem. Brick projects. Brick new private terracing apartments globe-lights and concrete colored intermix construction bricks. Drive quiet by the river. Harlem bridges start to sway out the windshield.

Drive toward the crowded power down the East Side Drive. And Buddy just be Buddy practicing for the long trip up to Angela.

About the level of 123d Street the Drive spread wider than it was and Buddy tense a bit like a pilot in a mission cockpit.

Check the gauges. Check the rearview mirror. Check the sideview mirror. Watch them cars ahead. The radio be playing loud and nice.

Wrapped up my money
and I couldn't find my way.
So I changed them bills to silver
And I rolled another game
so two could play
so two could pay.
And things ain't never been the same
since then
since when you came
you blew my lonely game with
love like a nickel and a dime
making changes all the time
love like a nickel love like a dime
making changes all the time.

Static. Buddy snap to. The drive be under a stone shed tunnel now. Radio song turn to static. Buddy feel a shivering. He see in the rearview mirror a large black car. A hearse and yellow headlights follow him. And snakestyle behind the hearse more of them. Largedarkcars and yellow lights.

Buddy feel fear.

Not able to switch lanes because there be no room for him. Broad daylight and they in this tunnel and this largedarkcar with yellowlights and other largedarkcars with yellowhearseheadlights be following right after Buddy.

They leave the tunnel to the broad daylight again but still the funeral procession following close right after him and Buddy feel panic.

Why they following after him? Where they going on the Drive? No cemeteries in this direction anywhere. This direction take you to the midtown city center of the power. Where's the cemetery for the funeral behind him? Buddy switch lane. The largedark car behind him switch lane behind him and the other yellow headhearse-lit large dark cars switch into line following after Buddy.

Him Buddy start to sweat. Another stoneshed tunnel upahead and under it the first hearse pull next to Buddy make Buddy feel like a midget. Look up and see the gargoyle gladioli flowers of the funeral like watercolor swords ready to ram another any corpse around.

Buddy frantic want to separate himself from this funeral procession. Find the next exit and leave the Drive entirely. On the midtown Manhattan sidestreet from the highway Buddy wheel the car to the curb and halt the engine underneath a No Parking Anytime sign. Scared sitting in a small sweat. Buddy don't want to drive no more. Get out and stretch his legs. (Illegal because the sign means on your seat and off your feet.)

From the East River walking west across Forty-ninth Street. Buddy want to cross Second Avenue. He look up north and see the midtown city see the carhorizon taxicolored truckcolored carcolored steel flowers for the funeral. He see the midtown city cemetery and the cold flowers the carsteel flowers filling up the land of stone.

Buddy turn to snatch his car and move it home.

TEN

Angela send him a letter:

Dear Buddy,

How are you?

I am fine. I am staying at St. Margaret's in Middlebrook, New York. It's this home for girls again.

How is your father? I hope he is feeling better.

If you want to, you can write me here. They let me get my mail if the letters are all right. The sisters are very nice, and they read my mail before I can read it.

We eat, sleep, and go to school and everything all in the same one building.

If I don't get in trouble, I can have a visitor at the end of the month. Do you think you can come and see me?

Love,
Angela

ELEVEN

Buddy read the letter again and again. Figure the sisters must be censoring the mail, or else Angela be brain damage from when her father hit her in the head. Buddy not sure what to think, but he have hope that it be censorship. End of the month leave him one week to wait until he see her.

He start a garden. Shovel clear some walkway for the garden. Buy cement and mix it with a strong rose coloring for Angela. She will walk around the earth the color of a rose. He pour the cement mix into a S shape in the yard and around it be planting roses and chrysanthemums, a pear tree and some marigold.

Buddy like working in the dirt. He like the feel of soil under the fingernails and mud changing shape in the palm of a hand or the slight chill shiver of a slow moving earthworm.

His relatives, and even sometimes his mother far away in Barbados, they all send him, send Buddy, food money and money for clothes. Treat him like a little man. He take all the clothes money and spend it ordering seeds from a garden catalog his father always use to use, with color photographs of fruit trees and things like that.

The backyard seem like a flower island in the middle of the block. Buddy stare at the fencing separate the people keep every yard too small. Keep every yard a secret angry under the windows. The alley cats the only living action yard to yard.

Then Buddy get himself a plan and go around to make it happen. Buddy want to tear the separating fences down. At first the people tell him when he talk to them they worry that the junkies will rob and steal out stuff from the new back openspace. But Buddy argue how the back be just as hard to enter as the front of houses. So everybody try it.

Pretty soon the neighbors break the backyard open. Pull the fencing down. Stretch the yard into a park they all will share. Have a great big smoky BarBcue to celebrate. Working the ground with neighbors. Planning the backyard park so there be different things that you can use it for. Buddy be less alone and busy. They have a huge dump of sand somebody bring in and even the older kids spread into it. Have a ball. The men plan how to share the hose they have for water-play when summer start.

Things looking up. People on the block say hello and talk awhile.

Buddy spend all the money he hold on work stuff, seed, tools, paint. He be losing weight.

He write to Angela:

Last night it rain, and I go walking out. I notice how the sidewalk looks blue when it rain. So I buy some strong blue paint to paint the sidewalk strong blue all the time. Then a taxi fly by and I been thinking about your father and I look at the steps lead to the parlor. They probably look better black and yellow. Done that today. Then I buy some slick gray paint to trim the windows. I would like to paint the street a bloody red where cars go through.

But the people on the block don't really dig all this painting that I do. They come around complaining. Yak. Yak.

Tell me what they feed you. Good cooking is hard to come by. Do you know how? To cook?

See you soon.
Buddy

Dear Angela:

I be the first one there on Saturday, see for myself what's happening to you.

Yesterday I make this table. Be like the Japanese. The table seem like a triangle. One point be the food and the other points be for you and me. It stand 15 inches high, from off the floor. Like I said, you can call me Slim. I hope you slim the same. Otherwise, it be uncomfortable.

Stain it what they call a rosewood coloring. I got this thing for roses, and for you. When the table be finish, I put it next to the big floor pillows where *you* can lie down listen to the phonograph, which I still ain't finish put together, but I have in mind because of you.

Love,
Buddy

TWELVE

Saturday arrive. Buddy driving up to Angela. Drive by houses, drive by parkside, drive by gasoline station, drive by the state police, drive by highway over the highway, drive by byways by the highway, drive by other people, other cars, traveling in the same, the opposite direction. Cross across them. Drive by boats. Drive by pond and river. Drive by train and railroad track.

Take a long time getting there.

Angela see Buddy and her heart beat hard.

She say, "You looking skinny."

He say, "You watch out. You be like a heavyweight."

"Sister Frances, this is Buddy Rivers."

"How you, Sister?"

Buddy see the sister trying to hide her face from the light. Seem like she shave her face.

"Sister Mary this my friend, Buddy Rivers."

"How you, Sister Mary?"

Buddy notice Sister Mary look like a football fullback off the field.

"Sister Margaret, this be Buddy Rivers. He my friend from Brooklyn."

Buddy think she look all right and wonder why the Sister Margaret be a nun.

Angela introduce Buddy to every single sister this and that. Buddy think the bunch of them be like some fallen angels. Fallen out of life.

"Ain no priests up here, Angela?"

"Why you asking me?"

"The sisters need some boyfriends. Something make them act alive.

I come up and be a altar boy! Get this heavy incense. Throw it all around the chapel. Everybody be high."

"Buddy, stop that."

"Stop what? How you like it up here, nothing but the sisters and the girls?"

"Let's go where we can really talk."

"Where's that?"

"You have to go outside. No place inside where you can be alone. Even for a minute. Even in my room I have four other girls in there with me. Everybody have the same deal. Five to a room."

They go outside. Buddy feel like a fool to ask in case they have a rule against his holding her hand. But he don't want to get his Angela in trouble. So they move out separated stiff.

Angela continue. Almost whisper in a hurry.

"Last week one of them attack me."

"One of who? The sisters?"

"No, not yet. But I hear about a sister on the third floor try to kiss another sister."

Buddy say, "Try to kiss her?" He start to laughing. "Angela you better be serious."

"I am serious," she say, laughing. "Half the girls be going with the other half. They don't let you do nothing else."

"Jesus K. Christ, what you be doing?"

"Well, I write my letters to you, you know. But they be no boys up here and we can't see none except once a month, if we be good. One of my friends, she ask the sister can they pray for all the people who in love. The sister say that's no kind of prayer for anybody in a chapel."

"Dig that."

"And another friend of mine. She suppose to get out when her birthday come. But the sister tell her she have to stay here unless she write her boyfriend and break up with him."

"Why?"

"The sister say they be too serious."

"Damn. What they think Jesus was into?"

"Well I don't know what they think. Except it seem like they want us to turn into nuns like them. Buddy, I don't want to be no nun."

"Why you even have to say that Angela."

Angela don't answer right away. Buddy waiting for the answer. Look at her face and feel himself not strong enough to help.

Angela go on. "They have this system. Points. More times you go to Mass the more points you be collecting. Points mean you get privileges. Like boys once a month. Or going home for a weekend. So you try for points. Next thing you know you start feeling like already you a nun. I'm fourteen and I think about what be happening when I grow up. Do I want to be like my mother. Do I want to be a nun. And I don't know between my mother and a nun. I don't know no more."

Angela sound funny. Hoarse. Buddy feel scare that she will cry.

"Angela! I break you outa here!"

"What you mean? What you saying?"

"Listen baby, I mean liberation. Here and now! All you gotta do is follow me!"

Tears come from Angela.

And Buddy feel himself whirl around and run back to the building.

Angela running after him.

Buddy bolting room by room trying to find a signal.

Find the dining room bell. And ring the bell and ring the bell and ring the bell. All the sisters run to the parlor look like overheated penguins.

All the girls run to the parlor, look like children.

Buddy ring the bell like bells be going outa style.

Bell, bell, bell.

He make a speech: "In the name of the Father, in the name of the Son, in the name of the Mother who got together with the Father and got that Son, I liberate my Angela, here and now. This is Eastertime in Middlebrook. Love is rising up. Love is rising up. I tell you, Jesus was a one hundred percent, hip to the living, female-loving dude. A loving dude."

Buddy make his speech, the nuns come flying at him. Gray robes, black and shapeless clouds of cloth material.

Buddy dodge among the nuns, and cry out, "Peace, peace, sister. Find yourself a priest."

Everything be all confuse, the sisters grabbing at each other, wide sleeves flapping furious, headpiece falling off.

The girls thrash to the doorway. Sisters like obstacles to impede and block their passage. The girls in sweaters, sisters in robes. Buddy yelling, "Peace, find yourself a priest."

Buddy grab Angela and tackle through three sisters, their weight bewildering their movements. Buddy say, "Sing, Angela, you be singing. This is liberation!" Angela not say nothing, stay close behind Buddy. Reach the doorsill. Start they running out to the car. Get inside, discover other girls be hiding in the car, waiting for the lift, waiting for liberation.

Buddy start the car, the car take off, they on they way. And speeding.

Tears continue from her eyes and Buddy standing still in front of Angela. Hands at his side.

Angela say, "Buddy, next weekend they let me go home. Visit my family for the weekend. Buddy. You want me to come to you then?"

Buddy answer her *yes*. His head feel hot. His eyes feel hot. His body cold. They plan together what will happen. When she leave her parents Sunday for the trip back up to Middlebrook. Then instead she will come to the house of Buddy and his father. Then they will then they will then they will do what they have to do. For liberation.

THIRTEEN

Buddy believing that alive mean *go*. He do it. He go there. Do this. Do that. Not so much the speed, but the pattern. Do it. Go there. Make a pattern. Break a pattern. Back and forwards, round and round. Curve and drift. Stop to start. Start to stop. Blur and solid:

> *When I'm alone with you*
> *All my worries taking flight*
> *All my sadness out of sight*
> *When I'm alone with you*
> *When I'm alone with you*
> *When I'm alone*
> *With you alone.*

Buddy trying to prepare for love inside the house of his father. He nail together and he sand things smooth. Clean and clear. Write down write up long list of things he wish that he could spread around for Angela to see. Then he sit down quiet thinking songs and thinking of his father. Think-how they Angela and Buddy have to find a way to stay together.

Angela come back to Brooklyn with a paper bag. When she reach the building where her family live she feel a freezing terror. But she go inside. Her brothers and her sister have been sent away and so the house seem hopeless ugly.

Angela sit down in the parlor on the couch. She waiting for her mother or her father when he will get off from working.

She check the refrigerator. Find no food. No stuff for snacking. One piece of meat be frozen rocky. Bread seem rocky. Milk smell sour. Only thing available is beer. A couple six-packs and a saucer holding gray beans leftover.

On the stove, a big pot bubbling steady full of peas and hambone.

"Angela! What you doing here?"

Her mother shut the front door and immediately call out.

"Hello, Ma." Angela leave the kitchen and walk into the parlor where her mother have snap on one of the big lamps no one hardly use.

"They kick you out, or what?"

"I'm just visiting for the weekend."

"Visiting! Hah. Freeloading be closer to the truth. They give you money? or do you expect that we will feed you for free?"

Angela want to sit down and be deaf. Be dumb. Be blind. She have no heart to argue with her mother. She miss her brothers and her sister. Now she realize she have no home. Her family be parents beat you in the head or hate you. She mean the father mother family. Her sister and her brothers make another family where she love and care. Angela trying to think how she can come around the hatred of her mother. How she can have a home that be a happy place be better than the upstate "home" for girls.

"Well, Miss Angela, you have in mind to sit on your behind and watch me slave a little bit?"

"Oh, Ma. Look, if you want me to do something tell me straight."

"Now you criticize the way I talk?"

"I only mean why we have to fight? Tell me what you want me to be doing. Period. I'll do it."

"If you so smart about the way I should be talking you don't need me to tell you nothing at all. For all I care you can go on and sit there, or stand upside down. I'm going out."

"Ma, you want me to go back upstate?"

"You got yourself into that mess."

"Ma, Daddy put me in the hospital. He beat me."

"I don't care what you do but do it out my sight. Don't let me hear you say no words about your father."

"Ma, I be going back upstate tonight. Right now."

"Well, what you waiting for? You see anybody stop you?"

Angela look at her mother long. She look around the room. Small room. Big empty dust feeling to the furniture. Dust.

Angela pick up the paper bag. Finally she take the housekey from her pocket. Put it on the television. "Okay, Ma, I'm going now," she say. And Angela go. She leave for good.

FOURTEEN

Angela hope Buddy be home. They have plan for Sunday. But the day is now. Friday.

She walk the avenue toward the subway and his house. Somebody come up from behind and hug around her close and large.

"Hey, where you going Angela?"

"See you." She turn around and into Buddy arms. Repeat. "See you."

They quick discuss the scene. They figure that tonight be safe enough. The nuns think Angela be visiting her parents and her parents think that Angela be traveling back to Middlebrook. Things seem temporary cool. Both Buddy and Angela feel excited trembling almost almost ready for the liberation they have scheme together.

"You have any money?"

Buddy nod his head.

"Maybe we should pick some food up."

"Okay. Let's go buy some bananas, some potato chips, some ice cream, and some soda. What you want?"

"I like a hamburger, some tissues and some soap."

"You need any of them — ah, what you may call female things?"

"If I do, I get them on my own time, Mr. Rivers!"

"Don't say I didn't ask you!"

"Angela, what you think about this store?"

Got burglar gates and great big locks. You can't hardly go inside the place. Place be halfway burn. Ashes on the floor.

"Look like a jail where food be taken out on bail."

Angela answer nothing.

Inside the store, they nudge each other when they see a roach slip by. Buy what they want. Buddy crumple up his dollar bills before he turn them over to the man.

"Don't be right to give them something green and pretty."

They run back to Buddy block.

"Come on, come on, let's get inside! We got one night."

Angela start laughing when she see the steps. Black and yellow just like Buddy wrote. They take them two at a time, two at a time.

First thing Angela notice when she step in the door, she smell sawdust, airplane glue and paint. Angela just standing by the door, make her eyes roam around the house.

Her eyes be roaming around the house.

The house very surprising. From the street it look like a three-floor brownstone. The outside stone steps take you to the front door, and that front door take you inside. And then, the big surprising part of the house begin because you see no hallway. No hallway. There be indoor stairs lead to a third floor. The indoor stairs be part of the living room on the second floor where you be standing inside the house.

The third floor be like a balcony, tore back from the downstairs living room and overlook that living room.

Most of the living room reach from the second floor, where you standing, to the roof. And, in a funny place, not really in the center of the ceiling of the roof, there be a stain-glass skylight, blue and red and purple and plain light, high up in the ceiling/roof of the living room.

So the house seem huge inside it. Huge and high. With the stairways zigzag on the side. Some of the steps unstained, unpainted. Maybe two piece of furniture in the living room. A easy chair. A portable TV.

Planks of lumber lean against the walls, and one window almost floor to ceiling, with a brand-new sticker on the corner of it. The other window be broken brick by brick. And temporary cardboard block the air until the wall will hold a longer pane of glass.

The wall be plaster rough. Some paper stripping curl toward the floor, and other parts be painted blue already.

Angela feel like she walking in a magazine before the final photograph be taken of the house. Before everything be finish.

No hallway. Angela stare hard to see a house where people live without a hallway. That mean every part of the house is real. It belong to somebody, and be part of how you live, not how you get to where you live, and be.

Buddy calling "Come on, Sister Angela." Buddy pound down the stairs, drop the package, and pound back up. "See how much weight you gain."

Buddy lift her to his shoulder, tell her, "Hold on."

Buddy walking tiptoe tremble, make believe the weight will kill him. Start to groaning. Groan all the way down the stairs, out to the garden, where he stand her up.

"Let me watch you walking on the concrete. How you like it?"

Angela see flowers not yet blooming any color. See the narrow pretty strip of path. A strong rose concrete way among the growing flowers. See the mud, the warm rich earth, a natural brown.

"Walk with me, Buddy."

"Not enough room, Angela."

"How can you make something so narrow, there be no room for two of us?"

"I guess I didn't think you come here, really."

"Dance with me, Buddy, then we can fit it."

Buddy move to Angela move to Buddy, like one person, moving on the concrete running red through the brown earth.

"They be some hard buttons on your coat."

"Well, I'm allergic to the wool you wearing. How you like it?"

"Here is really nice. I really like it."

"You want a soda?"

"I like a soda, but I like to wash my hands and wash my face, and then I like to come back out here."

"It be dark soon, Angela, we can come back out here, maybe later."

Buddy think about tomorrow. But don't even want to *say* tomorrow.

"Buddy, where the bathroom? I never see a house like this."

Buddy bend down to the floor, hold a knob there. When he come up, part of the wall come up with him. "There you go."

"Why you have a door like that?"

"Be good exercise, bend down, pull up, bend down, open it up. You get use to it. Everything in this house be like this."

She go in the bathroom. Whole room like the doorway to it. Seem like wood venetian blinds. Dark wood strips look like they comb down smooth, or almost smooth together, like venetian blinds. The soap, the shower curtain, bathtub mat, the towel and the washcloth, the toothbrush and the box of baby powder, everything except the mirror and the walls, be crazy orange. Angela uneasy. Real quick wash her hands and face with orange soap, and dry her hands and face on orange towels, smelling clean and good.

"Buddy, something happen to me! You better come on in, and see!"

Buddy calling, "What you doin?"

"My face turn orange in the bathroom. That be some really sneaky soap."

Buddy lift up the door, go inside look at Angela. Her face seem orange in the mirror. She look at him.

"You have the same disease."

Buddy step behind her, bring his face down to her face. They see each other in the mirror, orange.

"You better let me see how bad it is. It may be spreading."

"You always try to be so smart."

Buddy say, "Square business. It look serious to me. Better check it out."

He look close to her neck. Buddy say, "Oh, oh — you can see for yourself, you got a bad case of the orange."

Angela turn from the mirror, start to tickling him.

"Hey, woman, I'm a break my neck."

Buddy try to escape the tickling, bang his elbow on the sink, knock his head against the towel rack. Buddy say "shh . . . ."

Whip off the light. Whisper, "Here, hold on to this." Give Angela a piece of towel. "Don't make no noise, just hold on to the towel."

Buddy pull Angela slowly, quietly out the bathroom to the dining room — what use to be dining room. Buddy give Angela all the towel. He say, "Here, hold this on your eyes."

Press the lightswitch, make like a purple light on everything. "Okay. You can look now. Here, come here. You choose a record."

Buddy lift up the phonograph cabinet door and, smiling, show his Angela the phonograph, the albums pile together, thick. The room not finish yet, but almost.

One corner there the wires hang down from the ceiling, and no light. Toolbox and some tools beneath the music cabinet.

"Let me take your coat."

Buddy put the coats inside a large wood box built like a trunk against the wall. He lift the lid and fold the coats and pack them out of sight.

The music be the only sound. He dancing with her, slow enough to hear her breathe.

She say, "I wish we could just stay here."

"We can. A little while. Tonight."

They sit down on the mattress in the corner, flat against the floor.

"You think we get in trouble, Buddy?"

"I don't know. I'm glad you're here."

They be quiet holding close together. He kiss her mouth, her arm.

Her fingers teasing on his neck and trace the fire down his back, his back a bone and skin discovery she making, stroke by stroke.

And they undress themselves. Feel him feel her wet and lose the loneliness the words between them.

"What do you call it?" Buddy ask her.

"Well I call it making love."

"We make some love."

They make some love and then they fall asleep.

FIFTEEN

Next morning they legs be tangle together. Angela wake up and look at Buddy lying naked there beside her. She kiss Buddy face, lean on one elbow looking at his head.

Buddy waken. He turn over, rest her warm against his chest.

"Angela, I thought you was a virgin. But maybe you should of told me that you was a virgin. I mean I'm sorry. Are you all right?"

Angela say, "For real. It dint hurt no more after that one time I told you."

Buddy smiling say, "I'm glad you all right."

Angela laughing. "Well, you all right too, Buddy."

Suddenly Buddy sit up, exclaim, "You could be pregnant!" Turn around and hug her hard. "Hey, you know that one thing? Could be we have a baby coming soon!"

Angela answer him by saying, "That be fine with me. So long we be both together, taking care of business."

"Well, of course," he say excited. "Start with two of us, and go right on ahead, the two of us be taking care of three of us."

"What time is it?"

"Time we better move on outa here. Sometime soon the sisters *and* the police *and* your parents figure things through and we be trapped by them."

"Well, let's eat some bananas and some ice cream and then you tell me what we need to take so I can help you pack."

Buddy tell her while they dress themselves. They take the food, the toolbox, a saw, his portable radio, extra batteries, some soap and towels, can-opener, kaleidoscope, playing cards, picnic jug of water, all the blankets they can find, two pillows, paper, ballpoint pens, drafting supplies for Buddy to fool with, flashlight, candles, and matches.

They quickly load the car and slowly lock the house.

Get to the corner. Make two left turns. Drive down the street where you can still see iron trolley tracks from years ago. Drive from the neighborhood they know. Make a right turn put them on Bushwick Avenue. Look out for cops. Take the road into the cemetery. Leads them to the reservoir brick house.

Just before they reach the house they see a military burial ground. Seem like all them same white crosses turning death to boredom. White crosses. Here and there a dime-store flagstick. Eight inches high, stuck into the earth. Its small flag leaking slight and lonely color to the lonely formal ground.

Buddy say, "A flag is not a flower growing on you. When I die, I want something to grow on right on top of me, you know?"

Angela be silent. She don't want to think about the end of nothing. Everything just really starting up.

When he stop the car, Buddy raise the hood, pretend he fooling with the radiator, and Angela act swift. Make several fast trips to unload the car on the side away from the highway eyes, the side of the reservoir house where she will wait for Buddy.

He drive the car two miles farther on, take off the tags, and hike back to where she waiting.

Angela sit among the things sad and scared. She listen to the traffic while she hypnotize herself by studying the sunlight in the water.

Finally Buddy come back like a silhouette approaching her. He kiss her forehead and then swamp her with blankets wrap around her. Leave her looking like a tepee.

Buddy take a hammer and a wedge. Break into the house. Look around. Break up the cobwebs. Saw some, drill some openings into the boards that covering the windows. Let in some air and light.

Must be a toolshed people have forgot about. Buddy rake the floor to clear it. Find a spigot, fill a pail with soap and water. Slosh the floor to weight the dust down. Make things smell better.

When he go out until the floor will dry, he find that Angela have scale the fence and be halfway in the water.

"Angela! The cars be seeing you that way!"

She laugh at him, and after a while, come back.

"We stay here long enough, we could figure how to swim here safe without nobody seeing us. Like at night. But now you never know."

"They don't have no guards around here?"

"I never seen one. Come on inside and dig the house."

"Hey, so much stuff! So much equipment, this is really outasight. You probably knew you could work it out, didn't you? Can you use them things some way?"

"First thing I need to do is find some wood. And maybe buy some glass and screens. Then I could show you better."

They talk to keep the house around them. His voice her voice shape him and her familiar (shapes) inside the unfamiliar house. They talk but standing still talk trying to imagine how they can stay and move and sleep and change where they are standing now, inside.

"We have enough money for about two weeks. If we find a store nearby, we can take turns going so they don't know that we together."

"I want everyone to know. Oh, shit, to hell with it. To hell with it. With everyone. I wish we had a rug, right here."

Buddy recognize that Angela be just as scare as him, and worrying. He think about what to say.

"We can use a blanket, baby. Put a blanket down. Let's try it."

"Buddy, open up the door so we can see the reservoir and count the birds and watch for the police."

Use up a hour spreading things out comfortable. Then notice that the blanket they been walking on be mess up from the shoes. So they make a rule. Like Orientals they will leave they shoes outside the house. They will leave the outside mess outside. They lay another blanket down, a clean blanket, down on the floor for Angela.

After that they go outside to work together. Shovel a latrine. Make up a bathroom in the bushes at the bottom of the hill.

For a bed, Buddy bang two benches together that he find. Angela figuring that things will be all right. They will eat out of cans and use the water from the spigot. So they settle in.

"I hope they don't be no rats around here. Buddy, why you frowning up like that?"

"I worry about my father. How he is. Don't want him dying by himself alone. Don't want him dying. I worry about myself, I may be a father soon myself, depending on you, and I worry what we doing here. How long can we hold out?"

"You think your father, you think he will die, Buddy?"

"I don't know what I think. You realize how long it's been since I hear him speak to me, or tell me anything? He don't even know you. Never even seen you, Angela, you. Sometime I think how I will like to give him to you — give you to him. You two meeting, eating oranges or peaches. Can you picture that?"

"I can taste it happening, sometime I think maybe your father would adopt me."

"Listen, Angela, don't start no sister business here with me."

"Okay, Mr. Rivers." They wrestling each other, ticklefighting on the floor.

"If my father was me, he probably take a pencil and scheme some changes for the house."

"Why don't you do that?"

"If I do, what will you be doing?"

"Oh, I play the radio. Figure something out I have in mind."

First thing Buddy draw is trees. He have the tree between the highway and the house. But still, you know, the highway is there, the house is there, and now you have the trees. Nothing cut into nothing else. But things be differently together. From the highway, things seem different. From the house, the road seem different. But no interference. No elimination. No taking out the highway or the house. The trees be added on, be something more. And the same be better with the trees.

Next he mark in some plants, some vegetables, and some flowers. Then he have the whole roadside of the house be brick completely. Except for near the bottom where he draw a wall-to-wall long narrow window as wide as the house is wide. So when he and Angela lie down they can see outside but not be seen unless somebody crawl up on his stomach.

On the reservoir waterside the house be absolutely glass with blinds for when they need them. And then there be a fireplace. Buddy not sure about how practical really is a fireplace, and so instead he draw a big potbelly stove, then he scratch that out. Then he try a radiator. Then he scratch out the radiator and then he go back to drawing in the fireplace.

Part of the time, Angela watch. Finally, out loud, she say, "No furniture in that house."

"See, I think a house, a home should mean like the table and the chairs. You build them in. Build in the table like the floor, the doors, the window, and the wall. That way, nothing really loose. Everything is tight, and you can trust it."

"I feel pretty loose, right now. You trust me?"

"I like you better than some table and a chair."

"But you can't nail me down."

"Don't want nobody nail nobody down. I'm only talking about furniture. People move keep moving all around. That be interesting. But let them things stay quiet. Things stay in they place. The same place all the time."

"What you have against people if they sit tight and have like the telephone to do the traveling."

"Well, look, I don't mind the telephone except it be like television and the whole world is a box-up make-believe to make you think you into what be really happening but all the time you into nothing really but that box. I have this other plan."

"Hey, this other plan better be something we can eat. Plus something we can drink. I choose you who will go for soda."

Buddy taking odds and lose on the third show, to Angela. While he go away, Angela comb out her Afro, fool with the radio, and make some notes.

> *Wine grow ready on the vine*
> *My baby write me letters on his hand*
> *Night bring the river and the seed*
> *Love is all the land we need*
>
> *The wine grow ready on the vine*

SIXTEEN

Come back to tuna fish and root beer. Eat and drink away the hunger and the worry.

"What you think," Angela ask Buddy, "Suppose everybody hold a radio. And you already dig how many kinds of sound you maybe hear that way. Depending how you feel, where you be going to, or where you come from, or what you feel like doing."

Buddy close and folding Angela inside his arms to rock with her. They swaying slow.

"I know what I feel like doing."

"Turn it on the radio."

"Damn, Angela."

"Do it, Buddy, please?"

"It? What you mean."

"Find the music on the radio. The music for what you feel."

Buddy take the radio. He turn and turn until he find a solo horn and strings, a strong drum under them.

They make some love. Buddy drop into a dreaming. Leave his large hands like protection and support around the brown surprising sturdy breasts of Angela.

THE DREAM

Start on uptown Fulton Street around three o'clock and the streets suddenly be full of children suddenly free from school and crowds and

throngs of blackbrown yellow redskin children wearing white shirts/
blueskirt uniforms/armysurplus/leftover cousinspringcoats. Crowds and
crowds from seven years old up to seventeen. Into every attitude
and face. Into every natural style and pace of fights and chase and
rap and argument. A hundred and a hundred and ten thousand blackbrown yellow redskin kids suddenly spill into the streets suddenly fill
the streets suddenly free from school.

Buddy father be walking the other way alone. His arm around a
brown bag of groceries and Buddy father walking careful not to hurt
the hundred thousand kids swarm at him surging in the opposite
direction thick to circle by the stranger man his groceries. The
darkbrown muscle of his motion.

The dream continue around five o'clock on midtown Forty-ninth
Street/Fifth Avenue and suddenly them neighborhoods be full of hundreds and ten thousands hundreds of white folks suddenly leaving the
towers suddenly leaving floor to ceiling windowwalls walltowall carpets cafeterias lounge areas bigbathrooms easychairs desks sofabed and
couch great conference tables heavy leather books addingmachines
typewriters desks magazines furnaces that work hot water air condi-
tioning sculpture fountains and 43,785,619 suddenly empty rooms
with doors and locks and keys.

Buddy father walking the other way alone up the subway stairs. The
thousand other people pushing down (the stairs) Buddy father walking
careful not to let himself be hurt. The hundreds rush against around
him on his arrival for the night and they be leaving.

The dream continue around midnight, and the empty towers echo
harsh from emptiness. Other people women wash the office floors,
dust, straighten things. Other men sweep the corridors and rearrange
the furniture and distribute a next day supply of comfortable items.
Buddy father laugh among these other few men and other few women
friends spending the night with him in the otherwise empty towers
where he watchman of the night.

The dream continue around dawn and Buddy father working at his
pocket drawing pad. Buddy father the nightwatchman at the top on
the terrace roof of an otherwise empty skyscraper and now Buddy
father draw the inside of the building that he guard and fill the empty
tower full of people that he know.

The people and the family of the men and women who do clean and straighten up the towers for the other (morning) folk.

The children from the Brooklyn streets. The relatives of cleaning people Brooklyn children fill his father drawing of the empty towers now a skyscraper glowing full of life at night and through the night.

The dream continue bright from Buddy father drawing pad into another dream and all the crowded, cold, the peeling painted rickety and rusted the unlit shamble Brooklyn housing slide invisible into the Hudson River slide collapsing from a river pier of several thousand splinters. Meanwhile all the families all the Brooklyn people reach the evening empty towers and fill them up with cribs and toys and parties on the intercom and blankets on the leather couch and turnip greens cook steaming in the cafeteria.

Buddy wake from his dream kiss sleeping Angela and she wake up.

He try to talk about his dream but some of it run disappearing from his mind. Buddy tell his Angela about the high-rent houses of apartments and the vacancies, about the Empire State Building and the vacancies, the space no human being use, the cityspace for life where there be emptiness. He try to tell his Angela about the city emptiness at five o'clock, the waste, the rooms no body use at night.

So Angela ask Buddy what he think would really happen if the Brooklyn people use the emptiness, take over space no body else will use inside the city, inside the tower buildings.

Buddy say, "Well, we could share them office buildings. I mean it's pretty wild, you stop to think about it, all them office building empty more than all night long, and all them rich apartments in them rich apartment houses, empty, and the other terrible small houses fall apart, burn up, burn down, and babies dying sick, cold, or sleeping in a orange crate. Don't make no sense."

"But suppose the office folk don't want nobody in they buildings after five."

"Then they could stay up where they living anyhow and do your thing about the telephone. I mean they just use machines, just put them up in the garage, or something, and don't have to use no office in the city. Or, you know what? We could compromise. At first, just use the office that nobody renting anyhow."

"I like it, Buddy. But how you think the businessmen be sharing in the daytime with the folks from Brooklyn?"

"They learn. Even business people, they can learn. From the get-go Brooklyn folks know how to share. They teach them other people nice."

"Buddy, you some heavy dreaming head."

"No. You be the only dream around here, Angela. The only dream."

SEVENTEEN

Buddy and Angela lying quiet.

Listen to the traffic 50 mph. The afternoon turn twilight. They decide to bathe each other clean. Too cold to strip completely so they wash each other one part at a time. Pouring water in the big sink drainaway. His legs. The fingers of her hands. And then they trade on washing hair. Her laughing screams. His laughing howl. The icy water shrink the Afros to a brilliant squeaky tangling of black hair.

Go out and wander by the reservoir. Disturb the pigeons. Breathe in the early grass. The highway gasoline. Feel strong. Feel clean. Go out and wander.

When they think about the new house that they leave behind them it seem small almost impossible so small and unpredictable. Not really safe.

Buddy say he miss the lot of people on the corners out the windows. How they living now by hiding out he miss the action of the people streets and subways and the bus.

He have been at home and out of school and Angela have been away and out of town so long they sure now that the best part of the city is the people mingle bump and spin together various.

Angela say nothing. Walk beside him quiet. Near to evening no one near enough to hear them.

"Angela, you lonely?"

He hold Angela around her shoulder. She slightly leaning on his side. They walking on.

Buddy stop.

"You come on with me. We take some flowers from a grave we find, and bring them back and plant them by the house, right here, to-night."

"I feel spooky doing that."

"We the only spooks out here. I hope."

"Suppose somebody catch us."

"Somebody catch us, you and me, you think they think about some flowers we have borrow from a grave? Last thing people think about is flowers. And if they be after us, they not after no flowers, Angela, stolen or otherwise. Listen, tomorrow we should borrow trees! Trees. Evergreen stuff. Take it to the concrete. Stand it on a stoop. Borrow trees tomorrow."

Buddy run and snatch a branch and swinging on a tree.

Angela run and catch him hold him tight around his ankles.

"Hey, let go!"

Angela let go and flying wild among the cemetery stones. Buddy after her.

They body dodge the headstones.

Running free.

Out of breath they slow and start to search for flowers they could carry back with them and plant again outside the house.

Buddy have to use a flashlight. Mostly finding imitation this and that in plastic. Or else they finding dead plants left to shrivel in the graveyard.

Angela whisper urgent: "Wait, Buddy. Over here. What's that?"

They see some moss in the moonlight look like old tinsel lying down. Look like a growing snowflake. Buddy loosen the earth under and around the patch and then he lift two handfuls clinging soil.

Now Angela shine the flashlight careful so they quickly reach the reservoir and then the house and plant the small green moss almost invisible beside the doorway.

The benchbed seem too hard. They try to sleep together huddling in the highway house.

> *Well I never come home*
> *my love sing love and the*
> *oversea sky*
> *I never come home.*

Well I know I'm not ready to die
my heart like the wind
want to roam
I know I'm not ready to die.

They try to sleep in the house. They give it up and go out to the ground.

You be different from the dead. All them tombstones tearing up the ground, look like a little city, like a small Manhattan, not exactly. Here is not the same.

Here, you be bigger than the buildings, bigger than the little city. You be really different from the rest, the resting other ones.

Moved in his arms, she make him feel like smiling. Him, his head an Afro-bush spread free beside the stones, headstones thinning in the heavy air. Him, a ready father, public lover, privately alone with her, with Angela, a half an hour walk from the hallway where they start out to hold themselves together in the noisy darkness, kissing, kissed him, kissed her, kissing.

Cemetery let them lie there belly close, their shoulders now undressed down to the color of the heat they feel, in lying close, their legs a strong disturbing of the dust. His own where, own place for loving made for making love, the cemetery where nobody guard the dead.

His mouth warm on her lips. They wrap up together shivering strong and tired. Angela dream.

DREAM

See suddenly different neighborhoods.

The city split by sound.

Jazz sound territory. Blues. Country and Western turf.

Supermarket Muzak. Heavy classical and not so heavy not so classical. And the hospital. A silent zone.

All the people be like Angela who hold a radio. Use it like a compass on a music map. Tune the dial to what you want. Some hard rock coming very soft. You go the right direction then the sound grow louder on the radio.

If you don't, it don't. When the sound reach very loud you be along with all those other folk who want to hear the same sound at the same time. In a park. A office building. A ocean liner.

You never know where you will end up or who you maybe meet there where you going.

Could be like calypso. Buddy dancing on the way.

Call out. Is it louder? Is it louder? Maybe thirty thousand people in the street with Buddy dancing on the way. And everybody have a radio. That make a big fantastic street sound by itself.

People laugh and talk. Men help young Mommas cross the street. Lift up they strollers. Be like a protest marching only now the people getting into music. Really moving into it.

One time on a Sunday she and Buddy follow along to the entrance to the Zoo. There be these twelve-year-olds have put together a steel washtub/broomstick group and everyone stay listening and dance. Another time she and Buddy finish up on Fulton Street. All the trucks be detour. And Sparrow and the Duke of Iron real professionals play in the open air. A superparty.

And for some silence there be stations on the radio like a seashell on your ear. Sound like the wind can blow away your mind.

A whistle windsound.

People follow it. Be like a Sunday service. Everybody whisper. Put they fingers to they lips. Follow the silence into someplace like a hospital, a church, a beach, a rooftop, a playground. People like a Quaker meeting silent several hundred silent standing or for example in a library some sit and read or write some meditate.

Or on the grass like a seashell of silence the thousands standing and sit there.

THE LAST PAGE

Morning and they do not move.

Arms around and head and cheek the skin and temperature of touch. Buddy hold his Angela but closer now and near enough to hear her breathing regular. Here is how they feel a happiness. Angela awaken looking to his open eyes.

"I hope I'm pregnant, Buddy."

"Hey, Angela. We make that sure enough. And soon."

And so begins a new day of the new life in the cemetery.

An Interest in Life

by Grace Paley

MY HUSBAND gave me a broom one Christmas. This wasn't right. No one can tell me it was meant kindly.

"I don't want you not to have anything for Christmas while I'm away in the Army," he said. "Virginia, please look at it. It comes with this fancy dustpan. It hangs off a stick. Look at it, will you? Are you blind or crosseyed?"

"Thanks, chum," I said. I had always wanted a dustpan hooked up that way. It was a good one. My husband doesn't shop in bargain basements or January sales.

Still and all, in spite of the quality, it was a mean present to give a woman you planned on never seeing again, a person you had children with and got onto all the time, drunk or sober, even when everybody had to get up early in the morning.

I asked him if he could wait and join the Army in a half hour, as I had to get the groceries. I don't like to leave kids alone in a three-room apartment full of gas and electricity. Fire may break out from a nasty remark. Or the oldest decides to get even with the youngest.

"Just this once," he said. "But you better figure out how to get along without me."

"You're a handicapped person mentally," I said. "You should've been institutionalized years ago." I slammed the door. I didn't want to see him pack his underwear and ironed shirts.

I never got further than the front stoop, though, because there was

Mrs. Raftery, wringing her hands, tears in her eyes as though she had a monopoly on all the good news.

"Mrs. Raftery!" I said, putting my arm around her. "Don't cry." She leaned on me because I am such a horsy build. "Don't cry, Mrs. Raftery, please!" I said.

"That's like you, Virginia. Always looking at the ugly side of things. 'Take in the wash. It's rainin'!' That's you. You're the first one knows it when the dumb-waiter breaks."

"Oh, come on now, that's not so. It just isn't so," I said. "I'm the exact opposite."

"Did you see Mrs. Cullen yet?" she asked, paying no attention.

"Where?"

"Virginia!" she said, shocked. "She's passed away. The whole house knows it. They've got her in white like a bride and you never saw a beautiful creature like that. She must be eighty. Her husband's proud."

"She was never more than an acquaintance; she didn't have any children," I said.

"Well, I don't care about that. Now, Virginia, you do what I say now, you go downstairs and you say like this — listen to me — say, 'I hear, Mr. Cullen, your wife's passed away. I'm sorry.' Then ask him how he is. Then you ought to go around the corner and see her. She's in Witson & Wayde. Then you ought to go over to the church when they carry her over."

"It's not my church," I said.

"That's no reason, Virginia. You go up like this," she said, parting from me to do a prancy dance. "Up the big front steps, into the church you go. It's beautiful in there. You can't help kneeling only for a minute. Then round to the right. Then up the other stairway. Then you come to a great oak door that's arched above you, then," she said, seizing a deep, deep breath, for all the good it would do her, "and then turn the knob slo-owly and open the door and see for yourself: Our Blessed Mother is in charge. Beautiful. Beautiful. Beautiful."

I sighed in and I groaned out, so as to melt a certain pain around my heart. A steel ring like arthritis, at my age.

"You are a groaner," Mrs. Raftery said, gawking into my mouth.

"I am not," I said. I got a whiff of her, a terrible cheap wine lush.

My husband threw a penny at the door from the inside to take my notice from Mrs. Raftery. He rattled the glass door to make sure I looked at him. He had a fat duffel bag on each shoulder. Where did he acquire so much worldly possession? What was in them? My grandma's goose feathers from across the ocean? Or all the diaper-service diapers? To this day the truth is shrouded in mystery.

"What the hell are you doing, Virginia?" he said, dumping them at my feet. "Standing out here on your hind legs telling everybody your business? The Army gives you a certain time, for God's sakes, they're not kidding." Then he said, "I beg your pardon," to Mrs. Raftery. He took hold of me with his two arms as though in love and pressed his body hard against mine so that I could feel him for the last time and suffer my loss. Then he kissed me in a mean way to nearly split my lip. Then he winked and said, "That's all for now," and skipped off into the future, duffel bags full of rags.

He left me in an embarrassing situation, nearly fainting, in front of that old widow, who can't even remember the half of it. "He's a crock," said Mrs. Raftery. "Is he leaving for good or just temporarily, Virginia?"

"Oh, he's probably deserting me," I said, and sat down on the stoop, pulling my big knees up to my chin.

"If that's the case, tell the Welfare right away," she said. "He's a bum, leaving you just before Christmas. Tell the cops," she said. "They'll provide the toys for the little kids gladly. And don't forget to let the grocer in on it. He won't be so hard on you expecting payment."

She saw that sadness was stretched world-wide across my face. Mrs. Raftery isn't the worst person. She said, "Look around for comfort, dear." With a nervous finger she pointed to the truckers eating lunch on their haunches across the street, leaning on the loading platforms. She waved her hand to include in all the men marching up and down in search of a decent luncheonette. She didn't leave out the six longshoremen loafing under the fish-market marquee. "If their lungs and stomachs ain't crushed by overwork, they disappear somewhere in the world. Don't be disappointed, Virginia. I don't know a man living'd last you a lifetime."

Ten days later Girard asked, "Where's Daddy?"

"Ask me no questions, I'll tell you no lies." I didn't want the children to know the facts. Present or past, a child should have a father.

"Where *is* Daddy?" Girard asked the week after that.

"He joined the Army," I said.

"He made my bunk bed," said Phillip.

"The truth shall make ye free," I said.

Then I sat down with pencil and pad to get in control of my resources. The facts, when I added and subtracted them, were that my husband had left me with fourteen dollars, and the rent unpaid, in an emergency state. He'd claimed he was sorry to do this, but my opinion is, out of sight, out of mind. "The city won't let you starve," he'd said. "After all, you're half the population. You're keeping up the good work. Without you the race would die out. Who'd pay the taxes? Who'd keep the streets clean? There wouldn't be no Army. A man like me wouldn't have no place to go."

I sent Girard right down to Mrs. Raftery with a request about the whereabouts of Welfare. She responded RSVP with an extra comment in left-handed script: "Poor Girard . . . he's never the boy my John was!"

Who asked her?

I called on Welfare right after the new year. In no time I discovered that they're rigged up to deal with liars, and if you're truthful it's disappointing to them. They may even refuse to handle your case if you're too truthful.

They asked sensible questions at first. They asked where my husband had enlisted. I didn't know. They put some letter writers and agents after him. "He's not in the United States Army," they said. "Try the Brazilian Army," I suggested.

They have no sense of kidding around. They're not the least bit lighthearted and they tried. "Oh no," they said. "That was incorrect. He is not in the Brazilian Army."

"No?" I said. "How strange! He must be in the Mexican Navy."

By law, they had to hound his brothers. They wrote to his brother who has a first-class card in the Teamsters and owns an apartment house in California. They asked his two brothers in Jersey to help me. They have large families. Rightfully they laughed. Then they wrote to Thomas, the oldest, the smart one (the one they all worked so hard for years to keep him in college until his brains could pay off). He was the one who sent ten dollars immediately, saying, "What a bastard! I'll send something time to time, Ginny, but whatever you do, don't tell the authorities." Of course I never did. Soon they began to guess they were better people than me, that I was in trouble because I deserved it, and then they liked me better.

But they never fixed my refrigerator. Every time I called I said patiently, "The milk is sour . . ." I said, "Corn beef went bad." Sitting in that beer-stinking phone booth in Felan's for the sixth time (sixty cents) with the baby on my lap and Barbie tapping at the glass door with an American flag, I cried into the secretary's hardhearted ear, "I bought real butter for the holiday, and it's rancid . . ." They said, "You'll have to get a better bid on the repair job."

While I waited indoors for a man to bid, Girard took to swinging back and forth on top of the bathroom door, just to soothe himself, giving me the laugh, dreamy, nibbling calcimine off the ceiling. On first sight Mrs. Raftery said, "Whack the monkey, he'd be better off on arsenic."

But Girard is my son and I'm the judge. It means a terrible thing for the future, though I don't know what to call it.

It was from constantly thinking of my foreknowledge on this and other subjects, it was from observing when I put my lipstick on daily, how my face was just curling up to die, that John Raftery came from Jersey to rescue me.

On Thursdays, anyway, John Raftery took the tubes in to visit his mother. The whole house knew it. She was cheerful even before breakfast. She sang out loud in a girlish brogue that only came to tongue for grand occasions. Hanging out the wash, she blushed to recall what a remarkable boy her John had been. "Ask the sisters around the corner," she said to the open kitchen windows. "They'll never forget John."

That particular night after supper Mrs. Raftery said to her son, "John, how come you don't say hello to your old friend Virginia? She's had hard luck and she's gloomy."

"Is that so, Mother?" he said, and immediately climbed two flights to knock at my door.

"Oh, John," I said at the sight of him, hat in hand in a white shirt and blue-striped tie, spick-and-span, a Sunday-school man. "Hello!"

"Welcome, John!" I said. "Sit down. Come right in. How are you?

You look awfully good. You do. Tell me, how've you been all this time, John?"

"How've I been?" he asked thoughtfully. To answer within reason, he described his life with Margaret, marriage, work, and children up to the present day.

I had nothing good to report. Now that he had put the subject around before my very eyes, every burnt-up day of my life smoked in shame, and I couldn't even get a clear view of the good half hours.

"Of course," he said, "you do have lovely children. Noticeable-looking, Virginia. Good looks is always something to be thankful for."

"Thankful?" I said. "I don't have to thank anything but my own foolishness for four children when I'm twenty-six years old, deserted, and poverty-struck, regardless of looks. A man can't help it, but I could have behaved better."

"Don't be so cruel on yourself, Ginny," he said. "Children come from God."

"You're still great on holy subjects, aren't you? You know damn well where children come from."

He did know. His red face reddened further. John Raftery has had that color coming out on him boy and man from keeping his rages so inward.

Still he made more sense in his conversation after that, and I poured fresh tea to tell him how my husband used to like me because I was a passionate person. That was until he took a look around and saw how in the long run this life only meant more of the same thing. He tried to turn away from me once he came to this understanding, and make me hate him. His face changed. He gave up his brand of cigarettes, which we had in common. He threw out the two pairs of socks I knitted by hand. "If there's anything I hate in this world, it's navy blue," he said. Oh, I could have dyed them. I would have done anything for him, if he were only not too sorry to ask me.

"You were a nice kid in those days," said John, referring to certain Saturday nights. "A wild, nice kid."

"Aaah," I said, disgusted. Whatever I was then, was on the way to where I am now. "I was fresh. If I had a kid like me, I'd slap her cross-eyed."

The very next Thursday John gave me a beautiful radio with a record player. "Enjoy yourself," he said. That really made Welfare speechless. We didn't own any records, but the investigator saw my burden was lightened and he scribbled a dozen pages about it in his notebook.

On the third Thursday he brought a walking doll (twenty-four inches) for Linda and Barbie with a card inscribed, "A baby doll for a couple of dolls." He had also had a couple of drinks at his mother's, and this made him want to dance. "La-la-la," he sang, a ramrod swaying in my kitchen chair. "La-la-la, let yourself go . . ."

"You gotta give a little," he sang, "live a little . . ." He said, "Virginia, may I have this dance?"

"Sssh, we finally got them asleep. Please, turn the radio down. Quiet. Deathly silence, John Raftery."

"Let me do your dishes, Virginia."

"Don't be silly, you're a guest in my house," I said. "I still regard you as a guest."

"I want to do something for you, Virginia."

"Tell me I'm the most gorgeous thing," I said, dipping my arm to the funny bone in dish soup.

He didn't answer. "I'm having a lot of trouble at work," was all he said. Then I heard him push the chair back. He came up behind me, put his arms around my waistline, and kissed my cheek. He whirled me around and took my hands. He said, "An old friend is better than rubies." He looked me in the eye. He held my attention by trying to be honest. And he kissed me a short sweet kiss on my mouth.

"Please sit down, Virginia," he said. He kneeled before me and put his head in my lap. I was stirred by so much activity. Then he looked up at me and, as though proposing marriage for life, he offered — because he was drunk — to place his immortal soul in peril to comfort me.

First I said, "Thank you." Then I said, "No."

I was sorry for him, but he's devout, a leader of the Fathers' Club at his church, active in all the lay groups for charities, orphans, etc. I knew that if he stayed late to love with me, he would not do it lightly but would in the end pay terrible penance and ruin his long life. The responsibility would be on me.

So I said no.

And Barbie is such a light sleeper. All she has to do, I thought, is wake up and wander in and see her mother and her new friend John with his pants around his knees, wrestling on the kitchen table. A vision like that could affect a kid for life.

I said no.

Everyone in this building is so goddamn nosy. That evening I had to say no.

But John came to visit, anyway, on the fourth Thursday. This time he brought the discarded dresses of Margaret's daughters, organdy party dresses and glazed cotton for every day. He gently admired Barbara and Linda, his blue eyes rolling to back up a couple of dozen oohs and ahs.

Even Phillip, who thinks God gave him just a certain number of hellos and he better save them for the final judgment, Phillip leaned on John and said, "Why don't you bring your boy to play with me? I don't have nobody who to play with." (Phillip's a liar. There must be at least seventy-one children in this house, pale pink to medium brown, English-talking and gibbering in Spanish, rough-and-tough boys, the Lone Ranger's bloody pals, or the exact picture of Supermouse. If a boy wanted a friend, he could pick the very one out of his neighbors.)

Also, Girard is a cold fish. He was in a lonesome despair. Sometimes he looked in the mirror and said, "How come I have such an ugly face? My nose is funny. Mostly people don't like me." He was a liar too. Girard has a face like his father's. His eyes are the color of those little blue plums in August. He looks like an advertisement in a magazine. He could be a child model and make a lot of money. He is my first child, and if he thinks he is ugly, I think I am ugly.

John said, "I can't stand to see a boy mope like that. . . .What do the sisters say in school?"

"He doesn't pay attention is all they say. You can't get much out of them."

"My middle boy was like that," said John. "Couldn't take an interest. Aaah, I wish I didn't have all that headache on the job. I'd grab Girard by the collar and make him take notice of the world. I wish I could ask him out to Jersey to play in all that space."

"Why not?" I said.

"Why, Virginia, I'm surprised you don't know why not. You know I can't take your children out to meet my children."

I felt a lot of strong arthritis in my ribs.

"My mother's the funny one, Virginia." He felt he had to continue with the subject matter. "I don't know. I guess she likes the idea of bugging Margaret. She says, 'You goin' up, John?' 'Yes, Mother,' I say. 'Behave yourself, John,' she says. 'That husband might come home and hack-saw you into hell. You're a Catholic man, John,' she says. But I figured it out. She likes to know I'm in the building. I swear, Virginia, she wishes me the best of luck."

"I do too, John," I said. We drank a last glass of beer to make sure of a peaceful sleep. "Good night, Virginia," he said, looping his muffler neatly under his chin. "Don't worry. I'll be thinking of what to do about Girard."

I got into the big bed that I share with the girls in the little room. For once I had no trouble falling asleep. I only had to worry about Linda and Barbara and Phillip. It was a great relief to me that John had taken over the thinking about Girard.

John was sincere. That's true. He paid a lot of attention to Girard, smoking out all his sneaky sorrows. He registered him into a wild pack of cub scouts that went up to the Bronx once a week to let off steam. He gave him a Junior Erector Set. And sometimes when his family wasn't listening he prayed at great length for him.

One Sunday, Sister Veronica said in her sweet voice from another life, "He's not worse. He might even be a little better. How are *you*, Virginia?" putting her hand on mine. Everybody around here acts like they know everything.

"Just fine," I said.

"We ought to start on Phillip," John said, "if it's true Girard's improving."

"You should've been a social worker, John."

"A lot of people have noticed that about me," said John.

"Your mother was always acting so crazy about you, how come she didn't knock herself out a little to see you in college? Like we did for Thomas?"

"Now, Virginia, be fair. She's a poor old woman. My father was a weak earner. She had to have my wages, and I'll tell you, Virginia, I'm not sorry. Look at Thomas. He's still in school. Drop him in this jungle and he'd be devoured. He hasn't had a touch of real life. And here I am with a good chunk of a family, a home of my own, a name in the building trades. One thing I have to tell you, the poor old woman is sorry. I said one day (oh, in passing — years ago) that I might marry you. She stuck a knife in herself. It's a fact. Not more than an eighth of an inch. You never saw such a gory Sunday. One thing — you would have been a better daughter-in-law to her than Margaret."

"Marry me?" I said.

"Well, yes . . . Aaah — I always liked you, then . . . Why do you think I'd sit in the shade of this kitchen every Thursday night? For God's sakes, the only warm thing around here is this teacup. Yes, sir, I did want to marry you, Virginia."

"No kidding, John? Really?" It was nice to know. Better late than never, to learn you were desired in youth.

I didn't tell John, but the truth is, I would never have married him. Once I met my husband with his winking looks, he was my only interest. Wild as I had been with John and others, I turned all my wildness over to him and then there was no question in my mind.

Still, face facts, if my husband didn't budge on in life, it was my fault. On me, as they say, be it. I greeted the morn with a song. I had a hello for everyone but the landlord. Ask the people on the block, come or go — even the Spanish ones, with their sad dark faces — they have to smile when they see me.

But for his own comfort, he should have done better lifewise and moneywise. I was happy, but I am now in possession of knowledge that this is wrong. Happiness isn't so bad for a woman. She gets fatter, she gets older, she could lie down, nuzzling a regiment of men and little kids, she could just die of the pleasure. But men are different, they have to own money, or they have to be famous, or everybody on the block has to look up to them from the cellar stairs.

A woman counts her children and acts snotty, like she invented life, but men *must* do well in the world. I know that men are not fooled by being happy.

"A funny guy," said John, guessing where my thoughts had gone. "What stopped him up? He was nobody's fool. He had a funny thing about him, Virginia, if you don't mind my saying so. He wasn't much distance up, but he was all set and ready to be looking down on us all."

"He was very smart, John. You don't realize that. His hobby was crossword puzzles, and I said to him real often, as did others around here, that he ought to go out on the '$64 Question.' Why not? But he laughed. You know what he said? He said, 'That proves how dumb you are if you think I'm smart.' "

"A funny guy," said John. "Get it all off your chest," he said. "Talk it out, Virginia; it's the only way to kill the pain."

By and large, I was happy to oblige. Still I could not carry through about certain cruel remarks. It was like trying to move back into the dry mouth of a nightmare to remember that the last day I was happy was the middle of a week in March, when I told my husband I was going to have Linda. Barbara was five months old to the hour. The boys were three and four. I had to tell him. It was the last day with anything happy about it.

Later on he said, "Oh, you make me so sick, you're so goddamn big and fat, you look like a goddamn brownstone, the way you're squared off in front."

"Well, where are you going tonight?" I asked.

"How should I know?" he said. "Your big ass takes up the whole goddamn bed," he said. "There's no room for me." He bought a sleeping bag and slept on the floor.

I couldn't believe it. I would start every morning fresh. I couldn't believe that he would turn against me so, while I was still young and even his friends still liked me.

But he did, he turned absolutely against me and became no friend of mine. "All you ever think about is making babies. This place stinks like the men's room in the BMT. It's a fucking *pissoir*." He was strong on truth all through the year. "That kid eats more than the five of us put together," he said. "Stop stuffing your face, you fat dumbbell," he said to Phillip.

Then he worked on the neighbors. "Get that nosy old bag out of here," he said. "If she comes on once more with 'my son in the building trades' I'll squash her for the cat."

Then he turned on Spielvogel, the checker, his oldest friend, who only visited on holidays and never spoke to me (shy, the way some bachelors are). "That sonofabitch, don't hand me that friendship crap, all he's after is your ass. That's what I need — a little shitmaker of his using up the air in this flat."

And then there was no one else to dispose of. We were left alone fair and square, facing each other.

"Now, Virginia," he said, "I come to the end of my rope. I see a black wall ahead of me. What the hell am I supposed to do? I only got one life. Should I lie down and die? I don't know what to do any more. I'll give it to you straight, Virginia, if I stick around, you can't help it, you'll hate me . . ."

"I hate you right now," I said. "So do whatever you like."

"This place drives me nuts," he mumbled. "I don't know what to do around here. I want to get you a present. Something."

"I told you, do whatever you like. Buy me a rattrap for rats."

That's when he went down to the House Appliance Store, and he brought back a new broom and a classy dustpan.

"A new broom sweeps clean," he said. "I got to get out of here," he said. "I'm going nuts." Then he began to stuff the duffel bags, and I went to the grocery store but was stopped by Mrs. Raftery, who had to tell me what she considered so beautiful — death — then he kissed and went to join some army somewhere.

I didn't tell John any of this, because I think it makes a woman look too bad to tell on how another man has treated her. He begins to see her through the other man's eyes, a sitting duck, a skinful of flaws. After all, I had come to depend on John. All my husband's friends were strangers now, though I had always said to them, "Feel welcome."

And the family men in the building looked too cunning, as though they had all personally deserted me. If they met me on the stairs, they carried the heaviest groceries up and helped bring Linda's stroller down, but they never asked me a question worth answering at all.

Besides that, Girard and Phillip taught the girls the days of the week: Monday, Tuesday, Wednesday, Johnday, Friday. They waited for him once a week, under the hallway lamp, half asleep like bugs in the sun, sitting in their little chairs with their names on in gold, a birth present from my mother-in-law. At fifteen after eight he punctually came, to read a story, pass out some kisses, and tuck them into bed.

But one night, after a long Johnday of them squealing my eardrum split, after a rainy afternoon with brother constantly raising up his hand against brother, with the girls near ready to go to court over the proper ownership of Melinda Lee, the twenty-four-inch walking doll, the doorbell rang three times. Not any of those times did John's face greet me.

I was too ashamed to call down to Mrs. Raftery, and she was too mean to knock on my door and explain.

He didn't come the following Thursday either. Girard said sadly, "He must've run away, John."

I had to give him up after two weeks' absence and no word. I didn't know how to tell the children: something about right and wrong, goodness and meanness, men and women. I had it all at my fingertips, ready to hand over. But I didn't think I ought to take mistakes and truth away from them. Who knows? They might make a truer friend in this world somewhere than I have ever made. So I just put them to bed and sat in the kitchen and cried.

In the middle of my third beer, searching in my mind for the next step, I found the decision to go on "Strike It Rich." I scrounged some paper and pencil from the toy box and I listed all my troubles, which must be done in order to qualify. The list when complete could have brought tears to the eye of God if He had a minute. At the sight of it my bitterness began to improve. All that is really necessary for survival of the fittest, it seems, is an interest in life, good, bad, or peculiar.

As always happens in these cases where you have begun to help yourself with plans, news comes from an opposite direction. The doorbell rang, two short and two long — meaning John.

My first thought was to wake the children and make them happy. "No! No!" he said. "Please don't put yourself to that trouble. Virginia, I'm dog-tired," he said. "Dog-tired. My job is a damn headache. It's too much. It's all day and it scuttles my mind at night, and in the end who does the credit go to?

"Virginia," he said, "I don't know if I can come any more. I've been wanting to tell you. I just don't know. What's it all about? Could you answer me if I asked you? I can't figure this whole thing out at all."

I started the tea steeping because his fingers when I touched them were cold. I didn't speak. I tried looking at it from his man point of view, and I thought he had to take a bus, the tubes, and a subway to see me; and then the subway, the tubes, and a bus to go back home at 1 A.M. It wouldn't be any trouble at all for him to part with us forever. I thought about my life, and I gave strongest consideration to my children. If given the choice, I decided to choose not to live without him.

"What's that?" he asked, pointing to my careful list of troubles. "Writing a letter?"

"Oh no," I said, "it's for 'Strike It Rich.' I hope to go on the program."

"Virginia, for goodness' sakes," he said, giving it a glance, "you don't have a ghost. They'd laugh you out of the studio. Those people really suffer."

"Are you sure, John?" I asked.

"No question in my mind at all," said John. "Have you ever seen that program? I mean, in addition to all of this — the little disturbances of man" — he waved a scornful hand at my list — "they *suffer*. They live in the forefront of tornadoes, their lives are washed off by floods — catastrophes of God. Oh, Virginia."

"Are you sure, John?"

"For goodness' sake . . ."

Sadly I put my list away. Still, if things got worse, I could always make use of it.

Once that was settled, I acted on an earlier decision. I pushed his cup of scalding tea aside. I wedged myself onto his lap between his hard belt buckle and the table. I put my arms around his neck and said, "How come you're so cold, John?" He has a kind face and he knew how to look astonished. He said, "Why, Virginia, I'm getting warmer." We laughed.

John became a lover to me that night.

Mrs. Raftery is sometimes silly and sick from her private source of cheap wine. She expects John often. "Honor your mother, what's the matter with you, John?" she complains. "Honor. Honor."

"Virginia dear," she says. "You never would've taken John away to Jersey like Margaret. I wish he'd've married you."

"You didn't like me much in those days."

"That's a lie," she says. I know she's a hypocrite, but no more than the rest of the world.

What is remarkable to me is that it doesn't seem to conscience John as I thought it might. It is still hard to believe that a man who sends out the Ten Commandments every year for a Christmas card can be so easy buttoning and unbuttoning.

Of course we must be very careful not to wake the children or disturb the neighbors who will enjoy another person's excitement just so far, and then the pleasure enrages them. We must be very careful for ourselves too, for when my husband comes back, realizing the babies are in school and everything easier, he won't forgive me if I've started it all up again — noisy signs of life that are so much trouble to a man.

We haven't seen him in two and a half years. Although people have suggested it, I do not want the police or Intelligence or a private eye or anyone to go after him to bring him back. I know that if he expected to stay away forever he would have written and said so. As it is, I just don't know what evening, any time, he may appear. Sometimes, stumbling over a blockbuster of a dream at midnight, I wake up to vision his soft arrival.

He comes in the door with his old key. He gives me a strict look and says, "Well, you look older, Virginia." "So do you," I say, although he hasn't changed a bit.

He settles in the kitchen because the children are asleep all over the rest of the house. I unknot his tie and offer him a cold sandwich. He raps my backside, paying attention to the bounce. I walk around him as though he were a Maypole, kissing as I go.

"I didn't like the Army much," he says. "Next time I think I might go join the Merchant Marine."

"What Army?" I say.

"It's pretty much the same everywhere," he says.

"I wouldn't be a bit surprised," I say.

"I lost my cuff link, goddamnit," he says, and drops to the floor to look for it. I go down too on my knees, but I know he never had a cuff link in his life. Still I would do a lot for him.

"Got you off your feet that time," he says, laughing. "Oh yes, I did." And before I can even make myself half comfortable on that polka-dotted linoleum, he got onto me right where we were, and the truth is, we were so happy, we forgot the precautions.

About the Authors

PETER BEAGLE was born in New York City on April 20, 1939. He was graduated in 1959 from the University of Pittsburgh and also studied at Stanford University. His first novel, A Fine and Private Place, was published in 1960. With "Lila, the Werewolf," The Last Unicorn, and "Come, Lady Death," it was collected in the 1978 volume The Fantasy Worlds of Peter Beagle. His novel The Innkeeper's Song was published in 1993. Beagle's nonfiction includes The California Feeling (1969) and The Garden of Earthly Delights (1982), a study of Hieronymus Bosch. He lives in California.

GLORIA KURIAN BRODER, born and raised in Detroit, was graduated from the University of Michigan. Her short stories have appeared in Harper's, Carleton Miscellany, Kingfisher, Ploughshares and 96 Inc. She is the coauthor of a screenplay based on one of her short stories and produced under the auspices of the American Film Institute. With her husband, Bill Broder, she wrote the novel Remember This Time (1983). "Elena, Unfaithful," which originally appeared in 1971, was her first published story. She lives in Sausalito, California.

HAROLD BRODKEY was born on October 25, 1930, in Staunton, Illinois. A graduate of Harvard, he has taught at Cornell University, at Washington University in Saint Louis, and at the City College of New York. He won the Prix de Rome for 1959/60, a Brandeis University Creative Arts Award in 1974, and a Guggenheim Fellowship in 1987. He received first prize in the 1975 and 1976 O. Henry Award collections, and in 1978 his work was included in both the O. Henry and Best American Short Stories collections. First Love and Other Sorrows, a collection originally published in 1958, was reissued in March 1986; Women and Angels, a second collection, was published in 1985 by the Jewish

Publication Society of America. *The Runaway Soul*, a novel, was published in 1989. The novel *Profane Friendship* appeared in 1994. "Innocence" first appeared in *American Review*. Brodkey's work has been published in *The New Yorker, Esquire, Antaeus, Partisan Review, American Poetry Review, New American Review*, and *Discovery*. He lives in New York City.

WILLA CATHER was born in Virginia in 1873. When she was nine, her family moved to Nebraska, which was to be an essential source for her fiction. Early in her career she taught school and worked as a journalist for the *Pittsburgh Daily Leader*, before moving to New York in 1906 to work for six years as an editor on the staff of *McClure's* magazine. Her first book, *April Twilights* (1903), was a collection of poems; it was followed by a short-story collection, *The Troll Garden* (1905), and her first novel, *Alexander's Bridge* (1912). During the next thirty-five years, until her death in 1947, Cather published eleven more novels, three collections of stories, and two volumes of essays. "Coming, Aphrodite!" is from her collection of short stories *Youth and the Bright Medusa* (1920). Her other works include *O Pioneers!* (1913); *The Song of the Lark* (1915); *My Antonia* (1918); *One of Ours* (1922), for which she was awarded a Pulitzer Prize; and *A Lost Lady* (1923). *My Mortal Enemy* (1926), *Death Comes for the Archbishop* (1927), and *Lucy Gayheart* (1935) are among her later works.

JOHN CHEEVER was born in Quincy, Massachusetts, on May 27, 1912. He attended Thayer Academy and began writing professionally at the age of sixteen. His short stories frequently appeared in *The New Yorker* and over the years were published in several collections. *The Stories of John Cheever* (1979) won a National Book Critics Circle Award, a MacDowell Medal, and a 1979 Pulitzer Prize. His novels are *The Wapshot Chronicle* (1957), which received a 1958 National Book Award; *The Wapshot Scandal* (1964); *Bullet Park* (1969); *Falconer* (1977); and *Oh What a Paradise It Seems* (1982). In 1965 Cheever was awarded the Howells Medal for Fiction by the American Academy of Arts and Letters. He died on June 18, 1982, shortly after accepting the National Medal for Literature.

NICHOLAS DELBANCO was born in London in 1942 and became a U.S. citizen in 1955. He was graduated from Harvard in 1963 and received a master's degree in English and comparative literature from Columbia University in 1966. He is the author of books of nonfiction and more than ten novels, among them *Small Rain* (1975) and the Sherbrookes trilogy (*Possession*, 1977; *Sherbrookes*, 1978; and *Stillness*, 1980). *Running in Place: Scenes from the South of France*, a memoir, appeared in 1989 and a collection of short fiction, *The Writers' Trade, and Other Stories* was published in 1990. *In the Name of Mercy*, a novel, appeared in 1995. Among his awards are an NEA Creative Writing Fellowship and a Guggenheim Fellowship. He was a founding director of the Bennington

Writing Workshops and now directs the master's degree program in writing at the University of Michigan. "The Consolation of Philosophy" was first published in 1979 and appeared in his 1983 collection *About My Table and Other Stories*.

F. SCOTT FITZGERALD, named for his ancestor who wrote "The Star-Spangled Banner," was born in Saint Paul, Minnesota, in 1896. He attended Princeton for four years, but did not earn a degree. His first novel, *This Side of Paradise*, published in 1920, was an immediate critical and commercial success. In 1917, while in the army, in Montgomery, Alabama, he met Zelda Sayre. Their marriage—postponed until he could support her—took place in 1920. This background in part informs " 'The Sensible Thing' "; it was written in 1924 and appeared in Fitzgerald's 1926 collection *All the Sad Young Men*. His work, produced over a period when the Fitzgeralds often lived and traveled extensively abroad, includes the novels *The Beautiful and the Damned* (1922), *The Great Gatsby* (1925), and *Tender Is the Night* (1934). Other short-story collections include *Flappers and Philosophers* (1920), *Tales of the Jazz Age* (1922), and *Taps at Reveille* (1935). Fitzgerald's last years were spent in Hollywood working as a screenwriter, an experience that provides the backdrop for his novel *The Last Tycoon*, unfinished at the time of his death in 1940, but published in 1941, edited by Edmund Wilson.

IAN FRAZIER was born in Cleveland in 1951. In 1973 he received his bachelor's degree from Harvard University, where he wrote for the *Harvard Lampoon*. His pieces have appeared in *The Atlantic*, *The New Republic*, and *The New Yorker*, where he is a staff writer. *Dating Your Mom*, a collection of Frazier's humor pieces, was published in 1986. *Nobody Better, Better Than Nobody*, appeared in 1987. *Family*, a memoir, was published in 1994. He lives in New York City.

GAIL GODWIN was born in Birmingham, Alabama, in 1937 and grew up in Asheville, North Carolina. She received her bachelor's degree in journalism from the University of North Carolina at Chapel Hill, was a reporter for the *Miami Herald*, and then lived and worked in London. Following her return to the United States in 1966, she earned a master's degree and a doctorate. Her first novel, *The Perfectionists* (1970), was published while she was a student at the University of Iowa. In 1972 *Glass People* was published, followed by *The Odd Woman* (1974), *Violet Clay* (1978), *A Mother and Two Daughters* (1982), *The Finishing School* (1985), *A Southern Family* (1987), and two story collections, *Dream Children* (1976) and *Mr. Bedford and the Muses* (1983). Recent novels include *Father Melancholy's Daughter* (1991) and *The Good Husband* (1994). "St. George," originally published in 1969, is collected here for the first time. Godwin's achievements include a Guggenheim Fellowship (1975) and an award in literature from the American Academy and Institute of Arts and Letters (1981). She lives in Woodstock, New York.

DASHIELL HAMMETT was born in Maryland on May 27, 1894. He served in both World Wars and worked at a variety of jobs, including clerk, stevedore, ad manager, and private detective with the Pinkerton Agency. He is known as the father of the hard-boiled detective novel. The most famous of these is *The Maltese Falcon* (1930), which introduced the Sam Spade character and was made into a classic film. *The Thin Man*, which introduced Nick and Nora Charles, followed in 1932. Hammett's other novels include *Red Harvest* (1929), *The Dain Curse* (1929), and *The Glass Key* (1931). *The Big Knockover* (edited by Lillian Hellman), a collection of his works that includes the autobiographical "Tulip," was published in 1966, five years after his death. A second posthumous collection, *The Continental Op* (edited by Steven Marcus), appeared in 1974.

NATHANIEL HAWTHORNE, the descendant of a well-known Puritan family, was born in Salem, Massachusetts, on July 4, 1804. His first collection, *Twice-Told Tales*, appeared in 1837. In the period that followed, he worked in the Boston Custom House and lived for a while at Brook Farm, a utopian community that provided the background for his novel *The Blithedale Romance* (1852). After marrying Sophia Peabody in 1842, he lived in Concord and wrote the stories collected in *Mosses from an Old Manse* (1846), including "Rappaccini's Daughter." *The Scarlet Letter*, begun after he lost a job as surveyor of the port of Salem, was published in 1850. *The House of the Seven Gables* appeared in 1851. From 1853 to 1857 Hawthorne served as the American consul at Liverpool. He toured Europe in the period that followed; *The Marble Faun*, begun in Florence and completed in England, appeared in 1860. Hawthorne died in May 1864, and was buried in the Sleepy Hollow Cemetery at Concord, New Hampshire.

MARK HELPRIN was born in 1947 and spent part of his childhood in New York's Hudson River Valley. He has served in the Israeli infantry and air force and the British merchant navy and holds degrees from Harvard University (1969) and the Harvard Center for Middle Eastern Studies. His first book, *A Dove of the East and Other Stories*, appeared in 1975. Another collection, *Ellis Island and Other Stories* (1981), was the winner of a 1982 National Jewish Book Award, as well as the Prix de Rome, and was nominated for both the PEN/Faulkner Award and the American Book Award for fiction. *Refiner's Fire: The Life and Adventures of Marshall Pearl, a Foundling* was published in 1977. Helprin's second novel, *Winter's Tale*, appeared in 1983. The novel *A Soldier of the Great War* appeared in 1991; *Memoir from Antproof Case* was published in 1995. He lives in New York state.

ERNEST HEMINGWAY was born in Oak Park, Illinois, in 1899, the son of a doctor. As a teenager, he wrote for the *Kansas City Star* and at the age of eighteen left for Europe to serve as a volunteer for an ambulance unit during World War I. After the war he returned to reporting, working in Paris as the French correspondent for the *Toronto Star*. Two collections—*Three Stories and Ten Poems* (1923) and *In Our Time* (1925)—were followed by his first novels, *The Torrents of Spring* (1926) and *The Sun Also Rises* (1926). A *Farewell to Arms* was published in 1929; *To Have and Have Not* followed in 1937. Two of his nonfiction works are *Death in the Afternoon* (1932), an homage to bullfighting, and *Green Hills of Africa* (1935), about big-game hunting. Hemingway's support of the Loyalists in the Spanish Civil War provided the background for his novel *For Whom the Bell Tolls* (1940). He was a war correspondent during World War II, then lived in Cuba for many years. *Across the River and into the Trees* was published in 1950. Hemingway won a Pulitzer Prize for his novella *The Old Man and the Sea* (1952), and was later awarded the 1954 Nobel Prize in Literature. He died in 1961, a suicide. His several posthumous publications include A *Moveable Feast, Islands in the Stream*, and *The Garden of Eden*.

HENRY JAMES was born in New York City in 1843. His father was a writer and theologian; his brother, the philosopher William James. He was educated privately in the United States and Europe, and attended Harvard Law School. He frequently traveled and lived abroad, and in 1876 made his permanent home in London. Over the course of a long and richly gifted, productive writing life, he produced twenty novels and 112 tales. *Daisy Miller*, one of the tales, was published in 1878 (James later dramatized it); it revealed, among his other work of this period, his discovery of one of his essential subjects—the imprint of Europe on America. His other works include *Roderick Hudson* (1876), *The American* (1877); *The Portrait of a Lady* (1881), *The Bostonians* (1886), *The Princess Casamassima* (1866), *The Aspern Papers* (1888), *The Turn of the Screw* (1898), *The Wings of the Dove* (1902), *The Ambassadors* (1903), and *The Golden Bowl* (1904). He is also celebrated for the critical prefaces he wrote for the reissue of his novels. James became a British subject in 1915, and died the following year. In 1976 he was named to Westminster Abbey's Poets' Corner, an honor shared by few Americans.

JUNE JORDAN was born in New York City in 1936. She studied at Barnard College and the University of Chicago and has taught at Sarah Lawrence College, the City College of New York, and Yale University. A poet and essayist as well as a novelist, she has written, among other books, *Fannie Lou Hamer* (1971); *New Days: Poems of Exile and Return* (1974); *Things That I Do in the Dark: Selected Poems, 1954–1977* (1981); and *Living Room: New Poems, 1980–1984* (1985). *His Own Where* was first published as a young-adult novel, in 1971. The recipient of the Achievement Award for International Reporting from the National Association of Black Journalists (1984) and of the Prix de Rome in 1970, Jordan was an NEA fellow in creative writing in 1982 and a New York Foundation of the Arts fellow in poetry in 1985. She is now on the faculty of the University of California at Berkeley.

CARSON MCCULLERS was born on February 19, 1917, in Columbus, Georgia. She attended schools there, and later studied at Columbia University and at New York University. Her first novel, *The Heart Is a Lonely Hunter*, appeared in 1940; *Reflections in a Golden Eye* followed in 1941. *The Ballad of the Sad Café*, a collection, was published in 1951. McCullers adapted her 1946 novella *The Member of the Wedding* for the 1950 stage production, and it won the New York Drama Critics' Circle Award. Her novel *Clock without Hands* was published in 1961, and a posthumous collection of her writing, *The Mortgaged Heart*, was published in 1971. McCullers was awarded Guggenheim Fellowships in 1942 and 1946 and was also a fellow of the American Academy of Arts and Letters. She died in 1967.

LARRY MCMURTRY was born in Wichita Falls, Texas, in 1936 and grew up near there. He was graduated from North Texas State University in Denton in 1958, received a master's degree from Rice University in 1960, and studied at Stanford University on a Wallace Stegner Fellowship. His first novel, *Horseman, Pass By* (1961), received the Texas Institute of Letters Fiction Award. *Leaving Cheyenne*, his second novel, appeared in 1963. Subsequent works include *The Last Picture Show* (1966), *Moving On* (1970), *All My Friends Are Going to Be Strangers* (1972), *Terms of Endearment* (1975), and the epic *Lonesome Dove*, which won a 1986 Pulitzer Prize. Recent titles include *The Late Child* and *Dead Man's Walk*, both published in 1995. *Texasville*, linked by setting and characters to *The Last Picture Show*, appeared in 1987.

BERNARD MALAMUD was born in Brooklyn, New York, on April 26, 1914. He was graduated from the City College of New York in 1936 and received a master's degree from Columbia University in 1942. He taught nighttime English classes in the New York City high schools from 1940 until 1949 and later served on the faculty at Oregon State University and at Bennington College. His books include *The Natural* (1952); *The Assistant* (1957); *The Magic Barrel* (1958), for which he won a National Book Award; *The Fixer* (1967), which won both the 1967 National Book Award in fiction and a Pulitzer Prize; *Dubin's Lives* (1979); and *God's Grace* (1982). Recipient of the Rosenthal Award from the National Institute of Arts and Letters in 1958, Malamud won the Gold Medal for Fiction from the American Academy and Institute of Arts and Letters in 1983. He died on March 18, 1986.

BOBBIE ANN MASON was born in Mayfield, Kentucky. She was graduated from the University of Kentucky in 1962 and received a master's degree from the State University of New York at Binghamton in 1966 and a doctorate from the University of Connecticut in 1972. Her collection *Shiloh and Other Stories* (1982) won the PEN/Hemingway Award for first fiction in 1983 and was nominated for a National Book Critics Circle Award, the PEN/Faulkner Award, and an American Book Award. Mason's stories have appeared in *The New Yorker*, *The Atlantic*, *Redbook*, *The North American Review*, and *The Virginia Quarterly Review*. Her novel *In Country* was published in 1985. *Feather Crowns*, also a novel, appeared in 1993. She was the recipient of a literary award from the American Academy and Institute of Arts and Letters in 1984. Mason lives in Kentucky.

HERMAN MELVILLE was born in New York in 1819, to a distinguished family in financial decline. His father died when he was twelve, and not long thereafter, he dropped out of school. He worked at a variety of jobs—clerking in a bank, working at a fur-cap store, teaching—and in 1839, out of work and with prospects evidently exhausted, he set sail for Liverpool. Two years later, still unable to find satisfying work at home, he joined a whaling crew bound for the South Seas. The land and sea adventures of this seagoing period—1839 to 1844—were the source materials drawn upon in Melville's early novels, as well as in his masterpiece, *Moby-Dick* (1851). Although *Typee* (1846), *Omoo* (1847), and his other early novels were successful, the critical and popular response to *Moby-Dick* was largely hostile, and the reception given *Pierre* (1852) was even more so. In the difficult period that followed, Melville wrote and published, usually anonymously, stories that were published as *The Piazza Tales* in 1856; the story appearing here was its preface. *The Confidence-Man* (1857) failed to rescue either his literary or economic fortunes. From 1866 to 1885, he worked as a customs inspector in New York City. Melville died in New York, poor and virtually forgotten, in 1891. His novella *Billy Budd* went unpublished until 1924. The towering quality of his achievement was realized posthumously.

SUSAN MINOT was born in 1957 in Manchester, Massachusetts. She was graduated from Brown University and received her master's degree from Columbia University. Chapters from her first novel, *Monkeys* (1986), originally appeared in *The New Yorker* and *Grand Street*, and her work has been published in *The Pushcart Prize*. "Lust" appeared originally in *The Paris Review* and was included in the 1985 O. Henry Award collection, as well as in *The Best American Short Stories 1984*. *Lust and Other Stories* appeared in 1989 and *Folly*, a novel, was published in 1992. In December 1987 Minot was awarded France's Prix Femina Etranger Award, for *Monkeys*. She lives in New York City.

JOHN O'HARA, the son of a physician, was born on January 31, 1905, in Pottsville, Pennsylvania (a town similar to "Gibbsville," where many of his stories are set). After graduation from the Niagara Preparatory School, he worked as a reporter, went to Montana, then to Chicago, where he held a variety of jobs (engineer and amusement-park guard among them). He came back east, where he worked again as a writer for newspapers and magazines, including the *New York Daily Mirror*, *Time*, and *Collier's* magazines, the *New York Herald-Tribune*, and the *Pittsburgh Bulletin-Index*. O'Hara's literary reputation was established with the publication of his first novel, *Appointment in Samarra*, in 1934. In 1935 he published his first collection, *The Doctor's Son and Other Stories*, and his second novel, *Butterfield 8*. Between 1934 and 1970 he published a dozen novels—*Hope of Heaven*, *A Rage to Live*, *Ten North Frederick*, and *From the Terrace* among them—and more than ten collections of columns, stories, and novellas. "Imagine Kissing Pete" first appeared in 1960 in *The New Yorker*. O'Hara won a National Book Award for *Ten North Frederick* (1956) and the Gold Medal Award of Merit from the American Academy of Arts and Letters. He died in Princeton, New Jersey, on April 11, 1970.

GRACE PALEY was born in New York City in 1922 and attended Hunter College and New York University. Her first book of short stories, *The Little Disturbances of Man*, was published in 1959. Its title is drawn from the story appearing here, "An Interest in Life." *Enormous Changes at the Last Minute* appeared in 1975, followed in 1985 by *Later the Same Day*. Her *Collected Stories* appeared in 1994. Paley has taught at Columbia and Syracuse universities and is currently on the faculty of Sarah Lawrence College. In 1970 she received an award for short-story writing from the National Institute of Arts and Letters and was elected in 1980 to the American Academy and Institute of Arts and Letters. Her stories have appeared in numerous publications, including *The New Yorker*, *The Atlantic*, and *Esquire*. She lives in New York City and Vermont.

DOROTHY PARKER was born in West End, New Jersey, in 1893. A poet as well as a short-story writer, she was also well known as a member of the Algonquin Round Table, the nearly legendary literary group. Early in her career she wrote drama criticism for *Vanity Fair*, and later became a book critic for *The New Yorker*. Her reputation was established by her first, best-selling book of verse, *Enough Rope* (1926). Parker's other poetry volumes include *Death and Taxes* (1931) and *Not So Deep as a Well* (1936). Her story "A Telephone Call" first appeared in 1928. Her short-story collections include *Laments for the Living* (1930) and *Here Lies* (1939). She was coauthor (with Arnaud d'Usseau) of a 1953 play, *Ladies of the Corridor*. Parker died in 1967.

DAMON RUNYON was born in Manhattan, Kansas, in 1884. He attended public schools in Pueblo, Colorado, and had a long, varied career as a reporter on newspapers in Denver, San Francisco, and, for most of the balance of his working life, New York. He served in the Spanish-American War and was a war correspondent for the Hearst newspapers in Mexico (1912) and during World War I (1917–1918). His several collections of stories include *Guys and Dolls* (1931), which served as the basis for the successful Broadway musical of the same name. Among Runyon's other collections are *Blue Plate Special* (1934), *Take It Easy* (1938), and *My Wife Ethel* (1939). He died on December 10, 1946.

SUSAN FROMBERG SCHAEFFER was born in Brooklyn, New York, in 1941. She attended the University of Chicago, where she received her bachelor's degree (1961), and her master's (1963) and doctorate (1966), both with honors. The author of numerous novels—*Anya* (1974), *Time in Its Flight* (1978), *The Madness of a Seduced Woman* (1983), *The Injured Party* (1986), *Buffalo Afternoon* (1989), and *First Nights* (1993) among them—she has also written several books of poetry, including *The Witch and the Weather Report* (1972) and *Granite Lady* (1974), which was nominated for a National Book Award. *Anya* won Schaeffer both the Edward Lewis Wallant Award and the Friends of Literature Award in 1974. She was also the winner of an O. Henry Award in 1978 and held a Guggenheim Fellowship in 1985/86. She lives in Brooklyn and taught for many years at Brooklyn College. "Bluebeard's Second Wife" was published in this collection for the first time.

ISAAC BASHEVIS SINGER, born in Radzymin, Poland, on July 14, 1904, was a student at the Rabbinical Seminary in Warsaw from 1920 to 1927. He worked for Hebrew and Yiddish publications in Poland before moving to the United States in 1935 and becoming an American citizen in 1943. From 1935 on he wrote for the *Jewish Daily Forward*. Singer wrote in Yiddish but his work has long appeared in English translation. His novels and story collections, twenty-three in all, include *The Family Moskat* (1950), *Gimpel the Fool* (1957), *The Spinoza of Market Street* (1961), *Yentl, the Yeshiva Boy* (1983), and *Love and Exile* (1984). He twice won a National Book Award, in 1970 and 1974. A fellow of the Jewish Academy of Arts and Sciences, the American Academy and Institute of Arts and Letters, and the Polish Institute of Arts and Sciences in America, Singer was also a member of the American Academy of Arts and Sciences. In 1978 he was awarded the Nobel Prize for Literature. He lived in New York City. He died in 1991.

WILBUR DANIEL STEELE was born in Greensboro, North Carolina, on March 17, 1886, and grew up in Denver. He was graduated in 1907 from the University of Denver and subsequently studied art in Boston, Paris, and New York City. His nearly two hundred stories are collected in several volumes, including *Land's End* (1918) and *Tower of Sand* (1929). His novels include *That Girl from Memphis* (1945), *Diamond Wedding* (1950), and *The Way to the Gold*

(1955). The settings in his fiction include the Far West, parts of the South, and New England. The recipient of several O. Henry Awards, Steele also wrote several plays. In 1935 he collaborated with Anthony Brown on *How Beautiful with Shoes*, a dramatic version of the story that appears here. He died on May 26, 1970.

JOHN UPDIKE was born in Shillington, Pennsylvania, on March 18, 1932. He was graduated from Harvard University in 1954 and then studied at the Ruskin School of Drawing and Fine Art in England. Upon returning to the United States in 1955, he spent two years on the staff of *The New Yorker*, where his work has steadily appeared. Between 1958 and 1986 he published some thirty books—novels, short-story collections, poetry, and critical essays and reviews. Among his novels are *The Poorhouse Fair* (1959), *The Centaur* (1963; National Book Award), *Couples* (1968), *The Coup* (1978), and the Rabbit series: *Rabbit, Run* (1960), *Rabbit Redux* (1971), *Rabbit Is Rich* (1981), and *Rabbit at Rest* (1990). *Rabbit Is Rich* won a National Book Critics Circle Award, an American Book Award, and a Pulitzer Prize. *Rabbit at Rest* was awarded a Pulitzer Prize as well. Updike won the Rosenthal Award of the National Institute of Arts and Letters in 1960 and in 1981 was awarded a MacDowell Medal. "Here Come the Maples," one of several linked stories recounting the dissolution of a marriage, is taken from *Problems and Other Stories* (1979).

EUDORA WELTY was born in 1909 in Jackson, Mississippi, where she has spent most of her life. She attended the Mississippi State College for Women and earned her bachelor's degree in 1929 at the University of Wisconsin. Her novels include *Delta Wedding*, *The Ponder Heart*, *Losing Battles*, and *The Optimist's Daughter*, which won a 1973 Pulitzer Prize. Her reputation as a writer of the first rank also stands on her short stories, gathered in such collections as *A Curtain of Green* (1941), *The Wide Net and Other Stories* (1943), *The Golden Apples* (1949), and *The Bride of the Innisfallen* (1955). *The Collected Stories of Eudora Welty* was published in 1980, and *One Writer's Beginnings*, a memoir, in 1985. Among the many awards she has received are the National Institute of Arts and Letters Gold Medal (1972), the National Medal for Literature (1980), and the Presidential Medal of Freedom (1980).

EDITH WHARTON was born in 1862 to a prominent New York family. She was educated privately at home and in Europe. In 1885 she married Edward Robbins Wharton, and in 1907 they settled in France, where, even after their divorce in 1913, she resided for many years. In the years abroad, she formed lasting friendships with Henry James and other significant literary figures. Her first book of stories—*The Greater Inclination*, in which "Souls Belated" appears—was published in 1899. With *The House of Mirth* in 1905, her reputation as an important writer was established. Other titles followed: *Ethan Frome* (1911), *The Custom of the Country* (1913), and *The Age of Innocence* (1920), for which she won a Pulitzer Prize. Her other books include *The Valley of Decision* (1902), her collections *Xingu and Other Stories* (1916), *Certain People* (1930), and *Ghosts* (1937), and a travel book, *Italian Backgrounds* (1905). Wharton also wrote poetry and criticism. In 1915 she was awarded the Cross of the Legion of Honor by the French government for services volunteered as a relief worker in World War I. She died in France in 1937.

Acknowledgements

T HIS PROJECT had many friends, among them Al Silverman, Jennifer Josephy, Maron Waxman, Wendy Weil, David Willis McCullough, Gloria Norris, Alice Van Straalen, Larry Shapiro, Jill Sansone, Anne Close, Phyllis Robinson, Sarah Pence, Michael Brandon, Noirin Lucas, and Kathy Kiernan. I am grateful to Hilary Sterne for her assistance in preparing the notes on the authors. My gratitude goes also to the many others who were generous with time and suggestions, as well as to the publishers, agents, authors, and other individuals listed below, who granted permission to reprint previously copyrighted material as indicated.

"Coming, Aphrodite!" from *Youth and the Bright Medusa* by Willa Cather. Copyright 1920 by Willa Cather and renewed 1948 by the Executors of the Estate of Willa Cather. Reprinted by permission of Alfred A. Knopf, Inc.

"Up in Michigan" from *The Short Stories of Ernest Hemingway*. Copyright 1938 Ernest Hemingway. Copyright renewed © 1966 Mary Hemingway. Reprinted by permission of Scribner, an imprint of Simon & Schuster, Inc.

" 'The Sensible Thing' " from *All the Sad Young Men* by F. Scott Fitzgerald. Copyright 1924 Colorato Corporation; copyright renewed © 1952 Frances Scott Fitzgerald Lanahan. Reprinted by permission of Scribner, an imprint of Simon & Schuster, Inc.

"A Telephone Call" from *The Portable Dorothy Parker*, introduction by Brendan Gill. Copyright 1928, renewed © 1956 by Dorothy Parker. All rights reserved. Reprinted by permission of Viking Penguin, a division of Penguin Books USA, Inc.

"How Beautiful with Shoes" by Wilbur Daniel Steele. Copyright 1932, © renewed 1959 by Wilbur Daniel Steele. Reprinted by permission of Harold Matson Company, Inc. First published in *Harper's Magazine*.

"The Pacific" by Mark Helprin. Copyright © 1986 by Mark Helprin. Reprinted by permission of the Wendy Weil Agency, Inc. First published in *The Atlantic*.

"Elena, Unfaithful" by Gloria Kurian Broder. Copyright © 1971 by Gloria Kurian Broder. Reprinted by permission of the author. First published in *Harper's Magazine*.

"The Consolation of Philosophy" from *About My Table and Other Stories* by Nicholas Delbanco. Copyright © 1979, 1983 by Nicholas Delbanco. Reprinted by permission of William Morrow and Company, Inc.

"Bluebeard's Second Wife" by Susan Fromberg Schaeffer. Copyright © 1988 by Susan Fromberg Schaeffer. Reprinted by permission of the author.

"Dating Your Mom" from *Dating Your Mom* by Ian Frazier. Copyright © 1978, 1986 by Ian Frazier. Reprinted by permission of Farrar, Straus and Giroux, Inc. First published in *The New Yorker*.

"Residents and Transients" from *Shiloh and Other Stories* by Bobbie Ann Mason. Copyright © 1982 by Bobbie Ann Mason. Reprinted by permission of HarperCollins Publishers, Inc.

"His Own Where" by June Jordan. Copyright © 1971 by June Jordan. Reprinted by permission of HarperCollins Publishers, Inc.

"An Interest in Life" from *The Little Disturbances of Man* by Grace Paley. Copyright 1959 by Grace Paley. Reprinted by permission of the author.